A MATTER OF TIME

THE UNAUTHORIZED BACK TO THE FUTURE LEXICON

By Rich Handley

Layout and Design by Paul C. Giachetti

Cover and Interior Illustrations by Pat Carbajal

Foreword by Stephen Clark

D1059792

HASSLEIN•BOOKS

New York

Writer and editor: Rich Handley
Layout and design: Paul C. Giachetti
Cover and interior illustrations: Patricio Carbajal
Foreword: Stephen Clark

ISBN-13: 978-0-578-11344-9
Library of Congress Cataloging-in-Publication Data
First Edition: November 2012
10 9 8 7 6 5 4 3 2 1

CONTENTS◄▪▪▪

ACKNOWLEDGMENTS ◄▐▌▐▌

A Heavy Dose of Timely Thanks

"Get out of town! I didn't know you did anything creative!"

—**Marty McFly**

In 2009, following the release of my *Planet of the Apes* books, I received an e-mail from writer **Greg Mitchell**, who suggested I give the *Back to the Future* films the same treatment.

Back to the Future? Hmm. I've always loved the films, sure, but that seemed like light fare for an entire book. Greg reminded me that there were also the simulator ride, cartoons, comics, card game, video games and novels. Interest piqued, I told him I'd give it some thought, though I didn't have some of those materials. As I pondered the pitch, I was amazed to receive several snail-mail and e-mail packages from Greg, containing everything I lacked.

Sometime later, **Paul Giachetti** and I decided to expand Hasslein Books, and Greg's suggestion came up. "Heavy," said Paul. "There's that word again," I replied. "Why are things so heavy in the future? Is there a problem with the Earth's gravitational pull?" That discussion resulted in my writing a lexicon, and Greg a timeline. You now hold the first volume in your hands, and it's all due to Greg, as I would never have thought of the idea on my own. Thanks, Greg—your suggestion put the "great" in "great Scott."

Cue flashback effect: Paul and I worked together years ago, as the managing editor and art director of a magazine at a B2B publishing firm. As often happens in a "soldiers under fire in a foxhole" situation, Paul and I bonded and formed a very efficient working unit. When it came to creating Hasslein Books, he was the only partner I would have considered. His eye for visuals, unrepentant geekiness and dedication to keeping me on task—when I'd rather be reading comics, posting on Facebook and watching *Star Trek*, *Babylon 5* and *James Bond* DVDs—resulted in this lexicon's amazing design. So thanks, Paul—without you, I simply couldn't do this.

Thanks also to my supportive wife, **Jill**, without whom I couldn't do pretty much anything else. She's the enchantment under my sea. She's my density—I mean, my destiny.

Several other people also deserve thanks, and I sincerely hope I don't overlook anyone who helped out over the past two years. My humblest apologies if I have inadvertently left anyone off the list. If so, then I'm a butthead.

- **Pat Carbajal** (patart-pat.blogspot.com), the cover and interior illustrator for Hasslein's reference books, who consistently reaches into our heads and pulls out exactly what we want for every commission. For this volume, he produced not only another phenomenal cover, but also 27 astounding full-page illustrations—one for each letter of the alphabet, plus an extra sketch for the 0-9 section. His drawings so blow me away that I react like 1955 Doc Brown discovering the need for 1.21 jigowatts of electricity, every single time he turns in his work. Pat deserves extra thanks for "Carbajalizing" the headshots of the entire Hasslein team, over on hassleinbook.com's About page.

- **Stephen Clark** (BTTF.com), a leading authority on the *Back to the Future* series, who maintains the official *BTTF* Web site and Facebook group. Stephen contributed to the trilogy's Blu-ray boxset, among other projects, and selflessly helped me track down some elusive early-draft film scripts—without letting me reimburse him for his troubles, mind you. And, of course, he also wrote the excellent foreword to this book.

- **Robert Ring** (scifiblock.com), who read through the manuscript with a fine-toothed comb, and helped me clean up and tighten the text (which it needed). He was invaluable in making this a better book, and I very much appreciate his assistance and friendship.

- **Joseph F. Berenato** (criticalmess.net), a writer, graphic artist and self-proclaimed coffee junkie (and a co-author of Hasslein's upcoming book, *It's Alive: The Unauthorized Universal Monsters Chronology*, with Jim and Becky Beard) who graciously offered his expert proofreading and fact-checking skills. Without Joe's help, I would never have known that *Black Taboo* was an actual porn film! (I'm not sure what that says about him.)

- **Steve Cafarelli** (monkeygripmusic.com), a long-time friend who offered his services as Web designer when Paul and I decided to subject our Web site to a complete facelift (an offer that he has likely since regretted, given our frequent requests for site tweaks). To say that Steve's redesign left us speechless is not entirely accurate, since we couldn't stop gushing about it, but he took an amateurish-looking site in need of a mercy killing and turned it into a polished, professional portal, on which I'm proud to have my name.

- **Steven Greenwood**, the founder of an amazing resource known as Futurepedia (backtothefuture.wikia.com), who has probably forgotten more about *Back to the Future* than most people will ever know about the subject. Steve has been very supportive of my efforts with this lexicon, and his Wikia page has been an invaluable tool.

In addition, I thank the amazing cast and crew of the *Back to the Future* trilogy and its various spinoffs, as well as the following individuals, who contributed in ways large and small: Vivek Bhat, Keith Connor, Steve Czarnecki, Nelson Dewey, Johnny Dodd, Stephen Griffiths, Danny Hall, Pablo Hidalgo, A.J. Locascio, Luis-Gabriel Leal Ramirez, Dan Madsen, Tom Mason, the late Dwayne McDuffie, James and Michael McFadden, Toni McQuilken, Alex Purves, Jon Primrose, Stephen Procter, Katherine Ramos, Lisa Ravner, Jorge Rivera, Hartriono "Ben" Sastrowardoyo, Tom Silknitter, Kristen Sheley, James Sleeth, Lou Tambone and Aaron Harvey Waud.

Finally, a big thumbs-up goes to the DeLorean Motor Co., for designing what just might be the coolest-looking vehicle of all time. The way I see it, if you're going to build a time machine into a car, why not do it with some style?

v

FOREWORD ◄|||||

To Be Continued...!

by Stephen Clark

"Your future is whatever you make it, so make it a good one!"

—Emmett L. Brown

Back to the Future. Those four simple words, placed in this exact order, usually evoke a number of emotions and comments. "Oh, I love that film!" one person might exclaim. "Michael J. Fox was great in that!" another may state. "Best time-travel flick ever!" says another, before spouting out a number of now-classic lines, such as "You made a time machine... out of a DeLorean?!", "Think, McFly, think!", "Great Scott!!!" and "What are *you* lookin' at, butthead?"

Back to the Future was the biggest film of 1985, spending 11 weeks at the top of the U.S. box office—something completely unheard of in today's market. Eventually pulling in a domestic haul of $210,609,762, the movie placed solidly within the top-ten biggest films of all time.

It made an overnight movie star out of Michael J. Fox, who was already a bona fide television star thanks to his top-five smash-hit television series, *Family Ties*, and it added another legendary character to Christopher Lloyd's seemingly bottomless toolbox after NBC had canceled *Taxi* a few years earlier. The soundtrack produced the mega-hit "The Power of Love," the first song to hit #1 on the *Billboard* Hot 100 chart for Huey Lewis and the News. DeLoreans were suddenly a collector's item after the company had gone out of business three years earlier. And "skitching" (hitching a ride by holding onto an automobile while riding a skateboard) quickly became a dangerous new activity for teenagers to engage in.

Two days after it opened nationwide, I saw *Back to the Future* on Friday, July 5, 1985, with my longtime girlfriend and high-school sweetheart. I was a mere 20 years old back in the summer of 1985, working part-time in my dad's fast-food restaurant and taking some summer courses while wrapping up my sophomore year in college.

Back to the Future would prove to be the final movie we saw together before I proposed to her at a Rick Springfield concert four short days later. Little did I or my soon-to-be fiancée know that we were about to see a film which would ultimately impact both of our lives for many, many years to come.

Being a huge fan of time travel, I absolutely adored the film and was quite intrigued with how everything worked out in a logical and scientific manner. All its story setups eventually received their payoffs for the audience, which is one of the many traits for which *Back to the Future* is still widely recognized today.

We all know that Michael J. Fox was a true delight to behold throughout the film, and he was definitely a big reason why these two

"Alex P. Keaton" fans chose to go see this film that day. However, since no other actors appeared in the original trailer other than Fox, I went into the theater entirely oblivious to who else was in the cast. The fact that Christopher Lloyd was in it had completely flown beneath my radar until that magical moment when Doc Brown first emerged from inside of the DeLorean Time Machine and gleefully exclaimed, "Marty! You made it!"

"Oh, wow! It's Reverend Jim!!!" I boldly blurted out, a bit too loudly, during the screening. Having been a faithful *Taxi* viewer since 1978, I knew I was in for a real treat from that moment on.

Once Marty arrived in 1955, I easily recognized Lea Thompson as Tom Cruise's girlfriend from 1983's *All the Right Moves*, and I knew Crispin Glover as one of Jason Voorhees' many helpless victims from 1984's *Friday the 13th: The Final Chapter*. I just hadn't immediately connected the dots that these were the same actors I had seen earlier in the McFly house as Marty's 1985 parents. The film also introduced me to one of Hollywood's best-kept secrets— the undeniably talented Tom Wilson, who years later would become a lifelong friend. Indeed, I was experiencing ingenious filmmaking in its truest form as the story unfolded, engaging me every single step along the incredible 116-minute adventure.

As was common for me back in the days of $2.50 non-matinée screenings (I still have our original ticket stubs), I saw it a second time a few weeks later before this endearing movie temporarily faded from my consciousness, while school, work and my pending nuptials inhabited those spaces inside my brain... until the following summer rolled around.

Then, one day in June 1986, while browsing the magazine shelves at the bookstore in my local mall, I accidentally stumbled across the July '86 issue (#108) of *Starlog* magazine—an event that ultimately paved the path for a very unique journey which I would eventually travel. For you see, that issue contained the brilliantly penned essay *"The Other Marty McFly?"* by the late, great Disney Imagineer Bruce Gordon, and it toggled on a switch rooted deep inside of me.

Gordon's three-page article basically proposed the theory that Marty McFly's action of returning to his own era ten minutes early at the end the film caused him to switch places with himself from a parallel universe, allowing us to briefly see this other-dimensional Marty. The clincher to his incredible theory was that not only did we clearly see this "other" Marty McFly at the end of the film, when Doc was shot a second time (from our point of view), but we could also actually catch a brief glimpse of "Marty II" during the parking-lot scene at the beginning of the movie.

"Uh, WHAT???!!!!!"

Well, that's all it took to reel me in! I immediately purchased the magazine and headed straight to my local video rental store to rent the movie—which, I was aware, had just been released on VHS a few weeks earlier. I spent the better part of a weekend satisfying the inescapable urge to watch the parking-lot scene frame by frame (a very difficult task on VHS, even by today's standards) to locate this elusive "second Marty," and to discover all the other juicy nuggets Gordon identified that I had somehow managed to miss during my two theatrical viewings almost an entire year earlier.

✓ "Twin Pines Mall" was changed to "Lone Pine Mall"? Check!
✓ The cement ledge on the clock tower was correctly broken in 1985 at the end of the film, but not at the beginning? Check!
✓ "Marty II" was standing off in the shadows when Doc first got shot? No check!

Countless hours later, using my top-of-the-line RCA VCR, I was empty-handed and just couldn't locate this mysterious figure whom the author claimed was there. Eventually, I gave up and once again forgot about *Back to the Future* for a few more years... until 1989.

By the time I learned that year that not just one, but two *Back to the Future* sequels, filmed back to back, were headed my way, that switch inside me was permanently toggled to "ON." Like many other fans, I devoured every piece of information I could get my hands on regarding the sequels. I had a friend who owned something called a LaserDisc player, which handled frame-by-frame advancement much better, and I finally discovered the elusive "Marty II" (a quick movement of a silhouetted figure off in the background, the exact moment Doc tossed his pistol to the ground).

By this time, I was picking up every issue of *Starlog* the moment it hit stands, as though it were my last meal. I became a charter member of the Official *Back to the Future* Fan Club, whose four quarterly magazines were worn out cover-to-cover a day after landing in my mailbox. *Cinefex* magazine was around, too, but that was just about all that was available within my grasp, in terms of Hollywood film news. There was also Movietime, an entertaining and informative TV channel that provided a great deal of film news and trailers for upcoming movies. The only online service I could access back then was a film-related BBS list through CompuServe, but everyone I encountered there had no more information about the films than I had already gleaned from *Starlog*, *Cinefex*, Movietime and the Official Fan Club.

The two sequels eventually came and went, leaving me joyously thrilled yet incredibly thirsty for a whole lot more—even though I was fully aware that the filmmakers had sworn there would never be any more sequels. A week after *Back to the Future Part III* debuted in theaters, Movietime became E! Entertainment Television, and I suddenly felt "in the know" once more. I soon learned about Universal Studios Florida and its plans to launch *Back to the Future... The Ride*, and I also heard about the first of many horrible Universal Studios back-lot fires that torched the original Courthouse Square sets.

In 1991, when my wife—whom Tom Wilson calls the most patient and understanding female on the entire planet—surprised me at Christmas with a trip to Orlando the following month to celebrate our fifth wedding anniversary, this then-25-year-old man was just like a kid on his first trip to Disney World! *Back to the Future... The Ride* fully engulfed me into the *Back to the Future* phenomenon like no other experience up to that point, and I simply could not get enough.

I returned from that trip so excited about the films and motion-simulator ride that I decided I wanted to somehow become involved in its continuance. I discovered, while visiting the *Back to the Future* gift shop, that a comic book had recently been issued by Harvey Comics, and that later that same year, CBS would be airing the second season of an animated series based on the films, with live-action wraparounds hosted by Christopher Lloyd as Doc Brown. In the course of a two-year span, *Back to the Future* fans were treated to two sequels, a theme-park attraction and a Saturday morning cartoon series. Life was really good!

But the steady stream of new content quickly halted once the final thirteen episodes of the animated series' second season aired in 1992. The Fan Club magazines had already ceased production, as had the comic books, and it soon became lonely again in Hill Valley.

In the letters section of one of the comics' final issues, I came across a note from a fellow fan who wished there was another fan club now that the official one had gone defunct. Even though I was just a good ole' Southern boy from Alabama, I thought, "Hey, now that's something I can probably do. Why not at least give it a shot?"

Over the course of a year or so, I made a number of calls to Universal, and on one persistent day, back in the summer of 1992, I somehow found myself transferred to writer-producer Bob Gale's office at Universal. Bob was serving as the animated series' executive producer, as well as the director for the second and final season. One thing led to another, his office connected me with another similarly minded mega-fan from Southern California named Bob Boyce, and the two of us formed a brand-new fan club. At its peak, our amateur quarterly fanzine, the *Hill Valley Telegraph*, had a circulation of approximately 500.

By 1994, Boyce had long moved on to other interests, and I took the reins solo. The Internet was suddenly exploding, and our feeble efforts quickly moved online. "*Back to the Future...* The Web Page" debuted in 1995 as a supplement to our fanzine, hosted on a single dial-up account at a local ISP named Traveller Internet Services. By late 1996, all of our print efforts were taken online due to the instant nature of the Internet. This Web page was the precursor to BTTF.com, which launched in January 1997 and still operates at that address to this very day.

Since then, BTTF.com has evolved from being merely a "fan site" to being heavily involved with a number of very high-profile *Back to the Future* products, projects and events as a peer service. Among the highlights, we've served as:

- Writers of the "Did You Know That? Universal Animated Anecdotes" feature for all three films on the *Back to the Future— The Complete Trilogy* DVDs (2002), updated on the *Back to the Future 25th Anniversary Trilogy* Blu-ray discs (2010).

- Content and continuity consultants on Universal's official DVD Web site, BTTFmovie.com, for the *Back to the Future—The Complete Trilogy* DVD promotion (2002).

- Producers of the independent documentary *Looking Back at the Future* (2006), which later appeared in re-edited form on the

Back to the Future 2-Disc Special Edition DVD (2009) as the featurette "Looking Back to the Future."

- Photo consultants on *E! True Hollywood Story: Michael J. Fox* (2006).

- The grass-roots campaign behind *Back to the Future* being added to the Library of Congress' National Film Archive (2007), later highlighted in the documentary *These Amazing Shadows* (2011).

- Content and continuity consultants on the *Back to the Future... The Ride* segment featured on the *Back to the Future 2-Disc Special Edition* DVD (2009).

- Partners with AMC Theaters and Looney Labs to promote *Back to the Future: The Card Game*. All ticket holders for the *Back to the Future* 25th Anniversary theatrical re-release (2010) received a free bonus game card sponsored solely by BTTF.com.

- Copywriters, packaging designers, product authenticators and various other consulting jobs (2000 to present) for multiple licensees on their officially licensed *Back to the Future* products, including companies such as Diamond Select Toys, Looney Labs, Sun Star Diecasting America, Telltale Games and Welly Die Casting Fty.

- Coordinators for countless sci-fi conventions, car shows and film festivals in which we have appeared with a vast majority of the cast and crew (2001 to present).

One low point came in 2007, when Universal Orlando and Universal Studios Hollywood announced that they would be shuttering both *Back to the Future... The Ride* attractions that year. The Hollywood edition was honored with a closing-day ceremony for fans, which was attended by Bob Gale and Christopher Lloyd—a bittersweet event that I simply could not coerce myself into attending. This was the end of an era and would certainly mark the beginning of the end—or so I thought.

Over the years, interest in *Back to the Future* has been a motion-simulator ride in itself, as there have been lots of peaks and valleys along this incredible journey—with perhaps a few more valleys than peaks. Still, the series has endured the test of time. While the films were produced during the mid-to-late 1980s, they have certainly aged quite well over time, and still rest fondly within the hearts of millions of fans of all ages across the globe.

In 2010, *Back to the Future* reached the quarter-century milestone—one celebrated by hundreds of fans who flocked to various filming locations in and around Los Angeles a few weeks after the series debuted on Blu-ray. The event was called "We're Going Back!" (www.weregoingback.com), and planning for a "sequel" is currently underway for 2015.

After all the celebration hoopla ended following the 2010 milestone, I thought "Surely, this has to have been the pinnacle. We've had a really good ride, but interest in the series will certainly spiral down a speedy slope now that the 25th anniversary has come and gone." Thankfully, I was terribly wrong.

In 2011 came Nike's massive campaign to benefit the Michael J. Fox Foundation for Parkinson's Research (www.michaeljfox.org) by selling 1,500 pairs of officially licensed, screen-accurate replicas of the Nike Mags that Marty McFly sported throughout the 2015

portions of *Back to the Future Part II*. The eBay auction resulted in the largest charity auction in the company's history, ultimately generating more than $4.7 million raised for MJFF during the 10-day event.

2012 marked another pinpoint in time that fans thought would never happen: Mattel is producing an officially licensed, screen-accurate replica of Marty's futuristic pink hoverboard for release this Christmas. Early prototypes proved to be a rousing success in Mattel's booth this year at the annual San Diego Comic-Con.

We also learned this year that a full restoration of the original DeLorean Time Machine "A" car is currently underway by a team of professional restoration specialists who are huge fans of the series. Upon completion of the authentic restoration in the near future, this Hollywood treasure will be placed on permanent display at Universal Studios Hollywood for all the world to see.

As we quickly spin forward in time toward the series' 30th anniversary in 2015 and beyond, there are still a plethora of very pleasant surprises which lie ahead for *Back to the Future* fans. Rich Handley's *A Matter of Time: The Unauthorized Back to the Future Lexicon* is a prime example of this, standing as a testament to the endurance this series still has today, and the grip it holds in the hearts and minds of its legions of fans.

I won't spoil the pages ahead for you, but do trust me when I say that you're about to embark upon an incredible journey of unmatched research and creativeness, all pooled together into this one reference guide. I'm very thankful that there are people like Rich out there who have the knowledge and energy to tackle such a project as this, and I'm sure you'll feel the same way once you fully digest the following pages. Good luck, time-travel volunteers!

Stephen Clark has been actively and intimately involved with the Back to the Future *franchise in various capacities over the past two decades. Since 1995, he has operated the Internet's very first and longest-running* Back to the Future *Web site, BTTF.com. The officially sanctioned site is recognized by the films' cast, crew and fans worldwide as the central hub for all things related to* Back to the Future, *including official news, upcoming events and licensed merchandise. BTTF.com duly promotes the* Back to the Future *brand and the careers of its cast and crew through various online ventures and trade-show appearances. Additionally, the site offers consulting services for licensees developing new officially licensed products from the timeless film series.*

INTRODUCTION

This Sucker's Electrical

by Rich Handley

"Hey, hey, I've seen this one. I've seen this one. This is a classic!"
—**Marty McFly**

I love a good comedy, and as a teenager growing up in the 1980s, I certainly had my fill. Just off the top of my head, we had *Better Off Dead*, *One Crazy Summer*, *Weird Science*, *Fast Times at Ridgemont High*, *Vacation*, *Beetlejuice*, *Ghostbusters*, *Sixteen Candles*, *The Breakfast Club*, *Ferris Bueller's Day Off*—the list was endless.

But few movies define a generation like *Back to the Future* did. When you think about music from that era, images of Prince, Cyndi Lauper, Duran Duran, Michael Jackson and Culture Club come to mind—they *are* the '80s scene. And when it comes to movies, *Back to the Future* is at the top of the list.

I was in high school when *Back to the Future* debuted in 1985—and it had me at "Hello, McFly." I saw the film a few times at the theater, and later re-watched it repeatedly on network TV, as well as on VHS. My girlfriend back then loved the film, too, so I have fond memories of watching it with her.

In short, *Back to the Future* blew me away. The concept, the cast, the humor, the recurring gags, the costumes, the stunts, Claudia Wells (hey, I was a male teen)—I was hooked. Eighties films fueled my teen imagination, and whenever *Back to the Future* was on, this sucker was electrical. When Francis Ford Coppola's *Peggy Sue Got Married* hit theaters the following year, with Kathleen Turner portraying a clearly-too-old female analog to Marty McFly, I enjoyed it for what it was... but it was certainly no *Back to the Future*, much as it tried to be.

I was finishing up college when the sequels were released, back to back. Sadly, we lost Claudia as Jennifer and, worse, the brilliant Crispin Glover as George, and in any other series, such cast changes might have proved catastrophic. Still, I was astounded at how much I enjoyed them. All too often, comedy sequels tend to be cringeworthy cash-grabs, unworthy of the celluloid on which they were filmed—but that wasn't the case with *Back to the Future*. That same giddy feeling I experienced from the first movie, at age

17, returned for both *Parts II* and *III*, and I walked out of each viewing with a big grin on my face, as though I, too, had traveled back in time to my high school days.

It's rare that comedy sequels manage to re-capture the magic of their progenitors, as anyone who paid to see the disastrous *Police Academy, Revenge of the Nerds* and *Look Who's Talking* followups knows all too painfully well. But the *BTTF* trilogy indisputably pulled it off. Between the multi-colored sci-fi future of 2015, the dark "Biffhorrific" alternate 1985, the nostalgic revisiting of the first film's 1955 sequences, and the sentimental Spaghetti Western riff in 1885, the sequels hit it out of the park, scene after scene.

In recent years, I became acquainted with writer Greg Mitchell, who had read my *Planet of the Apes* books and suggested that I give *Back to the Future* the same treatment. As explained in this book's acknowledgments, I asked if he'd be interested in writing a chronology, while I tackled the lexicon. (I'm not stupid—a person would have to be *nuts* to write a *Back to the Future* timeline. So being naturally lazy, I chose the encyclopedia... keep reading to find out how THAT worked out for me.)

Greg—like Doc Brown, faced with the choice of whether or not to read a warning about Libyan nationalists murdering him in the future—figured, "What the hell?" and accepted the assignment. His book, *Back in Time: The Unauthorized Back to the Future Chronology*, will be out sometime in 2013.

When writing a book of this type, it's imperative to have enthusiasm for the project. Done properly, it involves repeated viewings and re-viewings, readings and re-readings, combined with countless hours of research, rewriting, interpolation, extrapolation and interviews—it's a huge undertaking, make no mistake, and with three such books now under my belt, I guarantee my next one will be no easier.

So why do it, you may wonder?

Quite simply, because it's so damned fun. What's not to enjoy about dissecting, devouring and utterly absorbing all you can about your favorite fictional universes? And how can someone NOT be fascinated by *Back to the Future*, in particular? Doc and Marty were like Kirk and Spock, Butch and Sundance, Han and Chewie, and Apollo and Starbuck (new or old), in that there was an amazing chemistry between them. Their friendship wasn't just a concept on paper; it was alive, brimming with electricity, due in no small part to the phenomenal performances of Michael J. Fox and Christopher Lloyd. And the trilogy's secondary cast—Biff, George, Lorraine, Jennifer, Clara, Mr. Strickland and even Einstein—remain, to this day, among cinema's most beloved characters.

Plus, hey, I love time-travel stories when they're done right, and it really doesn't get more right than the *Back to the Future* movies. All three reside on the top tier, alongside *Time After Time, Star Trek IV: The Voyage Home, Bill and Ted's Excellent Adventure, Somewhere in Time, Escape From the Planet of the Apes* and the first two *Terminator* flicks, as the best of the genre.

No matter what era Doc and Marty visited, every individual they encountered was hilarious and well-acted, every joke spot-on, every observation keen, and every parallel and payoff from one generation to the next brilliant. I discover something new with every viewing, even after all these years. Watching the *Back to the*

Future trilogy (and I watched it a LOT while writing this lexicon, as you can imagine), I sometimes wonder what drug Bob Gale and Robert Zemeckis were on while writing it, because I definitely want some. I can't think of a single trilogy as consistently witty, or as unceasingly electric. There's no *Highlander II, Godfather III, Alien IV* or *Star Trek V* in the bunch. How many film series can make THAT claim?

What amazed me, while compiling this encyclopedia, was just how much lore comprises the *BTTF* franchise. Oh, sure, I knew the films like the back of my hand, I'd experienced the simulator ride several times, and I was a bit familiar with the animated series, having watched a few episodes when they'd aired on TV. But I'd never read the comics or played the video games, and I'd never perused the early-draft scripts or novelizations. So I'd mistakenly assumed that this would be a project of smaller scope than either of my *POTA* books, and that Greg would be the one writing the larger volume. It soon became apparent, however, just how wrong I was. *A Matter of Time,* as it turns out, would make for quite an effective paperweight.

Like the *Apes* lexicon, this one is designed for anal-retentive, die-hard fans, as well as those who simply love the movies. If it showed up or was mentioned onscreen or in print, it's here—every character, place and gadget, no matter how obscure, from not only the films but also the cartoons, video games, card game, comics, novels, Universal Studios ride, screenplays and Happy Meals (the boxes, not the burgers), as well as obscure TV commercials and music videos.

It was a lot of work to go through it all, to be sure. But I didn't mind it, because revisiting *Back to the Future* reminded me how much fun it is to laugh my ass off. Even during some of the more ridiculous shenanigans of the animated series (and, believe me, there were some major doozies in the cartoon—even scenes in which Einstein drove a car or cooked hot dogs were not its silliest moments), I still cracked up regularly while watching it. The cartoon was wacky and absurd, but it was also entertaining and fun. Universal should really consider putting it out on DVD.

The true gem, I found, is Telltale Games' *BTTF* video game, which is such a worthy successor to the trilogy that I think of it as *Back to the Future Part IV.* If you haven't played the game, go order your copy right now. Trust me, you won't regret it. It's uproariously funny, the storyline is complex and well-conceived, the gameplay is great fun, the new characters seem right out of the movies themselves, and the voice actors (particularly A.J. Locascio and James Arnold Taylor as Marty and young Doc, respectively) are perfectly cast. I defy anyone to listen to Locascio's astoundingly accurate impression of Michael J. Fox and not fall over laughing.

Locascio, Taylor and their fellow video game actors join the ranks of the time-honored cast and crew who made *Back to the Future* the great pleasure it remains. If there's a finer comedy troupe from the '80s than Bob Gale, Robert Zemeckis, Michael J. Fox, Christopher Lloyd, Lea Thompson, Crispin Glover, Tom Wilson, James Tolkan, Mary Steenburgen, Claudia Wells and Elisabeth Shue, I surely can't think of one. These immensely talented individuals have given fans countless hours of electrified enjoyment over the past three decades, reminding us, time and again, what it was like to be a teenager in 1985, with our future not yet written.

ABBREVIATION KEY

Unlocking the Code to Time Travel

"Please excuse the crudity of this model. I didn't have time to build it to scale or paint it."

—Emmett L. Brown

This encyclopedia draws information not only from the *Back to the Future* films and TV series, but also from a variety of other sources, many of them obscure. For each entry in the lexicon, four-character codes indicate the source materials in which that information can be found.

Some codes feature additional lower-case suffixes, denoting that the entry was culled from the script, novelization or comic book adaptation of a film or TV episode, rather than from the onscreen episode or movie itself. In addition, codes for entries related to the animated series, comics and Telltale Games video game contain an episode or issue number.

Some view the films and their spinoff tales as taking place in the same universe, while others consider them separate. This lexicon does not take a stance on that debate, instead utilizing an all-inclusive approach: If it occurred or was mentioned in the cartoons, comics, games or novels—or even in a commercial or music video containing *Back to the Future* elements—it's covered here. Since all entries indicate their sources via the four-letter codes, readers are free to reject any aspects of the franchise they prefer not to include.

By way of example, **[BTF1-s1]** would indicate that a particular entry originated in the first film's draft-one screenplay, while **[BFAN-17]** would signify that the source was the animated series' 17th episode.

The symbols and codes are detailed below. To avoid redundancy, the notes accompanying the entries frequently employ shortened forms of the film titles (*BTTF1*, *BTTF2* and *BTTF3*), while *Back to the Future Part II* and *Back to the Future Part III* often drop the word "Part," for the sake of brevity, and the franchise's name as a whole is shortened simply to *BTTF*. Additional details about each story, including descriptions, credits and release dates, can be found in Appendix I.

CODE	STORY
ARGN	*BTTF*-themed TV commercial: Arrigoni
BFAN	*Back to the Future: The Animated Series*
BFCG	*Back to the Future: The Card Game*
BFCL	*Back to the Future* comic book (limited series)
BFCM	*Back to the Future* comic book (monthly series)
BFHM	*BTTF*-themed McDonald's Happy Meal boxes
BTFA	*Back to the Future Annual* (Marvel Comics)
BTF1	Film: *Back to the Future*
BTF2	Film: *Back to the Future Part II*
BTF3	Film: *Back to the Future Part III*
BUDL	*BTTF*-themed TV commercial: Bud Light
CHEK	*BTTF*-themed music video: O'Neal McKnight, "Check Your Coat"
CHIC	Photographs hanging in the Doc Brown's Chicken restaurant at Universal Studios
CITY	*BTTF*-themed music video: Owl City, "Deer in the Headlights"
CLUB	*Back to the Future Fan Club Magazine* (Fan Clubs Inc., four issues)
DCTV	*BTTF*-themed TV commercial: DirecTV
ERTH	*The Earth Day Special*
GALE	Interviews and commentaries: Bob Gale and/or Robert Zemeckis
GARB	*BTTF*-themed TV commercials for Garbarino
HUEY	*BTTF*-themed music video: Huey Lewis and the News, "The Power of Love"
LIMO	*BTTF*-themed music video: The Limousines, "The Future"
MCDN	*BTTF*-themed TV commercial: McDonald's
MITS	*BTTF*-themed TV commercial: Mitsubishi Lancer
MSFT	*BTTF*-themed TV commercial: Microsoft
NIKE	*BTTF*-themed TV commercial: Nike
NTND	Nintendo *Back to the Future: The Ride* Mini-Game
PIZA	*BTTF*-themed TV commercial: Pizza Hut

CODE	STORY
PNBL	Data East *Back to the Future* pinball game
REAL	Real life (not from any *Back to the Future* source)
RIDE	Simulator: *Back to the Future—The Ride*
SCRM	2010 Scream Awards: *Back to the Future* 25th Anniversary Reunion (broadcast)
SCRT	2010 Scream Awards: *Back to the Future* 25th Anniversary Reunion (trailer)
SIMP	Simulator: *The Simpsons Ride*
SLOT	*Back to the Future* Video Slots
STLZ	Unused *BTTF* footage of Eric Stoltz as Marty McFly
STRY	*Back to the Future Storybook*
TEST	Screen tests: Crispin Glover, Lea Thompson and Thomas F. Wilson
TLTL	Telltale Games' *Back to the Future—The Game*
TOPS	Topps' *Back to the Future II* trading-card set
TRIL	*Back to the Future: The Official Book of the Complete Movie Trilogy*
UNIV	Universal Studios Hollywood promotional video

SUFFIX	MEDIUM
-b	*BTTF2*'s Biff Tannen Museum video (extended)
-c	Credit sequence to the animated series
-d	Film deleted scene
-n	Film novelization
-o	Film outtake
-p	1955 phone book from *BTTF1*
-v	Video game print materials or commentaries
-s1	Screenplay (draft one)
-s2	Screenplay (draft two)
-s3	Screenplay (draft three)
-s4	Screenplay (draft four)
-sp	Screenplay (production draft)
-sx	Screenplay (*Paradox*)

THE LEXICON◄▐▐▐▌

What the Hell's a Jigowatt?!

"Who the hell is John F. Kennedy?"

—Sam Baines

3 - D

(CENTER, WITH MATCH AND SKINHEAD)

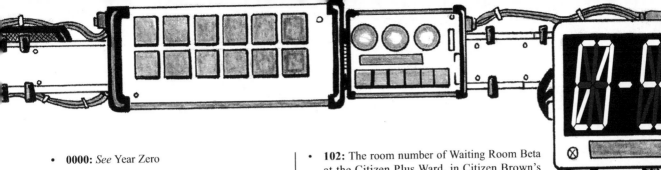

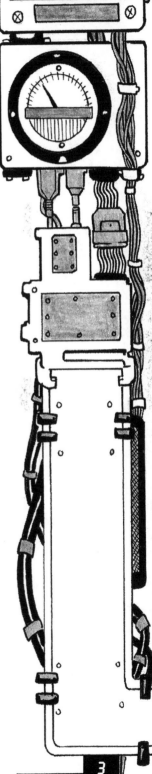

- **0000:** *See* Year Zero

- **000010034:** A serial number on the first of two tickets purchased by Jules Brown, enabling his parents, Emmett and Clara Brown, to book a 2091 passenger solar sailship to Mars to celebrate their second honeymoon [**BFAN-9**].

- **000010035:** A serial number on the second of two tickets that Jules Brown purchased for Emmett and Clara Brown so that they could celebrate their second honeymoon aboard a Mars-bound passenger solar sailship in 2091 [**BFAN-9**].

- **09011885:** Emmett Brown's California driver's license number, circa 1985 [**BTF1**].

- **097568:** A number printed on a movie ticket for the film *The Virtuous Husband*, which Emmett Brown and Edna Strickland went to see on their first date in 1931, in Citizen Brown's dystopian timeline [**TLTL-3**].

- **099986627:** An ID number listed on one of Café 80's menus in 2015, alongside a logo for a thumbprint-activated payment device and the phrase "Pay Up" [**BTF2**].

- **099986671:** An ID number listed on one of Café 80's menus in 2015, alongside a logo for a thumbprint-activated payment device and the phrase "Pay Up" [**BTF2**].

- **1:** The designation of a television camera used on the set of the *Mr. Wisdom* children's TV show [**BFAN-26**].

- **10:** The street address of Oliver Brown, Emmett Brown's uncle, in Milwaukee, Wisconsin, in the early 20th century. At age four, young Emmett spent time living with Oliver at this address [**BFAN-11**].

- **10:** The street address of the Hill Valley Apartments, circa 1931 [**TLTL-1**].

- **10:** *See* 1809 Mason Street

- **101:** A room at the Citizen Plus Ward, adjacent to Waiting Room Beta, in Citizen Brown's dystopian timeline. Marty McFly was incarcerated in this room while awaiting reconditioning [**TLTL-4**].

- **102:** The room number of Waiting Room Beta at the Citizen Plus Ward, in Citizen Brown's dystopian timeline. Jennifer Parker awaited reconditioning in this room [**TLTL-4**].

- **10261985:** Marty McFly's California driver's license number, circa 1985 [**BTF1**].

- **103:** A room adjacent to Room 102 at the Citizen Plus Ward, in Citizen Brown's dystopian timeline. While awaiting reconditioning, Biff Tannen was incarcerated in this room [**TLTL-4**].

- **112:** The street address of D. Levin, an ice cream shop located in Boston, Massachusetts, circa 1897 [**BFAN-8**].

- **11249 Business Center Road:** The Hill Valley street address of CusCo Industries, at which Marty McFly worked in 2015 [**BTF2, BFCG**].

- **1131 Park Lane:** *See* 3793 Oakhurst Street

- **1191 South Kelsey:** The street address of Emmett Brown's residence in 1944. The apartment, 3B, was located above a gas station [**BFAN-17**].

- **1.21 jigowatts:** A measurement of electricity. When Marty McFly was stranded in 1955, Emmett Brown lacked plutonium to power the time-traveling DeLorean in order to return the youth to his own era. However, Marty showed Doc a flyer indicating that Hill Valley's Clock Tower would be struck by lightning within a week, thereby producing the 1.21 jigowatts required to enable time travel. Armed with that foreknowledge, the scientist was able to harness the lightning and send Marty back to the future [**BTF1**].

  > **NOTE:** *In an early-draft script for BTTF1, the power required was 4,200 rads. This was changed to "1.21 jigowatts"—a misspelling and mispronunciation of "gigawatts," with a hard "g" instead of soft—in a later draft, either inadvertently or for comedic intent. Doc's handwritten letter to Marty in BTTF3 also used the "jigowatt" spelling, as did Marvel Comics' BTTF Annual and signage at Universal Studios' Back to the Future: The Ride.*

  > *Not coincidentally, the time reading on Einstein's chronometer after his one-minute time-traveling adventure read 1:21.*

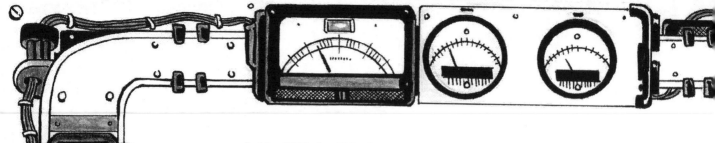

In May 2010, the ABC television series FlashForward *paid homage to this measurement in episode 19, "Course Correction." When the machine used in that series to cause a worldwide blackout was revealed, the term "1.21 GW" appeared on an overhead display.*

- **1.21 kilokarls:** A measurement of stimulation levels used to recondition inmates at the Citizen Plus Ward, in Citizen Brown's dystopian timeline [**TLTL-4**].

    NOTE: This was an in-joke referencing Doc's "1.21 jigowatts" line.

    On the TV series Lost, *character Karl Martin was subjected to very similar reconditioning. It's unknown whether the term "kilokarls" (a nonexistent real-world measurement) referred to that character.*

- **1.21 kilowatts:** The amount of power required to run the rotary engine of the full-scale Rocket-Powered Drill invented by Emmett Brown in 1931 [**TLTL-2**].

    NOTE: This measurement also paid homage to Doc's "1.21 jigowatts" line.

- **121 Park, A618-942308:** The street address of Ito. T. Fujitsu and his wife, Siva, in 2015 [**BTF2**].

- **1223 098 541 04290 327 486:** The number of a bank account at City Trust and Savings Bank, circa 1958. A check for $1,182,000 was drawn from this account to pay Biff Tannen his first winnings in the Bifforrific timeline, after he began betting at the Valley Racing Association using sporting-event results listed in *Grays Sports Almanac*. The check, #2634, was issued from the bank's main branch, located at the corner of Third and Main, and was signed by Tim Matthews [**BTF2**].

- **136113966:** The number of Emmett Brown's bar-coded license plate after he had the DeLorean upgraded in 2015 [**BTF1**].

- **15-Tube Mechanical Home Butler:** A type of robot created by Emmett Brown. In one timeline, the Home Butler became a common household appliance by 1985, making the scientist wealthy and successful [**BTF1-s1**].

- **161:** The house number of Jennifer Parker's family in Hill Valley, circa 1985 [**BTF3**].

- **1640 Riverside Drive:** The street address of Emmett Brown's family mansion, circa 1955. Doc's phone number was Klondike 5-4385. While stranded in that year, Marty McFly lived at this address for approximately a week, while he and Doc devised a way to repair the time-stream damage Marty had caused and jury-rig a way to send the youth back to the future [**BTF1**].

    NOTE: In BTTF1's draft-one screenplay, Brown lived at 788 West Spruce, with a phone number of Madison 3489.

- **1646 John F. Kennedy Drive:** The street address of Emmett Brown's garage apartment, circa 1985, located near a Burger King, a Toys "R" Us and other businesses [**BTF1**].

    NOTE: Between 1955 and 1985, Riverside Drive was renamed John F. Kennedy Drive—hence, the different street name in the 1955 phone book and on Brown's 1985 driver's license. Doc spent his family fortune pursuing time-travel experiments. Thus, the change in his address from 1640 to 1646 could indicate that the land on which his home once stood was broken up into smaller lots, one of which (1646) contained the sole remainder of his original home—the garage.

    In BTTF1's draft-one screenplay, Doc lived at 2980 Monroe Avenue.

- **17100:** The street address of ACI, a business located in Artesia, California [**BFAN-12**].

- **1711 Sycamore Street:** The street address of George McFly's family in 1955 [**BTF1**].

    NOTE: The house used to film these scenes was located at 1711 Bushnell Avenue.

- **1727 Sycamore Street:** The street address of Lorraine Baines' family in 1955 [**BTF1**].

    NOTE: The house used to film these scenes was located at 1727 Bushnell Avenue.

- **1800 Sycamore Street:** The street address of a house across the street from Lorraine Baines' family home in 1955 [**BTF1**].

    NOTE: The house used to film these scenes was located at 1800 Bushnell Avenue.

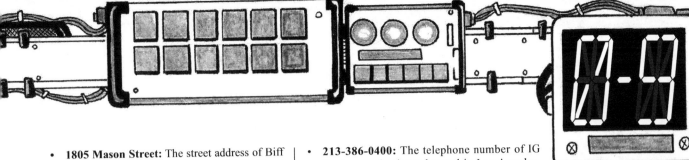

- **1805 Mason Street:** The street address of Biff Tannen's next-door neighbors in 1955. On at least one occasion, Biff intimidated a group of neighborhood children by tossing their ball onto the roof of this house [**BTF2**].

    NOTE: The house used to film these scenes was located at 1805 Bushnell Avenue.

- **1809 Mason Street:** The street address of Biff Tannen's childhood home in Hill Valley, circa 1955, where he lived with his grandmother, Gertrude Tannen. The house, in need of repairs and repainting, had a number of tacky and racist lawn decorations, as well as a handwritten sign warning others against trespassing [**BTF2**].

    NOTE: Despite Biff's address being 1809, the number above his front door was 10, and BTTF2's novelization cited his address as 2311 Mason Street. The house used to film these scenes was located at 1809 Bushnell Avenue.

- *1984 (a.k.a. Nineteen Eighty-Four):* A dystopian novel by George Orwell, concerning a society (known as Oceania) ruled by an oligarchical dictatorship known as the Party that used pervasive government surveillance and public mind control to oppress the masses [**REAL**].

    Edna Strickland read this book as an elderly woman in 1986, while angrily yelling at passersby from her apartment window [**TLTL-1**]. In an alternate timeline, she utilized the Party's tactics to subjugate Hill Valley's citizens [**TLTL-3, TLTL-4**].

- **1JV3 983:** The license plate number of an automobile owned by Jennifer Parker's father, circa 1985 [**BTF1**].

- **2:** The contestant number of a couple who took part in a jitterbug competition that Emmett Brown entered after traveling back to the 1940s [**BFAN-17**].

- **2:** The designation of a television camera used on the set of the *Mr. Wisdom* children's TV show [**BFAN-26**].

- *2015 Sports Almanac: 50 Years of Sports Statistics 1965-2014: See* Grays Sports Almanac: Complete Sports Statistics 1950-2000

- **213-386-0400:** The telephone number of IG Systems, a business located in Los Angeles, California [**BFAN-12**].

- **213-865-0735:** The telephone number of ACI, a business located in Artesia, California [**BFAN-12**].

- **213-889-2444:** The telephone number of Beverly Ho, a contact person at a business whose help-wanted ad Emmett Brown read in 1991 while searching for a job [**BFAN-12**].

    NOTE: Her surname, obstructed onscreen, may have had additional letters.

- **220:** The street address of a building in Courthouse Square, circa 2015, outside an alley in which Emmett Brown hid an unconscious Jennifer Parker while he and Marty McFly saved Marty's and Jen's future children from disaster [**BTF2**].

- **22KK53:** The street number of a building near the P.K. Rata Recycling Center, located in an alley in which Emmett Brown parked the flying DeLorean in 2015 [**BTF2**].

- **2311 Mason Street:** *See* 1809 Mason Street

- **2317:** The street address of Marty McFly's former home in Biffhorrific 1985, occupied in that reality by an African-American family [**BTF2-s1**]. When the McFlys owned the house, its street number was 9303 [**BTF2**].

    NOTE: The family was unnamed onscreen in Back to the Future II, *though the children, Loretta and Harold, were identified in the end credits. The novelization identified the father as Lewis, while the movie's first-draft screenplay named the wife Louise.*

- **23251:** The street address of a company listed in a 1991 help-wanted ad that Emmett Brown read while trying to find a job. The business was located at 23251 Mulholland Drive, in Woodland Hills, California, 91365 [**BFAN-12**].

- **237:** A proposition being debated in 2015 regarding the legalization of bionics. Upon visiting Hill Valley in that year, Marty McFly passed a poster urging Hill Valley's citizen's to vote "yes" to 237 [**BTF2**].

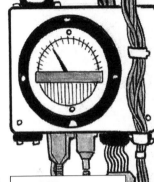

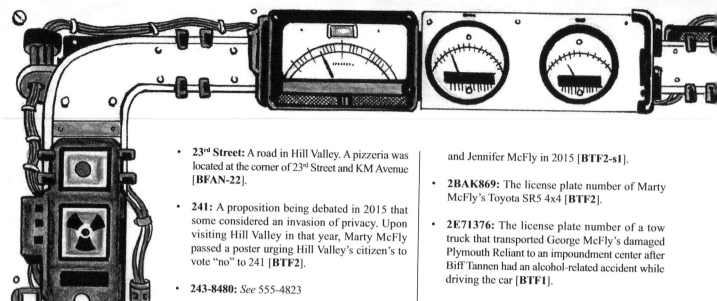

- **23rd Street:** A road in Hill Valley. A pizzeria was located at the corner of 23rd Street and KM Avenue [**BFAN-22**].

- **241:** A proposition being debated in 2015 that some considered an invasion of privacy. Upon visiting Hill Valley in that year, Marty McFly passed a poster urging Hill Valley's citizen's to vote "no" to 241 [**BTF2**].

- **243-8480:** *See* 555-4823

- **24-Hour Cloning Shack:** A business located in Hill Valley, circa 2091, not far from the McFly Space Center [**BFAN-9**].

- **24-Hour Hill Valley Bike Hut:** A business in Hill Valley specializing in bicycle parts, circa 1992, open 24 hours a day [**BFAN-23**].

- **25:** The street address of a business in Hill Valley. Emmett Brown read an ad for this company in a 1991 newspaper help-wanted section while trying to find a job. The address was 25 Carson, and the contact person listed was named Mel [**BFAN-12**].

    NOTE: *The name of Mel's company was obstructed from view.*

- **2634:** The number of a check for $1,182,000, issued in 1958 by City Trust and Savings Bank for Biff Tannen's first winnings in the Bifforrific timeline, after he began betting at the Valley Racing Association using sporting-event results listed in *Grays Sports Almanac*. The check was issued from the bank's main branch, located at the corner of Third and Main. It was signed by Tim Matthews, and was drawn on account #1223 098 541 04290 327 486 [**BTF2**].

- **27th Floor:** A level at Biff Tannen's Pleasure Paradise, a high-rise casino in Biffhorrific 1985. In that reality, Biff lived in the building's penthouse apartment on the 27th floor, with his wife, Lorraine [**BTF2**].

- **2920 Pearl Street:** Biff Tannen's street address in 1967, which he shared with his pet German Shepherd, Chopper. The small tract house had an attached garage and a picket fence [**BTF2-s1**].

- **2980 Monroe Avenue:** *See* 1646 Riverside Drive

- **299-6-4484:** The Hilldale phone number of Marty

and Jennifer McFly in 2015 [**BTF2-s1**].

- **2BAK869:** The license plate number of Marty McFly's Toyota SR5 4x4 [**BTF2**].

- **2E71376:** The license plate number of a tow truck that transported George McFly's damaged Plymouth Reliant to an impoundment center after Biff Tannen had an alcohol-related accident while driving the car [**BTF1**].

- **2H67820:** The license plate number of a white van in Hill Valley used by the 1985 re-election campaign of Mayor Goldie Wilson [**BTF1**].

- **2 left, 8 right, 18 left, 32 right:** The combination to a locker at the Citizen Plus Ward, in Citizen Brown's dystopian timeline. Marty McFly's guitar and other belongings were stored within this locker during his incarceration at that facility [**TLTL-4**].

- **2nd:** *See* Second Street

- **301 South Street:** The address of Hanley Park Cemetery in Biffhorrific 1985 [**BTF2-s1**].

- **3:15:** A scheduled stop of the Cheyenne Express in Hill Valley, during the late 1800s. In 1875, outlaw Thaddeus Tannen tied Genevieve Parker to the tracks of this train stop, forcing her husband, Wendel Parker, to sign over the deed to their home, the Parker BTQ Ranch [**BFAN-16**].

- **320:** The suite address of ACI, a business located at 17100 Pioneer Boulevard, in Artesia, California, 90701 [**BFAN-12**].

- **3345:** The street address of IG Systems, a business located in Los Angeles, California [**BFAN-12**].

- **33559:** A portion of the license plate number of a car belonging to Reginald, the drummer of Marvin Berry and the Starlighters [**BTF1**].

    NOTE: *The two characters at the beginning of the number were obscured by shadow.*

- **3563:** Irving "Kid" Tannen's mugshot number following his arrest by Officer Danny Parker in 1931. This number appeared on a plaque bearing Tannen's card used by Emmett Brown to compile data for his Mental Alignment Meter [**TLTL-4**].

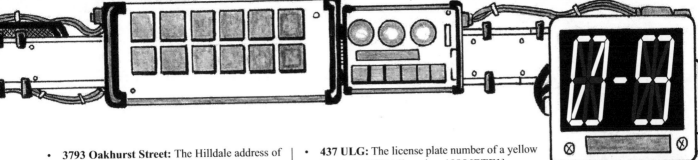

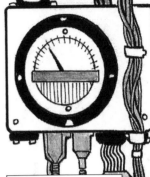

- **3793 Oakhurst Street:** The Hilldale address of Marty and Jennifer McFly in 2015 [**BTF2**].

  NOTE: In BTTF2's draft-one screenplay, the address given was 1131 Park Lane.

- **3B:** Emmett Brown's apartment number at 1191 South Kelsey in 1944. The residence was located above a gas station [**BFAN-17**].

- **3-D:** A member of Biff Tannen's gang, along with Match and Joey ("Skinhead"). 3-D and his friends often trailed Biff, following his lead in bullying and intimidating others, including George McFly [**BTF1, BTF2**]. His nickname derived from his tendency to wear three-dimensional cinematic glasses [**BTF1-n**].

  When Biff took a disliking to Marty McFly (who was stranded in 1955), 3-D and his fellow goons helped Biff try to run Marty over with a car. This resulted in the vehicle hitting a manure truck, and the four thugs being buried in animal dung. During the chase, 3-D saw Marty construct a 1980s skateboard from a child's wood-crate scooter, and decided to steal the idea and market it as a toy called a Roller Board [**BTF1-s4**].

  In Biffhorrific 1985, in which Biff Tannen was wealthy and corrupt, 3-D remained at Biff's side, along with Skinhead and Match, serving as his major enforcers [**BTF2**].

  NOTE: Though 3-D was not named onscreen, his nickname appeared in BTTF1's credits, fourth-draft screenplay and novelization. The first three script drafts called him Gums, as he lacked his two front teeth.

  It is unknown whether 3-D's plan to "invent" the skateboard panned out.

- **3D 22 30:** The license number of a vehicle parked outside the Sisters of Mercy Soup Kitchen when Marty McFly visited that establishment in 1931 [**TLTL-1**].

- **3N 48679:** The license plate number of a car in the neighborhood of George McFly's family, circa 1955 [**BTF1**].

  NOTE: Since the vehicle was parked in front of George's home, it may have belonged to the McFlys.

- **4,200 rads:** *See* 1.21 jigowatts

- **437 ULG:** The license plate number of a yellow Honda in Hill Valley, circa 1985 [**BTF1**].

- **4401:** The street address of KCET, a business in Los Angeles, California. The company was located at 4401 Sunset [**BFAN-12**].

- **444:** The street address of Pakk, a business located in Boston, Massachusetts, circa 1897 [**BFAN-8**].

- **46800 40203 64600 00203:** The bar-code number of Marty McFly's CusCo Industries employee credit card in 2015, which he used to complete an illegal transaction with Douglas J. Needles, resulting in Marty being fired from his job. This same bar-code number appeared on a retail receipt that Marty received after purchasing *Grays Sports Almanac: Complete Sports Statistics 1950-2000* at Blast From the Past [**BTF2**].

- **4S 28359:** The license plate number of a red automobile owned by an elderly couple in 1955. Marty McFly requested roadside help from the couple after becoming stranded in their era. However, the husband—a man named Wilbur—refused to stop, due to his wife's panicking at the sight of Marty's futuristic radiation suit [**BTF1**].

- **4x4:** *See* SR5 4x4

- **501:** The suite address of IG Systems, a business located in Los Angeles, California, at 3345 Wilshire [**BFAN-12**].

- **5253:** The identification number of a green police car, license plate number 814692, on the back of which Marty McFly hitched a skateboard ride to school in 1985 [**BTF1**].

- **555-4823:** The telephone number of Jennifer Parker's grandmother, circa 1985 [**BTF1**].

  NOTE: In BTTF1's novelization, the number was 243-8480. Onscreen, the number conformed to Hollywood's frequent use of the "555" prefix for fictitious phone numbers.

- **555-FLUX:** A telephone number used by Walter Wisdom as part of a scheme to sell Emmett Brown's DeLorean—which the fraudulent scientist had stolen—on television, for $999,995. The last four digits referred to the vehicle's Flux Capacitor [**BFAN-15**].

CODE	STORY
NIKE	*BTTF*-themed TV commercial: Nike
NTND	Nintendo *Back to the Future—The Ride* Mini-Game
PIZA	*BTTF*-themed TV commercial: Pizza Hut
PNBL	Data East *BTTF* pinball game
REAL	Real life
RIDE	Simulator: *Back to the Future—The Ride*
SCRM	2010 Scream Awards: *Back to the Future* 25th Anniversary Reunion (broadcast)
SCRT	2010 Scream Awards: *Back to the Future* 25th Anniversary Reunion (trailer)
SIMP	Simulator: *The Simpsons Ride*
SLOT	*Back to the Future Video Slots*
STLZ	Unused *BTTF* footage of Eric Stoltz as Marty McFly
STRY	*Back to the Future Storybook*
TEST	Screen tests: Crispin Glover, Lea Thompson and Tom Wilson
TLTL	Telltale Games' *Back to the Future—The Game*
TOPS	Topps' *Back to the Future II* trading-card set
TRIL	*BTTF: The Official Book of the Complete Movie Trilogy*
UNIV	Universal Studios Hollywood promotional video

SUFFIX	MEDIUM
-b	*BTTF2*'s Biff Tannen Museum video (extended)
-c	Credit sequence to the animated series
-d	Film deleted scene
-n	Film novelization
-o	Film outtake
-p	1955 phone book from *BTTF1*
-v	Video game print materials or commentaries
-s1	Screenplay (draft one)
-s2	Screenplay (draft two)
-s3	Screenplay (draft three)
-s4	Screenplay (draft four)
-sp	Screenplay (production draft)
-sx	Screenplay (*Paradox*)

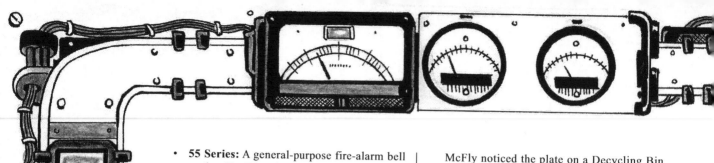

- **55 Series:** A general-purpose fire-alarm bell produced by Edwards Signaling [**REAL**]. Emmett Brown used such an alarm as a telephone ringer at his home in 1985 [**BTF1**].

    NOTE: The use of a "55" alarm bell in BTTF1's opening scenes foreshadowed Marty McFly's adventures in 1955.

- **56:** Biff Tannen's jersey number during his high school senior year, when he played for Hill Valley High School's football team. Since Biff repeated that year, he wore that number for an extended period of time [**BTF2-b**].

- **5A 71 09:** The license plate number of a Hill Valley Police Department vehicle into which Marty McFly nearly crashed the DeLorean in 1931. The police car, driven by Offcer Danny Parker, was involved in a shootout with a car full of gangsters, and the DeLorean's sudden arrival between the vehicles almost caused a pile-up [**TLTL-1**].

    NOTE: This same license plate number also appeared on a truck down the street from the police car.

- **6:** The street address of an apartment next to Hill Billiards, circa 1931 [**TLTL-1**].

- **61:** The team player number of Kelp, a dim-witted athlete who attended college with Marty McFly and Jennifer Parker [**BFAN-4**].

- **6-12-93-3:** The space-time coordinates of Steven Marble's workspace at the Institute of Future Technology's Anti-Gravitic Laboratory, where the scientist worked to develop a hoverbike [**RIDE**].

- **633CSI:** A model of BMW convertible sold in 2015. Griff Tannen owned such a car, the rear headlights of which he smashed while trying to hit Marty McFly with a baseball bat [**BTF2**].

- **65:** The speed limit of a road running outside Lyon Estates in 1955 [**BTF1**].

- **687523:** The ID number assigned to Biff Tannen during his incarceration at the Citizen Plus Ward, in Citizen Brown's dystopian timeline [**TLTL-4**].

- **6H 96472:** The 1955 license plate number of Biff Tannen's Ford Super Deluxe convertible [**BTF1, BTF2**], which Biff called Shiela. Marty

McFly noticed the plate on a Decycling Bin shelf in Citizen Brown's dystopian timeline, and used it to snap Biff out of his brainwashed state [**TLTL-3**].

- **6S 48405:** The license plate number of a motor vehicle belonging to Sam Baines in 1955. While spying on Sam's undressing daughter, Lorraine, George McFly fell to the ground from a nearby tree and was hit by this vehicle. After Marty McFly changed history by pushing George out of the way, Sam hit Marty instead [**BTF1**].

    NOTE: This same license number appeared on a car that had previously almost hit Marty as he entered Courthouse Square in 1955.

- **7-23-30:** A sequence of numbers written on a note underneath the bar of Irving "Kid" Tannen's speakeasy, El Kid, in 1931. Betting on those numbers at the bar's roulette wheel opened a secret passage leading to a nearby barber shop [**TLTL-2**].

- **726 BXG:** The license plate number of a blue Jeep CJ-7, on the back of which Marty McFly hitched a skateboard ride to school [**BTF1**].

- **733i:** A model of BMW produced in the 1980s [**REAL**]. After Marty McFly changed history by making his parents more successful, George McFly drove a BMW 733i [**BTF1**].

- **75 Ohm Matching Transformer:** A type of electrical device used to prevent speakers from exhibiting an undesirable mains hum due to a ground loop [**REAL**]. After traveling back to 1955, Marty McFly asked Emmett Brown if he had such a device, so that he could plug in his video camera. Given the different era, Doc did not understand the question [**BTF1-d**].

- **766825:** The license plate number of a crashed police car littering the streets of Lyon Estates in Biffhorrific 1985, in which the housing development was a slum area being bought up by Biff Tannen [**BTF2**].

- **788 West Spruce:** *See* 1646 Riverside Drive

- **7-Eleven:** An international chain of convenience stores [**REAL**]. A branch of 7-Eleven operated in Courthouse Square, circa 2015 [**BTF2**].

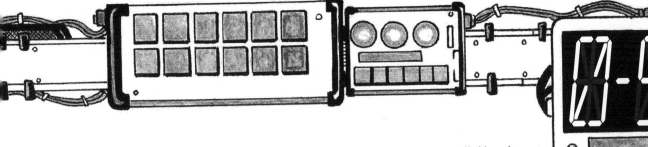

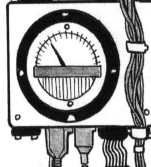

- **8:** The street address of Hill Billiards, circa 1931, which appeared on the pool hall's façade as a stylized eight-ball [**TLTL-1**].

- **814692:** The license plate number of a green police car, #5253, on the back of which Marty McFly hitched a skateboard ride in 1985 [**BTF1**].

- **818-500-3291:** The fax number of Computec, a business located in Glendale, California [**BFAN-12**].

- **818-500-8924:** The telephone number of Computec, a business located in Glendale, California [**BFAN-12**].

- **818-710-1800:** The toll-free San Fernando Valley, California, phone number of Steve Garfield, an employee of a business called THOR [**BFAN-12**].

  > *NOTE: This is a functioning telephone number for the Thor Agency, an actual employment company located in Calabasas, Calif.*

- **840-3851:** The telephone number of Biff's Automotive Detailing, circa 1985 [**BTF1**].

- **849-5680:** The telephone number of both Harry Kaven Realtor and The Third Eye, circa 1955 [**BTF1**].

  > *NOTE: Why both businesses shared the same phone number is unknown, but this could indicate they were owned by the same party.*

- **86 1147:** A number printed on a file folder outside Room 103 at the Citizen Plus Ward, in Citizen Brown's dystopian timeline [**TLTL-4**].

- **86 3258:** A number printed on a file folder outside Waiting Room Beta at the Citizen Plus Ward, in Citizen Brown's dystopian timeline [**TLTL-4**].

- **86 9014:** A number printed on a file folder outside Room 101 at the Citizen Plus Ward, in Citizen Brown's dystopian timeline [**TLTL-4**].

- **88 miles per hour:** The necessary speed to activate the Flux Capacitor in Emmett Brown's DeLorean. This velocity, when combined with 1.21 jigowatts of electricity—generated either by a nuclear reaction or via a bolt of lightning—

resulted in the car being propelled into the past or future [**BTF1**].

  > *NOTE: Adult Swim's TV series* Robot Chicken *spoofed this scenario in the sketch "87 MPH," in which Marty McFly was pulled over by police a mile short of achieving 88 miles per hour.*

- **88 Oriole Road, A6TB-94:** The street address of Douglas J. Needles, circa 2015 [**BTF2-n**].

  > *NOTE: Needles' address appeared on Marty McFly's vidphone as ending in "A6T." The novelization elaborated on this, adding "B-94."*

- **'86s:** A nickname describing the 1986 model of golf carts used by Hill Valley's populace in Citizen Brown's dystopian timeline. All of the town's citizens drove such vehicles, rather than cars or trucks [**TLTL-3**].

- **'89 Firebird Converter:** A model of Freeway Flyer converted from a classic Firebird automobile, in use circa 2015 [**BTF2**].

  > *NOTE: This name appeared in production materials included on BTTF2's Blu-ray release.*

- **'89 Mustang Converter:** A model of Freeway Flyer converted from a classic Mustang automobile, in use circa 2015 [**BTF2**].

  > *NOTE: This name appeared in production materials included on BTTF2's Blu-ray release.*

- **8H 25638:** The license plate number of a car belonging to a neighbor living across the street from Biff Tannen in 1955 [**BTF2**].

- **8L VX2:** The number of a license plate discarded in a Decycling Bin in Citizen Brown's dystopian timeline. This was on a nearby shelf as Marty McFly battled a brainwashed Biff Tannen [**TLTL-3**].

- **8N 39742:** The license plate number of Emmett Brown's cream-colored Packard in 1955. Marty McFly borrowed this car to convince George McFly to ask Lorraine Baines to the Enchantment Under the Sea Dance, and again when attending the dance himself [**BTF1**].

CODE	STORY
NIKE	*BTTF*-themed TV commercial: Nike
NTND	Nintendo *Back to the Future—The Ride* Mini-Game
PIZA	*BTTF*-themed TV commercial: Pizza Hut
PNBL	Data East *BTTF* pinball game
REAL	Real life
RIDE	Simulator: *Back to the Future—The Ride*
SCRM	2010 Scream Awards: *Back to the Future* 25th Anniversary Reunion (broadcast)
SCRT	2010 Scream Awards: *Back to the Future* 25th Anniversary Reunion (trailer)
SIMP	Simulator: *The Simpsons Ride*
SLOT	*Back to the Future Video Slots*
STLZ	Unused *BTTF* footage of Eric Stoltz as Marty McFly
STRY	*Back to the Future Storybook*
TEST	Screen tests: Crispin Glover, Lea Thompson and Tom Wilson
TLTL	Telltale Games' *Back to the Future—The Game*
TOPS	Topps' *Back to the Future II* trading-card set
TRIL	*BTTF: The Official Book of the Complete Movie Trilogy*
UNIV	Universal Studios Hollywood promotional video

SUFFIX	MEDIUM
-b	*BTTF2's* Biff Tannen Museum video (extended)
-c	Credit sequence to the animated series
-d	Film deleted scene
-n	Film novelization
-o	Film outtake
-p	1955 phone book from *BTTF1*
-v	Video game print materials or commentaries
-s1	Screenplay (draft one)
-s2	Screenplay (draft two)
-s3	Screenplay (draft three)
-s4	Screenplay (draft four)
-sp	Screenplay (production draft)
-sx	Screenplay (*Paradox*)

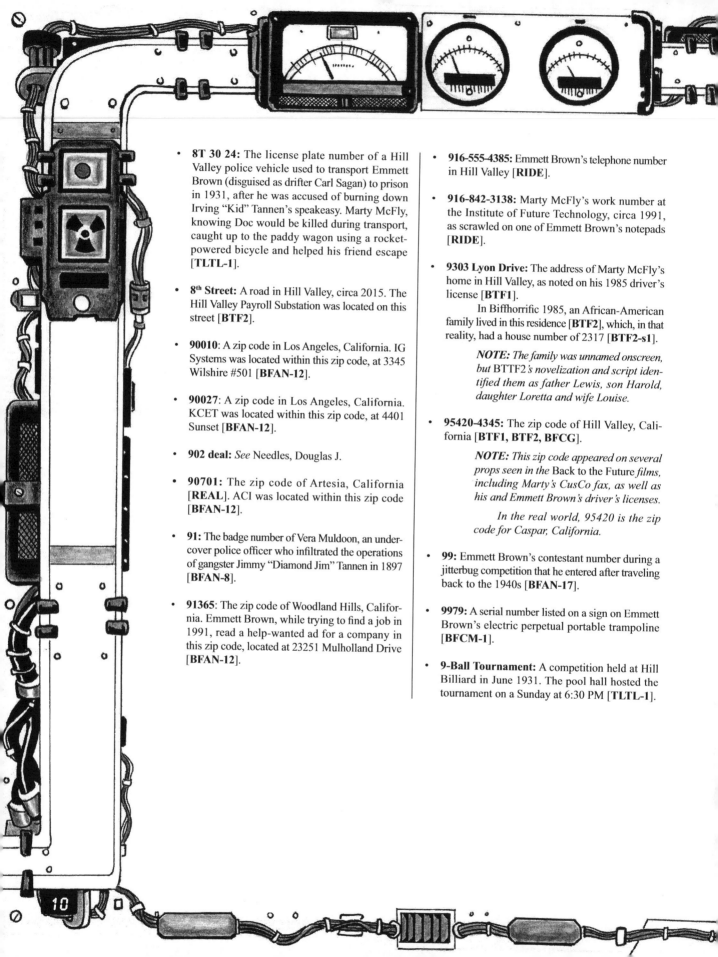

- **8T 30 24:** The license plate number of a Hill Valley police vehicle used to transport Emmett Brown (disguised as drifter Carl Sagan) to prison in 1931, after he was accused of burning down Irving "Kid" Tannen's speakeasy. Marty McFly, knowing Doc would be killed during transport, caught up to the paddy wagon using a rocket-powered bicycle and helped his friend escape [**TLTL-1**].

- **8th Street:** A road in Hill Valley, circa 2015. The Hill Valley Payroll Substation was located on this street [**BTF2**].

- **90010:** A zip code in Los Angeles, California. IG Systems was located within this zip code, at 3345 Wilshire #501 [**BFAN-12**].

- **90027:** A zip code in Los Angeles, California. KCET was located within this zip code, at 4401 Sunset [**BFAN-12**].

- **902 deal:** *See* Needles, Douglas J.

- **90701:** The zip code of Artesia, California [**REAL**]. ACI was located within this zip code [**BFAN-12**].

- **91:** The badge number of Vera Muldoon, an undercover police officer who infiltrated the operations of gangster Jimmy "Diamond Jim" Tannen in 1897 [**BFAN-8**].

- **91365:** The zip code of Woodland Hills, California. Emmett Brown, while trying to find a job in 1991, read a help-wanted ad for a company in this zip code, located at 23251 Mulholland Drive [**BFAN-12**].

- **916-555-4385:** Emmett Brown's telephone number in Hill Valley [**RIDE**].

- **916-842-3138:** Marty McFly's work number at the Institute of Future Technology, circa 1991, as scrawled on one of Emmett Brown's notepads [**RIDE**].

- **9303 Lyon Drive:** The address of Marty McFly's home in Hill Valley, as noted on his 1985 driver's license [**BTF1**].

  In Biffhorrific 1985, an African-American family lived in this residence [**BTF2**], which, in that reality, had a house number of 2317 [**BTF2-s1**].

  > ***NOTE:*** *The family was unnamed onscreen, but BTTF2's novelization and script identified them as father Lewis, son Harold, daughter Loretta and wife Louise.*

- **95420-4345:** The zip code of Hill Valley, California [**BTF1, BTF2, BFCG**].

  > ***NOTE:*** *This zip code appeared on several props seen in the* Back to the Future *films, including Marty's CusCo fax, as well as his and Emmett Brown's driver's licenses.*
  >
  > *In the real world, 95420 is the zip code for Caspar, California.*

- **99:** Emmett Brown's contestant number during a jitterbug competition that he entered after traveling back to the 1940s [**BFAN-17**].

- **9979:** A serial number listed on a sign on Emmett Brown's electric perpetual portable trampoline [**BFCM-1**].

- **9-Ball Tournament:** A competition held at Hill Billiard in June 1931. The pool hall hosted the tournament on a Sunday at 6:30 PM [**TLTL-1**].

AMPLIFIER

- **A:** A brand of alcohol served at the El Kid speakeasy in 1931 [**TLTL-2**].

- **A1-E15:** A number listed on a binder located at a monitoring station at the Citizen Plus Ward, in Citizen Brown's dystopian timeline [**TLTL-4**].

- **A1 Liquors:** A store in Hill Valley, circa 1986, that sold beer, liquor and wine. The shop was owned by a man named Mr. Figgins [**TLTL-1**].

- *Aaaargh! My Leg!*: A stunt-heavy movie helmed by Hollywood producer D.W. Tannen, filmed sometime in or before 1926 [**BFAN-11**].

  > *NOTE: Given that the first feature-length motion picture with synchronized dialogue sequences was* The Jazz Singer, *in 1927,* Aaaargh! My Leg! *was likely a silent film.*

- *Abbott and Costello Meet the Mummy*: A 1955 comedy film directed by Charles Lamont [**REAL**]. The Pohatchee Drive-in Theater listed this movie on its marquee that year [**BTF3**].

- **Abraham Jones, Junk Dealer:** A business in Hill Valley, circa 1952, run by an African-American teamster named Abraham Jones [**BTF1-s2**].

  > *NOTE: It's unknown whether Abraham Jones, Junk Dealer was connected to A. Jones Manure Hauling (from* BTTF3*) and D. Jones Manuring Hauling (from the first two films).*

- **Abrams Brokerage Company:** A business in Courthouse Square, circa 1985, that offered bail bonds, located near the intersection of Main Street and Hill Street. Marty McFly passed this company while hitching a skateboard ride to school [**BTF1**].

- **Access 12E:** A section of Skyway 35, a road for flying vehicles that passed through Hill Valley, circa 2015 [**RIDE**].

- *Accountant Weekly, The*: A magazine title that Marty McFly made up as a ruse to lure Arthur McFly (his grandfather) out of a gangster's safe house in 1931. After finding the building in which Artie was hidden, Marty claimed to be offering a free subscription to this publication [**TLTL-1**].

- **accu-lock:** A method used by drivers in 2015 to tail other vehicles without letting those drivers become aware of being followed [**BTF2-s1**].

- **ACI:** A business located at 17100 Pioneer Boulevard, Suite 320, in Artesia, California, 90701. In 1991, Emmett Brown read a help-wanted ad for this company. Its telephone number was 213-865-0735. The position posted was for a programmer/analyst [**BFAN-12**].

- **Acme.com:** A company at which a nerdy IT worker named TechFly worked in 2001, where he faced technological setbacks due to faulty Microsoft software, and endured bullying from his manager, Mister Biff. Robert L. Muglia, Microsoft's senior vice-president, witnessed TechFly's poor working conditions after traveling back in time with Emmett Brown in order to gain insights into Microsoft's failures [**MSFT**].

  > *NOTE: Acme Corp., featured in Warner Bros.' Wile E. Coyote and Road Runner cartoons, is a fictional manufacturer of outlandish products that inevitably fail at the worst moments. In the real world, Acme.com is a Web site run by ACME Laboratories.*

- **Acme Anti-Gravity Inc.:** A business located in Hill Valley, circa 2585 [**BFCL-1**].

- *Acme Robotics*: A scientific journal, a page of which hung in the lab of Emmett Brown [**BFCM-1**].

  > *NOTE: The page in question was reminiscent of a* Playboy *magazine centerfold, with a robot striking an erotic pose.*

- **Adaline's:** A business in Hill Valley, circa 1885 [**BTF3**].

- **Adods:** A sportswear manufacturer in an alternate 1986. In that timeline, Biff Tannen and his brothers, Cliff and Riff, wore Adods running suits [**TLTL-2**].

  > *NOTE: This company was named after German sports clothing maker Adidas.*

- **aerial acceleration cable:** A component of 21st-century flying vehicles. When Emmett Brown's DeLorean was shot while evading police in Biffhorrific 1985, the aerial acceleration cable was damaged, preventing the vehicle from reaching 88 miles per hour and attaining time travel [**BTF2-s1**].

- **aerial-nav circuit chip:** A component of Emmett Brown's DeLorean time circuits [**BTF3-s1**].

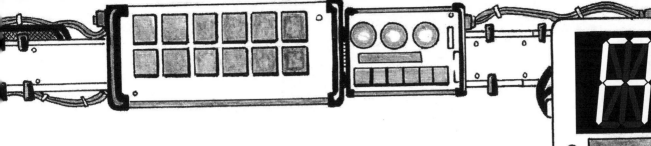

- **aerodynamic kits:** A service offered at Texaco's Hill Valley gas station, circa 2015, for use with flying vehicles [**BTF2**].

- **Aero-Mobile:** A type of flying car designed by Emmett Brown [**BTF1-s1**].

   > *NOTE: Mentioned in BTTF1's initial-draft screenplay, this was a precursor to the flying DeLorean seen onscreen. The second draft changed the spelling to "Aeromobile."*

   > *Episode 2 of Telltale Games' video game introduced another of Doc's flying vehicles, the Rocket Car, which he conceived in 1931. This may imply Doc was responsible for the widespread use of flying cars by 2015.*

- **Afton:** A neighborhood in Hill Valley, circa 2015, as indicated on a Courthouse Square map. A local hover-bus route, Q23-A6-1, passed through Hilldale and Afton [**BTF2**].

- **Agent Brown:** A chemical-warfare compound proposed in 1955, named after Emmett Brown. Doc's boss at the time, Dean Wooster, requested that Emmett help him and colleagues Cooper and Mintz develop the compound, but he refused [**BTF3-s1**].

- **Agnes:** A citizen of Hill Valley in Citizen Brown's dystopian timeline. A rebellious sort, Agnes risked reprisals by joking that she hoped the courthouse would be struck by lightning. George McFly spied on her conversations for the government via video monitors in his home [**TLTL-3**].

- **Agro-Waste Fuel Conversion System:** An invention of Emmett Brown that transformed ordinary manure into clean-burning fuel pellets. A single marble-sized pellet could heat a typical house for an entire winter, but the odor was overwhelming [**RIDE**].

- **Agro-Waste Manure:** A type of fertilizer created by the Agro-Waste Fuel Conversion System. The Institute of Future Technology had a supply of this substance in its Anti-Gravitic Laboratory [**RIDE**].

- **"Ain't We Got Fun?":** A foxtrot published in 1921, with music by Richard A. Whiting and lyrics by Raymond B. Egan and Gus Kahn [**REAL**].

Lounge singer Sylvia "Trixie Trotter" Miskin sang this tune at the El Kid speakeasy in 1931, accompanied by "Cue Ball" Donnely on piano. This song put Officer Danny Parker—who was emotionally inspired by Trotter's musical talents—in the mood to party [**TLTL-2**].

- **Airborne Personal Transport Device:** A flying vehicle conceived by Emmett Brown in an alternate 1931, as a follow-up to a previous failed invention known as the Rocket Car. This vehicle was powered by super-ionized static electricity [**TLTL-4**].

- **Airlock 7:** An entryway permitting the passage of people into and out of Robot City, a domed station in the Asteroid Belt of Earth's solar system, circa 2585 [**BFCL-1**].

- **Airplane Flight Pilot Facsimulation Level 1:** A video game simulation created by Emmett Brown, and programmed into his ELB Life-on-the-Edge Facsimulator, with simultions for low-altitude flights, dogfights and other aeronautic scenarios. While playing out this level, Doc was badly burned when his simulated aircraft crashed—an indication that the program was a bit too realistic [**BFAN-19**].

- **Air Traffic Control:** An agency in 2015 Hill Valley that directed the flow of flying vehicles through the air [**BTF2-sx**].

- **A. Jones Manure Hauling:** A business operating in Hill Valley, circa 1885 [**BTF3**], and a predecessor of 20th-century company D. Jones Manure Hauling [**BTF1, BTF2**].

   > *NOTE: It's unknown whether A. Jones and D. Jones were connected to Abraham Jones, Junk Dealer, mentioned in BTTF1's second-draft screenplay.*

- **Al:** An employee at a Hill Valley barber shop, circa 1931, who was associated with gangster Irving "Kid" Tannen [**TLTL-1**].

- **Ales, Richard, Professor:** An employee at the Institute of Future Technology [**RIDE**].

   > *NOTE: This individual, identified on signage outside Back to the Future: The Ride, was named after an executive at Universal Studios.*

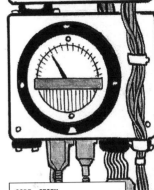

CODE	STORY
NIKE	*BTTF*-themed TV commercial: Nike
NTND	Nintendo *Back to the Future—The Ride* Mini-Game
PIZA	*BTTF*-themed TV commercial: Pizza Hut
PNBL	Data East *BTTF* pinball game
REAL	Real life
RIDE	Simulator: *Back to the Future—The Ride*
SCRM	2010 Scream Awards: *Back to the Future 25th Anniversary Reunion* (broadcast)
SCRT	2010 Scream Awards: *Back to the Future 25th Anniversary Reunion* (trailer)
SIMP	Simulator: *The Simpsons Ride*
SLOT	*Back to the Future Video Slots*
STLZ	Unused *BTTF* footage of Eric Stoltz as Marty McFly
STRY	*Back to the Future Storybook*
TEST	Screen tests: Crispin Glover, Lea Thompson and Tom Wilson
TLTL	Telltale Games' *Back to the Future—The Game*
TOPS	Topps' *Back to the Future II* trading-card set
TRIL	*BTTF: The Official Book of the Complete Movie Trilogy*
UNIV	Universal Studios Hollywood promotional video

SUFFIX	MEDIUM
-b	*BTTF2's* Biff Tannen Museum video (extended)
-c	Credit sequence to the animated series
-d	Film deleted scene
-n	Film novelization
-o	Film outtake
-p	1955 phone book from *BTTF1*
-v	Video game print materials or commentaries
-s1	Screenplay (draft one)
-s2	Screenplay (draft two)
-s3	Screenplay (draft three)
-s4	Screenplay (draft four)
-sp	Screenplay (production draft)
-sx	Screenplay (*Paradox*)

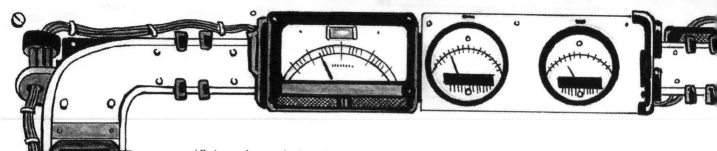

- **Ali:** An employee at the Crestview Service Center. One day, Ali and three other auto mechanics shared Bud Light beers while on break, speculating about what they would do if able to time-travel. Ali indicated he would invent fire and then copyright it, while another worker, Kidus, said he would travel to the past and murder his father.

   As they discussed the topic, Emmett Brown's flying DeLorean appeared on a nearby lift. Kidus suddenly vanished upon vowing patricide, having erased himself from history due to never having been born, and the DeLorean disappeared a moment later. Due to the temporal alteration, the others' knowledge of Kidus' existence was retroactively erased [**BUDL**].

- *Aliens Who I Have Known & Loved*: The autobiography of Biff Tannen, describing what he believed to have been a visit from extraterrestrials in 1967—though the "aliens" were actually Marty McFly and Jules and Verne Brown in disguise, aboard the flying DeLorean [**BFAN-23**].

   NOTE: In keeping with Biff Tannen's usual motif, the book's title was grammatically incorrect.

- **All Citizen's Bank:** A business in Courthouse Square in Citizen Brown's dystopian timeline [**TLTL-3**].

- **Allen, Marilyn:** An employee at the Institute of Future Technology, in charge of priority clearances [**RIDE**].

   NOTE: This individual, identified on signage outside Back to the Future: The Ride, *was named after an employee at Universal Studios.*

- **All-Natural Overhaul:** A service offered by rejuvenation clinics (a type of business popular in 2015, at which customers could restore their lost youth). Emmett Brown visited such a clinic while living in that era, and received an All-Natural Overhaul, consisting of skin-wrinkle removal, hair repair, blood changing, and the replacement of his spleen and colon, thereby adding 30 or 40 years to his life [**BTF2**].

- **Allosaurus:** A large theropod dinosaur from the late Jurassic period, approximately 155 to 150 million years ago [**REAL**].

   When Emmett, Jules and Verne Brown inadvertently prevented the extinction of the dinosaurs, changing history so that such species replaced mankind as Earth's dominant animal lifeform, the trio later discovered Allosauruses among those living in the altered 20th century. One individual, a police officer named Tannen, bore an uncanny resemblance to Biff Tannen [**BFAN-3, BFCM-2**]. In that reality, Hill Valley was known as Dinocity [**BFHM**].

   NOTE: The officer's name, not spoken onscreen, appeared in the comic book adaptation of the episode "Forward to the Past."

- **Allstate Insurance:** A U.S.-based personal line insurer [**REAL**] that maintained an office in Courthouse Square, as early as 1955 and at least until 1985 [**BTF1**].

- **Al's Tattoo & Art Studio:** A business that operated in Hill Valley until sometime in or before 1955, when it relocated to Burbank. By 1955, its windows were painted over, with the messages "Out of Business" and "Al Has Moved—So Long, Hill Valley" scrawled on the glass, as well as a "For Sale" sign from Harry Kaven Realtor [**BTF1**].

- **Alt:** A brand of caffeinated beverage sold in Citizen Brown's dystopian timeline [**TLTL-4**].

   NOTE: Alt's logo design was similar to that of Tab, a diet soft drink produced by Coca-Cola Co. (See also entry for Tab.)

   In Microsoft's Windows platform, a combination of the Alt and Tab keyboard strokes enables a user to alternate between windows and tasks—just as a time traveler alternates between realities.

- **Amazine Barcanine:** A business or brand name advertised on a billboard during an 1897 National League pennant game between the Baltimore Orioles and the Boston Beaneaters [**BFAN-8**].

   NOTE: The store's sign was difficult to read; as such, this spelling might not be entirely accurate.

- *Amazing Spider-Man, The*: An American comic book series published by Marvel Comics from 1963 to present [**REAL**]. After Emmett Brown inadvertently changed time so that dinosaurs never became extinct, a dino-version of the comic was apparently still published, featuring a reptilian analog of the fictional superhero [**BFCM-2**].

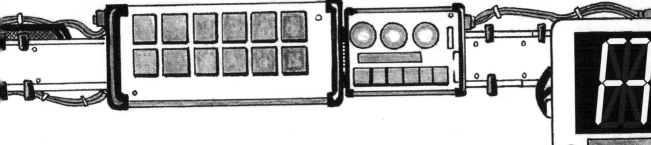

- **Amazing Stories:** An American science fiction magazine founded by Experimenter Publishing in 1926, which remained in print until 2005 [**REAL**]. While attending high school, George McFly read the October-November 1953 issue of this publication, featuring "The Big Tomorrow," by Paul Lohrman, as well as other works by H.L. Gold, R.W. Krepps, Richard Matheson, Robert Sheckley and Vern Fearing [**BTF1**].

- **Amazon Jungle:** A moist broadleaf rainforest covering most of South America's Amazon Basin, lush with a wide variety of plant and animal life [**REAL**].

  When Marty McFly was afflicted with athlete's foot fungus, he and Emmett Brown journeyed into the jungle's past, in 1532, to procure a *Bufo marinus*—an extinct toad that secreted a curative acidic substance from its sweat glands. In so doing, they encountered Spanish conquistador Capitan Biffando de la Tanén, an ancestor of Biff Tannen who sought the legendary City of Gold [**BFAN-7a**].

  Doc later revisited the rainforest to research the depletion of banana plants and other flora [**BFAN-20**].

  > *NOTE: In reality, the* Bufo marinus *is not extinct.*

- **American Civil War:** A war fought on U.S. soil from 1861 to 1865, when eleven Southern slave states, led by Jefferson Davis, seceded to form the Confederate States of America. The federal government, supported by 25 states known collectively as the Union, fought until the Confederates surrendered, and slavery was outlawed [**REAL**].

  In 1864, the Confederate forces of General Beauregard Tannen were wiped out by Union soldiers commanded by General Ulysses S. Clayton—until Jules and Verne Brown changed time by convincing both sides to shake hands and embrace peace, thereby preventing bloodshed [**BFAN-1**].

- **American College of Technological Science & Difficult Math (ACTS&DM):** A university for gifted students of science. While attending this college, Emmett Brown was the roommate and fraternity brother of Walter Wisdom. Their close bond ended, however, during the Inter-Collegiate Science Invent-Off, in which students competed by submitting their latest inventions. Doc entered

the Perpetual-Motion Hula Hoop, which utilized a battery and internal gyros to eliminate stress and injuries, while Wisdom created a Doggie-Diaper to prevent lawn and sidewalk cleanup. Jealous of Doc's invention, Walter claimed it as his own and attained great fame and fortune [**BFAN-15**].

> *NOTE: Doc referred to the university as the plural "American College of Technological Sciences & Difficult Math," but a sign at the school's front gate used the singular form, "Science."*

- **American Inquirer:** A tabloid newspaper published in 1992. After being brought to life from the video game *BraveLord and Monstrux*, the demon Monstrux greatly enjoyed this magazine—as snack food, not as reading material [**BFAN-19**].

  > *NOTE: The newspaper's name was based on that of the* National Enquirer.

- **American Legion Auxiliary:** a U.S.-based, non-profit patriotic service organization for female volunteers [**REAL**] that operated a chapter in Hill Valley [**BTF1**].

- **American Psychiatry:** A magazine published circa 1931, a copy of which Emmett Brown had in his laboratory, which he used as research for his Mental Alignment Meter [**TLTL-4**]. The April 1931 issue featured a cover story titled "Unlocking the Secrets of the Mind" [**TLTL-5**].

- **American Tourister:** A popular brand of suitcase [**REAL**]. Emmett Brown owned an American Tourister suitcase, which he planned to bring with him on the DeLorean's maiden time-travel voyage. The arrival of Libyan terrorists caused Marty McFly to make the trip instead, however, resulting in Marty's arrival in 1955 with Doc's suitcase in tow. Among its contents: a hairdryer that Marty used to intimidate George McFly into asking Lorraine Baines to the Enchantment Under the Sea Dance [**BTF1-s4**].

- **amplifier:** An electronic device designed to increase the loudspeaker volume of an electric or acoustic guitar, as well as modify tone by adding electronic effects and emphasizing or de-emphasizing particular frequencies [**REAL**].

  Emmett Brown kept a giant amplifier in his garage home, which Marty McFly used to practice his guitar. When Marty set all of the gauges on maximum, an overload in its circuits sent the

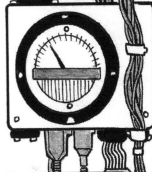

CODE	STORY
NIKE	*BTTF*-themed TV commercial: Nike
NTND	Nintendo *Back to the Future—The Ride* Mini-Game
PIZA	*BTTF*-themed TV commercial: Pizza Hut
PNBL	Data East *BTTF* pinball game
REAL	Real life
RIDE	Simulator: *Back to the Future—The Ride*
SCRM	2010 Scream Awards: *Back to the Future* 25th Anniversary Reunion (broadcast)
SCRT	2010 Scream Awards: *Back to the Future* 25th Anniversary Reunion (trailer)
SIMP	Simulator: *The Simpsons Ride*
SLOT	*Back to the Future Video Slots*
STLZ	Unused *BTTF* footage of Eric Stoltz as Marty McFly
STRY	*Back to the Future Storybook*
TEST	Screen tests: Crispin Glover, Lea Thompson and Tom Wilson
TLTL	Telltale Games' *Back to the Future—The Game*
TOPS	Topps' *Back to the Future II* trading-card set
TRIL	*BTTF: The Official Book of the Complete Movie Trilogy*
UNIV	Universal Studios Hollywood promotional video

SUFFIX	MEDIUM
-b	*BTTF2*'s Biff Tannen Museum video (extended)
-c	Credit sequence to the animated series
-d	Film deleted scene
-n	Film novelization
-o	Film outtake
-p	1955 phone book from *BTTF1*
-v	Video game print materials or commentaries
-s1	Screenplay (draft one)
-s2	Screenplay (draft two)
-s3	Screenplay (draft three)
-s4	Screenplay (draft four)
-sp	Screenplay (production draft)
-sx	Screenplay (*Paradox*)

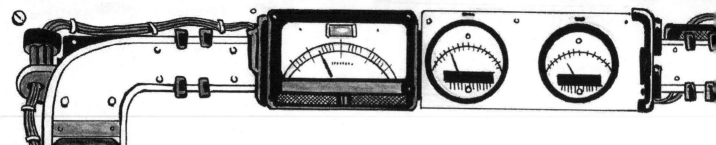

teen flying across the room [BTF1]. Marty later repaired the amplifier, with a great deal of effort [TLTL-1].

In Citizen Brown's dystopian timeline, a similar amplifier was utilized as part of Citizen Plus Program reconditioning [TLTL-4].

- **Anderson Sisters, The:** A singing group that traveled with the United Service Organizations (USO) to help raise U.S. troop morale during World War II, along with emcee Bobby Dawson and comedian Jerry "Odie" Cologne. The sisters—a redhead, a blonde and a brunette—finished each other's sentences while speaking. The brunette had a decidedly masculine voice [BFAN-17].

  NOTE: This trio was drawn to resemble The Andrews Sisters, a close-harmony singing group of the swing and boogie-woogie eras that frequently performed for U.S. soldiers.

- **Andrade, Claudia:** An ambiguous systems administrator at the Institute of Future Technology [RIDE].

  NOTE: This individual, identified on signage outside Back to the Future: The Ride, was named after a dispatcher in Universal Studios' Technical Services Department. It's unknown what being an "ambiguous systems administrator" entailed.

- **Andromeda Galaxy:** A spiral galaxy located 2.5 million light-years from Earth, also known as M31 [REAL]. Daphne, a mid-20s beatnik associate of Emmett Brown who sometimes attended parties thrown at the scientist's mansion in the 1950s, claimed to be from "the ninth system of the Andromeda Galaxy" [BTF1-s4].

- **Annual Convention of the Home Inventors and Mad Geniuses:** An event at which scientists could present their latest innovations. Emmett Brown presented his ELB Pediatric Policer at one such conference [BFAN-26].

- **Antanneny, Bifficus:** A burly ancestor of Biff Tannen who lived in ancient Rome, circa 36 A.D., under Emperor Tiberius Julius Caesar Augustus [BFAN-5, BFHM].

  When Marty McFly angered the Roman officer by spilling food on his tunic, Bifficus challenged Marty (who was traveling under the alias "Marticus") to a chariot race at the Circus Maximus, calling him an unus pullus ("chicken") and a "tuum de gluteus maximus" ("butthead"). Antanneny's powerful chariot, pulled by a pair of massive, blue horses, was covered in steel spikes.

  Realizing that Bifficus had to win in order for Caligula's rise and the Roman Empire's fall to occur as recorded, Emmett Brown advised Marty to purposely lose the race. Post-race, Antanneny asked Tiberius to feed Marty to the lions, but the time-travelers escaped in Doc's DeLorean, and the soldier fell into a barrel of manure [BFAN-5].

  NOTE: The emperor was not named onscreen, but in 36 A.D., the leader of the Roman Empire—and Caligula's predecessor—was Tiberius Julius Caesar Augustus.

- **Anthony:** A pseudonym that Marty McFly used while testing out the Personal Phone Helmet at the 1931 Hill Valley Exposition's House of Tomorrow exhibit. Assuming a false voice and the name Anthony, Marty dialed a nearby exhibit—the Phone Booth of the Future—and asked for Oliver Klozoff. Sylvia "Trixie Trotter" Miskin, who answered the phone, was not amused by the joke [TLTL-5].

  NOTE: This practical joke played on the phonetic similarity between Oliver Klozoff and the phrase "all of her clothes off."

- **Anti-Gravitic Laboratory:** Emmett Brown's personal lab at the Institute of Future Technology (IFT), located on Level 2, in Sector 2. Within this room, Doc produced a number of scientific innovations, including the Eight-Passenger DeLorean Time-Travel Vehicle [RIDE].

- **Anytown:** A U.S. city containing a hospital to which Mother Nature—a physical manifestation of nature's nurturing characteristics—was transported after falling ill in 1990. Concerned about her health, Emmett Brown traveled to the future and found that it would be grim if Mother Nature could not be saved. Returning to the past, the scientist rushed to the hospital's emergency room, where he shared his foreknowledge with Mother Nature's physician, Douglas "Doogie" Howser [ERTH].

  NOTE: This unusual crossover occurred in a 1990 video from Time Warner titled The Earth Day Special, in which celebrities, either in character or as themselves,

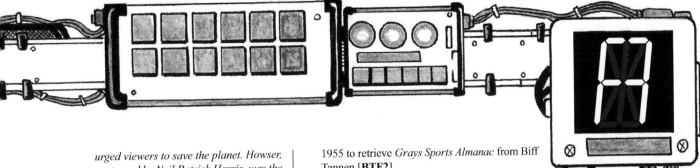

urged viewers to save the planet. Howser, portrayed by Neil Patrick Harris, was the title character of Doogie Howser, M.D., *an ABC television series airing from 1989 to 1993.*

- **Apatosaurus:** A genus of sauropod dinosaur, also called a Brontosaurus, that lived during the Jurassic Period, from approximately 154 million to 150 million years ago [**REAL**].

  While visiting prehistoric times to find something suitable to bring to school for show-and-tell, Verne Brown found an un-hatched Apatosaurus egg and brought it back with him to 1992, where it hatched and assumed Verne to be its mother. Verne and his brother, Jules Brown, named the animal Tiny [**BFAN-26**].

- **apian-powered aircraft:** An idea that Emmett Brown considered demonstrating at the 1931 Hill Valley Exposition, but ultimately rejected in favor of other innovations [**TLTL-v**].

  > *NOTE: Given the aircraft's designation, it would apparently have been powered by bees.*

- **Apocrypha:** The largest empire of North America, circa 2,991,299,129,912,991 A.D., located in former Canada and the northern United States. Apocrypha's queen offered Tannen the Barbarian great riches if he stole the Ruby Begonia for her.

  Tannen elicited help from Marty McFly and Emmett Brown in finding the jewel, in return for his assistance in freeing Doc's family from the queen's guards. When the trio delivered the ruby, however, they found the Browns well cared for, as the queen and Clara Clayton Brown had struck up a friendship [**BFCL-2**].

  > *NOTE: Many scientists believe Earth will cease to exist in approximately 7.6 billion years, with human life dying out within a billion years or so.*
  >
  > *The date "2,991,299,129,912,991" is "1992" (the year in which this* BTTF *comic book issue was published) in reverse, and repeated four times.*

- **Archer Space Patrol Walkie-Talkie:** A model of two-way citizens'-band (CB) transceivers sold by Radio Shack in the early 1980s [**REAL**]. Emmett Brown and Marty McFly used a set of these walkie-talkies to communicate while visiting

1955 to retrieve *Grays Sports Almanac* from Biff Tannen [**BTF2**].

- **Archimedes:** A horse belonging to Emmett Brown in 1885, during his time as a blacksmith in Hill Valley's Old West [**BTF3-sp, BTF3-n**]. Doc considered Archimedes his "trusty horse," and often rode this particular steed, such as while rescuing Clara Clayton from plummeting into the Shonash Ravine [**BTF3-n**].

  > *NOTE: Doc named the animal after Greek scientist and philosopher Archimedes of Syracuse.*

- **Arky, Mister:** Marty McFly's social-studies teacher at Hill Valley High School in 1985. A frustrated, embittered man of 55, Arky was paranoid about the looming threat of nuclear destruction and tried to instill that fear in his apathetic students. While visiting the 1950s, Marty briefly attended the younger Arky's class, where he discovered that the man was once energetic, dynamic and optimistic about the future, as disgusted with pessimism as he would later be with naïve optimism [**BTF1-s1, BTF1-s2, BTF1-n**].

  > *NOTE: By* BTTF1*'s third-draft screenplay, Mr. Arky was replaced by a woman called Mrs. Woods. Neither character appeared in the final version of the movie.*

- **Armstrong, Neil Alden:** An American astronaut and test pilot with the U.S. Air Force (USAF) and the National Aeronautics and Space Administration (NASA). The first person to set foot on the Moon, Armstrong commanded *Apollo 11*'s 1969 lunar landing [**REAL**]. Emmett Brown admired his work and kept a framed photograph of Armstrong in his home [**BTF1**].

- **Arnold:** A performing elephant in the Bob Brothers All-Star International Circus [**BFAN-18**].

- **Aroma Tanks:** A trio of containers attached to a Scent Dispenser used during the Personality Rebuild process utilized for Citizen Plus reconditioning, in Citizen Brown's dystopian timeline. The Scent Dispenser dispatched various substances into the air from the Aroma Tanks, in order to influence a person's reactions to stimuli. The tanks had a tendency to become clogged—a vulnerability that Marty McFly exploited while helping Emmett Brown escape from reconditioning [**TLTL-4**].

CODE	STORY
NIKE	*BTTF*-themed TV commercial: Nike
NTND	Nintendo *Back to the Future—The Ride* Mini-Game
PIZA	*BTTF*-themed TV commercial: Pizza Hut
PNBL	Data East *BTTF* pinball game
REAL	Real life
RIDE	Simulator: *Back to the Future—The Ride*
SCRM	2010 Scream Awards: *Back to the Future 25th Anniversary Reunion* (broadcast)
SCRT	2010 Scream Awards: *Back to the Future 25th Anniversary Reunion* (trailer)
SIMP	Simulator: *The Simpsons Ride*
SLOT	*Back to the Future Video Slots*
STLZ	Unused *BTTF* footage of Eric Stoltz as Marty McFly
STRY	*Back to the Future Storybook*
TEST	Screen tests: Crispin Glover, Lea Thompson and Tom Wilson
TLTL	Telltale Games' *Back to the Future—The Game*
TOPS	Topps' *Back to the Future II* trading-card set
TRIL	*BTTF: The Official Book of the Complete Movie Trilogy*
UNIV	Universal Studios Hollywood promotional video

SUFFIX	MEDIUM
-b	*BTTF2*'s Biff Tannen Museum video (extended)
-c	Credit sequence to the animated series
-d	Film deleted scene
-n	Film novelization
-o	Film outtake
-p	1955 phone book from *BTTF1*
-v	Video game print materials or commentaries
-s1	Screenplay (draft one)
-s2	Screenplay (draft two)
-s3	Screenplay (draft three)
-s4	Screenplay (draft four)
-sp	Screenplay (production draft)
-sx	Screenplay (Paradox)

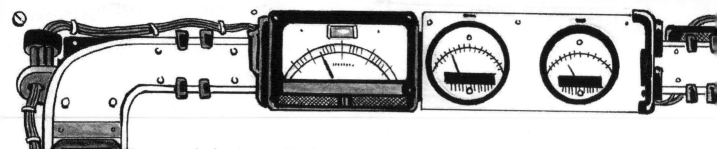

- **Arrigoni:** An Italian food and beverage manufacturer [**REAL**]. A pair of Italian teenagers, visiting the future in a time-traveling DeLorean, were amazed not by the futuristic marvels awaiting them, but rather by an Arrigoni vending machine, at which they stocked up on snacks and drinks before returning to the past. Their mother was equally amazed by their findings [**ARGN**].

- **Art Channel:** A television station in 2015 that broadcast ever-changing images of famous paintings, to serve as part of a home's décor [**BTF2-sx, BTF2-n**].

- **Artesia**: A city in California, zip code 90701. A business known as ACI was located in this city, at 17100 Pioneer Boulevard, Suite 320 [**BFAN-12**].

- **Art in Revolution:** A slogan on a jacket pin worn by Marty McFly in 1985 [**BTF1**].

- **Art's Yarn Barn:** A business located in Hill Valley, circa 1992, that sponsored a team competing in a bowling league at the Hill Valley Bowl-o-rama [**BFCL-3**].

- **Asimov, Isaac:** A renowned science fiction author who authored and edited more than 500 books during his lifetime [**REAL**]. Both Emmett Brown and George McFly were fans of his books [**TLTL-5**].

  Verne Brown referenced Asimov's works *Positronic Brain Surgery Made Easy*, "Robbie," *Robot Visions* and *I, Robot* while writing a school essay on the subject of robotics [**BFCL-1**].

  > *NOTE: The title* Positronic Brain Surgery Made Easy *is fictional, whereas the others are actual stories and novels written by Asimov.*

- **Asimov Library:** A public library located in Hill Valley, circa 2585 [**BFCL-1**].

  > *NOTE: Presumably, this library was named after writer Isaac Asimov.*

- **"Ask Edna":** An etiquette column published in the *Hill Valley Herald*, circa 1931, written by journalist Edna Strickland. The column doubled as a pro-temperance soapbox for Edna to speak out against liquor, organized crime and debauchery, as she believed the consumption of alcohol would inevitably lead to complete societal breakdown [**TLTL-1**].

- **Ask Mr. Foster:** An international travel agency. Its slogan: "Time to travel" [**REAL**]. The company operated an office in Courthouse Square as early as 1955, and at least until 1985 [**BTF1**].

- **Asparagus Tip O'Neil Pollo de Pope John Paul II Pie:** A menu item sold at Café 80's in 2015 [**BTF2**].

- **Assembly of Christ:** A church located in Courthouse Square, adjacent to Elmo's Ribs, and pastured by Reverend John Crump. Signs on the house of worship bore the mottos "Jesus Saves" and "Salvation Is Free." In 1985, while hitching a skateboard ride to school on the back of a Jeep CJ-7, Marty McFly passed this building. Later, upon returning from the past, he crashed Emmett Brown's DeLorean into the church's front wall [**BTF1**].

  > *NOTE: The church's name was based on that of Assemblies of God, a group of loosely-associated Pentecostal churches.*

- **Asterobotics:** A business located in Robot City, a domed station in the Asteroid Belt of Earth's solar system, circa 2585. The company provided positronic brain units [**BFCL-1**].

- **Asteroid Belt:** A region of Earth's solar system located between the orbits of Mars and Jupiter, occupied by numerous irregularly shaped minor planets (asteroids) [**REAL**].

  By 2585, mankind had established a domed station in the Asteroid Belt, known as Robot City, in which hundreds of robots served mankind by taking care of all manual labor so that humans could watch holovision programs. When Verne Brown showed an interest in robotics, Emmett Brown took their family on a journey to the 26th century, to visit Robot City so that Verne could see the technology in action [**BFCL-1**].

- *Astounding Science Fiction:* An American magazine later renamed *Analog Science Fiction and Fact* [**REAL**]. In 1955, George McFly enjoyed reading this publication [**BTF1**].

- **Atkins:** A city in the state of Nevada, in which the U.S. government performed aboveground atomic bomb testing in the 1950s. Emmett Brown and Marty McFly visited the base in 1952, hoping to harness a bomb blast's nuclear energy to power

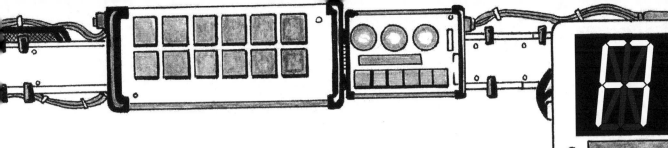

Doc's time machine and send Marty back to the future [**BTF1-s1**].

> *NOTE: The test-site sequence was cut from the final version of BTTF1 (the setting of which was changed to 1955), though storyboards were included as a Blu-ray extra. The first two script drafts set the base in the fictional Nevada city of Atkins, while the third moved it to New Mexico.*

- **Atlalanta:** *See* Atlantis

- **Atlantis:** A legendary island mentioned in Plato's dialogues, *Timaeus* and *Critias*, the existence of which has long been debated [**REAL**]. Emmett Brown had a travel sticker on his luggage bearing this fabled city's name, indicating he had visited Atlantis [**BFAN-9**].

  > *NOTE: The city's name first appeared onscreen misspelled as "Atlalanta," but was corrected in a subsequent shot to "Atlantis."*

- **Atlas:** A manufacturer that provided unbreakable and soundproof glass for the 1931 Hill Valley Exposition's House of Glass and Phone Booth of the Future exhibits [**TLTL-5**].

- **Atlas House of Glass:** A display at the 1931 Hill Valley Exposition. Presented by a company called Atlas, the House of Glass showcased a proposed modular living space for future families, along with a Future Furnishings display. During the event, the Emmett Brown from Citizen Brown's dystopian timeline kidnapped his younger self at the House of Glass in order to prevent Marty McFly from overwriting his version of history [**TLTL-5**].

- **Atmo-Processor:** A personal atmospheric enhancement unit created by Emmett Brown at the Institute of Future Technology, worn on a person's head and torso [**RIDE**].

  > *NOTE: This device was described on signage at Universal Studios' Back to the Future: The Ride.*

- **Atomic Gas:** *See* State Line Gas

- **Atomic Kid, The:** A 1954 black-and-white science fiction comedy starring Mickey Rooney and Robert Strauss, involving a uranium prospector accidentally exposed to radiation following an atomic bomb test [**REAL**].
  In 1955, Hill Valley's Essex Theater showed this film [**BTF1**], a screening of which Marty McFly attended while stranded in that year. He later deemed the movie to be "lame" [**BTF1-n**].

  > *NOTE: This movie's title was used as an in-joke referencing Marty's youth and the DeLorean's nuclear power source.*

- ***Atomic Science Weekly:*** A newspaper that Emmett Brown enjoyed reading [**BFCM-3**].

- **Atomic Wars, The:** A series of nuclear conflicts that Emmett Brown predicted would come to pass by the late 20th century. In 1955, upon seeing footage of his future self clad in a radiation suit, Doc assumed this to be due to fallout from the wars [**BTF1**].

- **AT&T:** An American multinational telecommunications corporation [**REAL**]. By 2015, AT&T still operated telephone booths in Hill Valley, and provided thumbprint ID systems for home security. Marty and Jennifer McFly used this function to secure their house, and also utilized AT&T as a home-telephone service provider [**BTF2**].

  > *NOTE: In the real world, phone booths became largely obsolete by the early 21st century, thanks to the advent of mobile phone services.*

- **Attel:** A manufacturer of hoverboards. Marty McFly used an Attel hoverboard to attach a trio of Flux Emitters to a time-traveling DeLorean stolen by Edna Strickland, so that Emmett Brown, flying overhead in a second car, could remotely control her vehicle [**TLTL-5**].

  > *NOTE: In the movies, the hoverboard was made by Mattel.*

- **Attila the Hun:** A despotic leader of the Hunnic Empire who led scourges across Europe throughout the fifth century [**REAL**]. P.T. Tannen's Villains Through History in Wax, an exhibit at the 1904 St. Louis World Exposition, contained a wax figure of his likeness, alongside statues of Ivan the Terrible and Bob the Nasty [**BFAN-25**].

- **Auto-Chef:** A robotic food-preparation device used in 2015. The ceiling-mounted appliance featured the face of a rotund, smiling chef, as well as

CODE	STORY
NIKE	*BTTF*-themed TV commercial: Nike
NTND	Nintendo *Back to the Future— The Ride* Mini-Game
PIZA	*BTTF*-themed TV commercial: Pizza Hut
PNBL	Data East *BTTF* pinball game
REAL	Real life
RIDE	Simulator: *Back to the Future—The Ride*
SCRM	2010 Scream Awards: *Back to the Future 25th Anniversary Reunion* (broadcast)
SCRT	2010 Scream Awards: *Back to the Future 25th Anniversary Reunion* (trailer)
SIMP	Simulator: *The Simpsons Ride*
SLOT	*Back to the Future Video Slots*
STLZ	Unused *BTTF* footage of Eric Stoltz as Marty McFly
STRY	*Back to the Future Storybook*
TEST	Screen tests: Crispin Glover, Lea Thompson and Tom Wilson
TLTL	Telltale Games' *Back to the Future—The Game*
TOPS	Topps' *Back to the Future II* trading-card set
TRIL	*BTTF: The Official Book of the Complete Movie Trilogy*
UNIV	Universal Studios Hollywood promotional video

SUFFIX	MEDIUM
-b	*BTTF2's* Biff Tannen Museum video (extended)
-c	Credit sequence to the animated series
-d	Film deleted scene
-n	Film novelization
-o	Film outtake
-p	1955 phone book from *BTTF1*
-v	Video game print materials or commentaries
-s1	Screenplay (draft one)
-s2	Screenplay (draft two)
-s3	Screenplay (draft three)
-s4	Screenplay (draft four)
-sp	Screenplay (production draft)
-sx	Screenplay (*Paradox*)

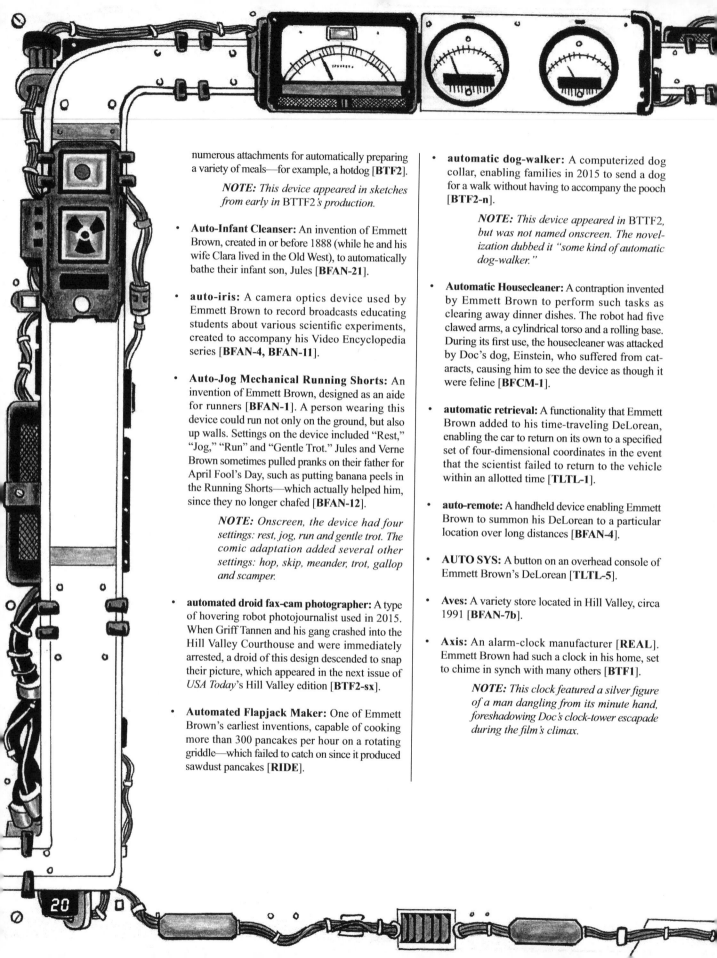

numerous attachments for automatically preparing a variety of meals—for example, a hotdog [**BTF2**].

> *NOTE: This device appeared in sketches from early in* BTTF2*'s production.*

- **Auto-Infant Cleanser:** An invention of Emmett Brown, created in or before 1888 (while he and his wife Clara lived in the Old West), to automatically bathe their infant son, Jules [**BFAN-21**].

- **auto-iris:** A camera optics device used by Emmett Brown to record broadcasts educating students about various scientific experiments, created to accompany his Video Encyclopedia series [**BFAN-4, BFAN-11**].

- **Auto-Jog Mechanical Running Shorts:** An invention of Emmett Brown, designed as an aide for runners [**BFAN-1**]. A person wearing this device could run not only on the ground, but also up walls. Settings on the device included "Rest," "Jog," "Run" and "Gentle Trot." Jules and Verne Brown sometimes pulled pranks on their father for April Fool's Day, such as putting banana peels in the Running Shorts—which actually helped him, since they no longer chafed [**BFAN-12**].

> *NOTE: Onscreen, the device had four settings: rest, jog, run and gentle trot. The comic adaptation added several other settings: hop, skip, meander, trot, gallop and scamper.*

- **automated droid fax-cam photographer:** A type of hovering robot photojournalist used in 2015. When Griff Tannen and his gang crashed into the Hill Valley Courthouse and were immediately arrested, a droid of this design descended to snap their picture, which appeared in the next issue of *USA Today*'s Hill Valley edition [**BTF2-sx**].

- **Automated Flapjack Maker:** One of Emmett Brown's earliest inventions, capable of cooking more than 300 pancakes per hour on a rotating griddle—which failed to catch on since it produced sawdust pancakes [**RIDE**].

- **automatic dog-walker:** A computerized dog collar, enabling families in 2015 to send a dog for a walk without having to accompany the pooch [**BTF2-n**].

> *NOTE: This device appeared in* BTTF2*, but was not named onscreen. The novelization dubbed it "some kind of automatic dog-walker."*

- **Automatic Housecleaner:** A contraption invented by Emmett Brown to perform such tasks as clearing away dinner dishes. The robot had five clawed arms, a cylindrical torso and a rolling base. During its first use, the housecleaner was attacked by Doc's dog, Einstein, who suffered from cataracts, causing him to see the device as though it were feline [**BFCM-1**].

- **automatic retrieval:** A functionality that Emmett Brown added to his time-traveling DeLorean, enabling the car to return on its own to a specified set of four-dimensional coordinates in the event that the scientist failed to return to the vehicle within an allotted time [TLTL-1].

- **auto-remote:** A handheld device enabling Emmett Brown to summon his DeLorean to a particular location over long distances [**BFAN-4**].

- **AUTO SYS:** A button on an overhead console of Emmett Brown's DeLorean [**TLTL-5**].

- **Aves:** A variety store located in Hill Valley, circa 1991 [**BFAN-7b**].

- **Axis:** An alarm-clock manufacturer [**REAL**]. Emmett Brown had such a clock in his home, set to chime in synch with many others [**BTF1**].

> *NOTE: This clock featured a silver figure of a man dangling from its minute hand, foreshadowing Doc's clock-tower escapade during the film's climax.*

BROWN, EMMETT

(LEFT, WITH CLARA, JULES AND VERNE)

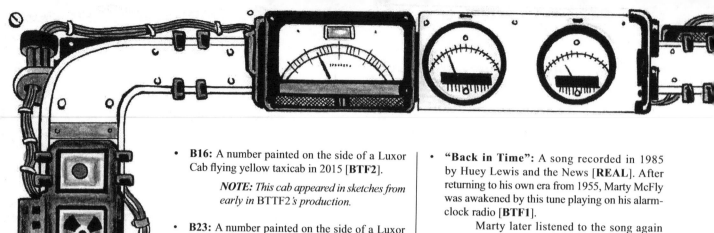

- **B16:** A number painted on the side of a Luxor Cab flying yellow taxicab in 2015 [**BTF2**].

  > *NOTE: This cab appeared in sketches from early in BTTF2's production.*

- **B23:** A number painted on the side of a Luxor Cab flying yellow taxicab in 2015 [**BTF2**].

  > *NOTE: This cab appeared in sketches from early in BTTF2's production.*

- **B25:** A number painted on the side of a Luxor Cab flying yellow taxicab in 2015. Biff Tannen hired this cab to follow Emmett Brown's DeLorean so he could steal the vehicle and alter history in his own favor [**BTF2**]. The driver of this cab, Fred, kept his pet parrot, Priscilla, with him in the car [**BTF2-n**].

- **B7:** A button on a security keypad used to access the Institute of Future Technology's Anti-Gravitic Laboratory [**RIDE**].

- **Babcock ("Old Buzzard"):** A college professor who taught a music-appreciation course attended by Marty McFly in 1991. The instructor gave Marty a C- on a test in this class, despite Marty having written an extra-credit report on the social significance of the Bonedaddys [**BFAN-4**].

- **Babs:** A pretty, brunette-haired friend of Lorraine Baines at Hill Valley High School, circa 1955. Lorraine, Babs and a third young woman, Betty, often hung out together [**BTF1, BTF2**].

  > *NOTE: This character was named in BTTF1's credits, script and novelization. In an early draft of that film's screenplay, Babs and Betty did not appear; instead, Lorraine (then called Eileen) hung out with a young woman named Madge.*

- **Baby Fist:** A punk-rock band in Citizen Brown's dystopian timeline. In that reality, Jennifer Parker wore a t-shirt emblazoned with the group's logo [**TLTL-3**].

- **Bacardi:** A popular brand of rum [**REAL**], among the alcoholic beverages stocked in Biff Tannen's penthouse bar in Biffhorrific 1985 [**BTF2**].

- **back-and-forth chair:** *See* rocking chair

- **"Back in Time":** A song recorded in 1985 by Huey Lewis and the News [**REAL**]. After returning to his own era from 1955, Marty McFly was awakened by this tune playing on his alarm-clock radio [**BTF1**].

  Marty later listened to the song again on a jukebook in Emmett Brown's abandoned laboratory, after the scientist vanished without a trace [**TLTL-1**].

  > *NOTE: Huey Lewis and the News recorded "Back in Time" specifically for the Back to the Future soundtrack. It was later used as the animated series' theme song.*

- ***Back to the Future***: A movie shown at the Hill Valley Theater in 1992 [**BFAN-22**].

  > *NOTE: It is unknown whether this is somehow the real BTTF movie or an unrelated film that happens to have the same name within the BTTF universe.*
  >
  > *Eric Stoltz was originally cast as Marty McFly, until being replaced by Michael J. Fox. The television series Fringe paid homage to this switch by featuring an alternate reality in which Stoltz starred in the film. It is unknown which actor starred in the version of Back to the Future existing within BTTF continuity, nor whether the movie featured McFly's exploits with Emmett Brown. (See also entries on Michael J. Fox, Alex P. Keaton, Taxi and Family Ties.)*

- **Bad Rap Bail Bonds:** A bail-bond dealer in Hill Valley, in Biffhorrific 1985 [**BTF2**].

- **Bailey, William:** A signature printed on the currency known as "Biff Bucks" [**BTF2**].

- **Baines, Eileen:** *See* McFly, Lorraine

- **Baines, Ellen:** A younger sister of Lorraine Baines, aunt of Marty McFly, and daughter of Sam and Stella Baines [**BTF2-s1**]. Stella was pregnant with Ellen when Marty McFly traveled back to 1955 and met the family in that era [**BTF1-s4, BTF1-n**].

  During the counterculture movement of the 1960s, Ellen found Hippie slang to be "groovy." A science fiction fan, she particularly enjoyed the TV series *Lost in Space* [**BTF2-s1**].

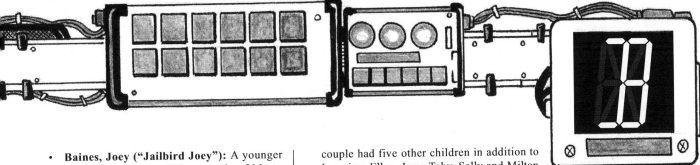

- **Baines, Joey ("Jailbird Joey"):** A younger brother of Lorraine Baines, uncle of Marty McFly, and son of Sam and Stella Baines [**BTF1, BTF2-s**].

    In 1985, "Jailbird" Joey was in prison, and failed to obtain his freedom despite several attempts at parole. When Marty traveled back to 1955, he learned that his toddler-aged uncle was happiest sitting in his playpen, so Marty's grandparents let him spend most of his time within its confines. Knowing the boy's later fate, Marty remarked that Joey should get used to being behind bars [**BTF1**]. In Biffhorrific 1985, Joey still ended up in prison [**BTF2**].

    By 2015, his incarceration status remained unchanged, though Lorraine continued to hold parties annually at parole time, hoping that her brother might one day be free [**BTF2-d**].

    ***NOTE:** Joey's crime has not been revealed.*

- **Baines, Lorraine:** *See* McFly, Lorraine

- **Baines, Milton ("Miltie"):** A younger brother of Lorraine Baines, uncle of Marty McFly, and son of Sam and Stella Baines. As a youth, Milton often donned a coonskin cap (popularized by the *Davy Crockett* installments of the television series *Walt Disney's Wonderful World of Color*), much to the frustration of his mother, who disliked when he wore it to the dinner table. When Marty traveled back to 1955, young Miltie was very impressed by Marty's claim that his family had two televisions—a rarity in the '50s [**BTF1-s4, BTF1-n**].

    ***NOTE:** In the film's novelization, Marty called the child Miltie, implying that was the name by which he knew his adult uncle. This was likely a reference to actor Milton Berle, also known as Uncle Miltie.*

- **Baines, Sally:** A younger sister of Lorraine Baines, aunt of Marty McFly, and daughter of Sam and Stella Baines [**BTF1-s4, BTF1-n, BTF2-s**]. In 1967, at age 19, Sally had friends named Jeanne and Mary Ann, with whom she went to see the film *To Sir, With Love*, starring Sidney Poitier [**BTF2-s1, BTF2-s2**].

- **Baines, Sam:** Marty McFly's maternal grandfather, and the mother of Marty's mother, Lorraine Baines. A gruff, no-nonsense man, he lived in Hill Valley with his wife, Stella. The couple had five other children in addition to Lorraine: Ellen, Joey, Toby, Sally and Milton [**BTF1, BTF2-s, BTF1-n, BTF2-s**].

    In 1955, Sam ran over George McFly with his car, after George fell into the street from a tree while spying on a disrobing Lorraine. Unaware of George's peeping activities, Sam brought the injured teen into his home, where Lorraine's nurturing personality caused her to develop feelings for him, and the two eventually wed and had children.

    When Marty traveled back to 1955, he inadvertently altered history by pushing George out of the way. Hence, Marty was struck by the car and nursed back to health instead, thus replacing George as the object of Lorraine's affections (and thereby preventing his own birth). Given Marty's unusual clothing and anachronistic questions, Sam deemed him an idiot, warning Lorraine that if she ever had any children like Marty, he'd disown her [**BTF1**].

    Sam strongly supported the Vietnam War, and believed the Hippie movement, in resisting the draft and protesting the conflict, to be ruining the United States. In fact, he wished he could send all Hippies—whom he considered "Commies"—to fight in the war, so that they could become "men." Thus, it greatly frustrated Sam when Lorraine joined a pro-peace movement, in opposition of his beliefs [**BTF2-s1**].

- **Baines, Stella:** Marty McFly's maternal grandmother, who lived in Hill Valley with her husband, Sam, and their six children: Lorraine, Ellen, Joey, Toby, Sally and Milton [**BTF1, BTF1-s, BTF1-n, BTF2-s**].

    After Sam ran over George McFly in 1955 and brought the injured teen into their home to convalesce, George and Lorraine developed feelings for one another and later wed. Their time-traveling son, Marty, unwittingly changed these events, however, by saving George's life and being struck by the car instead. Stella invited Marty to stay at their house while recovering, but Marty made a hasty retreat, uncomfortable with Lorraine's obvious romantic interest in him. After he left, Stella declared her future grandson to be odd [**BTF1**].

    ***NOTE:** Sam's cry of "Stella!" upon running Marty over referenced Tennessee Williams' A Streetcar Named Desire.*

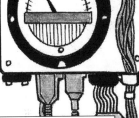

CODE	STORY
NIKE	*BTTF*-themed TV commercial: Nike
NTND	Nintendo *Back to the Future—The Ride* Mini-Game
PIZA	*BTTF*-themed TV commercial: Pizza Hut
PNBL	Data East *BTTF* pinball game
REAL	Real life
RIDE	Simulator: *Back to the Future—The Ride*
SCRM	2010 Scream Awards: *Back to the Future 25th Anniversary Reunion* (broadcast)
SCRT	2010 Scream Awards: *Back to the Future 25th Anniversary Reunion* (trailer)
SIMP	Simulator: *The Simpsons Ride*
SLOT	*Back to the Future Video Slots*
STLZ	Unused *BTTF* footage of Eric Stoltz as Marty McFly
STRY	*Back to the Future Storybook*
TEST	Screen tests: Crispin Glover, Lea Thompson and Tom Wilson
TLTL	Telltale Games' *Back to the Future—The Game*
TOPS	Topps' *Back to the Future II* trading-card set
TRIL	*BTTF: The Official Book of the Complete Movie Trilogy*
UNIV	Universal Studios Hollywood promotional video

SUFFIX	MEDIUM
-b	*BTTF2*'s Biff Tannen Museum video (extended)
-c	Credit sequence to the animated series
-d	Film deleted scene
-n	Film novelization
-o	Film outtake
-p	1955 phone book from *BTTF1*
-v	Video game print materials or commentaries
-s1	Screenplay (draft one)
-s2	Screenplay (draft two)
-s3	Screenplay (draft three)
-s4	Screenplay (draft four)
-sp	Screenplay (production draft)
-sx	Screenplay (Paradox)

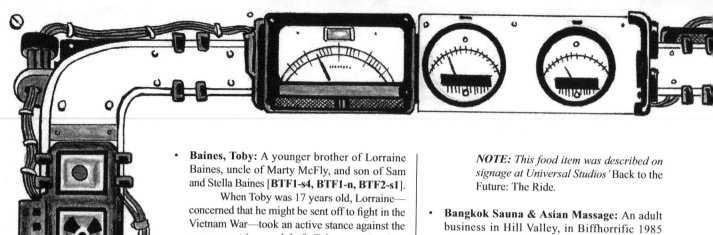

- **Baines, Toby:** A younger brother of Lorraine Baines, uncle of Marty McFly, and son of Sam and Stella Baines [**BTF1-s4, BTF1-n, BTF2-s1**].

    When Toby was 17 years old, Lorraine—concerned that he might be sent off to fight in the Vietnam War—took an active stance against the government-imposed draft. Toby wanted to join the conflict, hoping to "kick some Commie butt," but his mother preferred that he attend college (though Toby's poor academic grades made the latter outcome unlikely) [**BTF2-s1**].

- **Baines McFly, Lorraine:** *See* McFly, Lorraine

- **"Ballad of Davy Crockett, The":** A popular tune recorded by various artists, including Fess Parker [**REAL**]. In 1955, Roy's Records sold recordings of this song. In addition, Marty McFly heard the tune playing on a jukebook at Lou's Café after traveling to that era [**BTF1**].

- **balloon-mount:** A device invented by Emmett Brown, enabling him to attach a video camera to a hot-air balloon and document his travels in the contraption [**BFAN-2**].

- **Ballybowhill:** A village in County Dublin, Ireland [**REAL**]. Seamus and Maggie McFly hailed from this area before immigrating to the United States [**BTF3-n**].

- **Baltimore Orioles:** A National League baseball team [**REAL**]. In 1897, the team beat the Boston Beaneaters for the league pennant, after Pee Wee McFly struck out during a crucial third playoff game, coerced by gangster Jimmy "Diamond Jim" Tannen to throw the game. Marty McFly changed the game's outcome, however, by going back in time and enabling Pee Wee to instead win the game for his team [**BFAN-8**].

    NOTE: The Boston Beaneaters was the name by which the Atlanta Braves were known during that era. In real-world 1897, the team actually won the league pennant against the Orioles.

- **banana pizza:** A type of food that could be created using Emmett Brown's Digi-Chef digital food molecularizer. Banana pizza was made by combining bananas and pizza at the molecular level, resulting in banana-shaped pizza wrapped in a yellow peel [**RIDE**].

NOTE: This food item was described on signage at Universal Studios' Back to the Future: The Ride.

- **Bangkok Sauna & Asian Massage:** An adult business in Hill Valley, in Biffhorrific 1985 [**BTF2**].

- **Bank of America Corp.:** An American banking and financial-services firm [**REAL**]. The company maintained an office in Courthouse Square as early as 1955, and at least until 1985 [**BTF1**]. In 1931, the branch went by the institution's prior name, Bank of Italy [**TLTL-1**].

    NOTE: In BTTF1's novelization, this was called the Hill Valley Bank.

- **Bank of Elmdale:** *See* Hill Valley Courthouse

- **Bank of Italy (BI):** A financial institution founded in 1904 by Amadeo Giannini, which later became the Bank of America [**REAL**]. A Bank of Italy branch was located in Hill Valley in 1931, [**TLTL-1**], which in 1985 was known as Bank of America [**BTF1**].

- **Barbara's Bush Pie Gorbachev Goulash:** A menu item sold at Café 80's in 2015 [**BTF2**].

- **Barbie:** A fashion doll manufactured by Mattel, first sold in 1959 [**REAL**]. A Barbie doll was among the items for sale at Blast From the Past, an antique and collectibles shop in 2015 Hill Valley [**BTF2**].

- **Barney:** An easily excitable deputy law-enforcement official in California's Hill County, circa 1992, who served under Sheriff Andy Taylor. Barney had a southern drawl and a high-pitched, nervous-sounding voice [**BFAN-22, BFAN-23**].

    NOTE: Sheriff Andy Taylor, portrayed by late actor Andy Griffith, appeared on The Danny Thomas Show; The Andy Griffith Show; Gomer Pyle, U.S.M.C.; Mayberry R.F.D.; *and* Return to Mayberry. *Barney spoke similarly to—and was drawn to resemble—actor Don Knotts, who worked alongside Griffith as Deputy Barney Fife.*

- **Bartholomew:** A beatnik poet who, in the 1950s, attended parties thrown at Emmett Brown's mansion, where he sat quietly in a zen position,

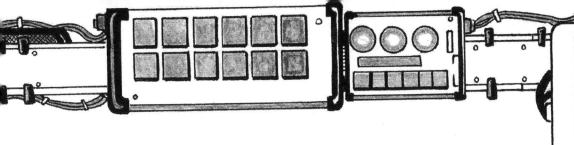

offering such nuggets of wisdom as "Hydrogen is like life: It's a gas." Other beatniks in attendance hung on Bartholomew's every word [**BTF1-s4**].

- **Bart Spray Paint:** A brand of paint sold in Hill Valley in Citizen Brown's dystopian timeline. Jennifer Parker used this product to paint graffiti on public property [**TLTL-3**].

    > **NOTE:** *This brand name paid homage to* The Simpsons, *the opening credits of which featured main character Bart Simpson engaging in graffiti-tagging.*

- **Bash-'Em-Up Bumper Cars:** An amusement-park ride typically operated in Hill Valley as part of its annual Founder's Day celebration [**BFAN-22**].

- **Bath House:** A small stand in Hill Valley, circa 1885, that featured outdoor showers and barber services [**BTF3**].

- **Bathysphere:** An unpowered, spherical deep-sea submersible designed by engineer Otis Barton, and used by naturalist William Beebe for a series of dives off Bermuda's coast between 1930 and 1934 [**REAL**].

    The Bathysphere was featured at the 1931 Hill Valley Exposition as part of the Enlightenment Under the Sea display, presented by French diver Jacques Douteux, with attendees invited to ride the submersible in a large water-filled tank. During the event, an alternate-reality Emmett Brown (from Citizen Brown's dystopian timeline) kidnapped his younger self in order to prevent Marty McFly from overwriting the dystopian version of history, and hid young Emmett inside the Bathysphere. Marty discovered the truth, however, and rescued his friend [**TLTL-5**].

- **Battle of the Bands:** An annual event held at Hill Valley High School, at which local student musical groups competed for a chance to perform at an upcoming school dance. Marty McFly and his band, the Pinheads, entered the Battle of the Bands in 1985, but were quickly disqualified by the unimpressed judges for being "too darn loud" [**BTF1**].

    > **NOTE:** *The judge who dismissed the band was portrayed by Huey Lewis—in the singer's acting debut—who recorded "Back in Time" and "The Power of Love" for the film's soundtrack.*

- **Battlestar Galactica:** A 1978 science fiction television series created by Glen A. Larson that has spawned several sequels and "reimagined" follow-up shows [**REAL**].

    In an effort to convince George McFly to ask Lorraine Baines to the Enchantment Under the Sea Dance, Marty McFly posed as an extraterrestrial named Darth Vader, from the planet Vulcan [**BTF1**], and claimed to receive a transmission from the *Battlestar Galactica* [**BTF1-n, BTF1-d**].

- **BBH:** A word of graffiti scrawled on the wall of Hill Valley High School, circa 1985 [**BTF1**].

- **Bean Bag:** A booth at the Hill Valley Festival in 1885. According to a sign on the booth, a score of two out of three earned a player a prize [**BTF3**].

- **Bears:** A professional football team in a league known as the IFL, circa 2015. That season was the Bears' best in 30 years, showing the rest of the league that they were no longer has-beens [**BTF2-n**].

    > **NOTE:** *This team would appear to be an evolution of the NFL's Chicago Bears, given their more than 30-year history. It's unknown what the acronym "IFL" stood for, though it was may have been short for "International Football League," given that "NFL" is short for "National Football League."*

- **"Beat It":** A popular song from Michael Jackson's 1982 album *Thriller* [**REAL**]. When Marty McFly visited the Café 80's in 2015, this song was playing at the restaurant [**BTF2**].

- **Beatles, The:** A British rock-and-roll band of the 1960s, among the most commercially and critically successful groups in music history [**REAL**].

    Emmett Brown, after traveling back to 1964, photographed the Beatles during a press conference welcoming the band to the United States. Snapping a picture from the front row, Doc commented, "Let it be" [**RIDE**].

    The Beatles' music, like all rock-and-roll, was deemed illegal by Edna Strickland in Citizen Brown's dystopian timeline [**TLTL-3**].

- **Bed Head Casual:** A hairstyle offered at The Combformist, a Hill Valley business in Citizen Brown's dystopian timeline [**TLTL-v**].

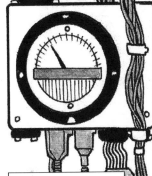

CODE	STORY
NIKE	*BTTF*-themed TV commercial: Nike
NTND	Nintendo *Back to the Future— The Ride* Mini-Game
PIZA	*BTTF*-themed TV commercial: Pizza Hut
PNBL	Data East *BTTF* pinball game
REAL	Real life
RIDE	Simulator: *Back to the Future—The Ride*
SCRM	2010 Scream Awards: *Back to the Future* 25th Anniversary Reunion (broadcast)
SCRT	2010 Scream Awards: *Back to the Future* 25th Anniversary Reunion (trailer)
SIMP	Simulator: *The Simpsons Ride*
SLOT	*Back to the Future Video Slots*
STLZ	Unused *BTTF* footage of Eric Stoltz as Marty McFly
STRY	*Back to the Future Storybook*
TEST	Screen tests: Crispin Glover, Lea Thompson and Tom Wilson
TLTL	Telltale Games' *Back to the Future—The Game*
TOPS	Topps' *Back to the Future II* trading-card set
TRIL	*BTTF: The Official Book of the Complete Movie Trilogy*
UNIV	Universal Studios Hollywood promotional video

SUFFIX	MEDIUM
-b	*BTTF2*'s Biff Tannen Museum video (extended)
-c	Credit sequence to the animated series
-d	Film deleted scene
-n	Film novelization
-o	Film outtake
-p	1955 phone book from *BTTF1*
-v	Video game print materials or commentaries
-s1	Screenplay (draft one)
-s2	Screenplay (draft two)
-s3	Screenplay (draft three)
-s4	Screenplay (draft four)
-sp	Screenplay (production draft)
-sx	Screenplay (*Paradox*)

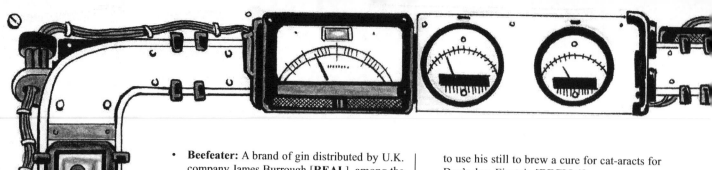

- **Beefeater:** A brand of gin distributed by U.K. company James Burrough [**REAL**], among the alcoholic beverages stocked in Biff Tannen's penthouse bar in Biffhorrific 1985 [**BTF2**].

- **Bee Gees:** A pop and disco musical group of the 1960s and 1970s, consisting of brothers Barry, Robin and Maurice Gibb [**REAL**]. A Bee Gees album was among the items for sale at Blast From the Past, an antique and collectibles shop in 2015 Hill Valley [**BTF2**].

- **Bell, John Jr.:** A Hollywood professional, circa 2015, who helped director Max Spielberg create *Jaws 19*, according to the film's poster [**BTF2**].

    NOTE: John Bell worked as an ILM visual effects art director on BTTF2 and BTTF3.

- **Bell, Mickey:** One of several professionals who helped to compile material for *Grays Sports Almanac: Complete Sports Statistics 1950-2000* [**BTF2**]

    NOTE: This individual was named on the book's title page.

- **Bellman Retrospective, A:** An exhibit offered by the Hill Valley Museum of Art in 2015 [**BTF2**].

- **Ben:** A name painted on Hill Valley High School's wall, circa 1985 [**BTF1**].

- **Bender:** One of three crash-test dummies, along with Fender and Li'l Fender, used in a safety video at the Institute of Future Technology's Anti-Gravitic Laboratory, to instruct Time-Travel Volunteers how to avoid being injured while operating Emmett Brown's Eight-Passenger DeLorean Time-Travel Vehicle. The dummies banged their heads, had limbs severed by closing doors and were strangulated by cameras caught in a safety restraint—and also broke rules regarding flash photography, eating and smoking—as a warning to those watching the video [**RIDE**].

- **Benedict, Arnie ("Eggs"):** A diminutive gangster operating in Chicago's South Side, circa 1927, who violently defended his territory with armed goons. The mob boss, who operated a speakeasy and employed the forced services of pharmacist Jim McFly to brew liquor for him during the Prohibition Era, was duped by Emmett Brown and Marty McFly into believing they were East Coast gangsters. In reality, they simply wanted

to use his still to brew a cure for cat-aracts for Doc's dog, Einstein [**BFCM-1**].

    NOTE: This character's name was based on that of Benedict Arnold, a reputedly traitorous general of the American Revolutionary War, as well as eggs Benedict, a dish consisting of half an English muffin topped with poached eggs, bacon or ham, and Hollandaise sauce. He was drawn to resemble Edward G. Robinson, a Hollywood film actor famous for playing numerous gangster characters.

- **Ben-Hur, Judah:** A well-muscled slave in ancient Rome, circa 36 A.D. After Jules and Verne Brown prevented Judah's master from whipping him in a bath house, Judah expressed his gratitude by leading them through catacombs in order to rescue their father, Emmett Brown.

    With Judah's help, the Browns and Marty McFly escaped certain death by returning to their DeLorean. The slave then escaped servitude using a chariot, with which Marty had previously raced against gladiator Bifficus Antanneny [**BFAN-5**].

    NOTE: Judah Ben-Hur was a fictional character in Lew Wallace's 1880 novel, Ben-Hur: A Tale of the Christ, as well as the 1959 Charlton Heston film, Ben-Hur, based on that book. The Back to the Future version adopted Heston's appearance and speaking pattern.

- **Benny:** A wild bald eagle cared for in 1888 by Windjammer Diefendorfer, a kindly old man who fitted Benny with a toupée. Marty McFly encountered the animal while visiting that era [**BFAN-21**].

- **Benny:** A construction worker in Hill Valley, circa 1952. She and a co-worker, Kenny, were assigned to demolish a skyscraper using dynamite. Emmett Brown, convinced he was a superhero called Mega Brainman, tried to rescue the building's occupants, unaware it had previously been condemned and evacuated, and was caught in the explosion—which he somehow survived [**BFAN-24**].

- **Benny, Jack:** An American actor, comedian and vaudevillian of film, radio and television [**REAL**]. When Marty McFly tried to convince Emmett Brown, in 1955, that he was from the future, the scientist challenged him to name the president in 1985. Marty replied Ronald Reagan, but Brown

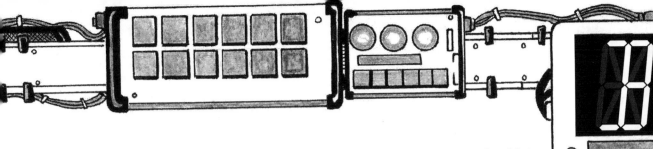

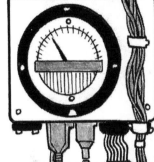

scoffed at the notion, mockingly asking if Benny was the secretary of the treasury [**BTF1**].

- **Bension, Ron:** An employee at the Institute of Future Technology [**RIDE**].

  > *NOTE: This individual, identified on signage outside* Back to the Future: The Ride, *was named after an executive at Universal Studios.*

- **Bermuda Triangle:** A portion of the western North Atlantic Ocean in which numerous surface vessels and aircraft have vanished under mysterious circumstances, giving rise to supernatural explanations [**REAL**].

  In an alternate 1964, the escapades of scientist Dr. Feldstein in the Bermuda Triangle resulted in all U.S. states (87 in that timeline) banning time-travel experiments [**BTF1-s1**].

  > *NOTE: The nature of Feldstein's Bermuda Triangle exploits is unknown.*

- **Bernie:** A newsstand robot operating a kiosk in Hill Valley, circa 2015. Marty McFly tried to purchase a copy of *Grays Sports Almanac* from Bernie, but his poor credit rating prevented him from paying via thumbprint [**BTF2-s2**].

- **Berry, Chuck:** An American singer and guitarist of rock-and-roll music [**REAL**]. His cousin, Marvin Berry, was the front man of Marvin Berry and the Starlighters. When Marvin's band performed at the Enchantment Under the Sea Dance in 1955, Marty McFly joined the band on guitar, playing Chuck's song "Johnny B. Goode" three years before its release. Amazed, Marvin called his cousin, who was looking for a new sound [**BTF1**].

  > *NOTE: Thus, Marty indirectly introduced Chuck Berry to his own music—played on the same Gibson guitar with which Berry himself often performed.*
  >
  > *Adult Swim's TV series* Robot Chicken *spoofed this scenario in the sketch "Calling Chuck Berry," which showed the ramifications of Marvin's call: Chuck Berry, furious at hearing someone playing a song he had just finished laying down, stormed the dance, ready to kill Marty, only to meet Lorraine Baines. Lorraine, excited at meeting a rock star, pushed aside George*

  McFly to be with him—the end result being Marty turning African-American.

- **Berry, Marlin:** A descendant of Chuck Berry and Marvin Berry in one possible timeline, circa 2015 [**BFCG**].

- **Berry, Marvin:** A guitarist of the 1950s, and the front man of Marvin Berry and the Starlighters, who performed at the Enchantment Under the Sea Dance in 1955. When Marvin injured his hand while helping Marty McFly out of the band's locked car trunk, Marty—determined to have the group perform so that his parents would kiss and fall in love—filled in for Marvin on guitar. The musician was so awed by Marty's rock-and-roll sound that he called his cousin, Chuck Berry, to hear it [**BTF1**].

  > *NOTE: In the film's first-draft screenplay, the band was called Lester Moon and the Midnighters. The second draft dubbed the group Marvin Berry and the Starlighters. By the third draft, this had changed to Marvin Moon and the Midnighters, which was eventually changed back to Marvin Berry and the Starlighters.*

- **Bertha:** A uniformed maid who worked for George and Lorraine McFly in 1985, in an altered timeline in which they were happy and successful [**BTF1-s3, BTF1-s4**].

- **Best Litter Columnist:** An award that Edna Strickland won for her writing for *Cat Lover's Quarterly* magazine [**TLTL-1**].

- **Betty:** A blonde-haired friend of Lorraine Baines at Hill Valley High School, circa 1955. Lorraine, Betty and a third young woman, Babs, often hung out together [**BTF1**].

  > *NOTE: This character was named in BTTF1's credits, script and novelization. In an early screenplay draft, Babs and Betty did not appear; instead, Lorraine (then called Eileen) hung out with a girl named Madge.*
  >
  > *Betty was originally slated to return with Babs in* Back to the Future II, *but actress Cristen Kauffman was unavailable.*

- **Beyer's & Co.:** A company that produced a wheat-based food product called Tantalizing Tasties,

CODE	STORY
NIKE	*BTTF*-themed TV commercial: Nike
NTND	Nintendo *Back to the Future—The Ride* Mini-Game
PIZA	*BTTF*-themed TV commercial: Pizza Hut
PNBL	Data East *BTTF* pinball game
REAL	Real life
RIDE	Simulator: *Back to the Future—The Ride*
SCRM	2010 Scream Awards: *Back to the Future* 25th Anniversary Reunion (broadcast)
SCRT	2010 Scream Awards: *Back to the Future* 25th Anniversary Reunion (trailer)
SIMP	Simulator: *The Simpsons Ride*
SLOT	*Back to the Future Video Slots*
STLZ	Unused *BTTF* footage of Eric Stoltz as Marty McFly
STRY	*Back to the Future Storybook*
TEST	Screen tests: Crispin Glover, Lea Thompson and Tom Wilson
TLTL	Telltale Games' *Back to the Future—The Game*
TOPS	Topps' *Back to the Future II* trading-card set
TRIL	*BTTF: The Official Book of the Complete Movie Trilogy*
UNIV	Universal Studios Hollywood promotional video

SUFFIX	MEDIUM
-b	*BTTF2*'s Biff Tannen Museum video (extended)
-c	Credit sequence to the animated series
-d	Film deleted scene
-n	Film novelization
-o	Film outtake
-p	1955 phone book from *BTTF1*
-v	Video game print materials or commentaries
-s1	Screenplay (draft one)
-s2	Screenplay (draft two)
-s3	Screenplay (draft three)
-s4	Screenplay (draft four)
-sp	Screenplay (production draft)
-sx	Screenplay (*Paradox*)

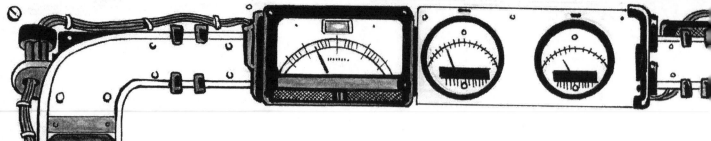

circa 1955. This product was advertised on the back cover of the August 1954 issue of *Tales From Space* [**BTF1**].

> ***NOTE:*** *Beyer's & Co. and Tantalizing Tasties were a fictional manufacturer and breakfast cereal mentioned in RKO Radio Pictures' 1938 film,* Everybody's Doing It.

- **B.G.:** A producer at a local Hill Valley television station who helped Emmett Brown record Video Encyclopedia entries for his Science Journal broadcasts [**BFAN-23**].

> ***NOTE:*** *B.G.'s initials were the same as those of Bob Gale, the co-writer and producer of the* Back to the Future *trilogy.*

- **Bias V -150V:** A toggle on Emmett Brown's giant guitar amplifier, and part of the device's Driver Adjust system [**BTF1**].

- **Biff:** A menu item sold at Café 80's in 2015 [**BTF2**].

- **Biff Buck:** A type of currency used in the Biffhorrific timeline, featuring Biff Tannen's likeness instead of that of a U.S. president. Biff Bucks were available in numerous denominations, including $5, $50 and $100, and were signed by William Bailey and Richard Thomas. All such bills contained the same serial number: L 894944210 B [**BTF2**].

> ***NOTE:*** *The term "Biff Buck" is frequently used by fans, but may not be the currency's official designation.*

- **Biff City:** Marty McFly's nickname for an alternate 1985 in which Biff Tannen was a corrupt and powerful criminal who ruled Hill Valley from a penthouse apartment above Biff Tannen's Pleasure Paradise [**BTF2-s1**].

> ***NOTE:*** Back to the Future: The Official Book of the Complete Movie Trilogy *dubbed this darker Hill Valley as "Biffhorrific." Another moniker, "Hell Valley," was scrawled on the city's greeting sign in the film, while the film's second-draft screenplay called it "Tannen Valley."*

- **BiffCo Enterprises:** A corporation founded by Biff Tannen in the Biffhorrific timeline, after he became an overnight millionaire thanks to future foreknowledge gleaned from *Grays Sports Almanac*, a magazine given to him by his future

self, containing 50 years of sports statistics. Holdings of BiffCo Enterprises included the San Andreas Nuclear Power Plant, Biff's Pleasure Palace, Biff's Realty, the Biff Tannen Museum, Biff Tannen's Pleasure Paradise and BiffCoToxic Waste Disposal. Hugely successful, BiffCo Enterprises changed the face of Hill Valley in that reality, making its focus on industrialization and debauchery [**BTF2-b**].

- **BiffCo Realty:** A business owned by Biff Tannen that, in Biffhorrific 1985, purchased all of the homes in Emmett Brown's neighborhood so that Biff could use the land to erect a toxic-waste dump [**BTF2-s1**].

- **BiffCo Toxic Waste Disposal:** A garbage landfill business owned by Biff Tannen in Biffhorrific 1985, as part of his BiffCo Enterprises corporation [**BTF2-b**].

- **Biffhorrific:** A nickname describing a dark, lawless version of 1985 in which Biff Tannen was a corrupt and powerful criminal who ruled Hill Valley from a penthouse apartment above Biff Tannen's Pleasure Paradise [**TRIL**].

> ***NOTE:*** *The name "Biffhorrific" was used by the film crew while BTTF2 was produced. Other monikers for this alternate Hill Valley included "Hell Valley" (scrawled on the city's greeting sign), "Biff City" (mentioned in the movie's first-draft screenplay) and "Tannen Valley" (in the second-draft script).*

- **Biffingham, Lord, Earl of Tannenshire:** A tyrannical, obese English nobleman, circa 1367, and an ancestor of Biff Tannen. Lord Biffingham captured local women as wives, imprisoning them in the towers of his home, Castle Biffingham.

To that end, the evil earl kidnapped time-traveler Clara Clayton Brown; locked her husband, Emmett Brown, in a dungeon; and challenged the scientist to a joust. Clara, assisted by Jennivere McFly—an ancestor of Marty McFly, also held captive in the tower—rescued Doc, along with Jenny's husband, Harold McFly, in a homemade hot-air balloon, thwarting the tyrant's marriage plans [**BFAN-2**].

Before going to sleep at the end of each day, Lord Biffingham turned on his "knight light" [**BFHM**].

> ***NOTE:*** *It's unclear what the "knight*

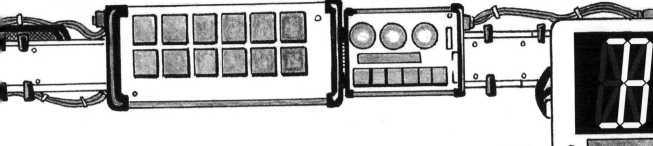

light" was, since it could not have been an electrical device.

- **Biff's:** A name on a large neon sign adorning the top of Biff Tannen's Pleasure Paradise [**BTF2**].

- **Biff's Alien Souvenirs:** A roadside stand located in Hill Valley, operated by Biff Tannen. Believing he'd been visited by extraterrestrials in 1967 (the "aliens" were actually Marty McFly and Jules and Verne Brown in disguise, aboard the flying DeLorean), Biff sold bumper stickers, a beverage known as Jupiter Juice, and his autobiography, *Aliens Who I Have Known & Loved*, at the souvenir kiosk. This venture failed to earn much business, however [**BFAN-23**].

- **Biff's Automotive Detailing:** A business owned by Biff Tannen in an altered version of 1985, in which George McFly was confident and successful, and Biff—George's former bully— was docile, friendly and subservient [**BTF1**]. Its motto: "To make your car spiffy in a jiffy, just call Biff-y!" [**TLTL-v**].

- **Biff's Pleasure Palace:** A biker bar attached to Biff Tannen's Pleasure Paradise in Biffhorrific 1985 [**BTF2**].

- **Biff's Realty:** A real-estate firm owned by Biff Tannen in Biffhorrific 1985. Intent on developing the land on which Lyon Estates stood, Biff—via Biff's Realty—bought out most of the houses in the development, terrorizing their owners into selling their homes [**BTF2**].

- **Biffster:** A nickname used by Marty McFly to describe relatives of Biff Tannen, many of whom shared similar physical characteristics and personality traits [**BFAN-4**]. Given the tendency for Biffsters to be abusive and rude, Emmett Brown suspected the presence of rogue Neanderthal genes in their DNA [**TLTL-2**].

  > *NOTE: For a list of all known Biffsters, see Appendix III.*

- **Biff Tannen Museum:** A monument to Biff Tannen's achievements, attached to Biff Tannen's Pleasure Paradise in the Biffhoriffic 1985. The museum played a video for passersby, recounting the Tannen family's history, mixing in a good deal of propaganda to gloss over any negative aspects of that history [**BTF2, BTF2-b**].

- **Biff Tannen's Pleasure Paradise:** A high-rise casino in Biffhorrific 1985, in which Biff Tannen was a corrupt and powerful criminal kingpin. The Pleasure Paradise was built on the site of the former Hill Valley Courthouse. A gaudy, loud, neon-lit eyesore, the casino contained two adjoining businesses, Biff's Pleasure Palace (a biker bar) and the Biff Tannen Museum (a monument to his achievements). Biff and his wife, Lorraine, lived in the building's penthouse apartment on the 27th floor [**BTF2**].

- **Big-Brain Bus:** A large, green vehicle shaped like a human brain, and used by scientist Walter Wisdom, the host of children's TV series *Mr. Wisdom*, to visit local malls under the guise of meeting young fans. In reality, he sought only to merchandise his TV show and make money off of children with his mobile Mr. Wisdom Discount Lab [**BFAN-15**].

  > *NOTE: This series' title paid homage to scientist Donald Jeffrey Herbert Kemske, better known to TV audiences as Mr. Wizard, of* Watch Mr. Wizard *and* Mr. Wizard's World *fame.*

- **Big City First National Bank:** A financial institution for which Emmett and Clara Brown pretended to work in order to gain access to the *Mr. Wisdom* studio set. Once inside, they rescued Tiny, Verne Brown's pet Apatosaurus, which had been captured and sold by Biff Tannen to TV host Walter Wisdom [**BFAN-26**].

- **Big Pictures:** A business that ran deliveries to Hill Valley in 1991 [**BFAN-12**].

  > *NOTE: This company's name was visible on the side of a delivery truck that almost ran over Emmett Brown. Since the top half of the first word was cut off onscreen, it's possible it may have been something other than "Big."*

- **Big Star:** A business located in Hill Valley, circa 1991 [**BFAN-7b**].

- **Bill:** One of several names that Marty McFly and Verne Brown urged Jules Verne to adopt, since Verne (who'd been named in the novelist's honor) hated the name Verne [**BFAN-21**].

- **Bill:** A sports radio announcer who, with a fellow broadcaster named Bob, narrated a 1955

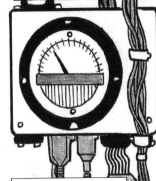

CODE	STORY
NIKE	*BTTF*-themed TV commercial: Nike
NTND	Nintendo *Back to the Future— The Ride* Mini-Game
PIZA	*BTTF*-themed TV commercial: Pizza Hut
PNBL	Data East *BTTF* pinball game
REAL	Real life
RIDE	Simulator: *Back to the Future—The Ride*
SCRM	2010 Scream Awards: *Back to the Future 25th Anniversary Reunion* (broadcast)
SCRT	2010 Scream Awards: *Back to the Future 25th Anniversary Reunion* (trailer)
SIMP	Simulator: *The Simpsons Ride*
SLOT	*Back to the Future Video Slots*
STLZ	Unused *BTTF* footage of Eric Stoltz as Marty McFly
STRY	*Back to the Future Storybook*
TEST	Screen tests: Crispin Glover, Lea Thompson and Tom Wilson
TLTL	Telltale Games' *Back to the Future—The Game*
TOPS	Topps' *Back to the Future II* trading-card set
TRIL	*BTTF: The Official Book of the Complete Movie Trilogy*
UNIV	Universal Studios Hollywood promotional video

SUFFIX	MEDIUM
-b	*BTTF2's* Biff Tannen Museum video (extended)
-c	Credit sequence to the animated series
-d	Film deleted scene
-n	Film novelization
-o	Film outtake
-p	1955 phone book from *BTTF1*
-v	Video game print materials or commentaries
-s1	Screenplay (draft one)
-s2	Screenplay (draft two)
-s3	Screenplay (draft three)
-s4	Screenplay (draft four)
-sp	Screenplay (production draft)
-sx	Screenplay (*Paradox*)

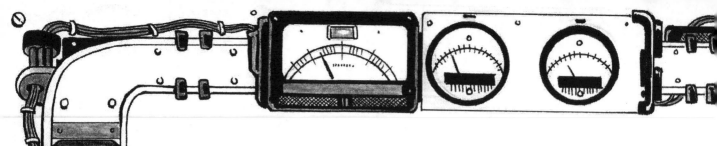

UCLA/Washington State football game in which Washington beat UCLA thanks to a field goal by Jim Decker. An elderly Biff Tannen from 2015—having traveled back to 1955 to give his younger self a copy of *Grays Sports Almanac*—tuned into this sportscast to convince younger Biff to bet on games listed in that book, and thus become wealthy and corrupt [**BTF2-n**].

- **Billy Spaceboy:** A floating robot that greeted group-tour visitors to the McFly Museum of Aeronautics in 2091. The mechanical tour guide had a "B" on its chest and a warm, calming voice [**BFAN-9**].

- **Billy Spaceboy Junior Cadet Wings:** A free gift provided to all children visiting the McFly Museum of Aeronautics who refrained from chewing plutonium spitwads while on site [**BFAN-9**].

- **binocular helmet:** A type of headgear invented by Emmett Brown, enabling his son, Verne, to spot objects from great distances. The blue helmet contained a pair of large yellow lenses that slid down over a wearer's eyes [**BFHM**].

- **bionics:** The application of biological methods and systems found in nature to engineering and modern technology [**REAL**].

  According to a *USA Today* report, a professional sports pitcher was suspended in 2015 for using an uncalibrated bionic arm. Griff Tannen also had a number of bionic implants, some of which were said to have short-circuited, making him unstable and dangerous. That year, a proposition known as 237 was under consideration to legalize the technology's use [**BTF2**].

- **Bird's Eye:** An international frozen-food brand owned by Pinnacle Foods [**REAL**]. The McFly family often ate Bird's Eye mixed vegetables for dinner, much to Marty McFly's disgust [**BTF1-s4, BTF1-n**].

- **Birky, Kurt:** A time-flux designer at the Institute of Future Technology, stationed in the East Wing [**RIDE**].

  NOTE: This individual, identified on signage outside Back to the Future: The Ride, *was named after an executive at Universal Studios.*

- **B.J.:** The initials of an attorney-at-law operating in Chicago's South Side, circa 1927. His title and initials adorned his briefcase [**BFCM-1**].

  NOTE: This man was seated at a police station while Emmett Brown tried to spring Marty McFly from jail.

- **Black & Decker:** A manufacturer of power tools, accessories, hardware and home-improvement products [**REAL**]. In 2015, the company marketed the Hydrator, a device able to rehydrate pizza and other foods in mere seconds [**BTF2**].

- ***Black Taboo***: A pornographic film released on video in 1984, starring Tina Davis, Billy Dee and Tony El-ay [**BTF2**]. Biff Tannen owned a copy of this movie in Biffhorrific 1985 [**BTF2**].

- **Blast From the Past:** A shop in Courthouse Square, circa 2015, that sold antiques and collectibles, including a Frisbie flying disc; a bust of John F. Kennedy; VHS copies of *Jaws 2, Dragnet, National Lampoon's Animal House* and *Stand-up Reagan*; *BurgerTime* and *Jaws* video games for the Nintendo Entertainment System; a 1967 lava lamp; an unopened bottle of Pepsi; a Magnavox; a giant peanut; a soup tureen; a Macintosh computer made in 1984; bottles of Perrier water; a Roger Rabbit doll; Jimmy Carter presidential campaign posters; Barbie and Ken dolls; "Smiley" Happy Face buttons; a JVC Super VHS video camera; a Dustbuster; a Black 'n Decker clothes iron; a Ronald Reagan picture disc titled *The President's Album*; a Bee Gees album; a Guess jacket; and a magazine titled *Grays Sports Almanac: Complete Sports Statistics 1950-2000*.

  While in 2015, Marty McFly visited Blast From the Past and purchased the almanac, hoping to become wealthy by betting on future events. Emmett Brown discarded the magazine, however, enabling an elderly Biff Tannen to steal the book, along with Doc's DeLorean, and accomplish what Marty had planned to do [**BTF2**].

  NOTE: The Guess jacket on display was identical to the one Marty wore in 1985, including the "Art in Revolution" pin attached to it, which could indicate it to have been Marty's actual jacket.

- **Bluebird Motel:** A business in Courthouse Square. In 1955, Marty McFly passed a sign for the motel while preparing to drive the DeLorean back to the

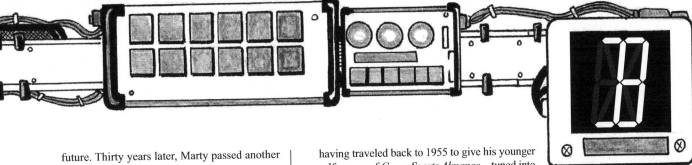

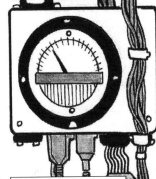

future. Thirty years later, Marty passed another sign for the motel [**BTF1**].

- **Blue Jays:** A professional baseball team based in Toronto, Ontario, Canada [**REAL**]. According to a *USA Today* report in 2015, the Blue Jays had recently fired their manager [**BTF2**].

- **Blue Nirvana:** A musical group that performed at a Vietnam War protest rally to which Lorraine McFly donated her time in 1967 [**BTF2-s1**].

- **"Blue Suede Shoes":** A rockabilly tune first recorded by Carl Perkins in 1955 and later covered by Elvis Presley [**REAL**].

    While visiting 1952, Marty McFly tried to change history and attain fame by performing "Blue Suede Shoes" for an agent at the Midwest Talent Agency, but the man decided it was not commercial enough and threw Marty out of his office. Reginald Washington, a band manager who overheard the performance, liked what he heard and asked Marty to play it again for a New York record executive. This meeting, however, never came to pass [**BTF1-s1**].

- **BMW:** A German manufacturer of automobiles and motorcycles [**REAL**]. After Marty McFly changed history by making his parents more successful, George McFly drove a BMW 733i [**BTF1**].

    One type of BMW convertible sold in 2015 was the 633CSI. Griff Tannen had a car of this model [**BTF2**].

- **Board Game Club:** An extracurricular activity enjoyed by Marty McFly in Citizen Brown's dystopian timeline. Marty's involvement with the Board Game Club furthered his reputation in that reality as a nerd [**TLTL-3**].

- **Bob:** A name scrawled in graffiti on the wall of Hill Valley High School, circa 1985 [**BTF1**].

    NOTE: *The name "Bob" appears many times throughout the* Back to the Future *saga, as an in-joke reference to* BTTF *creators Robert Zemeckis and Bob Gale.*

- **Bob:** A sports radio announcer who, with a fellow broadcaster named Bill, narrated a 1955 UCLA/Washington State football game in which Washington beat UCLA thanks to a field goal by Jim Decker. An elderly Biff Tannen from 2015—

having traveled back to 1955 to give his younger self a copy of *Grays Sports Almanac*—tuned into this sportscast to convince younger Biff to bet on games listed in that book, and thus become wealthy and corrupt [**BTF2-n**].

- **Bob Brothers All-Star International Circus, The:** A circus operating in 1933, co-owned by Robert and Bob Brothers. Acts included clowns, a human cannonball, aerialists, a bearded lady, acrobats, seals, elephants, lions, tigers and bears, as well as a band that played off-key. By 1992, the circus had been out of business for years.

    After seeing an old poster for this company in a comic book shop, Verne Brown and his friend Chris used Doc's DeLorean to travel back in time and see the show—which they found very disappointing. Verne and Chris helped the brothers keep the circus afloat by performing as trapeze artists, thereby preventing landlord Mac Tannen from taking over the business [**BFAN-18**].

- **Bobby:** A classmate of Verne Brown at Hill Valley Elementary School in 1991. One of his drawings hung in Verne's classroom [**BFAN-13**].

- **Bobs:** A business in Hill Valley, circa 1991 [**BFAN-6, BFAN-18**]. Emmett Brown recreated this business in miniature for a board game that he created [**BFAN-6**].

    NOTE: *The company's name was printed sans apostrophe.*

- **Boca Raton:** A city in Palm Beach County, Florida [**REAL**]. In 1985, twelve wooden crates filled with cocaine washed ashore near this city. Drug-enforcement agents, however, found no identification marks on the containers. A news story about this incident was playing on a television in Emmett Brown's garage as Marty McFly visited to check on the scientist [**BTF1**].

- **Boiling Bucket of Killer Goop, The:** An evil creature in the video game *BraveLord and Monstrux* that poured boiling liquid upon its adversaries. Monstrux turned the once-ordinary cauldron into a demon so that it would fight BraveLord for him [**BFAN-19**].

- **bojo:** A popular insult, circa 2015, analogous to "idiot" [**BTF2**].

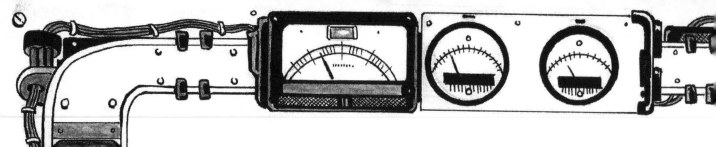

- **Bond, James:** One of several names that Verne Brown, having traveled back to before his birth, urged Emmett and Clara Brown to name him instead of Verne [**BFAN-21**].

    NOTE: James Bond, a fictional character created by Ian Fleming, has appeared in numerous novels, films and comics. Oddly, Doc seemed not to notice the incongruity of a person knowing who Bond was in 1888.

- **Bonedaddys, The:** A Los Angeles-based musical group [**REAL**]. Marty McFly wrote an extra-credit report on the group's social significance for a test in his music-appreciation college course, but still scored a C- on the exam [**BFAN-4**].

- **booster belt:** A device invented by Emmett Brown to wax the roof of his car without using a ladder. Verne Brown and his friend Chris, while working for the Bob Brothers All-Star International Circus in 1933, used the belts to safely perform as aerialists [**BFAN-18**].

- **booster-boots:** A type of footwear invented by Emmett Brown. Booster-boots increased a wearer's height by lifting that person off the ground, and also allowed the individual to outrun moving vehicles and jump over tall buildings. The boots were activated by adjusting a dial and clicking the heels. After being hit on the head by a wrestling announcer's microphone in 1952, Doc thought he was a superhero called Mega Brainman, and used the booster-boots as part of his costume [**BFAN-24**].

- **Booth, John Wilkes:** A stage actor who, in 1865, assassinated President Abraham Lincoln at Ford's Theatre, in Washington, D.C. [**REAL**]. Booth's image was among the visual stimuli used by Emmett Brown to evoke reactions from test subjects using his Mental Alignment Meter [**TLTL-4**].

    NOTE: Booth's last name was misspelled as "Boothe" during Doc's testing.

- **Booth A-113:** A booth at the 1931 Hill Valley Exposition, at which Ernest Philpott gave out free samples of his Professor Fringle's Algae-Cakes [**TLTL-5**].

- **Boot Hill Cemetery:** A burial ground in Hill Valley, located on Mt. Clayton, adjacent to the Delgado Mine, and the city's oldest graveyard.

Emmett Brown was buried here in 1885 after being murdered by Buford "Mad Dog" Tannen. His tombstone noted that he was mourned by his "beloved Clara" [**BTF3**].

    NOTE: In Paradox, a combined script for both film sequels, the Delgado Mine was adjacent to Oak Park Cemetery (where George McFly was buried in Back to the Future II), indicating that Boot Hill and Oak Park may have been the same burial ground, but in different eras.

    Mt. Clayton was named on Doc's hand-drawn map of the mine, which also indicated Boot Hill to have been the city's oldest cemetery. Boot Hill Cemetery has been the name of graveyards seen in several classic Western TV series, including Gunsmoke.

- **Bootsie:** A name that Jules and Verne Brown considered for a baby Apatosaurus that Verne had found while visiting prehistoric times. Eventually, they settled on the ironic name Tiny [**BFAN-26**].

- **Bosco:** A popular brand of chocolate syrup [**REAL**]. In 2015, Marty and Jennifer McFly had this product in their kitchen [**BTF2**].

- **Bostoid Pizza:** A takeout pizzeria located in Robot City, a domed station in the Asteroid Belt of Earth's solar system, circa 2585. The company promised not to charge customers if its robotic drivers failed to deliver orders within 30 seconds [**BFCL-1**].

- **Boston:** The capital city of Massachusetts [**REAL**]. In 2015, I-99's Hyperlane-Grid 4 contained an exit for flying cars that led to this city, as well as to Phoenix, London and Hill Valley [**BTF2**].

- **Boston Beaneaters:** A National League baseball team, circa 1897, managed by Frank Selee [**REAL**]. The team lost the pennant that year to the Baltimore Orioles, after Pee Wee McFly struck out during a crucial third playoff game, coerced by gangster Jimmy "Diamond Jim" Tannen to throw the game. Marty McFly changed the game's outcome, however, by traveling back in time and enabling Pee Wee to win the game [**BFAN-8**].

    NOTE: "Boston Beaneaters" was the name by which the Atlanta Braves were known

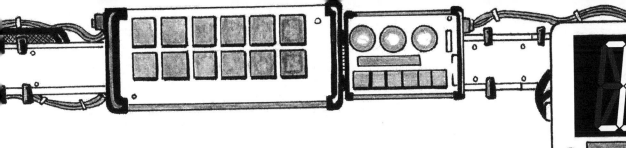

during that era. In 1897, the team won the league pennant against the Orioles.

- **Bot Shoppe, The:** A business located in Courthouse Square, circa 2015 [**BTF2**].

- **Bottoms Up:** A plastic-surgery franchise with offices in Courthouse Square, circa 2015. This business boasted board-certified implant surgeons, and advertised its products—such as the Super Inflatable "Tit" and the Headlight "Tit"—on Channel 63 [**BTF2**].

- **Brain Banger, The:** A ride at the Mega Monster Mountain amusement park. Verne Brown was very fond of this attraction, which consisted of a horizontal, circular platform that spun to create centrifugal force to hold riders against the wall [**BFAN-25**].

  > **NOTE:** *The Brain Banger was similar to a real-life ride called the Round-up.*

- **Brain Buster Brown:** The stage-name under which Emmett Brown briefly competed as a wrestler with the Small Town Professional Wrasslin organization in 1952, when he fought the reigning champion, Mad Maximus. Though Doc never wanted to be a fighter, he succumbed to peer pressure to accept the gig after tussling with a wrestling promoter over a potato at a Hoggly-Woggly supermarket. The scientist was no match for Maximus, however, and was quickly defeated during his only match [**BFAN-24**].

- **Brain-wave Analyzer:** An invention of Emmett Brown, built in or before 1955, enabling a wearer to telepathically hear others' thoughts. The analyzer consisted of a mass of vacuum tubes, rheostats, gauges, wiring and antennae. Doc abandoned the device after failing to discern what Marty McFly was thinking [**BTF1-n**]. Marty later tried the helmet on himself as Doc read a letter from his future self, stranded in 1885 [**BTF3**].

  When Doc's miscalculated time-tampering caused him to vanish in 1986, Hill Valley's government sold off his estate to make way for a parking garage. Biff Tannen was particularly interested in the analyzer [**TLTL-1**].

  A similar-looking device called a Citizen Plus Helmet was used to brainwash inmates at the Citizen Plus Ward, in Citizen Brown's dystopian timeline, to make them obedient members of society. In that reality, rather than reading minds,

the helmet reprogrammed them [**TLTL-4**].

  > **NOTE:** *It's unclear if the Deep-Thought Mind-Reading Helmet, from the animated series, was intended to be the same device featured in BTTF1—called a Brain-wave Analyzer in that movie's novelization—or a separate attempt at telepathy. Back to the Future: The Ride introduced a third such device, the Deep-Thinking Mind-Reading Helmet, while the Telltale Games video game revealed a fourth, the Mind Mapping Helmet.*

  > *Doc's pride in the animated version would seem to indicate it was more successful than its film counterpart, but the analyzer may have worked, unbeknownst to Doc, as his guesses (that Marty had traveled a long distance, that he was selling newspapers and that he was with the Coast Guard Youth Auxiliary) were not off the mark—Marty had traveled a great distance in time, he'd read a newspaper before seeking out Doc and he'd told the Baines family he was in the Coast Guard. Thus, Doc may have successfully read fragments of these memories.*

  > *Reinforcing this possibility, the novelization added another guess—that Marty was selling peanut brittle for the Boy Scouts—referencing a scene from earlier in the book involving George McFy and a pushy neighbor with a Girl Scout daughter, as well as George's peanut brittle.*

- **Brain Wave Analyzer**: A patented invention of Emmett Brown, used to monitor a person's brain patterns. When Doc started becoming forgetful in 1991, he plugged himself in to this device to make sure his brain was healthy—and found, thanks to an April Fool's Day joke perpetrated by his sons, Jules and Verne, that his brain was full to 99.99 percent capacity. To conserve what little thought he believed remained, he opted to give up science—a vow he later dropped once the prank was exposed [**BFAN-12**].

  > **NOTE:** *Although this device was identically named to Doc's telepathy helmet (sans the hyphen), its form and function greatly differed.*

- **"Brainwaves and You":** An academic article published in or before 1931, discussing theta-band transmissions and other topics. That year,

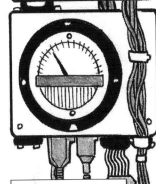

CODE	STORY
NIKE	*BTTF*-themed TV commercial: Nike
NTND	Nintendo *Back to the Future—The Ride* Mini-Game
PIZA	*BTTF*-themed TV commercial: Pizza Hut
PNBL	Data East *BTTF* pinball game
REAL	Real life
RIDE	Simulator: *Back to the Future—The Ride*
SCRM	2010 Scream Awards: *Back to the Future 25th Anniversary Reunion* (broadcast)
SCRT	2010 Scream Awards: *Back to the Future 25th Anniversary Reunion* (trailer)
SIMP	Simulator: *The Simpsons Ride*
SLOT	*Back to the Future Video Slots*
STLZ	Unused *BTTF* footage of Eric Stoltz as Marty McFly
STRY	*Back to the Future Storybook*
TEST	Screen tests: Crispin Glover, Lea Thompson and Tom Wilson
TLTL	Telltale Games' *Back to the Future—The Game*
TOPS	Topps' *Back to the Future II* trading-card set
TRIL	*BTTF: The Official Book of the Complete Movie Trilogy*
UNIV	Universal Studios Hollywood promotional video

SUFFIX	MEDIUM
-b	*BTTF2*'s Biff Tannen Museum video (extended)
-c	Credit sequence to the animated series
-d	Film deleted scene
-n	Film novelization
-o	Film outtake
-p	1955 phone book from *BTTF1*
-v	Video game print materials or commentaries
-s1	Screenplay (draft one)
-s2	Screenplay (draft two)
-s3	Screenplay (draft three)
-s4	Screenplay (draft four)
-sp	Screenplay (production draft)
-sx	Screenplay (*Paradox*)

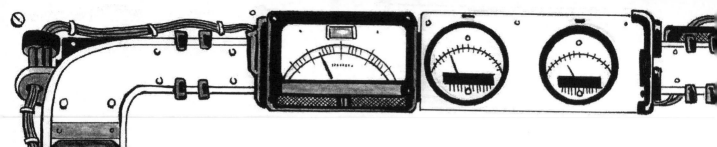

Emmett Brown—while studying the human mind as research for his Mental Alignment Meter—had a copy of this article in his office at the Hill Valley Courthouse [**TLTL-5**].

- **Brat Police:** A type of police force invented by Marty McFly in 1967. Upon seeing his older siblings, David and Linda, as fighting children (ages 5 and 2 ½), Marty (who'd been picked on by Dave when he was younger) told them that children who tease smaller kids were jailed by the Brat Police, and were then killed and fed to wolves. This left young David and Linda terrified—and well-behaved [**BTF2-s1**].

- *BraveLord:* A well-muscled fictional hero in the video game *BraveLord and Monstrux,* who protected a medieval kingdom called Pectoria from his arch-nemesis, the demon Monstrux. BraveLord fought evil and vehemently hated Brussels sprouts.

    When a power surge at Super Mega Arcade World brought the two enemies to life, Verne Brown was disappointed to learn that his hero was more concerned with preening his "massive pecs" than stopping Monstrux from taking over the real world—and that he was terrified at the sight of a kitten. What's more, since he lacked his magic belt, the warrior refused to fight the demon outside the game.

    As such, Verne and his friends were forced to defeat the monster themselves, after which he sent BraveLord and Monstrux back to cyberspace [**BFAN-19**].

    > ***NOTE:*** *BraveLord was drawn to resemble He-Man, from* Masters of the Universe, *and spoke like Kevin Nealon's "Franz" spoof of Arnold Schwarzenegger from* Saturday Night Live—*even calling Marty McFly "girly."*

- *BraveLord and Monstrux:* An interactive video game in which the warrior BraveLord battled the demon Monstrux, to prevent the latter from conquering the kingdom of Pectoria. Verne Brown played the game so often that he shirked his responsibilities—until a power surge at Super Mega Arcade World caused the two fictional characters to enter the real world [**BFAN-19**].

- **Braves:** A shop containing Western frontier memorabilia at the Pohatchee Drive-in Theater, located outside Hill Valley in 1955. Before traveling back to 1885, Marty McFly obtained supposedly authentic cowboy garb from Braves, similar to how cowboys dressed in classic Western films—but upon arriving in the Old West, he soon realized how ridiculous and anachronistic he actually looked [**BTF3**].

- **Bravo Tango Delta 629:** *See* BTD629

- **Brent Super Market:** A business listed in the Hill Valley phone book, circa 1955 [**BTF1-p**].

- **Brey Otto Upholstering:** A business listed in the Hill Valley phone book, circa 1955 [**BTF1-p**].

- **Brides Pond:** An area of Hill Valley, circa 1885, as indicated on a map hanging at the Hill Valley Railroad Station [**BTF3**].

- **Broadway Florist:** A flower shop specializing in weddings, funerals, parties and corsages, located on Main Street, in Courthouse Square, near the intersection of Hill Street. In 1985, Marty McFly passed this store while hitching a skateboard ride to school [**BTF1**].

- **Brooklyn Dodgers:** A Major League Baseball team later known as the Los Angeles Dodgers, and sometimes nicknamed the Bums [**REAL**]. The Dodgers were Emmett Brown's favorite baseball team in 1955 [**BTF1-n**].

- **Brothers, Bob:** A co-owner (with his brother, Robert Brothers) of the Bob Brothers All-Star International Circus, which performed at the Hill Valley Fairgrounds in 1933. The two brothers served as emcees, spoke very loudly and frequently completed each other's sentences. Verne Brown and his friend Chris helped the duo keep their circus from going bankrupt—and from being taken over by landlord Mac Tannen—by helping to raise public interest, and by performing in the circus as aerialists [**BFAN-18**].

    > ***NOTE:*** *The brothers were named after* Back to the Future *creators Robert Zemeckis and Bob Gale.*

- **Brothers, Robert:** A co-owner (with his brother, Bob Brothers) of the Bob Brothers All-Star International Circus [**BFAN-18**].

- **Brown:** A popular last name in Hill Valley and its surrounding cities [**BTF1-p**].

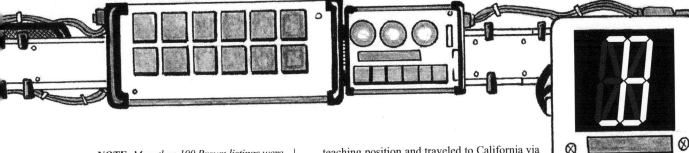

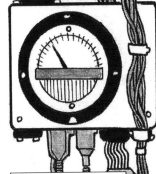

NOTE: More than 100 Brown listings were included in the 1955 telephone directory that Marty McFly accessed in BTTF1 while searching for Emmett Brown's address in that era. It's especially interesting to note that a woman named "Clara C. Brown" was among them, given that Doc's future wife, not introduced until BTTF3, was Clara Clayton Brown. Oddly, no Browns were listed beyond Fred Brown, and Doc's first name was misspelled.

Due to the sheer volume of names and street addresses listed in the fictional phone book (which covered a pair of two-page spreads), it would be impractical and bulky to incorporate all of that information into this lexicon. A scan of the actual prop page used in the film, containing the Brown listings, can be viewed in Appendix V.

- **BROWN:** The license plate of Emmett Brown's chauffeur-driven golfcart in Citizen Brown's dystopian timeline, circa 1986 [**TLTL-3**].

- **Brown, Alfred Co.:** A general contractor listed in the 1955 Hill Valley phone book [**BTF1-p**].

- **Brown, Burt:** The owner of the Brown Burt Flower Market, circa 1955 [**BTF1-p**].

- **Brown, Clarabelle Clayton ("Clara"):** The wife of Emmett Brown, and the mother of Jules and Verne Brown. A schoolteacher, she was hired to work in the Hill Valley schoolhouse in 1885 [**BTF3**] after being widowed in Silver City [**BTF3-s1**].

  Born in 1855 to pioneers Daniel Clayton and Martha O'Brien [**BFAN-13**], she had an uncle named Ulysses S. Clayton, who served as a general in the Union Army during the American Civil War [**BFAN-1**], as well as a beloved uncle known as Jumping Jehosaphat [**BFAN-21**].

  Originally from New Jersey, Clara enjoyed an active childhood, including climbing and horseback-riding [**BTF3-n**]. At age 11, she contracted diphtheria and was quarantined for three months. To keep her occupied, her father bought her a telescope so she could see everything out the window. This evolved into a lifelong passion for astronomy and the works of Jules Verne, including *From the Earth to the Moon* [**BTF3**]. Years later, following several unfortunate events back east, Clara accepted the Hill Valley

teaching position and traveled to California via locomotive, intending to build a new life for herself [**BTF3-n**].

  Shortly after her arrival, however, the horse of Clara's rented buckboard became spooked by a snake, carrying her over the side of the Shonash Ravine, to her death. The landform was then renamed the Clayton Ravine in her honor. The story of her death became a legend among Hill Valley's schoolchildren, some of whom wished their teachers would suffer the same fate.

  Emmett Brown (living in that era as a blacksmith) altered history when he saved her life, preventing her from going down with the wagon. The two became immediately infatuated with one another, their bond deepening as they discovered a mutual interest in science and the writings of Jules Verne. After years of being alone, Doc realized he loved her—but, unable to stay for risk of further damaging history, he forced himself to say goodbye to her.

  Doc revealed his future origins, but she mistook his claim of time-travel for a lie, and cast him aside. The next morning, she decided to leave Hill Valley and her pain behind. As her train pulled out of the station, she overheard a salesman describing a heartbroken man he'd met at the Palace Saloon, and realized it had been Emmett. Stopping the train, she ran back to find him, but he and Marty McFly had already departed by the time she reached Doc's stable. She noticed a model that Emmett had built to plan his return to the future, and realized he'd told her the truth.

  Clara set out on horseback to catch up with them, and found the duo using a stolen locomotive to push Doc's DeLorean up to 88 miles per hour. The train's engine was too loud for them to hear her calling out, so Clara climbed aboard the moving train but lost her footing and nearly fell under the locomotive's wheels. Stunned to see her behind him, Doc rescued her from death a second time, staying with her as Marty and the DeLorean vanished into the future. The two eventually married and had two sons, whom they named Jules and Verne [**BTF3**].

  Over the next few years, Doc converted a train engine car into another time machine, which he christened the *Jules Verne Train* [**RIDE**]. When the boys were young, Doc and Clara brought them briefly to 1985, so they could pick up Doc's dog, Einstein, and say a proper goodbye to Marty before returning to the past [**BTF3**].

  Eventually, the Brown family relocated

CODE	STORY
NIKE	*BTTF*-themed TV commercial: Nike
NTND	Nintendo *Back to the Future—The Ride* Mini-Game
PIZA	*BTTF*-themed TV commercial: Pizza Hut
PNBL	Data East *BTTF* pinball game
REAL	Real life
RIDE	Simulator: *Back to the Future—The Ride*
SCRM	2010 Scream Awards: *Back to the Future* 25th Anniversary Reunion (broadcast)
SCRT	2010 Scream Awards: *Back to the Future* 25th Anniversary Reunion (trailer)
SIMP	Simulator: *The Simpsons Ride*
SLOT	*Back to the Future Video Slots*
STLZ	Unused *BTTF* footage of Eric Stoltz as Marty McFly
STRY	*Back to the Future Storybook*
TEST	Screen tests: Crispin Glover, Lea Thompson and Tom Wilson
TLTL	Telltale Games' *Back to the Future—The Game*
TOPS	Topps' *Back to the Future II* trading-card set
TRIL	*BTTF: The Official Book of the Complete Movie Trilogy*
UNIV	Universal Studios Hollywood promotional video

SUFFIX	MEDIUM
-b	*BTTF2*'s Biff Tannen Museum video (extended)
-c	Credit sequence to the animated series
-d	Film deleted scene
-n	Film novelization
-o	Film outtake
-p	1955 phone book from *BTTF1*
-v	Video game print materials or commentaries
-s1	Screenplay (draft one)
-s2	Screenplay (draft two)
-s3	Screenplay (draft three)
-s4	Screenplay (draft four)
-sp	Screenplay (production draft)
-sx	Screenplay (*Paradox*)

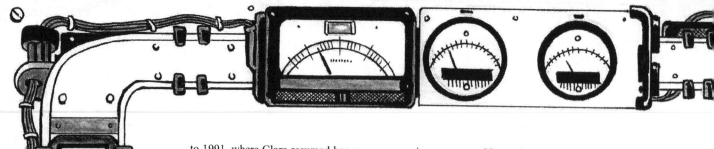

to 1991, where Clara resumed her career as an English teacher at Hill Valley Elementary School. She acclimated to the future remarkably well, her life made easier by her husband's inventions [**BFAN-1 to BFAN-26, BFCM-1 to BFCM-4, BFCL-1 to BFCL-3**].

Clara and her sons became great fans of the television show *Northern Exposure*. When Emmett inadvertently caused a city-wide brown-out, she rigged up the family TV to a workout bicycle so that they would not miss an episode [**BFAN-22**]. She and her husband sometimes gazed at the Moon's Sea of Tranquility through a telescope on the roof of their home [**BFAN-9**]; as a child, she'd often enjoyed gazing at the Moon, and had nicknamed the Copernicus crater "Little Sunshine" [**BTF3-n**].

Clara also had a fascination with horticulture and maintained a garden that she dubbed "Clara's Veggie Patch" [**BFAN-26**]. She and Doc genetically engineered a massive strain of corn that they named Super-Growth Mondo-Corn, a single ear of which nearly filled their garage [**BFAN-21**].

During this period of her life, she embarked on a number of adventures and faced numerous dangers, including being kidnapped by Lord Biffingham, the Earl of Tannenshire in 1367 [**BFAN-2**]; being stranded in space while traveling to Mars aboard the *MSC Marty* in 2091 [**BFAN-9**]; being sent to Debtor's Prison in 1845, along with the owners of Fedgewick Toys [**BFAN-10**]; attending a performance of William Shakespeare's *Hamlet* starring its original cast [**BFAN-16**]; visiting the Eiffel Tower, in Paris, France [**BFAN-21**]; meeting Bill Hill, Hill Valley's "Old Pioneer" [**BFAN-22**]; attending the 1904 St. Louis World Exposition, where she and Emmett recorded themselves singing "Meet Me in St. Louis, Louis" [**BFAN-25**]; being caught in the line of fire of a duel between Buford Tannen and another gunslinger [**BFAN-c**]; and befriending the queen of Apocrypha in 2,991,299,129,912,991 A.D. [**BFCL-2**].

Doc named his sailboat the S.S. *Clara* in honor of their love [**BFAN-14**].

> ***NOTE:** Clara's full first name, Clarabelle, was revealed in the episode "Brothers."*

> *Clara was portrayed by Mary Steenburgen, who had played Amy Robbins a decade prior, in Nicholas Meyer's* Time After Time. *The two roles were remark-*

ably similar, both involving an intelligent, career-minded woman falling in love with a time-traveling scientist from another era, initially disbelieving his story, and ultimately traveling with him to his own time after narrowly avoiding death; the characters even shared a few lines of dialog.

Mount Clayton, indicated on Doc's map of the Delgado Mine, may have been named after Clara as well. However, since he made the map before she arrived in Hill Valley and died at the Shonash Ravine, it's doubtful that Hill Valley's citizens would have named a mountain after her, since they would not yet have known her.

For a full list of Clara's known relatives, see Appendix III.

- **Brown, Doc:** An alias used by Emmett Brown while visiting Chicago's South Side, in 1927, to find a cure for cat-aracts for his dog, Einstein. The scientist posed as Doc Brown, a brewmaster for Martin "Zipper" McFly (Marty McFy's criminal alias), in order to locate a Prohibition Era still and use it to ferment medicine from juniper berries.

  When mob boss Arnie "Eggs" Benedict recognized his name from a brand of celery tonic, Doc explained that he was no longer producing the soda, having turned to brewing "hooch" (alcohol). This earned Eggs' trust, enabling Doc to access his still and save his pet [**BFCM-1**].

  > ***NOTE:** Doc Brown's Celery Tonic (now called Cel-Ray) has been in production since 1868. The soda was particularly popular in the 1920s.*

- **Brown, Eckhart, Judge:** *See* Brown, Erhardt, Judge

- **Brown, Emil & Co.:** A printing company listed in the Hill Valley phone book, circa 1955 [**BTF1-p**].

- **Brown, Emmett Lathrop, Doctor ("Doc," "Daredevil Emmett," "The Streak," "Brain Buster," "Mega Brainman," "First Citizen Brown"):** An eccentric, absent-minded scientist and inventor from a wealthy Hill Valley family of Germanic descent. Many of his inventions, such as the Brain-wave Analyzer, proved to be failures, but he persevered, despite a reputation for wreaking havoc during experiments. Brown was fascinated and inspired by the works of previous pioneering

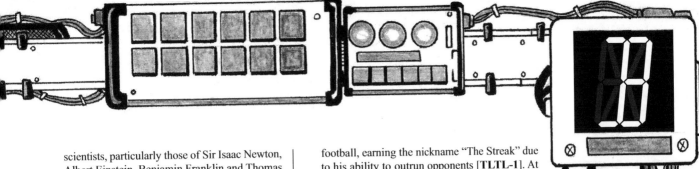

scientists, particularly those of Sir Isaac Newton, Albert Einstein, Benjamin Franklin and Thomas Edison [**BTF1**].

Doc loved animals, though he was not above using them to further his research. These included a monkey known as Shemp [**BTF1-s1, BTF1-s2**]; dogs named Einstein [**BTF1**], Newton [**BTF2-s1**] and Copernicus [**BTF2, BTF3**]; and horses called Archimedes, Newton and Galileo, which he owned while living in the Old West [**BTF3-sp, BTF3-n**].

Emmett's mother was Sarah Lathrop, whose maiden name became his middle name [**BTF3-s1**]. His father was prominent Hill Valley judge Erhardt Brown [**TLTL-1**], a German immigrant who'd changed their family name from von Braun to Brown during World War I [**BTF3**]. Emmett may have been named after a rag doll that Sarah had owned as a child, which she'd named Emma [**BTF3-s1**].

Emmett grew up a child prodigy. In 1926, he already knew several languages, the elements of the periodic table, numerous constellations of the Northern Hemisphere and a large chunk of the encyclopedia. That year, he spent time at the home of his Uncle Oliver, in Milwaukee, Wisconsin, where he fell into a lake. Surrounded by fish, he panicked and nearly drowned, instilling a lifelong, deep-seated fear of fishing. History changed when Doc's future sons, Jules and Verne, altered the timeline to prevent him from developing such a phobia.

In the resultant new timeline, Doc enjoyed a brief career as a Hollywood stunt actor and marketing sensation known as "Daredevil Emmett." This began when he inadvertently performed a stunt routine during the filming of a movie at Roris von Hinklehofen's Flying Circus, when the line of his fishing pole snagged a passing stunt plane. Impressed, Hollywood talent scout Harvey Wannamaker hired the youth and made him a star, with Oliver as his manager.

As Daredevil Emmett, Brown became a much-loved child icon, his name and likeness adorning comic books, soda, soup, nuts, trading cards, record albums and other products. But when Emmett nearly died during a stunt for D.W. Tannen's film *Raging Death Doom*, a fearful Oliver halted his nephew's acting career. By the 1990s, Doc's contribution to Hollywood was forgotten to all but the most ardent film buffs [**BFAN-11**].

As a youth, Emmett often played sandlot football, earning the nickname "The Streak" due to his ability to outrun opponents [**TLTL-1**]. At age 11, he read Jules Verne's *Twenty Thousand Leagues Under the Sea* and decided to devote his life to science. The following year, upon devouring Verne's *Journey to the Center of the Earth*, he attempted to travel to the Earth's core. He didn't get far, but the author's work had a profound effect on his life, nonetheless [**BTF3**].

Young Emmett sometimes spent summers on the farm of another uncle, Abraham Lathrop [**BTF3-sx**], and worked on the ranch of a local businessman named Statler [**BTF3-sp**]. He learned how to ride, shoot and rope, instilling in him a desire to be a cowboy [**BTF3-sx, BTF3-sp**]. He also watched many Saturday matinees of Western films, starring such actors as Roy Rogers and Tim Holt [**BTF3-n**].

Emmett was educated at a boy's school. Since Jules Verne had been sketchy in his novels when creating female characters, Emmett came to idealize women, and had little experience interacting with them as a teenager [**TLTL-4**].

The young scientist attended Hill Valley High School, where he was twice voted most likely to violate the laws of Newtonian physics [**BFAN-12**]. During his teen years, he spent much of his time at pool halls [**BFCM-4**].

In 1931, at age 17, Emmett worked as a clerk at the Hill Valley Courthouse. His father, Judge Brown, expected him to follow in his footsteps, but the teen longed to be a scientist and inventor—an aspiration of which Erhardt did not approve. In a laboratory in his room, Emmett designed a device called a Rocket-Powered Drill. He built a prototype and applied for a patent with the U.S. Patent Office, but never received a response and eventually abandoned the project.

When a future version of Doc, disguised as drifter Carl Sagan, was wrongfully imprisoned for arson in 1931, Marty McFly traveled from 1985 to that year to elicit young Emmett's help in freeing the older scientist. Marty convinced young Brown to build the drill under the pretense that he worked for the Patent Office, then took the device to break Doc out of jail. Emmett was crestfallen to learn that he'd been duped [**TLTL-1**].

Still, this incident gave Emmett the courage to leave the legal profession and devote himself entirely to science, much to his father's displeasure. Among his early inventions was a flying vehicle called a Rocket Car, which proved faulty, crashing onto a rooftop during its test

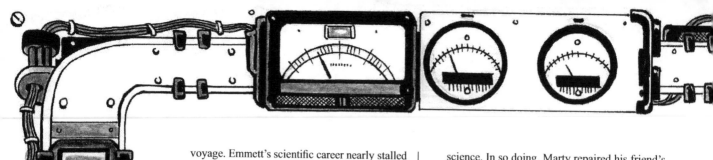

voyage. Emmett's scientific career nearly stalled at this point, until he saw the film *Frankenstein*, starring Boris Karloff. This instilled in him a passion that would remain with him for his entire life—until Marty accidentally altered time, causing Emmett to fall in love with (and later marry) Edna Strickland, thus preventing the budding scientist from seeing the film [**TLTL-2**].

In this new reality, Emmett abandoned science, and Hill Valley thus became a pristine, self-sustaining, walled utopia with extremely strict rules of propriety. As benevolent dictator First Citizen Brown, Doc (manipulated by Edna's conservative philosophies) promoted civil and social engineering, using Hill Valley as a prototype to show how technology could be utilized to shape a more efficient, orderly society. Under his rule, Hill Valley's citizens were mandated to live as vegetarians, wear ID badges and follow strict dress codes. Although he intended good for the city, Edna's single-minded obsession with curtailing vice and subversion had perverted his ideals. Thanks to Marty's intervention, the elder Brown came to realize his mistakes—but before he could fix the timeline, Edna subjected him to hypnotic re-conditioning [**TLTL-3**].

Marty helped old Doc escape, then returned to 1931 with him to end young Emmett's affair with Edna. In the interim, young Emmett, guided by Edna's self-righteousness, had built a Mental Alignment Meter, enabling him to read and interpret the subconscious desires of the human mind, in order to ascertain if an individual was good or bad. The contraption, which he'd planned to display at that year's Hill Valley Exposition, would ultimately start him on the path toward becoming Citizen Brown.

Unable to convince young Emmett that Edna wasn't right for him, Marty sought help from Sylvia "Trixie Trotter" Miskin, to trick Edna into believing Emmett had cheated on her. The ruse worked, and the couple split up—but by this time, the older Brown had grown smitten with Edna once more and resented Marty's attempt to change his past. At the last second, Brown betrayed Marty, stranding him in 1931 and instead allying himself with Edna [**TLTL-4**].

Citizen Brown kidnapped his younger self at the expo, hiding him in various exhibits to keep Marty away from him, and to prevent the young scientist from exhibiting a flying car. Marty found young Emmett and helped him carry out the exhibit as planned, re-sparking his passion for

science. In so doing, Marty repaired his friend's damaged relationship with his father, who was amazed at the sight of his son flying; thereafter, Erhardt fully supported Emmett's scientific pursuits. With teenage Emmett's career as an inventor restored and Citizen Brown's dystopian timeline eliminated, Marty and the elder Brown returned to their own era [**TLTL-5**].

After high school, Doc attended the American College of Technological Science & Difficult Math (ACTS&DM), a university for the scientifically gifted. His roommate and fraternity brother was Walter Wisdom, with whom he formed a close bond. The friendship ended during the Inter-Collegiate Science Invent-Off, in which students competed by submitting their inventions. Jealous of Doc's submission, the Perpetual-Motion Hula Hoop, Walter claimed it as his own, attaining the fame and fortune that should have been Brown's [**BFAN-15**].

During World War II, Doc worked on the Manhattan Project, a U.S.-led research and development program. This resulted in the creation of the world's first atomic bomb [**GALE**].

In 1952, Doc had a short wrestling career with the Small Town Professional Wrasslin organization—very short, as he lost his only match to the reigning champion, Mad Maximus. During this match, he fought under the stage-name Brain Buster Brown. Hit on the head by a microphone, he briefly believed himself to be a superhero, Mega Brainman, a "friend to the friendless, champion to the championless, superhero to the superheroless." A second knock on the skull eventually cured Doc of the delusion [**BFAN-24**].

That same year, Emmett's colleague Charles urged him to invest in the fledgling Xerox Corp. Convinced that the company had no future—since few would know how to pronounce its name (Doc mispronounced it as "X-rox")—Brown turned down the offer, missing out on a profitable investment opportunity [**BTF1-s1**].

Brown purchased the Cusimano Brothers Gearworks Factory that year from a man named Fredman, for $1.85 million, and launched Emmett Brown Enterprises so he could follow his dream of inventing a Photo-Electric Chemical Power Converter that could efficiently convert radiation into electrical energy [**BTF1-s2**]. The company later evolved into Dr. E. Brown Enterprises, offering atomic engineering and technical guidance, as well as clock and refrigerator repair

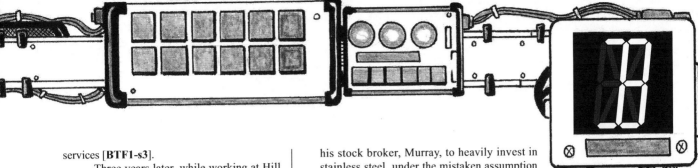

services [**BTF1-s3**].

Three years later, while working at Hill Valley University [**BTF2-s1**] under Dean Wooster, Doc dated the administrator's daughter, Jill Wooster. The dean, along with colleagues Cooper and Mintz, pressured Doc into taking part in one of three projects: developing the Edsel automobile, creating a chemical-warfare compound (to be dubbed Agent Brown in his honor) or helping to build the aforementioned company, Xerox. When Emmett refused all three opportunities, Dean Wooster put an end to his affair with Jill [**BTF3-s1**].

In 1955, while standing on his toilet to hang a clock, Brown slipped and hit his head, knocking himself unconscious. When he awoke, he had a vision of a device capable of facilitating time travel, which he dubbed the Flux Capacitor. This single invention would utterly change his life, though it would take thirty years and most of his family's fortune to fund research into making it a reality. After his home burnt to the ground (possibly due to arson), Doc moved into his garage, using the insurance money to continue his work.

In 1985, Emmett's decades of toil paid off, when he finally built a working time machine from a DeLorean DMC-12 sports car. Powered by electricity, the device required an enormous amount of energy to break the time barrier—1.21 jigowatts, to be exact, which he realized he could generate via plutonium.

Obtaining the radioactive substance required that he scam a group of Libyan nationalists. Hired to build them a nuclear bomb, he kept the plutonium and instead delivered a shiny case filled with used pinball-machine parts. The terrorists found him, however, and gunned him down at the Twin Pines Mall before he could embark on his maiden voyage.

Marty McFly witnessed the murder and cried out in anger, attracting the Libyans' notice. When they tried to kill him as well, the youth escaped in the DeLorean, propelling him to 1955—on the same day that Doc had invented time travel. Marty tracked down Brown's younger self, eliciting his help in going back to the future. The scientist deemed the task impossible, but Marty's foreknowledge of a lightning strike at the town's Clock Tower gave Doc the idea of harnessing the bolt's energy into the Flux Capacitor. [**BTF1**]

After viewing the DeLorean, Brown told

his stock broker, Murray, to heavily invest in stainless steel, under the mistaken assumption that all automobiles would be made from this material in the future [**BTF1-s4**].

Marty tried to warn his friend of his eventual murder, writing a note urging him to take precautions when the time came. Doc refused to look at it, fearful of the damage he could cause by knowing the future, but eventually gave in and read it anyway, enabling him to later wear a bullet-proof vest and survive the ordeal [**BTF1**].

Around 1980, Doc entertained the notion that all mammals spoke a common language, but this research proved fruitless. Other failed schemes included mining gold by superheating the Earth's surface, as well as determining everyone's predetermined age by studying the composition of their fingernails. He also published a paper claiming a baby's sex could be ascertained prior to conception. Most of his ideas received little notice, so he continued working privately, hoping to create something that would earn his peers' acclaim [**BTF1-n**]. Ultimately, this culminated in the creation of his DeLorean time machine [**BTF1**].

Emmett first met Marty when the latter was 13 or 14 years old. Marty had heard Doc described as a dangerous crackpot and lunatic, and was curious why people felt this way. Sneaking into Brown's laboratory, he was fascinated by the equipment within. Finding him in the lab, Doc was delighted to learn that Marty thought he was cool, and that the youth accepted him for what he was. Since both were the black sheep in their respective environments, a friendship formed. Doc offered Marty a part-time job helping with experiments, tending to his lab and watching Einstein [**GALE**]. He, in turn, paid Marty 50 dollars per week, providing him with free beer and access to his vintage record collection [**BTF1-s4**].

In 1985, following Marty's maiden voyage of the DeLorean time machine, Doc traveled 30 years into the future to experience time travel for himself [**BTF1**]. While in 2015, he performed a hover-conversion on the car, enabling it to fly, and added a Mr. Fusion Home Energy Reactor to fuel the vehicle more cleanly. In addition, the aging scientist visited a rejuvenation clinic to receive an All-Natural Overhaul, consisting of skin-wrinkle removal, hair repair, blood changing and the replacement of his spleen and colon. In so doing, he added approximately 30 or 40 years to his lifespan [**BTF2**].

CODE	STORY
NIKE	*BTTF*-themed TV commercial: Nike
NTND	Nintendo *Back to the Future—The Ride* Mini-Game
PIZA	*BTTF*-themed TV commercial: Pizza Hut
PNBL	Data East *BTTF* pinball game
REAL	Real life
RIDE	Simulator: *Back to the Future—The Ride*
SCRM	2010 Scream Awards: *Back to the Future* 25th Anniversary Reunion (broadcast)
SCRT	2010 Scream Awards: *Back to the Future* 25th Anniversary Reunion (trailer)
SIMP	Simulator: *The Simpsons Ride*
SLOT	*Back to the Future Video Slots*
STLZ	Unused *BTTF* footage of Eric Stoltz as Marty McFly
STRY	*Back to the Future Storybook*
TEST	Screen tests: Crispin Glover, Lea Thompson and Tom Wilson
TLTL	Telltale Games' *Back to the Future—The Game*
TOPS	Topps' *Back to the Future II* trading-card set
TRIL	*BTTF: The Official Book of the Complete Movie Trilogy*
UNIV	Universal Studios Hollywood promotional video

SUFFIX	MEDIUM
-b	*BTTF2*'s Biff Tannen Museum video (extended)
-c	Credit sequence to the animated series
-d	Film deleted scene
-n	Film novelization
-o	Film outtake
-p	1955 phone book from *BTTF1*
-v	Video game print materials or commentaries
-s1	Screenplay (draft one)
-s2	Screenplay (draft two)
-s3	Screenplay (draft three)
-s4	Screenplay (draft four)
-sp	Screenplay (production draft)
-sx	Screenplay (*Paradox*)

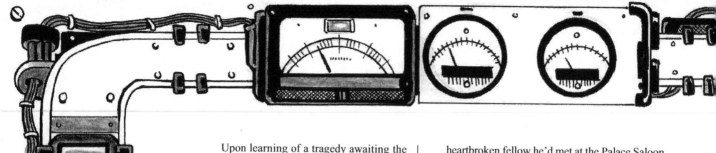

CODE	STORY
ARGN	*BTTF*-themed TV commercial: Arrigoni
BFAN	*Back to the Future: The Animated Series*
BFCG	*Back to the Future: The Card Game*
BFCL	*Back to the Future* comic book (limited series)
BFCM	*Back to the Future* comic book (monthly series)
BFHM	*BTTF*-themed McDonald's Happy Meal boxes
BTFA	*Back to the Future Annual* (Marvel Comics)
BTF1	Film: *Back to the Future*
BTF2	Film: *Back to the Future Part II*
BTF3	Film: *Back to the Future Part III*
BUDL	*BTTF*-themed TV commercial: Bud Light
CHEK	*BTTF*-themed music video: O'Neal McKnight, "Check Your Coat"
CHIC	Photographs hanging in the Doc Brown's Chicken restaurant at Universal Studios
CITY	*BTTF*-themed music video: Owl City, "Deer in the Headlights"
CLUB	*Back to the Future* Fan Club Magazine
DCTV	*BTTF*-themed TV commercial: DirecTV
ERTH	*The Earth Day Special*
GALE	Interviews and commentaries: Bob Gale and/or Robert Zemeckis
GARB	*BTTF*-themed TV commercials for Garbarino
HUEY	*BTTF*-themed music video: Huey Lewis and the News, "The Power of Love"
LIMO	*BTTF*-themed music video: The Limousines, "The Future"
MCDN	*BTTF*-themed TV commercial: McDonald's
MITS	*BTTF*-themed TV commercial: Mitsubishi Lancer
MSFT	*BTTF*-themed TV commercial: Microsoft

Upon learning of a tragedy awaiting the McFly family, however, Doc returned to 1985 to warn his younger friend [**BTF1**]. Doc had discovered that Marty McFly Jr.—Marty's future son with Jennifer Parker—was being pressured to help Griff Tannen rob the Hill Valley Payroll Substation, which would end in Marty Jr. being jailed, along with his sister, Marlene. The scientist devised a plan by which Marty Sr. would pose as his son and refuse to take part in the theft. The plan worked, but set off events culminating in an elderly Biff Tannen stealing the DeLorean and giving his younger self an almanac containing future sports statistics, thereby enabling him to become a wealthy, powerful criminal kingpin. Realizing their error, Emmett and Marty retrieved the book and restored the timeline, but soon thereafter, Doc became stranded in 1885 when the DeLorean was struck by lightning [**BTF2**].

In 1885, Doc forged a new career as a blacksmith, enjoying the wonders of the Old West. Though considered eccentric, he became a valued member of Hill Valley society, performing favors for Mayor Hubert and others. When he fixed a horseshoe for Buford "Mad Dog" Tannen, his happy life came to a halt, as the horse threw a shoe, causing the outlaw to break a bottle of whiskey, and then to shoot the horse in anger. Blaming Doc for the loss, Tannen demanded that the blacksmith pay him $80, but Brown refused, for which Buford shot him in the back.

Upon finding Doc's gravestone in 1955, Marty learned of his friend's fate and traveled back to rescue him. The situation became more complicated when Doc met newly arrived schoolteacher Clara Clayton. In the original timeline, Clara's horse had been spooked by a snake, carrying her to her death over the side of the Shonash Ravine. But this time, Emmett saved her life, preventing her from going down with the wagon.

The two grew infatuated with one another as they discovered a mutual interest in science and the writings of Jules Verne. After years of being alone, Doc realized he loved her—but, unable to stay for risk of further damaging history, he forced himself to say goodbye. The inventor revealed his future origins to her, but she mistook his claim of time-travel for a manipulative lie and cast him aside.

The next morning, Clara decided to leave Hill Valley, but as her train pulled out of the station, she overheard a salesman describing a heartbroken fellow he'd met at the Palace Saloon and Hotel, and realized the man was describing Emmett. Stopping the locomotive, she ran back to find him, but he and Marty had already departed by the time she reached Doc's stable. There, upon seeing a model built to plan their return to the future, she realized Doc had told her the truth.

Clara set out on horseback to catch up with the time-travelers, and found them using a stolen locomotive to push the DeLorean up to 88 miles per hour. The train's engine was too loud for them to hear her calling out, so Clara climbed aboard the moving train—but she lost her footing and nearly fell under the locomotive's wheels. Stunned to see her behind him, Doc rescued her from death a second time, staying with her as Marty and the car vanished. The two eventually married and had two sons, whom they named Jules and Verne [**BTF3**].

Over the next several years, Doc converted a train engine car into another time machine, which he christened the *Jules Verne Train* [**RIDE**]. When the boys were young, Doc and Clara brought them briefly to 1985, to pick up Einstein and say a proper goodbye to Marty [**BTF3**].

Eventually, the Browns relocated to 1991, where Emmett made all of their lives easier by filling their home with his many eccentric inventions [**BFAN-1**]. Doc also purchased a sailboat, which he christened the *S.S. Clara* [**BFAN-14**]. During this period of his life, Doc and his family shared many time-traveling adventures, often accompanied by Marty and Einstein [**BFAN-1 to BFAN-26, BFCM-1 to BFCM-4, BFCL-1 to BFCL-3**].

Brown formed a think-tank called the Institute of Future Technology (IFT), serving as its chief inventive officer. Within this facility, scientists and inventors created numerous innovations, including the Eight-Passenger DeLorean Time-Travel Vehicle [**RIDE**]. Eventually, Doc ran out of funding and had no choice but to sell the institute. Herschel "Krusty the Clown" Krustofski purchased the facility, which the entertainer used to create his Krustyland theme park [**SIMP**].

At some point, Doc attended the Annual Convention of the Home Inventors and Mad Geniuses. At this event, he presented his ELB Pediatric Policer to his colleagues [**BFAN-26**].

Doc also created a database to educate future scientists, with help from a television producer known as B.G. [**BFAN-23**] and

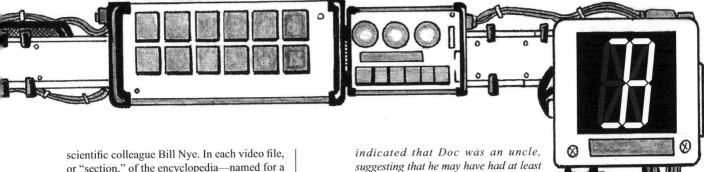

scientific colleague Bill Nye. In each video file, or "section," of the encyclopedia—named for a letter of the English alphabet—Nye demonstrated a different type of experiment, with Brown narrating [**BFAN-1 to BFAN-26**].

Brown briefly worked at Chez Crossé as a parking attendant in 1991, after Jules and Verne played an April Fool's Day joke by convincing him that his brain was nearly full, and that he thus needed to abandon science. Fired for crashing a customer's car, he tried his hand at other jobs as well, including as a chef at Tony's Pizza, and at the Luau Lunch Hut as a piano player. In time, the boys revealed the truth and he once more resumed his scientific pursuits [**BFAN-12**].

NOTE: The above lexicon entry is, by necessity, not all-inclusive. Doc, as one of Back to the Future*'s primary protagonists, was involved in nearly all iterations of the mythos, and was usually the main focus, along with Marty. To include every detail of his adventures would thus be impractical. The entire lexicon, taken as a whole, should be considered when examining Doc's life.*

In particular, his animated adventures are not described here in detail; to learn more about those tales, see Appendix I. For an exhaustive list of Doc's inventions, see Appendix II. And for a full list of his various aliases and known relatives, see Appendix III.

Emmett's character varied wildly from one film screenplay draft to the next, as he evolved from being a drug-using video bootlegger, known as "Prof. Brown," to a womanizing beatnik socialite. His middle name, Lathrop, was revealed in the animated episodes "Put on Your Thinking Caps, Kids! It's Time for Mr. Wisdom!" and "Hill Valley Brown-Out."

After BTTF1 was completed, actor Christopher Lloyd proposed a sequel in which he would play evil and heroic versions of Emmett Brown, who would become a diabolical villain in the future. Although such a sequel was never written or filmed, the premise was revisited in Telltale Games' BTTF video game, in which Lloyd portrayed both Doc and Citizen Brown.

BTTF2's first-draft screenplay

indicated that Doc was an uncle, suggesting that he may have had at least one sibling. No information about such a relative is available, however.

- **Brown, Emmett Jr.:** The fictional son of Emmett Brown and Sylvia "Trixie Trotter" Miskin, born out of wedlock. Emmett Jr. did not actually exist, as he was created as a ruse by Trixie and Marty McFly to end Emmett's relationship with Edna Strickland by making Edna think Emmett had cheated on her. Trixie's photo of Emmett Jr. was actually a snapshot of Emmett himself as a young child [**TLTL-4**].

- **Brown, Erhardt, Judge:** The father of Emmett Brown, and a judge at the Hill Valley Courthouse in 1931 [**TLTL-1**]. His wife (Doc's mother) was Sarah Lathrop [**BTF3-s1**]. Born Erhardt von Braun, he changed his family's surname to Brown during World War I [**BTF3**].

Judge Brown, considered the most learned, incorruptible and just judge in the city's history, was a strict disciplinarian with regard to his son. Emmett worked for him as a courthouse clerk at age 17 and took his duties very seriously for fear of his father's wrath. Eventually, Emmett's interest in science caused a rift between the two men, when the youth asserted his right to pursue his dreams, instead of following his father into the legal sector [**TLTL-1**].

A severe man of German descent, Erhardt had a thick accent, a large mustache, spectacles and a corpulent shape. He was hired to serve on Hill Valley Criminal Court in 1916, and remained in that position for at least the next 15 years. An immigrant, he came to America against his father's wishes, unable to speak English and with only $2 to his name. Erhardt became a judge later in life, and demanded that his son follow in his footsteps. After seeing Emmett demonstrate his flying car at the 1931 Hill Valley Exposition, however, the judge grew fiercely proud of his son's accomplishments and thereafter supported his scientific pursuits—even going so far as to set up the Erhardt Brown Scholarship for Young Scientists [**TLTL-5**].

The book *Hill Valley Historical Society, 1865-1990* noted that "his justice was severe, but his heart was incorruptible" [**TLTL-v**]. He died sometime before Marty McFly was born [**TLTL-3**].

NOTE: Supplemental materials included

CODE	STORY
NIKE	*BTTF*-themed TV commercial: Nike
NTND	Nintendo *Back to the Future—The Ride* Mini-Game
PIZA	*BTTF*-themed TV commercial: Pizza Hut
PNBL	Data East *BTTF* pinball game
REAL	Real life
RIDE	Simulator: *Back to the Future—The Ride*
SCRM	2010 Scream Awards: *Back to the Future* 25th Anniversary Reunion (broadcast)
SCRT	2010 Scream Awards: *Back to the Future* 25th Anniversary Reunion (trailer)
SIMP	Simulator: *The Simpsons Ride*
SLOT	*Back to the Future Video Slots*
STLZ	Unused *BTTF* footage of Eric Stoltz as Marty McFly
STRY	*Back to the Future Storybook*
TEST	Screen tests: Crispin Glover, Lea Thompson and Tom Wilson
TLTL	Telltale Games' *Back to the Future—The Game*
TOPS	Topps' *Back to the Future II* trading-card set
TRIL	*BTTF: The Official Book of the Complete Movie Trilogy*
UNIV	Universal Studios Hollywood promotional video

SUFFIX	MEDIUM
-b	*BTTF2*'s Biff Tannen Museum video (extended)
-c	Credit sequence to the animated series
-d	Film deleted scene
-n	Film novelization
-o	Film outtake
-p	1955 phone book from *BTTF1*
-v	Video game print materials or commentaries
-s1	Screenplay (draft one)
-s2	Screenplay (draft two)
-s3	Screenplay (draft three)
-s4	Screenplay (draft four)
-sp	Screenplay (production draft)
-sx	Screenplay (*Paradox*)

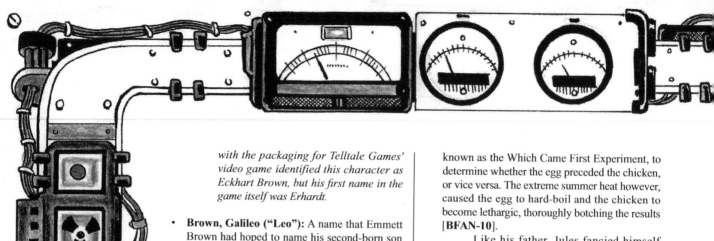

with the packaging for Telltale Games' video game identified this character as Eckhart Brown, but his first name in the game itself was Erhardt.

- **Brown, Galileo ("Leo"):** A name that Emmett Brown had hoped to name his second-born son ("Leo" for short), in honor of astronomer Galileo Galilei. Instead, he and his wife, Clara Clayton Brown, named the child Verne [**BFAN-21**].

- **Brown, Goodman:** An alias used by Emmett Brown while living among the Puritans of Salem, Massachusetts, in 1692. As Goodman Brown, Doc was responsible for removing others' trash—which he deemed a fascinating way to explore the culture. In so doing, he introduced a recycling program to the Puritans [**BFAN-4**].

- **Brown, Jehosaphat:** A name that Clara Clayton Brown had hoped to name her second-born son, in honor of her beloved uncle. Instead, she and her husband, Emmett, named the child Verne [**BFAN-21**].

- **Brown, Jules Eratosthenes ("Julie"):** The oldest son of Emmett and Clara Clayton Brown, born sometime after 1885, during Hill Valley's frontier period. He and his younger brother, Verne, first met Doc's friends Marty McFly and Jennifer Parker while visiting 1985 with their parents aboard the *Jules Verne Train*. Doc had named the locomotive after the two boys [**BTF3, RIDE**].

  Once the Browns relocated to the 20th century, Jules attended Hill Valley Elementary School, where he greatly disliked a school administrator called Vice-Principal Strickland [**BFAN-12, BFAN-26**]. He and Verne experienced a number of adventures and faced various challenges during their youth, frequently traveling into the past and future aboard their father's time-traveling DeLorean, with or without his permission [**BTF3, BFAN-1 to BFAN-26, BFCM-1 to BFCM-4, BFCL-1 to BFCL-3**]

  A dedicated scholar even from a young age, Jules often sought to increase his knowledge, and found complex science and mathematics more fun than the video games and childhood diversions that Verne enjoyed. At age two, he drew a DNA molecule on his Etch A Sketch toy. His intelligence intimidated Verne, who was far less into studying [**BFAN-1**].

  In 1991, Jules conducted a research project

known as the Which Came First Experiment, to determine whether the egg preceded the chicken, or vice versa. The extreme summer heat however, caused the egg to hard-boil and the chicken to become lethargic, thoroughly botching the results [**BFAN-10**].

Like his father, Jules fancied himself an inventor. In 1991, he created the Cerebrum Observator, a device built from an otoscope, a medical examination device used to look into a person's ears. This enabled him to view an individual's thoughts and dreams [**BFAN-11**].

He also created a hovercase, utilizing hoverboard antigravity technology to enable a user to travel with a loaded briefcase without having to lift it [**BFAN-20**]. Another invention was the J.E.B. Cross-time Headliner, which combined an old-style teletype machine with a Flux Capacitor, enabling him to print up newspaper pages from any desired era, in order to learn about history. Jules built the device as an anniversary gift for his parents [**BFAN-9**].

In addition, Jules invented the Robogriddle, a cooking contraption utilizing five robotic arms to automatically produce flapjacks at high speed, from batter-pouring to table service [**BFAN-16**]. He also devised the Uniview, a helmet and lenses connected to a long tube, enabling a wearer to watch television without annoying others [**BFAN-11**].

Among his most ambitious creations was the Jules Brown Money-Tree, a synthetic tree containing leaves resembling U.S. paper currency, which he created intending to make his family wealthy, as well as buy the friendships of other children. The money-tree was a follow-up to his multi-motif leaf tree, a synthetic variety containing striped and polka-dotted leaves, as well as pink hearts, yellow moons and green clovers, designed to resemble cheap upholstery.

The multi-motif leaf tree took weeks to cultivate and was very sensitive—when Verne yelled loudly, all of its leaves fell off. Therefore, Jules instead turned to creating the money-tree. To protect it, he also built an anti-pilfering security system, comprising wired sensors, sirens and a spring-loaded boxing glove. For a time, the tree brought the Browns fame and notoriety, causing the U.S. government to investigate whether he was the kingpin of an international counterfeiting racket. Ultimately, the money leaves shriveled, making it useless as a source of legal tender.

Emmett Brown later created a homemade chlorophyll and enzyme booster for Jules, in

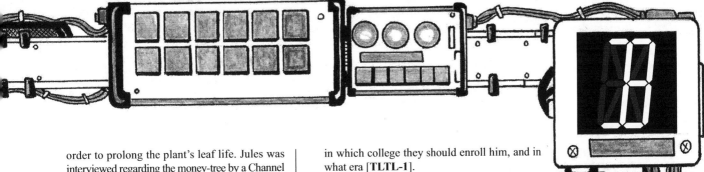

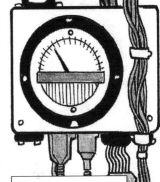

order to prolong the plant's leaf life. Jules was interviewed regarding the money-tree by a Channel 91 television reporter named Tammy, as well as by the newspaper *USA Hooray* [**BFAN-20**].

Jules and Verne witnessed the American Civil War after Verne stole Doc's DeLorean and traveled back to 1864 Chattanooga. Verne became a drummer-boy under the Confederate Army's General Beauregard Tannen. Emmett and Jules followed him back and met their ancestor, General Ulysses S. Clayton, of the Union Army. Jules and Verne convinced both armies to shake hands and embrace peace, preventing bloodshed [**BFAN-1**].

Jules liked to tease his brother about being intellectually inferior, though sometimes his jibing went too far. On one occasion, he convinced Verne that he was adopted (which he wasn't), causing the younger Brown to steal the DeLorean and go back in time to find his "real" father, whom he erroneously believed to be Benjamin Franklin [**BFAN-6**].

Jules had a strong crush on Franny Philips [**BFAN-20, BFAN-26**], and was often excluded by another classmate, Jackson, who considered him too nerdy to play with. When Jules created the money-tree, both children became much nicer to him—though Franny came to genuinely like him, no longer interested only in what he could buy for her [**BFAN-20**].

Jules loved amusement parks, and was particularly fond of the Gut Twister and the Spleen Splitter, rides at Mega Monster Mountain [**BFAN-25**]. He was also a fan of baseball, and owned a baseball card bearing the image of Pee Wee McFly, from an 1897 championship game [**BFAN-8**]. However, he intensely disliked *The Half Show*, a popular children's television program featuring characters that he dismissed as "juvenile martial-arts mutations" [**BFAN-20**].

During a trip to 1845 London, Jules and Verne met an orphaned street urchin named Reginald, forced to work as a pickpocket for a thug named Murdock. Reg picked Jules' pocket, stealing a watch fob once owned by Jules' great-grandfather, which contained the keys to Doc's DeLorean. To retrieve the watch, the boys worked alongside Reg as pickpockets, eventually convincing the child to give up his life of crime [**BFAN-10**]. The boys also helped Roman slave Judah Ben-Hur escape servitude in 36 A.D. [**BFAN-5**].

When Jules was in his early teens, his parents had already begun research to determine in which college they should enroll him, and in what era [**TLTL-1**].

> ***NOTE:*** *Jules' middle name, revealed in the episode "Go Fly a Kite," was derived from Eratosthenes of Cyrene, a Greek mathematician and poet known for coining the phrase "geography." His nickname, "Julie," was spoken in "Dickens of a Christmas" (though Jules preferred not to be called by that name).*

- **Brown, Vernon Newton ("Verne," "Vernie"):** The youngest son of Emmett and Clara Clayton Brown, born sometime after 1885, during Hill Valley's frontier period. He and his older brother, Jules, first met Doc's friends Marty McFly and Jennifer Parker while visiting 1985 with their parents aboard the *Jules Verne Train*. Doc had named the locomotive after the two boys [**BTF3, RIDE**].

Once the Browns relocated to the 20th century, Verne attended Hill Valley Elementary School, where he greatly disliked a school administrator called Vice-Principal Strickland [**BFAN-12, BFAN-26**]. He and Jules experienced a number of adventures and faced various challenges during their youth, frequently traveling into the past and future aboard their father's time-traveling DeLorean, with or without his permission [**BTF3, BFAN-1 to BFAN-26, BFCM-1 to BFCM-4, BFCL-1 to BFCL-3**]

An expert video game player, Verne was especially skilled at a monster-battling game called *The Legend of Gruno*. His father encouraged his game-playing, knowing it enhanced his hand-eye coordination [**BFAN-1**]. He also enjoyed *BraveLord and Monstrux*—until a power surge at Super Mega Arcade World caused the game's fictional characters to enter the real world. Verne was disappointed to learn that his hero, BraveLord, was more concerned with preening his "massive pecs" than stopping Monstrux from taking over the world—and that he was terrified of kittens [**BFAN-19**].

Another game Verne played was *Intergalactic Space Feud*, in which three-headed aliens tried to vaporize players. Once tired of the game, he tossed it to the side of the road [**BFAN-13**]. Verne's video game addiction sometimes caused him problems. A neighbor, Jörg Johannsen, hired him to mow the lawn, but he often ignored the chore in favor of playing video games. This caused the Johannsens' grass

CODE	STORY
NIKE	*BTTF*-themed TV commercial: Nike
NTND	Nintendo *Back to the Future—The Ride* Mini-Game
PIZA	*BTTF*-themed TV commercial: Pizza Hut
PNBL	Data East *BTTF* pinball game
REAL	Real life
RIDE	Simulator: *Back to the Future—The Ride*
SCRM	2010 Scream Awards: *Back to the Future* 25th Anniversary Reunion (broadcast)
SCRT	2010 Scream Awards: *Back to the Future* 25th Anniversary Reunion (trailer)
SIMP	Simulator: *The Simpsons Ride*
SLOT	*Back to the Future* Video Slots
STLZ	Unused *BTTF* footage of Eric Stoltz as Marty McFly
STRY	*Back to the Future* Storybook
TEST	Screen tests: Crispin Glover, Lea Thompson and Tom Wilson
TLTL	Telltale Games' *Back to the Future—The Game*
TOPS	Topps' *Back to the Future II* trading-card set
TRIL	*BTTF: The Official Book of the Complete Movie Trilogy*
UNIV	Universal Studios Hollywood promotional video

SUFFIX	MEDIUM
-b	*BTTF2*'s Biff Tannen Museum video (extended)
-c	Credit sequence to the animated series
-d	Film deleted scene
-n	Film novelization
-o	Film outtake
-p	1955 phone book from *BTTF1*
-v	Video game print materials or commentaries
-s1	Screenplay (draft one)
-s2	Screenplay (draft two)
-s3	Screenplay (draft three)
-s4	Screenplay (draft four)
-sp	Screenplay (production draft)
-sx	Screenplay (*Paradox*)

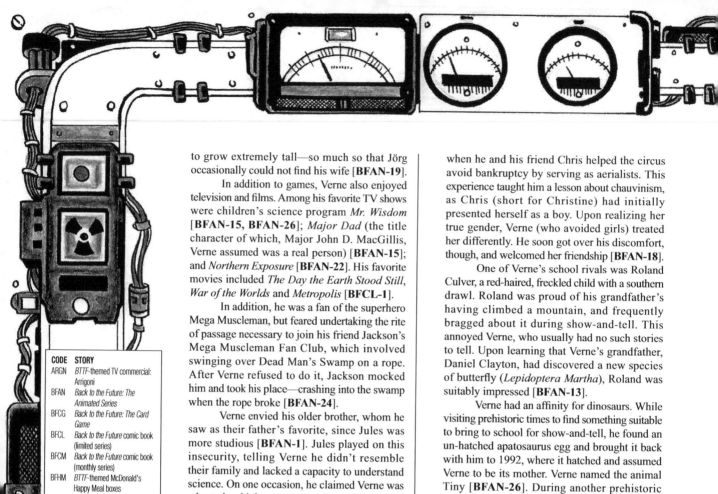

to grow extremely tall—so much so that Jörg occasionally could not find his wife [**BFAN-19**].

In addition to games, Verne also enjoyed television and films. Among his favorite TV shows were children's science program *Mr. Wisdom* [**BFAN-15, BFAN-26**]; *Major Dad* (the title character of which, Major John D. MacGillis, Verne assumed was a real person) [**BFAN-15**]; and *Northern Exposure* [**BFAN-22**]. His favorite movies included *The Day the Earth Stood Still*, *War of the Worlds* and *Metropolis* [**BFCL-1**].

In addition, he was a fan of the superhero Mega Muscleman, but feared undertaking the rite of passage necessary to join his friend Jackson's Mega Muscleman Fan Club, which involved swinging over Dead Man's Swamp on a rope. After Verne refused to do it, Jackson mocked him and took his place—crashing into the swamp when the rope broke [**BFAN-24**].

Verne envied his older brother, whom he saw as their father's favorite, since Jules was more studious [**BFAN-1**]. Jules played on this insecurity, telling Verne he didn't resemble their family and lacked a capacity to understand science. On one occasion, he claimed Verne was adopted, which was untrue. Verne concluded that Benjamin Franklin was his biological father, after finding a photo of himself with the inventor from 1752. Journeying back in time to meet the man, he interrupted his kite-flying experiments, preventing Franklin from discovering the nature of electricity. This altered history, plunging the world into darkness, until Verne's family restored the timeline by manufacturing another lightning storm for Franklin to study [**BFAN-6**].

A mischievous child, Verne had an uncanny knack for impersonating his mother, and sometimes called his school in her voice to excuse himself from attending [**BFAN-13**]. In 1991, he played an April Fool's Day joke on his father, convincing him that his brain was nearly full, and that he needed to give up science. Another day, he placed banana peels in Doc's Auto-Jog Mechanical Running Shorts—which actually helped, since they no longer chafed [**BFAN-12**].

While visiting Chattanooga in 1864, Verne became a drummer-boy under Confederate Army General Beauregard Tannen, during the American Civil War. Verne introduced the Tannen clan to the term "butthead," by uttering the phrase in Beauregard's presence [**BFAN-1**].

Verne briefly performed with the Bob Brothers All-Star International Circus in 1933, when he and his friend Chris helped the circus avoid bankruptcy by serving as aerialists. This experience taught him a lesson about chauvinism, as Chris (short for Christine) had initially presented herself as a boy. Upon realizing her true gender, Verne (who avoided girls) treated her differently. He soon got over his discomfort, though, and welcomed her friendship [**BFAN-18**].

One of Verne's school rivals was Roland Culver, a red-haired, freckled child with a southern drawl. Roland was proud of his grandfather's having climbed a mountain, and frequently bragged about it during show-and-tell. This annoyed Verne, who usually had no such stories to tell. Upon learning that Verne's grandfather, Daniel Clayton, had discovered a new species of butterfly (*Lepidoptera Martha*), Roland was suitably impressed [**BFAN-13**].

Verne had an affinity for dinosaurs. While visiting prehistoric times to find something suitable to bring to school for show-and-tell, he found an un-hatched apatosaurus egg and brought it back with him to 1992, where it hatched and assumed Verne to be its mother. Verne named the animal Tiny [**BFAN-26**]. During another prehistoric voyage, he befriended a pteranodon that he called "Donny," which gave him and his family rides on its back and in its talons [**BFAN-3**].

In 1992, Verne's parents enrolled him in classes at the Hill Valley Dance Academy, under the tutelage of an instructor named Dorothy, who had little patience for his inability to master the waltz. While visiting 1944, he met Dorothy's younger self, who developed a crush on him [**BFAN-17**]. Verne also took part in his school's Drama Club, an extracurricular group that performed theatrical productions. When the club produced *Sleeping Beauty*, he dreaded appearing in it, for fear that he'd have to kiss fellow student Beatrice Spalding [**BFAN-26**].

Verne hated his name, and asked Marty to help him find a way to rename author Jules Verne, so that his own identity would be changed as well. Among their suggested alternates were Bill, James Bond, Charles Dickens, Frank, Hammer, Luke Perry, Raphael, Bart Simpson, Dr. Seuss and Mark Twain. The attempt failed, and both Vernes retained their original names [**BFAN-21**].

When Verne was in his early teens, his parents had already begun research to determine in which college they should enroll him, and in what era [**TLTL-1**].

In one possible future, Verne traveled back

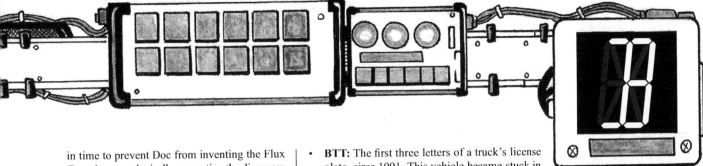

in time to prevent Doc from inventing the Flux Capacitor, paradoxically preventing the discovery of time travel in the first place. [**BFCG**]

> *NOTE: Verne's middle name (Newton) and nickname (Vernie) were established in the episode "Brothers." The name Newton paid homage to physicist and astronomer Sir Isaac Newton, a personal hero of his father.*
>
> *In the episode "Marty McFly PFC," Verne's dance instructor referred to him as Vernon Brown. That name has appeared in no other* Back to the Future *lore, however, and would seem inconsistent with Doc having named him after author Jules Verne, who was not named Vernon.*

- **Brown & Bigelow Advertising Co.:** A business listed in the 1955 Hill Valley phone book, owned by Russell T. Campbell [**BTF1-p**].

- **Brown Burt Flower Market:** A business listed in the 1955 Hill Valley phone book, owned by Burt Brown [**BTF1-p**].

- **Brown Car Auto Repair:** A business listed in the 1955 Hill Valley phone book [**BTF1-p**].

- **Brown Floral Co.:** A business listed in the 1955 Hill Valley phone book [**BTF1-p**].

- **Bruno's Bakery:** A business in Hill Valley, circa 1955, as indicated on a drawing made by Emmett Brown that year as he calculated Marty McFly's return to 1985 [**BTF1**].

- **B.S. Gideon:** A manufacture of corsets. In 1885, a Hill Valley business known as the M. Fennigot Millinery sold this company's products [**BTF3-n**].

- **BTD629:** The California license plate number of a 1979 Plymouth Reliant owned by Marty McFly's family in 1985. The car was damaged during an alcohol-related accident when George McFly's boss, Biff Tannen, borrowed and crashed the vehicle [**BTF1**].

> *NOTE: A tow-truck dispatcher referred to the license plate as "Bravo Tango Delta 629," in keeping with typical phonetic-alphabet conventions.*

- **BTT:** The first three letters of a truck's license plate, circa 1991. This vehicle became stuck in traffic after Emmett Brown inadvertently drove a tractor onto a busy road [**BFAN-12**].

> *NOTE: The remainder of the license plate was obstructed from view, but it's likely the next letter would have been an "F"—resulting in an in-joke reference to "BTTF," the common acronym for* Back to the Future.

- **Bub:** A student who ran for class president at Hill Valley High School in 1955. Marty McFly passed his campaign poster while retrieving *Grays Sports Almanac* from Gerald Strickland's office [**BTF2**].

- **Buchanan, R.M.:** A citizen of Hill Valley listed on Arthur McFly's ledger at the 1931 Hill Valley Exposition [**TLTL-2**].

- **Buck:** A member of Buford Tannen's gang in 1885. The shortest outlaw in the group, he wore his hat flattened [**BTF3-s1, BTF3-sx**].

> *NOTE: This character, unnamed onscreen, was identified in BTTF3's screenplays.*

- **Buck:** A wild beaver cared for by Windjammer Diefendorfer, which Marty McFly encountered while visiting 1888. The kindly old man fitted Buck's teeth with braces [**BFAN-21**].

- **Buck:** An individual murdered by Irving "Kid" Tannen sometime in or before 1931. Kid's bartender, Zane Williams, illustrated a caricature of Buck for the Wall of Honor at the gangster's speakeasy, El Kid [**TLTL-v**].

- **Buckingham Palace:** The official residence and workplace of the British monarchy, located in Westminster, England [**REAL**]. After Emmett Brown visited this site, a photo commemorating the occasion was displayed at Doc Brown's Chicken [**CHIC**].

- ***Buck Rogers*:** A fictional series about Anthony "Buck" Rogers, introduced in Philip Francis Nowlan's 1928 novella *Armageddon 2419 A.D.*, and continued in various comic strips, movies, radio shows and TV series [**REAL**].

  Upon seeing Emmett Brown's flying DeLorean in 1931, Officer Daniel Parker thought it something out of *Buck Rogers*, and reported the

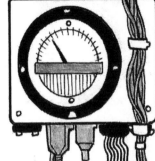

CODE	STORY
NIKE	*BTTF*-themed TV commercial: Nike
NTND	Nintendo *Back to the Future— The Ride* Mini-Game
PIZA	*BTTF*-themed TV commercial: Pizza Hut
PNBL	Data East *BTTF* pinball game
REAL	Real life
RIDE	Simulator: *Back to the Future—The Ride*
SCRM	2010 Scream Awards: *Back to the Future 25th Anniversary* Reunion (broadcast)
SCRT	2010 Scream Awards: *Back to the Future 25th Anniversary* Reunion (trailer)
SIMP	Simulator: *The Simpsons Ride*
SLOT	*Back to the Future Video Slots*
STLZ	Unused *BTTF* footage of Eric Stoltz as Marty McFly
STRY	*Back to the Future Storybook*
TEST	Screen tests: Crispin Glover, Lea Thompson and Tom Wilson
TLTL	Telltale Games' *Back to the Future—The Game*
TOPS	Topps' *Back to the Future II* trading-card set
TRIL	*BTTF: The Official Book of the Complete Movie Trilogy*
UNIV	Universal Studios Hollywood promotional video

SUFFIX	MEDIUM
-b	*BTTF2*'s Biff Tannen Museum video (extended)
-c	Credit sequence to the animated series
-d	Film deleted scene
-n	Film novelization
-o	Film outtake
-p	1955 phone book from *BTTF1*
-v	Video game print materials or commentaries
-s1	Screenplay (draft one)
-s2	Screenplay (draft two)
-s3	Screenplay (draft three)
-s4	Screenplay (draft four)
-sp	Screenplay (production draft)
-sx	Screenplay (*Paradox*)

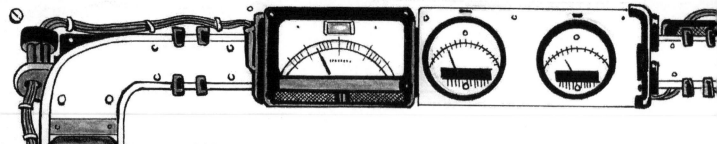

sighting to his chief, resulting in Parker being demoted and sent for psychiatric care. This altered history prevented Danny from marrying Betty Lapinski—and, thus, their granddaughter, Jennifer Parker, from being born [**TLTL-2**].

- **Budweiser:** An American-style lager produced by Anheuser-Busch [**REAL**]. In 1985, Marty McFly passed a van bearing Budweiser's logo while hitching a skateboard ride to school [**BTF1**].

    In 2012, four employees of the Crestview Service Center shared Bud Lites while on break, speculating about what they would do if able to time-travel. One mechanic, Ali, said he would invent and copyright fire, while another, Kidus, indicated he would go back and murder his father. As Emmett Brown's flying DeLorean suddenly appeared on a nearby lift, Kidus vanished, having erased himself from history due to his never having been born, and the vehicle disappeared a moment later. Because of the temporal alteration, the others forgot their missing friend had ever existed [**BUDL**].

- ***Bufo marinus*:** An immense, remarkably shy species of toad native to South America's Amazon Jungle until its extinction. The toad secreted an acidic substance from its sweat glands that could cure athlete's foot fungus—though in large doses, the secretion could be fatal [**REAL**].

    The *Bufo marinus* had a variety of skin tones, including blue, green, purple and orange, and was susceptible to the high-pitched tone of a tuning fork. When Marty McFly contracted athlete's foot, he and Emmett Brown visited the Amazon rainforest in 1532, in order to procure such a toad. Upon returning to their own era, they brought back several specimens to repopulate the extinct species [**BFAN-7a**].

    NOTE: *The* Bufo marinus, *also called a cane toad, is not extinct in the real world.*

- **b'up to go:** A brand or product name printed on the side of a box stored at the Sisters of Mercy Soup Kitchen during Irving Tannen's ownership [**TLTL-1**].

- **Burger King:** A global chain of fast-food hamburger restaurants [**REAL**]. Emmett Brown's home in 1985 was littered with multiple food wrappers, the result of his living in a garage apartment next-door to a Burger King. David McFly worked at this restaurant until his brother,

Marty, altered history by making Dave (and the rest of his family) more successful [**BTF1**].

> ***NOTE:*** *The Burger King seen onscreen is located on Victory Boulevard, in Burbank, California.*
>
> *In* BTTF1*'s third-draft screenplay, Dave worked at McDonald's rather than Burger King.*

- ***BurgerTime:*** A 1982 arcade game created by Data East that was also ported to several home computers and consoles [**REAL**]. A Nintendo Entertainment System (NES) version was among the items for sale at Blast From the Past, an antique and collectibles shop in 2015 Hill Valley [**BTF2**].

- **Burke, PFC:** A soldier at a U.S. government aboveground atomic bomb testing site in Atkins, Nevada. Emmett Brown and Marty McFly visited the base in 1952, in order to harness a bomb blast's nuclear energy to power a time machine and send Marty back to the future [**BTF1-s2**].

    > ***NOTE:*** *The nuclear test-site sequence was cut from the final version of* BTTF1 *(the setting of which was changed to 1955), though storyboards were included as a Blu-ray extra. The first two script drafts set the base in the fictional Nevada city of Atkins, while the third moved it to New Mexico.*

- **Burning Demon of Deathly Doom, The:** An evil creature in the video game *BraveLord and Monstrux* that could shoot flame at adversaries from three candles. Monstrux turned the once-ordinary candelabra into a demon so that it would fight BraveLord for him [**BFAN-19**].

- **Burns, Geo:** A pirate acquainted with Mac the Black, circa 1697. His signature was tattooed on Mac's chest [**BFAN-14**].

- **Burns, George:** An American comedian, writer and actor, born Naftaly Birnbaum, whose career spanned the vaudeville, radio, television and film media [**REAL**]. Burns announced a comeback in 2091 [**BFAN-9**].

    > ***NOTE:*** *Actor George Burns, still alive when the episode aired in 1991, died five years later, at age 100. Had he lived until 2091, he'd have been nearly two centuries old.*

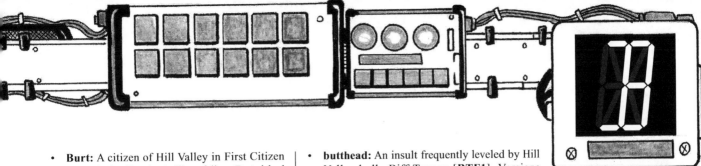

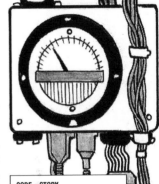

- **Burt:** A citizen of Hill Valley in First Citizen Brown's timeline. A rebellious fellow, Burt risked reprisals by calling the dystopian society "a joke." George McFly spied on Burt's conversations for the government via video monitors in his home [**TLTL-3**].

- **Business Center Road:** A street in Hill Valley. CusCo Industries was located at 11249 Business Center Road [**BTF2, BFCG**].

- **Butch:** A name that Jules and Verne Brown considered for a baby Apatosaurus that Verne had found while visiting prehistoric times. Eventually, they settled on the ironic name Tiny [**BFAN-26**].

- **Butler, Brett Morgan:** A Major League Baseball centerfielder for numerous teams, who played for the Los Angeles Dodgers from 1991 to 1994 [**REAL**]. When Emmett Brown researched the game of baseball, Butler appeared in one of the scientist's instructional videos, explaining the Magnus effect and the physics of throwing a curveball [**BFAN-8**].

- **Butterfield:** A racehorse that competed in 1931. Butterfield was among several horses mentioned during a radio broadcast as Marty McFly and Emmett Brown attempted to steal liquor from Irving "Kid" Tannen's speakeasy [**TLTL-1**].

  NOTE: Ruby Butterfield provided voices for several Telltale Games video games, including the Sam & Max *lines. Telltale presumably named the horse after the actor.*

- **butthead:** An insult frequently leveled by Hill Valley bully Biff Tannen [**BTF1**]. Versions of the term had previously been employed by Biff's ancestors as far back as the ancient Roman Empire, when Bifficus Antanneny called Marticus (Marty McFly's alias in that era) a "tuum de gluteus maximus" (a rough translation of the term in Latin) [**BFAN-5**].

  General Beauregard Tannen later utilized the phrase "buttocksbrain," until 1864, when a time-traveling Verne Brown introduced him to the word "butthead" [**BFAN-1**]. Officer Tannen, an allosaurus police officer in Dinocity—an alternate version of Hill Valley inhabited by sapient dinosaurs—used the term "tailhead" [**BFAN-3, BFHM**]. And in 2585, Governor Tannen, one of Biff's descendants, had an android servant programmed to slap people around and call them "butthead" for him [**BFCL-1**].

  NOTE: BTTF1's screenplay had Biff calling people "asshole" (in drafts one to three) and "dipshit" (in draft four).

- **buttocksbrain:** An insult used by Beauregard Tannen, circa 1864, analogous to his descendant Biff Tannen's pet phrase, "butthead" [**BFAN-1**].

- **Byrd, Richard Evelyn, Rear Admiral:** A U.S. naval officer who helped pioneer the aviation and polar-exploration fields [**REAL**]. Emmett Brown kept a small figure of the admiral atop his camera that moved back and forth, so that those being photographed could "watch the Byrdie" [**BFAN-25**].

CODE	STORY
NIKE	*BTTF*-themed TV commercial: Nike
NTND	Nintendo *Back to the Future—The Ride* Mini-Game
PIZA	*BTTF*-themed TV commercial: Pizza Hut
PNBL	Data East *BTTF* pinball game
REAL	Real life
RIDE	Simulator: *Back to the Future—The Ride*
SCRM	2010 Scream Awards: *Back to the Future 25th Anniversary Reunion* (broadcast)
SCRT	2010 Scream Awards: *Back to the Future 25th Anniversary Reunion* (trailer)
SIMP	Simulator: *The Simpsons Ride*
SLOT	*Back to the Future Video Slots*
STLZ	Unused *BTTF* footage of Eric Stoltz as Marty McFly
STRY	*Back to the Future Storybook*
TEST	Screen tests: Crispin Glover, Lea Thompson and Tom Wilson
TLTL	Telltale Games' *Back to the Future—The Game*
TOPS	Topps' *Back to the Future II* trading-card set
TRIL	*BTTF: The Official Book of the Complete Movie Trilogy*
UNIV	Universal Studios Hollywood promotional video

SUFFIX	MEDIUM
-b	*BTTF2*'s Biff Tannen Museum video (extended)
-c	Credit sequence to the animated series
-d	Film deleted scene
-n	Film novelization
-o	Film outtake
-p	1955 phone book from *BTTF1*
-v	Video game print materials or commentaries
-s1	Screenplay (draft one)
-s2	Screenplay (draft two)
-s3	Screenplay (draft three)
-s4	Screenplay (draft four)
-sp	Screenplay (production draft)
-sx	Screenplay (*Paradox*)

CEEGAR

(CENTER, WITH STUBBLE AND BUCK)

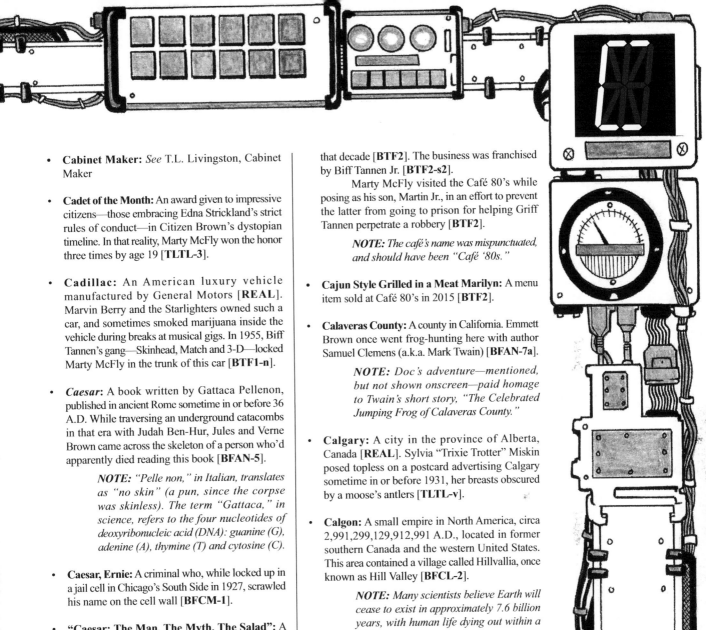

- **Cabinet Maker:** *See* T.L. Livingston, Cabinet Maker

- **Cadet of the Month:** An award given to impressive citizens—those embracing Edna Strickland's strict rules of conduct—in Citizen Brown's dystopian timeline. In that reality, Marty McFly won the honor three times by age 19 [**TLTL-3**].

- **Cadillac:** An American luxury vehicle manufactured by General Motors [**REAL**]. Marvin Berry and the Starlighters owned such a car, and sometimes smoked marijuana inside the vehicle during breaks at musical gigs. In 1955, Biff Tannen's gang—Skinhead, Match and 3-D—locked Marty McFly in the trunk of this car [**BTF1-n**].

- *Caesar:* A book written by Gattaca Pellenon, published in ancient Rome sometime in or before 36 A.D. While traversing an underground catacombs in that era with Judah Ben-Hur, Jules and Verne Brown came across the skeleton of a person who'd apparently died reading this book [**BFAN-5**].

    > NOTE: *"Pelle non," in Italian, translates as "no skin" (a pun, since the corpse was skinless). The term "Gattaca," in science, refers to the four nucleotides of deoxyribonucleic acid (DNA): guanine (G), adenine (A), thymine (T) and cytosine (C).*

- **Caesar, Ernie:** A criminal who, while locked up in a jail cell in Chicago's South Side in 1927, scrawled his name on the cell wall [**BFCM-1**].

- **"Caesar: The Man, The Myth, The Salad":** A proposed extra-credit report for Marty McFly's college history class. As research, Marty accompanied Emmett Brown to the year 36 A.D., hoping to meet the Roman emperor firsthand [**BFAN-5**].

    > NOTE: *The emperor was unnamed onscreen, though historically, the Empire's leader was Tiberius Julius Caesar Augustus. Caesar salad was created by Italian-Mexican restaurateur Caesar Cardini in 1924, with no connection to Julius Caesar.*

- **Café 80's:** An eatery in 2015 Hill Valley, located on the site of the former Lou's Café. The diner featured video simulacra of Michael Jackson, Ronald Reagan and Ayatollah Khomeini suggesting menu items, as well as a wide range of memorabilia from that decade [**BTF2**]. The business was franchised by Biff Tannen Jr. [**BTF2-s2**].

    Marty McFly visited the Café 80's while posing as his son, Martin Jr., in an effort to prevent the latter from going to prison for helping Griff Tannen perpetrate a robbery [**BTF2**].

    > NOTE: *The café's name was mispunctuated, and should have been "Café '80s."*

- **Cajun Style Grilled in a Meat Marilyn:** A menu item sold at Café 80's in 2015 [**BTF2**].

- **Calaveras County:** A county in California. Emmett Brown once went frog-hunting here with author Samuel Clemens (a.k.a. Mark Twain) [**BFAN-7a**].

    > NOTE: *Doc's adventure—mentioned, but not shown onscreen—paid homage to Twain's short story, "The Celebrated Jumping Frog of Calaveras County."*

- **Calgary:** A city in the province of Alberta, Canada [**REAL**]. Sylvia "Trixie Trotter" Miskin posed topless on a postcard advertising Calgary sometime in or before 1931, her breasts obscured by a moose's antlers [**TLTL-v**].

- **Calgon:** A small empire in North America, circa 2,991,299,129,912,991 A.D., located in former southern Canada and the western United States. This area contained a village called Hillvallia, once known as Hill Valley [**BFCL-2**].

    > NOTE: *Many scientists believe Earth will cease to exist in approximately 7.6 billion years, with human life dying out within a billion years or so.*

- **Calidarium:** *See* Thermae

- **California Raisins:** A fictional rhythm-and-blues group used for advertising purposes during the 1980s, comprising anthropomorphized Claymation raisin characters [**REAL**]. Upon returning from the past in the DeLorean, Marty McFly disturbed a homeless man named Red, who was lying on a bench containing a California Raisins ad [**BTF1**].

- **Caligula, Emperor:** The leader of the Roman Empire from 37 A.D. to 41 A.D., following the reign of Tiberius Caesar [**REAL**]. When Emmett Brown and Marty McFly visited ancient Rome in 36 A.D., Marty accidentally offended a Roman officer, Bifficus Antanneny, by spilling food on

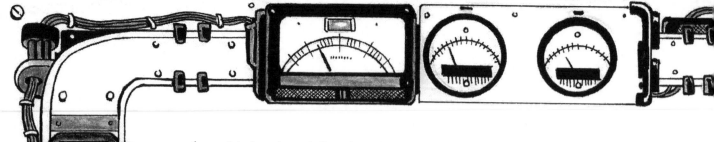

the man's tunic, and was challenged to a chariot race. Realizing that Antanneny had to win in order for Caligula's rise and the Empire's fall to occur as history recorded (his power was vital to Caligula becoming the next emperor), Doc advised Marty to purposely lose [**BFAN-5**].

> *NOTE: Tiberius was not named onscreen, though historically, he led the Roman Empire in 36 A.D., and was Caligula's predecessor.*

• **Callahan:** An executive at a company that employed George McFly in the 1980s. He promoted a worker named Jenkins over George, who chalked this up to Jenkins playing golf with the man [**BTF1-s2**].

• **Callahan, Harry, Agent:** A name that Marty McFly considered as an alias while visiting Hill Valley in 1931 to save Emmett Brown from being killed by gangster Irving "Kid" Tannen's mob [**TLTL-1**].

> *NOTE: Clint Eastwood portrayed fictional police detective Harold Francis "Dirty Harry" Callahan in the films* Dirty Harry, Magnum Force, The Enforcer, Sudden Impact *and* The Dead Pool.

• **Calvin Klein, Inc.:** A popular fashion brand, founded in 1968 [**REAL**].
  As a teenager, Marty McFly wore Calvin Klein underwear. When Marty was struck by a car in 1955 belonging to his grandfather (Sam Baines), Marty's mother (Lorraine Baines) noticed his underwear and assumed "Calvin Klein" to be his name. He continued to use the name throughout his stay in that era [**BTF1**].
  In Citizen Brown's dystopian timeline, Jennifer Parker found it amusing that Marty wore this brand of underwear [**TLTL-4**].

• **Camaro Z28:** *See* Toyota SR5 4x4

• **Campbell, Russell T.:** The owner of Brown & Bigelow Advertising Co., a business listed in the 1955 Hill Valley phone book [**BTF1-p**].

• **Camp Fire Girls of America:** An American youth organization established in 1910 to help young women. The organization has been co-ed since 1975 [**REAL**]. Camp Fire Girls of America operated a chapter in Hill Valley [**BTF1**].

• **cancer:** A broad group of diseases involving unregulated cell growth within an animal's body, in which the cells divide and grow uncontrollably, thereby forming malignant tumors [**REAL**]. According to an October 2015 report in *USA Today*, cholesterol was being researched as a possible cure for cancer [**BTF2**].

• **Canine Cafeteria:** An invention of Emmett Brown consisting of a hot plate used to warm up dog food. The Canine Cafeteria incorporated an alarm clock to automatically activate at meal times and announce "chow time," thereby summoning a pooch to receive a meal of sawdust dog food [**RIDE**].

• **Canine Retrieval Apparatus:** An invention of Emmett Brown built to rescue dogs from great heights. The scientist conceived the device at age 17, after his future pet, Einstein, became trapped atop Hill Valley's Clock Tower [**TLTL-v**].

• **Canton, John:** An employee at the Institute of Future Technology, stationed in the West Wing [**RIDE**].

> *NOTE: This individual, identified on signage outside* Back to the Future: The Ride, *was named after the 18th-century English physicist.*

• **Canyon Road:** A street leading to Hill Valley's Gannon Canyon. In 1967, Marty McFly drove the DeLorean along this road while trying to return to 1985, as the earlier era's Emmett Brown used power lines strung above Gannon Canyon to generate the electricity necessary to power the vehicle's Flux Capacitor [**BTF2-s1**].

• **Capacitor Drive:** A component of the Flux Capacitor, a device invented by Emmett Brown to enable time travel. It was vital to disconnect the Capacitor Drive before opening the device [**BTF1**].

• **Capone:** A citizen of Chicago, Illinois, who served time in a South Side jail, sometime in or before 1927. During his incarceration, he scrawled "Capone wuz heer" on a cell wall [**BFCM-1**].

> *NOTE: This may have been Alphonse Gabriel "Al" Capone, a notorious real-life criminal operating in Chicago during that era.*

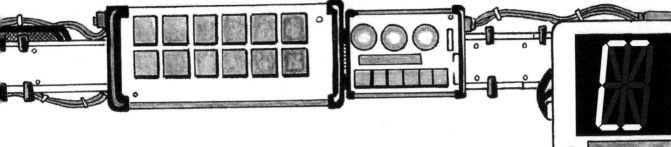

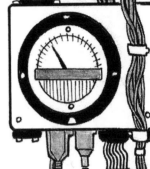

- **Cara:** One of two names (along with Sara) that a barbed-wire salesman mistook for Clara Clayton's in 1885, while telling a fellow traveler about his conversation with Emmett Brown at the Palace Saloon and Hotel. Clara, overhearing the tale, realized how much Emmett loved her and exited the train to find him [**BTF3-n**].

- **Caribbean, The:** A region southeast of the Gulf of Mexico, consisting of the Caribbean Sea, its islands and the surrounding coasts [**REAL**]. Determined to get a tattoo against his mother's wishes, Verne Brown used the family DeLorean to visit this area, in 1697, where he and Marty McFly posed as pirates [**BFAN-14**].

  > *NOTE: It's unknown which Caribbean island Marty and Verne visited, as there are thousands.*

- **Carmody, Jim:** An employee at the Institute of Future Technology, stationed in the West Wing [**RIDE**].

  > *NOTE: This individual, identified on signage outside* Back to the Future: The Ride, *was named after a Universal Studios employee.*

- **Carnegie, Dale:** A prominent lecturer who authored the best-selling book *How to Win Friends and Influence People*, first published in 1936 [**REAL**]. At age 16, George McFly memorized entire sections of that work, hoping to carve out a new life for himself based on the book's positive attitude. Such efforts, however, proved to be a failure [**BTF1-n**].

- **Carnegie Hall:** A concert venue in Manhattan, New York [**REAL**]. "Cue Ball" Donnely, a mobster in Irving "Kid" Tannen's gang, hoped someday to quit the speakeasy business and become a musician at Carnegie Hall [**TLTL-2**].

- **Carrillo, Jose:** An employee at the Institute of Future Technology, assigned as the facility's hilltop affairs colleague [**RIDE**].

  > *NOTE: This individual, identified on signage outside* Back to the Future: The Ride, *was named after an employee at Universal Studios.*

- **Carson:** A street in or near Hill Valley [**BFAN-12**].

- **Carson Ravine:** *See* Clayton Ravine

- **Carson Spur:** A short branch line of the Central Pacific Railroad in 1885, located in Hill Valley, three miles from Shonash Ravine, near an abandoned silver mine. Marty McFly and Emmett Brown, attempting to return to their own era by having a steam locomotive push the damaged DeLorean up to 88 miles per hour, loaded up the vehicle at this point [**BTF3**].

- **Carruthers, Lou:** *See* Caruthers, Lou

- **Cars of the Future:** An attraction at the 1931 Hill Valley Exposition, held in the North Tent and sponsored by Statler DeSoto [**TLTL-4**].

- **Carter, James Earl Jr. ("Jimmy"):** The 39th President of the United States, from 1977 to 1981 [**REAL**]. Several promotional materials from Carter's presidential campaign were among the items for sale at Blast From the Past, an antique and collectibles shop in 2015 Hill Valley [**BTF2**].

- **Caruthers, Lou:** The middle-aged proprietor of Lou's Café, an eatery in Courthouse Square, circa 1955. A crotchety, sarcastic man, Lou teased Marty McFly for wearing a "life preserver" after the teen traveled back in time wearing 1980s apparel, and had little patience when Marty ordered a Tab and a Pepsi Free, neither of which was yet available in the 1950s. Among his employees was future mayor Goldie Wilson [**BTF1**].

  > *NOTE: Lou's last name was spelled "Carruthers" on the Blu-ray trivia track for BTTF1—the same spelling used in the movie's revised fourth-draft screenplay. Prior drafts, however, spelled it "Caruthers." In the film's first draft, his name was Dick Wilson and the diner was called Wilson's Café.*

- **Castle Biffingham:** A fortress in Tannenshire, England, owned by Lord Biffingham, the Earl of Tannenshire, circa 1367. The tyrannical Biffingham locked women away in the castle's towers (including Jennivere McFly and Clara Clayton Brown), while imprisoning male captives in his dungeons. The castle was guarded by several beefy, ugly, dim-witted soldiers [**BFAN-2**].

- **cat-aracts:** A canine eye disease causing a dog to see all objects and individuals as feline. If not treated with a by-product of fermented juniper berries, the illness could lead to blindness. When Einstein, Emmett Brown's dog, contracted the

CODE	STORY
NIKE	*BTTF*-themed TV commercial: Nike
NTND	Nintendo *Back to the Future—The Ride* Mini-Game
PIZA	*BTTF*-themed TV commercial: Pizza Hut
PNBL	Data East *BTTF* pinball game
REAL	Real life
RIDE	Simulator: *Back to the Future—The Ride*
SCRM	2010 Scream Awards: *Back to the Future 25th Anniversary Reunion* (broadcast)
SCRT	2010 Scream Awards: *Back to the Future 25th Anniversary Reunion* (trailer)
SIMP	Simulator: *The Simpsons Ride*
SLOT	*Back to the Future Video Slots*
STLZ	Unused *BTTF* footage of Eric Stoltz as Marty McFly
STRY	*Back to the Future Storybook*
TEST	Screen tests: Crispin Glover, Lea Thompson and Tom Wilson
TLTL	Telltale Games' *Back to the Future—The Game*
TOPS	Topps' *Back to the Future II* trading-card set
TRIL	*BTTF: The Official Book of the Complete Movie Trilogy*
UNIV	Universal Studios Hollywood promotional video

SUFFIX	MEDIUM
-b	*BTTF2*'s Biff Tannen Museum video (extended)
-c	Credit sequence to the animated series
-d	Film deleted scene
-n	Film novelization
-o	Film outtake
-p	1955 phone book from *BTTF1*
-v	Video game print materials or commentaries
-s1	Screenplay (draft one)
-s2	Screenplay (draft two)
-s3	Screenplay (draft three)
-s4	Screenplay (draft four)
-sp	Screenplay (production draft)
-sx	Screenplay (*Paradox*)

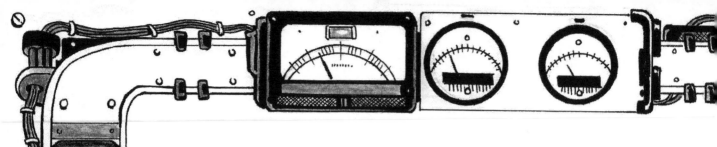

illness, he began attacking people and things around him, until Doc and Marty McFly visited 1927 Chicago to find a liquor still with which to ferment a cure [**BFCM-1**].

> *NOTE: In humans, a cataract (no hyphen) is a clouding of the lens or its envelope, varying from slight to complete opacity. "Cat-aracts" is not an actual illness.*

- ***Cat Lover's Quarterly:*** A magazine for fans of felines. Edna Strickland once wrote for *Cat Lover's Quarterly*, and proudly displayed a trio of editorial trophies from that magazine, one of which was for "Best Litter Columnist" [**TLTL-1**].

- ***Cattle Queen of Montana:*** A 1954 motion-picture Western starring Barbara Stanwyck and Ronald Reagan [**REAL**]. The Essex Theater, in Courthouse Square, showed this film in 1955 [**BTF1**].

> *NOTE: In the initial draft of BTTF1's script, the theater, then known as the Orpheum, was playing* The Quiet Man, *starring John Wayne and Maureen O'Hara.*

- **CBS News Bomb Headquarters:** A temporary area at a U.S. military base, established in 1955 so that the news organization could cover the aboveground detonation of an atomic bomb [**BTF1-s3**].

- **CD:** A simply named kiosk at the 1992 St. Louis World Exposition, at which visitors could listen to the recorded singing of previous fairs' visitors. Emmett and Clara Brown, having traveled back in time to attend the 1904 exposition, recorded themselves singing "Meet Me in St. Louis, Louis" at that event's Music Pavilion, built on the same spot on which the CD booth would later be located. Their sons, Jules and Verne Brown, heard the recording at the 1992 exposition [**BFAN-25**].

- **Ceegar:** A member of Buford Tannen's gang in 1885. The tallest outlaw in the group, he was named for his habit of smoking stogies [**BTF3-s1, BTF3-sx**].

> *NOTE: This character, unnamed onscreen, was identified in BTTF3's screenplays.*

- **Ceja, Ramiro:** An employee at the Institute of Future Technology, stationed in the West Wing [**RIDE**].

> *NOTE: This individual, identified on signage outside* Back to the Future: The

Ride, was named after a Universal Studios employee.

- **Central Pacific 7:** The caboose of Locomotive No. 131. In 1885, Emmett Brown boarded the train via this car so that he and Marty McFly could use it to push the damaged DeLorean up to 88 miles per hour and return to their own era [**BTF3**].

- **Central Pacific Railroad (CPR):** A railroad network running between California and Utah, later part of the Union Pacific Railroad [**REAL**]. In 1885, a CPR passenger and freight train, Locomotive No. 131, stopped at the Hill Valley Railroad Station, as well as at other stops leading up to the end of the line at San Francisco. Marty McFly and Emmett Brown hijacked this train in order to use it to push the damaged DeLorean up to 88 miles per hour, thereby sending them back to their own era [**BTF3**].

- **Century 22:** A real-estate office located in Courthouse Square, circa 2015 [**BTF2-n**].

> *NOTE: This business' name was based on that of real-estate agent franchise Century 21.*

- **Cerebrum Observator:** An invention of Jules Brown, built from an otoscope—a medical examination device used to look into a person's ears—enabling Jules to view an individual's thoughts and dreams [**BFAN-11**].

- **Chambers, Deborah:** A librarian at Hill Valley High School, circa 1955. Chambers served as a school-appointed chaperone to that year's Enchantment Under the Sea Dance. At the function, she set about getting "wallflowers" to get up and dance, telling them that a body in motion was more enticing than one standing still [**BTF1-n**].

> *NOTE: Miss Chambers' sexually inappropriate advice to the students played on the popular "repressed librarian" stereotype.*

- **Channel 109:** A television station broadcast in 2015. Marty McFly Jr. sometimes watched this channel's programming [**BTF2**].

- **Channel 18:** A TV station in 2015, the broadcasts of which Marty McFly Jr. enjoyed watching [**BTF2**].

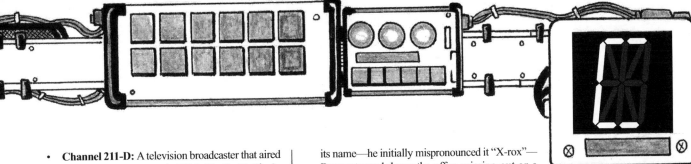

- **Channel 211-D:** A television broadcaster that aired ESPN sports coverage in 2015. Martin McFly Jr. was a frequent viewer of this channel [**BTF2-sx, BTF2-n**].

- **Channel 24:** A 2015 television station that Marty McFly Jr. sometimes watched [**BTF2**].

- **Channel 63:** A television station broadcast in 2015, among Martin McFly Jr.'s favorites. Plastic-surgery franchise Bottoms Up advertised its products, such as the Super Inflatable "Tit," on this station [**BTF2**].

- **Channel 87:** A TV station that Marty McFly Jr. enjoyed watching in 2015 [**BTF2**].

- **Channel 91:** A television station received in Hill Valley. Biff Tannen liked to watch news programs on this channel, though he sometimes fell asleep during broadcasts [**BFAN-20**].

- **Channel 92:** A local television station in Hill Valley that aired episodes of *Mr. Wisdom*, a children's science series starring host Walter Wisdom, as well as the *He-Boy Gladiator Show* [**BFAN-26**]. Biff Tannen Jr. enjoyed viewing cartoons on this station—when he could wrest the TV remote control from his father [**BFAN-20**].

- **Channel 93:** A local Hill Valley television station that televised the town's annual Founder's Day Tractor-Pull Contest [**BFAN-22**].

- **Chapel O Love:** A business that performed cheap weddings, located in Las Vegas, Nevada [**BTF2-n**]. In a future timeline in which Marty McFly was considered a failure, he and Jennifer Parker were married at the Chapel O Love—much to the horror of the younger Jennifer, who viewed photos from the wedding after traveling forward to the year 2015 [**BTF2**].

- **"Chapel O' Love":** The first big hit of Marty McFly's rock band, Marty and the Pinheads. This song, a cover of the Dixie Cups' 1964 classic "Chapel of Love," peaked at #11 on the rock-and-roll charts in 1994 [**BFCG**].

- **Charles:** A colleague of Emmett Brown who, in 1952, tried to convince the scientist to become a major stockholder and employee of the fledgling Xerox Corp. Convinced that the company had no future since few would know how to pronounce its name—he initially mispronounced it "X-rox"—Brown turned down the offer, missing out on a profitable investment opportunity [**BTF1-s1**].

> *NOTE: Charles was likely Charles Peter McColough, one of Xerox's co-founders.*

- **Charles II, King:** The last Habsburg King of Spain, circa the late 17th century [**REAL**]. A musketeer in his employ arrested Marty McFly in 1697 while the latter was posing as pirate Mac the Black [**BFAN-14**].

- **Charlie:** The night watchman at Hill Valley City Hall in 1955. Since he and Emmett Brown shared a passion for the Old West, Charlie let the scientist bend the rules by accessing records after-hours, as he was more lenient with those who had interests similar to his own [**BTF3-n**].

- **Charlie ("Checkerboard Charlie," "Checkers"):** A gangster murdered by Irving "Kid" Tannen, sometime in or before 1931. Following the man's death, Kid's bartender, Zane Williams, drew a caricature of him for their speakeasy's Wall of Honor, with the caption "Checkerboard Charlie, removed from the board" [**TLTL-2**].

- **Chase, W.H.:** A citizen of Hill Valley who was listed on Arthur McFly's ledger at the 1931 Hill Valley Exposition [**TLTL-2**].

- **Cha's Feess:** A cigar and tobacco dealer located in Hill Valley, circa 1885 [**BTF3**].

> *NOTE: This company's name was apparently short for Charles Feess, a real-world cigar manufacturer prominent in the 19th century.*

- **Chattanooga:** A city in Tennessee [**REAL**]. Verne Brown, stealing his father's DeLorean, visited Chattanooga in 1864, where he encountered General Beauregard Tannen and was put to work as a drummer-boy in the Confederate Army during the American Civil War. Emmett and Jules Brown followed him back in time, along with Marty McFly, and met the boys' ancestor, General Ulysses S. Clayton, of the Union Army. Although history initially recorded a battle between Clayton's and Tannen's forces, Jules and Verne convinced both armies to shake hands and embrace peace, thereby preventing bloodshed [**BFAN-1**].

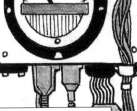

CODE	STORY
NIKE	*BTTF*-themed TV commercial: Nike
NTND	Nintendo *Back to the Future—The Ride* Mini-Game
PIZA	*BTTF*-themed TV commercial: Pizza Hut
PNBL	Data East *BTTF* pinball game
REAL	Real life
RIDE	Simulator: *Back to the Future—The Ride*
SCRM	2010 Scream Awards: *Back to the Future 25th Anniversary Reunion* (broadcast)
SCRT	2010 Scream Awards: *Back to the Future 25th Anniversary Reunion* (trailer)
SIMP	Simulator: *The Simpsons Ride*
SLOT	*Back to the Future Video Slots*
STLZ	Unused *BTTF* footage of Eric Stoltz as Marty McFly
STRY	*Back to the Future Storybook*
TEST	Screen tests: Crispin Glover, Lea Thompson and Tom Wilson
TLTL	Telltale Games' *Back to the Future—The Game*
TOPS	Topps' *Back to the Future II* trading-card set
TRIL	*BTTF: The Official Book of the Complete Movie Trilogy*
UNIV	Universal Studios Hollywood promotional video

SUFFIX	MEDIUM
-b	*BTTF2*'s Biff Tannen Museum video (extended)
-c	Credit sequence to the animated series
-d	Film deleted scene
-n	Film novelization
-o	Film outtake
-p	1955 phone book from *BTTF1*
-v	Video game print materials or commentaries
-s1	Screenplay (draft one)
-s2	Screenplay (draft two)
-s3	Screenplay (draft three)
-s4	Screenplay (draft four)
-sp	Screenplay (production draft)
-sx	Screenplay (*Paradox*)

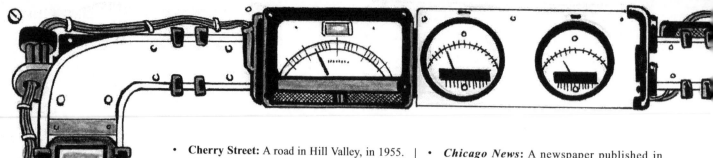

- **Cherry Street:** A road in Hill Valley, in 1955. While visiting that year, Marty McFly conducted a test run with the DeLorean and discovered that Cherry Street had a rise like a speed bump. This enabled him to later avoid crashing the car [**BTF1-n**].

- **Cheryl:** A name scrawled in graffiti on the wall of Hill Valley High School, circa 1985 [**BTF1**].

- **Chester:** A bartender employed at Hill Valley's Palace Saloon and Hotel, circa 1885. Chester knew the regular patrons by name, and seemed concerned for their welfare—particularly Emmett Brown, whom he knew could not hold his liquor. A young man named Joey assisted Chester at the bar [**BTF3**].

- **Chevrolet Nova:** A compact automobile produced by General Motors between 1962 and 1988 [**REAL**]. In 1985, George McFly drove such a vehicle, which Biff Tannen borrowed and crashed after driving while intoxicated. This put a crimp in Marty McFly's plans, as he'd intended to borrow the car to take his girlfriend, Jennifer Parker, for a weekend trip to the Lake [**BTF1**].

- **Cheyenne Express:** A train line running out of Cheyenne, Wyoming, circa 1875, with stops in several cities, including Hill Valley. In 1875, outlaw Thaddeus Tannen tied Genevieve Parker to the tracks of this train line, forcing her husband, Wendel Parker, to sign over the deed to their home, the Parker BTQ Ranch [**BFAN-16**].

- **Chez Crossé:** A business in Hill Valley, circa 1991. Emmett Brown briefly worked here as a parking attendant after his sons, Jules and Verne, played an April Fool's Day joke by convincing him that his brain was nearly full, and that he needed to give up science. He was soon fired for crashing a customer's car [**BFAN-12**].

- **Chicago:** The largest city in the U.S. state of Illinois [**REAL**]. When Einstein, Emmett Brown's dog, contracted a canine disease called cat-aracts, Doc and Marty McFly visited 1927 Chicago to find a liquor still with which to ferment a cure. They posed as East Coast mobsters Martin "Zipper" McFly and Doc Brown, in order to access the still of crime boss Arnie "Eggs" Benedict, and also met Mugsy Tannen, an ancestor of Biff Tannen, as well as Jim McFly, one of Marty's forebearers [**BFCM-1**].

- *Chicago News:* A newspaper published in Chicago, Illinois, circa 1927. Marty McFly read this publication while visiting that era with Emmett Brown [**BFCM-1**].

- **Chicken-Head, King:** A nickname given by Marty McFly to the chieftain of a tribe that guarded the legendary City of Gold, in South America's Amazon Jungle. The king and his people protected the golden city from Spanish conquistador Biffando de la Tanén and other would-be conquerors. Marty gave the king this name due to the brightly colored bird that he wore on his head. Chicken-Head, in turn, called him Dances With Frogs, having witnessed Marty doing just that [**BFAN-7a**].

- **Chico:** A name scrawled in graffiti on the wall of Hill Valley High School, circa 1985 [**BTF1**].

- **chipmunk stew:** A meal prepared by soldiers of the Confederate Army serving under General Beauregard Tannen during the American Civil War. The stew contained chipmunk meat, dirt and other ingredients. Verne Brown found it disgusting [**BFAN-1**].

- **chloroform:** An organic liquid compound once used as an anesthetic [**REAL**]. After posing as Darth Vader of the planet Vulcan in order to convince George McFly to ask Lorraine Baines to the Enchantment Under the Sea Dance, Marty McFly utilized chloroform to put George to sleep. He used too strong a dose, however, causing George to sleep for most of the day and miss school [**BTF1-d**].

    Marty again used chloroform to render Irving "Kid" Tannen's employee, Matches, unconscious so he could rescue Arthur McFly from Tannen's mob. Arthur—who'd also been subjected to chloroform, by Kid's gang—babbled as though drunk throughout the ordeal [**TLTL-2**].

    First Citizen Brown, an older version of Emmett Brown from an alternate timeline, used chloroform to render his younger self unconscious, while trying to prevent Marty McFly from altering history to erase his reality [**TLTL-5**].

- **Chocolate-Dipped Cheese Balls:** A brand of snack food that Emmett Brown enjoyed [**BFCM-4**].

- **cholesterol:** An essential structural component of mammalian cell membranes. This organic chemical substance was classified as a waxy steroid of fat

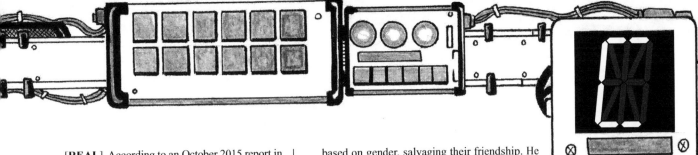

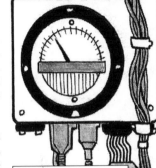

[REAL]. According to an October 2015 report in *USA Today*, cholesterol was being researched as a possible cure for cancer [BTF2].

- **Chopper:** Biff Tannen's pet German Shepherd in 1967 [BTF2-s1].

- **Chow Blower, The:** A ride at the Mega Monster Mountain amusement park. Verne Brown was very fond of this attraction, in which riders in parachute-equipped seats were propelled from the mouth of a giant, mechanical squatting man, as though vomited [BFAN-25].

- **Chow Hut:** A restaurant in Hill Valley, circa 1991. Among its menu items was the Super Double-Grease Bomb Burger, of which Marty McFly and Verne Brown were quite fond [BFAN-17].

- **Chris:** *See* Christine ("Chris")

- **Christ:** A religious title often synonymous with Jesus of Nazareth, the central figure of Christianity [REAL]. Christ's birth was among events that Emmett Brown considered witnessing via his time-traveling DeLorean [BTF1].

  > *NOTE: Doc entered "Dec. 25, 0000" into the time circuits as the date of Christ's birth. However, he was in error for a number of reasons. First, the year of Jesus' birth is generally considered to have occurred a few years BC, and not in December. Second, and most important, there is no year 0000 on either the Julian or Gregorian calendars—the year following 1 BC, on both, is 1 AD. It's unknown to when Doc would have traveled had he actually attempted to visit the so-called Year Zero.*

- **Christine ("Chris"):** A young girl in Hill Valley who pretended to be male in order to befriend Verne Brown, by dressing in masculine clothing and calling herself Chris. Verne was amazed at Chris' prowess at baseball—but was confused by non-masculine aspects of her personality, such as a fondness for a girl-centric comic book called *Mega-Cindy*.

  When Verne brought Chris to 1933 to attend the Bob Brothers All-Star International Circus, the two ended up performing as aerialists. Upon learning that Chris was short for Christine (as opposed to Christopher), Verne was initially angry at the deception, but learned not to discriminate based on gender, salvaging their friendship. He later invited her to play ball with his friends, and to take part in the Brown family's semi-annual water-balloon fight [BFAN-18].

- **Chronometric Analyzer:** A diagnostic device built in 1931 by Emmett Brown's future self. The scientist created the contraption using parts from a hardware store in that era, in order to analyze and repair the DeLorean's malfunctioning time circuits [TLTL-4].

- **Chronometric Clock:** A scientific innovation featured at the 1931 Hill Valley Exposition, consisting of various rotating rings and spheres atop a trio of pillars [TLTL-5]. The contraption was also called a Cosmic Clock [TLTL-v].

- **Church of Our Lady of the Desert:** A religious institution based near the border of Nevada and Utah, circa 1952. Emmett Brown and Marty McFly passed a bus carrying several priests and nuns from this church while traveling to a nuclear test site in Atkins, Nevada [BTF1-s2].

- **Ciabatta:** A brand of alcohol served at Irving "Kid" Tannen's speakeasy in 1931 [TLTL-2].

- **Cinegog:** *See* Roxy, The

- **Circus Maximus:** An open-air stadium in ancient Rome during the reign of Emperor Tiberius Julius Caesar Augustus [REAL]. Bifficus Antanneny and Marty McFly competed here in a chariot race in 36 A.D., after Marty spilled food on Antanneny's tunic [BFAN-5].

- **Circus Peanuts:** A peanut-shaped marshmallow confection, typically made with orange coloring and artificial banana flavor [REAL]. In Citizen Brown's dystopian timeline, many items were deemed illegal, including Circus Peanuts [TLTL-3].

- **Citizen Brown:** *See* First Citizen Brown

- **Citizen Plus Helmet:** A type of machinery used to brainwash inmates at the Citizen Plus Ward to make them obedient members of society, in Citizen Brown's dystopian timeline. The helmet was designed very similarly to Emmett Brown's Brain-wave Analyzer—but instead of reading minds, it reprogrammed them [TLTL-4].

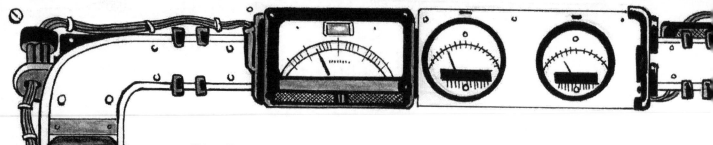

Citizen Plus Program: A government re-education initiative in Citizen Brown's dystopian timeline that encouraged Hill Valley's wayward inhabitants to become better citizens. The program used hypnotherapy to tame negative urges and make obedience automatic, by making it impossible for a person to break rules without feeling physically ill to the point of vomiting.

Those in the program were provided with a digital watch that performed a variety of functions, including emitting a signal inducing the wearer to carry out post-hypnotic suggestions, such as committing acts of violence against those deemed dangerous by the state. The first Citizen Plus graduate was Biff Tannen, who, after re-conditioning, reformed from his criminal ways, becoming an obedient, model citizen—since he had no choice but to do so [**TLTL-3**].

Marty McFly almost received this reconditioning as well, but managed to escape before his mind could be altered [**TLTL-4**].

NOTE: The program utilized techniques similar to those seen in Stanley Kubrick's film adaptation of Anthony Burgess' dystopian novella, A Clockwork Orange.

Citizen Plus Treatment Agreement: A contract signed by Hill Valley citizens undergoing the Citizen Plus Program in Citizen Brown's dystopian timeline. Under the terms of the agreement, members agreed to be incarcerated until the completion of the the procedure [**TLTL-3**].

Citizen Plus Treatment Chamber: A room in which Hill Valley citizens underwent Citizen Plus reconditioning in Citizen Brown's dystopian timeline [**TLTL-3**].

Citizen Plus Ward: A complex in Hill Valley, in Citizen Brown's dystopian timeline. In this ward, Edna Strickland subjected the town's citizens to brainwashing in order to make them model members of society [**TLTL-4**].

Citizen Reading Room: A business in Courthouse Square in Citizen Brown's dystopian timeline [**TLTL-3**].

City: A business located in Hill Valley, circa 2015 [**RIDE**].

City Archives: A branch of Hill Valley's municipal government, circa 1955, located in the basement of Hill Valley City Hall. Emmett Brown and Marty McFly consulted the archives after finding a gravestone in Boot Hill Cemetery revealing that Doc had been murdered by Buford Tannen in 1885, in an effort to learn more about this event so that Marty could travel back in time and prevent its occurrence [**BTF3-n**].

City of Gold: A legendary city in South America's Amazon Jungle, located atop a high plateau, and accessible only via a narrow land bridge. Spanish conquistador Biffando de la Tanén sought this fabled city in 1532. Upon meeting Marty McFly and Emmett Brown, he believed them to have the same goal, and hoped they would lead him to it. The City of Gold was considered a sacred secret to a local tribe that protected its location from outsiders. Doc and Marty thwarted Biffando's attempt to raid the city, then destroyed the bridge to make further attacks impossible [**BFAN-7a**].

City of the Future, The: *See* Cleveland

City Trust and Savings Bank: A financial institution in Hill Valley that issued a check for $1,182,000 to Biff Tannen in 1958. The check covered his first winnings in the Bifforrific timeline, after he began betting at the Valley Racing Association, using sporting-event results listed in *Grays Sports Almanac*. The check, #2634, was issued from the bank's main branch, located at the corner of Third and Main. It was signed by Tim Matthews, and was drawn on account #1223 098 541 04290 327 486 [**BTF2**].

Civic Ordinance 181B: A legal mandate in Citizen Brown's dystopian timeline making it illegal to possess or consume alcohol [**TLTL-3**].

Civic Ordinance 2XM: A legal mandate in Citizen Brown's dystopian timeline deeming many items and goods illegal, including weapons, cigarettes, bubblegum, dogs and Circus Peanuts [**TLTL-3**].

Civic Ordinance 9-Triple-E: A legal mandate in Citizen Brown's dystopian timeline requiring that every citizen wear khaki pants and orange polo shirts each week on Polo Shirt Thursday [**TLTL-3**].

Civic Ordinance C-64: A legal mandate in Citizen Brown's dystopian timeline making it illegal to attempt to destroy public landmarks [**TLTL-3**].

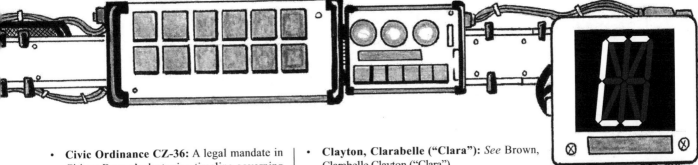

- **Civic Ordinance CZ-36:** A legal mandate in Citizen Brown's dystopian timeline governing home cleanliness. Those found to have dust mites were ordered to vacate their houses, and were publicly humiliated by having the front door marked with yellow Caution tape until a cleanup crew could remove the dust [**TLTL-3**].

- **Civic Ordinance WB-714:** A legal mandate in Citizen Brown's dystopian timeline requiring every citizen to wear an ID tag bearing his or her name [**TLTL-3**].

- *Civil War, The*: A book about the history of the American Civil War. After Verne Brown was trapped in that era, Einstein—his family dog—found a photo in this volume showing Verne as a drummer-boy in the Confederate Army, under General Beauregard Tannen [**BFAN-1**].

- **Clancy's Chowder House:** An Irish restaurant located in Boston, Massachusetts, circa 1897. The Boston Beaneaters celebrated Pee Wee McFly's victory at this eatery following that year's National League pennant game against the Baltimore Orioles [**BFAN-8**].

- **CLARA:** A name stamped on a metal broach worn by Clara Clayton in 1885. The schoolteacher gave the ornament to Emmett Brown as a symbol of her love, but he later returned it to her before going back to his own era [**BTF3**].

- *Clara*, S.S.: A small sailboat owned by Emmett Brown, named after his wife, Clara. In 1992, while searching for Jamaica aboard the *Clara* using a route followed by privateer Henry Morgan, Doc became stranded on an island in the Caribbean, where he was besieged by pirates [**BFAN-14**].

  NOTE: The outcome of this encounter, which occurred during a live-action segment of the animated series, is unrecorded.

- **Clara's Veggie Patch:** A garden that Clara Clayton Brown maintained at the Brown family's farm in Hill Valley, circa 1991. A sign in the patch warning "all critters" to keep out failed to protect the crops, as Tiny—Verne Brown's pet Apatosaurus—tore up the entire garden (though Clara attributed the devastation to gophers) [**BFAN-26**].

- **Class of 1984:** A slogan on a sweatshirt worn by Linda McFly, denoting her year of high school graduation [**BTF1**].

- **Clayton, Clarabelle ("Clara"):** *See* Brown, Clarabelle Clayton ("Clara")

- **Clayton, Daniel ("Dan," "Danny"):** The father of Clarabelle Clayton Brown, and father-in-law of Emmett Brown. Doc met Daniel and his wife, Martha O'Brien, while visiting the year 1850, five years prior to Clara's birth. At the time, the two were traveling the Oregon Trail as part of a wagon train.

  Bookwormish and nebbishy, Daniel had a large collection of jarred insects and was often distracted by reading. After Martha joined the wagon train, he could barely focus on anything else, but his introverted nature kept her from noticing him (though she did aggressively pursue Marty McFly, who was visiting that era with her descendants, Jules and Verne Brown).

  When Martha was endangered by an attacking bear in Wyoming, Daniel bravely boarded a makeshift hang-glider built by Doc Brown (their future son-in-law) and rescued her. Falling immediately in love with Daniel, Martha married him that same day [**BFAN-13**].

- **Clayton, Grandpa:** An ancestor of Clara Clayton Brown. Clara's husband, Emmett Brown, carried a watch fob once owned by this individual, which Doc used as a keychain to hold the keys to his DeLorean [**BFAN-10**].

- **Clayton, Polly:** An ancestor of Clara Clayton Brown [**BFAN**].

  NOTE: This character was slated to appear in the Back to the Future *animated series, but was ultimately dropped before the series aired. No further details are available.*

- **Clayton, Ulysses S., General:** An officer in the Union Army during the American Civil War, with a large nose and a long, grey mustache. Clayton's descendants included a niece, Clara Clayton Brown, and her two sons, Jules and Verne Brown. Ulysses suffered from rheumatism, and was subjected by his physician to a device called an electrical-magnetical machine.

  Although his forces initially wiped out those of Confederate Army General Beauregard Tannen in 1864, history changed when Verne convinced the two armies to stop fighting and shake hands, thereby preventing the slaughter [**BFAN-1**].

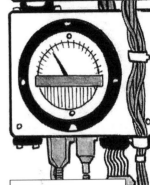

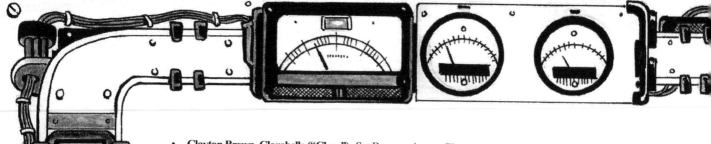

- **Clayton Brown, Clarabelle ("Clara"):** *See* Brown, Clarabelle Clayton ("Clara")

- **Clayton Cliff:** *See* Clayton Ravine

- **Clayton Ravine:** The name given to Hill Valley's Shonash Ravine (its original Native-American designation) following the death of Clara Clayton in one possible timeline. After Marty McFly and Emmett Brown prevented Clara's death, the ravine was instead named Eastwood Ravine, in honor of Clint Eastwood (Marty's alias in 1885), who was believed to have died in Clara's place [**BTF3**].

    Marty and Jennifer Parker often visited this location in order to make out in private [**BTF3-s1**].

    In First Citizen Brown's dystopian timeline, Emmett Brown maintained a secret laboratory near this ravine [**TLTL-4**].

    NOTE: Paradox, a combined screenplay for both sequel films, dubbed this area Carson Ravine. BTTF3's first-draft screenplay called it Clayton Cliff.

- **CLB NightVision Prototype 85:** A helmet invented by Emmett Brown and stored in his time-traveling DeLorean, enabling a wearer to see in the dark [**BFAN-1**].

- **Clemens, Samuel Langhorne ("Mark Twain"):** An American author and humorist whose works included *The Adventures of Tom Sawyer* and *Adventures of Huckleberry Finn* [**REAL**]. Emmett Brown once went frog-hunting with him in Calaveras County, California [**BFAN-7a**].

    Clemens' *nom de plume,* "Mark Twain," was one of several names that Marty McFly and Verne Brown urged Jules Verne to adopt, since Verne (who'd been named in Jules Verne's honor) hated the name Verne [**BFAN-21**].

    Twain visited Hill Valley sometime before 1885, telling a number of tall tales to the patrons of the Palace Saloon and Hotel. The bartender, Chester, later compared Emmett Brown's claim of being from the future to Twain's stories [**BTF3-sp, BTF3-n**].

    NOTE: Doc's frog-hunting adventure paid homage to Twain's short story, "The Celebrated Jumping Frog of Calaveras County," implying that the story's events may have actually occurred in Back to the Future *history.*

- **Cleopatra ("Cleo"):** A much-beloved pig owned by farmer Mac Tannen in 1933. Tannen was unusually attached to the animal, treating it more as a person than as a beast—unsurprisingly, given that Cleo walked on her hind legs; could carry items with her front legs, as though she had arms; displayed modesty when seen naked; and appeared to understand English [**BFAN-18**].

- **Cleveland:** A city in the U.S. state of Ohio, located on the southern shore of Lake Erie [**REAL**]. After Marty McFly altered time, Cleveland became a beautiful, clean and modern city by the 1980s. Known as the City of the Future in this timeline, Cleveland featured streamlined skyscrapers and flying cars [**BTF1-s1**].

- **Click-o-bot:** A type of robot utilized by the human citizens of Robot City, a domed station in the Asteroid Belt of Earth's solar system, circa 2585. Click-o-bots enabled lazy humans to remotely change holovision channels without having to move from the reclining position [**BFCL-1**].

- **Clock Tower, The:** A local monument atop the Hill Valley Courthouse that was struck by lightning in 1955 [**BTF1**], remaining nonfunctional until at least 2015 [**BTF2**].

    The tower was first constructed in 1885 and was partially funded by proceeds from the Hill Valley Festival, held in September of that year. Emmett Brown (who'd become stranded in the Old West) and Marty McFly (who'd gone back to rescue him, under the alias Clint Eastwood) were present at the clock's unveiling. A photograph of them standing next to the clock was later preserved by the Hill Valley Historical Society [**BTF3**].

    In 1931, Edna Strickland launched a campaign called the Clock Tower Fund, to commission a sculptor to place ornamental gargoyle statues on either side of the clock face, in order to inspire citizens to do their civic duty [**TLTL-2**].

    On the night of the damaging storm in 1955, Emmett Brown wired up the Clock Tower in order to harness the bolt's electrical energy so he could send Marty and the DeLorean back to the future. Thirty years later, a grassroots campaign led by the Hill Valley Preservation Society, known as the Save the Clock Tower Fund, attempted to raise the money necessary to repair the existing clock, as an alternative to Mayor Goldie Wilson's plans to replace it [**BTF1**].

    Despite the Preservation Society's efforts,

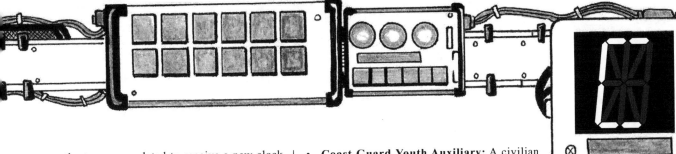

the tower was slated to receive a new clock sometime between 1985 and 1990 [**TLTL-v**]. By 2015, however, the clock remained un-repaired, and a similar grassroots campaign was launched to prevent this from taking place, by a group devoted to preserving it as an historic landmark [**BTF2**].

In Citizen Brown's dystopian timeline, the damaged clock was dismantled in 1976, and a new, larger, more modern version was installed as the window to Brown's mayoral office [**TLTL-3**].

- **Clock Tower Fund:** A campaign launched by Edna Strickland in 1931 to commission a sculptor to place ornamental gargoyle statues on either side of the clock face in Courthouse Square, so as to inspire citizens to do their civic duty [**TLTL-2**].

In 1985, a similar grassroots campaign—the Save the Clock Tower Fund—attempted to raise money to repair the clock, which had been damaged by lightning in 1955 [**BTF1**].

- **Close-Eye**: A red-haired pioneer who, in 1850, traveled in a wagon train with Martha O'Brien and Daniel Clayton. The leader of the expedition, who looked and spoke like John Wayne, entrusted Close-Eye with the group's valuables [**BFAN-13**].

- **Clothestime:** A discount retailer of junior-sized women's sportswear, dresses and accessories [**REAL**]. In the 1980s, Clothestime operated a shop in Hill Valley, across the street from the Twin Pines Mall [**BTF1**].

- **clothing-conversion coordinates:** A term coined by Emmett Brown regarding a camera built to create optical illusions of those photographed, enabling his family to appear to wear clothing appropriate to various eras without having to change their attire. Before snapping a photo to generate the period-attire illusion, Doc first had to enter the clothing-conversion coordinates of those traveling through time [**BFAN-10**].

- **Clyde:** The assistant of P.T. Tannen, the proprietor of P.T. Tannen's Villains Through History in Wax exhibit and, later, P.T. Tannen's House of Curiosity, both at the 1904 St. Louis World Exposition. The British man, mustached and small in stature, helped Tannen to kidnap Marty McFly as an exhibit in the House of Curiosity [**BFAN-25**].

- **C. Merchant, Doctor:** A medical office in Hill Valley, circa 1885 [**BTF3**].

- **Coast Guard Youth Auxiliary:** A civilian volunteer support group for the U.S. Coast Guard [**REAL**]. When Marty McFly visited Emmett Brown in 1955, the scientist, using a telepathy helmet called the Brain-wave Analyzer, guessed that Marty—who wore a jacket resembling a life preserver—was seeking donations for this organization [**BTF1**].

- **Cobb, David C.:** An employee at the Institute of Future Technology, stationed in the East Wing [**RIDE**].

> *NOTE: This individual, identified on signage outside* Back to the Future: The Ride, *was named after Universal Studios' creative director.*

- **Cocoa-Cup:** A consumer product sold in 1931. Its slogan: "Sleep tight with Cocoa-Cup." A billboard for this product, featuring a painting of the Moon, was mounted behind Hill Valley's Sisters of Mercy Soup Kitchen. The sign was damaged when the test flight of Emmett Brown's Rocket Car failed, causing the flying vehicle to crash into it [**TLTL-2**].

> *NOTE: The visual of the vehicle sticking out of the Moon paid homage to an iconic image from* A Trip to the Moon, *a 1902 silent film (considered the first science fiction movie) adapting Jules Verne's novel* From the Earth to the Moon *and H. G. Wells' novel* The First Men in the Moon. *Both Wells' and Verne's works are heavily referenced throughout the BTTF mythos.*
>
> *Cocoa-Cup is not an actual product in the real world.*

- **Cocoa Krispies:** A brand of breakfast cereal manufactured by Kellogg Co. [**REAL**]. Marty McFly's family had a box of this cereal in their kitchen in 1985 [**BTF1**].

- **Code 27:** A code phrase used by the crew of the *MSC Marty*, signifying a catastrophe aboard the passenger solar sailship [**BFAN-9**].

- **Codiga, Richard, Professor:** An employee at the Institute of Future Technology [**RIDE**].

> *NOTE: This individual's name appeared on signage outside* Back to the Future: The Ride.

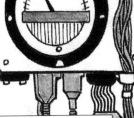

CODE	STORY
NIKE	*BTTF*-themed TV commercial: Nike
NTND	Nintendo *Back to the Future—The Ride* Mini-Game
PIZA	*BTTF*-themed TV commercial: Pizza Hut
PNBL	Data East *BTTF* pinball game
REAL	Real life
RIDE	Simulator: *Back to the Future—The Ride*
SCRM	2010 Scream Awards: *Back to the Future* 25th Anniversary Reunion (broadcast)
SCRT	2010 Scream Awards: *Back to the Future* 25th Anniversary Reunion (trailer)
SIMP	Simulator: *The Simpsons Ride*
SLOT	*Back to the Future Video Slots*
STLZ	Unused *BTTF* footage of Eric Stoltz as Marty McFly
STRY	*Back to the Future Storybook*
TEST	Screen tests: Crispin Glover, Lea Thompson and Tom Wilson
TLTL	Telltale Games' *Back to the Future—The Game*
TOPS	Topps' *Back to the Future II* trading-card set
TRIL	*BTTF: The Official Book of the Complete Movie Trilogy*
UNIV	Universal Studios Hollywood promotional video

SUFFIX	MEDIUM
-b	*BTTF2's* Biff Tannen Museum video (extended)
-c	Credit sequence to the animated series
-d	Film deleted scene
-n	Film novelization
-o	Film outtake
-p	1955 phone book from *BTTF1*
-v	Video game print materials or commentaries
-s1	Screenplay (draft one)
-s2	Screenplay (draft two)
-s3	Screenplay (draft three)
-s4	Screenplay (draft four)
-sp	Screenplay (production draft)
-sx	Screenplay (*Paradox*)

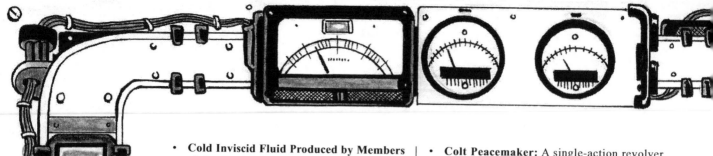

- **Cold Inviscid Fluid Produced by Members of the Genus *Apis Mellifera*:** An affectionate nickname that Emmett Brown sometimes called his wife, Clara Clayton Brown—in essence, "Honey" [**BFAN-4**].

- **Cole, Nat King:** A big-band and jazz musician of the early 20th century, born Nathaniel Adams Coles [**REAL**]. In 1955, Roy's Records, located in Courthouse Square, displayed Cole's album *Unforgettable* in its front window [**BTF1**].

- **ColecoVision:** A home video game console released in 1982 by Coleco Industries [**REAL**]. While visiting the House of Tomorrow exhibit at the 1931 Hill Valley Exposition, Marty McFly quipped that it was missing a ColecoVision [**TLTL-5**].

- **Colfax:** A city in Placer County, California [**REAL**]. When a speakeasy in Colfax was destroyed by an arsonist in 1931, journalist Edna Strickland claimed drifter Carl Sagan (Emmett Brown's alias in that era) had committed the crime, given Doc's prior arrest for torching Irving "Kid" Tannen's Hill Valley speakeasy. In reality, Edna herself had been responsible for both blazes, as well as a third in Georgetown [**TLTL-2**].

- **Collins, Phil:** A British musician, actor and long-time member of progressive rock band Genesis [**REAL**]. Collins' music, like all rock-and-roll, was deemed illegal by Edna Strickland in Citizen Brown's dystopian timeline [**TLTL-3**].

- **Cologne, Jerry ("Odie"):** A comedian who traveled with the United Service Organizations (USO) to help raise U.S. troop morale during World War II, along with emcee Bobby Dawson and singing group The Anderson Sisters [**BFAN-17**].

  > ***NOTE:*** *Odie Cologne was the name of a cartoon skunk on the 1960 animated series,* King Leonardo and his Short Subjects. *His name was a play on the phrase "eau de cologne."*

- **Colorado River:** A river running through the Southwestern United States [**REAL**]. When Emmett Brown conducted experiments to locate water in Nevada's desert, an attempt to use a divining rod brought him to Hoover Dam and the Colorado River [**BFAN-22**].

- **Colt Peacemaker:** A single-action revolver with a revolving cylinder able to hold up to six metallic cartridges, introduced in 1885 by Colt's Patent Firearms Manufacturing Co. [**REAL**]. The company operated a booth at the Hill Valley Festival that year to promote the Peacemaker, inviting passersby to shoot at moving targets [**BTF3**]. Salesman Elmer H. Johnson manned the kiosk [**BTF3-sp**].

  Marty McFly—thanks to his experience playing the Wild Gunman video game in his own era—scored excellently at the booth. When Marty was later challenged to a duel by Buford Tannen, Johnson gave the youth a free Peacemaker, hoping to be able to brag that it was this weapon that had killed the outlaw (though he planned to reclaim the revolver if Marty lost) [**BTF3**].

- **Combformist, The:** A hair stylist in Courthouse Square in Citizen Brown's dystopian timeline [**TLTL-3**]. Hair styles offered included the Sheepish Schoolboy, the Day-Trader Casual, the Bed Head Casual and the Nouveau Riche [**TLTL-v**].

- **Come-and-Get-It Lunchbox:** An invention of Emmett Brown, designed to loudly summon its owner at mealtime. This innovation incorporated the ELB Lunchbox Burglar Deterrent, an extendable arm and mallet that attacked anyone attempting to steal it. Walter Wisdom, Doc's unscrupulous college roommate, stole the invention in 1992, intending to claim it as his own, but Doc regained the device, discrediting Wisdom during a live television broadcast [**BFAN-15**].

- **Comet Kahooey:** A comet—an icy body in Earth's solar system displaying a visible atmosphere when close to the Sun—viewable in the sky over Hill Valley every 25 years. Strange events were purported to accompany its 1967 arrival, such as busses running late, unusual sounds and noises, and the town becoming a large magnetic field; the latter, however, was caused by Emmett Brown's Flying Observatory, which achieved lift by creating a negative magnetic charge. The town's citizens, including Biff Tannen, thus panicked when the next visit occurred in 1992, fearful that it heralded the arrival of extraterrestrials [**BFAN-23**].

  > ***NOTE:*** *The comet's name was based on that of Comet Kohoutek, which was much hyped in 1973 but ultimately disappointed*

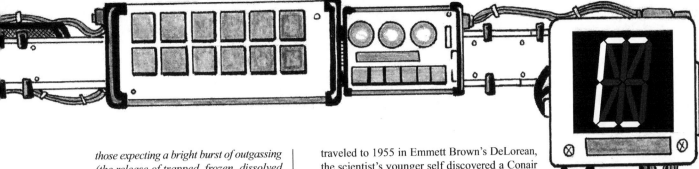

those expecting a bright burst of outgassing (the release of trapped, frozen, dissolved or absorbed gas).

- **Como, Ws.A.:** A citizen of Hill Valley listed on Arthur McFly's ledger at the 1931 Hill Valley Exposition [**TLTL-2**].

- **Compton**: A street in or near Hill Valley [**BFAN-12**].

- **Compton, Brian:** The project CFO of the Institute of Future Technology [**RIDE**].

  > *NOTE: This individual, identified on signage outside* Back to the Future: The Ride, *was named after Universal Studios' CFO and CIO when the ride was produced.*

- **Compton's Flyer:** A racehorse that competed in 1931. Compton's Flyer was among several horses mentioned during a radio broadcast as Marty McFly and Emmett Brown attempted to steal liquor from Irving "Kid" Tannen's speakeasy [**TLTL-1**].

  > *NOTE: This horse's name paid homage to thoroughbred racehorse Compton Flyer.*

- **Compu-Fax:** A satellite news service that provided articles to *USA Today*, circa 2015. Compu-Fax produced a story in October of that year, covering Martin McFly Jr.'s arrest for robbing the Hill Valley Payroll Substation [**BTF2**].

- **Compu-Serve:** A payment option offered at the Texaco gas station in 2015 Hill Valley [**BTF2**].

- **Computec**: A business located in Glendale, California. In 1991, Emmett Brown read a help-wanted ad for this company. Its telephone number was 818-500-3291, and its fax number was 818-500-8924. The contact person listed was named Eve [**BFAN-12**].

- **Compu-Vend:** A computerized vendor featured at Hill Valley's 7-Eleven branch, circa 2015, that offered maps and routes for local hover buses and express trams across the Mid-Valley region and downtown Hill Valley [**BTF2**].

- **Conair Corp.:** A manufacturer of personal-care products, health and beauty goods, and small appliances [**REAL**]. After Marty McFly

traveled to 1955 in Emmett Brown's DeLorean, the scientist's younger self discovered a Conair hairdryer in his older counterpart's suitcase, and wondered if people in the future no longer used towels [**BTF1-s4, BTF1-d, BTF1-n**].

Marty later utilized the dryer to simulate a futuristic weapon while posing as an extraterrestrial (Darth Vader of the planet Vulcan) to convince George McFly to ask Lorraine Baines to the Enchantment Under the Sea Dance [**BTF1**].

- **Condon, Joe:** A fictional crime reporter featured in "The River Pirates," a comic book story published in *Headline Comics* #67 (September/October 1954) [**REAL**]. Biff Tannen's friend 3-D owned this comic in 1955 [**BTF1**].

- **Container Pack:** A brand-name of foam products sold in Citizen Brown's dystopian timeline [**TLTL-3**].

- **Continuuophone:** A scientific invention displayed at the 1931 Hill Valley Exposition, also known as a theremin—an electronic musical instrument controlled without physical contact from a player. Visitors to the event's Theremin Booth could stand on a pad and move around, and thereby produce various musical sounds [**TLTL-5**].

- **Converse Chuck Taylor All-Stars:** A type of canvas and rubber footwear produced by Converse, introduced in 1917 [**REAL**]. Marty McFly wore such shoes while visiting 1955, as his 1985 Nike sneakers presented an anachronism [**BTF1**].

- **COOL SYS 1:** A button on an overhead console of Emmett Brown's DeLorean [**TLTL-5**].

- **COOL SYS 2:** A button on an overhead console of Emmett Brown's DeLorean [**TLTL-5**].

- **Cooper:** A university colleague of Emmett Brown in 1955. He, along with Dean Wooster and fellow colleague Mintz, requested that Doc, as a member of their staff, agree to take part in one of three projects: developing the Edsel automobile, creating a chemical-warfare compound (which would be dubbed Agent Brown in his honor) or helping to build a new company called Xerox. Emmett, however, refused [**BTF3-s1**].

CODE	STORY
NIKE	*BTTF*-themed TV commercial: Nike
NTND	Nintendo *Back to the Future—The Ride* Mini-Game
PIZA	*BTTF*-themed TV commercial: Pizza Hut
PNBL	Data East *BTTF* pinball game
REAL	Real life
RIDE	Simulator: *Back to the Future—The Ride*
SCRM	2010 Scream Awards: *Back to the Future 25th Anniversary Reunion* (broadcast)
SCRT	2010 Scream Awards: *Back to the Future 25th Anniversary Reunion* (trailer)
SIMP	Simulator: *The Simpsons Ride*
SLOT	*Back to the Future Video Slots*
STLZ	Unused *BTTF* footage of Eric Stoltz as Marty McFly
STRY	*Back to the Future Storybook*
TEST	Screen tests: Crispin Glover, Lea Thompson and Tom Wilson
TLTL	Telltale Games' *Back to the Future—The Game*
TOPS	Topps' *Back to the Future II* trading-card set
TRIL	*BTTF: The Official Book of the Complete Movie Trilogy*
UNIV	Universal Studios Hollywood promotional video

SUFFIX	MEDIUM
-b	*BTTF2*'s Biff Tannen Museum video (extended)
-c	Credit sequence to the animated series
-d	Film deleted scene
-n	Film novelization
-o	Film outtake
-p	1955 phone book from *BTTF1*
-v	Video game print materials or commentaries
-s1	Screenplay (draft one)
-s2	Screenplay (draft two)
-s3	Screenplay (draft three)
-s4	Screenplay (draft four)
-sp	Screenplay (production draft)
-sx	Screenplay (*Paradox*)

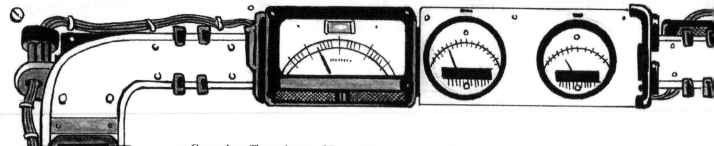

- **Copernicus:** The canine pet of Emmett Brown in 1955, named after Renaissance scientist Nicholas Copernicus [**BTF1-n, BTF3**]. The mutt was the third in line of Doc's pets named after famous thinkers [**BTF1-n**].

  > *NOTE: In* BTTF1*'s third-draft screenplay, Copernicus was identified as a Saint Bernard, though onscreen, the dog (like Doc's later pet, Einstein) appeared to be a mixed-breed. He appeared in* BTTF1 *unnamed, but was called Copernicus in the movie's screenplay and novelization; the name was later spoken aloud in* Back to the Future III.

- **Copernicus:** An impact crater on Earth's moon, located in eastern Oceanus Procellarum [**REAL**]. As a child suffering from diphtheria, with only a telescope that her father had given her to keep her occupied, Clara Clayton nicknamed the crater Little Sunshine [**BTF3-n**].

- **CORE MNTR:** A button on an overhead console of Emmett Brown's DeLorean [**TLTL-5**].

- **Corleone, Michael, Agent ("Mike"):** A name that Marty McFly considered as an alias while visiting Hill Valley in 1931 to save Emmett Brown from being killed by gangster Irving "Kid" Tannen's mob [**TLTL-1**].

  > *NOTE: Michael Corleone, a character in Mario Puzo's novels* The Godfather *and* The Sicilian, *was portrayed by Al Pacino in Francis Ford Coppola's* Godfather *trilogy.*

- **Cosmic Clock:** *See* Chronometric Clock

- **Country Club Dance:** A high-society event held in Hill Valley. In 1992, Marty McFly's snobbish friend Liz invited him to be her date, but instead attended the dance with a rich boy named Milton Van Conrad III [**BFAN-25**].

- **County Asylum:** A mental-health facility located in or near Hill Valley. Otis Peabody was taken to this institution in 1955 for observation, after claiming a "space zombie" had damaged his barn. In reality, the "alien" had been Marty McFly clad in a radiation suit, his "spacecraft" a time-traveling DeLorean [**BTF1-n**].

- **County General:** A hospital in Hill Valley. When George McFly was critically injured in a car accident in 1973, County General was inaccessible, and so he was taken instead to Hill Valley Community Hospital [**BTF2-s1**].

- **Courageous Clyde:** An alias used by Marty McFly in 1926, in Hollywood, California. As Courageous Clyde, Marty walked a tightrope erected across Upper Yosemite Falls, as part of a scene created for producer D.W. Tannen's stunt film *Raging Death Doom*, starring Daredevil Emmett Brown. Marty managed to maintain his balance, thanks to bubblegum placed on the bottom of each shoe [**BFAN-11**].

- **Court 3:** A slamball court in Hill Valley, circa 2015 [**BTF2-s2**].

  > *NOTE: In an early draft of* Back to the Future II, *Marty McFly met Griff Tannen here, rather than at the Café 80's.*

- **Courthouse Challenge Deportment Award:** An honorific given to exemplary citizens of Hill Valley in Citizen Brown's dystopian timeline. In that reality, Marty McFly was among the award's winners [**TLTL-3**].

- **Courthouse of the Future:** An attraction at the 1931 Hill Valley Exposition in Citizen Brown's dystopian timeline, sponsored by Hal's Hardware. The display predicted what the courthouse would look like 50 years later [**TLTL-4**].

- **Courthouse Square:** The central point of downtown Hill Valley, comprising a grassy square surrounded by numerous local businesses and agencies, as well as a large central Clock Tower [**BTF1**].

  The appearance of Courthouse Square evolved drastically between 1885 and 2585 as the nature of those businesses changed. However, the area still remained recognizable from one era to the next [**BTF1, BTF2, BTF3, BFAN-1 to BFAN26**].

- **Courthouse Square Exit:** An exit off I-99 (a highway for flying cars, circa 2015, located among the clouds above California), accessible via Hyperlane-Grid 4 [**BTF2**].

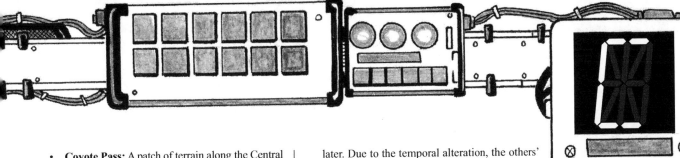

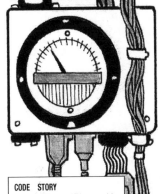

- **Coyote Pass:** A patch of terrain along the Central Pacific Railroad line in 1885, near Carson Spur and accessible via Gale Ridge. When Marty McFy and Emmett Brown failed to hijack Locomotive No. 131 before it left the Hill Valley Railroad Station, they were forced to change plans by cutting off the train at Coyote Pass [**BTF3**].

- **CPCTR MAIN:** A button on an overhead console of Emmett Brown's DeLorean [**TLTL-5**].

- **CPR Kid:** *See* Lester

- **crag:** A slang term, circa 2015, analogous to "ass." Example of usage: "Are you kirgo? We could get our crags numped!" [**BTF2-sx, BTF2-n**].

- **Craig:** One of at least two boyfriends of Linda McFly (another being Greg) in a time-altered 1985 in which the McFly family was confident and successful [**BTF1**].

- **Cranford, Jeff, E.S.C.:** A Hollywood professional, circa 2015, who helped director Max Spielberg create *Jaws 19*, according to the film's poster [**BTF2**].

  > **NOTE:** *Jeffrey Cranford worked as a production assistant on* BTTF2*, and as an apprentice editor on* BTTF3*.*

- **Crash Repel and Avoidance System Hardware (C.R.A.S.H.):** A technology created by Emmett Brown at the Institute of Future Technology, enabling his eight-seat DeLorean to push off any vehicles in danger of colliding with it [**RIDE**].

  > **NOTE:** *This device was described on signage at Universal Studios'* Back to the Future: The Ride*.*

- **Crestview Service Center:** An automotive garage. One day, four auto mechanics shared Bud Lights while on break, speculating about what they would do if able to time-travel. One worker, Ali, indicated he would invent and copyright fire, while another, Kidus, said he would travel to the past and murder his father.

  As they discussed the topic, Emmett Brown's flying DeLorean suddenly appeared on a nearby lift. The patricidal Kidus vanished, having erased himself from history due to never having been born, and the car disappeared moments later. Due to the temporal alteration, the others' knowledge of Kidus' existence was retroactively erased [**BUDL**].

- **Cretaceous period:** A geologic period ranging from 145.5 million to 65.5 million years ago, ending with the extinction of the dinosaurs [**REAL**].

  Emmett Brown, while visiting the year 3 million B.C.—which he deemed "smack dab in the middle of the Cretaceous period," despite that era having ended more than 60 million years prior—inadvertently prevented the mass-extinction event, thus eliminating mankind's evolution as a species and allowing the dinosaurs to flourish as an advanced society [**BFAN-3**], with Hill Valley replaced by Dinocity [**BFHM**].

  > **NOTE:** *Scientists believe the dinosaurs' extinction took place 65.5 million years ago, so their continued existence in 3 million B.C. is inexplicable—as is Doc's knowledge gap.*

- **CRM 114:** A designation on a label attached to Emmett Brown's giant guitar amplifier, indicating the lock keyhole used to activate the device [**BTF1**].

  > **NOTE:** *The serial number CRM 114 also appeared in two films from director Stanley Kubrick—2001: A Space Odyssey, on the spacecraft* Discovery*; and* Dr. Strangelove or: How I Learned to Stop Worrying and Love the Bomb*, on a B-52's message decoder.*

- **Crockett, Sonny, Agent:** A name that Marty McFly considered as an alias while visiting Hill Valley in 1931 to save Emmett Brown from being killed by gangster Irving "Kid" Tannen's mob [**TLTL-1**].

  > **NOTE:** *James "Sonny" Crockett, a character on* Miami Vice*, was portrayed by Don Johnson on television, and by Colin Farrell in a film adaptation of the TV series.*

- **Cro-Magnon:** The first early modern humans, who lived during the European Upper Paleolithic era [**REAL**]. Emmett Brown, having fallen for his sons' April Fool's Day prank to make him think he'd used up most of his brain power, traveled to

CODE	STORY
NIKE	*BTTF*-themed TV commercial: Nike
NTND	Nintendo *Back to the Future—The Ride* Mini-Game
PIZA	*BTTF*-themed TV commercial: Pizza Hut
PNBL	Data East *BTTF* pinball game
REAL	Real life
RIDE	Simulator: *Back to the Future—The Ride*
SCRM	2010 Scream Awards: *Back to the Future 25th Anniversary Reunion* (broadcast)
SCRT	2010 Scream Awards: *Back to the Future 25th Anniversary Reunion* (trailer)
SIMP	Simulator: *The Simpsons Ride*
SLOT	*Back to the Future Video Slots*
STLZ	Unused *BTTF* footage of Eric Stoltz as Marty McFly
STRY	*Back to the Future Storybook*
TEST	Screen tests: Crispin Glover, Lea Thompson and Tom Wilson
TLTL	Telltale Games' *Back to the Future—The Game*
TOPS	Topps' *Back to the Future II* trading-card set
TRIL	*BTTF: The Official Book of the Complete Movie Trilogy*
UNIV	Universal Studios Hollywood promotional video

SUFFIX	MEDIUM
-b	*BTTF2*'s Biff Tannen Museum video (extended)
-c	Credit sequence to the animated series
-d	Film deleted scene
-n	Film novelization
-o	Film outtake
-p	1955 phone book from *BTTF1*
-v	Video game print materials or commentaries
-s1	Screenplay (draft one)
-s2	Screenplay (draft two)
-s3	Screenplay (draft three)
-s4	Screenplay (draft four)
-sp	Screenplay (production draft)
-sx	Screenplay (*Paradox*)

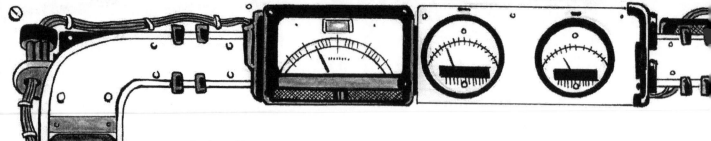

the time of the Cro-Magnon to be free of science and thereby conserve his remaining power. Bored with the proto-humans' simple minds, he soon returned to his own era [**BFAN-12**].

- **CRS-43-PG-159 4A2/YM27/6AX:** A series of numbers and letters stenciled on the side of Jennifer Parker's graffiti paint box in Citizen Brown's dystopian timeline. Using these paints, Jennifer protested Brown's oppressive rules by vandalizing public property [**TLTL-3**].

- **Crump:** A classmate of Marty McFly at Hill Valley High School in 1985, in Mister Arky's class. He didn't like to contribute to class discussions [**BTF1-s1**].

- **Crump, John, Reverend:** The pastor of an Assembly of Christ church located in Courthouse Square, circa 1985 [**BTF1**].

- **Crumrine, Paul:** A writer for the *Hill Valley Telegraph* who, in the Biffhorrific timeline, reported George McFly's death and Emmett Brown's committment to an asylum. Once the timeline was restored, Crumrine instead wrote about both men receiving civic awards [**BTF2**].

  > **NOTE:** *In the real world, writer Paul Crumrine wrote the book* Navigating the Yellow Stream, *as well as the short story "Found Scribbled on a Roll of Toilet Paper." He also contributed to* Weird Tales #336.

- **Crusher:** A surly mutt whose owner, Wilkins, frequented the Hogshead Tavern in 1845 London. Crusher had an eye-patch (like Wilkins), as well as a spiked collar and an angry disposition, and often crushed bones in his yellow teeth [**BFAN-10**].

- **CTRL ALT:** A button on an overhead console of Emmett Brown's DeLorean [**TLTL-5**].

- **CTRL CMPTR:** A button on an overhead console of Emmett Brown's DeLorean [**TLTL-5**].

- **CTRL INSTR:** A button on an overhead console of Emmett Brown's DeLorean [**TLTL-5**].

- **CTRL SERV:** A button on an overhead console of Emmett Brown's DeLorean [**TLTL-5**].

- **Cuba:** An island nation in the Caribbean, consisting of the main island of Cuba, Isla de la Juventud and several archipelagos [**REAL**]. In an altered timeline, Cuba became one of 87 states of the United States by the year 1964 [**BTF1-s1**].

- **Cubs:** A Major League Baseball team based in Chicago, Illinois [**REAL**]. In 2015, the team won the World Series in five games against a Miami team [**BTF2**].

  > **NOTE:** *When* BTTF2 *was released in 1989, no Major League team played in Miami, or elsewhere in Florida. In 1993, however, the Florida Marlins—later renamed the Miami Marlins—were formed, making it possible for a Miami team to beat the Cubs in 2015.*

- **Cubs:** A local children's sports team in Hill Valley. In 1985, a neighbor of George McFly whose daughter was on the Cubs pressured George into buying an entire case of peanut brittle, in order to support her team's fundraising efforts. Uncomfortable with confrontation, George agreed to the purchase [**BTF1-d**]. This neighbor's name was Howard [**BTF1-s4**].

  > **NOTE:** *This scene, explaining why the McFlys had so much peanut brittle in the first movie, was cut from the final film, but was included as a deleted scene on the Blu-ray release. In the fourth-draft screenplay, and in the novelization, the daughter was selling Girl Scout Cookies.*

- **Cue Ball:** *See* Donnely ("Cue Ball")

- **Culver, Roland:** A red-haired, freckled classmate of Verne Brown at Hill Valley Elementary School in 1991. He had a southern U.S. accent and did poorly in arithmetic.

  Roland was proud of his grandfather's achievement of having climbed a mountain, and bragged about it during show-and-tell. This annoyed Verne, who usually had no such stories to tell. But upon learning that Verne's grandfather, Daniel Clayon, had discovered a new species of butterfly (*Lepidoptera Martha*), Roland was suitably impressed [**BFAN-13**].

- **Cummins, Erin:** A Hollywood professional, circa 2015, who helped director Max Spielberg create *Jaws 19*, according to the film's poster [**BTF2**].

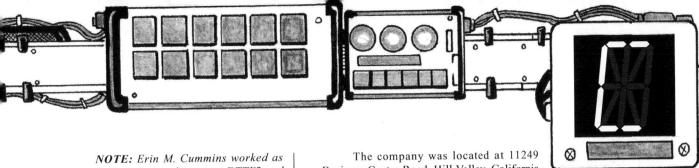

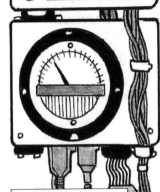

NOTE: Erin M. Cummins worked as an assistant art director on BTTF2 *and* BTTF3.

- **Cupid's:** An adult book store in Courthouse Square, located near the intersection of Main Street and Hill Street, and specializing in adult books, films and magazines [**BTF1**].

- **CusCo Industries:** A company at which Marty McFly worked in 2015, until his boss, Ito T. Fujitsu, fired him for engaging in fraudulent activities with Douglas J. Needles. Fujitsu, monitoring a conversation between McFly and Needles, discovered the illegal transaction. After calling Marty to announce his termination, Fujitsu then faxed him a message announcing, "You're fired!!!" [**BTF2**].

The company was located at 11249 Business Center Road, Hill Valley, California 95420-4345 [**BTF2, BFCG**]. Emmett Brown recreated this business in miniature for a board game that he created [**BFAN-6**].

- **Cusimano:** A student in Mister Arky's class at Hill Valley High School in 1952. He didn't like to contribute to class discussions [**BTF1-s1**].

- **Cusimano Brothers Gearworks Factory:** A business in Hill Valley, circa 1952. Emmett Brown purchased the plant from a man named Fredman for $1.85 million, so that he could launch Emmett Brown Enterprises and follow his dream of inventing a Photo-Electric Chemical Power Converter that could efficiently convert radiation into electrical energy [**BTF1-s2**].

CODE	STORY
NIKE	*BTTF*-themed TV commercial: Nike
NTND	Nintendo *Back to the Future— The Ride* Mini-Game
PIZA	*BTTF*-themed TV commercial: Pizza Hut
PNBL	Data East *BTTF* pinball game
REAL	Real life
RIDE	Simulator: *Back to the Future—The Ride*
SCRM	2010 Scream Awards: *Back to the Future* 25th Anniversary Reunion (broadcast)
SCRT	2010 Scream Awards: *Back to the Future* 25th Anniversary Reunion (trailer)
SIMP	Simulator: *The Simpsons Ride*
SLOT	*Back to the Future Video Slots*
STLZ	Unused *BTTF* footage of Eric Stoltz as Marty McFly
STRY	*Back to the Future Storybook*
TEST	Screen tests: Crispin Glover, Lea Thompson and Tom Wilson
TLTL	Telltale Games' *Back to the Future—The Game*
TOPS	Topps' *Back to the Future II* trading-card set
TRIL	*BTTF: The Official Book of the Complete Movie Trilogy*
UNIV	Universal Studios Hollywood promotional video

SUFFIX	MEDIUM
-b	*BTTF2*'s Biff Tannen Museum video (extended)
-c	Credit sequence to the animated series
-d	Film deleted scene
-n	Film novelization
-o	Film outtake
-p	1955 phone book from *BTTF1*
-v	Video game print materials or commentaries
-s1	Screenplay (draft one)
-s2	Screenplay (draft two)
-s3	Screenplay (draft three)
-s4	Screenplay (draft four)
-sp	Screenplay (production draft)
-sx	Screenplay (*Paradox*)

DEEP-THOUGHT MIND-READING HELMET

(OR BRAIN-WAVE ANALYZER)

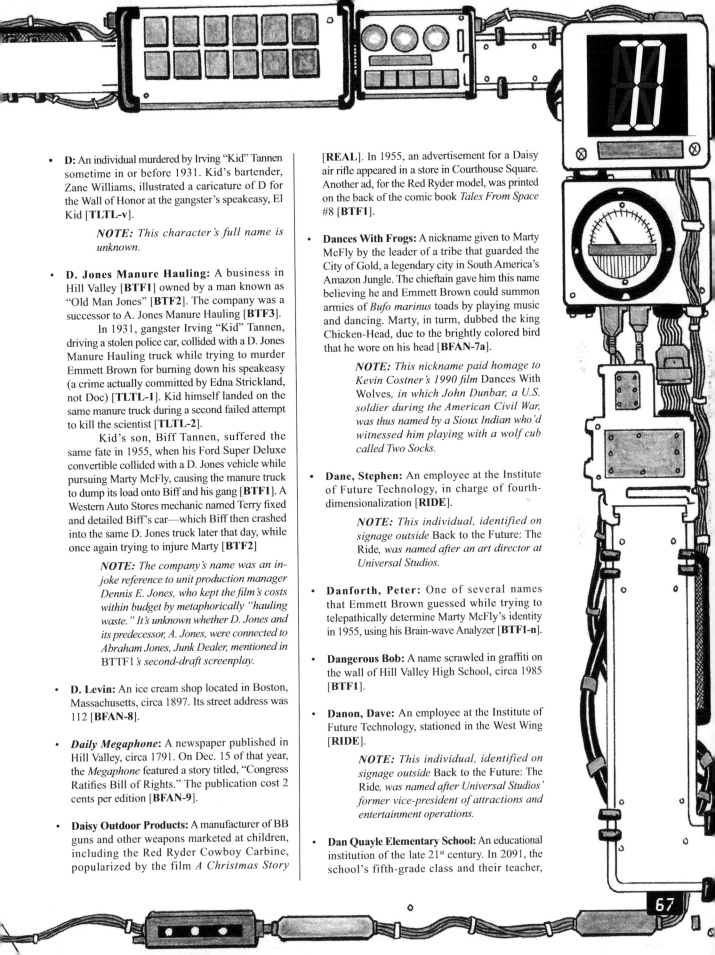

- **D:** An individual murdered by Irving "Kid" Tannen sometime in or before 1931. Kid's bartender, Zane Williams, illustrated a caricature of D for the Wall of Honor at the gangster's speakeasy, El Kid [**TLTL-v**].

  > *NOTE: This character's full name is unknown.*

- **D. Jones Manure Hauling:** A business in Hill Valley [**BTF1**] owned by a man known as "Old Man Jones" [**BTF2**]. The company was a successor to A. Jones Manure Hauling [**BTF3**].

  In 1931, gangster Irving "Kid" Tannen, driving a stolen police car, collided with a D. Jones Manure Hauling truck while trying to murder Emmett Brown for burning down his speakeasy (a crime actually committed by Edna Strickland, not Doc) [**TLTL-1**]. Kid himself landed on the same manure truck during a second failed attempt to kill the scientist [**TLTL-2**].

  Kid's son, Biff Tannen, suffered the same fate in 1955, when his Ford Super Deluxe convertible collided with a D. Jones vehicle while pursuing Marty McFly, causing the manure truck to dump its load onto Biff and his gang [**BTF1**]. A Western Auto Stores mechanic named Terry fixed and detailed Biff's car—which Biff then crashed into the same D. Jones truck later that day, while once again trying to injure Marty [**BTF2**]

  > *NOTE: The company's name was an in-joke reference to unit production manager Dennis E. Jones, who kept the film's costs within budget by metaphorically "hauling waste." It's unknown whether D. Jones and its predecessor, A. Jones, were connected to Abraham Jones, Junk Dealer, mentioned in BTTF1's second-draft screenplay.*

- **D. Levin:** An ice cream shop located in Boston, Massachusetts, circa 1897. Its street address was 112 [**BFAN-8**].

- *Daily Megaphone*: A newspaper published in Hill Valley, circa 1791. On Dec. 15 of that year, the *Megaphone* featured a story titled, "Congress Ratifies Bill of Rights." The publication cost 2 cents per edition [**BFAN-9**].

- **Daisy Outdoor Products:** A manufacturer of BB guns and other weapons marketed at children, including the Red Ryder Cowboy Carbine, popularized by the film *A Christmas Story*

[**REAL**]. In 1955, an advertisement for a Daisy air rifle appeared in a store in Courthouse Square. Another ad, for the Red Ryder model, was printed on the back of the comic book *Tales From Space #8* [**BTF1**].

- **Dances With Frogs:** A nickname given to Marty McFly by the leader of a tribe that guarded the City of Gold, a legendary city in South America's Amazon Jungle. The chieftain gave him this name believing he and Emmett Brown could summon armies of *Bufo marinus* toads by playing music and dancing. Marty, in turm, dubbed the king Chicken-Head, due to the brightly colored bird that he wore on his head [**BFAN-7a**].

  > *NOTE: This nickname paid homage to Kevin Costner's 1990 film* Dances With Wolves, *in which John Dunbar, a U.S. soldier during the American Civil War, was thus named by a Sioux Indian who'd witnessed him playing with a wolf cub called Two Socks.*

- **Dane, Stephen:** An employee at the Institute of Future Technology, in charge of fourth-dimensionalization [**RIDE**].

  > *NOTE: This individual, identified on signage outside* Back to the Future: The Ride, *was named after an art director at Universal Studios.*

- **Danforth, Peter:** One of several names that Emmett Brown guessed while trying to telepathically determine Marty McFly's identity in 1955, using his Brain-wave Analyzer [**BTF1-n**].

- **Dangerous Bob:** A name scrawled in graffiti on the wall of Hill Valley High School, circa 1985 [**BTF1**].

- **Danon, Dave:** An employee at the Institute of Future Technology, stationed in the West Wing [**RIDE**].

  > *NOTE: This individual, identified on signage outside* Back to the Future: The Ride, *was named after Universal Studios' former vice-president of attractions and entertainment operations.*

- **Dan Quayle Elementary School:** An educational institution of the late 21st century. In 2091, the school's fifth-grade class and their teacher,

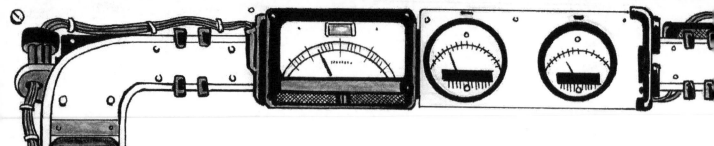

Mrs. Phillips, visited the McFly Museum of Aeronautics, in Hill Valley [**BFAN-9**].

> ***NOTE:*** *James Danforth "Dan" Quayle was the 44th Vice-President of the United States, under President George H. W. Bush. Less than a year after this episode aired, Quayle was widely lambasted for misspelling the word "potato" at an elementary-school spelling bee hosted in Trenton, New Jersey.*

- **Daphne:** A mid-20s beatnik who sometimes attended parties thrown at Emmett Brown's mansion in the 1950s. This attractive young woman wore heavy avant-garde makeup and claimed to be from the ninth system of the Andromeda Galaxy [**BTF1-s4**].

- ***Daredevil Brown:*** A newspaper comic strip published in 1926, featuring the fictional exploits of four-year-old Hollywood stunt actor Daredevil Emmett Brown [**BFAN-11**].

- **Daredevil Brown:** A brand of soda produced in 1926, named after Hollywood actor Daredevil Emmett Brown [**BFAN-11**].

- **Daredevil Nuts:** A brand of canned nuts sold in 1926, featuring the likeness of Daredevil Emmett Brown [**BFAN-11**].

- **Daredevil Soup:** A brand of canned soup produced in 1926, marketing the popularity of Daredevil Emmett Brown [**BFAN-11**].

- **Dark Ages, The:** A historical periodization denoting Europe's economic and cultural deterioration following the Roman Empire's decline [**REAL**]. Upon learning that his older self had become stranded in 1885, the 1955 version of Emmett Brown mused that he was lucky he hadn't ended up in the Dark Ages, where he would likely have been executed as a heretic [**BTF3**].

- **Darth Vader:** *See* Vader, Darth

- **Data:** *See* Unger, Rafe ("Data")

- **data-fax court:** A 21st-century legal institution in the United States. In 2015, Martin McFly Jr. was tried in a data-fax court after being arrested for robbing the Hill Valley Payroll Substation [**BTF2**].

> ***NOTE:*** *The nature of a data-fax court is unknown.*

- **Dave:** A wild horned deer cared for by Windjammer Diefendorfer, circa 1888. The kindly old man helped Dave by removing several hats attached to its horns. Marty McFly encountered the animal while visiting that era [**BFAN-21**].

- **Dave's:** A variety store in Hill Valley, circa 1991. Emmett Brown recreated this business in miniature for a board game that he created [**BFAN-6**].

- **da Vinci, Leonardo:** An employee at the Institute of Future Technology, in charge of extravaganza development [**RIDE**].

> ***NOTE:*** *This individual, identified on signage outside* Back to the Future: The Ride, *was named after the Renaissance painter and sculptor.*

- **Davoyan, Leon:** A computational systems maven at the Institute of Future Technology [**RIDE**].

> ***NOTE:*** *This individual, identified on signage outside* Back to the Future: The Ride, *was named after a Universal Studios technician.*

- **Dawson, Bobby ("Doodles"):** An emcee with the United Service Organizations (USO) who helped raise U.S. troop morale during World War II. Between introducing singers and other acts, Dawson frequently urged attendees to buy U.S. war bonds [**BFAN-17**].

> ***NOTE:*** *Dawson was drawn to resemble comedian Bob Hope, who performed similar tasks during wartime, and also utilized Hope's usual speaking and joking styles.*

- **Day, Dan A.:** A person buried at the Boot Hill Cemetery, near the entrance of the abandoned Delgado Mine [**BTF3**].

- ***Day the Earth Stood Still, The:*** A classic science fiction movie filmed in 1951, directed by Robert Wise [**REAL**]. Verne Brown had a poster of this film hanging in his bedroom when he was a child [**BFCL-1**].

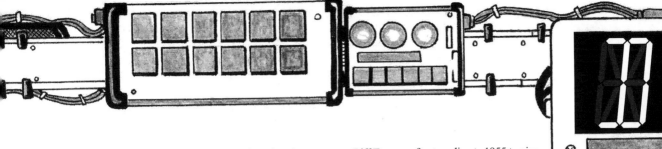

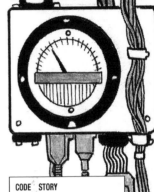

- **Day-Trader Casual:** A hairstyle offered at The Combformist, a Hill Valley business in Citizen Brown's dystopian timeline [**TLTL-v**].

- **DCMTAXI:** A model of flying taxicab, in use circa 2015 [**BTF2**].

- **Deacon's Hill Tunnel:** *See* River Road Tunnel

- **dead file:** A slang term popular in 2015, analogous to "dead duck," and used to denote trouble (as in "You're a dead file, McFly!") [**BTF2-sx, BTF2-n**].

- **Dead Man's Swamp:** A patch of wetland in or near Hill Valley. In order to join the Mega Muscleman Fan Club, Verne Brown's friends undertook a rite of passage that involved swinging over the swamp on a rope. Verne feared doing so, but a bully named Jackson pressured him into jumping anyway. After Verne stood his ground and refused to do it, Jackson took his place and crashed into the swamp when the rope broke, earning the other children's derisive laughter [**BFAN-24**].

- **Deadwood Kid, The:** An outlaw sought by the U.S. government in 1885. A Wanted poster for this individual hung in the office of M.R. Gale, the editor of the *Hill Valley Telegraph* [**BTF3**].

- **Debtor's Prison:** A number of correctional facilities in London, England, in which those unable to pay their bills were incarcerated [**REAL**]. One section of a particular debtor's prison, known as the Tannen Wing, housed citizens whose homes or businesses were foreclosed by landlord Ebiffnezer Tannen. In 1845, after Marty McFly visited Tannen disguised as the Ghost of Christmas, the frightened miser freed all of the inmates and cleared their debts [**BFAN-10**].

    NOTE: This episode paid homage to the 1843 novella A Christmas Carol, *by English author Charles Dickens, in which Ebenezer Scrooge endured a similar experience.*

- **Decker:** A business in Hill Valley, circa 1992 [**BFAN-18**].

- **Decker, Jim:** A college football player for UCLA in 1955. That year, Decker kicked a field goal in the final seconds of a game against Washington State, enabling UCLA to win with a score of 19 to 17 [**REAL**].

Biff Tannen, after traveling to 1955 to give his younger self a copy of *Grays Sports Almanac*, used this game to prove the book's ability to predict the future, by reading the game's published results and then listening to those same scores on the radio. Impressed, young Biff accepted the gift and began betting on sports events, thereby becoming an immensely wealthy and powerful man [**BTF2**].

- **Decycling Bin:** A public station in Citizen Brown's dystopian timeline, located outside Emmett Brown's mayoral office. The final resting place for all contraband confiscated in Hill Valley, the Decycling Bin ensured that "socially toxic" items—such as weapons, alcohol, cigarettes, bubblegum, dogs and Circus Peanuts—would never find their way back into the hands of the general public, since they were shunted down a chute to the former basement of Irving "Kid" Tannen's speakeasy [**TLTL-3**].

- **Dee Dee's Delight:** An adult business in Hill Valley, in Biffhorrific 1985, that featured nude barmaids [**BTF2**].

- **Deep-Thinking Mind-Reading Helmet:** An invention of Emmett Brown that harnessed electromagnetic impulses created by synaptic responses from the cerebrum and the cerebellum, transmitting mind waves into the helmet's interpreting circuitry, thus translating the impulses into written language [**RIDE**].

    NOTE: Other telepathy helmets created by Doc include the Brain-wave Analyzer, from BTTF1; the Brain Wave Analyzer, from the animated series; the Deep-Thought Mind-Reading Helmet, also seen in the animated series; and the Mind Mapping Helmet, from the Telltale Games video game.

- **Deep-Thought Mind-Reading Helmet:** An invention of Emmett Brown that enabled a wearer to hear the unspoken thoughts of others [**BFAN-1**].

    NOTE: It's unclear if this device, mentioned in the animated episode "Brothers," was the same helmet featured in the first Back to the Future *film—called a Brain-wave Analyzer in the movie's novelization—or a separate attempt at telepathy. The animated series also featured a device called a Brain Wave Analyzer.*

CODE	STORY
NIKE	*BTTF*-themed TV commercial: Nike
NTND	Nintendo *Back to the Future—The Ride* Mini-Game
PIZA	*BTTF*-themed TV commercial: Pizza Hut
PNBL	Data East *BTTF* pinball game
REAL	Real life
RIDE	Simulator: *Back to the Future—The Ride*
SCRM	2010 Scream Awards: *Back to the Future 25th Anniversary Reunion* (broadcast)
SCRT	2010 Scream Awards: *Back to the Future 25th Anniversary Reunion* (trailer)
SIMP	Simulator: *The Simpsons Ride*
SLOT	*Back to the Future Video Slots*
STLZ	Unused *BTTF* footage of Eric Stoltz as Marty McFly
STRY	*Back to the Future Storybook*
TEST	Screen tests: Crispin Glover, Lea Thompson and Tom Wilson
TLTL	Telltale Games' *Back to the Future—The Game*
TOPS	Topps' *Back to the Future II* trading-card set
TRIL	*BTTF: The Official Book of the Complete Movie Trilogy*
UNIV	Universal Studios Hollywood promotional video

SUFFIX	MEDIUM
-b	*BTTF2*'s Biff Tannen Museum video (extended)
-c	Credit sequence to the animated series
-d	Film deleted scene
-n	Film novelization
-o	Film outtake
-p	1955 phone book from *BTTF1*
-v	Video game print materials or commentaries
-s1	Screenplay (draft one)
-s2	Screenplay (draft two)
-s3	Screenplay (draft three)
-s4	Screenplay (draft four)
-sp	Screenplay (production draft)
-sx	Screenplay (*Paradox*)

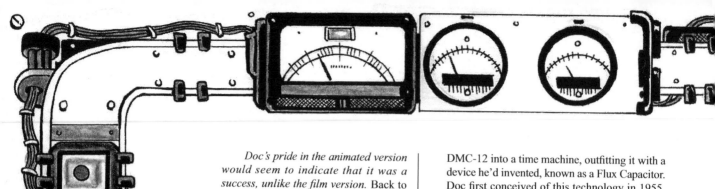

Doc's pride in the animated version would seem to indicate that it was a success, unlike the film version. Back to the Future: The Ride *introduced a similarly named device, the Deep-Thinking Mind-Reading Helmet, while the Telltale Games video game revealed another, the Mind Mapping Helmet.*

- **degaussing unit:** An illegal technology that, according to a *USA Today* report, Martin McFly Jr. had in his possession when arrested for robbery in 2015 [**BTF2**].

  NOTE: Degaussing is the process of decreasing or eliminating a magnetic field.

- **del Caliche, Loraine:** A name scrawled in graffiti on the wall of Hill Valley High School, circa 1985 [**BTF1**].

- **Delgado Highway:** A road running through Hill Valley, circa 1985. The Del-Wood Plaza Complex was located at the corner of Delgado Highway and Woodman Road [**BTF3-s1**].

- **Delgado Mine:** An abandoned mining operation in the Hill Valley area, located on Mt. Clayton, adjacent to Boot Hill Cemetery. While stranded in 1885, Emmett Brown buried his time-traveling DeLorean in the Delgado Mine, leaving instructions for Marty McFly detailing how to find the vehicle in 1955 and return to his own era [**BTF3**].

  NOTE: Mt. Clayton was indicated on Doc's hand-drawn map of the mine.

- **DeLorean, Marty:** An alias used by Marty McFly while visiting 1967. Jailed for not having a draft card, Marty, disguised as a Hippie, claimed that his name was Marty DeLorean, in the hope that Emmett Brown would hear of his arrest and, having met Marty and seen the car in 1955, would understand the name's significance—which he did [**BTF2-s1**].

- **DeLorean DMC-12:** A silver-colored, stainless-steel sports car produced by DeLorean Motor Co. in 1981 and 1982. The vehicle featured gull-wing doors and a fiberglass underbody, to which brushed stainless-steel panels were affixed [**REAL**].

  In 1985, Emmett Brown converted a DMC-12 into a time machine, outfitting it with a device he'd invented, known as a Flux Capacitor. Doc first conceived of this technology in 1955, after falling off his toilet and striking his head. The car ran on gasoline, but a nuclear reaction was required to generate the 1.21 jigowatts of electricity needed to power the Flux Capacitor.

  To that end, Doc stole a case of plutonium from Libyan nationalists, who'd hired him to build them a bomb. As he prepared to embark on his maiden voyage, the terrorists tracked him down to the Twin Pines Mall, assassinating him in cold blood. Marty jumped into the car to avoid a similar fate, and found himself stranded in 1955. There, he sought assistance from Brown's younger self to fix the vehicle so he could return to his own era. In so doing, Marty managed to prevent Doc's murder, by warning him of his fate in a letter [**BTF1**].

  Doc resumed his research upon Marty's return, steering the DeLorean thirty years into the future, to 2015. There, he performed a hover-conversion on the car, enabling it to fly, and also added a Mr. Fusion Home Energy Reactor to fuel the vehicle more cleanly.

  While in 2015, the scientist learned of a danger facing Marty's future children, and brought his friend forward in time to help them. Biff Tannen stole the vehicle and journeyed back to 1955, intending to alter time by giving his younger self an almanac filled with future sports statistics. Marty and Doc fixed Biff's time tampering and retrieved the DeLorean, but the car was struck by lightning, sending it to 1885, and rendering it incapable of flight or time travel. Doc hid the car in the Delgado Mine, leaving instructions for Marty to locate it [**BTF2**].

  Unbeknownst to Marty and Doc at the time, an exact duplicate of the DeLorean was created by the lightning strike, propelling it far into the future. The scientist discovered this fact while visiting 2025 aboard the *Jules Verne Train*, and recovered the car in time to stop Griff Tannen from using it to vandalize the time stream [**TLTL-1**].

  Stranded in 1955, Marty again elicited help from Brown's younger self. Following older Doc's map, the duo located the damaged DeLorean, then repaired it so Marty could return to his own year once more. Upon discovering that Doc would die in 1885, however, he traveled back to save his friend instead. The vehicle's fuel line was ruptured in that year, making the car un-drivable. The 1885 Doc devised a way to use a locomotive to push

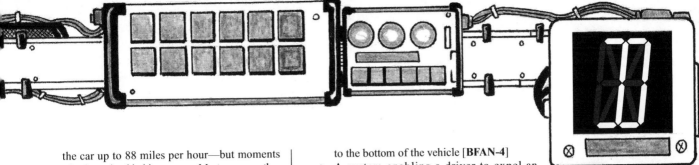

the car up to 88 miles per hour—but moments after he arrived in his own era, Marty saw another train fast approaching. Unable to save the car, he jumped to safety as the DeLorean was destroyed [**BTF3**].

Since DeLoreans are collector's items, parking the vehicle on a street made it vulnerable to thievery. To that end, following the first vehicle's destruction, the scientist built a second, larger version that could fold up at the pull of a lever, down to the size of a suitcase, and be reconfigured into different models. This DeLorean, which had voice-activated time circuits, was programmed to open only at the sound of Doc's voice or Einstein's bark. Since the car-suitcase weighed 2,796 pounds, he also designed a remote-control crane to carry it for him (which, during testing, exploded) [**BFAN-1**].

Doc also built an Eight-Passenger DeLorean Time-Travel Vehicle, an experimental, energy-efficient, convertible upgrade from the original car, capable of carrying eight occupants in two rows of four. This version, designed at the Institute of Future Technology's Anti-Gravitic Laboratory, was used by a team of scientists and Time-Travel Volunteers to study history [**RIDE**].

Doc created a number of add-on systems for the DeLorean, including:

- A slingshot that extended from beneath the hood at the pull of a lever, hammering two metal stakes into the ground, thereby anchoring a thick rubber-band with which Doc could propel the flying car into the air [**BFAN-3**]
- A device for launching the vehicle out of Doc's garage, which was designed like a giant pinball-machine's ball-serving mechanism [**BFAN-17**]
- Another launch system, consisting of a massive boxing glove attached to a tension-loaded spring that punched the rear of the car, causing it to quickly accelerate [**BFAN-8**]
- An inflatable raft affixed to the vehicle's bottom in the event of a water landing, which was activated by a pull cord beneath a dashboard panel, enabling the car to rise to the surface and travel back to shore [**BFAN-4**]
- A system for reconfiguring the DeLorean as a covered wagon, for use during the Hill Valley Pioneer Days Parade [**BFAN-13**]
- A handheld auto-remote device enabling Doc to summon the car to his location over long distances [**BFAN-4**]
- A large set of extendable chain cutters attached

to the bottom of the vehicle [**BFAN-4**]
- A system enabling a driver to expel an occupant by extending the passenger seat through the door, discarding that person on the ground [**BFAN-7b**]
- The ELB Autogroom 5000, a robotic shaving and grooming system built into the dashboard [**BFAN-7b**]
- The ELB Super-Sniffer Snout 4000, which amplified Einstein's canine sniffing ability via a large, nose-like contraption attached on one end to the dog's snout, and on the other to the front of the DeLorean [**BFAN-20**]
- A pair of robotic arms inside the trunk that could pick up items and automatically place them within the vehicle's storage compartment [**BFAN-7b**]
- An automatic-retrieval feature enabling the car to return to specified four-dimensional coordinates in the event that Doc failed to return to the vehicle within an allotted span of time [**TLTL-1**]

Other individuals known to drive time-traveling DeLoreans have included a pair of Italian teenagers who discovered an Arrigoni vending machine in the future [**ARGN**]; two men who journeyed back from 2152 to 2011, where they crashed head-on into a Porsche and had an out-of-body experience before dying [**LIMO**]; and two others who traveled from 1989 to 2015, where they dined at a futuristic Pizza Hut [**PIZA**]. When another DeLorean suddenly appeared at an auto repair shop, its mere presence altered time by negating the existence of a mechanic who had wished he owned a time machine so that he could murder his father [**BUDL**].

NOTE: Back to the Future—The Card Game *referred to this vehicle as the Time Car.*

The time machine was originally conceived as being constructed from a refrigerator, but Robert Zemeckis and Steven Spielberg changed it to a car, fearing that children, upon seeing the movie, might suffocate after climbing into a fridge.

The filmmakers chose a DeLorean to pay homage to the gull-wing doors of Klaatu's spaceship in The Day the Earth Stood Still.

In October 2011, DeLorean Motor Co. announced that it would again begin

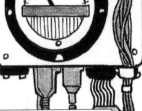

CODE	STORY
NIKE	*BTTF*-themed TV commercial: Nike
NTND	Nintendo *Back to the Future—The Ride* Mini-Game
PIZA	*BTTF*-themed TV commercial: Pizza Hut
PNBL	Data East *BTTF* pinball game
REAL	Real life
RIDE	Simulator: *Back to the Future—The Ride*
SCRM	2010 Scream Awards: *Back to the Future 25th Anniversary Reunion* (broadcast)
SCRT	2010 Scream Awards: *Back to the Future 25th Anniversary Reunion* (trailer)
SIMP	Simulator: *The Simpsons Ride*
SLOT	*Back to the Future Video Slots*
STLZ	Unused *BTTF* footage of Eric Stoltz as Marty McFly
STRY	*Back to the Future Storybook*
TEST	Screen tests: Crispin Glover, Lea Thompson and Tom Wilson
TLTL	Telltale Games' *Back to the Future—The Game*
TOPS	Topps' *Back to the Future II* trading-card set
TRIL	*BTTF: The Official Book of the Complete Movie Trilogy*
UNIV	Universal Studios Hollywood promotional video

SUFFIX MEDIUM

-b	*BTTF2*'s Biff Tannen Museum video (extended)
-c	Credit sequence to the animated series
-d	Film deleted scene
-n	Film novelization
-o	Film outtake
-p	1955 phone book from *BTTF1*
-v	Video game print materials or commentaries
-s1	Screenplay (draft one)
-s2	Screenplay (draft two)
-s3	Screenplay (draft three)
-s4	Screenplay (draft four)
-sp	Screenplay (production draft)
-sx	Screenplay (*Paradox*)

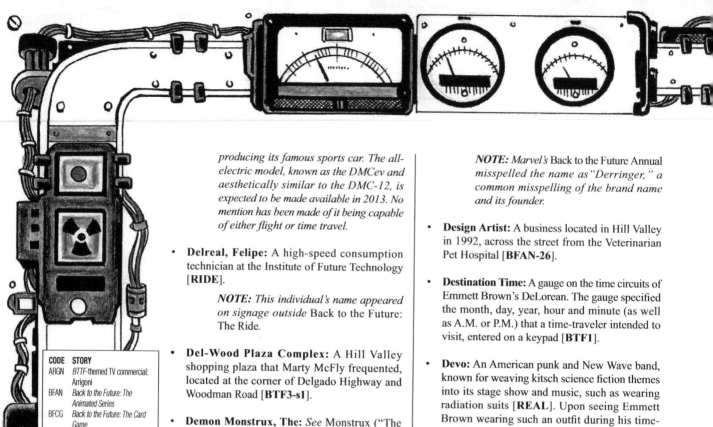

producing its famous sports car. The all-electric model, known as the DMCev and aesthetically similar to the DMC-12, is expected to be made available in 2013. No mention has been made of it being capable of either flight or time travel.

- **Delreal, Felipe:** A high-speed consumption technician at the Institute of Future Technology [**RIDE**].

  NOTE: This individual's name appeared on signage outside Back to the Future: The Ride.

- **Del-Wood Plaza Complex:** A Hill Valley shopping plaza that Marty McFly frequented, located at the corner of Delgado Highway and Woodman Road [**BTF3-s1**].

- **Demon Monstrux, The:** *See* Monstrux ("The Demon Monstrux")

- **Dennis:** A domestic servant of a wealthy woman from Hill Valley. When Emmett Brown inadvertently caused a citywide brown-out in 1992, Dennis was unable to charge his employer's electric golf cart [**BFAN-22**].

- **Denver:** The capital city of Colorado [**REAL**]. In October 2015, the slamball playoffs were held in Denver, according to *USA Today* [**BTF2**].

- **Denver Broncos:** A professional football team in the American Football Conference's West Division [**REAL**]. Emmett Brown had a clock in his home bearing the team's helmet design, set to chime in synch with many others [**BTF1**].

- **Department of Social Services:** A state agency in Calfornia [**REAL**]. The Department of Social Services maintained a branch in Courthouse Square, with its offices located inside the Hill Valley Courthouse [**BTF1**].

- **Derby & Dias:** A brand of bourbon sold at Hill Valley's Palace Saloon and Hotel, circa 1885 [**BTF3**].

- **Deringer:** A single-shot pistol created by Henry Deringer [**REAL**]. Buford Tannen tried to kill Emmett Brown in 1885 using such a gun, but Marty McFly disarmed him with a Frisbie pie plate [**BTF3**].

NOTE: Marvel's Back to the Future Annual *misspelled the name as "Derringer," a common misspelling of the brand name and its founder.*

- **Design Artist:** A business located in Hill Valley in 1992, across the street from the Veterinarian Pet Hospital [**BFAN-26**].

- **Destination Time:** A gauge on the time circuits of Emmett Brown's DeLorean. The gauge specified the month, day, year, hour and minute (as well as A.M. or P.M.) that a time-traveler intended to visit, entered on a keypad [**BTF1**].

- **Devo:** An American punk and New Wave band, known for weaving kitsch science fiction themes into its stage show and music, such as wearing radiation suits [**REAL**]. Upon seeing Emmett Brown wearing such an outfit during his time-travel experiments at the Twin Pines Mall, Marty McFly mistook the garb for a "Devo suit" [**BTF1**].

- **DeVos, David C.:** An employee at the Institute of Future Technology, stationed in the West Wing [**RIDE**].

  NOTE: This individual, identified on signage outside Back to the Future: The Ride, *was named after a Universal Studios employee who served as the ride's pre-show director.*

- **Dewey, Nelson ("Fatty"):** A gangster operating in Chicago's South Side, circa 1927. A wanted poster for this individual hung in a jail in which Marty McFly was briefly incarcerated [**BFCM-1**].

  NOTE: This character was named after artist Nelson Dewey, who illustrated the Back to the Future *comic book series for Harvey Comics.*

- **Diagnostic Modules:** A set of devices invented by Emmett Brown for troubleshooting problems with his DeLorean's time circuits. The scientist used these modules to determine why the circuits malfunctioned, stranding Doc and Marty McFly in 1931.

  When Edna Strickland stole a duplicate DeLorean and tried to burn down the Palace Saloon and Hotel in 1876, Doc utilized an additional invention, Flux Synchronization Modules, to sync up the two vehicles' Diagnostic

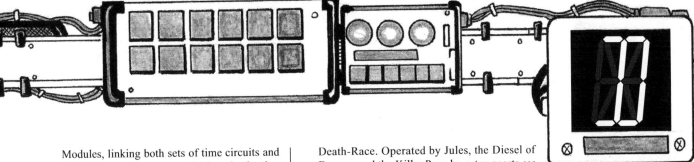

Modules, linking both sets of time circuits and overriding the alternate car's time destination [**TLTL-5**].

- **Diana, Queen:** *See* Queen Diana

- **Diane:** A citizen of Hill Valley who dated a man named Jack in 1986. Edna Strickland, a spinster who spied on people from her apartment and yelled at them via a bullhorn, publicly taunted the couple for hanging out behind a tree [**TLTL-1**].

  > *NOTE: The names Jack and Diane paid homage to John Cougar Mellencamp's 1982 hit song, "Jack & Diane," in which the titular couple hid behind a shady tree, presumably to have sex.*

- **Diatribe:** A small empire in North America, circa 2,991,299,129,912,991 A.D., located in former northwestern Canada [**BFCL-2**].

  > *NOTE: Many scientists believe Earth will cease to exist in approximately 7.6 billion years, with human life dying out within a billion years or so.*

- **Dickens, Charles:** A Victorian English writer who authored numerous masterpiece novels, including *A Christmas Carol*, *Oliver Twist* and *A Tale of Two Cities* [**REAL**]. His name was among those that Marty McFly and Verne Brown urged author Jules Verne to rename himself, in the hope that young Verne would no longer be named "Verne" in the novelist's honor [**BFAN-21**].

- **Diefendorfer, Windjammer, Doctor ("Windy"):** A kindly old physician living in Hill Valley's Old West period. The diminutive doctor had mismatched eyes—one squinty, the other protruding. A neighbor and friend of Emmett and Clara Brown in that era, he loved animals and spent his time nursing sick creatures back to health before returning them to their natural habitats.

  Diefendorfer's "cures" were often quite eccentric, such as giving a beaver dental braces and fitting a bald eagle with a toupee. In 1888, he helped the Browns through the delivery of their son Verne, while an older version of Verne waited in an adjoining room [**BFAN-21**].

- **Diesel of Doom:** A model train used by Jules and Verne Brown to stage games of Turboliner

Death-Race. Operated by Jules, the Diesel of Doom raced the Killer Porsche, a toy sports car remote-controlled by Verne [**BFAN-2**].

- **Diet Pepsi Free:** *See* Pepsi Free

- **Digi-Chef:** A digital food molecularizer created by Emmett Brown at the Institute of Future Technology, able to combine various foods (bananas and pizza, for example) into a single substance (banana pizza, in this case) at the molecular level [**RIDE**].

  > *NOTE: This device was described on signage at Universal Studios' Back to the Future: The Ride.*

- **Dinocity:** A version of Hill Valley in a reality in which dinosaurs never went extinct, and thus replaced humans as Earth's dominant animal lifeform [**BFHM**]. The city contained massive structures befitting dinosaurs' larger size, and housing businesses similar to human culture, including lounges, restaurants, stores, apartment buildings and more. Dinocity arose when Emmett, Jules and Verne Brown inadvertently diverted the mass-extinction event of the Cretaceous period. By restoring the normal timeline, however, the trio prevented Dinocity from existing [**BFAN-3**].

  > *NOTE: The city appeared in the animated episode "Forward to the Past," but was named only on a McDonald's Happy Meal box based on that episode.*

- **dino plane:** A flying machine operated by citizens of Dinocity, a version of Hill Valley from a reality in which dinosaurs never went extinct [**BFHM**].

- **dinosaur:** Earth's dominant terrestrial vertebrates from the late Triassic period until the end of the Cretaceous period. The extinction of most dinosaur species occurred during a massive catastrophic event millions of years ago [**REAL**].

  Emmett Brown and his sons, Jules and Verne, inadvertently thwarted that mass-extinction event while visiting the year 3 million B.C., thereby enabling dinosaurs to evolve into a thriving society, with mankind erased from existence. In so doing, the Browns were briefly captured by a Tyrannosaurus police officer [**BFAN-3, BFCM-2**]. In that version of reality, Hill Valley was known as Dinocity [**BFHM**].

  During a separate voyage to the

CODE	STORY
NIKE	*BTTF*-themed TV commercial: Nike
NTND	Nintendo *Back to the Future— The Ride* Mini-Game
PIZA	*BTTF*-themed TV commercial: Pizza Hut
PNBL	Data East *BTTF* pinball game
REAL	Real life
RIDE	Simulator: *Back to the Future—The Ride*
SCRM	2010 Scream Awards: *Back to the Future 25th Anniversary Reunion* (broadcast)
SCRT	2010 Scream Awards: *Back to the Future 25th Anniversary Reunion* (trailer)
SIMP	Simulator: *The Simpsons Ride*
SLOT	*Back to the Future Video Slots*
STLZ	Unused *BTTF* footage of Eric Stoltz as Marty McFly
STRY	*Back to the Future Storybook*
TEST	Screen tests: Crispin Glover, Lea Thompson and Tom Wilson
TLTL	Telltale Games' *Back to the Future—The Game*
TOPS	Topps' *Back to the Future II* trading-card set
TRIL	*BTTF: The Official Book of the Complete Movie Trilogy*
UNIV	Universal Studios Hollywood promotional video

SUFFIX	MEDIUM
-b	*BTTF2*'s Biff Tannen Museum video (extended)
-c	Credit sequence to the animated series
-d	Film deleted scene
-n	Film novelization
-o	Film outtake
-p	1955 phone book from *BTTF1*
-v	Video game print materials or commentaries
-s1	Screenplay (draft one)
-s2	Screenplay (draft two)
-s3	Screenplay (draft three)
-s4	Screenplay (draft four)
-sp	Screenplay (production draft)
-sx	Screenplay (*Paradox*)

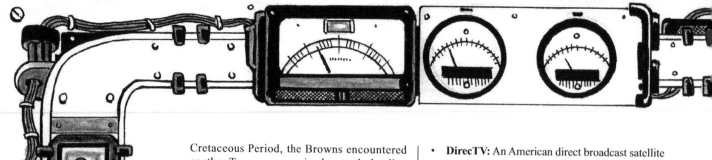

Cretaceous Period, the Browns encountered another Tyrannosaurus, inadvertently landing the DeLorean on its head. As the car accelerated to time-travel, the resulting flames ignited the dinosaur's tail [**BFAN-c**].

Marty McFly and Verne later visited 1 zillion B.C. in order to find an interesting item for Verne's classroom show-and-tell. During this adventure, Verne stole the un-hatched egg of an Apatosaurus, which hatched in 1992, mistaking Verne for its mother. Verne and Jules named the animal Tiny [**BFAN-26**].

In addition, a team of time-travel volunteers from 1991 were almost consumed by a Tyrannosaurus while pursuing Biff Tannen to stop him from stealing the DeLorean. The dinosaur swallowed the volunteers' car—a prototype Eight-Passenger DeLorean Time Travel Vehicle—but both parties escaped unscathed [**RIDE**].

> *NOTE: Scientists place dinosaurs' extinction at around 65.5 million years ago, so their existence in 3 million B.C. is inexplicable. Furthermore, the Earth is believed to be only 4.2 billion years old, and "zillion" is not an actual number, making "1 zillion B.C." a fictional date.*
>
> *In LJN's* Back to the Future *video games, dinosaurs were among the obstacles Marty had to face while making his way through Hill Valley. Their presence was unexplained, and had nothing to do with the films' events, on which the games were supposedly based.*

- **Dinosaurus Humongous:** A name given by Walter Wisdom to Tiny, Verne Brown's pet Apatosaurus, which Biff Tannen had stolen and sold to Wisdom. As the TV personality prepared to unveil the animal during a ratings-grabbing special episode, Verne and his family rescued Tiny, replacing the creature with a fake-looking substitute, thereby publicly humiliating both Wisdom and Biff [**BFAN-26**].

- **dinotarian:** A term used by a race of intelligent dinosaurs that evolved after Emmett Brown inadvertently prevented the dinosaurs' extinction in 3 million B.C. The word was analogous to "humanitarian," describing one who showed kindness and sympathy toward all beings [**BFAN-3**].

- **DirecTV:** An American direct broadcast satellite service provider and broadcaster [**REAL**]. After sending Marty McFly back to the future in 1955, Emmett Brown realized he forgot to advise his friend to sign up for DirecTV HD instead of cable once he returned to 1985 [**DCTV**].

> *NOTE: This occurred in a 2007 commercial for DirecTV, featuring Christopher Lloyd as Doc Brown. It's inconceivable that Doc's 1955 self would have had foreknowledge of DirecTV's future services. Furthermore, although the company was founded in 1985 as Hughes Electronics Corp., its satellite service was not launched until 1994.*

- **Discovery Program:** A series of American scientific space missions launched by the National Aeronautics and Space Administration (NASA) in 1992, to explore Earth's solar system [**REAL**].

The Hill Valley Space Center and Air-Sickness Clinic housed a facility used by NASA as part of this program, at which Emmett Brown was suited up for a trip into outer space, in order to help a local cable company overhaul its communications satellite—in return for free cable service, including premium channels [**BFAN-15**].

> *NOTE: This might explain Doc's fascination with DirecTV.*

- **DISP1:** A button on an overhead console of Emmett Brown's DeLorean [**TLTL-5**].

- **DISP2:** A button on an overhead console of Emmett Brown's DeLorean [**TLTL-5**].

- **disposable paper garments:** A type of clothing that Emmett Brown, in 1955, assumed everyone would be wearing in the future, until discovering that his future self would still be wearing cotton boxer shorts in the 1980s [**BTF1-d**].

- **Dixon, Mark:** A redheaded prankster at Hill Valley High School who sometimes bullied George McFly [**BTF1-s4, BTF1-n**].

At the Enchantment Under the Sea Dance in 1955, Dixon locked George in a phone booth, making him late for a staged fight with Marty McFly in the school's parking lot, in which George was supposed to "rescue" Lorraine Baines from Marty's sexual advances. George thus arrived to find not Marty, but Biff Tannen, who was trying

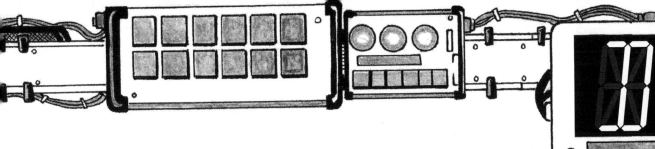

to rape Lorraine at the time [**BTF1-d**].

George knocked Biff unconscious and escorted Lorraine to the dance, but Dixon forcibly cut in while the two were slow-dancing. George initially accepted the tormenting per usual, but quickly mustered the courage to push Mark out of the way and protect Lorraine, which made her realize she loved him [**BTF1**].

> *NOTE: Dixon's phone-booth prank gave George the opportunity to face his fears—by punching Biff—while his cutting in at the dance enabled George to reinforce his newfound confidence. Had Dixon not done these things, George would have arrived before Biff, and would have remained the weak, cowardly individual he was in the original timeline. In essence, Dixon was responsible for George becoming a better man.*

- **Doc:** A character on a daytime television series, circa 1991. After falling for an April Fool's Day joke perpetrated by his sons, Jules and Verne—intended to make him think his brain was nearly full—Emmett Brown watched an episode of this mindless show.

  In the episode, "Doc" spent his time cutting paper doll chains in an easy chair, while his wife chastised him for wasting his life. Deeming the show unrealistic, Doc Brown turned off the TV and began the same activity in his own easy chair, while his wife, Clara, similarly castigated him. Emmett never noticed the ironic similarity as his reality mimicked fiction [**BFAN-12**].

- **Doc Black Brownboard:** *See* Doc Brown Blackboard

- **Doc Brown:** *See* Brown, Emmett Lathrop, Doctor

- **Doc Brown Blackboard:** An invention of Emmett Brown, consisting of a large, pink-framed viewscreen that, at the pull of a handle, produced moving images designed to look as though drawn with chalk, accompanied by voice narration. The distracted scientist sometimes mistakenly called it the Doc Black Brownboard [**BFAN-3**].

- **Doc Brown's Celery Tonic:** A brand of soft drink similar to ginger ale, derived from celery seed extract [**REAL**].

  While visiting Chicago's South Side in 1927 to find a cure for cat-aracts for his dog, Einstein,

Emmett Brown posed as a brewmaster for Martin "Zipper" McFly (Marty McFly's criminal alias in that era). When Mob boss Arnie "Eggs" Benedict mistook Doc for the beverage's creator, Doc lied that he'd given up producing the soda so he could instead brew hooch [**BFCM-1**].

> *NOTE: Doc Brown's Celery Tonic (now called Cel-Ray) has been sold since 1868. The soda was particularly popular in the 1920s.*

- **Doc Brown's Chicken:** A restaurant at Universal Studios Hollywood, claiming to serve "the finest chicken of all time" [**REAL**]. Doc Brown's served four types of fried chicken on its lunch and dinner menus, and featured framed photographs of Emmett Brown holding up pieces of chicken at various worldwide landmarks and historical event sites, [**UNIV**] including the U.S. Capitol Building, the Pyramids at Giza, Buckingham Palace, Stonehenge, the Eiffel Tower, the Taj Mahal, Hollywood and more [**CHIC**].

> *NOTE: This is an actual restaurant at Universal Studios, located near the former* Back to the Future: The Ride *attraction, and featuring an actor other than Christopher Lloyd portraying Doc.*

- **Doc Brown's Extradimensional Storage Closet:** *See* Extradimensional Storage Closet

- **Doctor Frinkle's Algae Cakes:** *See* Professor Fringle's Algae-Cakes

- **Doggie-Diapers:** An invention of Walter Wisdom, created while the scientist was attending the American College of Technological Science & Difficult Math. The Doggie-Diapers, designed to prevent lawn and sidewalk cleanup, were intended to be Wisdom's entry in the Inter-Collegiate Science Invent-Off contest. However, upon seeing Emmett Brown's submission—a Perpetual-Motion Hula Hoop—Wisdom discarded the diapers, stole the hula hoop and claimed it as his own, attaining fame and fortune as a result [**BFAN-15**].

- **Doggy Dip for Fleas and Ticks:** A pet-care product created to eliminate insects from an animal's fur. Biff Tannen used this product during his infrequent baths [**BFCL-3**].

> *NOTE: This would seem to indicate that Biff suffered from fleas and/or ticks.*

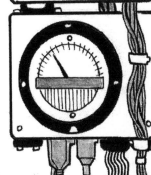

CODE	STORY
NIKE	*BTTF*-themed TV commercial: Nike
NTND	Nintendo *Back to the Future— The Ride* Mini-Game
PIZA	*BTTF*-themed TV commercial: Pizza Hut
PNBL	Data East *BTTF* pinball game
REAL	Real life
RIDE	Simulator: *Back to the Future—The Ride*
SCRM	2010 Scream Awards: *Back to the Future* 25th Anniversary Reunion (broadcast)
SCRT	2010 Scream Awards: *Back to the Future* 25th Anniversary Reunion (trailer)
SIMP	Simulator: *The Simpsons Ride*
SLOT	*Back to the Future Video Slots*
STLZ	Unused *BTTF* footage of Eric Stoltz as Marty McFly
STRY	*Back to the Future Storybook*
TEST	Screen tests: Crispin Glover, Lea Thompson and Tom Wilson
TLTL	Telltale Games' *Back to the Future—The Game*
TOPS	Topps' *Back to the Future II* trading-card set
TRIL	*BTTF: The Official Book of the Complete Movie Trilogy*
UNIV	Universal Studios Hollywood promotional video

SUFFIX MEDIUM

-b	*BTTF2*'s Biff Tannen Museum video (extended)
-c	Credit sequence to the animated series
-d	Film deleted scene
-n	Film novelization
-o	Film outtake
-p	1955 phone book from *BTTF1*
-v	Video game print materials or commentaries
-s1	Screenplay (draft one)
-s2	Screenplay (draft two)
-s3	Screenplay (draft three)
-s4	Screenplay (draft four)
-sp	Screenplay (production draft)
-sx	Screenplay (*Paradox*)

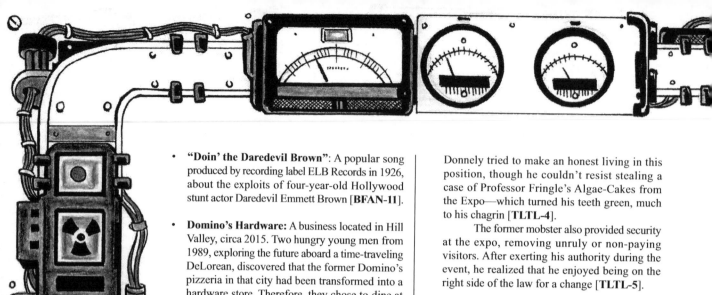

- **"Doin' the Daredevil Brown"**: A popular song produced by recording label ELB Records in 1926, about the exploits of four-year-old Hollywood stunt actor Daredevil Emmett Brown [**BFAN-11**].

- **Domino's Hardware:** A business located in Hill Valley, circa 2015. Two hungry young men from 1989, exploring the future aboard a time-traveling DeLorean, discovered that the former Domino's pizzeria in that city had been transformed into a hardware store. Therefore, they chose to dine at Pizza Hut, which was still in business [**PIZA**].

- **Domino's Pizza:** The second-largest pizzeria chain in the United States [**REAL**]. Sometime between 1989 and 2015, its Hill Valley location was transformed into a hardware store known as Domino's Hardware [**PIZA**].

- **Donaldson:** A friend of Marty McFly at Hill Valley High School. Donaldson liked to take drugs, and sometimes invited Marty over to his house to join him in getting high. When his brother got married in 1985, Donaldson asked Marty to provide pirated pornographic films for a party held in the brother's honor [**BTF1-s1**].

  NOTE: In BTTF1's initial-draft screenplay, Marty was a video bootlegger.

- **Donnely ("Cue Ball"):** A baldheaded cook at the Sisters of Mercy Soup Kitchen, circa 1931, and a member of Irving "Kid" Tannen's gang, along with Zane Williams and Matches. Cue Ball enjoyed being a cook, and took pride in his secret soup recipe—which wasn't very tasty. Secretly, he helped Kid deliver alcohol (illegal during the Prohibition Era) to the gangster's hidden speakeasy, El Kid [**TLTL-1**].

  Donnely resented having to perform manual labor, such as moving crates and cleaning up blood, and felt more like a butler than a gangster. A skilled pianist, he often performed at El Kid, accompanied by lounge singer Sylvia "Trixie Trotter" Miskin. Secretly, Cue Ball longed to leave criminal life behind and perform as a musician at Carnegie Hall. Ultimately, he was arrested, along with his fellow gangsters, when policeman Danny Parker raided the speakeasy [**TLTL-2**].

  Cue Ball avoided prison time by testifying against Kid—as he put it, "exhibiting an admirable sense of self-preservation." He later obtained employment as a truck driver at the 1931 Hill Valley Exposition, working for Arthur McFly.

Donnely tried to make an honest living in this position, though he couldn't resist stealing a case of Professor Fringle's Algae-Cakes from the Expo—which turned his teeth green, much to his chagrin [**TLTL-4**].

The former mobster also provided security at the expo, removing unruly or non-paying visitors. After exerting his authority during the event, he realized that he enjoyed being on the right side of the law for a change [**TLTL-5**].

  NOTE: The names of Kid's lackeys in the Telltale Games video game corresponded to those of Biff Tannen in the films, possibly denoting family relations. In Cue Ball's case, his analog was Biff's short-haired friend, Joey ("Skinhead").

- **Donny:** A pteranodon that lived circa 3 million B.C., in what would later be Hill Valley. The friendly, flying pterosaur, dubbed "Donny" by Verne Brown, happily gave the boy and his family rides on its back and in its talons during their visit to the Cretaceous period.

  Donny had purple skin, green tailfeathers and tufts, and a large, smiling, yellow beak with a red band around it, similar to that of a toucan. He was presumably killed during a mass-extinction event when a large meteor struck the Earth's surface moments after the Brown family returned to their own era [**BFAN-3**].

- **"Donut City":** A song recorded by musician Eddie Van Halen in 1984 [**REAL**]. In an effort to convince George McFly to ask Lorraine Baines to the Enchantment Under the Sea Dance in 1955, Marty McFly posed as an alien called Darth Vader, from the planet Vulcan, and threatened to melt George's brain if he didn't ask her out. Marty played a loud cassette tape of "Donut City" to enhance the effect [**BTF1**].

  NOTE: This song was recorded for the soundtrack of The Wild Life, a film starring Lea Thompson (Lorraine) and Eric Stoltz (the actor originally cast as Marty).

- **Doris:** An employee at Lou's Café, circa 1955. When Marty McFly tried to pay for a cup of coffee using a 1978 20-dollar bill, owner Lou Caruthers assumed it to be counterfeit and told Doris to call the police [**BTF1-s3**].

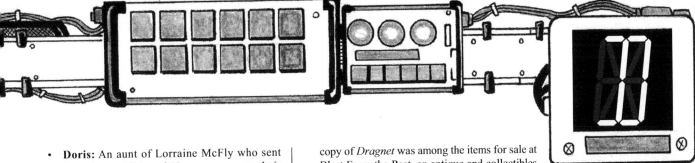

Doris: An aunt of Lorraine McFly who sent Lorraine's children $50 every year on their birthdays. A sick woman, Doris spent time in a hospital in 1967. Her husband was named Mickey [**BTF2-s1**].

Dorothy: A dance instructor at the Hill Valley Dance Academy, circa 1992. A proper, assertive woman, she was often frustrated by Verne Brown's inability to master the waltz. While exploring 1944 with Marty McFly, Verne encountered Dorothy's younger self as she tended to Hill Valley's Victory Garden with her sister, Rosie. Bespectacled and short, the youthful Dorothy developed a crush on Verne [**BFAN-17**].

Douteux, Jacques, Professor: A famous French diver from the Oceanic Institute, who hosted the Enlightenment Under the Sea display at the 1931 Hill Valley Exposition. Douteux, clad in a deep-sea diving suit, had an extremely thick French accent.

Citizen Brown—an alternate version of Emmett Brown who led an oppressive, dystopian Hill Valley, and hoped to thwart Marty McFly from erasing that timeline—posed as Douteux during the expo in order to hide his younger self within the diver's Bathysphere and keep him away from Marty's influence [**TLTL-5**].

NOTE: This character's name was a pun on that of French marine explorer and researcher Jacques Cousteau.

Downtown Renovation Project: An initiative launched in Citizen Brown's dystopian timeline in 1976, under which the first major additions were made to the Hill Valley Courthouse since its construction. The building was expanded with an additional 128 offices in the new flanking wings, and a new mayoral office was added to the original Clock Tower space. In addition, the lightning-damaged clock was dismantled, and a new, modern clock was installed as the window to Brown's mayoral office [**TLTL-3**].

Draft Resister's Odyssey, A: A speech delivered by Marty DeLorean (an alias of Marty McFly) at a Vietnam War protest rally to which Lorraine McFly donated her time in 1967 [**BTF2-s1**].

Dragnet: A 1987 comedy film starring Dan Aykroyd and Tom Hanks, based on the popular television and radio crime drama [**REAL**]. A VHS copy of *Dragnet* was among the items for sale at Blast From the Past, an antique and collectibles shop in 2015 Hill Valley [**BTF2**].

Drama Club: An extracurricular group at Hill Valley Elementary School that performed various theatrical productions. In 1992, the club produced a version of *Sleeping Beauty*. Verne Brown dreaded having to appear in the production, for fear that he'd have to kiss fellow student Beatrice Spalding [**BFAN-26**].

Dr. Apple Bakery: A business located in Hill Valley, circa 1991 [**BFAN-7b**].

Dr. E. Brown Enterprises: A company owned and operated by Emmett Brown [**BTF1**], offering atomic engineering, technical guidance, and clock and refrigerator repair [**BTF1-s3**]. The inventor operated a white GMC van bearing the firm's name, advertising 24-hour scientific services. In 1985, Doc used the vehicle to transport his DeLorean time machine to the Twin Pines Mall for testing purposes [**BTF1**].

Driver Adjust: The designation of a panel on Emmett Brown's giant guitar amplifier, containing several toggles, labeled "HV Filiment," "LV Filiment," "Bias V -150V," "LV Plate," "Klystron HV" and "PA Plate" [**BTF1**].

Dr. Pepper: A popular brand of carbonated soft drink [**REAL**]. The family of Emmett Brown had cans of this soda in their home [**BFCM-4**].

Dr. Seuss: The pen-name of American writer Theodor Seuss Geisel, an author of dozens of children's books. These included *Green Eggs and Ham*, *How the Grinch Stole Christmas!* and *The Cat in the Hat* [**REAL**].

The name "Dr. Seuss" was among those that Marty McFly and Verne Brown urged author Jules Verne to rename himself, in the hope that young Verne would no longer be named "Verne" in the novelist's honor [**BFAN-21**].

Drying Mode: A 21st-century innovation enabling wet clothing to dry itself by means of high-powered blasts of hot air, produced by fans hidden inside the garments [**BTF2**].

Dukes of Hazzard, The: An American TV series that aired on CBS from 1979 to 1985, featuring

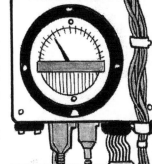

CODE	STORY
NIKE	*BTTF*-themed TV commercial: Nike
NTND	Nintendo *Back to the Future—The Ride* Mini-Game
PIZA	*BTTF*-themed TV commercial: Pizza Hut
PNBL	Data East *BTTF* pinball game
REAL	Real life
RIDE	Simulator: *Back to the Future—The Ride*
SCRM	2010 Scream Awards: *Back to the Future* 25th Anniversary Reunion (broadcast)
SCRT	2010 Scream Awards: *Back to the Future* 25th Anniversary Reunion (trailer)
SIMP	Simulator: *The Simpsons Ride*
SLOT	*Back to the Future* Video Slots
STLZ	Unused *BTTF* footage of Eric Stoltz as Marty McFly
STRY	*Back to the Future* Storybook
TEST	Screen tests: Crispin Glover, Lea Thompson and Tom Wilson
TLTL	Telltale Games' *Back to the Future—The Game*
TOPS	Topps' *Back to the Future II* trading-card set
TRIL	*BTTF: The Official Book of the Complete Movie Trilogy*
UNIV	Universal Studios Hollywood promotional video

SUFFIX	MEDIUM
-b	*BTTF2*'s Biff Tannen Museum video (extended)
-c	Credit sequence to the animated series
-d	Film deleted scene
-n	Film novelization
-o	Film outtake
-p	1955 phone book from *BTTF1*
-v	Video game print materials or commentaries
-s1	Screenplay (draft one)
-s2	Screenplay (draft two)
-s3	Screenplay (draft three)
-s4	Screenplay (draft four)
-sp	Screenplay (production draft)
-sx	Screenplay (*Paradox*)

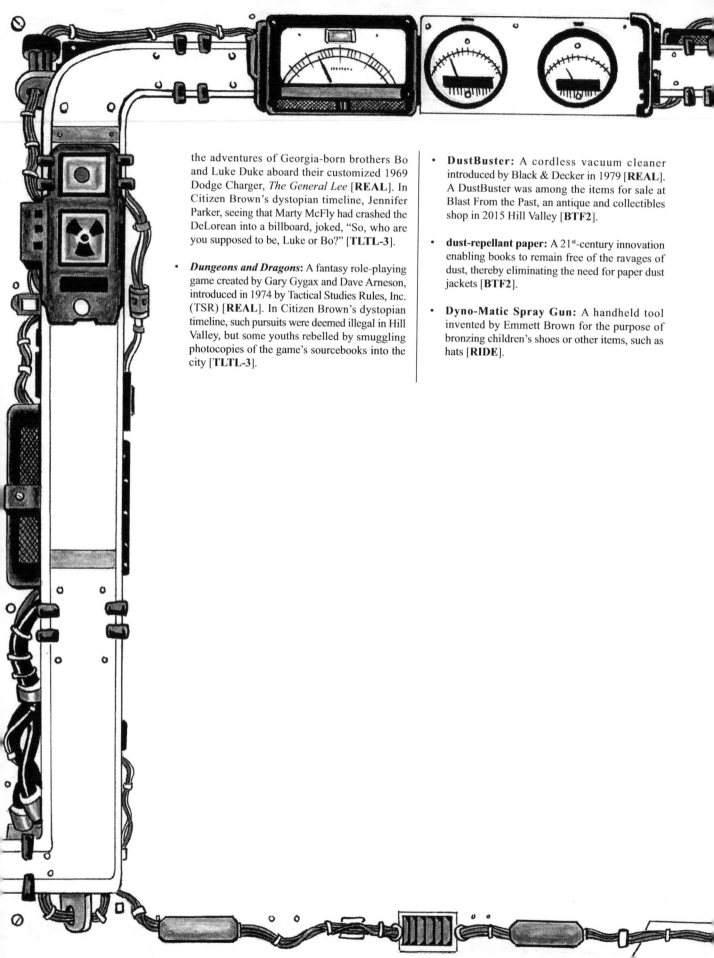

the adventures of Georgia-born brothers Bo and Luke Duke aboard their customized 1969 Dodge Charger, *The General Lee* [**REAL**]. In Citizen Brown's dystopian timeline, Jennifer Parker, seeing that Marty McFly had crashed the DeLorean into a billboard, joked, "So, who are you supposed to be, Luke or Bo?" [**TLTL-3**].

- ***Dungeons and Dragons***: A fantasy role-playing game created by Gary Gygax and Dave Arneson, introduced in 1974 by Tactical Studies Rules, Inc. (TSR) [**REAL**]. In Citizen Brown's dystopian timeline, such pursuits were deemed illegal in Hill Valley, but some youths rebelled by smuggling photocopies of the game's sourcebooks into the city [**TLTL-3**].

- **DustBuster:** A cordless vacuum cleaner introduced by Black & Decker in 1979 [**REAL**]. A DustBuster was among the items for sale at Blast From the Past, an antique and collectibles shop in 2015 Hill Valley [**BTF2**].

- **dust-repellant paper:** A 21st-century innovation enabling books to remain free of the ravages of dust, thereby eliminating the need for paper dust jackets [**BTF2**].

- **Dyno-Matic Spray Gun:** A handheld tool invented by Emmett Brown for the purpose of bronzing children's shoes or other items, such as hats [**RIDE**].

EINSTEIN
(LEFT, WITH ALBERT EINSTEIN)

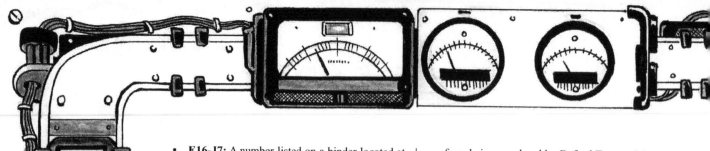

- **E16-J7:** A number listed on a binder located at a monitoring station at the Citizen Plus Ward, in Citizen Brown's dystopian timeline [**TLTL-4**].

- **E4:** A button on a security keypad used to access the Institute of Future Technology's Anti-Gravitic Laboratory [**RIDE**].

- **Eagle GT:** *See* Goodyear Tire and Rubber Co.

- **Earl Hays Publishing Co.:** A Los Angeles-based company that produced *Grays Sports Almanac: Complete Sports Statistics 1950-2000* [**BTF2**].

    NOTE: This company was named after The Earl Hays Press, a firm specializing in creating prop products and packaging, including book jackets, for the motion-picture industry since 1915.

- **Early Times:** A brand of Kentucky whiskey [**REAL**]. In 1955, Biff Tannen's gang spiked the punch at Hill Valley High School's Enchantment Under the Sea Dance with this and other liquors [**BTF2**].

- **"Earth Angel (Will You Be Mine)":** A doo-wop song recorded in 1954 by The Penguins [**REAL**]. The following year, Marvin Berry and the Starlighters performed this tune at the Enchantment Under the Sea Dance, with Marty McFly filling in for an injured Berry on guitar. It was during this song that George McFly and Lorraine Baines kissed for the first time [**BTF1**].

- **Eastern Auto Stores:** *See* Western Auto Stores

- **East Wing:** A section of the Institute of Future Technology, containing numerous offices and laboratories [**RIDE**].

- **Eastwood, Clint:** An American film actor and director known for his roles in numerous action films and so-called "Spaghetti Westerns" [**REAL**]. In Biffhorrific 1985, the corrupt and powerful Biff Tannen enjoyed watching Eastwood's film *A Fistful of Dollars*, and was particularly impressed when Eastwood's character, the Man With No Name, used a piece of metal hidden beneath his poncho as a bulletproof vest during a quick-draw [**BTF2**].

    Marty McFly was also a fan of Eastwood's movies, particularly *A Fistful of Dollars*. After visiting 1885 in order to save Emmett Brown

from being murdered by Buford Tannen, Marty was reminded of the film's climactic scene. During a deadly duel with Tannen, Marty, using the alias Clint Eastwood and clad similarly to The Man With No Name, defeated the outlaw just as Eastwood's character had defeated Ramón Rojo: by hiding a steel chest plate beneath his pancho to deflect Buford's bullets.

Marty and Doc later stole a locomotive to push the damaged DeLorean up to 88 miles per hour so they could return to their own era. This resulted in the train falling into the Shonash Ravine. The canyon was renamed the Eastwood Ravine in Marty's honor, since he was thought to have perished during the explosion [**BTF3**].

While visiting 1931 to save Emmett Brown from being killed by Irving "Kid" Tannen's gang, Marty McFly considered using the alias Harry Callahan, a fictional police detective in Eastwood's five *Dirty Harry* films [**TLTL-1**].

    *NOTE: Posters from two of Eastwood's earliest films (*Tarantula *and* Revenge of the Creature*) were displayed at the Pohatchee Drive-in Theater in* Back to the Future III.

- **Eastwood Ravine:** A name given to Hill Valley's Shonash Ravine (its original Native-American designation) in honor of Clint Eastwood, Marty McFly's alias in 1885, believed to have perished in a locomotive accident at the cliff. Prior to Marty's visit to that era, the area had been renamed Clayton Ravine, in the memory of Clara Clayton, who had fallen to her death after losing control of her wagon's horses [**BTF3**].

    Marty and Jennifer Parker often visited this location in order to make out in private [**BTF3-s1**].

    In First Citizen Brown's dystopian timeline, Emmett Brown maintained a secret laboratory near this ravine [**TLTL-4**].

    NOTE: Paradox, a combined screenplay for both sequel films, dubbed this area Carson Ravine. BTTF3 *'s first-draft screenplay called it Clayton Cliff.*

- **E. Brown Industries:** A business in Courthouse Square in Citizen Brown's dystopian timeline [**TLTL-3**].

    NOTE: Presumably, this company was owned by Emmett Brown.

- **EB Stuart:** A business located in Boston, Massachusetts, circa 1897 [**BFAN-8**].

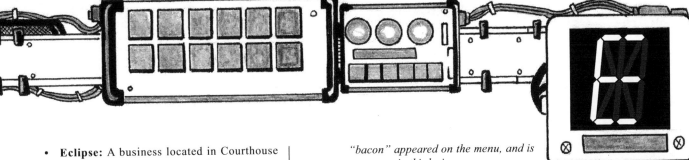

- **Eclipse:** A business located in Courthouse Square, circa 2015, that offered contemporary and traditional lighting [**BTF2**].

- **Edison, Thomas:** An employee at the Institute of Future Technology [**RIDE**].

    > **NOTE:** *This individual, identified on signage outside* Back to the Future: The Ride, *was named after the famous inventor.*

- **Edison, Thomas Alva, Doctor:** An American businessman and scientist known for his many inventions, including a phonograph and a long-lasting electric lightbulb [**REAL**]. Emmett Brown admired his work, and kept a framed photo of him in his home [**BTF1**].

    During a trip to the 1920s, Doc managed to meet his idol, and asked him to autograph a lightbulb. Edison wrote, "To Doc, The best! Thomas" [**BFAN-11, RIDE**].

- **Edna's Animal Patrol:** A group formed by Edna Strickland in Citizen Brown's dystopian timeline. Edna's Animal Patrol searched the city for stray animals—especially dogs—which, if found, were summarily removed [**TLTL-3**].

- **Edsel:** A model of automobile manufactured by Ford Motor Co. from 1958 to 1960 [**REAL**]. In 1955, while Emmett Brown worked as a university physics professor, his boss, Dean Wooster, and colleagues Cooper and Mintz requested that Doc help Ford develop the Edsel. Emmett, however, refused the assignment [**BTF3-s1**]. In 2015, a flying version of the Edsel was available [**BTF2-n**].

- **Edwards Signaling:** A manufacturer whose products included the 55 Series fire alarm bell [**REAL**]. In 1985, Emmett Brown used such an alarm as his home telephone ringer [**BTF1**].

- **EG:** A name scrawled in graffiti on the wall of Hill Valley High School, circa 1985 [**BTF1**].

- **Egan, Beverly:** A Hollywood professional, circa 2015, who helped director Max Spielberg create *Jaws 19*, according to the film's poster [**BTF2**].

- **Egg & Bacoon:** A menu item sold at Café 80's in 2015 [**BTF2**].

    > **NOTE:** *The misspelling of the word*

"bacon" *appeared on the menu, and is not a typo in this lexicon.*

- **Egypt:** *See* Great Pyramid of Giza, The; Great Sphinx of Giza, The

- **Eiffel Tower:** A puddle-iron lattice tower erected in Paris, France, in 1889 [**REAL**]. Emmett Brown recorded a portion of his Science Journal while he and Clara were visiting the famous landmark as tourists [**BFAN-21**]. After Doc visited this site, a photo commemorating the occasion was displayed at Doc Brown's Chicken [**CHIC**].

- **Eight-Passenger DeLorean Time-Travel Vehicle:** An experimental, energy-efficient, convertible upgrade from Emmett Brown's original time-traveling sports car, capable of carrying eight occupants in two rows of four. When Biff Tannen broke into the Institute of Future Technology's Anti-Gravitic Laboratory to steal the original time-traveling DeLorean, Doc Brown dispatched a team of Time-Travel Volunteers in the eight-passenger version to apprehend him.

    In order to catch Biff, the volunteers pursued him into the future and past, with instructions to accelerate up to 88 miles per hour and bump Biff's DeLorean upon finding him, thereby causing a time-travel vortex that would suck both vehicles back to the institute. Biff was thus apprehended and sent back to his own era [**RIDE**].

- **Einstein, Albert:** An employee at the Institute of Future Technology's director of audiotronics [**RIDE**].

    > **NOTE:** *This individual, identified on signage outside* Back to the Future: The Ride, *was named after the famous physicist.*

- **Einstein, Albert, Doctor:** A Nobel Prize-winning German theoretical physicist, known for his General Theory of Relativity [**REAL**]. Emmett Brown admired Einstein's work, and kept a framed photo of the man in his home. He also named his dog after Einstein [**BTF1**].

    During a trip through time, Doc had the chance to meet his idol—and brought his dog along for the ride, to meet his namesake [**RIDE**]. Doc also had a cookie jar shaped like the physicist's head [**BFAN-10**].

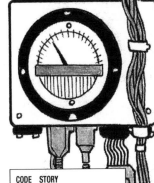

CODE	STORY
NIKE	*BTTF*-themed TV commercial: Nike
NTND	Nintendo *Back to the Future—The Ride* Mini-Game
PIZA	*BTTF*-themed TV commercial: Pizza Hut
PNBL	Data East *BTTF* pinball game
REAL	Real life
RIDE	Simulator: *Back to the Future—The Ride*
SCRM	2010 Scream Awards: *Back to the Future 25th Anniversary Reunion* (broadcast)
SCRT	2010 Scream Awards: *Back to the Future 25th Anniversary Reunion* (trailer)
SIMP	Simulator: *The Simpsons Ride*
SLOT	*Back to the Future Video Slots*
STLZ	Unused *BTTF* footage of Eric Stoltz as Marty McFly
STRY	*Back to the Future Storybook*
TEST	Screen tests: Crispin Glover, Lea Thompson and Tom Wilson
TLTL	Telltale Games' *Back to the Future—The Game*
TOPS	Topps' *Back to the Future II* trading-card set
TRIL	*BTTF: The Official Book of the Complete Movie Trilogy*
UNIV	Universal Studios Hollywood promotional video

SUFFIX	MEDIUM
-b	*BTTF2*'s Biff Tannen Museum video (extended)
-c	Credit sequence to the animated series
-d	Film deleted scene
-n	Film novelization
-o	Film outtake
-p	1955 phone book from *BTTF1*
-v	Video game print materials or commentaries
-s1	Screenplay (draft one)
-s2	Screenplay (draft two)
-s3	Screenplay (draft three)
-s4	Screenplay (draft four)
-sp	Screenplay (production draft)
-sx	Screenplay (*Paradox*)

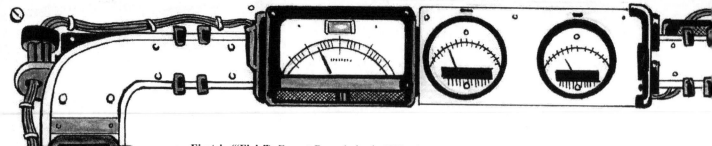

- **Einstein ("Einie"):** Emmett Brown's dog in 1985, named after scientist Albert Einstein. In 1985, Einie became the world's first time traveler, when Doc launched him one minute into the future in a converted DeLorean DMC-12 sports car, during Temporal Experiment Number One [**BTF1**]. Einstein's grandfather was a bloodhound, making Einie part bloodhound and, thus, an expert tracker [**BTF2-s1**].

  While visiting the year 2015, Emmett placed Einstein within a suspended-animation kennel for the duration of his stay. He later retrieved Einie, who remained with him as he helped Marty McFly prevent his children from going to prison. This chain of events culminated in the Biffhoriffic timeline, in which Biff Tannen was a powerful criminal kingpin who ruled Hill Valley. Einstein was left behind when Marty and Doc returned to 1955 to stop that grim version of history from occurring, and a lightning strike on the DeLorean propelled Doc and the car back to 1885, preventing him from returning for his dog [**BTF2**].

  While stranded in 1885, Emmett fell in love with and eventually married Clara Clayton. Several years later, the couple traveled to 1985 aboard a time-traveling locomotive that Doc named the *Jules Verne Train*, after their sons, Jules and Verne Brown. The family retrieved Einie and brought him to live with them in the past [**BTF3**]. Einstein remained with the Browns when they later relocated to the 20th century, accompanying them and Marty on a number of temporal adventures [**BFAN-1 to BFAN-26, BFCM-1 to BFCM-4, BFCL-1 to BFCL-3**].

  Einie traveled with Doc to 1931 when the scientist conducted research for a high school graduation gift for Marty. After Doc was wrongly arrested for arson in that year, the pooch survived for some time on the streets, until Emmett's 17-year-old self began caring for him. Just as the older scientist had previously done, the younger Emmett involved the dog in one of his experiments, to test his prototype Rocket Car.

  With history frequently changing due to Marty's and Doc's actions in that era, Einstein experienced a variety of existences, including living as a refugee in Citizen Brown's dystopian timeline, in which dogs were outlawed by Edna Strickland. Eventually, history was repaired and Einstein and Doc were reunited in their proper time [**TLTL-1 to TLTL-5**].

  In 1991, Einstein became romantically involved with a miniature poodle living next door to the Browns' farm [**BFAN-2**].

  The following year, Einie developed cataracts, a canine eye disease causing a dog to see all objects and individuals as feline—which, if not treated with a byproduct of fermented juniper berries, could lead to blindness. Einie began attacking everyone and everything around him, until Doc and Marty visited 1927 Chicago to find a liquor still with which to ferment a cure [**BFCM-1**].

  Doc built a device by which Einstein could send hotdogs to his lab at specified snack times—even from across the yard—at the push of a button [**BFAN-2**]. He also created a number of inventions to improve Einie's existence. These included:

  - An automated toaster, coffee maker and dog-food dispenser, used to serve both Doc and Einstein breakfast each morning [**BTF1**]
  - A pair of robotic gloves enabling Einie to use a computer, play cards and perform other manual tasks [**BFAN-1, BFAN-6, BFAN-22**]
  - A sensor that recognized the dog's paw-print, enabling him to enter the Brown family home unaided [**BFAN-2**]
  - A machine allowing Einstein to receive a robotic massage whenever he felt like being petted [**BFAN-2**]
  - A mechanical dog-washing tub [**BFAN-4**]
  - A pair of scissors, stored in the dog's collar, that could be activated at the press of a paw [**BFAN-7b**]
  - A contraption combining a baby stroller and a pulley, with which the mutt could raise himself to the roof for fresh air [**BFAN-9**]
  - The ELB Super-Sniffer Snout 4000, which amplified Einstein's canine sniffing ability via a large, nose-like contraption attached on one end to the dog's snout, and on the other to the front of Doc's DeLorean [**BFAN-20**]
  - The Canine Cafeteria, a type of hot plate used to warm up dog food, containing an alarm clock to automatically activate at meal times and announce "Chow time," thereby summoning a pooch to receive a meal of sawdust dog food [**RIDE**]
  - The Canine Retrieval Apparatus, built to rescue dogs from great heights, such as when stranded on a roof [**TLTL-v**]

    NOTE: *In early drafts of* BTTF1, *Einstein was first a Capuchin monkey and then a chimpanzee (both called Shemp), and later a Saint Bernard. Onscreen, the dog (like*

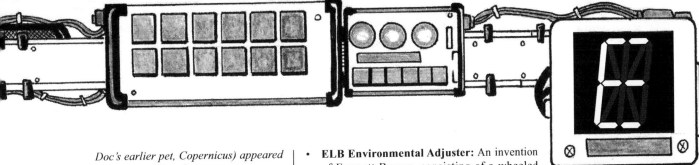

Doc's earlier pet, Copernicus) appeared to be a mixed-breed mutt.

Although Einstein was a normal dog on film, he was quite anthropomorphized in the cartoons, in which he could operate a computer, stand on two legs and drive the DeLorean and locomotive. He could also communicate with Marty via barking, which Marty could understand perfectly, as though Einie had spoken in English.

According to the film's Blu-ray trivia track, Einstein's naming may have been a "vague reference" to Edison, a dog owned by Caractacus Potts, an eccentric car inventor in the musical Chitty Chitty Bang Bang.

- **ejection seat:** A system designed to rescue occupants of an aircraft or other flying vehicle in the event of an emergency [**REAL**]. By 2015, drivers of flying cars were urged to fly safely, with the motto that "ejection seats save lives" [**BTF2**].

- **ELB:** The initials of Emmett Brown, which appeared on the front of his time-traveling locomotive, the *Jules Verne Train* [**BTF3, RIDE**]. Doc was fond of signing all of his memos and notes with a stylized "ELB" [**BTF2-n**].

  The scientist carved his initials onto a piece of wood in 1885, signifying the hidden location of his damaged flying DeLorean within the Delgado Mine, so that Marty McFly could locate it seventy years later and return to his own era [**BTF3**].

  NOTE: *Doc's hand-drawn map of the mine indicated that he'd initially planned to carve Marty's name, but used his own initials instead. The scientist used his initials on a variety of other inventions as well, as seen in the animated series and its comic book spinoff.*

- **ELB Aqua-Ammomatic:** A scientifically perfected water-balloon system created by Emmett Brown. The device could propel balloons more accurately, at greater distances and with a better burst ratio when heated to 82 degrees and expanded to a pressure of 1.2 pounds per square inch (psi) [**BFAN-18**].

- **ELB Autogroom 5000:** A robotic shaving and grooming system built into the dashboard of Emmett Brown's flying DeLorean [**BFAN-7b**].

- **ELB Environmental Adjuster:** An invention of Emmett Brown, consisting of a wheeled contraption with a large emitting dish, able to customize environmental conditions, such as thunder, lightning or fog. When Marty McFly "borrowed" the machine to produce special effects for a performance of The Pinheads, he inadvertently created horrific storms that nearly destroyed Hill Valley [**BFAN-12**].

  NOTE: *Onscreen, the device was called an Environmental Adjuster and had only three settings: thunder, lightning and fog. The episode's comic adaptation called it the ELB Environmental Adjuster, and added additional settings: wind, flood, earthquake, typhoon, hurricane, cyclone and gale.*

- **ELB Hot-Diggity Dogger:** An invention of Emmett Brown, able to boil and serve a thousand wieners per hour, apply mustard and ketchup, and supply a beverage. The contraption did not work properly, as it tended to soil a customer with hot dogs and soda. Doc also created Super-Sudsy Soap for its clean-up cycle [**BFAN-22**].

- **ELB Hovercraft:** A vehicle hastily assembled by Emmett Brown after his Environmental Adjuster nearly destroyed Hill Valley. Using the hovercraft, Doc managed to navigate deadly storms to reach and deactivate the device [**BFCM-4**].

- **ELB Life-on-the-Edge Facsimulator:** A patent-pending invention of Emmett Brown consisting of ultra-realistic video game simulations of racecars, airplanes and other scenarios, designed to help develop hand-eye coordination on a level equal to actual experience. The game included a simulator console, a chair and a large, photorealistic video screen. A local arcade wanted to purchase the setup, but that deal failed after Doc had a falling out with its owners [**BFAN-19**].

- **ELB Lunchbox Burglar Deterrent:** An add-on feature to the Come-and-Get-It Lunchbox, an invention of Emmett Brown designed to loudly summon its owner at mealtime. The burglar-deterring device consisted of an extendable arm and mallet to attack anyone attempting to steal the lunchbox [**BFAN-15**].

- **ELB Pediatric Policer:** A helmet-mounted device created by Emmett Brown that operated

CODE	STORY
NIKE	*BTTF*-themed TV commercial: Nike
NTND	Nintendo *Back to the Future—The Ride* Mini-Game
PIZA	*BTTF*-themed TV commercial: Pizza Hut
PNBL	Data East *BTTF* pinball game
REAL	Real life
RIDE	Simulator: *Back to the Future—The Ride*
SCRM	2010 Scream Awards: *Back to the Future* 25th Anniversary Reunion (broadcast)
SCRT	2010 Scream Awards: *Back to the Future* 25th Anniversary Reunion (trailer)
SIMP	Simulator: *The Simpsons Ride*
SLOT	*Back to the Future* Video Slots
STLZ	Unused *BTTF* footage of Eric Stoltz as Marty McFly
STRY	*Back to the Future Storybook*
TEST	Screen tests: Crispin Glover, Lea Thompson and Tom Wilson
TLTL	Telltale Games' *Back to the Future—The Game*
TOPS	Topps' *Back to the Future II* trading-card set
TRIL	*BTTF: The Official Book of the Complete Movie Trilogy*
UNIV	Universal Studios Hollywood promotional video

SUFFIX	MEDIUM
-b	*BTTF2*'s Biff Tannen Museum video (extended)
-c	Credit sequence to the animated series
-d	Film deleted scene
-n	Film novelization
-o	Film outtake
-p	1955 phone book from *BTTF1*
-v	Video game print materials or commentaries
-s1	Screenplay (draft one)
-s2	Screenplay (draft two)
-s3	Screenplay (draft three)
-s4	Screenplay (draft four)
-sp	Screenplay (production draft)
-sx	Screenplay (Paradox)

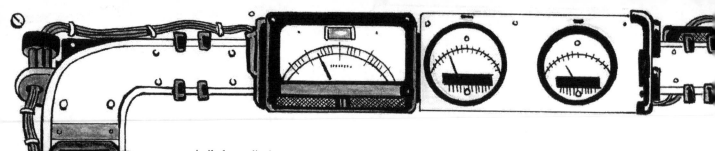

similarly to a lie detector, and could determine if a child was engaged in wrongdoing. The Pediatric Policer measured sudden changes in a wearer's blood pressure, skin temperature and pulse rate, triggering alarms in the event of bad behavior. Doc presented the contraption at the Annual Convention of the Home Inventors and Mad Geniuses [**BFAN-26**].

- **ELB Quick-o-Popper:** A room-sized popcorn popper invented by Emmett Brown, for use in popping the massive kernels of Doc's genetically engineered corn strain, which he dubbed Super-Growth Mondo-Corn [**BFAN-21**].

- **ELB Records:** A recording label, circa 1926, that produced a popular hit song called "Doin' the Daredevil Brown," about the exploits of four-year-old Hollywood stunt actor Daredevil Emmett Brown [**BFAN-11**].

- **ELB Sunshine Umbrella for Rainy-Day Tans:** An invention of Emmett Brown, intended for folks who enjoy walking in the rain. Once opened, the umbrella emanated a bright light and emitted a stream of water, simulating rain and sunshine. Walter Wisdom, Doc's unscrupulous college roommate, stole the invention in 1992, intending to claim it as his own, but Doc regained the device, discrediting Wisdom during a live television broadcast [**BFAN-15**].

- **ELB Super-Sniffer Snout 4000:** An invention of Emmett Brown that amplified the sniffing ability of his dog, Einstein, via a large, nose-like contraption attached on one end to the canine's snout, and on the other to the front of Doc's DeLorean [**BFAN-20**].

- **ELB Video Message Center:** A recording device invented by Emmett Brown. Attached to his refrigerator, the ELB Video Message Center enabled the scientist and his family to record and play back messages to each other [**BFAN-6**].

- **ELB Yo-Bub No-Stub Folding Chairs:** A type of seating invented by Emmett Brown. Each chair contained a sensor dish programmed to move it out of the way in the event that a passerby might be in danger of stubbing a toe. The chairs could walk unassisted, and could be summoned to follow a user via a single clap [**BFAN-22**].

- **Electric, General:** A fictional U.S. Army general. While serving as a soldier in 1944, Marty McFly and Verne Brown escaped that era by claiming an officer named General Electric had ordered them to put out a soldier's lights (that is, knock him unconscious) [**BFAN-17**].

    NOTE: The officer's name was a pun on General Electric Co., and the use of the "lights" phrase furthered the joke. (See also entry for "General Electric.")

- **electrical-magnetical machine:** An electrical generator once used for a variety of purposes, including curing rheumatism and improving leg strength [**REAL**]. The physician of Ulysses S. Clayton used such a device on the general during the American Civil War. Emmett Brown borrowed it to create a super-magnet, with which he attempted (and failed) to stop Clayton's forces and those of General Beauregard Tannen from fighting, by magnetically pulling away their weaponry [**BFAN-1**].

- **electric perpetual portable trampoline:** An invention of Emmett Brown, created to help his son, Jules, get sufficient exercise. The trampoline could fold up and fit into a person's pocket, and be activated to instantly unfold at the push of a button [**BFCM-1**].

    NOTE: Jules identified it as an electric portable perpetual trampoline, but a sign on the actual contraption switched the second and third words in the title.

- **Electro-guide boots:** A type of hover-technology-based footwear designed by Emmett Brown. Verne Brown often used the boots indoors, despite being repeatedly told not to do so, frequently creating havoc in the process [**BFAN-3**].

- **Electrokinetic Levitator:** An invention of Emmett Brown, built in 1931. This early-model flying vehicle was based on the scientist's failed Rocket Car, and was powered by a glowing, hovering coil known as the Static Accumulator [**TLTL-5**].

- **Electromagnetic Experiment:** A scientific project undertaken in the laboratory of Emmett Brown, with assistance from his son, Jules, involving the creation of a simple electromagnet [**BFAN-1**].

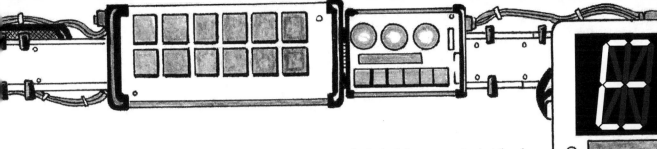

- **Electro Zapper:** A brand of electrical-discharge insect-control system used by Marty McFly's family in an alternate version of 1986 [**TLTL-2**].

- **Elektro-Pacifier:** A scientific innovation for police personnel, presented at the 1931 Hill Valley Exposition by Detective Daniel Parker, as part of the event's Future of Law Enforcement exhibit. This prototype weapon was designed to enable officers to stun fleeing criminals by shocking them from a distance [**TLTL-5**].

  > ***NOTE:*** *In effect, the device was a 1930s analog to a modern-day Taser.*

- **Eli:** A name mentioned in an inscription written on a wall of the Sisters of Mercy Soup Kitchen in 1931. According to the inscription, Eli thought a woman he knew was drinking too much, and urged her to get rid of her wine. Upon reading the scrawl, Marty McFly commented that Eli should mind his own business [**TLTL-1**].

- **Elite Barber Shop:** A haircutting establishment in Courthouse Square, circa 1955 [**BTF1**].

- **Eliza:** A name scrawled in graffiti on the wall of Hill Valley High School, circa 1985 [**BTF1**].

- **El Kid:** A Hill Valley speakeasy owned by gangster Irving "Kid" Tannen in the 1920s that illegally sold alcoholic beverages during the Prohibition era [**TLTL-1**]. The bar was built on the site of the Palace Saloon and Hotel, an establishment owned by Kid's ancestor, Beauregard B. Tannen, circa 1876 [**TLTL-5**].

  After the building burnt to the ground under suspicious circumstances, Tannen secretly resumed his operations in the cellar of the Sisters of Mercy Soup Kitchen. Emmett Brown, disguised in that era as drifter Carl Sagan, was arrested and jailed for the crime, after which Tannen's gang stormed the Hill Valley Police Station and murdered him. Upon learning of Doc's death from an old newspaper headline, Marty McFly traveled back in time to rescue his friend [**TLTL-1**].

  After pinpointing the speakeasy's hidden entrance, Marty listened as patrons provided coded passwords. Once inside, he posed as a member of the Sacramento Mob, enabling him to talk to the bar's occupants without raising suspicion. He met Kid's girlfriend, lounge singer Sylvia "Trixie Trotter" Miskin (Marty's future grandmother), as well as policeman Daniel Parker (a corrupt cop who lacked the courage to shut the place down), and tried to convince them both to help him put Tannen in prison. Eventually, Marty's efforts paid off, as Parker closed the speakeasy and arrested Tannen and his thugs. Zane Williams, the bartender, tried to avoid a raid by pressing a panic button, mechanically converting the place into an eatery called Kid's Ice Cream, but Parker was not fooled by the obvious ruse [**TLTL-2**].

  Years later, in Citizen Brown's dystopian timeline, Edna Strickland used the former speakeasy site to store contraband confiscated from Hill Valley's populace [**TLTL-3**].

- **Ellie-Mae:** A wild bear cared for by Windjammer Diefendorfer, circa 1888. Marty McFly encountered the animal while visiting that era, and found that the gentle creature was even more scared of him than he was of it [**BFAN-21**].

- **Ellison, Harlan:** A science fiction author with more than 1,000 writing credits to his name, including screenplays, books, novellas, essays, short stories and teleplays [**REAL**]. Verne Brown referenced his book *On Robots* while writing a school essay on the subject of robotics [**BFCL-1**].

  > ***NOTE:*** *On Robots is fictional, and was not written by Ellison in the real world.*

- **Elmdale High School:** *See* Hill Valley High School (HVHS)

- **Elmo's Ribs:** A shop in Hill Valley, located next to an Assembly of Christ church. Marty McFly passed this store while hitching a skateboard ride to school [**BTF1**].

- **Elroy:** An identity given by Jules and Verne Brown to a baby Apatosaurus that Verne found while visiting prehistoric times. To keep their father, Emmett Brown, from discovering the dinosaur's nature, the boys claimed to be playing a game called Martians at the Beach, and that Elroy was a human child who'd painted himself green. They later named the animal Tiny [**BFAN-26**].

- **El Sapo Coin Toss:** A booth at the Hill Valley Festival in 1885 [**BTF3**]. The game, despite its name, involved players tossing wooden discs into the open mouth of a large clay frog [**BTF3-n**].

- **Emergency Cash:** A label on a briefcase owned by Emmett Brown, containing U.S. currency from

CODE	STORY
NIKE	*BTTF*-themed TV commercial: Nike
NTND	Nintendo *Back to the Future—The Ride* Mini-Game
PIZA	*BTTF*-themed TV commercial: Pizza Hut
PNBL	Data East *BTTF* pinball game
REAL	Real life
RIDE	Simulator: *Back to the Future—The Ride*
SCRM	2010 Scream Awards: *Back to the Future 25th Anniversary Reunion* (broadcast)
SCRT	2010 Scream Awards: *Back to the Future 25th Anniversary Reunion* (trailer)
SIMP	Simulator: *The Simpsons Ride*
SLOT	*Back to the Future Video Slots*
STLZ	Unused *BTTF* footage of Eric Stoltz as Marty McFly
STRY	*Back to the Future Storybook*
TEST	Screen tests: Crispin Glover, Lea Thompson and Tom Wilson
TLTL	Telltale Games' *Back to the Future—The Game*
TOPS	Topps' *Back to the Future II* trading-card set
TRIL	*BTTF: The Official Book of the Complete Movie Trilogy*
UNIV	Universal Studios Hollywood promotional video

SUFFIX	MEDIUM
-b	*BTTF2*'s Biff Tannen Museum video (extended)
-c	Credit sequence to the animated series
-d	Film deleted scene
-n	Film novelization
-o	Film outtake
-p	1955 phone book from *BTTF1*
-v	Video game print materials or commentaries
-s1	Screenplay (draft one)
-s2	Screenplay (draft two)
-s3	Screenplay (draft three)
-s4	Screenplay (draft four)
-sp	Screenplay (production draft)
-sx	Screenplay (*Paradox*)

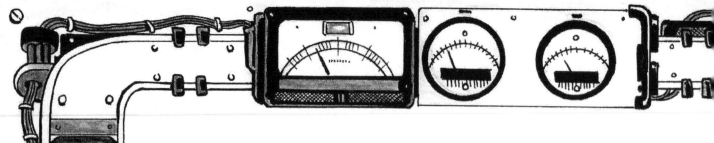

a number of eras throughout the 19th and 20th centuries, for use in the event of an unexpected need to travel into the past [**BTF2**].

- **EMIT MNTR:** A button on an overhead console of Emmett Brown's DeLorean [**TLTL-5**].

- **Emma:** A toy rag doll belonging to Sarah Lathrop, Emmett Brown's mother, when she was a little girl in 1885 [**BTF3-s1**].

  > **NOTE:** *The implication was that Sarah later named her son after the doll.*

- **Enchanted Tower, The:** A tall stone structure in Apocrypha, the largest empire of former North America, circa 2,991,299,129,912,991 A.D., and located in the Holy Park. Tannen the Barbarian elicited the help of Marty McFly and Emmett Brown in entering the tower, said to be enchanted (it was protected by an electric fence, far in advance of Tannen's primitive culture) after the queen of Apocrypha promised him great riches for stealing the Ruby Begonia. The gem was protected in a jewel vault located within the tower, guarded by a giant green serpent [**BFCL-2**].

  > **NOTE:** *Many scientists believe Earth will cease to exist in approximately 7.6 billion years, with human life dying out within a billion years or so.*

- **Enchantment Under the Sea Dance:** An annual student event held at Hill Valley High School. In 1955, George and Lorraine McFly fell in love at this dance. It was here, after their first kiss, that Lorraine realized she'd spend the rest of her life with George. Their son, Marty McFly, almost prevented this kiss—and, thus, his own birth—while stranded in the past, by unknowingly altering history so that Lorraine fell in love with him instead of George.

  In order to restore the timeline, Marty went to extreme lengths to urge George to ask Lorraine to the dance. In so doing, he managed to boost his father's self-confidence, giving George the courage to stand up to long-time bullies Biff Tannen and Mark Dixon. Thus, when Marty returned to his own era, he discovered that his parents were not only still together, but much happier, healthier and more successful than before.

  During the dance, Marty played guitar with the hired band, Marvin Berry and the Starlighters, and inspired the birth of rock and roll. In later years,

Lorraine would wax nostalgic about this night, to the annoyance of her children (particularly Linda McFly, who called it the Fish Under the Sea Dance), never knowing that her son was the same youth she'd met 30 years prior [**BTF1**].

After an elderly Biff Tannen changed history by giving his younger self a copy of *Grays Sports Almanac* so that he could bet on future sporting events and become a wealthy man, Marty returned to 1955 to retrieve the book. His search for Biff and the *Almanac* led to his revisiting the dance, where he made sure to avoid coming into contact with his earlier self. The situation was almost worsened, however, when Biff's cronies (3-D, Match and Skinhead) spotted the second Marty and tried to jump him [**BTF2**].

> **NOTE:** *BTTF1's initial-draft screenplay called the event the Springtime to Paris Dance, while the second draft changed it to the Springtime in Paris Dance. By the time of filming, it would become the Enchantment Under the Sea Dance.*

- *Encyclopedia Robotica:* A textbook about robots that Verne Brown referenced while writing a school essay on that subject [**BFCL-1**].

- **Engineer Dan Hobby Hut:** A toy and hobby store located in Hill Valley, owned by a heavyset man named Dan Philips. Two of Jules Brown's classmates, Franny Philips (Dan's daughter) and a boy named Jackson, frequented this shop [**BFAN-20**].

- **Enlightenment Under the Sea:** A display at the 1931 Hill Valley Exposition, offering a prediction of futuristic underwater exploration. The display was hosted by famous diver Jacques Douteux [**TLTL-5**].

  > **NOTE:** *The display's name was an in-joke reference to the Enchantment Under the Sea Dance.*

- **Ennis, J.M., Mayor:** The mayor of North Park, a town near Hill Valley, circa 1885 [**BTF3**].

  > **NOTE:** *A sign for this town, containing Ennis' name, was among those leaning against a sign shop located next to Marshal James Strickland's office.*

- *Enquisitor:* A tabloid periodical that Emmett Brown read while avoiding activities that might

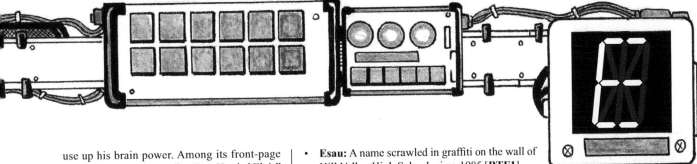

use up his brain power. Among its front-page headlines was "Mutant Alien Two-Headed Elvis" [**BFCM-4**].

> *NOTE: The magazine's name and content were based on those of* The National Enquirer. *Given the* Enquirer*'s reputation for fabricated stories, it's unlikely that the Mutant Alien Two-Headed Elvis existed.*

- **Entertainer, The:** A video-rental business located in Robot City, a domed station in the Asteroid Belt of Earth's solar system, circa 2585 [**BFCL-1**].

- **Entertainment and Sports Programming Network (ESPN):** A cable television network focused on sports-related programming [**REAL**]. In 2015, Hill Valley's citizens could watch ESPN's sports coverage on Channel 211-D [**BTF2-sx, BTF2-n**].

- **Entry Identi-Pad:** A home-security system used in 2015, requiring a home's occupant to provide a thumbprint prior to admittance [**BTF2**].

- **Environmental Adjuster:** *See* ELB Environmental Adjuster

- **Erhardt Brown Scholarship for Young Scientists:** A fund set up by Emmett Brown's father, Judge Erhardt Brown, to encourage youths to pursue a career in the sciences. Erhardt initially disapproved of his son's scientific interests, but grew proud upon seeing Emmett demonstrating a flying car prototype at the 1931 Hill Valley Exposition. Thereafter, he offered the scholarship to others considering the same path [**TLTL-5**].

- **Erlewine Chiquita:** A model of guitar, popular in 1985 [**REAL**]. Marty McFly had a yellow guitar of this type, on which he sometimes practiced before school using a giant amplifier erected at the home of his friend Emmett Brown [**BTF1**].

- **Errata:** A small empire in North America, circa 2,991,299,129,912,991 A.D., located in the former southern United States and Central America [**BFCL-2**].

> *NOTE: Many scientists believe Earth will cease to exist in approximately 7.6 billion years, with human life dying out within a billion years or so.*

- **Esau:** A name scrawled in graffiti on the wall of Hill Valley High School, circa 1985 [**BTF1**].

- **Eskimo Pie:** A popular brand name of foil-wrapped, chocolate-covered vanilla ice-cream bars [**REAL**]. A sidewalk cart selling Eskimo Pies was located near the scene of a motor-vehicle accident in 1955, in which Biff Tannen's Ford Super Deluxe convertible collided with a manure truck [**BTF1**].

- **Esmonde, Michael, Ph.D.:** An employee at the Institute of Future Technology, in charge of Meaux-Fleur Tronics [**RIDE**].

> *NOTE: This individual, identified on signage outside* Back to the Future: The Ride, *was named after an employee at Universal Studios.*

- **Essex Theater:** A movie theater in Courthouse Square [**BTF1, BTF2**], which was under construction as early as 1885, likely as a live theater [**BTF3**]. In 1931, the Essex showed the film *Shark* [**TLTL-1**].

In 1955, the theater was showing *Cattle Queen of Montana*, starring Barbara Stanwyck and Ronald Reagan. By 1985, the theater had become an X-rated venue, featuring such movies as *Orgy American Style* [**BTF1**]. In the Biffhorrific version of 1985, it was called the Hill Valley Theater of Live Sex Acts [**BTF2**].

By 2015, the theater was renovated as the Holomax Theater, which showed holographic movies, such as *Jaws 19*. The Holomax used a holographic projector to create three-dimensional images on the street in front of the theater, advertising the movies being shown [**BTF3**].

The Essex provided patrons with free dishware [**BTF1**].

- **Estrada Maria, Special Agent ("Señorita Maria"):** A beautiful young woman from Spain, living on an island in the Caribbean, who worked as a special agent for the Spanish Armada in 1697. Assigned to bring pirate Mac the Black to justice for stealing the fleet's flagship as his pirate vessel, Estrada posed as a local woman longing to meet the famed pirate. Marty McFly pretended to be Mac in order to impress her, and later helped her capture the man once his ruse was exposed [**BFAN-14**].

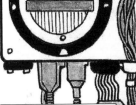

CODE	STORY
NIKE	*BTTF*-themed TV commercial: Nike
NTND	Nintendo *Back to the Future—The Ride* Mini-Game
PIZA	*BTTF*-themed TV commercial: Pizza Hut
PNBL	Data East *BTTF* pinball game
REAL	Real life
RIDE	Simulator: *Back to the Future—The Ride*
SCRM	2010 Scream Awards: *Back to the Future* 25th Anniversary Reunion (broadcast)
SCRT	2010 Scream Awards: *Back to the Future* 25th Anniversary Reunion (trailer)
SIMP	Simulator: *The Simpsons Ride*
SLOT	*Back to the Future* Video Slots
STLZ	Unused *BTTF* footage of Eric Stoltz as Marty McFly
STRY	*Back to the Future* Storybook
TEST	Screen tests: Crispin Glover, Lea Thompson and Tom Wilson
TLTL	Telltale Games' *Back to the Future—The Game*
TOPS	Topps' *Back to the Future II* trading-card set
TRIL	*BTTF: The Official Book of the Complete Movie Trilogy*
UNIV	Universal Studios Hollywood promotional video

SUFFIX	MEDIUM
-b	*BTTF2*'s Biff Tannen Museum video (extended)
-c	Credit sequence to the animated series
-d	Film deleted scene
-n	Film novelization
-o	Film outtake
-p	1955 phone book from *BTTF1*
-v	Video game print materials or commentaries
-s1	Screenplay (draft one)
-s2	Screenplay (draft two)
-s3	Screenplay (draft three)
-s4	Screenplay (draft four)
-sp	Screenplay (production draft)
-sx	Screenplay (*Paradox*)

NOTE: *Maria Estrada was named after the animated series' casting director.*

- **Eunice:** A middle-aged patron of the El Kid speakeasy in 1931. Her boyfriend, Ernest Philpott, drunkenly accused Marty McFly of staring at her, threatening to fight for her honor. Eunice told Ernie to let it go, calling him a "mean drunk," but he took a swing anyway and fell on his face. After gangster "Cue Ball" Donnely made Ernie leave to cool off, Eunice invited Marty to take his place, but the youth politely declined [**TLTL-2**].

- **eureka kookamunga:** An expression of excitement used by Emmett Brown when one of his inventions was successful [**BFAN-2**].

- **Eve:** A contact person listed for Computec, located in Glendale, California, in a 1991 help-wanted ad that Emmett Brown read while searching for a job [**BFAN-12**].

- **expandable pizza:** *See* rehydrated pizza

- **express tram:** A mode of public transportation used across the Mid-Valley region and downtown Hill Valley, circa 2015 [**BTF2**].

- **Extradimensional Storage Closet:** A room in Emmett Brown's lab, by which he could access multiple dimensions of time and space. The closet, controlled via a pan-dimensional field generator, was larger on the inside than outside. When Verne Brown accessed the closet while seeking a device able to deliver a sufficient electrical shock to restore his father's lost memory, the resultant power surge turned the closet inside out, damaging the fabric of the space-time continuum.

  This propelled the Browns and Marty McFly through the Seventh Dimension, causing them to randomly jump around time and space. As the family's house and other locales fell into the closet, Earth nearly collapsed into a black hole. Doc averted the crisis by using his DeLorean to restore the closet's proper configuration [**BFCL-3**].

  NOTE: In essence, Doc had his own TARDIS ("Time and Relative Dimensions in Space"), a time machine featured in British science fiction series Doctor Who.

- **Eyepatch:** An old-timer who frequented Hill Valley's Palace Saloon and Hotel in 1885, along with Jeb, Levi, Zeke, Toothless and Moustache. He had a thick mustache and a black patch over his left eye. When Marty McFly considered backing out of a duel with Buford Tannen, Eyepatch and Toothless branded Marty a coward [**BTF3-sx**].

  NOTE: The name "Eyepatch" appeared in BTTF3's production-draft screenplay. His birth name is unknown.

- **E-Z Credit Finance Company:** A business located in Courthouse Square, circa 2015 [**BTF2-n**].

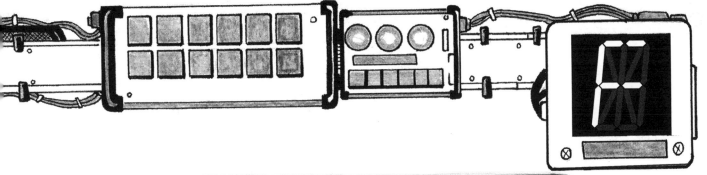

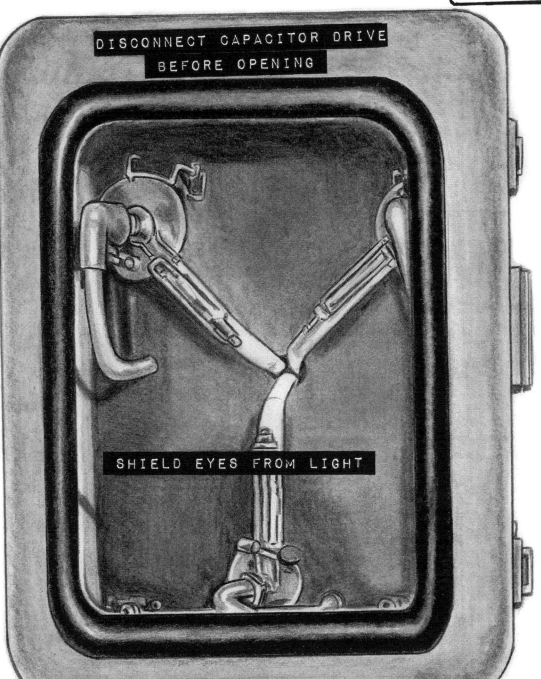

DISCONNECT CAPACITOR DRIVE
BEFORE OPENING

SHIELD EYES FROM LIGHT

FLUX CAPACITOR

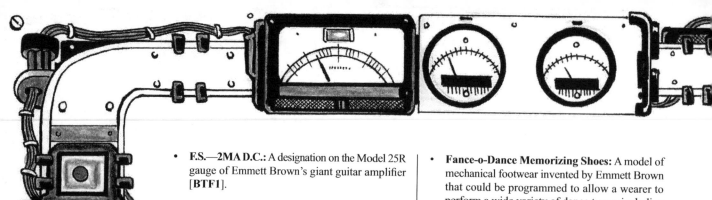

- **F.S.—2MA D.C.:** A designation on the Model 25R gauge of Emmett Brown's giant guitar amplifier [**BTF1**].

- **F1:** A parking area at Hill Valley's Twin Pines Mall. In 1985, Emmett Brown conducted Temporal Experiment Number One—the testing of a time-traveling DeLorean—in this section of the mall's parking lot [**BTF1**].

- **Facfax:** A division of the U.S. Postal Service, circa 2015, that provided mailboxes in Hill Valley able to fax a letter in half a second [**BTF2**].

    NOTE: Marty McFly passed a Facfax mailbox advertising "05 Second Service." Early production sketches of the mailbox, labeld "FaxMail," offered "30 Second Service."

- **Fairfax:** An incorporated town in Marin County, California [**REAL**]. In Citizen Brown's dystopian timeline, the inhabitants of Fairfax often laughed at Hill Valley's extreme societal model [**TLTL-3**].

- *Family Feud:* An American television game show created by Mark Goodson and Bill Todman, most notably hosted by Richard Dawson [**REAL**]. George McFly, in an effort to raise his family's morale, suggested that he, Lorraine and Marty try out for a game show, such as *The Price Is Right*. Marty, however, recommended *Family Feud*, since that would enable the entire family, including his uncle John, to take part [**TEST**].

- *Family Ties:* An American sitcom that aired on NBC from 1982 to 1989, starring actor Michael J. Fox as Alex P. Keaton [**REAL**]. In 2015, the Café 80's played an excerpt from an episode of this series on one of its many video monitors [**BTF2**].

    NOTE: Keaton, Marty and Fox all exist as characters within the BTTF mythos, while both Back to the Future *and* Family Ties *have both been mentioned as fictional series. To learn more about this seeming impossibility, see the entries for Alex P. Keaton, Michael J. Fox and* Back to the Future.

- *Family Vacations—1995-2005:* A videobook in the house of Marty and Jennifer McFly, circa 2015. When Jennifer's younger self from 1985 visited her future home, she saw this and other videobooks stored on a shelf [**BTF2-sx, BTF2-n**].

- **Fance-o-Dance Memorizing Shoes:** A model of mechanical footwear invented by Emmett Brown that could be programmed to allow a wearer to perform a wide variety of dance types, including the waltz, swing, fox trot, cha-cha or Bobby Van hopping dance. The shoes were customizable as pumps, loafers, sneakers, or pumps that looked like sneakers. Wearing the Fance-o-Dance shoes, Doc placed second in the Hill Valley High Jitterbug Jam.

    When Verne Brown had trouble waltzing, Doc considered lending him the shoes—which Verne thought looked goofy and smelled worse—but a malfunction precluded that option. Therefore, Verne and Marty McFly traveled back to 1944 to retrieve Doc's long-lost blueprints so he could repair them [**BFAN-17**].

- **Fanny, Aunt:** An aunt of Edna and Gerald Strickland [**TLTL-1**].

    NOTE: This individual may not have existed, as Edna mentioned her while expressing disbelief: "Student of history, my aunt Fanny!" The phrase "my aunt Fanny," denoting doubt, is a euphemism for "my ass," and may have been used in that vein.

- *Fantastic Story Magazine:* A science fiction pulp magazine published from 1950 to 1955 [**REAL**]. While attending high school, George McFly owned a copy of the Fall 1954 issue, featuring "Forgotten World," by Edmond Hamilton; "Trouble on Titan," by Arthur K. Barnes; "The Last Man in New York," by Paul MacNamara; and "Dames Is Poison," by Kelvin Kent [**BTF1**].

- **Fawn Hall's Slice Ollie North Platter:** A menu item sold at Café 80's in 2015 [**BTF2**].

- **Fargo, Frank ("Fearless Frank"):** A train conductor reputed to have successfully managed to reach 70 miles hour using a steam-powered locomotive, out past Verde Junction, sometime in or before 1885 [**BTF3**].

- **FaxMail:** *See* Facfax

- **Federal Bureau of Investigation (FBI):** An agency of the U.S. Department of Justice, serving as a federal criminal investigative body and an internal intelligence agency [**REAL**]. When Libyan nationalists stole a case of plutonium

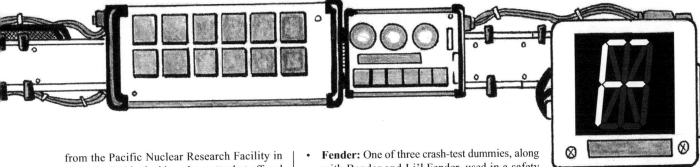

from the Pacific Nuclear Research Facility in 1985, the FBI looked into the matter but offered no comment to the press [**BTF1**].

When Jules Brown invented a money-tree, the bureau assigned two agents, Smith and Jones, to determine if the youth was a kingpin of an international counterfeiting racket [**BFAN-20**].

- **FedEx:** A U.S.-based logistics services firm originally known as Federal Express [**REAL**]. In 2585, the company was still in operation, with delivery routes to Robot City, a domed station in the Asteroid Belt of Earth's solar system [**BFCL-1**].

- **Fedgewick:** A short, kindly, bespectacled toymaker who owned a shop in London in 1845. His landlord, Ebiffnezer Tannen, ruthlessly made sure the rent was always paid on time. When Fedgewick was an hour late in making payment, Tannen foreclosed on his business and sent him and his wife to Debtor's Prison.

  There, the couple remained until Marty McFly, disguised as the Ghost of Christmas, frightened Tannen into freeing all of the inmates and clearing their debts. The Fedgewicks then celebrated by sharing a Christmas dinner with Marty and Emmett Brown [**BFAN-10**].

- **Fedgewick Toys:** A toystore located in London, England, in 1845. While visiting that era with Emmett Brown, Marty McFly followed a pretty woman into this establishment and promptly received a slap across the face after offending her.

  When landlord Ebiffnezer Tannen foreclosed on the shop's rent, the Fedgewicks, along with Clara Clayton Brown, were sent to Debtor's Prison. They were later freed after Marty McFly tricked Tannen into turning over a new leaf by posing as the Ghost of Christmas to scare him into clearing everyone's debts [**BFAN-10**].

- **Feldstein, Doctor:** A scientist whose 1964 escapades in the Bermuda Triangle, in an alternate timeline, resulted in the United States having 87 states, all of which banned time-travel experiments [**BTF1-s1**].

  NOTE: The nature of Feldstein's Bermuda Triangle exploits is unknown.

- **feline's nocturnal clothing:** An expression used by Emmett Brown to laud a person as superlative, analogous to "the cat's pajamas" [**BFAN-9**].

- **Fender:** One of three crash-test dummies, along with Bender and Li'l Fender, used in a safety video at the Institute of Future Technology's Anti-Gravitic Laboratory, to instruct Time-Travel Volunteers how to avoid being injured while operating Emmett Brown's Eight-Passenger DeLorean Time-Travel Vehicle. The dummies banged their heads, had limbs severed by closing doors and were strangulated by cameras caught in a safety restraint—and also broke rules regarding flash photography, eating and smoking—as a warning to those watching the video [**RIDE**].

- **Fender Musical Instruments Corp.:** A manufacturer of stringed instruments and amplifiers, such as solid-body electric guitars [**REAL**]. In 1955, Marvin Berry and the Starlighters used the company's Bassman amplifier while performing at the Enchantment Under the Sea Dance [**BTF1**].

- **Fepsi:** A brand of soft-drink advertised on a banner at the Small Town Professional Wrasslin organization in 1952 [**BFAN-24**].

  NOTE: This beverage's name was based on that of the soft drink Pepsi—which also existed in the BTTF universe. (See Pepsi entry.)

- **Ferris Wheel:** An amusement-park ride at the 1904 St. Louis World Exposition, employing the tension-spoke principle. Emmett and Clara Brown, after traveling back in time to attend the fair, enjoyed this attraction—Doc for the scientific principle behind it, Clara for the view [**BFAN-25**].

- **Fido:** A dog whose food dish was used to serve water at Oxen's Gore Tavern & Bed 'N' Breakfast, located in Hillvallia, a primitive village in former North America, circa 2,991,299,129,912,991 A.D. [**BFCL-2**].

  NOTE: Many scientists believe Earth will cease to exist in approximately 7.6 billion years, with human life dying out within a billion years or so.

- **Fido:** A small dog appearing in a retrospective video highlighting Emmett Brown's inventions. In the video, Fido enjoyed a meal of sawdust dog food warmed up in Doc's Canine Cafeteria device [**RIDE**].

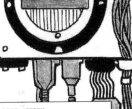

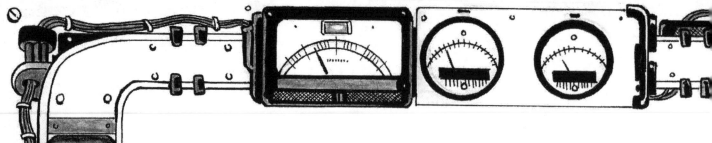

- **Figgins:** The owner of A1 Liquors, a store in Hill Valley, circa 1986 [**TLTL-1**].

- *Fired Up*: A greatest-hits album released by Marty McFly's rock band, Marty and the Pinheads, in 2015. This album went platinum, topping the rock-and-roll charts [**BFCG**].

- **First Citizen Brown:** Emmett Brown's title in a timeline in which Hill Valley was a pristine, self-sustaining, walled, dystopian society with very strict rules of propriety—the United States' first fully incorporated gated city, exempt from state legislation. As Citizen Brown, Doc (who'd fallen in love with Edna Strickland as a young man, and had thus devoted himself to her conservative philosophies instead of science) promoted civil and social engineering, using Hill Valley as a prototype for tomorrow's cities in order to show how technology could be utilized to shape a more efficient, orderly society.

  In this reality, Hill Valley's citizens were mandated to be vegetarians (though they could eat liver and bologna) and wear ID badges at all times. What's more, dress codes—such as Polo Shirt Thursday and Hawaiian Shirt Friday—were strictly enforced. Many items and genres were il-legalized, including weapons, alcohol, cigarettes, cigars, bubblegum, dogs, Circus Peanuts, science fiction, *Dungeons and Dragons*, skateboards, rock-and-roll music, pinball games, novelty items (such as X-ray specs, joy buzzers and trick gum), por-nographic films and magazines, public displays of affection, graffiti and more, including even men-tioning provocative words, such as "hormones."

  Although Brown's intentions were good, he was merely a pawn manipulated by Edna, whose single-minded obsession with curtailing vice and subversion had perverted his ideals. Upon meeting Marty McFly, Brown came to realize his mistake—but before he could fix the timeline, Edna subjected him to hypnotic re-conditioning, rendering him unable to act [**TLTL-3**]. Marty helped Brown escape, and the two worked to un-do the timeline damage by going back in time to prevent Doc and Edna from falling in love [**TLTL-4**]. Citizen Brown, however, came to resent Marty for wanting to wipe out his timeline, and instead worked against the youth's efforts, hoping to prevent Hill Valley from becoming a police state while still retaining his relationship with Edna. This proved disastrous, and Citizen Brown eventually faded from existence [**TLTL-5**].

- **First International Bank:** A business located near Emmett Brown's home in Hill Valley, circa 1985 [**BTF1**].

- **Fitzgibbon, Peter:** The Institute of Future Technology's chief regulator [**RIDE**].

  > ***NOTE:*** *This individual, identified on signage outside* Back to the Future: The Ride, *was named after an employee at Universal Studios.*

- **Fish Under the Sea Dance, The:** A name erroneously used by Linda McFly to describe the Enchantment Under the Sea Dance, where George and Lorraine McFly first fell in love [**BTF1**].

- *Fistful of Dollars, A*: A 1964 "Spaghetti Western" starring Clint Eastwood [**REAL**].

  In Biffhorrific 1985, the corrupt and powerful Biff Tannen enjoyed watching Eastwood's film *A Fistful of Dollars*, and was particularly impressed when Eastwood's character, the Man With No Name, used a piece of metal hidden beneath his poncho as a bulletproof vest during a quick-draw [**BTF2**].

  Marty McFly was also a fan of *A Fistful of Dollars*. After traveling to 1885 to save Emmett Brown from being murdered by Buford Tannen, Marty was reminded of the film's climactic scene. During a deadly duel with Tannen, Marty, using the alias Clint Eastwood and clad similarly to The Man With No Name, defeated the outlaw just as Eastwood's character had defeated Ramón Rojo: by hiding a steel chest plate beneath his pancho to deflect Buford's bullets [**BTF3**].

- **Flashback-o-Matic:** An invention of Emmett Brown enabling a user to recall forgotten memories by typing words onto an old-fashioned typewriter, thereby triggering a helmet-mounted projector to display the memories in question on a screen [**BFAN-17**].

- **Floeo:** A word of unknown meaning, scrawled in graffiti on the wall of Hill Valley High School, circa 1985 [**BTF1**].

- **Floozy of the Foothills:** *See* McFly, Sylvia

- **Florence Nightingale Effect:** A label given to the tendency for doctors, nurses and caregivers to develop romantic feelings toward their patients. This so-called effect was named for Florence

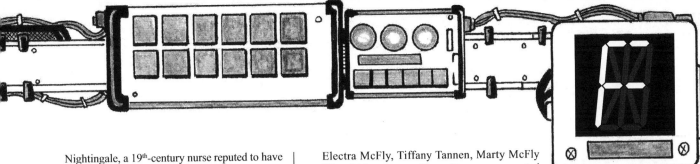

Nightingale, a 19th-century nurse reputed to have shown great concern for those under her care [**REAL**].

Lorraine Baines' attraction to George McFly stemmed from her feelings of guilt over her father, Sam Baines, hitting George with his car. This led to the two becoming married, despite their incompatibility—which Emmett Brown attributed to the Florence Nightingale Effect [**BTF1**].

- **Flores, Ben:** One of several professionals who helped to compile material for *Grays Sports Almanac: Complete Sports Statistics 1950-2000* [**BTF2**].

> *NOTE: This individual was named on the book's title page.*

- **Flux Capacitance Energy Converter:** *See* Flux Capacitor

- **Flux Capacitor:** An invention of Emmett Brown that facilitated time travel. Doc first conceived of the device on Nov. 5, 1955, after falling off a wet toilet while hanging a clock, causing him to strike his head on his sink. The Flux Capacitor required 1.21 jigowatts of electricity to trigger a temporal reaction, which could be achieved using either plutonium or a bolt of lightning.

  Receiving a vision of the Flux Capacitor following his head injury, Doc spent the next three decades—and his family's fortune—funding the contraption's development. His dream was finally achieved in 1985, when he converted a DeLorean DMC-12 sports car into a time machine, with the Flux Capacitor set to activate once the vehicle accelerated to 88 miles per hour.

  The system proved successful, propelling Doc's dog, Einstein, one minute into the future, but Libyan nationalists murdered Doc moments later. Marty McFly escaped the same fate by jumping into the DeLorean and flooring the accelerator. As the car's speed reached 88, this resulted in the Flux Capacitor's activation, sending him back to 1955—on the same day that Doc struck his head [**BTF1**].

  Doc later created another Flux Capacitor for his *Jules Verne Train* while living in the Old West, using technology found in that era [**BTF3, RIDE**].

  In a series of alternate timelines, the temporal tampering of various individuals—Clay Strickland, Darlene Needles, Clara Wilson, Jules McFly, Marlin Berry, Buffy Tannen,

Electra McFly, Tiffany Tannen, Marty McFly III and his own son, Verne Brown—prevented Doc from inventing the Flux Capacitor, thereby paradoxically eliminating the discovery of time travel in the first place [**BFCG**].

> *NOTE: The animated episode "Put on Your Thinking Caps, Kids! It's Time for Mr. Wisdom!" claimed the Flux Capacitor had been one of Doc's college dreams. However, BTTF1 clearly stated that Doc had conceived of the idea in 1955 (long after his student days) after falling off a toilet. (In the BTTF1's fourth-draft screenplay, Doc came up with the idea upon being hit over the head with a beer bottle by a young woman offended by his sexual advances.)*
>
> *In the first two script drafts, the time machine (then involving a refrigerator rather than a sports car) was enabled by a device called a Photo-Electric Chemical Power Converter. This was changed to the Flux Capacitance Energy Converter in draft three, the Temporal Field Capacitor in draft four, and the Flux Capacitor on film.*

- **Flux Catheter:** Biff Tannen's mis-reading of the term "Flux Capacitor" while thumbing through Emmett Brown's personal notebook [**TLTL-1**].

- **flux compression:** A function of the Flux Capacitor, as indicated on a drawing that Emmett Brown created upon first conceiving of the device [**BTF1**].

- **flux dispersal:** A function of Emmett Brown's Flux Capacitor, which made time travel possible. Brown chose a DeLorean DMC-12 to test the device, as the sports car's stainless-steel construction improved flux dispersal [**BTF1**].

- **Flux Emitters:** A trio of devices invented by Emmett Brown, used to enable his DeLorean to achieve time travel. The emitters were attached to the vehicle's hood on the front passenger's and driver's sides, as well as to the roof [**TLTL-5**].

- **Flux Override Modules:** *See* Flux Synchronization Modules

- **Flux Synchronization Modules:** A series of devices built by Emmett Brown for use

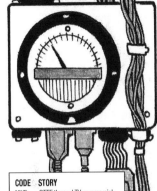

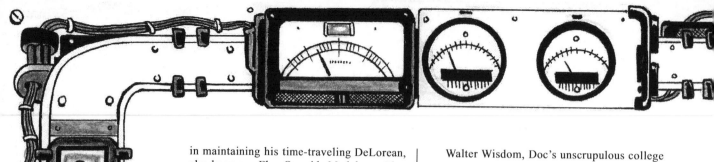

in maintaining his time-traveling DeLorean, also known as Flux Override Modules or Flux Synchronizers. When Edna Strickland stole a duplicate DeLorean and attempted to burn down the Palace Saloon and Hotel in 1876, the scientist utilized the Synchronizers to sync up the two vehicles' diagnostic modules, thereby making it possible to link both sets of time circuits and override the alternate car's time destination [**TLTL-5**].

- **Flux Synchronizers:** *See* Flux Synchronization Modules

- **flying bicycle:** A vehicle invented in 1931 by Marty McFly, using parts of Emmett Brown's Rocket-Powered Drill attached to the back of a bicycle. When Irving "Kid" Tannen tried to murder Emmett Brown for burning down his speakeasy, Marty used the flying bicycle to catch up to the gangster's car and rescue his friend [**TLTL-1**].

- **flying circuits:** A system that allowed Emmett Brown's DeLorean time machine to achieve flight, acquired when Doc visited 2015 and had the vehicle hover-converted. A lightning bolt in 1955 shorted out the time circuits, rendering the car no longer flight-worthy [**BTF3**].

- **Flying High Kite Store:** A business in Courthouse Square, circa 2015 [**BTF2**].

- **Flying Observatory:** A vehicle built by Emmett Brown in 1967, so he could view Comet Kahooey's arrival. Powered by a stationary bicycle, it resembled a flying saucer and achieved lift by creating a negative magnetic charge that disrupted magnetic fields throughout Hill Valley. In 1992, Biff Tannen mistook the vessel for a spacecraft and incited mass hysteria, convincing others that Doc was an extraterrestrial.

    To learn the truth, Marty McFly traveled back to 1967 with Jules and Verne Brown. Marty inadvertently damaged the craft, causing it to crash into a swamp, where it remained for the next 25 years. This changed history, preventing Doc from being accused of having alien origins [**BFAN-23**].

- **Fly Trap, Rehabilitation and Release Center:** An invention of Emmett Brown, intended as a humane alternative to a traditional fly-swatter. The device consisted of a glass capsule containing a miniature bed and an overstuffed chair for flies.

Walter Wisdom, Doc's unscrupulous college roommate, stole the invention in 1992, intending to claim it as his own, but Doc regained the device, discrediting Wisdom during a live television broadcast [**BFAN-15**].

- **Foggy Mountain Home for the Incurably Insane:** A mental-health facility in Hill Valley, circa 1931, to which Edna Strickland often delivered soup from the Sisters of Mercy Soup Kitchen [**TLTL-1**].

- **Foley, Agent:** A special agent with the Nuclear Regulatory Commission (N.R.C.) who investigated Emmett Brown's theft of plutonium in 1985, with his partner, Agent Reese [**BTF1-s1**].

    > **NOTE:** *As a running joke, Bob Gale and Robert Zemeckis have included police officers and agents named Reese and Foley in many scripts throughout their careers.*

- **Foley, Officer:** A member of the Hill Valley Police force, circa 2015, who patrolled the streets with her partner, Officer Reese, forming Unit N11-11. When Emmett Brown left Jennifer Parker asleep in an alleyway, Foley and Reese found her unconscious and assumed her to be a drug user. Mistaking Jennifer for her older self—and assuming she'd received rejuvenation therapy to retain her youth—the duo delivered Jen to the home she and Marty shared in that era [**BTF2**].

    Reese and Foley rarely agreed about anything, partly due to Reese's fanaticism regarding rules and regulations—everything had to be done entirely by the book, which Foley found annoying. What's more, Foley, a rookie cop who often empathized with those in poorer areas, like Hilldale, felt that Reese had lost her humanity after years spent on the job [**BTF2-n**].

- **Ford Motor Co.:** An American automaker founded in 1903 by Henry Ford [**REAL**]. In 1955, Biff Tannen drove a Ford Super Deluxe convertible. Three decades later, Marty McFly hitched a skateboard ride on the back of a Ford pick-up truck after discovering he was late for school one day [**BTF1**].

- **Ford Super Deluxe:** A classic convertible automobile produced by the Ford Motor Co. in the 1940s [**REAL**]. In 1955, Biff Tannen owned a black version of this model, license plate number 6H 96472. Twice during the same week, this car

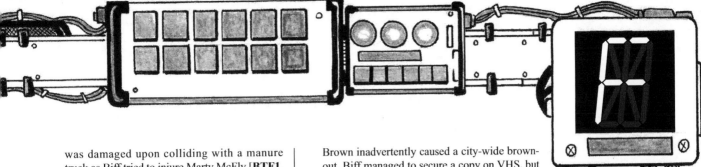

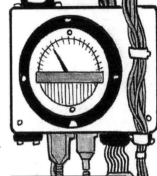

was damaged upon colliding with a manure truck as Biff tried to injure Marty McFly [**BTF1, BTF2**].

- **Forest Road:** A street in Hill Valley, on which a community center was located in 1955. The Hill Valley Women's Club held a bake sale at this site [**BTF2**].

- **FOR MARY:** The vanity license plate number of a green car in Hill Valley, circa 1985 [**BTF1**].

  > *NOTE: Marty McFly and Jennifer Parker passed this car while Jennifer consoled Marty over losing the Battle of the Bands audition. The license plate paid homage to Mary Radford, the longtime personal assistant to Frank Marshall, the* Back to the Future *trilogy's second unit director and executive producer.*

- **for Petri's sake:** An expression used by Emmett Brown to denote exasperation, analogous to "for Pete's sake" [**BFAN-5, BFAN-10**].

  > *NOTE: This phrase referred to German bacteriologist Julius Richard Petri, the inventor of the Petri dish. The comic adaptation of the episode "Roman Holiday" misspelled the name as "Petrie."*

- ***For Whom the Bell Tolls:*** A novel by Ernest Hemingway, first published in 1940 [**REAL**]. Lorraine Baines read this book while attending Hill Valley High School [**BTF1**].

- **Founder's Day:** An annual holiday celebrated in Hill Valley, honoring William Hill (a folkloric figure known as the Old Pioneer), and intended as a day for all citizens to work together. During the celebration, local businesses offered sales, while citizens built floats of the Old Pioneer and his mule, and also enjoyed a rock concert, Bash-'Em-Up Bumper Cars and other attractions (prior to the advent of electricity, the original founders had horseshoe tosses, quilting bees and greased-pig chases) [**BFAN-22**].

- **Founder's Day Tractor-Pull Contest:** An annual event held in Hill Valley, to honor the city's Founder's Day celebration. The contest, on which Biff Tannen and his friends often placed bets, was televised on Channel 93. In 1992, those viewing the event on TV missed the end after Emmett

Brown inadvertently caused a city-wide brown-out. Biff managed to secure a copy on VHS, but Doc used the video tape as a rope before Biff could view it [**BFAN-22**].

- **Fox, Michael J.:** A Canadian-American actor, producer and author of film and television [**REAL**]. Mistaking Emmett Brown for an extraterrestrial, Marty McFly—in response to Doc's insistence that he was human—sarcastically claimed he was Michael J. Fox. Verne Brown noted that Marty actually resembled him [**BFAN-23**].

  > *NOTE: The metafictional mention of Fox—who portrayed Marty in the* Back to the Future *trilogy—indicates that Fox and McFly co-existed in the same reality. This oddity is compounded by in-universe references to the film* Back to the Future *and the TV series* Family Ties *(starring Fox) and* Taxi *(starring Christopher Lloyd), as well as Alex P. Keaton, Fox's character on* Family Ties.

- **Fox Photo:** An American photo-store chain dealing in cameras, film and photographic equipment [**REAL**]. In 1985, a Fox Photo stand at Hill Valley's Twin Pines Mall was destroyed when a group of Libyan nationalists crashed a van into the booth [**BTF1**].

  > *NOTE: Fox Photo was an actual company in 1985, sold to Kodak the following year. Thus, the use of the name "Fox" was not a reference to actor Michael J. Fox.*

- ***Francis in the Navy:*** A 1955 comedy film in the "Francis the Talking Mule" series, directed by Arthur Lubin [**REAL**]. The Pohatchee Drive-in Theater listed this movie on its marquee that year [**BTF3**].

- **Frank:** One of several names that Marty McFly and Verne Brown urged Jules Verne to adopt, since Verne (who'd been named in the novelist's honor) hated the name Verne [**BFAN-21**].

- ***Frankenstein:*** A 1931 horror film from Universal Pictures, based on Mary Shelley's same-named novel, and starring Boris Karloff [**REAL**].

  In 1986, Marty McFly had a poster from this movie hanging in his bedroom. Upon visiting 1931, he discovered that the film was playing at Hill Valley's Town Theater. Seeing this movie

CODE	STORY
NIKE	*BTTF*-themed TV commercial: Nike
NTND	Nintendo *Back to the Future—The Ride* Mini-Game
PIZA	*BTTF*-themed TV commercial: Pizza Hut
PNBL	Data East *BTTF* pinball game
REAL	Real life
RIDE	Simulator: *Back to the Future—The Ride*
SCRM	2010 Scream Awards: *Back to the Future 25th Anniversary Reunion* (broadcast)
SCRT	2010 Scream Awards: *Back to the Future 25th Anniversary Reunion* (trailer)
SIMP	Simulator: *The Simpsons Ride*
SLOT	*Back to the Future Video Slots*
STLZ	Unused *BTTF* footage of Eric Stoltz as Marty McFly
STRY	*Back to the Future Storybook*
TEST	Screen tests: Crispin Glover, Lea Thompson and Tom Wilson
TLTL	Telltale Games' *Back to the Future—The Game*
TOPS	Topps' *Back to the Future II* trading-card set
TRIL	*BTTF: The Official Book of the Complete Movie Trilogy*
UNIV	Universal Studios Hollywood promotional video

SUFFIX	MEDIUM
-b	*BTTF2*'s Biff Tannen Museum video (extended)
-c	Credit sequence to the animated series
-d	Film deleted scene
-n	Film novelization
-o	Film outtake
-p	1955 phone book from *BTTF1*
-v	Video game print materials or commentaries
-s1	Screenplay (draft one)
-s2	Screenplay (draft two)
-s3	Screenplay (draft three)
-s4	Screenplay (draft four)
-sp	Screenplay (production draft)
-sx	Screenplay (*Paradox*)

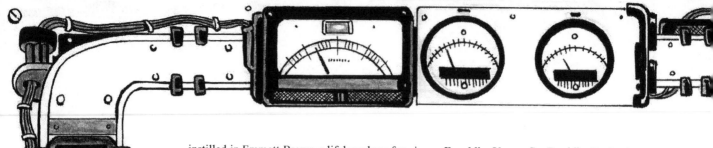

instilled in Emmett Brown a lifelong love for science, but history changed when he fell in love with Edna Strickland and instead spent the evening with her [**TLTL-1**].

* **Frankie:** A thief who robbed the Hill Valley Savings & Loan in 1991, along with a fellow criminal named Sidney. He had light-brown skin and long dark, unkempt hair. With no getaway car available, the two thugs stole the nearest parked car—the flying DeLorean of Emmett Brown, in which Doc's dog, Einstein, was resting.

  The vehicle's voice-activated time circuits mistook their conversation as a destination, and brought them to Sydney, Australia, in 1790. There, they were imprisoned in a jail run by Mongo P. Tannen, but Einstein freed them, returned to the future and delivered them to the police.

  Before embarking on a life of crime, Frankie attended chef school, to which he sometimes considered returning [**BFAN-7b**].

* **Franklin, Benjamin:** An employee at the Institute of Future Technology's director of audiotronics [**RIDE**].

  > *NOTE: This individual, identified on signage outside* Back to the Future: The Ride, *was named after the famous inventor.*

* **Franklin, Benjamin ("Ben Jr.," "Benny"):** A name that Verne Brown called himself after running away from home and traveling back to 1752, under the mistaken belief that his father was actually inventor Benjamin Franklin [**BFAN-6**].

  > *NOTE: Verne also went by the name "Verne Franklin," according to Doc's computer system.*

* **Franklin, Benjamin, Doctor:** An American author, printer, inventor and politician, and one of the United States' Founding Fathers. Among his innovations were bifocal lenses, lightning rods, printing presses, the Franklin stove and more [**REAL**].

  Emmett Brown admired Franklin's work and kept a framed photograph within his home [**BTF1**]. Doc met his idol in 1752 after following Verne Brown back in time to that year, when Verne became mistakenly convinced that Ben Franklin was his father. While there, Emmett inspired Franklin to invent the rocking chair [**BFAN-6**].

* **Franklin, Verne:** *See* Franklin, Benjamin

* **Franny's Fine Fans:** A business located in Hill Valley, circa 1991, that sold air-moving devices [**BFCM-4**].

* **Fred:** A cab driver in 2015 who kept a pet parrot, Priscilla, on his shoulder while driving. Fred often talked to the bird—which not only responded, but also advised him if he was about to make a mistake, such as charging the wrong fare. Biff Tannen, upon learning that Emmett Brown had invented a time machine, hailed Fred's cab to follow Doc's DeLorean so Biff could steal the vehicle and change history in his favor. Fred decided Biff was crazy, and regretted taking the fare [**BTF2-n**].

* **Fred:** A soldier who fought in the American Civil War, circa 1864. He had a nephew who served in the opposing army [**BFAN-1**].

  > *NOTE: Fred's name was heard as soldiers from both forces threw down their arms and embraced. It's unclear whether he served in the Confederate or Union Army.*

* **Fred:** *See* Red

* **Fredman:** The proprietor of the Cusimano Brothers Gearworks Factory, a Hill Valley business. In 1952, Emmett Brown purchased the plant from Fredman for $1.85 million, so that he could launch Emmett Brown Enterprises and follow his dream of inventing a Photo-Electric Chemical Power Converter [**BTF1-s2**].

* **Fredman:** A schoolmate of Marty McFly at Hill Valley High School. She and Marty sometimes endured detention together with Vice-Principal Gerald Strickland. When she coughed during one such detention, Strickland warned her that any further outbursts would earn her five additional detention sessions [**BTF1-s3**].

* **Freeway Flyer:** A class of flying machines used in 2015, including the Six-Wheel Van, the '89 Mustang Converter, the '89 Firebird Converter and a type of pick-up truck [**BTF2**].

  > *NOTE: This name appeared in production materials included on* BTTF2's *Blu-ray release.*

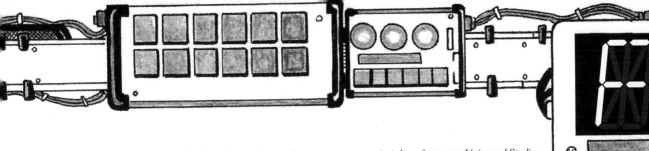

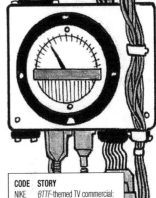

- **Fremont Press Printing:** A business located near Emmett Brown's home in Hill Valley, circa 1985 [**BTF1**].

- **French Kiss:** A Baldwin-based punk-rock band that beat out Marty McFly's high school rock group, The Pinheads, for a gig at Hill Valley High School's 1985 dance [**BTF1-s2**].

- **French Poodle Clock:** A type of vintage alarm clock produced by the California Clock Co. [**REAL**]. Emmett Brown had such a clock in his home, set to chime in synch with many others [**BTF1**].

- **French's:** An American manufacturer of mustard and other products [**REAL**]. The McFly family sometimes ate French's instant mashed potatoes for dinner, much to Marty McFly's disappointment [**BTF1-s4, BTF1-n**].

- **Fresh Produce:** A roadside business along a highway outside Hill Valley, circa 1931. Marty McFly passed this store while helping Emmett Brown escape from a police vehicle stolen by Irving "Kid" Tannen, who planned to murder the scientist [**TLTL-1**].

- **Freud, Sigismund Schlomo ("Sigmund"), Doctor:** An Austrian neurologist who founded the discipline of psychoanalysis [**REAL**]. Emmett Brown created a robotic version of Freud as part of his Mechanical Psychoanalyst, an invention consisting of a bed wired up to monitor its occupant, with the android Freud seated nearby, asking questions about a patient's innermost feelings. Doc considered the device a failure, since the questions proved to be annoying rather that curative [**BFCL-3**].

- **Friedman:** A bank-loan officer who agreed to provide Emmett Brown with a small-business loan so he could keep the Institute of Future Technology (IFT) open during hard times. Before this could happen, however, Doc's colleague, Professor John I.Q. Nerdelbaum Frink Jr., ran him over with the DeLorean. Frink had traveled back in time to find out why the institute had been replaced by the Krustyland theme park, ironically becoming the instrument of that replacement [**SIMP**].

  NOTE: This character appeared in The Simpsons Ride, *in queue footage intended*

as an in-joke reference to Universal Studios Florida's replacement of Back to the Future: The Ride *with that attraction.*

- **Frigidarium:** *See* Thermae

- **Frink, Johnathan I.Q. Nerdelbaum Jr., Professor ("John"):** A highly intelligent but socially inept scientist who was a friend and colleague to Emmett Brown. When he learned that Doc's Institute of Future Technology had been replaced by the Krustyland theme park, he traveled two years back in time via Doc's DeLorean to find out why.

  At that moment, Doc was securing a small-business loan from a bank-loan officer named Friedman, so he could keep the IFT open for several more years. In a moment of irony, Frink accidentally ran over the man, leaving Doc with no choice but to sell the facility to Krusty the Clown [**SIMP**].

  NOTE: This character, from television's The Simpsons, *appeared in queue footage in* The Simpsons Ride, *as an in-joke reference to Universal Studios Florida's replacement of* Back to the Future: The Ride *with that attraction.*

- **Frisbie Pie Co.:** A baking company founded in 1871 by William Russell Frisbie that sold pies in metal tins with an airfoil shape. Toy manufacturer Wham-O marketed a flying disc known as a Frisbee, named after the pie plates [**REAL**].

  Marty McFly, while attending the 1885 Hill Valley Festival, was amused to read the phrase "Frisbie's Pies" on one such tin. He later used the plate to disarm Buford Tannen, preventing him from murdering Emmett Brown [**BTF3**].

  Edna Strickland, while using the alias Mary Pickford, had a Frisbie tin hanging outside her home in an alternate 1931 [**TLTL-5**]. What's more, a Frisbee was among the items for sale at Blast From the Past, an antique and collectibles shop in 2015 Hill Valley [**BTF2**].

- **Frog:** A name scrawled in graffiti on the entrance to Lyon Estates in Biffhorrific 1985, in which the housing development was a slum. This individual was apparently romantically involved with a person named Slappy [**BTF2**].

- ***From the Earth to the Moon:*** A science fantasy novel written by Jules Verne, published in 1865

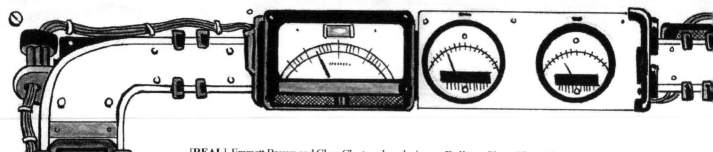

[REAL]. Emmett Brown and Clara Clayton shared a love for this book, which helped to deepen their romantic bond [BTF3].

> *NOTE: Telltale Games' video game featured a visual of a rocket sticking out of the Moon, which paid homage to* A Trip to the Moon, *a 1902 silent film adaptation of* From the Earth to the Moon.

- **Frosted Krispies:** A brand of breakfast cereal manufactured by Kellogg Co. [REAL]. Marty McFly's family had a box of this cereal in their kitchen in 1985 [BTF1].

- **frug:** A word used by the prudish Edna Strickland in place of actual profanities, as in "What the frug?" [TLTL-5].

- **Fruit-bearing Helicopter:** A scientific innovation described by the House of Tomorrow exhibit at the 1931 Hill Valley Exposition. According to a narrated recording played at the exhibit, future homes would have fresh fruit baskets, replenished daily by fleets of such vehicles [TLTL-5].

> *NOTE: This prediction proved to be remarkably accurate, given the Garden Center fruit dispenser featured in* Back to the Future II.

- **FUEL MNTR:** A button on an overhead console of Emmett Brown's DeLorean [TLTL-5].

- **Fujitsu, Ito. T. ("The Jits"):** The Japanese supervisor of Marty McFly and Douglas J. Needles at CusCo until Marty's termination in 2015. Fujitsu had a wife, Siva, but no children. He enjoyed Jao and Thai food, and disliked beer and Mexican cuisine. "The Jits," as his staff called him, sometimes monitored communications between his employees, in order to catch them violating company policies.

    While listening to a conversation between Marty and Needles, Fujitsu learned of an illegal transaction the two had planned. After calling Marty to announce his termination, Fujitsu also faxed him several messages stating, "You're fired!!!" [BTF2]. Marty suspected that Needles may have set him up to take the fall [BTF2-n].

> *NOTE: It's unknown whether The Jits also fired Needles.*

- **Fujitsu, Siva:** The wife of Ito. T. Fujitsu. The couple lived at 121 Park, A618-942308, and had no children [BTF2].

- **Full-Body Oven Mits:** An invention of Emmett Brown, consisting of human-sized, heat-resistant gloves capable of protecting a wearer even from the heat of molten lava. Doc used these mits to protect his family and Marty McFly after Walter Wisdom tricked them into crashing the *Jules Verne Train* into Krakatoa's soon-to-erupt volcano in 1883 [BFAN-15].

- **Full-course Food Pellets:** A type of pill created by Emmett Brown that, when added to water, provided a complete meal. Verne Brown often brought four such pellets with him for lunch while attending Hill Valley Elementary School [BFAN-26].

- **Funicello Sisters, The:** A pair of twin aerialists who worked for the Bob Brothers All-Star International Circus until 1933, when the trapeze performers quit to pursue careers as telephone operators. To keep the circus from losing business due to their departure, Verne Brown and his friend Chris temporarily replaced them, performing as the Stupendous Chris and Verne [BFAN-18].

- **FUSION:** A word on the front license plate of Emmett Brown's flying DeLorean [PNBL].

> *NOTE: Doc's car featured a front license plate only in the BTTF pinball game. Onscreen, a plate appeared only on the rear of the vehicle, and contained the phrase "OUTATIME" (when initially constructed) and later a bar code (following hover-conversion). What's more, the FUSION tag was on an Illinois license plate, whereas the car bore a California plate on film.*

- **Fusion Bar:** A tavern located in Courthouse Square, circa 2015 [BTF2-n].

- **Fusion Gold:** A type of fuel offered at Texaco's Hill Valley gas station, circa 2015, priced at $6.95 per gallon [BTF2].

- **Fusion Industries:** A corporation involved in trash collection, circa 2015, and the manufacturer of the Mr. Fusion Home Energy Reactor [BTF2].

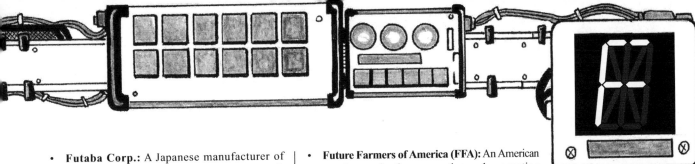

- **Futaba Corp.:** A Japanese manufacturer of electronic remote-control devices [**REAL**]. Emmett Brown used a Futaba handheld remote to steer his time-traveling DeLorean during Temporal Experiment Number One [**BTF1**].

- **Future Boy:** A derisive nickname that Emmett Brown skeptically dubbed Marty McFy upon first meeting the time-traveling youth in 1955 [**BTF1**].

- **Future City of Hill Valley:** A display at the 1931 Hill Valley Exposition, sponsored by Hal's Hardware. This attraction predicted that by 1981, Hill Valley would look very futuristic, with 10 million citizens living in a network of burrows extending a mile underground, affording them plenty of space to work, play and raise families.

   The exhibit claimed inhabitants would be able to take pleasure-rides in an elevated "super-train of tomorrow," and that agricultural advances would feed the burgeoning population, with artificial rainstorms summoned at the push of a button, to drench Hill Valley's crops. This, it predicted, would be followed by an artificial rainbow, to assure people that their needs were taken care of [**TLTL-4**].

   NOTE: None of the display's extrapolations proved to be at all accurate.

- **Future Farmers of America (FFA):** An American youth organization promoting and supporting agricultural education via middle and high school classes [**REAL**]. The organization operated a chapter in Hill Valley [**BTF1**].

- **Future Furnishings:** A display at the 1931 Hill Valley Exposition, featured in tandem with the Atlas House of Glass (a futuristic, modular living space), and offering a prediction of how homes might someday be laid out. Its slogan: "For a push-button world" [**TLTL-5**].

- **Future of Law Enforcement, The:** A display at the 1931 Hill Valley Exposition, featuring a number of prototype weapons and tools for police officers. The exhibit was presented by Detective Daniel Parker [**TLTL-5**].

   NOTE: "The Future of Law Enforcement" was the title of the pilot episode of RoboCop: The Series *and its spinoff comic book from Marvel Comics.*

- **Futuristic Potatoes in a Flavorful Glamour Reagan Scramble:** A menu item sold at Café 80's in 2015 [**BTF2**].

- **FXD:** *See* Nemotech FXD

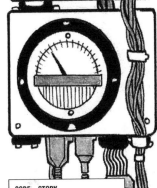

CODE	STORY
NIKE	*BTTF*-themed TV commercial: Nike
NTND	Nintendo *Back to the Future—The Ride* Mini-Game
PIZA	*BTTF*-themed TV commercial: Pizza Hut
PNBL	Data East *BTTF* pinball game
REAL	Real life
RIDE	Simulator: *Back to the Future—The Ride*
SCRM	2010 Scream Awards: *Back to the Future 25th Anniversary Reunion* (broadcast)
SCRT	2010 Scream Awards: *Back to the Future 25th Anniversary Reunion* (trailer)
SIMP	Simulator: *The Simpsons Ride*
SLOT	*Back to the Future Video Slots*
STLZ	Unused *BTTF* footage of Eric Stoltz as Marty McFly
STRY	*Back to the Future Storybook*
TEST	Screen tests: Crispin Glover, Lea Thompson and Tom Wilson
TLTL	Telltale Games' *Back to the Future—The Game*
TOPS	Topps' *Back to the Future II* trading-card set
TRIL	*BTTF: The Official Book of the Complete Movie Trilogy*
UNIV	Universal Studios Hollywood promotional video

SUFFIX	MEDIUM
-b	*BTTF2's* Biff Tannen Museum video (extended)
-c	Credit sequence to the animated series
-d	Film deleted scene
-n	Film novelization
-o	Film outtake
-p	1955 phone book from *BTTF1*
-v	Video game print materials or commentaries
-s1	Screenplay (draft one)
-s2	Screenplay (draft two)
-s3	Screenplay (draft three)
-s4	Screenplay (draft four)
-sp	Screenplay (production draft)
-sx	Screenplay (*Paradox*)

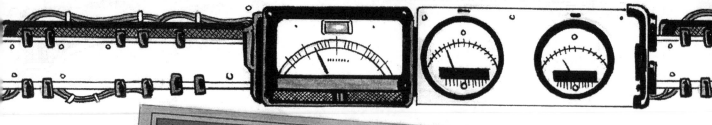

★ G R A Y S ★

SPORTS
ALMANAC

COMPLETE SPORTS STATISTICS

1950–2000

INCLUDING
BASEBALL, FOOTBALL
BOXING, HORSERACING
AND MORE!

GRAYS SPORTS ALMANAC

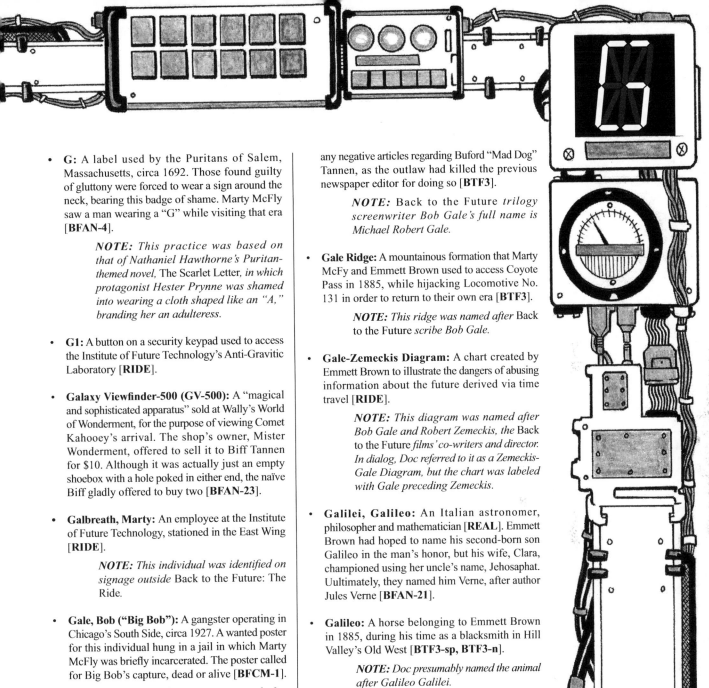

- **G:** A label used by the Puritans of Salem, Massachusetts, circa 1692. Those found guilty of gluttony were forced to wear a sign around the neck, bearing this badge of shame. Marty McFly saw a man wearing a "G" while visiting that era [**BFAN-4**].

    NOTE: This practice was based on that of Nathaniel Hawthorne's Puritan-themed novel, The Scarlet Letter, *in which protagonist Hester Prynne was shamed into wearing a cloth shaped like an "A," branding her an adulteress.*

- **G1:** A button on a security keypad used to access the Institute of Future Technology's Anti-Gravitic Laboratory [**RIDE**].

- **Galaxy Viewfinder-500 (GV-500):** A "magical and sophisticated apparatus" sold at Wally's World of Wonderment, for the purpose of viewing Comet Kahooey's arrival. The shop's owner, Mister Wonderment, offered to sell it to Biff Tannen for $10. Although it was actually just an empty shoebox with a hole poked in either end, the naïve Biff gladly offered to buy two [**BFAN-23**].

- **Galbreath, Marty:** An employee at the Institute of Future Technology, stationed in the East Wing [**RIDE**].

    NOTE: This individual was identified on signage outside Back to the Future: The Ride.

- **Gale, Bob ("Big Bob"):** A gangster operating in Chicago's South Side, circa 1927. A wanted poster for this individual hung in a jail in which Marty McFly was briefly incarcerated. The poster called for Big Bob's capture, dead or alive [**BFCM-1**].

    NOTE: This character was named after Bob Gale, who co-wrote the Back to the Future *films.*

- **Gale, Bob, Dr.:** An employee at the Institute of Future Technology's director of audiotronics [**RIDE**].

    NOTE: This individual, identified on signage outside Back to the Future: The Ride, *was named after the co-writer of the* Back to the Future *films.*

- **Gale, M.R.:** The editor of *The Hill Valley Telegraph* in 1885. Gale was reluctant to publish any negative articles regarding Buford "Mad Dog" Tannen, as the outlaw had killed the previous newspaper editor for doing so [**BTF3**].

    NOTE: Back to the Future trilogy screenwriter Bob Gale's full name is Michael Robert Gale.

- **Gale Ridge:** A mountainous formation that Marty McFy and Emmett Brown used to access Coyote Pass in 1885, while hijacking Locomotive No. 131 in order to return to their own era [**BTF3**].

    NOTE: This ridge was named after Back to the Future *scribe Bob Gale.*

- **Gale-Zemeckis Diagram:** A chart created by Emmett Brown to illustrate the dangers of abusing information about the future derived via time travel [**RIDE**].

    NOTE: This diagram was named after Bob Gale and Robert Zemeckis, the Back to the Future *films' co-writers and director. In dialog, Doc referred to it as a Zemeckis-Gale Diagram, but the chart was labeled with Gale preceding Zemeckis.*

- **Galilei, Galileo:** An Italian astronomer, philosopher and mathematician [**REAL**]. Emmett Brown had hoped to name his second-born son Galileo in the man's honor, but his wife, Clara, championed using her uncle's name, Jehosaphat. Uultimately, they named him Verne, after author Jules Verne [**BFAN-21**].

- **Galileo:** A horse belonging to Emmett Brown in 1885, during his time as a blacksmith in Hill Valley's Old West [**BTF3-sp, BTF3-n**].

    NOTE: Doc presumably named the animal after Galileo Galilei.

- **galloping Galileo:** An expression used by Emmett Brown to denote shock or surprise [**BFAN-3, BFAN-11, BFAN-13, BFAN-15, BFAN-20, BFAN-21**].

    NOTE: This phrase referred to Italian astronomer Galileo Galilei. In the comic book adaptation of "Forward to the Past," Doc used the phrase "Great galloping Galileo."

- **gallopin' jigowatts:** A phrase used by Emmett Brown, denoting surprise [**BFCM-4**].

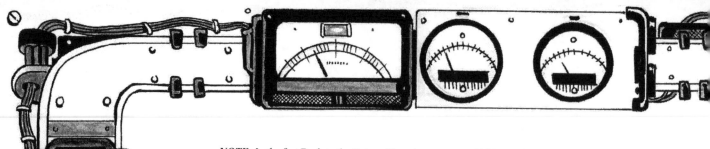

NOTE: *In the first* Back to the Future *film, Doc repeatedly yelled "1.21 jigowatts!" Although the correct spelling of the word is "gigawatt," the film's screenplay spelled it "jigowatt," which is also how actor Christopher Lloyd pronounced it.*

- **Game Grid**: A 1980s computer video game, the film version of which Marty McFly considered superior [**TLTL-3**].

  NOTE: Game Grid *is a fictional title. In the film* Tron *and its spinoff video games, the Game Grid was a simulation environment in which programs fought in various gladiatorial games, including Light Cycle, Disc Arena and the Ring Game.*

- **Game of Life, The:** A Milton Bradley board game, also called LIFE, simulating players' travels through life, including college, employment, marriage, children and retirement [**REAL**]. The McFly family had the game in their home in 1985 [**BTF1**].

- **Gannon Canyon:** A gorge in Hill Valley. In order to send Marty McFly back to 1985, the 1967 version of Emmett Brown used power lines strung above Gannon Canyon to generate the necessary electricity for the DeLorean's Flux Capacitor [**BTF2-s1**].

- **Gannon Canyon Museum:** An institution that sold Native American artifacts in Hill Valley, circa 1967. The small building was located along Canyon Road [**BTF2-s1**].

- **garb:** A slang term used in 2015, meaning "to speak about" [**BTF2-n**].

- **Garbarino:** A retail electronics store chain in Argentina [**REAL**]. Emmett Brown discovered the retailer's Buenos Aires location after traveling to the year 2011. Amazed at the many modern gadgets available there for purchase, he became a television commercial spokesperson for the company [**GARB**].

- **Garber, Mary Ellen ("Meg"):** *See* Baines McFly, Lorraine

- **Garcia, Thomas A.:** An employee at the Institute of Future Technology, in charge of cryogenic studies [**RIDE**].

NOTE: *This individual, identified on signage outside* Back to the Future: The Ride, *was named after an employee at Universal Studios.*

- **Garden Center:** A floating fruit basket used in home kitchens, circa 2015. Calling out "Fruit" or "Hey, fruit" would summon the Garden Center to descend from the ceiling, offering a variety of fresh fruit items. Once a selection was made, the user would say "Retract," and the device would then ascend out of sight. Marty and Jennifer McFly had a Garden Center in their home that was sometimes slow to respond [**BTF2**].

- **Garfield, Steve:** A contact person at THOR, a business listed in a 1991 help-wanted ad that Emmett Brown read while searching for a job. His telephone number was 818-710-1800 [**BFAN-12**].

- **Gary, Mark, A.S.C.:** A Hollywood professional, circa 2015, who helped director Max Spielberg create *Jaws 19*, according to the film's poster [**BTF2**].

- **Gastrosensory Slider:** A section of the control panel used to recondition inmates' minds at the Citizen Plus Ward, in Citizen Brown's dystopian timeline. Pushing this slider forced a subject to endure stomach discomfort. Marty McFly, posing as a security guard, manipulated this control while trying to help Emmett Brown escape the complex; in so doing, he inadvertently caused his friend a great deal of pain [**TLTL-4**].

- **Gates, Katherine:** An employee at the Institute of Future Technology, in charge of creative illusions [**RIDE**].

  NOTE: *This individual's name appeared on signage outside* Back to the Future: The Ride.

- **Gault, Bob:** An employee at the Institute of Future Technology, stationed in the East Wing [**RIDE**].

  NOTE: *This individual, identified on signage outside* Back to the Future: The Ride, *was named after Universal Studios' president and CEO.*

- **Gaynor's Hideaway:** A business in Courthouse Square, circa 1985 [**BTF1**].

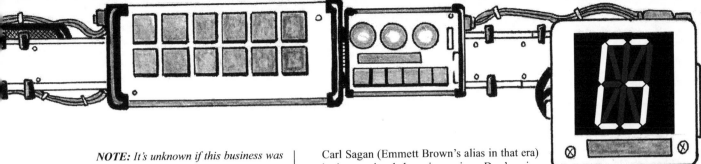

NOTE: It's unknown if this business was related to Hansen, Misetich & Gaynor, mentioned on a 1955 billboard advertising the building of Lyon Estates. Both were named after Albert N. Gaynor, a member of the art department that helped to create the Back to the Future *films. The novelization noted that its customers were enjoying drinks, implying that Gaynor's Hideaway was either a bar or a lounge.*

- **General Electric:** An American corporation involved in numerous industries, including consumer goods [**REAL**]. Emmett Brown had a coffee maker manufactured by this company, set to automatically brew at specified times each day [**BTF1**].

  NOTE: Universal Pictures, which produced the Back to the Future *films, became a subsidiary of General Electric from 2004 until it was sold to cable provider Comcast in 2010. In essence, the inclusion of the coffee maker served as prophetic product placement for the company's own goods. (See also entries for "Electric, General" and "G.E. Superconductors.")*

- **Gen'l Mercantile:** A business in Hill Valley, circa 1885, that sold boots, shoes, clothing and fancy dry goods [**BTF3**].

- *George & Lorraine 50th Anniversary:* A videobook in the house of Marty and Jennifer McFly, circa 2015. When Jennifer's younger self from 1985 visited her future home, she saw this and other videobooks stored on a shelf [**BTF2-sx, BTF2-n**].

- **George F. McFly Memorial Wing:** An emergency facility at the Hill Valley Community Hospital, christened in 2015 in honor of George McFly [**BTF2-s1**].

  NOTE: Although George's middle name was stated in BTTF2 as being Douglas, that movie's first-draft screenplay indicated his middle initial to be F.

- **Georgetown:** A city in El Dorado County, California [**REAL**]. When a speakeasy in Georgetown was destroyed by an arsonist in 1931, journalist Edna Strickland claimed drifter

Carl Sagan (Emmett Brown's alias in that era) had committed the crime, given Doc's prior arrest for torching Irving "Kid" Tannen's Hill Valley speakeasy. In reality, Edna herself was responsible for both blazes, as well as a third in Colfax [**TLTL-2**].

- **G.E. Superconductors:** A business operating in 2015 [**BTF2-sx, BTF2-s1**].

  NOTE: Given the name, the firm would appear to have grown out of General Electric.

- **GF:** A produce supplier in Citizen Brown's dystopian timeline. A box from this company was among the trash in an alley in which Jennifer Parker sometimes spray-painted graffiti [**TLTL-3**].

- **GH:** A business located in Hill Valley, circa 2015 [**RIDE**].

- **Ghost of Christmas:** A disguise used by Marty McFly to frighten miser Ebiffnezer Tannen into changing his ways. Donning a robe and bringing Tannen around 1845 London on a hoverboard, Marty showed him many images of poverty and inequity, including children forced to work on Christmas Eve. Tannen was unmoved, however, until viewing a 3-D monster film similar to *Godzilla* [**BFAN-10**].

  NOTE: Marty based his ghost disguise on the Ghosts of Christmas Past, Present and Yet to Come, who haunted Ebenezer Scrooge in Charles Dickens' 1843 novella A Christmas Carol. *When Tannen asked which one he was, Marty improvised, "All of the above."*

- **giant amplifier:** *See* amplifier

- **Gibson ES-345:** A type of semi-acoustic electric guitar produced by Gibson Guitar Corp., an American manufacturer of guitars and other instruments [**REAL**]. In 1955, musician Marvin Berry played a red ES-345 while performing with his band, Marvin Berry and the Starlighters. Marty McFly filled in for Berry at the Enchantment Under the Sea Dance when the guitarist injured his hand [**BTF1**].

  NOTE: Although Berry utilized an ES-345 in 1955, this model was not introduced until 1959. In 1955, Gibson offered an

CODE	STORY
NIKE	*BTTF*-themed TV commercial: Nike
NTND	Nintendo *Back to the Future—The Ride* Mini-Game
PIZA	*BTTF*-themed TV commercial: Pizza Hut
PNBL	Data East *BTTF* pinball game
REAL	Real life
RIDE	Simulator: *Back to the Future—The Ride*
SCRM	2010 Scream Awards: *Back to the Future* 25th Anniversary Reunion (broadcast)
SCRT	2010 Scream Awards: *Back to the Future* 25th Anniversary Reunion (trailer)
SIMP	Simulator: *The Simpsons Ride*
SLOT	*Back to the Future Video Slots*
STLZ	Unused *BTTF* footage of Eric Stoltz as Marty McFly
STRY	*Back to the Future Storybook*
TEST	Screen tests: Crispin Glover, Lea Thompson and Tom Wilson
TLTL	Telltale Games' *Back to the Future—The Game*
TOPS	Topps' *Back to the Future II* trading-card set
TRIL	*BTTF: The Official Book of the Complete Movie Trilogy*
UNIV	Universal Studios Hollywood promotional video

SUFFIX	MEDIUM
-b	*BTTF2*'s Biff Tannen Museum video (extended)
-c	Credit sequence to the animated series
-d	Film deleted scene
-n	Film novelization
-o	Film outtake
-p	1955 phone book from *BTTF1*
-v	Video game print materials or commentaries
-s1	Screenplay (draft one)
-s2	Screenplay (draft two)
-s3	Screenplay (draft three)
-s4	Screenplay (draft four)
-sp	Screenplay (production draft)
-sx	Screenplay (*Paradox*)

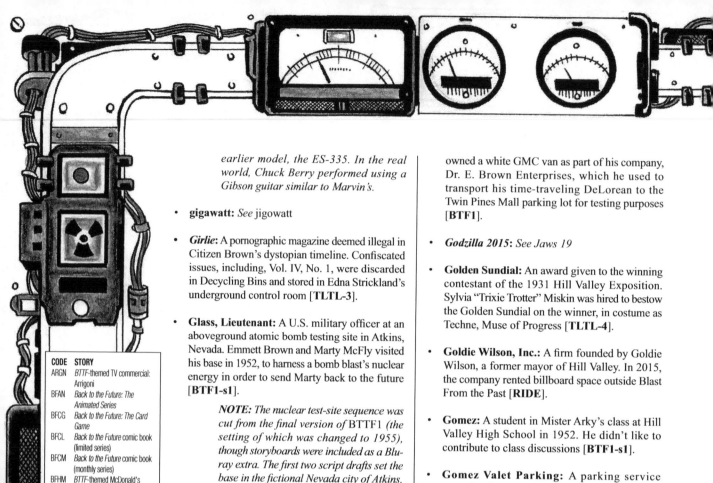

earlier model, the ES-335. In the real world, Chuck Berry performed using a Gibson guitar similar to Marvin's.

- **gigawatt:** *See* jigowatt

- *Girlie*: A pornographic magazine deemed illegal in Citizen Brown's dystopian timeline. Confiscated issues, including, Vol. IV, No. 1, were discarded in Decycling Bins and stored in Edna Strickland's underground control room [**TLTL-3**].

- **Glass, Lieutenant:** A U.S. military officer at an aboveground atomic bomb testing site in Atkins, Nevada. Emmett Brown and Marty McFly visited his base in 1952, to harness a bomb blast's nuclear energy in order to send Marty back to the future [**BTF1-s1**].

    NOTE: The nuclear test-site sequence was cut from the final version of BTTF1 (the setting of which was changed to 1955), though storyboards were included as a Blu-ray extra. The first two script drafts set the base in the fictional Nevada city of Atkins, while the third moved it to New Mexico.

- **Gleason, Jackie:** A popular American actor and comedian, best known for his role as Ralph Kramden on *The Honeymooners* [**REAL**]. In 1985, Marty McFly's father, George McFly, enjoyed watching that series while eating dinner. While in 1955, Marty discovered that the family of his mother, Lorraine Baines, also watched Gleason's show at dinnertime [**BTF1**].

    NOTE: The episode shown in both eras was "The Man From Space"—which, in the real world, aired on Dec. 31, 1955, almost two months after Marty's arrival in the past.

- **Glee Club Car Wash:** An event held in 1955 at Hill Valley High School. Marty McFly passed a poster advertising the car wash while trying to retrieve *Grays Sports Almanac* from Vice-Principal Gerald Strickland's office [**BTF2**].

- **Glendale:** A city in Los Angeles County, California [**REAL**]. A company known as Computec was located in this city [**BFAN-12**].

- **GMC:** A truck and van manufacturer marketed by General Motors Co. [**REAL**]. Emmett Brown owned a white GMC van as part of his company, Dr. E. Brown Enterprises, which he used to transport his time-traveling DeLorean to the Twin Pines Mall parking lot for testing purposes [**BTF1**].

- *Godzilla 2015*: *See Jaws 19*

- **Golden Sundial:** An award given to the winning contestant of the 1931 Hill Valley Exposition. Sylvia "Trixie Trotter" Miskin was hired to bestow the Golden Sundial on the winner, in costume as Techne, Muse of Progress [**TLTL-4**].

- **Goldie Wilson, Inc.:** A firm founded by Goldie Wilson, a former mayor of Hill Valley. In 2015, the company rented billboard space outside Blast From the Past [**RIDE**].

- **Gomez:** A student in Mister Arky's class at Hill Valley High School in 1952. He didn't like to contribute to class discussions [**BTF1-s1**].

- **Gomez Valet Parking:** A parking service operating in 2015, employees of which wore a dapper blazer and tie [**BTF2-s1**].

    NOTE: In BTTF2's first-draft script, Marty McFly worked for this company, rather than for CusCo.

- **Goodwill Industries:** A local business in Courthouse Square, circa 1985, located next to Statler Toyota, on the former site of Ruth's Frock Shop [**BTF1**].

- **Goodyear Tire and Rubber Co.:** A tire manufacturer for automobiles and other vehicles [**REAL**]. Emmett Brown used Goodyear's Eagle GT tires on the DeLorean DMC-12 sports car that he converted into a time machine [**BTF1**].

- **Gorbachev Goulash Rambo:** A menu item sold at Café 80's in 2015 [**BTF2**].

- **Gordos Blowtorch Repairs Servyce:** A business that operated in Hill Valley, circa 1991 [**BFAN-10**].

    NOTE: A thermometer in the home of Emmett Brown advertised this business. The thermometer misspelled "service" and "repair," and mis-punctuated "Gordo's."

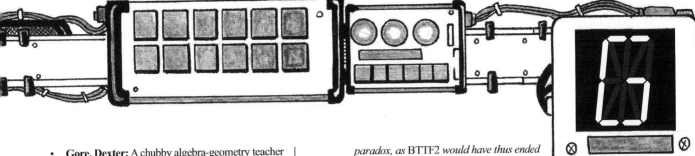

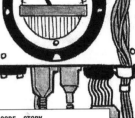

- **Gore, Dexter:** A chubby algebra-geometry teacher at Hill Valley High School, circa 1955. Gore served as a school-appointed chaperone to the Enchantment Under the Sea Dance that year, but was more interested in refreshments than dancing [**BTF1-n**].

- **Gormé, Eydie:** An early-20th-century singer of ballads and swing tunes [**REAL**]. In 1955, Roy's Records, located in Courthouse Square, displayed her album *Eydie in Dixlieland* in its front window [**BTF1**].

- *Grays Sports Almanac: Complete Sports Statistics 1950-2000*: A magazine containing the results of five decades' worth of sporting events. Published by Earl Hays Publishing Co., the book was edited by Paul Grumrine, and compiled by Ben Flores, Tom Hoffarth, Sharon Jaeger, Norman Rubinstein and Mickey Bell.

  Marty McFly purchased the almanac at the Blast From the Past antique shop in 2015, hoping to become rich by betting on games for which he knew the outcome. Discovering Marty's intention, Emmett Brown discarded the magazine in order to protect the timeline. Biff Tannen, who'd witnessed the exchange, stole the almanac and Doc's DeLorean, traveled to 1955 and gave the book to his younger self. This changed history by making Biff a powerful, dangerous millionaire. Marty and Doc restored the timeline, however, by following him back to 1955 and retrieving the almanac, which Marty then destroyed by setting it ablaze [**BTF2**].

  The Institute of Future Technology later obtained the almanac and returned it to Blast From the Past in 2015. Emmett Brown feared that the same thing would happen, however, so he purchased the book and threw it back into the trash [**RIDE**].

  > *NOTE: The almanac's editor and compilers were named on the book's title page.*

  > *In* Back to the Future II*'s first-draft screenplay, Marty purchased the almanac at an "infostore" called The Library, rather than at Blast From the Past. In that script, the book was titled* 2015 Sports Almanac: 50 Years of Sports Statistics 1965-2014. *In the film's novelization, it was called* Grey's Sports Almanac 1950-2000.

  > *IFT removing the almanac from the past would seem to have created a major* paradox, *as BTTF2 would have thus ended differently. It could be that the 2015 visit seen in the ride may have preceded the film's events, and that either the shop's staff found the book in the trash and simply put it back in the window for sale—thereby enabling it to be available for Marty to purchase—or the store may simply have had more than one copy of the almanac.*

  > *What's more, Doc's decision to discard it a second time would hardly prevent a recurrence anyway, given that the almanac was presumably just one copy from a larger print run, and not the only one produced.*

- **great balls of combustion manifested in light and heat:** An expression used by Emmett Brown to denote surprise, analogous to "great balls of fire" [**BFAN-5**].

- **Greater Hill Valley Medfield Basin:** A site in Hill Valley, at which Emmett Brown inadvertently broke every window while testing an untried scientific invention in 1961 [**BFAN-3**].

- **great galloping Galileo:** *See* galloping Galileo

- **Great Pyramid of Giza, The:** The largest and oldest of the three pyramids in Egypt's Giza Necropolis, considered one of the Seven Wonders of the Ancient World [**REAL**].

  Its builders initially designed the structure to balance point-down, with its width increasing with elevation. When Emmett Brown knocked it over after bumping into it with the *Jules Verne Train*, however, the pyramid flipped over and landed point-up—a design that pleased its builders more than the original concept [**BFAN-15**].

  After Doc visited this site, a photo commemorating the occasion was displayed at Doc Brown's Chicken [**CHIC**].

- **Great Satan Special:** *See* Hostage Special

- **Great Satan Special Pepsi Pie:** A menu item sold at Café 80's in 2015 [**BTF2**].

- *Great Scientists of the Twentieth Century*: A television documentary that aired in 1992. Emmett Brown looked forward to watching this broadcast, hoping he might be among those mentioned [**BFAN-15**].

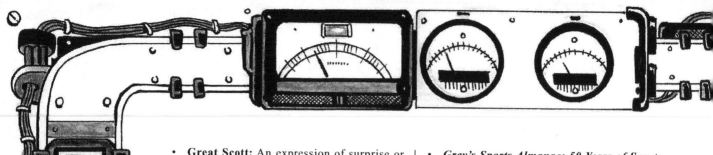

Great Scott: An expression of surprise or amazement frequently used by Emmett Brown [**BTF1**].

> *NOTE: The film's novelization substituted the phrase "Jumping Jehovah," while Doc's preferred phrase in the animated series was "Jumping Jigowatts."*

Great Sphinx of Giza, The: The largest statue on Earth, depicting a reclining sphinx (a mythical creature with a lion's body and a human head), located on Egypt's Giza Plateau [**REAL**]. After traveling 3,000 years into the past, Emmett and Verne Brown angered the ancient Egyptians by placing a large fake nose, mustache and eyeglasses on the statue's face [**BFAN-4**]. When Emmett Brown's Extradimensional Storage Closet malfunctioned in 1992, warping the fabric of spacetime, one door of his house now opened to Egypt, near the site of the Sphinx [**BFCL-3**].

Greek Theatre: An amphitheater located in Los Angeles' Griffith Park, built in 1929 and managed by the Nederlander Organization [**REAL**]. In 1985, as a group of teenagers visited the venue to attend a Loverboy rock concert, a time-traveling DeLorean suddenly arrived outside the entrance. As the excited teens ran toward the vehicle, the occupant—clad in a radiation suit—switched the car's time circuits to bring him to the site of the 2010 Scream Awards [**SCRM**].

Greetings From the Moon: A phrase appearing on a postcard hanging on Marty McFly's bedroom wall in 1986 [**TLTL-1**].

> *NOTE: This postcard's slogan paid homage to* Bright Side of the Moon, *a* Sam and Max *video game produced by Telltale Games.*

Greg: One of at least two boyfriends of Linda McFly (another being Craig) in a time-altered 1985 in which the McFly family was confident and successful [**BTF1**].

Greta: A holographic robot that welcomed travelers to the Tunnel Tubeway, a form of high-speed public travel used in Hill Valley, circa 2091. Greta greeted each car at the Tubeway's entrance and requested its destination, after which the system carried the vehicle to the proper coordinates in mere seconds [**BFAN-9**].

Grey's Sports Almanac: 50 Years of Sports Statistics 1950-2000: *See Grays Sports Almanac: Complete Sports Statistics 1950-2000*

Griffith, D.W.: An American pioneer film director whose works included *The Birth of a Nation* and *Intolerance* [**REAL**]. At age seven, D.W. lived in Hill Valley's Old West, where he witnessed Marty McFly defeating Buford Tannen by using a stove door as a shield during a duel. Amazed at such ingenuity, the child asked Marty how he came up with the idea. Marty replied that he'd seen it in a Clint Eastwood movie, and that the boy would eventually find out what a movie was [**BTF3-sx, BTF3-sp, BTF3-sn**].

> *NOTE: David Llewelyn Wark "D. W." Griffith was a pioneering film director of the early 20th century. Since he was born in 1875, his age at the time of* BTTF3 *(set in 1885 onscreen and in 1888 in an early screenplay titled* Paradox*) does not jibe with actual history.*

grip-shoes: A type of footwear sold by Nike in 2015, enabling a wearer to run up curved walls [**BTF2-s1**]. Grip shoes were used on slamball courts, enabling players to run around spherical courts, on walls and upside-down [**BTF2-s2**].

Groby Road Bridge: A Hill Valley structure washed out by a storm in 1973. When George McFly was critically injured that year in a car accident, County General was thus inaccessible, so he was treated at Hill Valley Community Hospital [**BTF2-s1**].

Grossman, Lev, Doctor: A scientist who offered a presentation at the 1931 Hill Valley Exposition [**TLTL-5**].

> *NOTE: Novelist and journalist Lev Grossman writes about science and technology in the real world.*

Ground Round: A racehorse that competed in 1931. Ground Round was among several horses mentioned during a radio broadcast as Marty McFly and Emmett Brown attempted to steal liquor from Irving "Kid" Tannen's speakeasy [**TLTL-1**].

> *NOTE: Ground Round Grill & Bar is an American casual dining restaurant franchise, founded by Howard Johnson's*

CODE	STORY
ARGN	*BTTF*-themed TV commercial: Arrigoni
BFAN	*Back to the Future: The Animated Series*
BFCG	*Back to the Future: The Card Game*
BFCL	*Back to the Future comic book (limited series)*
BFCM	*Back to the Future comic book (monthly series)*
BFHM	*BTTF*-themed McDonald's Happy Meal boxes
BTFA	*Back to the Future Annual (Marvel Comics)*
BTF1	Film: *Back to the Future*
BTF2	Film: *Back to the Future Part II*
BTF3	Film: *Back to the Future Part III*
BUDL	*BTTF*-themed TV commercial: Bud Light
CHEK	*BTTF*-themed music video: O'Neal McKnight, "Check Your Coat"
CHIC	Photographs hanging in the Doc Brown's Chicken restaurant at Universal Studios
CITY	*BTTF*-themed music video: Owl City, "Deer in the Headlights"
CLUB	*Back to the Future Fan Club Magazine*
DCTV	*BTTF*-themed TV commercial: DirecTV
ERTH	*The Earth Day Special*
GALE	Interviews and commentaries: Bob Gale and/or Robert Zemeckis
GARB	*BTTF*-themed TV commercials for Garbarino
HUEY	*BTTF*-themed music video: Huey Lewis and the News, "The Power of Love"
LIMO	*BTTF*-themed music video: The Limousines, "The Future"
MCDN	*BTTF*-themed TV commercial: McDonald's
MITS	*BTTF*-themed TV commercial: Mitsubishi Lancer
MSFT	*BTTF*-themed TV commercial: Microsoft

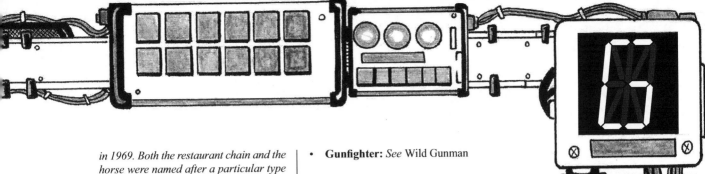

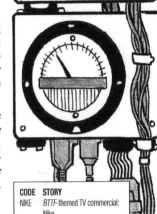

in 1969. Both the restaurant chain and the horse were named after a particular type of ground beef.

- **Grumrine, Paul:** The editor of *Grays Sports Almanac: Complete Sports Statistics 1950-2000* [**BTF2**].

    NOTE: This individual was named on the book's title page.

- **Guess:** An American clothing manufacturer, founded in 1981 [**REAL**]. In 1985, high school student Marty McFly wore a two-tone blue and grey denim Guess Marciano jacket with bottom cinching, adorned with an "Art in Revolution" decorative pin [**BTF1**]. That same jacket, including the pin, was among the items available for sale at Blast From the Past, an antique and collectibles shop in 2015 Hill Valley [**BTF2**].

- **guitar amplifier:** *See* amplifier

- **Gums:** *See* 3-D

- **Gunfighter:** *See* Wild Gunman

- **Gunthar, Sergeant:** A soldier at a U.S. government aboveground atomic bomb testing site in Atkins, Nevada, which Emmett Brown and Marty McFly visited in 1952, in order to harness a bomb blast's nuclear energy to power a time machine and send Marty back to the future [**BTF1-s1**].

    NOTE: The nuclear test-site sequence was cut from the final version of BTTF1 (the setting of which was changed to 1955), though storyboards were included as a Blu-ray extra. The first two script drafts set the base in the fictional Nevada city of Atkins, while the third moved it to New Mexico.

- **Gut Twister, The:** A ride at the Mega Monster Mountain amusement park. Jules Brown was very fond of this attraction, which consisted of two vertically moving arms, each ending in a car filled with occupants [**BFAN-25**].

CODE	STORY
NIKE	*BTTF*-themed TV commercial: Nike
NTND	Nintendo *Back to the Future—The Ride* Mini-Game
PIZA	*BTTF*-themed TV commercial: Pizza Hut
PNBL	Data East *BTTF* pinball game
REAL	Real life
RIDE	Simulator: *Back to the Future—The Ride*
SCRM	2010 Scream Awards: *Back to the Future* 25th Anniversary Reunion (broadcast)
SCRT	2010 Scream Awards: *Back to the Future* 25th Anniversary Reunion (trailer)
SIMP	Simulator: *The Simpsons Ride*
SLOT	*Back to the Future Video Slots*
STLZ	Unused *BTTF* footage of Eric Stoltz as Marty McFly
STRY	*Back to the Future Storybook*
TEST	Screen tests: Crispin Glover, Lea Thompson and Tom Wilson
TLTL	Telltale Games' *Back to the Future—The Game*
TOPS	Topps' *Back to the Future II* trading-card set
TRIL	*BTTF: The Official Book of the Complete Movie Trilogy*
UNIV	Universal Studios Hollywood promotional video

SUFFIX	MEDIUM
-b	*BTTF2*'s Biff Tannen Museum video (extended)
-c	Credit sequence to the animated series
-d	Film deleted scene
-n	Film novelization
-o	Film outtake
-p	1955 phone book from *BTTF1*
-v	Video game print materials or commentaries
-s1	Screenplay (draft one)
-s2	Screenplay (draft two)
-s3	Screenplay (draft three)
-s4	Screenplay (draft four)
-sp	Screenplay (production draft)
-sx	Screenplay (*Paradox*)

HOVERBOARDS

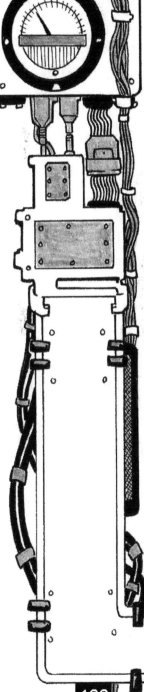

- **Hack:** *See* Unger, Rafe ("Data")

- **Haircut Omatic:** A hair-grooming helmet designed by Emmett Brown, containing comb, brush and scissors attachments. The device had three settings— "high school football buzz cut," "bald-man wash and wax" and "executive clean-cut and trim"—but sometimes malfunctioned, creating a series of constantly changing haircuts, including punk, beehive, bouffant, powdered-wig and other male and female styles. Marty McFly discovered this aspect upon donning the device before Doc had perfected it [**BFAN-25**].

- **hairdryer:** A handheld electrical device used to dry a person's hair [**REAL**]. In 1985, Emmett Brown owned a hairdryer manufactured by Conair [**BTF1-s4**].

    When Marty McFly traveled back to 1955, Brown, while looking through his older self's suitcase, was befuddled by the concept of a hairdryer, wondering if people still used towels in 1985. Marty later utilized the device to simulate a futuristic "heat ray" gun while posing as an extraterrestrial to convince George McFly to ask Lorraine Baines to the Enchantment Under the Sea Dance [**BTF1-d**].

- **HAL 9000:** An employee at the Institute of Future Technology's director of audiotronics [**RIDE**].

    NOTE: This individual or entity, identified on signage outside Back to the Future: The Ride, *paid homage to the computer of Arthur C. Clarke's* 2001: A Space Odyssey *and its three sequels.*

- **Half Show, The:** A television series broadcast in Hill Valley, circa 1992. The show—the characters of which Jules Brown described as "juvenile martial-arts mutations"—was extremely popular with children [**BFAN-20**].

    NOTE: The Half Show was apparently similar to Teenage Mutant Ninja Turtles, *often described as "heroes in a half-shell."*

- **Hal's Bike Shop:** A business in Courthouse Square, circa 1955 [**BTF1**].

- **Hal's Hardware:** A business in Hill Valley, established in 1895. Hal's Hardware sponsored the Courthouse of the Future attractive at the 1931 Hill Valley Exposition [**TLTL-4**].

- **Hamiltonian Operator:** A term in quantum mechanics referring to the operator (a function acting on the space of physical states) corresponding to a system's total energy [**REAL**].

    When Marty McFly visited 1931 to rescue Emmett Brown from jail, he encountered the scientist's 17-year-old self, who was unable to solve the equation for Ivanov's Conundrum, which began with "H to the A, multiplied by the inverse of A." Marty asked the older Doc about this equation, and was told the answer—that H equaled the Hamiltonian Operator [**TLTL-1**].

- *Hamlet* (a.k.a. *The Tragical History of Hamlet, Prince of Denmark*): A tragedy written by William Shakespeare, sometime between 1599 and 1601. The play involved a Danish prince who feigned insanity in order to avenge his father's murder [**REAL**]. Emmett Brown and his wife, Clara, attended a performance of *Hamlet* starring its original cast, using their DeLorean to visit Shakespeare's era [**BFAN-16**].

- **Hammer:** One of several names that Marty McFly and Verne Brown urged Jules Verne to adopt, since Verne (who'd been named in the novelist's honor) hated the name Verne [**BFAN-21**].

    NOTE: Rap star Stanley Kirk Burrell— better known as MC Hammer—was very popular during Verne's childhood.

- **Hampton:** A British butler who, in 1931, worked at Emmett Brown's family mansion in Hill Valley [**TLTL-5**].

- **Handy's Houseware Hut**: A business located in Hill Valley, circa 1991, that sold mattresses and other home products [**BFAN-12**].

- **Hanley Park Cemetery:** *See* Oak Park Cemetery

- **Hansen & Misetich:** A painting and decorating business in Hill Valley, circa 1955 [**BTF1**].

- **Hansen, Misetich & Gaynor:** A business in Hill Valley that oversaw the construction of Lyon Estates in 1955 [**BTF1**].

    NOTE: Presumably, this business was connected to Hansen & Misetich. Both were named after Albert N. Gaynor, a member of the art department that helped to create the Back to the Future *films. The construction*

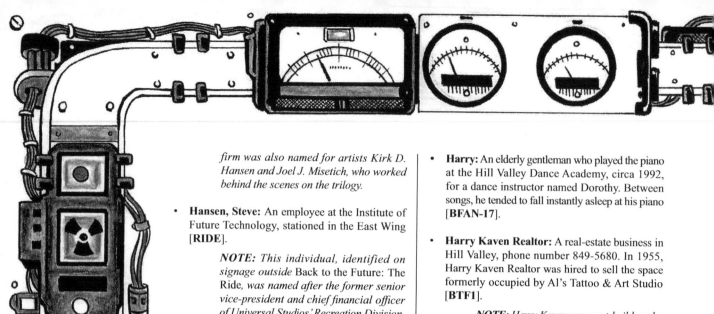

firm was also named for artists Kirk D. Hansen and Joel J. Misetich, who worked behind the scenes on the trilogy.

- **Hansen, Steve:** An employee at the Institute of Future Technology, stationed in the East Wing [**RIDE**].

    NOTE: This individual, identified on signage outside Back to the Future: The Ride, *was named after the former senior vice-president and chief financial officer of Universal Studios' Recreation Division.*

- **Happy Dinet:** A restaurant located in Hill Valley, circa 1991 [**BFAN-7b**].

    NOTE: This business' name would appear to be a misspelling of "dinette."

- **Happy Face ("Smiley"):** A stylized representation of a smiling human face, common in popular culture, and marketed as "Smiley" in 1972 by Franklin Loufrani [**REAL**]. Several Smiley buttons were among the items for sale at Blast From the Past, an antique and collectibles shop in 2015 Hill Valley [**BTF2**].

- **Hardware Hut:** A business located in Hill Valley. Emmett Brown sometimes purchased supplies at this store for his experiments. Its owner was a very short man with a bald head and a New England accent [**BFAN-22**].

- **Harold:** A seven-year-old African-American youth who lived in Marty McFly's former home in Lyon Estates, in Biffhorrific 1985. He and his sister, Loretta, lived with their parents, Lewis and Louise. Marty—unaware that time had changed, and that he thus didn't live there anymore—climbed into the window of what was once his bedroom, causing young Loretta to scream, and Lewis to furiously chase him out of the house with a baseball bat, mistaking Marty as one of Biff's enforcers, sent to bully them into selling their house [**BTF2**].

    NOTE: The family was unnamed onscreen, though Loretta and Harold were identified in the end credits. BTTF2's novelization identified the father as Lewis, while the movie's first-draft script named the wife Louise.

- **Harrison:** *See* Needles, Douglas J.

- **Harry:** An elderly gentleman who played the piano at the Hill Valley Dance Academy, circa 1992, for a dance instructor named Dorothy. Between songs, he tended to fall instantly asleep at his piano [**BFAN-17**].

- **Harry Kaven Realtor:** A real-estate business in Hill Valley, phone number 849-5680. In 1955, Harry Kaven Realtor was hired to sell the space formerly occupied by Al's Tattoo & Art Studio [**BTF1**].

    NOTE: Harry Kaven was a set-builder who worked on the Back to the Future *films.*

- **hasta la bye-bye:** Biff Tannen's unique misconstruing of the phrase "hasta la vista" [**RIDE**].

- **Hat Hut:** A shop at the Mega Monster Mountain amusement park that sold a variety of souvenir headwear [**BFAN-25**].

- **Havoline:** A motor oil brand marketed by Texaco [**REAL**]. The Texaco station in 2015 Hill Valley sold Havoline oil [**BTF2**].

- **Hawaiian Shirt Thursday:** A mandate of Hill Valley's dress code in Citizen Brown's dystopian timeline. On this day each week, citizens were required to wear identical Hawaiian shirts [**TLTL-3**].

- **Hay, Clifford C., Dr.:** The Institute of Future Technology's director of audiotronics [**RIDE**].

    NOTE: This individual, identified on signage outside Back to the Future: The Ride, *was named after Clifford Hay, who helped to design the ride.*

- **Haysville:** A town located near Hill Valley, circa 1885. When Marty McFly visited that era, he discovered that the local marshal had traveled to Haysville to attend the hanging of outlaw Stinky Lomax [**BTF3**].

    In an alternate timeline in which Edna Strickland changed history by preventing Hill Valley from being founded, Haysville was built 25 miles from where Hill Valley would have been located [**TLTL-5**].

- *Haysville Herald:* A newspaper published in the town of Haysville, in an alternate timeline in

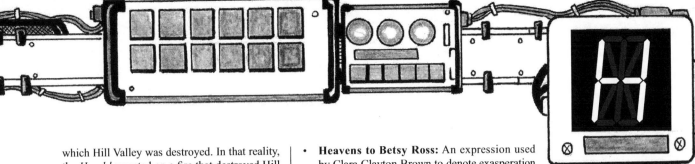

which Hill Valley was destroyed. In that reality, the *Herald* reported on a fire that destroyed Hill Valley in 1876, due to Edna Strickland accidentally burning down the entire town [**TLTL-5**].

- **Haysville Mercantile Deliveries:** An alternate version of Hill Valley Mercantile Deliveries, in a timeline created when Edna Strickland accidentally burned down Hill Valley. That reality's William McFly worked for this business in 1931 [**TLTL-5**].

- **Headlight "Tit":** A breast-enhancement product offered by Bottoms Up, a plastic-surgery franchise, circa 2015. The company offered the Headlight "Tit" as a two-for-one sale [**BTF2**].

- *Headline Comics:* A comic book published in the 1950s, containing "stories from true police and FBI cases" [**REAL**]. In 1955, Biff Tannen's friend 3-D owned the September/October 1954 issue, #67, titled "The River Pirates," about crime reporter Joe Condon [**BTF1**].

- **Headroom, Max:** A fictional artificial-intelligence (AI) character portrayed by actor Matt Frewer. Max Headroom was featured on several 1980s television series, and was known for his stuttering, electronically sampled voice [**REAL**].

  At the Café '80s, a theme restaurant in 2015 Hill Valley, computer simulations of Ronald Reagan, Michael Jackson and Iranian Grand Ayatollah Khomeini greeted visitors, each featuring Max Headroom's mannerisms and stylish appearance [**BTF2**].

- **heat ray:** A fictional handheld weapon that Marty McFly conceived in 1955 while posing as Darth Vader, from the planet Vulcan, in order to convince George McFly to ask Lorraine Baines to the Enchantment Under the Sea Dance. The so-called "heat ray" was actually a 1980s Conair hairdryer from Emmett Brown's suitcase [**BTF1-d**].

- **Heat-Seeking Rat Trap:** An invention of Emmett Brown, comprising a motorized windup mousetrap on wheels with a miniaturized dish for tracking vermin [**BFAN-15**].

- **"Heaven Is One Step Away":** A song recorded by Eric Clapton in 1985 [**REAL**]. This tune was playing on the radio as Marty McFly disturbed a sleeping bum named Red upon returning from the past in the DeLorean [**BTF1**].

- **Heavens to Betsy Ross:** An expression used by Clara Clayton Brown to denote exasperation [**BFAN-6**].

  NOTE: *This patriot was historically credited with creating the first American flag. Clara's use of this phrase in "Go Fly a Kite" was ironic, as 1752 (Ross' birth year) was the same year that Clara's son, Verne Brown, visited in that episode.*

- **Heavens to Kepler:** An expression used by Emmett Brown to express sincerity, analogous to "Heavns to Betsy" [**BFAN-6, BFAN-10**].

  NOTE: *This phrase referenced German mathematician Johannes Kepler.*

- **heavy:** A slang term meaning "of great significance or profundity." Marty McFly often used this term when confronted with something he considered amazing or astounding. Variation: "heavy-duty" [**BTF1**].

- *Heavy:* The title of a rock-and-roll album among the contraband confiscated by Edna Strickland in Citizen Brown's dystopian timeline [**TLTL-3**].

  NOTE: *This was an in-joke reference to Marty McFly's pet phrase, "heavy."*

- **heavy-duty:** A variation of the phrase "heavy," sometimes used by Marty McFly to express amazement [**BTF1**].

- *He-Boy Gladiator Show:* A children's television series that aired on Channel 92, circa 1992, and was filmed at a studio in Hill Valley. Biff Tannen Jr. was a fan of this series [**BFAN-26**].

  NOTE: *This series' title was based on that of the* He-Man and the Masters of the Universe *franchise.*

- **Hell Hole:** An adult business in Hill Valley, in Biffhorrific 1985 [**BTF2**].

- **Hell Valley:** A nickname for Hill Valley in Biffhorrific 1985, in which Biff Tannen was a corrupt and powerful criminal who ruled the city from a penthouse apartment above his casino, Biff Tannen's Pleasure Paradise. In that reality, someone painted an "E" over the "I" in "Hill Valley" on the city's welcome sign [**BTF2**].

  NOTE: *The book* Back to the Future:

CODE	STORY
NIKE	*BTTF*-themed TV commercial: Nike
NTND	Nintendo *Back to the Future—The Ride* Mini-Game
PIZA	*BTTF*-themed TV commercial: Pizza Hut
PNBL	Data East *BTTF* pinball game
REAL	Real life
RIDE	Simulator: *Back to the Future—The Ride*
SCRM	2010 Scream Awards: *Back to the Future* 25th Anniversary Reunion (broadcast)
SCRT	2010 Scream Awards: *Back to the Future* 25th Anniversary Reunion (trailer)
SIMP	Simulator: *The Simpsons Ride*
SLOT	*Back to the Future* Video Slots
STLZ	Unused *BTTF* footage of Eric Stoltz as Marty McFly
STRY	*Back to the Future* Storybook
TEST	Screen tests: Crispin Glover, Lea Thompson and Tom Wilson
TLTL	Telltale Games' *Back to the Future—The Game*
TOPS	Topps' *Back to the Future II* trading-card set
TRIL	*BTTF: The Official Book of the Complete Movie Trilogy*
UNIV	Universal Studios Hollywood promotional video

SUFFIX	MEDIUM
-b	*BTTF2*'s Biff Tannen Museum video (extended)
-c	Credit sequence to the animated series
-d	Film deleted scene
-n	Film novelization
-o	Film outtake
-p	1955 phone book from *BTTF1*
-v	Video game print materials or commentaries
-s1	Screenplay (draft one)
-s2	Screenplay (draft two)
-s3	Screenplay (draft three)
-s4	Screenplay (draft four)
-sp	Screenplay (production draft)
-sx	Screenplay (*Paradox*)

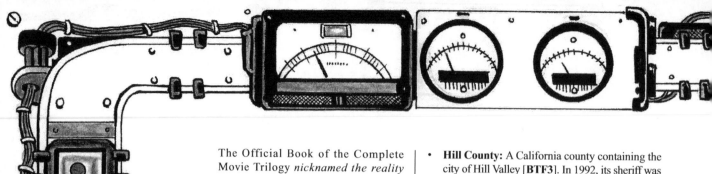

The Official Book of the Complete Movie Trilogy *nicknamed the reality "Biffhorrific." Another moniker, "Biff City," appeared in* BTTF2's *first-draft script, while the second draft called it "Tannen Valley."*

- **Helter Skelter:** A brand of hair dye used by Jennifer Parker in Citizen Brown's dystopian timeline. In this reality, Jennifer was a nonconformist punk-rocker who dyed her hair black, purple and yellow [**TLTL-3**].

  NOTE: A helter skelter is an amusement-park ride with a spiral slide built around a high tower. The term was used by murderer Charles Manson to predict an apocalyptic racial war between blacks and whites.

- **Henderson ("Happy-Feet"):** A vaudeville entertainer murdered by Irving "Kid" Tannen, in or before 1931. Kid's bartender, Zane Williams, illustrated a caricature of Happy-Feet Henderson for the Wall of Honor at the gangster's speakeasy, El Kid [**TLTL-v**].

- **Henry's Favorite Zodiac Paste With Red, White and Blue Sauce:** A menu item sold at Café 80's in 2015 [**BTF2**].

- ***Here Come the Robots:*** A textbook about robotics that Verne Brown referenced while writing a school essay on that subject [**BFCL-1**].

- **Hill, William ("Bill," "The Old Pioneer"):** The mule-riding founder of Hill Valley. A statue of the pioneer and his pack animal adorned the city [**BTF2-s1**].

  A revered folkloric figure, Bill Hill was honored each year during Hill Valley's Founder's Day celebration. When Emmett Brown caused a citywide brown-out on Founder's Day in 1992, a mob formed and society began breaking down. Clara Clayton Brown thus traveled back in time to bring the Old Pioneer to the future, so that he could reveal how the holiday was celebrated in the past, before the advent of electricity. With the crisis averted, she returned the grizzled old gentleman to his own era [**BFAN-22**].

- **Hill Billiards:** A pool hall in Hill Valley, circa 1931. The street address on its main front door was 8, printed as a stylized eight-ball [**TLTL-1**].

- **Hill County:** A California county containing the city of Hill Valley [**BTF3**]. In 1992, its sheriff was Andy Taylor, who worked with a deputy named Barney [**BFAN-22**].

  NOTE: Sheriff Andy Taylor, portrayed by late actor Andy Griffith, appeared on The Danny Thomas Show; The Andy Griffith Show; Gomer Pyle, U.S.M.C.; Mayberry R.F.D.; *and* Return to Mayberry. *Barney spoke similarly to—and was drawn to resemble—actor Don Knotts, who worked alongside Griffith as Deputy Barney Fife.*

- **Hilldale:** A high-class, suburban section of Hill Valley, circa 1985. By 2015, the area had degenerated, becoming a breeding ground for tranks, lobos and zipheads. Marty and Jennifer McFly lived here with their children, Marty Jr. and Marlene.

  Marty's teen self, upon time-traveling to 2015, was initially excited to learn that he'd end up in Hilldale. However, he soon discovered how poorly the area had fared in the three decades since his era, and was rather disappointed [**BTF2**].

- **Hilldale Waste Recylcing Station H 14 D:** A recycling facility located outside the entrance to the Hilldale housing development in 2015 [**BTF2**].

- **Hill Street—400:** A Hill Valley roadway populated by numerous local shops, and intersecting Main Street in Courthouse Square. Lou's Café was located on the corner of these two streets [**BTF1**].

- **Hill Valley:** A suburban town in California [**BTF1**], located in Hill County [**BTF2, BFAN-22**], in the vicinity of Los Angeles and Laguna Hills [**BFAN-12**]. Its zip code was 95420-4345 [**BTF2**], its slogan "Hill Valley—A Nice Place to Live" [**BTF1**].

  Hill Valley was founded in 1850 by settlers traveling the Oregon Trail as part of a wagon train. Clara Clayton's parents, Daniel Clayton and Martha O'Brien, were among that group [**BFAN-13**].

  The town was incorporated in 1865 [**TLTL-3**], and celebrated its 20th anniversary of townhood at the 1885 Hill Valley Festival, which was marked by the construction of the Hill Valley Courthouse, atop which was erected a large Clock Tower. The Shonash Ravine Bridge was built the following year, during the summer of 1886 [**BTF3**]. Hill Valley greatly increased its population in 1906, when a large number of displaced persons

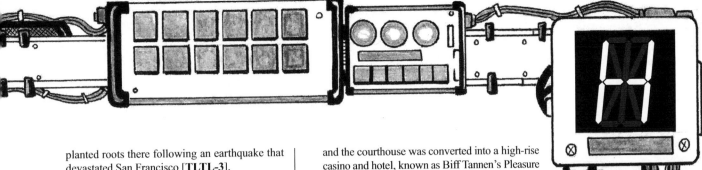

planted roots there following an earthquake that devastated San Francisco [**TLTL-3**].

The McFly, Brown, Baines, Parker, Tannen and Strickland families all had a long history as residents of Hill Valley. At the center of the city was Courthouse Square. Built around the courthouse and clock, the square contained numerous restaurants, shops and other businesses. At various points throughout its history, it also featured parkland, gardens, a gazebo and a manmade lake, with its aesthetic, character and socioeconomic status evolving from one generation to the next [**BTF1, BTF2, BTF3, BFAN-1 to BFAN-26, TLTL-1 to TLTL-5**].

Over time, the once-beautiful Hill Valley degenerated from a clean and upbeat town, in the 1950s, to a dirty, graffiti-littered and economically depressed suburban slum, by the 1980s. During this period, several businesses in Courthouse Square closed, some without replacement [**BTF1**]. By 2015, the downtown area experienced a revival, with the addition of many new businesses, and with the courthouse converted into the Courthouse Mall [**BTF2**].

By 2585, robotics were fully integrated into Hill Valley society, with a variety of automata performing almost all manual labor. This freed the city's population to concentrate on artistic and intellectual pursuits [**BFCL-1**]. Farther into the future—in 2,991,299,129,912,991 A.D., by which time North American civilization had degenerated to barbarism—the former Hill Valley was now a primitive village known as Hillvallia [**BFCL-2**].

Hill Valley's history and appearance were altered on a number of occasions, due to the temporal tamperings of Emmett Brown, Marty McFly and others. One major change occurred when Biff Tannen stole Doc's DeLorean in 2015 and traveled back to 1955, where he gave his younger self a copy of *Grays Sports Almanac: Complete Sports Statistics 1950-2000*. By knowing the outcomes of a half-century's worth of sporting events, Biff was able to repeatedly win large sums of money from betting on the results.

During the next three decades, Biff became an immensely wealthy and powerful criminal, who owned the police and ruled Hill Valley through fear and violence. In this "Biffhorrific" reality, Hill Valley transformed into a cesspool of sin and corruption, filled with adult entertainment, bars, a toxic-waste dump, biker-gang hangouts, casinos and filth. Hill Valley High School was burned down, teen gangs terrorized the streets,

and the courthouse was converted into a high-rise casino and hotel, known as Biff Tannen's Pleasure Paradise. Marty and Doc eventually discovered what Biff had done and repaired the timeline, restoring the city to its prior state [**BTF2**].

In another instance, Doc and his sons, Jules and Verne Brown, inadvertently prevented the extinction of the dinosaurs millions of years in the past, enabling the creatures to replace mankind as Earth's dominant animal lifeform. In that reality, Hill Valley evolved into a thriving society of sapient dinosaurs [**BFAN-3**], known as Dinocity [**BFHM**].

Marty brought about yet another change when he inadvertently caused 17-year-old Emmett Brown to fall in love with Edna Strickland in 1931. Smitten with the conservative Edna, the younger Brown abandoned science, embracing instead her conservative philosophies. With Edna by his side as his wife, Hill Valley became a pristine, self-sustaining, walled utopia with very strict rules of propriety—and with Doc as its benevolent dictator.

As First Citizen Brown, Doc promoted civil and social engineering, using Hill Valley as a prototype to show how technology could be utilized to shape a more efficient, orderly society. Under his rule, Hill Valley's citizens were mandated to live as vegetarians, wear ID badges and follow strict dress codes. Although he intended only good for the city, Edna's single-minded obsession with curtailing vice and subversion had perverted his ideals [**TLTL-3**].

Thanks to Marty's intervention, the elder Brown came to realize his mistakes, and agreed to help restore the timeline. The two returned to 1931 to break up Edna and young Emmett, hoping to eliminate the dystopian reality. However, the former dictator grew smitten with the younger Edna, and resented Marty's attempt to change his past. Ultimately, Brown betrayed Marty, allying instead with Edna [**TLTL-4**].

When Citizen Brown's attempt to stop Marty failed, Edna fled to 1876, where she accidentally burnt the entire city to the ground, starting with the Palace Saloon and Hotel. In the resultant timeline, Hill Valley was replaced by a new town, known as Haysville. Marty and Doc (now restored to his former, non-dictatorial self) followed her back to ascertain what she'd done. Upon learning of the 1876 fire, they headed her off before she could ignite the town, once again protecting Hill Valley's original appearance and character [**TLTL-5**].

NOTE: The first film's third-draft

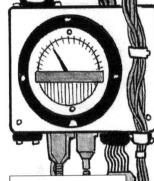

CODE	STORY
NIKE	*BTTF*-themed TV commercial: Nike
NTND	Nintendo *Back to the Future— The Ride* Mini-Game
PIZA	*BTTF*-themed TV commercial: Pizza Hut
PNBL	Data East *BTTF* pinball game
REAL	Real life
RIDE	Simulator: *Back to the Future—The Ride*
SCRM	2010 Scream Awards: *Back to the Future* 25th Anniversary Reunion (broadcast)
SCRT	2010 Scream Awards: *Back to the Future* 25th Anniversary Reunion (trailer)
SIMP	Simulator: *The Simpsons Ride*
SLOT	*Back to the Future* Video Slots
STLZ	Unused *BTTF* footage of Eric Stoltz as Marty McFly
STRY	*Back to the Future* Storybook
TEST	Screen tests: Crispin Glover, Lea Thompson and Tom Wilson
TLTL	Telltale Games' *Back to the Future—The Game*
TOPS	Topps' *Back to the Future II* trading-card set
TRIL	*BTTF: The Official Book of the Complete Movie Trilogy*
UNIV	Universal Studios Hollywood promotional video

SUFFIX	MEDIUM
-b	*BTTF2*'s Biff Tannen Museum video (extended)
-c	Credit sequence to the animated series
-d	Film deleted scene
-n	Film novelization
-o	Film outtake
-p	1955 phone book from *BTTF1*
-v	Video game print materials or commentaries
-s1	Screenplay (draft one)
-s2	Screenplay (draft two)
-s3	Screenplay (draft three)
-s4	Screenplay (draft four)
-sp	Screenplay (production draft)
-sx	Screenplay (*Paradox*)

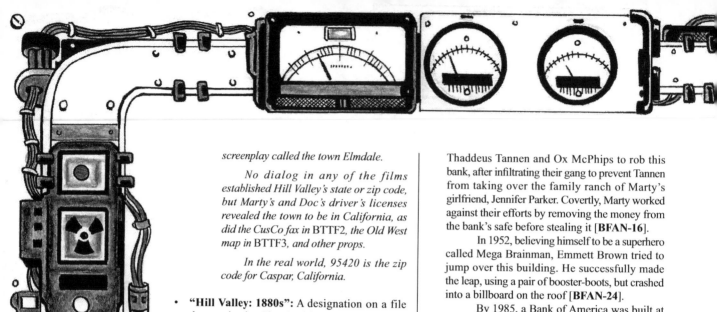

screenplay called the town Elmdale.

No dialog in any of the films established Hill Valley's state or zip code, but Marty's and Doc's driver's licenses revealed the town to be in California, as did the CusCo fax in BTTF2, the Old West map in BTTF3, and other props.

In the real world, 95420 is the zip code for Caspar, California.

- **"Hill Valley: 1880s":** A designation on a file drawer in the City Archives, located in the basement of Hill Valley City Hall. In 1955, Emmett Brown and Marty McFly accessed the records contained in this drawer after finding a gravestone revealing that Doc had been murdered in 1885 by Buford Tannen [**BTF3-n**].

- **Hill Valley 4-H Clubs:** The Hill Valley chapter of the 4-H Clubs [**BTF2**], a youth organization administered by the U.S. Department of Agriculture's National Institute of Food and Agriculture [**REAL**].

- **Hill Valley Airport:** A facility at which aircraft could take off and land, located near the Clayton Ravine [**BTF3-sx**].

- **Hill Valley Apartments:** A group of rooms for rent, circa 1931, located above the Hill Valley Bakery. The street address on its main front door was 10. These apartments served as a safe house for Irving "Kid" Tannen's gang. Arthur McFly lived here against his will while in Tannen's forced employ, until young Emmett Brown, working for his father, Judge Erhardt Brown, served him a subpoena to appear at the Hill Valley Courthouse [**TLTL-1**].

- **Hill Valley Army/Navy Store:** A business in Hill Valley, circa 1955. Emmett Brown and Marty McFly procured tools and supplies here before setting out to excavate Doc's DeLorean, buried since 1885 in the abandoned Delgado Mine [**BTF3-n**].

- **Hill Valley Bakery:** An eatery that served fresh bread and other comestibles, established in 1905. In 1931, the Hill Valley Apartments were located above the bakery [**TLTL-1**].

- **Hill Valley Bank:** A financial institution in Hill Valley, circa 1875. Marty McFly helped outlaws Thaddeus Tannen and Ox McPhips to rob this bank, after infiltrating their gang to prevent Tannen from taking over the family ranch of Marty's girlfriend, Jennifer Parker. Covertly, Marty worked against their efforts by removing the money from the bank's safe before stealing it [**BFAN-16**].

In 1952, believing himself to be a superhero called Mega Brainman, Emmett Brown tried to jump over this building. He successfully made the leap, using a pair of booster-boots, but crashed into a billboard on the roof [**BFAN-24**].

By 1985, a Bank of America was built at this location [**BTF1**].

- **Hill Valley Beach and Unsynchronized Swimming Center:** An outdoor area along Hill Valley's shoreline. In 1992, Emmett Brown used a Geiger counter to search for buried money in the sand on this beach, then spent the next week trying to locate his lost DeLorean keys [**BFAN-16**].

- **Hill Valley Bowl-o-rama:** A bowling alley at which Emmett Brown's family found themselves after a power surge to Doc's Extradimensional Storage Closet caused them to jump randomly around in time and space [**BFCL-3**].

- **Hill Valley Bulldogs:** A sports team of Hill Valley High School, circa 1955. A book cover for one of George McFly's textbooks bore an image of the team's bulldog mascot. Among their rivals was a team called the Indians [**BTF1**].

  NOTE: A Bulldogs vs. Indians poster hung in the school's hall when Marty McFly and Emmett Brown visited the facility to find Marty's parents. Bob Gale's junior high school team was the Bulldogs, while Gale's high school team was the Indians.

- **Hill Valley Bureau of Discipline:** The main government building of Hill Valley in Citizen Brown's dystopian timeline [**TLTL-3**].

- **Hill Valley Chamber of Commerce:** A network of local companies and organizations formed to further business interests in Hill Valley [**BTF1**].

- ***Hill Valley Chronicle*:** A newspaper published in Hill Valley. In 1952, this periodical ran an article about Emmett Brown's Small Town Professional Wrasslin match with Mad Maximus [**BFAN-24**].

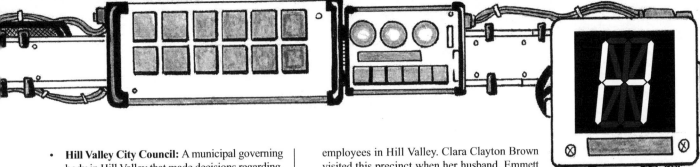

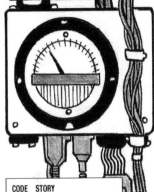

- **Hill Valley City Council:** A municipal governing body in Hill Valley that made decisions regarding, among other things, the approval of construction on hospitals, power plants and other facilities [**BTF2-s1**].

- **Hill Valley City Hall:** The administration building of Hill Valley's municipal government, circa 1955. Located within its basement was the City Archives. Emmett Brown and Marty McFly, upon finding a gravestone in Boot Hill Cemetery revealing that Doc had been murdered by Buford Tannen in 1885, consulted the archives to learn more about this event. The building would have been closed, but Doc was friendly with Charlie, the night watchman, who shared his passion for the Old West and let him bend the rules by accessing records after-hours [**BTF3-n**].

- **Hill Valley College:** An educational institution located in Hill Valley. Marty McFly and Jennifer Parker attended this school in 1991 [**BFAN-4, BFAN-12**].

- **Hill Valley Community Center:** An institution at which George McFly was slated to receive an award in Biffhorrific 1973, for his role as a long-time civic activist against the policies of BiffCo. This ceremony was interrupted, however, by George's murder at the hands of Biff Tannen [**BTF2**].

- **Hill Valley Community Hospital:** A vast medical complex built in 1973. Although many considered the hospital unnecessary and expensive, and though the City Council wanted to sell off the land to build a nuclear power plant, a lack of funding for the latter project ultimately facilitated the hospital's construction.

  When George McFly was critically injured in a car accident that same year, County General was inaccessible, so he was taken instead to Hill Valley Community Hospital. George later stipulated in his will that his fortune be donated to this hospital for a new emergency facility, the George F. McFly Memorial Wing [**BTF2-s1**].

  NOTE: *Although George's middle name of Douglas was revealed in* BTTF2, *that movie's first-draft screenplay indicated his middle initial to be F.*

- **Hill Valley Community Police Station:** A precinct for police officers and other law-enforcement employees in Hill Valley. Clara Clayton Brown visited this precinct when her husband, Emmett Brown, went missing in 1991 [**BFCM-4**].

- **Hill Valley Courthouse:** A structure in Courthouse Square that, in 1985, contained the local offices of California's Department of Social Services. Erected atop the building was a large Clock Tower [**BTF1**].

  Built in 1885, the courthouse was nearly the site of a hanging that year, when Buford Tannen attempted to kill Marty McFly by stringing him up from the building's unfinished structure. Emmett Brown, however, prevented the murder [**BTF3**].

  In 1931, at age 17, Emmett had worked here as a clerk, filing paperwork and serving subpoenas for his father, Judge Erhardt Brown [**TLTL-1**]. While testing a prototype Rocket Car, he accidentally stranded Einstein (his future dog, which had visited the past with the scientist's older self) on the courthouse's roof [**TLTL-2**].

  That same year, after breaking up with Edna Strickland, Emmett nearly fell from the courthouse roof when he lost his footing while sulking on the Clock Tower's ledge. Marty, however, rescued him from plummeting to his death [**TLTL-4**].

  In 1955, the courthouse was struck by lightning, permanently stopping the clock at 10:04 P.M. On the night of that storm, Emmett Brown harnessed the lightning's 1.21 jigowatts of energy to power the Flux Capacitor of his time-traveling DeLorean, thereby enabling Marty McFly to return to his own era. Thirty years later, Mayor Goldie Wilson tried to replace the clock, but the Hill Valley Preservation Society worked hard to retain its damaged condition, sponsoring a Save the Clock Tower Fund [**BTF1**].

  In Biffhorrific 1985, in which Biff Tannen was corrupt and powerful, the former courthouse was now a high-rise casino, known as the Biff Tannen Pleasure Paradise. Adjoining the casino were related businesses, Biff's Pleasure Palace and the Biff Tannen Museum [**BTF2**].

  In Citizen Brown's dystopian timeline, the courthouse was replaced by a vast, well-protected government building, with Emmett Brown's mayoral office housed behind the refurbished clock face [**TLTL-3**].

  By 2015, the edifice was transformed into a shopping center called Courthouse Mall, containing numerous underground shops. The Clock Tower was still non-functional during this era, and some activists, such as former auto mechanic Terry,

CODE	STORY
NIKE	*BTTF*-themed TV commercial: Nike
NTND	Nintendo *Back to the Future—The Ride* Mini-Game
PIZA	*BTTF*-themed TV commercial: Pizza Hut
PNBL	Data East *BTTF* pinball game
REAL	Real life
RIDE	Simulator: *Back to the Future—The Ride*
SCRM	2010 Scream Awards: *Back to the Future 25th Anniversary Reunion* (broadcast)
SCRT	2010 Scream Awards: *Back to the Future 25th Anniversary Reunion* (trailer)
SIMP	Simulator: *The Simpsons Ride*
SLOT	*Back to the Future Video Slots*
STLZ	Unused *BTTF* footage of Eric Stoltz as Marty McFly
STRY	*Back to the Future Storybook*
TEST	Screen tests: Crispin Glover, Lea Thompson and Tom Wilson
TLTL	Telltale Games' *Back to the Future—The Game*
TOPS	Topps' *Back to the Future II* trading-card set
TRIL	*BTTF: The Official Book of the Complete Movie Trilogy*
UNIV	Universal Studios Hollywood promotional video

SUFFIX	MEDIUM
-b	*BTTF2*'s Biff Tannen Museum video (extended)
-c	Credit sequence to the animated series
-d	Film deleted scene
-n	Film novelization
-o	Film outtake
-p	1955 phone book from *BTTF1*
-v	Video game print materials or commentaries
-s1	Screenplay (draft one)
-s2	Screenplay (draft two)
-s3	Screenplay (draft three)
-s4	Screenplay (draft four)
-sp	Screenplay (production draft)
-sx	Screenplay (*Paradox*)

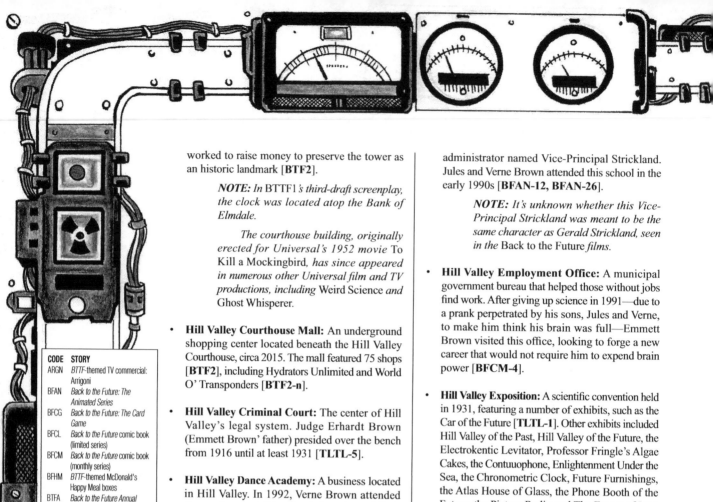

worked to raise money to preserve the tower as an historic landmark [**BTF2**].

> **NOTE:** *In* BTTF1*'s third-draft screenplay, the clock was located atop the Bank of Elmdale.*

> *The courthouse building, originally erected for Universal's 1952 movie* To Kill a Mockingbird, *has since appeared in numerous other Universal film and TV productions, including* Weird Science *and* Ghost Whisperer.

- **Hill Valley Courthouse Mall:** An underground shopping center located beneath the Hill Valley Courthouse, circa 2015. The mall featured 75 shops [**BTF2**], including Hydrators Unlimited and World O' Transponders [**BTF2-n**].

- **Hill Valley Criminal Court:** The center of Hill Valley's legal system. Judge Erhardt Brown (Emmett Brown' father) presided over the bench from 1916 until at least 1931 [**TLTL-5**].

- **Hill Valley Dance Academy:** A business located in Hill Valley. In 1992, Verne Brown attended dance classes at this school, but showed little prowess with the waltz, much to the frustration of his instructor, Dorothy [**BFAN-17**].

- **Hill Valley Department of Records:** An agency of Hill Valley's local government that stored the archived records of the Hill Valley Historical Society. After discovering his own gravestone in Boot Hill Cemetery, Emmett Brown accessed the department's files on Buford Tannen, recorded as having killed Doc in 1885 [**BTF3**].

- **Hill Valley Dreamers:** A local baseball team, circa 1992, that played at the Hill Valley Stadium and Swap-Meet Grounds. The team had a reputation for frequently losing, and thus drew few attendees to its games [**BFAN-25**].

- **Hill Valley Dump:** A refuse dumping site in Hill Valley, circa 2091. All vehicles entering the Tunnel Tubeway public-transit system without first registering their destination were automatically re-routed to the Violation Center—an exit tube into the Hill Valley Dump [**BFAN-9**].

- **Hill Valley Elementary School**: A primary education institution in Hill Valley, with an administrator named Vice-Principal Strickland. Jules and Verne Brown attended this school in the early 1990s [**BFAN-12, BFAN-26**].

> **NOTE:** *It's unknown whether this Vice-Principal Strickland was meant to be the same character as Gerald Strickland, seen in the* Back to the Future *films.*

- **Hill Valley Employment Office:** A municipal government bureau that helped those without jobs find work. After giving up science in 1991—due to a prank perpetrated by his sons, Jules and Verne, to make him think his brain was full—Emmett Brown visited this office, looking to forge a new career that would not require him to expend brain power [**BFCM-4**].

- **Hill Valley Exposition:** A scientific convention held in 1931, featuring a number of exhibits, such as the Car of the Future [**TLTL-1**]. Other exhibits included Hill Valley of the Past, Hill Valley of the Future, the Electrokentic Levitator, Professor Fringle's Algae Cakes, the Contuuophone, Enlightenment Under the Sea, the Chronometric Clock, Future Furnishings, the Atlas House of Glass, the Phone Booth of the Future, the Picture Radio and The Future of Law Enforcement [**TLTL-4**]. To promote the exposition, a large banner was displayed near the Hill Valley Courthouse [**TLTL-2**].

The expo was held at Hill Valley High School. Accountant Arthur McFly was put in charge of money and contestant registration, as well as the employment and termination of workers, while Ernest Philpott oversaw set-up. Sylvia "Trixie Trotter" Miskin was hired to portray Techne, Muse of Progress, presenting contestants and serving as an inspiration for innovation. "Cue Ball" Donnely delivered goods to the high school, and also provided security during the expo [**TLTL-4**].

Citizen Brown—an alternate version of Emmett Brown who became not a scientist, but the leader of a police state—attended the expo to thwart Marty McFly from erasing his timeline. To that end, Brown kidnapped his younger self, hiding him from Marty within various exhibits, hoping to prevent young Emmett from exhibiting his invention, a flying car, and thus change history by quelling his interest in science. Marty found his young friend, however, and helped him carry out the demonstration, thereby ensuring Brown's career in the sciences [**TLTL-5**].

The *Hill Valley Telegraph* covered the event, with a headline of "Hill Valley Expo Delights

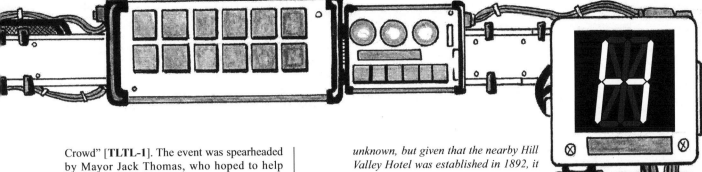

Crowd" [**TLTL-1**]. The event was spearheaded by Mayor Jack Thomas, who hoped to help the city become a magnet for big investors in the technology sector. It showcased cutting-edge technologies in order to burnish the city's reputation as a forward-thinking community. The venture folded after only three years, however, after an influenza exhibit leaked into the concession stand [**TLTL-4**]

> *NOTE: A sign inside the event bore the slogan "Hill Valley Science and Technology Exposition." All exterior signage, however, simply read, "Hill Valley Exposition."*

- **Hill Valley Fairgrounds:** An area of land in Hill Valley used to host public venues, such as the Bob Brothers All-Star International Circus. The fairgrounds were located on a portion of the Tannen Farm, owned by Mac Tannen [**BFAN-18**].

- **Hill Valley Father and Son Big Mouth Bass Off:** An annual event in Hill Valley. In 1991, Emmett Brown refused to take his sons, Verne and Jules, to the Bass Off, due to a lifelong fear of fish. After the boys went back in time to alter history, preventing him from developing the phobia in the first place, the scientist happily took them on the fishing trip [**BFAN-11**].

- **Hill Valley Festival:** An outdoor event held in September 1885 to raise funds to construct the city's Clock Tower. The festival featured dancing, food, games and product demonstrations. During the celebration, Buford "Mad Dog" Tannen confronted Emmett Brown over a disputed bill for $80; this led to Doc's death at the outlaw's hands, until Marty McFly altered history by rescuing his friend from the past [**BTF3**].

- **Hill Valley Fire Department (HVFD):** An organization that provided emergency firefighting and rescue services for Hill Valley. The HVFD sponsored a Visitor's Day in 1955, and posted fliers around town, inviting citizens to attend [**BTF2**].

- **Hill Valley General Store:** A business operating in the late 1800s, during Hill Valley's Old West period, that sold a variety of merchandise—clothing, pots and pans, food, picture frames and more—in a small, confined space. Clara Clayton Brown shopped at this store after returning to this era [**BFHM**].

> *NOTE: The exact year of Clara's visit is*

unknown, but given that the nearby Hill Valley Hotel was established in 1892, it would appear her patronage occurred sometime near the turn of the 20th century.

- **Hill Valley Gifts:** A business in Courthouse Square, circa 2015 [**BTF2**].

- **Hill Valley Hardware:** A business located in Hill Valley, circa 1991. Emmett Brown considered this shop among his favorite places to visit [**BFAN-7b**]. Doc had a calendar from this store hanging in his laboratory [**BFCM-3**].

- *Hill Valley Herald*: A newspaper published in Hill Valley. In 1931, Edna Strickland was a reporter for this publication, as well as for the *Hill Valley Telegraph* [**TLTL-1**].

> A *Herald* headline on Apr. 1, 1991, read "Doc Brown Loses Mind," thanks to a prank pulled by Emmett Brown's sons, Jules and Verne [**BFCM-4**].

- **Hill Valley High Future Homemakers:** A club operating at Hill Valley High School, circa 1955. This group met weekly, on Wednesdays [**BTF1**].

> *NOTE: A poster for this club hung in the high school's hall when Marty McFly and Emmett Brown visited the school to find Marty's parents.*

- **Hill Valley High Jitterbug Jam:** A dance competition in which Emmett Brown once placed second thanks to one of his inventions, the Fance-o-Dance Memorizing Shoes, which enabled him to perform a variety of fancy steps [**BFAN-17**].

> *NOTE: Hill Valley's citizens apparently had a great fondness for dancing the jitterbug, given the existence of both the Hill Valley High Jitterbug Jam and the Hill Valley Jitterbugging Contest.*

- **Hill Valley High School (HVHS):** A public secondary education facility located in the town of Hill Valley [**BTF1**]. Its mascot was a greased pig [**BFAN-22**]. As early as 1955 and as late as 1985, its vice-principal was Gerald Strickland [**BTF1**].

> Marty McFly attended Hill Valley High in 1985, along with his girlfriend, Jennifer Parker. Three decades prior, Marty's parents, George McFly and Lorraine Baines McFly, had attended the school as well [**BTF1**]. Emmett Brown also

CODE	STORY
NIKE	*BTTF*-themed TV commercial: Nike
NTND	Nintendo *Back to the Future—The Ride* Mini-Game
PIZA	*BTTF*-themed TV commercial: Pizza Hut
PNBL	Data East *BTTF* pinball game
REAL	Real life
RIDE	Simulator: *Back to the Future—The Ride*
SCRM	2010 Scream Awards: *Back to the Future* 25th Anniversary Reunion (broadcast)
SCRT	2010 Scream Awards: *Back to the Future* 25th Anniversary Reunion (trailer)
SIMP	Simulator: *The Simpsons Ride*
SLOT	*Back to the Future* Video Slots
STLZ	Unused *BTTF* footage of Eric Stoltz as Marty McFly
STRY	*Back to the Future* Storybook
TEST	Screen tests: Crispin Glover, Lea Thompson and Tom Wilson
TLTL	Telltale Games' *Back to the Future—The Game*
TOPS	Topps' *Back to the Future II* trading-card set
TRIL	*BTTF: The Official Book of the Complete Movie Trilogy*
UNIV	Universal Studios Hollywood promotional video

SUFFIX	MEDIUM
-b	*BTTF2*'s Biff Tannen Museum video (extended)
-c	Credit sequence to the animated series
-d	Film deleted scene
-n	Film novelization
-o	Film outtake
-p	1955 phone book from *BTTF1*
-v	Video game print materials or commentaries
-s1	Screenplay (draft one)
-s2	Screenplay (draft two)
-s3	Screenplay (draft three)
-s4	Screenplay (draft four)
-sp	Screenplay (production draft)
-sx	Screenplay (*Paradox*)

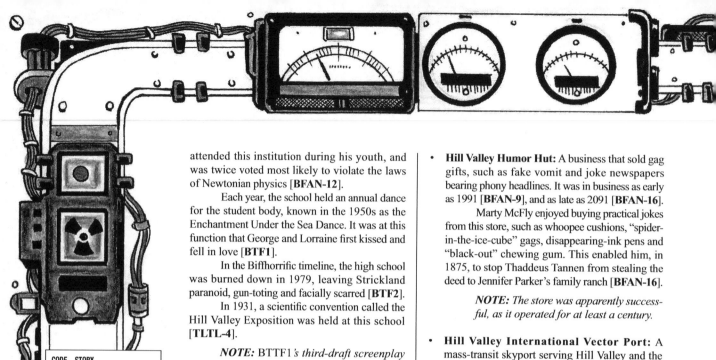

attended this institution during his youth, and was twice voted most likely to violate the laws of Newtonian physics [**BFAN-12**].

Each year, the school held an annual dance for the student body, known in the 1950s as the Enchantment Under the Sea Dance. It was at this function that George and Lorraine first kissed and fell in love [**BTF1**].

In the Biffhorrific timeline, the high school was burned down in 1979, leaving Strickland paranoid, gun-toting and facially scarred [**BTF2**].

In 1931, a scientific convention called the Hill Valley Exposition was held at this school [**TLTL-4**].

> **NOTE:** *BTTF1's third-draft screenplay called the school Elmdale High School.*
>
> *A deleted scene from* Back to the Future II *showed Marty viewing the school's burnt-out remains in the alternate 1985.*
>
> *The school used for Hill Valley High was actually Whittler High School, located in Whittler, California.*

- **Hill Valley Historical Society:** An institution established in 1875, devoted to preserving the city's history for posterity. It was also known as the Historical Society of Hill Valley [**TLTL-v**].

  After discovering his own gravestone in Boot Hill Cemetery, Emmett Brown accessed the Historical Society's records regarding Buford Tannen, who was recorded as having killed him in 1885 [**BTF3**].

- ***Hill Valley Historical Society, 1865-1990:*** A book produced by the Hill Valley Historical Society to celebrate the city's 125th anniversary, featuring portraits of numerous distinguished citizens of Hill Valley [**TLTL-v**].

- **Hill Valley Historical Society Archives:** An institution to which many of Emmett Brown's home and residence belongings were donated in 1986, when the scientist—stranded in 1931—was presumed dead or missing [**TLTL-v**].

- **Hill Valley Hotel:** A business operating in the late 1800s, during Hill Valley's Old West period. Established in 1892, this small, one-floor hotel had a wooden porch and a pair of swinging doors at its entrance. Emmett Brown visited the Hill Valley Hotel during a trip to that era, and noticed several oddities about it, including an upside-down clock hanging on its porch [**BFHM**].

- **Hill Valley Humor Hut:** A business that sold gag gifts, such as fake vomit and joke newspapers bearing phony headlines. It was in business as early as 1991 [**BFAN-9**], and as late as 2091 [**BFAN-16**].

  Marty McFly enjoyed buying practical jokes from this store, such as whoopee cushions, "spider-in-the-ice-cube" gags, disappearing-ink pens and "black-out" chewing gum. This enabled him, in 1875, to stop Thaddeus Tannen from stealing the deed to Jennifer Parker's family ranch [**BFAN-16**].

  > **NOTE:** *The store was apparently successful, as it operated for at least a century.*

- **Hill Valley International Vector Port:** A mass-transit skyport serving Hill Valley and the surrounding area, circa 2015 [**BTF2**].

- **Hill Valley Jitterbugging Contest:** A dance competition held in Hill Valley. The winners in 1944 were Verne Brown—who was visiting that era with Marty McFly—and a youthful version of Verne's future dance instructor, Dorothy. The event was emceed by Bobby "Doodles" Dawson [**BFAN-17**].

  > **NOTE:** *Hill Valley's citizens apparently had a great fondness for dancing the jitterbug, given the existence of both the Hill Valley High Jitterbug Jam and the Hill Valley Jitterbugging Contest.*

- **Hill Valley Junior Science Fair:** An event in which budding scientists could compete by presenting their innovations and inventions. In 1932, Emmett Brown submitted a videotape recorder with full 14-day programming capability. The device worked perfectly, but the television had yet to be invented [**BFAN-13**].

- **Hill Valley Livery Vehicle Hut:** A business that sold busses, trucks and other types of large vehicles, circa 1991. Biff Tannen purchased a custom-built, extra-deluxe Super-Winnelumbago at this establishment [**BFAN-20**].

- **Hill Valley Mall:** A shopping center located in Hill Valley. Its security guards were very persistent in pursuing troublemakers, such as Verne Brown [**BFAN-5**].

- **Hill Valley Mercantile Deliveries:** A commercial delivery company established in 1905. Marty McFly's great-grandfather, William McFly, worked for this business in 1931. When Edna Strickland

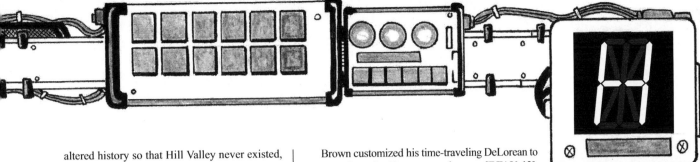

altered history so that Hill Valley never existed, this company was called Haysville Mercantile Deliveries—and Willie McFly was still an employee [**TLTL-5**].

- **Hill Valley Militia:** A citizen's military force that provided defense and emergency law enforcement in Hill Valley. When the city succumbed to mass hysteria during Comet Kahooey's arrival in 1992, over a possible extra-terrestrial invasion, the militia was among the organizations dispatched to the aliens' supposed hiding place—Emmett Brown's home [**BFAN-23**].

- **Hill Valley Museum of Art:** A museum that, in 2015, offered an exhibit called "A Bellman Retrospective" [**BTF2**].

- **Hill Valley of the Future:** An attraction at the 1931 Hill Valley Exposition, offering predictions of what the city would look like decades in the future [**TLTL-4**].

- **Hill Valley of the Past:** An attraction at the 1931 Hill Valley Exposition, exploring what the area containing the city was like during prehistoric times [**TLTL-4**].

- **Hill Valley Orphanage:** An organization for children without parents, circa 1931. Edna Strickland often delivered soup from the Sisters of Mercy Soup Kitchen to this establishment [**TLTL-1**].

- **Hill Valley Payroll Substation:** A financial institution in Hill Valley, located on 8th Street. Griff Tannen and his gang—Rafe "Data" Unger, Leslie "Spike" O'Malley and Chester "Whitey" Nogura—attempted to rob the Payroll Substation in 2015, and to set up Martin McFly Jr. to take the fall for the crime.

  Marty McFly Sr. prevented the incident, however, by time-traveling to 2015 with Emmett Brown, taking his son's place and refusing to take part in the robbery. Griff's gang tried to beat Marty up for this, chasing him through Courthouse Square on hoverboards, but ended up crashing through the Courthouse's glass window, for which the trio were arrested and jailed [**BTF2**].

- **Hill Valley Pioneer Days Parade:** A public event commemorating the United States' expansion in the 19th century. To take part in the parade, Emmett

Brown customized his time-traveling DeLorean to reconfigure itself as a covered wagon [**BFAN-13**].

- **Hill Valley Police Department (H.V.P.D.):** The local Hill Valley arm of California's law-enforcement agency [**BTF2, TLTL-1**]. By 2015, its members operated flying vehicles [**BTF2**].

- **Hill Valley Police Station:** The headquarters of the Hill Valley Police Department, built in 1891. In 1931, following the arsonist destruction of Irving "Kid" Tannen's speakeasy, Tannen's gang stormed the station and killed the arrested suspect—Emmett Brown, who was visiting that era posing as drifter Carl Sagan. Upon learning of this event from an article in the *Hill Valley Telegraph*, Marty McFly journeyed back in time to rescue his friend from the police station's jail cell [**TLTL-1**].

- **Hill Valley Power Station:** A facility that provided electricity to homes and businesses in Hill Valley. In 1991, Emmett Brown caused the power station to suffer a blackout, by over-taxing the grid with his scientific experiments [**BFAN-2**].

- **Hill Valley Preservation Society:** A civic group operating in Hill Valley. In 1985, the organization sponsored the Save the Clock Tower Fund, intended to halt an initiative sponsored by Mayor Goldie Wilson to replace the clock, which had been struck by lightning 30 years prior. The Preservation Society sought to keep the clock in its damaged condition, in order to preserve the town's history and heritage [**BTF1**].

- **Hill Valley Prison:** A penitentiary in which criminals were incarcerated behind electronic forcefields. In 2091, Griff Tannen and his grandson, Ziff Tannen, shared a cell at this complex [**BFAN-9**].

- **Hill Valley Railroad Station:** A stop along a Central Pacific Railroad line, circa 1885, at which Locomotive No. 131 dropped off and picked up passengers. Emmett Brown, while living in that era as a blacksmith, agreed to pick up Clara Clayton, the town's new teacher, at this station. He was delayed, however, resulting in her renting a buckboard and nearly plummeting to her death in the Shonash Ravine [**BTF3**].

- **Hill Valley Remedial School:** An educational institution for students with poor academic

CODE	STORY
NIKE	*BTTF*-themed TV commercial: Nike
NTND	Nintendo *Back to the Future—The Ride* Mini-Game
PIZA	*BTTF*-themed TV commercial: Pizza Hut
PNBL	Data East *BTTF* pinball game
REAL	Real life
RIDE	Simulator: *Back to the Future—The Ride*
SCRM	2010 Scream Awards: *Back to the Future* 25th Anniversary Reunion (broadcast)
SCRT	2010 Scream Awards: *Back to the Future* 25th Anniversary Reunion (trailer)
SIMP	Simulator: *The Simpsons Ride*
SLOT	*Back to the Future* Video Slots
STLZ	Unused *BTTF* footage of Eric Stoltz as Marty McFly
STRY	*Back to the Future Storybook*
TEST	Screen tests: Crispin Glover, Lea Thompson and Tom Wilson
TLTL	Telltale Games' *Back to the Future—The Game*
TOPS	Topps' *Back to the Future II* trading-card set
TRIL	*BTTF: The Official Book of the Complete Movie Trilogy*
UNIV	Universal Studios Hollywood promotional video

SUFFIX	MEDIUM
-b	*BTTF2*'s Biff Tannen Museum video (extended)
-c	Credit sequence to the animated series
-d	Film deleted scene
-n	Film novelization
-o	Film outtake
-p	1955 phone book from *BTTF1*
-v	Video game print materials or commentaries
-s1	Screenplay (draft one)
-s2	Screenplay (draft two)
-s3	Screenplay (draft three)
-s4	Screenplay (draft four)
-sp	Screenplay (production draft)
-sx	Screenplay (*Paradox*)

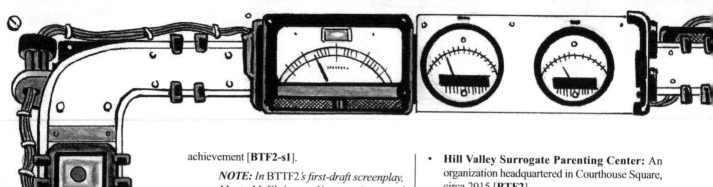

achievement [**BTF2-s1**].

> *NOTE: In* BTTF2*'s first-draft screenplay, Marty McFly's son, Norman (renamed Marty Jr. in the final movie) attended this school.*

- **Hill Valley Savings & Loan:** A bank that two thugs, named Sidney and Frankie, robbed in 1991. With no getaway car available, the thieves stole the nearest parked car: Emmett Brown's DeLorean, in which Doc's dog, Einstein, was resting. The vehicle's voice-activated time circuits mistook their conversation as a destination, and brought them to Sydney, Australia, circa 1790 [**BFAN-7b**].

- **Hill Valley Science and Technology Exposition:** *See* Hill Valley Exposition

- **Hill Valley Space Center and Air-Sickness Clinic:** A facility for amateur astronauts, housing a branch of NASA's Discovery Program. In 1992, Emmett Brown visited this space center to be suited up for a trip to outer space, in order to help a local cable company overhaul its communications satellite—in return for free cable service, including premium channels [**BFAN-15**].

- **Hill Valley Speedway:** A closed-circuit racing track that Marty McFly sometimes visited as a teenager. The speedway featured so-called "funny cars," of which Marty was reminded in 1955 after seeing the DeLorean fitted with 1950s tires and makeshift time circuits [**BTF3-n**].

- **Hill Valley Stadium and Swap-Meet Grounds:** A sports arena in Hill Valley, home to the Hill Valley Dreamers. Due to the baseball team's poor record, many of the stadium's seats often remained unoccupied [**BFAN-25**].

- **Hill Valley Stationers:** A stationary shop operating in Courthouse Square as early as 1931 [**TLTL-1**] and as late as 1955 [**BTF1**].

> *NOTE: This business, named Hill Valley Stationers onscreen, was called the Hill Valley Stationery Shop in* BTTF1*'s novelization.*

- **Hill Valley Stationery Shop:** *See* Hill Valley Stationers

- **Hill Valley Surrogate Parenting Center:** An organization headquartered in Courthouse Square, circa 2015 [**BTF2**].

- **Hill Valley Tar Pits:** A pool of natural asphalt, located at the future site of Hill Valley during prehistoric times [**TLTL-4**].

> *NOTE: Tar pits—caused by a sticky, black, viscous semi-solid substance called bitumen leaking to the Earth's surface—are known to exist only in a few places on Earth. California, the state containing Hill Valley, is among those places.*

- ***Hill Valley Telegraph:*** A local newspaper published in Hill Valley [**BTF1, BTF2, BTF3**], founded in 1871 [**TLTL-1**]. In 1885, its office was located just down the street from the Clock Tower. Its editor at that time was M.R. Gale [**BTF3**].

  The *Telegraph* reported on a number of notable events in the town's history, including the destruction by fire of Emmett Brown's mansion, the selling of 435 acres of land on the inventor's family estate to developers following bankruptcy, damage to the Clock Tower due to a lightning strike in 1955, and more [**BTF1**].

  Edna Strickland was once a reporter for this newspaper, and owned a complete collection of every issue from 1871 to 1986 [**TLTL-1**].

> *NOTE: Edna's newspapers, when knocked over by Marty McFly, all bore the same front-page headline: "Local Shopkeeper Robbed By Zombies."*

- ***Hill Valley Telegraph, March 1 – April 30, 1973:*** A hardbound collection of all *Telegraph* newspapers published during a two-month period of that year. Emmett Brown and Marty McFly consulted this book while researching George McFly's death at Biff Tannen's hands in the Biffhorrific timeline [**BTF2**].

- **Hill Valley Theater:** A movie theater in Hill Valley, that showed the film *Back to the Future* in 1992 [**BFAN-22**].

> *NOTE: Eric Stoltz was originally cast as Marty McFly, until being replaced by Michael J. Fox. The television series* Fringe *paid homage to this switch by featuring an alternate reality in which Stoltz starred in the film. It's unknown which actor starred*

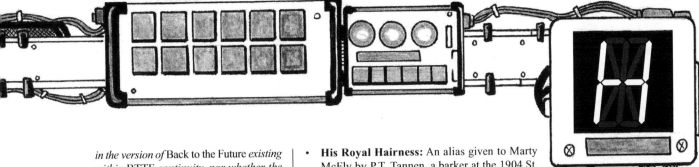

in the version of Back to the Future *existing within BTTF continuity, nor whether the movie featured McFly's exploits with Emmett Brown.*

- **Hill Valley Theater of Live Sex Acts:** An adult movie theater in the Biffhorrific version of Hill Valley, circa 1985 [**BTF2**].

- **Hill Valley Tourist Court:** A facility located along a highway, circa 1931. Marty McFly passed this building while trying to help Emmett Brown escape from a police vehicle stolen by Irving "Kid" Tannen, who planned to murder the scientist [**TLTL-1**].

- **Hill Valley Town Council:** The local elected government of Hill Valley [**BFCG**]. In one timeline, the council renamed Shonash Ravine as Clayton Ravine in 1885 following the death of Clara Clayton. In another, it chose the name Eastwood Ravine, in honor of Clint Eastwood (Marty McFly's alias in that era) [**BTF3, BFCG**].

- **Hill Valley Transit:** A business in Courthouse Square, circa 2015 [**BTF2**].

- **Hill Valley Transport:** A car service operating in 2015 [**BTF2**].

- **Hill Valley Unity:** A propaganda slogan used on government posters in Citizen Brown's dystopian timeline [**TLTL-3**].

- **Hill Valley University:** An educational facility at which Emmett Brown worked in 1967 as a science professor [**BTF2-s1**]. His boss at the college was Dean Wooster [**BTF3-s1**].

- **Hill Valley Women's Club:** An organization that held a bake sale in 1955, at a community center on Forest Road [**BTF2**].

- **Hillvallia:** A primitive village in former North America, circa 2,991,299,129,912,991 A.D., located in the empire of Calgon, on the site of former Hill Valley [**BFCL-2**].

    ***NOTE:** Many scientists believe Earth will cease to exist in approximately 7.6 billion years, with human life dying out within a billion years or so.*

- **His Royal Hairness:** An alias given to Marty McFly by P.T. Tannen, a barker at the 1904 St. Louis World Exposition, who made Marty the centerpiece of his attraction, PT. Tannen's House of Curiosity. Marty, having used one of Emmett Brown's inventions—the Haircut Omatic—faced ever-changing hairdos, including punk, beehive, bouffant, powdered-wig and other male and female styles. Tannen, realizing people would pay to see this, caged Marty and charged visitors admission to watch the changes [**BFAN-25**].

- **Historical Society of Hill Valley:** *See* Hill Valley Historical Society

- *History of Hill Valley: 1850-1930, A*: A hardbound book created by the Hill Valley Historical Society, containing an early 20th-century photograph of William McFly and his family. In 1955, Marty McFly and Emmett Brown came across this book and photo while researching how Buford Tannen murdered Doc in 1885 [**BTF3**].

- **Hitter:** A brand name of aluminum baseball bats, and a preferred weapon of Biff Tannen's crime family, the Tannen Gang, in an alternate version of 1986 [**TLTL-2**].

    In Citizen Brown's dystopian timeline, Biff Tannen used a Hitter bat to render George McFly unconscious so he could steal George's surveillance tapes for Edna Strickland. George's family utilized a different type of baseball bat, however, as McFlys *never* used aluminum bats [**TLTL-3**].

    ***NOTE:** Why the McFlys never use aluminum bats is unknown.*

- **HM Prison:** A penal facility in Sydney, Australia, circa 1790. The prison was run by warden Mongo P. Tannen. Two 20th-century thugs named Frankie and Sidney served time here after stealing Emmett Brown's DeLorean and ending up stranded in that era. Doc's dog, Einstein, freed them from captivity, then delivered them to the police in their own era [**BFAN-7b**].

    ***NOTE:** Presumably, "HM" stood for "His Majesty's," given the Australian setting.*

    In the animated series, Einstein was much smarter and more capable than his onscreen counterpart, and thus could stage prison breakouts and drive cars.

CODE	STORY
NIKE	*BTTF*-themed TV commercial: Nike
NTND	Nintendo *Back to the Future—The Ride* Mini-Game
PIZA	*BTTF*-themed TV commercial: Pizza Hut
PNBL	Data East *BTTF* pinball game
REAL	Real life
RIDE	Simulator: *Back to the Future—The Ride*
SCRM	2010 Scream Awards: *Back to the Future 25th Anniversary Reunion* (broadcast)
SCRT	2010 Scream Awards: *Back to the Future 25th Anniversary Reunion* (trailer)
SIMP	Simulator: *The Simpsons Ride*
SLOT	*Back to the Future Video Slots*
STLZ	Unused *BTTF* footage of Eric Stoltz as Marty McFly
STRY	*Back to the Future Storybook*
TEST	Screen tests: Crispin Glover, Lea Thompson and Tom Wilson
TLTL	Telltale Games' *Back to the Future—The Game*
TOPS	Topps' *Back to the Future II* trading-card set
TRIL	*BTTF: The Official Book of the Complete Movie Trilogy*
UNIV	Universal Studios Hollywood promotional video

SUFFIX	MEDIUM
-b	*BTTF2*'s Biff Tannen Museum video (extended)
-c	Credit sequence to the animated series
-d	Film deleted scene
-n	Film novelization
-o	Film outtake
-p	1955 phone book from *BTTF1*
-v	Video game print materials or commentaries
-s1	Screenplay (draft one)
-s2	Screenplay (draft two)
-s3	Screenplay (draft three)
-s4	Screenplay (draft four)
-sp	Screenplay (production draft)
-sx	Screenplay (*Paradox*)

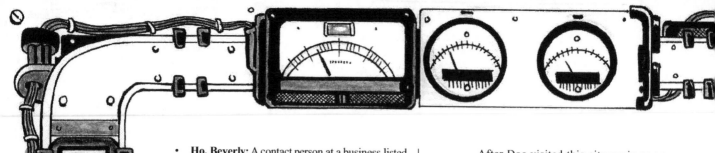

- **Ho, Beverly:** A contact person at a business listed in a 1991 help-wanted ad that Emmett Brown read while searching for a job. Her telephone number was 213-889-2444 [**BFAN-12**].

  NOTE: Her last name may have had more letters, as it was obstructed onscreen.

- **Hoffa, James Riddle ("Jimmy"):** An American labor union leader who vanished in 1975 under unknown circumstances. Hoffa was widely believed to have been related to organized crime, and his death the result of foul play [**REAL**]. In the Biffhorrific timeline, in which Biff Tannen was corrupt and powerful, Biff was photographed with Hoffa at teamster events [**BTF2-b**].

- **Hoffarth, Tom:** One of several professionals who helped to compile material for *Grays Sports Almanac: Complete Sports Statistics 1950-2000* [**BTF2**].

  NOTE: This individual was named on the book's title page.

- **Hoggly-Woggly:** A supermarket in Hill Valley, circa 1952. Emmett Brown sometimes shopped for groceries at this store [**BFAN-24**].

  NOTE: This market's name was based on that of the Piggly-Wiggly retail chain.

- **Hog Heaven:** A motorcycle shop located in Courthouse Square, near the intersection of Hill Street. In 1985, Marty McFly passed this business while hitching a skateboard ride to school on the back of a pick-up truck [**BTF1**].

- **Hogshead Tavern:** A pub in London, circa 1845. A pickpocketing street urchin named Reginald, who worked for a thug called Murdock, frequented this establishment. Emmett Brown visited the tavern while searching for Jules and Verne Brown, whom Murdock had pressed into service [**BFAN-10**].

- **Hollywood:** A district of Los Angeles, California, widely considered the historical center of the moviemaking industry [**REAL**].

  In 1926, Emmett Brown enjoyed a brief but successful Hollywood career as a silent film star known as Daredevil Emmett Brown. When he nearly died during a stunt for D.W. Tannen's film *Raging Death Doom*, his uncle and manager, Oliver Brown, put an immediate end to his nephew's acting career [**BFAN-11**].

After Doc visited this city again as an adult, a photo commemorating the occasion was displayed at Doc Brown's Chicken [**CHIC**].

- *Hollywood Gazette*: A newspaper published in Hollywood, California, that ran an article in 1926 about the exploits of stunt actor Daredevil Emmett Brown [**BFAN-11**].

- **hologram projector:** *See* three-dimensional holographic projector

- **holographic teacher:** A study aid used by Marty McFly to help him prepare for college exams. A hologram of a schoolteacher wearing a yellow blouse, a dark skirt and large glasses dictated lessons about various subjects—and seemed annoyed whenever Marty paid attention to something else, such as his guitar [**BFAN-1**].

- **Holomax:** A movie theater in 2015 Hill Valley that showed 3-D movies. In October of that year, the theater showed *Jaws 19*, directed by Max Spielberg, with a giant holographic shark "attacking" passersbys in order to promote the film [**BTF2**].

- **Holomax:** A brand-name of holovision systems sold in Robot City, a domed station in the Asteroid Belt of Earth's solar system, circa 2585 [**BFCL-1**].

- **holovision:** A type of electronic entertainment media popular in Robot City, a domed station in the Asteroid Belt of Earth's solar system, circa 2585. The average human living in that city spent nearly 98 percent of his or her waking time watching holovision, with a Click-o-bot standing by to change channels via remote control [**BFCL-1**].

- **Holt, Tim:** An American actor who appeared in numerous Western films between the 1930s and 1950s [**REAL**]. Emmett Brown watched Holt's films as a youth, sitting in Saturday matinees. Thus, when choosing clothing for Marty McFly to wear in 1885, Doc picked out an outfit that matched what he'd seen onscreen—but that was wildly out of fashion for the Old West, thus making Marty a laughing-stock [**BTF3-n**].

- **Holt's Diner:** A restaurant in Courthouse Square, circa 1955, that offered booth service [**BTF1**].

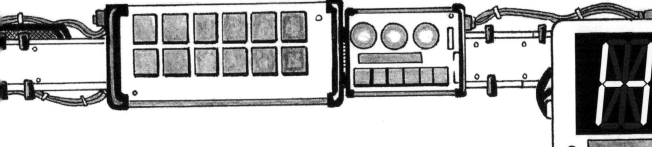

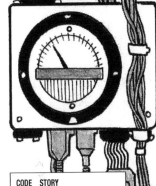

- **holy bovine:** An expression used by Emmett Brown to denote shock, analogous to "holy cow" [**BFAN-5, BFAN-12, MCDN**]. Doc used the expression from at least the age of four [**BFAN-11**]. His son, Jules Brown, also sometimes utilized the phrase [**BFAN-26**].

- **holy Marconi:** An exclamation favored by Emmett Brown for expressing surprise [**BFAN-3, BFAN-6**].

    NOTE: This phrase referred to Italian radio-telegraph inventor Guglielmo Marconi.

- **Holy Park, The:** An area of Apocrypha, the largest empire of former North America, circa 2,991,299,129,912,991 A.D., containing the Enchanted Tower [**BFCL-2**].

    NOTE: Many scientists believe Earth will cease to exist in approximately 7.6 billion years, with human life dying out within a billion years or so.

- **Home Ec Bake Sale:** An event held in 1955 at Hill Valley High School. Marty McFly passed a poster advertising this sale while trying to retrieve *Grays Sports Almanac* from Vice-Principal Gerald Strickland's office [**BTF2**].

- **Honest Joe Statler's Fine Horses:** A business in Hill Valley, circa 1885, that sold, bought and traded horses [**BTF3**].

- ***Honeymooners, The***: A classic American situation comedy that ran on CBS from 1955 to 1956, starring Jackie Gleason [**REAL**]. George McFly watched the series so often that his sons, David and Marty, could mockingly recite the lines by heart [**BTF1-n**].

    George was particularly amused by the episode "The Man From Space." While visting 1955, Marty discovered that his mother's parents, Sam and Stella Baines, watched that same episode when it was broadcast live [**BTF1**].

    NOTE: In the real world, "The Man From Space" aired on Dec. 31, 1955, almost two months after Marty's arrival in that year.

- **Hook, Captain:** A pirate acquainted with Mac the Black, circa 1697. His signature was tattooed on Mac's chest [**BFAN-14**].

    NOTE: Captain James Hook was the primary antagonist of J. M. Barrie's play Peter Pan; or, the Boy Who Wouldn't Grow Up *and its novelization,* Peter and Wendy.

- **Hoop Toss:** A booth at the Hill Valley Festival in 1885 [**BTF3**].

- **Hoover, Herbert Clark, President:** The 31st president of the United States [**REAL**]. Marty McFly passed several re-election posters for Hoover in 1931, promising "a chicken in every pot." After Marty and Emmett Brown made a number of mistakes in that era, Doc commented that they should return to their own time period before they got Hoover re-elected [**TLTL-2**].

    NOTE: Herbert Hoover was a single-term president, from 1929 to 1933.

- **Hoover Dam:** A concrete arch-gravity dam located on the border between Nevada and Arizona, in the Colorado River's Black Canyon [**REAL**]. When Emmett Brown conducted experiments to find water in Nevada's desert, an attempt to use a divining rod brought him to Hoover Dam and the Colorado River. He accidentally opened the reservoir while attempting to fill his canteen from a water spout, thereby causing a power failure [**BFAN-22**].

- **Hostage Special:** A tofu-based menu item offered at the Café 80's [**BTF2-n**]. The diner's Max Headroom-style video simulacrum of Ayatollah Khomeini interrupted a simulacrum of Ronald Reagan to demand that visitors try this special instead of the food suggested by Reagan [**BTF2**].

    NOTE: This was an in-joke reference to a diplomatic crisis between Iran and the United States from 1979 to 1981, in which 52 Americans were held hostage for 444 days by Islamist students and militants. The hostage-takers were backed by Khomeini, who took over the American Embassy in Tehran in support of the Iranian Revolution.

    In BTTF2's *novelization, as well as in a combined script for both sequel films, titled* Paradox, *the dish was called the Great Satan Special (referring to "Great Satan," a nickname for the United States among some Middle East countries). Onscreen, however, Khomeini yelled, "You must try the Hostage Special!"*

CODE	STORY
NIKE	*BTTF*-themed TV commercial: Nike
NTND	Nintendo *Back to the Future— The Ride* Mini-Game
PIZA	*BTTF*-themed TV commercial: Pizza Hut
PNBL	Data East *BTTF* pinball game
REAL	Real life
RIDE	Simulator: *Back to the Future—The Ride*
SCRM	2010 Scream Awards: *Back to the Future 25th Anniversary Reunion* (broadcast)
SCRT	2010 Scream Awards: *Back to the Future 25th Anniversary Reunion* (trailer)
SIMP	Simulator: *The Simpsons Ride*
SLOT	*Back to the Future Video Slots*
STLZ	Unused *BTTF* footage of Eric Stoltz as Marty McFly
STRY	*Back to the Future Storybook*
TEST	Screen tests: Crispin Glover, Lea Thompson and Tom Wilson
TLTL	Telltale Games' *Back to the Future—The Game*
TOPS	Topps' *Back to the Future II* trading-card set
TRIL	*BTTF: The Official Book of the Complete Movie Trilogy*
UNIV	Universal Studios Hollywood promotional video

SUFFIX	MEDIUM
-b	*BTTF2's* Biff Tannen Museum video (extended)
-c	Credit sequence to the animated series
-d	Film deleted scene
-n	Film novelization
-o	Film outtake
-p	1955 phone book from *BTTF1*
-v	Video game print materials or commentaries
-s1	Screenplay (draft one)
-s2	Screenplay (draft two)
-s3	Screenplay (draft three)
-s4	Screenplay (draft four)
-sp	Screenplay (production draft)
-sx	Screenplay (*Paradox*)

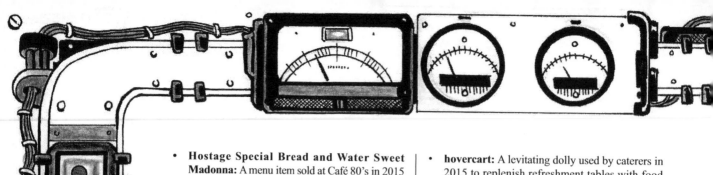

- **Hostage Special Bread and Water Sweet Madonna:** A menu item sold at Café 80's in 2015 [**BTF2**].

- **Hot Cocoa Ferraro Hostage Special, Bread and Water:** A menu item sold at Café 80's in 2015 [**BTF2**].

- **House of Glass:** *See* Atlas House of Glass

- **hoverbike:** An anti-gravitic, dual-mode, high-speed personal transport developed by Steven Marble, Ph.D., at the Institute of Future Technology's Anti-Gravitic Laboratory. The hoverbook utilized a substance called Tandemonium to remain stable at speeds of up to 38 miles per hour [**RIDE**].

- **hoverboard:** A type of anti-gravity skateboard popular in 2015. Mattel marketed a model for young children, while other brands offered greater power, included the Pit Bull, Rising Sun and No Tech models. Lower-end hoverboards ceased functioning while hovering over water; high power levels were required to operate in such a setting.

  While evading Griff Tannen's gang in a hoverboard chase, Marty McFly "borrowed" a pink board from a young girl. He later offered to return it, but she told him he could keep it, as she happily took Tannen's Pit Bull as her own [**BTF2**].

  The hoverboard came in handy during several of Marty's other adventures [**BFAN 1 to BFAN26, TLTL-5**], and ended up saving Clara Clayton's life after he traveled back to Hill Valley's Old West, in 1885. There, Emmett Brown used the toy to catch Clara before she could fall to her death from a speeding locomotive [**BTF3**].

  NOTE: At the end of Part II, Marty left the hoverboard near the Lyon Estates billboard. However, he had it with him at the beginning of Part III, indicating he and Doc must have retrieved it between films, en route to the scientist's home.

- **hover bus:** A mode of public transportation used across the Mid-Valley region and downtown Hill Valley, circa 2015 [**BTF2**].

- **hovercam:** A model of anti-gravity-based camera used at the Institute of Future Technology, harnessing sub-ether (faster-than-light) transmissions [**RIDE**].

- **hovercart:** A levitating dolly used by caterers in 2015 to replenish refreshment tables with food [**BTF2-s1**].

- **hovercase:** An invention of Jules Brown, utilizing hoverboard antigravity technology to enable a user to travel with a loaded briefcase, without having to lift it. The device was damaged when Jules' brother, Verne, ran over it with a bicycle [**BFAN-20**].

- **hover-conversion:** A service offered by Wilson Conversion Systems, circa 2015. The company advertised that it could hover-convert a road car into a skyway flier for only $39,999.95 [**BTF2**].

- **hovercycle:** A two-wheeled flying vehicle used in 2015. Emmett Brown nearly crashed his DeLorean into a hovercycle when he brought Marty McFly and Jennifer Parker into the future [**BTF2-d**].

- **hovering:** A term used in the early 21st century, referring to the act of driving a flying automobile. Those doing so erratically might be told to "Watch where you're hovering" [**RIDE**].

- **hover-ski:** A term used in 2015 to describe the act of riding a hoverboard over water. Hover-skiing required a board with extra power, such as a Pit Bull [**TOPS**].

- **hoverwheel:** A type of automobile wheel employing antigravity technology. Cars made in the 21st century used hoverwheels to attain flight. Emmett Brown outfitted his time-traveling DeLorean for flight via a conversion kit, including hoverwheels [**TLTL-3**].

- **Howard:** A 40-year-old, potbellied and unpleasant neighbor of George and Lorraine McFly [**BTF1-s4, BTF1-d, BTF1-n**], who only spoke to George when he needed something or was looking for someone to berate [**BTF1-n**].

  In 1985, Howard's daughter sold peanut brittle as a fundraiser for her local sports team, the Cubs. Howard, seeing George as a pushover, signed him up to buy a case without asking his permission. Uncomfortable with confrontations, George meekly agreed to the purchase, much to the disgust of his son, Marty [**BTF1-d, BTF1-s4**].

  NOTE: This scene, explaining why George was eating peanut brittle onscreen, was cut from BTTF1, but was included as a deleted

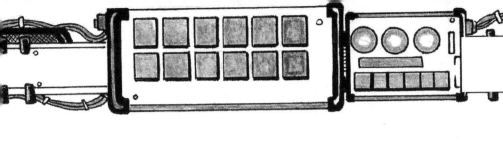

scene on the Blu-ray release. *In the movie's fourth-draft screenplay and novelization, Howard's daughter was selling Girl Scout Cookies, rather than peanut brittle.*

- *Howdy Doody*: A children's television program that aired on NBC from 1947 to 1960, featuring human and puppet characters, and utilizing circus and Western frontier themes [**REAL**]. In 1955, a broadcast of *Howdy Doody* awoke Emmett Brown from slumber after he fainted upon seeing Marty McFly moments after sending him back to the future [**BTF3**].

- **how in Herculaneum…?:** An expression used by Emmett Brown to denote confusion, analogous to "How the heck…?" [**BFAN-5**].

   NOTE: *Herculaneum was an ancient Roman town destroyed in 79 A.D. by volcanic gasses from Mount Vesuvius.*

- **Howser, Douglas, Doctor ("Doogie"):** A child prodigy with a genius I.Q. and eidetic intellect who, at age 16, graduated medical school and became a physician. When Mother Nature—a physical manifestation of nature's nurturing characteristics—became ill and was hospitalized in Anytown, Emmett Brown traveled into the future and discovered that it would be grim if she could not be saved. Returning to the past, the scientist rushed to the hospital's emergency room, where he shared his foreknowledge with Mother Nature's physician, Douglas "Doogie" Howser [**ERTH**].

   NOTE: *Howser, portrayed by Neil Patrick Harris, was the title character of* Doogie Howser, M.D., *an ABC TV series airing from 1989 to 1993. This unusual crossover occurred in a 1990 video from Time Warner, titled* The Earth Day Special, *in which numerous celebrities came together to urge viewers to save the planet.*

- *How to Cook*: A book in Emmett Brown's personal library, circa 1992 [**BFAN-17**].

- *How to Win Friends and Influence People*: A bestselling book written by Dale Carnegie, first published in 1936 [**REAL**].
   George McFly memorized entire sections at age 16, in an effort to carve out a new life for himself based on the author's positive attitude. When Biff Tannen began bullying him, George

tried being nice in an effort to defuse his hostility, but Biff responded by rubbing a hero sandwich in his face [**BTF1-n**].

- **Hubbard Avenue:** A road in Hill Valley, circa 1955, on which Statler Motors Studebaker was located [**BTF1**].

- **Hubbs, Larry:** A Hollywood producer, circa 2015, who helped director Max Spielberg create *Jaws 19*, according to the film's poster [**BTF2**].

   NOTE: *Lawrence A. Hubbs worked as a set director on BTTF2.*

- **Hubert, Mayor:** The highest-ranking member of Hill Valley's municipal government, circa 1885. A middle-age man, he had mutton-chop sideburns and wore a black hat.
   Hubert was a friend of Emmett Brown while Doc was stranded in that era. Thus, as a favor to the mayor, the scientist agreed to pick up the town's new schoolteacher, Clara Clayton, when she arrived by train.
   Mayor Hubert later presided over the dedication of the new Clock Tower at that year's Hill Valley Festival [**BTF3**].

   NOTE: *Hubert's last name is unknown. The role of Hubert was initially offered to former U.S. President Ronald Reagan, who'd been referenced in both of the prior films, but Reagan declined.*

- **Huey Lewis and the News:** An American rock band of the 1980s and 1990s. The group's hits included "The Power of Love" and "Back in Time" [**REAL**].
   In 1985, Marty McFly's band, the Pinheads, auditioned with "The Power of Love" at Hill Valley High School's Battle of the Bands competition. A fan of Huey Lewis, Marty had a poster of the group's album *Sports* hanging in his bedroom [**BTF1**].
   That same year, Huey Lewis and the News performed "The Power of Love" at a nightclub called Uncle Charlie's. While Emmett Brown attended the concert, a young couple fascinated with his DeLorean took the vehicle for a joyride [**HUEY**].

   NOTE: *One Battle of the Bands judge was portrayed by Huey Lewis—in the singer's acting debut—who dismissed the performance as being "too darn loud."*

CODE	STORY
NIKE	*BTTF*-themed TV commercial: Nike
NTND	Nintendo *Back to the Future—The Ride* Mini-Game
PIZA	*BTTF*-themed TV commercial: Pizza Hut
PNBL	Data East *BTTF* pinball game
REAL	Real life
RIDE	Simulator: *Back to the Future—The Ride*
SCRM	2010 Scream Awards: *Back to the Future 25th Anniversary Reunion* (broadcast)
SCRT	2010 Scream Awards: *Back to the Future 25th Anniversary Reunion* (trailer)
SIMP	Simulator: *The Simpsons Ride*
SLOT	*Back to the Future Video Slots*
STLZ	Unused *BTTF* footage of Eric Stoltz as Marty McFly
STRY	*Back to the Future Storybook*
TEST	Screen tests: Crispin Glover, Lea Thompson and Tom Wilson
TLTL	Telltale Games' *Back to the Future—The Game*
TOPS	Topps' *Back to the Future II* trading-card set
TRIL	*BTTF: The Official Book of the Complete Movie Trilogy*
UNIV	Universal Studios Hollywood promotional video

SUFFIX	MEDIUM
-b	*BTTF2*'s Biff Tannen Museum video (extended)
-c	Credit sequence to the animated series
-d	Film deleted scene
-n	Film novelization
-o	Film outtake
-p	1955 phone book from *BTTF1*
-v	Video game print materials or commentaries
-s1	Screenplay (draft one)
-s2	Screenplay (draft two)
-s3	Screenplay (draft three)
-s4	Screenplay (draft four)
-sp	Screenplay (production draft)
-sx	Screenplay (Paradox)

A third Huey Lewis song, "In the Nick of Time," was intended for the soundtrack, but was instead recorded by Patti LaBelle for the film Brewster's Millions.

The band was originally slated to appear in Back to the Future II, *as 60-year-old verisons of themselves in 2015, but this did not come to pass.*

- **humburger:** A vegetarian menu item at SoupMo, a restaurant in Citizen Brown's dystopian timeline. Humburgers were made from pressed roasted hummus [**TLTL-3**].

- **HV8851:** A file that Emmett Brown and Marty McFly accessed at the Hill Valley Historical Society while researching details regarding Doc's death in 1885. This file contained a photo of an outdoor scene, including a wooden fence [**BTF3**].

- **HV885-A:** A file at the Hill Valley Historical Society that Marty McFly and Emmett Brown read while searching for information pertaining to Buford Tannen's murder of Doc in 1885. This file contained a photo of Marty and Doc at that year's unveiling of the Clock Tower [**BTF3**].

- **HV Filiment:** A toggle on Emmett Brown's giant guitar amplifier, and part of the device's Driver Adjust system [**BTF1**].

- **H.V.R.C. 165.05:** A number on a "No Trespassing" sign posted outside the burnt-out Hill Valley High School in Biffhorrific 1985 [**BTF2-d**].

    NOTE: "H.V." likely referred to "Hill Valley," but the meaning of "R.C." is unclear.

- **Hyatas:** A Japanese market in Hill Valley, circa 2015, that sold all-natural, earth-grown fruits [**BTF2**].

- **Hydrator:** A cooking appliance manufactured by Black & Decker in 2015, enabling a family to rehydrate food in mere seconds. Marty and Jennifer McFly had a Hydrator in their home that could rehydrate a 15-inch Pizza Hut pizza in only two seconds [**BTF2**].

    NOTE: BTTF2's novelization indicated that the McFly family's Hydrator was an old model requiring 12 seconds to finish hydrating a pizza, but this does not match what occurred onscreen.

- **Hydrators Unlimited:** A business located in the Hill Valley Courthouse Mall, an underground shopping center beneath the courthouse, circa 2015 [**BTF2-n**].

- **Hydraulic Scrapbook:** An electronic scrapbook invented by Emmett Brown, used for preserving personal and family-history memorabilia, such as photographs and news clippings, with pneumatic cylinders to automatically turn the pages [**BTF1-s1**].

- **Hydrolunarsolarwinderator:** An invention of Emmett Brown, designed to be the world's most efficient generator. Doc created the contraption in 1992 to make amends for inadvertently causing a citywide brown-out in Hill Valley.

    Drawing energy from wind, water, sunlight and moonlight, the portable power plant transformed, at the press of a pedal, from a device small enough to fit in a wheelbarrow to an entire building that could be linked to a city's power lines in order to provide unlimited, free power.

    The generator worked—until it overheated, causing electrical appliances in the city to run amuck, including those not plugged in. This resulted in an angry mob, led by Biff Tannen, attempting to run the Browns out of town. Biff made the situation worse by pouring a bottle of soda on it, igniting a massive power surge. Doc, however, defused the situation before much damage resulted from Biff's blunder [**BFAN-22**].

- **Hyperlane-Grid 4:** An exit off I-99 (a highway for flying cars, circa 2015, located among the clouds above California) leading to Courthouse Square, with additional exits, including Phoenix, Boston and London [**BTF2**].

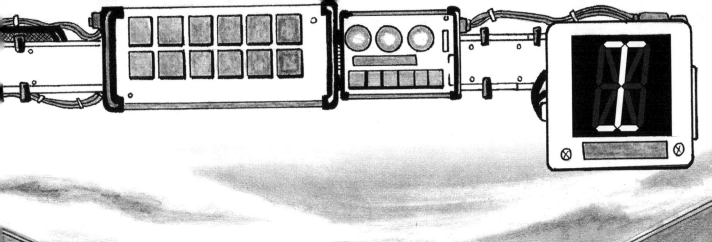

INSTITUTE OF FUTURE TECHNOLOGY

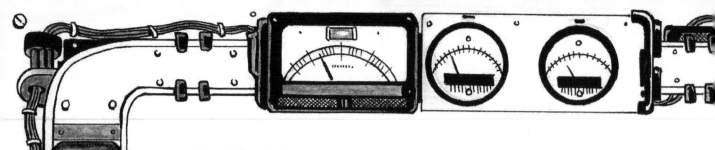

- **I-99:** A highway for flying cars, circa 2015, located among the clouds above California. Hyperlane-Grid 4 off I-99 led to the Courthouse Square Exit, in Hill Valley, as well as to Phoenix, Boston and London. When Emmett Brown brought Marty McFly and Jennifer Parker to 2015 to help their future children, Doc's DeLorean almost caused a vehicular accident on this road [**BTF2**].

- **Ibanez Black Strat:** A guitar brand manufactured by Japanese firm Hoshino Gakki [**REAL**]. Marty McFly played an Ibanez Black Strat while auditioning with the Pinheads for Hill Valley High School's 1985 Battle of the Bands [**BTF1**].

- **I Brake for Birds:** A bumper sticker on a car in Hill Valley, circa 2015. After stealing Emmett Brown's DeLorean in order to change history in his own favor, Biff Tannen hid behind this vehicle upon returning from the past, then faded from existence [**BTF2-d**].

  > *NOTE: Robert Zemeckis and Bob Gale have suggested that Biff's vanishing, unexplained onscreen, was caused by his wife Lorraine having shot him in 1996, thereby causing him to no longer exist in the future.*

- **Ice Cream:** An eatery at a shopping plaza in Hill Valley. Marty McFly sometimes rode his hoverboard past this store [**BFAN-c**].

  > *NOTE: The store's name is unknown, as only the words "Ice Cream" was visible on its sign. Similarly, the plaza in which it was located was simply labeled as "Shops."*

- **Ice Cream Clone, The:** A business in Hill Valley, circa 2015, that sold a type of ice cream said to be "better than the real thing" [**BTF2**].

- **Ice Cube:** One of several names that Verne Brown, having traveled back to before his birth, urged Emmett and Clara Brown to name him instead of Verne [**BFAN-21**].

  > *NOTE: Rap star O'Shea Jackson—better known as Ice Cube—was very popular during Verne's childhood.*

- **ID33727:** Emmett Brown's identification number at the physics department of the University of California (UC) Berkeley, where he conducted research on capacitor discharge as part of a project known as Temporal Dynamics Model 580 [**TLTL-1**].

- **identipad:** A thumbprint-activated home-security device, also called an identiplate and a thumb plate, used in 2015 to keep intruders out of a person's house [**BTF2-n**].

- **identiplate:** *See* identipad

- **"I Don't Care":** A popular song written by Jean Lenox, with music by Harry O. Sutton. "I Don't Care" was recorded by Eva Tanguay in 1922, and again in 1949 by Judy Garland [**REAL**].

  Sylvia "Trixie Trotter" Miskin sang this song at the El Kid speakeasy in 1931, accompanied by "Cue Ball" Donnely on piano. While Trixie performed, Marty McFly noticed that Danny Parker, a depressed policeman who regretted lacking the courage to arrest gangster Irving "Kid" Tannen, was emotionally affected by the mood of her music. To that end, Marty switched her lyrics sheet with that of "You Should Care" (a song with the same tune, written by Edna Strickland), inspiring Parker to care about his life once more, and to restore his honor by shutting down the speakeasy [**TLTL-2**].

  At some point, Trixie recorded the song on an album. Emmett Brown had a recording of the tune in his laboratory, which he found soothing [**TLTL-4**].

- **IFL:** A professional football league, circa 2015. Teams in this league included the Spacers and the Bears [**BTF2-n**].

  > *NOTE: It's unknown what the acronym "IFL" stood for, though it may have been short for "International Football League," given that "NFL" is short for "National Football League."*

- **IG Systems:** A business located in Los Angeles, California. Its street address was 3345 Wilshire #501, its telephone number was 213-386-0400, and its zip code was 90010. In 1991, Emmett Brown read a help-wanted ad for this firm while trying to find a job [**BFAN-12**].

- **I'm a Butthead:** A phrase handwritten on a sign that Biff Tannen mockingly hung from an employee's uniform at the Institute of Future Technology's Anti-Gravitic Laboratory, as the young thug broke into the facility to steal Emmett

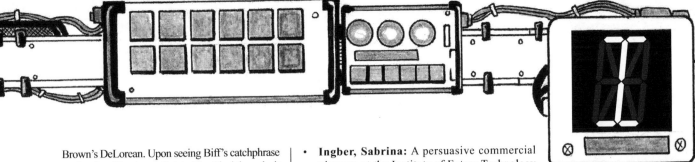

Brown's DeLorean. Upon seeing Biff's catchphrase on the sign, Doc immediately identified the culprit [**RIDE**].

- **Imperial:** A brand name advertised on signs at Lou's Café, circa 1955 [**BTF1**].

- **Independence Hall:** A building located in Independence National Historical Park, in Philadelphia, Pennsylvania. Established in 1753, the hall—originally known as the Pennsylvania State House—was the principal meeting place of the Second Continental Congress [**REAL**].

  In 1752, while the site was still under construction, Emmett Brown thought his son Verne had fallen from its roof. In asking two passersby for help, Doc called the building "Independence Hall," thereby introducing its future name [**BFAN-6**].

  > **NOTE:** *Verne's near-fall from the building's clock face paralleled* Back to the Future's *climax, complete with Doc hanging from a large clock hand.*

- **Indian Rocks State Park:** *See* Pohatchee Drive-in Theater

- **Indians:** A sports team that was a rival to the Hill Valley Bulldogs in 1955 [**BTF1**].

  > **NOTE:** *A Bulldogs vs. Indians poster hung in the school's hall when Marty McFly and Emmett Brown visited the facility to find Marty's parents. Bob Gale's junior high school team was the Bulldogs, while his high school team was the Indians.*

- **Inebriomatic:** A scientific innovation for police personnel, presented at the 1931 Hill Valley Exposition by Detective Daniel Parker, as part of the event's Future of Law Enforcement exhibit. This prototype device enabled officers to determine whether a person had been drinking, simply by having that individual breathe into it [**TLTL-5**].

  > **NOTE:** *In essence, the device was a 1930s analog to a modern-day breathalyzer.*

- **infostore:** A type of bookstore, circa 2015. Unlike 20th-century book sellers, infostores displayed only covers, with computer terminals behind them. Hill Valley contained an infostore called The Library [**BTF2-s1**].

- **Ingber, Sabrina:** A persuasive commercial virtuoso at the Institute of Future Technology [**RIDE**].

  > **NOTE:** *This individual, identified on signage outside* Back to the Future: The Ride, *was named after an employee at Universal Studios.*

- **Innuendo:** A small empire in North America, circa 2,991,299,129,912,991 A.D., located in the former northeastern United States and Canada [**BFCL-2**].

  > **NOTE:** *Many scientists believe Earth will cease to exist in approximately 7.6 billion years, with human life dying out within a billion years or so.*

- **input device:** A handheld computer interface used by Jules and Verne Brown. The two boys sometimes fought over whose turn it was to play with the input device, as Jules liked to utilize it to conduct science experiments, whereas Verne enjoyed using it to play video games [**BFAN-1**].

- **Institute of Future Technology (IFT):** A think-tank founded by Emmett Brown, who also served as the institute's chief inventive officer. Within this facility, scientists and inventors created numerous innovations, including the Eight-Passenger DeLorean Time-Travel Vehicle. Time travel was a frequent source of research for IFT's staff, with teams routinely sent into the past and future to study other eras.

  In 1991, Biff Tannen infiltrated the institute, having stowed away when one such team returned from 1955. Biff stole Doc's time-traveling DeLorean, but the scientist dispatched a team of Time-Travel Volunteers to pursue him in the eight-occupant version. Biff was apprehended and brought back to the institute so that he could be returned to his own era [**RIDE**].

  When Professor John I.Q. Nerdelbaum Frink Jr. visited Doc at the institute, he found the Krustyland theme park in its place. Curious, Frink traveled two years back in time via the DeLorean, to find Doc securing a small-business loan from a bank loan officer named Friedman, so he could afford to keep the IFT open. Frink accidentally ran over the man, however, leaving Doc no choice but to sell the facility to Krusty the Clown [**SIMP**].

  > **NOTE:** *The institute appeared in queue footage in* The Simpsons Ride *as an in-joke explaining Universal Studios' replacement*

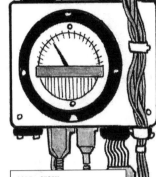

CODE	STORY
NIKE	*BTTF*-themed TV commercial: Nike
NTND	Nintendo *Back to the Future—The Ride* Mini-Game
PIZA	*BTTF*-themed TV commercial: Pizza Hut
PNBL	Data East *BTTF* pinball game
REAL	Real life
RIDE	Simulator: *Back to the Future—The Ride*
SCRM	2010 Scream Awards: *Back to the Future* 25th Anniversary Reunion (broadcast)
SCRT	2010 Scream Awards: *Back to the Future* 25th Anniversary Reunion (trailer)
SIMP	Simulator: *The Simpsons Ride*
SLOT	*Back to the Future* Video Slots
STLZ	Unused *BTTF* footage of Eric Stoltz as Marty McFly
STRY	*Back to the Future Storybook*
TEST	Screen tests: Crispin Glover, Lea Thompson and Tom Wilson
TLTL	Telltale Games' *Back to the Future—The Game*
TOPS	Topps' *Back to the Future II* trading-card set
TRIL	*BTTF: The Official Book of the Complete Movie Trilogy*
UNIV	Universal Studios Hollywood promotional video

SUFFIX	MEDIUM
-b	*BTTF2*'s Biff Tannen Museum video (extended)
-c	Credit sequence to the animated series
-d	Film deleted scene
-n	Film novelization
-o	Film outtake
-p	1955 phone book from *BTTF1*
-v	Video game print materials or commentaries
-s1	Screenplay (draft one)
-s2	Screenplay (draft two)
-s3	Screenplay (draft three)
-s4	Screenplay (draft four)
-sp	Screenplay (production draft)
-sx	Screenplay (*Paradox*)

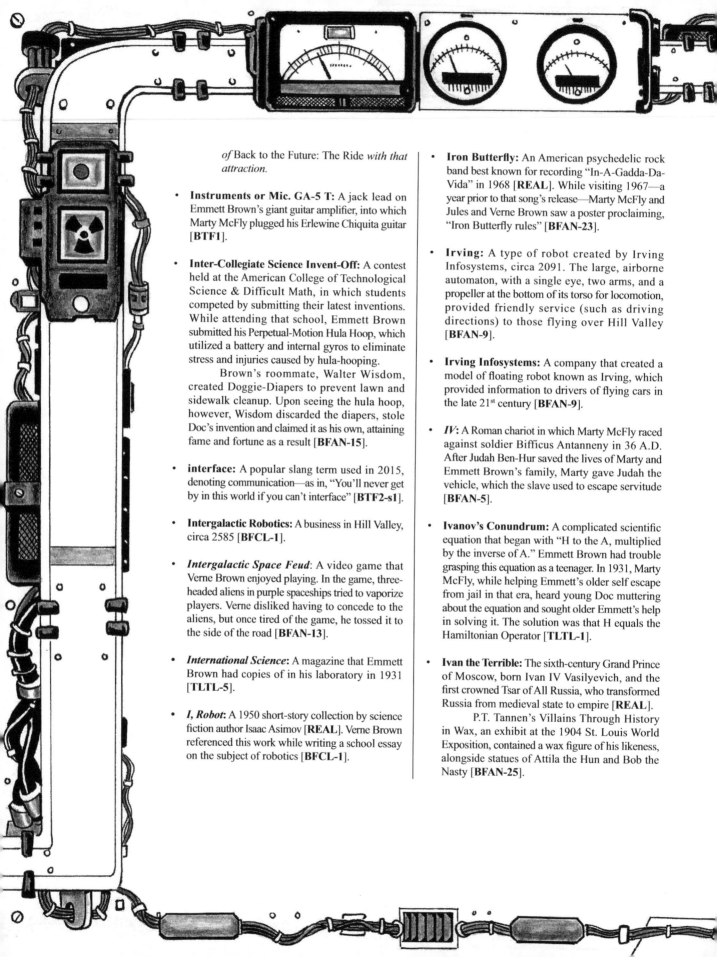

of Back to the Future: The Ride *with that attraction.*

- **Instruments or Mic. GA-5 T:** A jack lead on Emmett Brown's giant guitar amplifier, into which Marty McFly plugged his Erlewine Chiquita guitar [**BTF1**].

- **Inter-Collegiate Science Invent-Off:** A contest held at the American College of Technological Science & Difficult Math, in which students competed by submitting their latest inventions. While attending that school, Emmett Brown submitted his Perpetual-Motion Hula Hoop, which utilized a battery and internal gyros to eliminate stress and injuries caused by hula-hooping.

  Brown's roommate, Walter Wisdom, created Doggie-Diapers to prevent lawn and sidewalk cleanup. Upon seeing the hula hoop, however, Wisdom discarded the diapers, stole Doc's invention and claimed it as his own, attaining fame and fortune as a result [**BFAN-15**].

- **interface:** A popular slang term used in 2015, denoting communication—as in, "You'll never get by in this world if you can't interface" [**BTF2-s1**].

- **Intergalactic Robotics:** A business in Hill Valley, circa 2585 [**BFCL-1**].

- ***Intergalactic Space Feud***: A video game that Verne Brown enjoyed playing. In the game, three-headed aliens in purple spaceships tried to vaporize players. Verne disliked having to concede to the aliens, but once tired of the game, he tossed it to the side of the road [**BFAN-13**].

- ***International Science***: A magazine that Emmett Brown had copies of in his laboratory in 1931 [**TLTL-5**].

- ***I, Robot***: A 1950 short-story collection by science fiction author Isaac Asimov [**REAL**]. Verne Brown referenced this work while writing a school essay on the subject of robotics [**BFCL-1**].

- **Iron Butterfly:** An American psychedelic rock band best known for recording "In-A-Gadda-Da-Vida" in 1968 [**REAL**]. While visiting 1967—a year prior to that song's release—Marty McFly and Jules and Verne Brown saw a poster proclaiming, "Iron Butterfly rules" [**BFAN-23**].

- **Irving:** A type of robot created by Irving Infosystems, circa 2091. The large, airborne automaton, with a single eye, two arms, and a propeller at the bottom of its torso for locomotion, provided friendly service (such as driving directions) to those flying over Hill Valley [**BFAN-9**].

- **Irving Infosystems:** A company that created a model of floating robot known as Irving, which provided information to drivers of flying cars in the late 21st century [**BFAN-9**].

- ***IV***: A Roman chariot in which Marty McFly raced against soldier Bifficus Antanneny in 36 A.D. After Judah Ben-Hur saved the lives of Marty and Emmett Brown's family, Marty gave Judah the vehicle, which the slave used to escape servitude [**BFAN-5**].

- **Ivanov's Conundrum:** A complicated scientific equation that began with "H to the A, multiplied by the inverse of A." Emmett Brown had trouble grasping this equation as a teenager. In 1931, Marty McFly, while helping Emmett's older self escape from jail in that era, heard young Doc muttering about the equation and sought older Emmett's help in solving it. The solution was that H equals the Hamiltonian Operator [**TLTL-1**].

- **Ivan the Terrible:** The sixth-century Grand Prince of Moscow, born Ivan IV Vasilyevich, and the first crowned Tsar of All Russia, who transformed Russia from medieval state to empire [**REAL**].

  P.T. Tannen's Villains Through History in Wax, an exhibit at the 1904 St. Louis World Exposition, contained a wax figure of his likeness, alongside statues of Attila the Hun and Bob the Nasty [**BFAN-25**].

JULES VERNE TRAIN

- **J19:** A roadway exit in Hill Valley, circa 2015 [**RIDE**].

- **J8-P12:** A number listed on a binder located at a monitoring station at the Citizen Plus Ward, in Citizen Brown's dystopian timeline [**TLTL-4**].

- **Jack:** A citizen of Hill Valley who dated a woman named Diane in 1986. Edna Strickland, a spinster who spied on people from her apartment window, publicly taunted the couple via a bullhorn for hanging out behind a tree [**TLTL-1**].

     NOTE: The names Jack and Diane paid homage to John Cougar Mellencamp's 1982 hit song, "Jack & Diane," in which the titular couple hid behind a shady tree, presumably to have sex.

- **Jackson:** A classmate of Marty McFly at Hill Valley High School in 1985, in Mister Arky's class. He didn't like to contribute to class discussions [**BTF1-s1**].

- **Jackson:** A lanky friend—and occasional bully—of Verne Brown [**BFAN-20, BFAN-21, BFAN-24**].

Jackson often hosted swimming parties in his heated backyard pool, inviting many children, but excluding "brainiacs" like Verne's brother, Jules. A classmate of Jules at Hill Valley Elementary School, he often taunted the young genius—until Jules created a money-tree, a synthetic plant containing leaves resembling U.S. currency. Since this made Jules wealthy, Jackson allowed him to attend parties, as long as Jules provided refreshments. However, once the tree's money leaves shriveled, making it useless as legal tender, Jackson began snubbing Jules once more [**BFAN-20**].

Despite his friendship with Verne, Jackson sometimes teamed up with Biff Tannen Jr. to bully the younger boy, calling him "Verne the Worm" and other taunts [**BFAN-21**]. He and other neighborhood boys created the Mega Muscleman Fan Club, emulating the comic book exploits of their favorite superhero. Anyone looking to join the club had to prove his or her heroism by swinging over Dead Man's Swamp. Verne feared doing so, but Jackson pressured him into jumping anyway. After Verne stood his ground and refused to do so, Jackson took his place but crashed into the swamp when the rope broke, earning the other children's derision [**BFAN-24**].

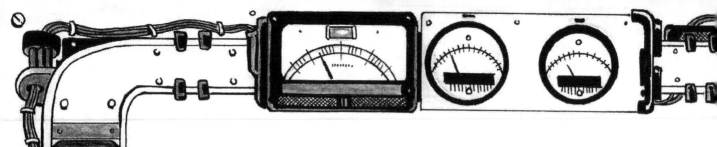

- **Jackson, Cooper:** An actor who appeared in the motion picture *Shark* in 1931, alongside costar Claire Stephens [**TLTL-1**].

- **Jackson, Michael Joseph:** An iconic pop musician of the 20th century, first as part of The Jackson 5, and later as a solo artist [**REAL**].

  In 2015, Marty McFly encountered a Max Headroom-style video simulacrum of Michael Jackson greeting customers at the Café 80's, reading various menu items. Later, upon ending up in Biffhorrific 1985, he discovered an African-American family living in his home, his bedroom occupied by a young girl named Loretta who had several Michael Jackson posters on her wall [**BTF2**].

  When Marty offended Buford Tannen at the Palace Saloon and Hotel in 1885, the outlaw fired several shots at his feet, yelling for him to "dance." Misunderstanding the order, Marty began dancing Jackson's signature move, the Moonwalk, much to the confusion of the bar's patrons [**BTF3**].

- **Jack's Pawn Shop:** A business in Hill Valley in Biffhorrific 1985. Open 24 hours a day, Jack's offered fast cash to those desperate to sell their belongings [**BTF2-s1**].

- **Jacobson & Field, Attorneys at Law:** A law office in Hill Valley, circa 1955 [**BTF2**].

  NOTE: When Marty McFly visited 1955 in the first movie, this business was called Orson and Tillich, Attorneys at Law. Why the firm changed names is unknown.

- **Jaeger, Sharon:** One of several professionals who helped to compile material for *Grays Sports Almanac: Complete Sports Statistics 1950-2000* [**BTF2**].

  NOTE: This individual was named on the book's title page.

- **Jamie's Bakery:** An eatery in Hill Valley, circa 1991 [**BFAN-6, BFAN-7b**]. Emmett Brown recreated this business in miniature for a board game that he created [**BFAN-6**].

- *Jane's Book of Sunk Ships:* A book from which an October 2015 edition of *USA Today* quoted statistics regarding ships sunk by whales [**BTF2**].

  NOTE: Jane's Fighting Ships, an annual reference book cataloging information about all known warships, arranged by nation, was launched in 1898 by John F. T. Jane.

- **Jason:** A representative of Hill Valley Community Hospital. In 2015, Jason introduced Lorraine McFly at a ceremony at which she donated money in George McFly's name for the construction of a new emergency facility [**BTF2-s1**].

- *Jaws:* A 1975 thriller directed by Steven Spielberg, based on Peter Benchley's same-named novel about a shark menacing a summer resort town [**REAL**]. A Nintendo Entertainment System (NES) video game based on the film was among the items for sale at Blast From the Past, an antique and collectibles shop in 2015 Hill Valley [**BTF2**].

- *Jaws 14: See Jaws 19*

- *Jaws 17:* A film reviewed by *USA Today* in October 2015. The newspaper deemed the film "*Jaws* without bite" [**BTF2**].

  NOTE: The "17" may have been a typo, as Jaws 19 *was in theaters that year, as seen in* Back to the Future II.

- *Jaws 19:* A 3-D sequel to *Jaws* that played in theaters in 2015. Its tagline: "This time it's really, *really* personal." Directed by Max Spielberg, *Jaws 19* played at Hill Valley's Holomax theater, with a giant holographic shark "attacking" passersby in order to promote the movie. According to the film's poster, *Jaws 19* was produced by Ark Kline, Larry Hubbs and Paul Sonskoid [**BTF2**].

  NOTE: The slogan to this fictional movie was an in-joke reference to the tagline for Jaws IV: The Revenge*: "This time, it's personal."*

  In Back to the Future II*'s first-draft script, the theater showed* Godzilla 2015 *rather than* Jaws 19. *In the movie's novelization, as well as in the combined script for both sequel films, titled* Paradox, *it was called* Jaws 14. *A* USA Today *newspaper seen in the film, meanwhile, contained a review of* Jaws 17.

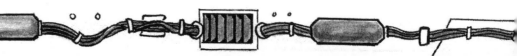

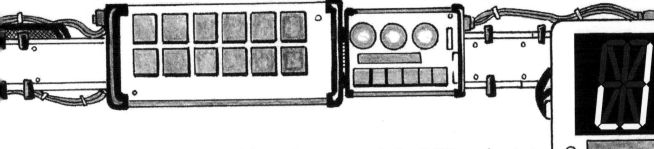

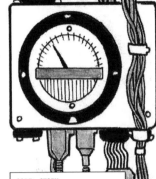

- **Jaws 2:** A 1978 sequel to Steven Spielberg's thriller film *Jaws*, directed by Jeannot Szwarc [**REAL**]. A VHS copy of *Jaws 2* was among the items for sale at Blast From the Past, an antique and collectibles shop in 2015 Hill Valley [**BTF2**].

- **Jay:** A contact person at a company listed in a 1991 help-wanted ad that Emmett Brown read while trying to find a job [**BFAN-12**].

- **Jaycees:** An American leadership-training and civic organization, also called the U.S. Junior Chamber [**REAL**]. Jaycees operated a chapter in Hill Valley in 1985 [**BTF1**].

- **JCPenney:** A chain of American mid-range department stores [**REAL**]. In 1985, Emmett Brown conducted experiments with his time-traveling DeLorean outside a JCPenney store at Hill Valley's Twin Pines Mall [**BTF1**].

    NOTE: In Telltale Games' BTTF video game, Marty McFly had a dream in which the store was called JPPinney.

- **J.D. Armstrong Realty:** A residential and commercial real-estate business in Courthouse Square, circa 1955 [**BTF1**]. The company sold bomb shelters for $1,350 [**BTF2**].

- **Jeanne:** A friend of Sally Baines during their teen years. In 1967, Sally, Jeanne and a third friend, Mary Ann, went to see the film *To Sir, With Love* [**BTF2-s1**].

- **Jeb:** An old-timer who frequented Hill Valley's Palace Saloon and Hotel in 1885, along with Levi, Zeke, Toothless, Eyepatch and Moustache [**BTF3-sp, BTF3-n**].

    Jeb had a droopy moustache and wore a black hat. Upon seeing Marty McFly dressed in non-authentic cowboy garb, Jeb joked that he looked like he'd stolen the garb from a dead Chinese man. When Marty later refused to fight Buford Tannon, Jeb warned him that he'd be branded a coward if he didn't face the outlaw [**BTF3**].

    NOTE: This character, unnamed onscreen, was identified as Jeb in BTTF3's novelization and storyboards, as well as in Paradox, *a combined script for both film sequels.*

On Sept. 2, 1885—one day prior to BTTF3's events—150 white miners had murdered their Chinese co-workers in Rock Springs, Wyoming. This may have been the source of Jeb's morbid humor.

- **J.E.B. Cross-time Headliner:** An invention of Jules Brown. The contraption combined an old-style teletype machine with a Flux Capacitor, enabling a user to print up newspaper pages from any desired era, in order to learn about history. The youth built the device as an anniversary gift for his parents, Emmett and Clara Brown [**BFAN-9**].

- **Jeep:** An automobile brand of the Chrysler Group [**REAL**]. When late for school one day, Marty McFly hitched a skateboard ride on the back of a blue Jeep CJ-7 [**BTF1**].

    NOTE: The Jeep was driven by Walter Scott, the stunt coordinator for all three Back to the Future *films, who also had cameos in Parts II and III, respectively, as the driver of a futuristic Jeep that Marty grabbed onto during the hoverboard chase scene, and as the conductor when Clara Clayton pulled the train cord.*

- **Jehosaphat ("Jumping Jehosaphat"):** A beloved uncle of Clara Clayton Brown, circa 1888, who made a name for himself working at county fairs, jumping from hot-air balloons into buckets of water, which earned him the nickname "Jumping Jehosaphat." Clara and her husband, Emmett Brown, discussed naming their second-born son after him, but instead decided on the name "Verne" [**BFAN-21**].

    NOTE: It's unclear whether Jehosaphat shared Clara's surname of Clayton.

- **Jenkins:** A coworker of George McFly who, in 1982, received a promotion that George was expecting to get—due not to his qualifications, but rather because Jenkins played golf with a company executive named Mr. Callahan [**BTF1-s2**].

- **Jenkins:** A corpulent schoolmate of Marty McFly at Hill Valley High School. He and Marty sometimes received detention together with Vice-Principal Gerald Strickland [**BTF1-s3**].

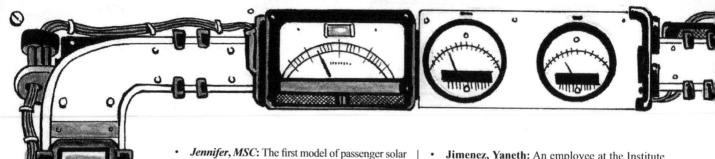

- **Jennifer, MSC:** The first model of passenger solar sailship built by McFly Space Cruises, named after Jennifer McFly. The decommissioned vessel was maintained at the McFly Museum of Aeronautics, in Hill Valley, for visitors to view. When the *MSC Marty* (named after Marty McFly) was stranded in space in 2091 due to sabotage, with Emmett Brown and Clara Clayton Brown on board, their sons, Jules and Verne, equipped the *Jennifer* with rocket packs and towed the *Marty* to safety [**BFAN-9**].

- **Jerr-Dan:** A manufacturer of towing and recovery equipment owned by Oshkosh Corp. [**REAL**]. In 1985, Marty McFly was awed by the sight of a Toyota 4x4 being transported to Statler Toyota aboard a Jerr-Dan tow-truck [**BTF1**].

- **Jet Burger:** A restaurant in Hill Valley, circa 2015 [**RIDE**].

- **Jet-drill:** *See* Rocket-Powered Drill

- **jigowatt:** Emmett Brown's unique pronunciation of the word "gigawatt." It took 1.21 jigowatts of electricity to power the Flux Capacitor of Emmett Brown's DeLorean. In 1985, he achieved this reaction via plutonium, but since that element was difficult to obtain in 1955, the scientist harnessed a bolt of lightning, from a storm that damaged the Hill Valley Courthouse's Clock Tower, to send Marty McFly and the DeLorean back to their proper era [**BTF1**].

  > *NOTE: Although the word is spelled "gigawatt," the* Back to the Future *screenplay misspelled it "jigowatt," either inadvertently or for comedic intent (so that actor Christopher Lloyd would purposely pronounce it using a soft instead of hard "g"). Doc's handwritten letter to Marty from 1885 used the "jigowatt" spelling, as did Marvel Comics'* BTTF Annual *and signage at Universal Studios'* Back to the Future: The Ride.

- **Jim:** A citizen of Hill Valley in Citizen Brown's dystopian timeline. Marty McFly passed Jim on a Polo Shirt Thursday, when the latter was wearing that day's mandated khaki pants and orange polo shirt [**TLTL-3**].

- **Jimenez, Yaneth:** An employee at the Institute of Future Technology, in charge of parcel and apparel dispersement [**RIDE**].

  > *NOTE: This individual, identified on signage outside* Back to the Future: The Ride, *was named after a Universal Studios employee.*

- **Jiminez, Ernest:** A bovine disc flipologist at the Institute of Future Technology [**RIDE**].

  > *NOTE: This individual, identified on signage outside* Back to the Future: The Ride, *was named after a Universal Studios employee.*

- **Jimmy:** A young child in Chattanooga, Tennessee, who served as a drummer boy to General Beauregard Tannen during the American Civil War, circa 1864. Verne Brown befriended Jimmy while visiting that era. He had scraggly red hair, a thick drawl and a single front tooth protruding outside his mouth, and he missed his mother's raspberry pie. His cousin Roy served in the opposing forces of the Union Army [**BFAN-1**].

- **Jimmy:** A Marty McFly impersonator aboard the *MSC Marty*, circa 2091. The British youth covered his red hair and pug nose with a mask of Marty's face, and played guitar onstage during the passenger solar sailship's cruises. Jimmy was considered the best Marty McFly impersonator in the entire Tri-Planet Area. He hated the job, however, particularly when guests approached him after performances [**BFAN-9**].

- **Jimmy:** A teenage boy in Hill Valley, circa 1992. Biff Tannen Jr. sometimes bullied him, and on one occasion knocked his frozen yogurt out of his hand [**BFAN-19**].

- **Joe:** The owner of Joe's Tonsorial Emporium. The elderly barber had a ring of grey hair, a grey mustache and a small pair of eyeglasses [**BFAN-8**].

- **Joe Morris Music Co.:** A publisher of sheet music, located at 1587 Broadway, in New York City [**REAL**]. "Cue Ball" Donnelly's piano sheet music for the song "My Melancholy Baby," which he used in 1931 while performing at the El Kid speakeasy, was published by this company [**TLTL-2**].

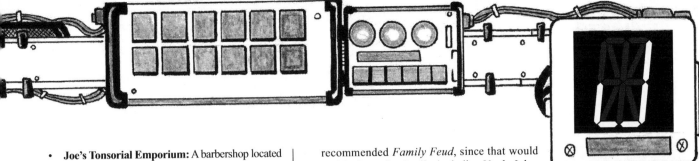

- **Joe's Tonsorial Emporium:** A barbershop located in Boston, Massachusetts, circa 1897. Gangster Jimmy "Diamond Jim" Tannen frequented this shop, conducting business while his hair was being cut [**BFAN-8**].

- **Joey:** An employee at Hill Valley's Palace Saloon and Hotel, circa 1885. The mustached young man assisted the establishment's bartender, Chester [**BTF3**].

- **Joey ("Skinhead"):** A member of Biff Tannen's gang in 1955, along with Match and 3-D. Joey had a buzz cut that inspired his nickname. He and his friends often trailed Biff, following his lead in bullying others [**BTF1, BTF2**].

  In Biffhorrific 1985, in which Biff Tannen was wealthy and corrupt, Skinhead remained at Biff's side, along with 3-D and Match, serving as Biff's major enforcers as Tannen became Hill Valley's billionaire crime boss [**BTF2**].

  > **NOTE:** *Though not named onscreen, this character was called Skinhead in BTTF1's credits, script and novelization. His birth name, Joey, was revealed in BTTF2.*
  >
  > *Actor J.J. Cohen, who played Skinhead, also portrayed a member of Douglas J. Needles' gang, possibly a clue that the two were related.*

- **Johann:** A person buried in Boot Hill Cemetery. Emmett Brown and Marty McFly took refuge behind his tombstone while blasting open the Delgado Mine [**BTF3**].

  > **NOTE:** *Johann's surname was not included on the gravestone.*

- **Johannsen, Jörg:** A Nordic-accented neighbor of Emmett and Clara Brown in Hill Valley, circa 1992. He and his wife hired Verne Brown to mow their lawn, but the boy's video game addiction sometimes kept him from carrying out the chore, causing the Johannsens' grass to grow extremely tall—so much so that Jörg occasionally could not find his wife [**BFAN-19**].

- **John:** An uncle of Marty McFly. George McFly, in an effort to raise his family's morale, suggested that he, Lorraine and Marty try out for a game show, such as *The Price Is Right*. Marty, however,

recommended *Family Feud*, since that would enable the entire family, including Uncle John, to take part [**TEST**].

  > **NOTE:** *John's surname is unknown. Since none of Lorraine's siblings were named John, he may have been George's brother.*

- **John:** A person buried at the Boot Hill Cemetery, near the entrance of the abandoned Delgado Mine [**BTF3**].

  > **NOTE:** *John's last name on the gravestone was obstructed, but the first two letters appeared to be "Mi."*

- **John:** A citizen of Hill Valley in Citizen Brown's dystopian timeline. Marty McFly passed John on a Polo Shirt Thursday, when the latter was wearing that day's mandated khaki pants and orange polo shirt. George McFly—who spied on citizens for the government via video monitors in his home— later overheard John discussing an illegal activity with an unnamed woman [**TLTL-3**].

- **John F. Kennedy Drive:** A street in Hill Valley, circa 1985, located a block past Riverside Drive, and known in 1955 as Maple [**BTF1**].

- **Johnny:** A citizen of Hill Valley who "woke up in a pile of his own sick, completely unable to remember the previous two weeks of his life." Edna Strickland printed his story on a handout titled "Lost Fortnight," which she used in 1931 to warn others about the evils of alcohol [**TLTL-2**].

- **"Johnny B. Goode":** A popular rock-and-roll song written and recorded by musician Chuck Berry in 1958 [**REAL**].

  In 1955, Chuck's cousin, Marvin Berry— the guitarist and lead vocalist of Marvin Berry and the Starlighters—performed this tune at Hill Valley High School's Enchantment Under the Sea Dance. Marty McFly filled in on guitar, introducing Hill Valley's youth to the concept of rock-and-roll. Marvin was so impressed by this song—which would not be released for another three years—that he called Chuck to hear Marty's performance, inspiring his cousin to try out a new sound [**BTF1**].

  Spying a microphone at Irving "Kid" Tannen's speakeasy in 1931, Marty stepped up

CODE	STORY
NIKE	*BTTF*-themed TV commercial: Nike
NTND	Nintendo *Back to the Future— The Ride* Mini-Game
PIZA	*BTTF*-themed TV commercial: Pizza Hut
PNBL	Data East *BTTF* pinball game
REAL	Real life
RIDE	Simulator: *Back to the Future—The Ride*
SCRM	2010 Scream Awards: *Back to the Future* 25th Anniversary Reunion (broadcast)
SCRT	2010 Scream Awards: *Back to the Future* 25th Anniversary Reunion (trailer)
SIMP	Simulator: *The Simpsons Ride*
SLOT	*Back to the Future Video Slots*
STLZ	Unused *BTTF* footage of Eric Stoltz as Marty McFly
STRY	*Back to the Future Storybook*
TEST	Screen tests: Crispin Glover, Lea Thompson and Tom Wilson
TLTL	Telltale Games' *Back to the Future—The Game*
TOPS	Topps' *Back to the Future II* trading-card set
TRIL	*BTTF: The Official Book of the Complete Movie Trilogy*
UNIV	Universal Studios Hollywood promotional video

SUFFIX	MEDIUM
-b	*BTTF2's* Biff Tannen Museum video (extended)
-c	Credit sequence to the animated series
-d	Film deleted scene
-n	Film novelization
-o	Film outtake
-p	1955 phone book from *BTTF1*
-v	Video game print materials or commentaries
-s1	Screenplay (draft one)
-s2	Screenplay (draft two)
-s3	Screenplay (draft three)
-s4	Screenplay (draft four)
-sp	Screenplay (production draft)
-sx	Screenplay (*Paradox*)

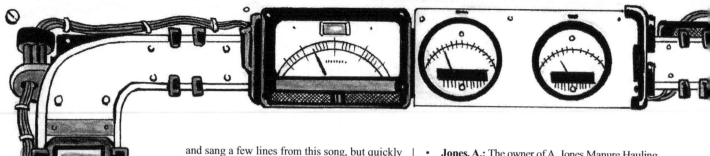

and sang a few lines from this song, but quickly thought better of it, seeing others' negative reaction to the anachronistic music [**TLTL-2**].

- **Johnson, Elmer H.:** A salesman for Colt's Patent Firearms Manufacturing Co., who demonstrated the Colt Peacemaker at the 1885 Hill Valley Festival. Johnson invited passersby to fire the revolver at a game of moving targets, and was astounded by Marty's shooting prowess (resulting from the youth's skill at the video game Wild Gunman). The salesman gave Marty a free Peacemaker to use during his duel with Buford Tannen, but noted that he'd reclaim the weapon if Marty lost [**BTF3-sp, BTF3-n**].

  NOTE: This character, unnamed onscreen in Back to the Future III, *was identified as Elmer H. Johnson in the film's novelization and production-draft screenplay (which misspelled his surname as "Johnshon" in one instance).*

- **Johnson, Martha:** A Hollywood professional, circa 2015, who helped director Max Spielberg create *Jaws 19*, according to the film's poster [**BTF2**].

  NOTE: Martha Johnson worked as a set director on BTTF2 and BTTF3.

- **John Stephenson's Gimick Shop:** A business located in Boston, Massachusetts, circa 1897 [**BFAN-8**].

  NOTE: This shop, identified on its storefront, was named after artist John Stevenson, who worked as a character designer on the Back to the Future *animated series. The word "gimmick" was misspelled on the sign.*

- **Jones:** An FBI agent who, along with fellow agent Smith, investigated Jules Brown's money-tree to determine if the youth was the kingpin of an international counterfeiting racket. Jones had a fondness for cream soda, crullers and *Garfield* [**BFAN-20**].

  NOTE: It is a common motif in fiction for pairs of characters to be named Smith and Jones, particularly with regard to government agents. This convention was utilized in The Matrix, as well as in promotional materials for the Men in Black films.

- **Jones, A.:** The owner of A. Jones Manure Hauling, circa 1885 [**BTF3**].

- **Jones, Abraham:** A teamster in Hill Valley, circa 1952, and the proprietor of a business called Abraham Jones, Junk Dealer [**BTF1-s2**].

- **Jones, D. ("Old Man Jones:"):** The owner of D. Jones Manure Hauling, circa 1955. Biff Tannen's car collided with a D. Jones truck twice within the same week [**BTF1, BTF2**].

- **Jones, Lieutenant:** A U.S. military officer at an aboveground atomic bomb testing site in Atkins, Nevada. Emmett Brown and Marty McFly visited his base in 1952, to harness a bomb blast's nuclear energy in order to send Marty back to the future [**BTF1-s1**].

  NOTE: The nuclear test-site sequence was cut from the final version of BTTF1 (the setting of which was changed to 1955), though storyboards were included as a Blu-ray extra. The first two script drafts set the base in the fictional Nevada city of Atkins, while the third moved it to New Mexico.

- **Jones, Tom:** An employee at the Institute of Future Technology, stationed in the West Wing [**RIDE**].

  NOTE: This individual, identified on signage outside Back to the Future: The Ride, *was named after a Universal Studios employee.*

- **Jordan, Bob:** A member of Marvin Berry and the Starlighters, who performed at the Enchantment Under the Sea Dance in 1955. A tall, imposing man, he did not take kindly to being called the racial slur "spook" [**BTF1-n**].

- ***Journal of the American Medical Association, The (JAMA):*** A weekly, peer-reviewed journal providing reviews, research, essays, news and other medical content [**REAL**]. Emmett Brown used this periodical to diagnose his pet, Einstein, with cat-aracts, a canine eye disease causing him to see objects and people as cats [**BFCM-1**].

- ***Journey to the Center of the Earth, A:*** A science fiction novel by author Jules Verne, published in 1864 [**REAL**].

  At age 12, after reading this book, Emmett

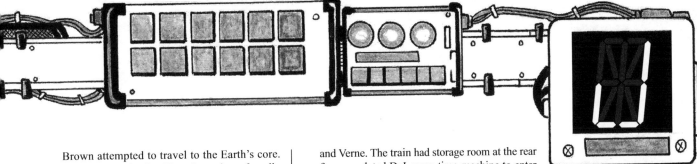

Brown attempted to travel to the Earth's core. He didn't get far, but Verne's work profoundly impacted his life [**BTF3**]. His fascination with this novel led to his inventing a rocket-powered drill [**TLTL-1**].

- **JPPinney:** *See* JCPenney

- **J. Teegarden:** A carpentry business in Hill Valley, circa 1885 [**BTF3**].

    > *NOTE: A sign for this business was among those leaning against a sign shop located next to Marshal James Strickland's office.*

- **Jules Brown Money-Tree:** A synthetic tree designed by Jules Brown, containing leaves resembling U.S. paper currency. Jules created the tree to make his family wealthy, and to buy the friendships of other children. To protect it, he built an anti-pilfering security system comprising wired sensors, sirens and a spring-loaded boxing glove.

    For a time, the money-tree brought fame and notoriety to Jules' family, causing the U.S. government to investigate whether he was the kingpin of an international counterfeiting racket. Ultimately, the tree's money leaves shriveled, making it useless as a source of legal tender. Emmett Brown later created a homemade chlorophyll and enzyme booster for Jules, in order to prolong the plant's leaf life [**BFAN-20**].

- *Jules Verne, Collected Works, Vol. I to Vol. IV:* A four-book hardbound collection of Verne's science fiction writings. Emmett Brown owned the complete series [**TLTL-1**].

- *Jules Verne Train:* A flying, time-traveling train built by Emmett Brown and modeled after the engine car of a late 19th-century locomotive. The *Jules Verne Train* was named after Jules and Verne Brown (Emmett's sons), as well as Jules Verne, his (and his wife Clara's) favorite science fiction author [**RIDE**].

    Doc built the train while living in Hill Valley's Old West period, using technology from that era. He later utilized the vehicle to retrieve his dog, Einstein, from 1985, and to say goodbye to Marty McFly before returning to the past [**BTF3**].

    After Doc and his family relocated to 1991, they lived on a farm in Hill Valley and kept the "time-train" hidden in a garage until needed. From time to time, the couple used the train to embark on a series of adventures with their children, Jules

and Verne. The train had storage room at the rear for an updated DeLorean time-machine to enter and exit [**BFAN-1 to BFAN-26, BFCM-1 to BFCM-4, BFCL-1 to BFCL-3**].

> *NOTE: The locomotive was not called the Jules Verne Train in either BTTF3 or the animated series, but was thus identified on signage outside Universal Studios' Back to the Future: The Ride attraction. Back to the Future—The Card Game referred to this vehicle as the Overpowered Locomotive and the Time Train.*
>
> *The front of the locomotive resembled Captain Nemo's submarine Nautilus, featured in Jules Verne's novels Twenty Thousand Leagues Under the Sea and The Mysterious Island.*

- **Julie:** A shapely young woman who lived near Emmett Brown's family in Hill Valley, circa 1991. A friend of Marty McFly, she had short, orange hair and thick, red glasses, and enjoyed reading on a swimming-pool raft [**BFAN-4**].

- **Jumping Jehovah:** *See* Great Scott

- **Jumping Jigowatts:** An expression used by Emmett Brown to denote surprise or shock [**BFAN-1, BFAN-6, BFAN-7a, BFAN-13, BFAN-19, BFAN-24, BFAN-26, BFCM-3, RIDE**]. Doc's son, Jules, sometimes used the phrase as well [**BFAN-11**].

    > *NOTE: Although the correct spelling of the word is "gigawatt," BTTF1's screenplay utilized the spelling "jigowatt," which is also how actor Christopher Lloyd pronounced it.*

- **Junior Brown Brigade:** A youth organization in Citizen Brown's dystopian timeline. In that reality, Marty McFly was the president of the Junior Brown Brigade [**TLTL-3**].

- **juniper berry:** The female seed cone produced by juniper plants [**REAL**]. A byproduct of fermenting the berries could cure cat-aracts, a canine eye disease causing a dog to see objects and individuals as cats [**BFCM-1**].

- **junk fax:** A term used in 2015, analogous to "junk mail" [**BTF2-n**].

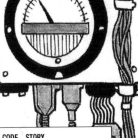

- **Junkmobile:** A powered go-cart consisting of a wheeled bathtub mounted to a snow sled, built by Emmett Brown for his son, Verne. The youth sometimes rode the vehicle to and from school [**BFAN-21, BFAN-22, BFAN-26**].

    NOTE: The Junkmobile, which appeared unnamed in the animated series, was so designated by McDonald's—which, in 1992, produced a plastic toy based on the vehicle for its Back to the Future-*themed Happy Meals. The toy Junkmobile differed somewhat from its cartoon counterpart.*

- **Jupiter Juice:** A type of beverage that Biff Tannen sold at an extra-terrestrial-themed roadside stand in Hill Valley, as part of a scheme to make money off passersby [**BFAN-23**].

- **Justerini & Brooks (J&B):** A brand of blended scotch whiskey [**REAL**]. J&B was among the alcoholic beverages stocked in Biff Tannen's penthouse bar in Biffhorrific 1985 [**BTF2**].

- **JVC:** A Japanese consumer and professional electronics corporation [**REAL**].

    Emmett Brown owned a JVC VideoMovie camera in 1985, with which Marty McFly recorded the testing of his time-traveling DeLorean during Temporal Experiment Number One. Marty later showed Doc's younger self the video in 1955, enabling the scientist to figure out a way to send the youth back to the future [**BTF1**].

    A similar video camera was among the items for sale at Blast From the Past, an antique and collectibles shop in 2015 Hill Valley [**BTF2**].

KLEIN, CALVIN

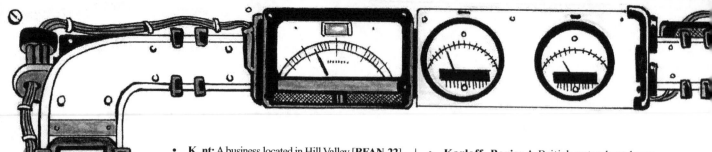

- **K_nt:** A business located in Hill Valley [**BFAN-22**].

  NOTE: The second letter of the store's name is unknown, as a street pole obscured it from view. The most likely candidate for the missing letter would be "e."

- **K9 Crunchies:** A brand of dog biscuits that Emmett Brown kept in his home for his dog, Einstein [**BFAN-15**].

- **Kahooey:** *See* Comet Kahooey

- **Kal Kan:** A popular brand name of dog food [**REAL**]. Emmett Brown kept a supply of the product in his home for his pet, Einstein, and invented an automatic contraption to open the cans and pour the contents into a bowl at appointed times. Sometimes, the scientist forgot to turn off the device while away from his home, resulting in a mess of uneaten dog food on the floor [**BTF1**].

  NOTE: The company, known as Kal Kan when Back to the Future *was filmed, changed its name to Whiskas in 1988.*

- **Kaminsky, Diva:** An employee at the Institute of Future Technology, in charge of carbon lifeform resources [**RIDE**].

  NOTE: This individual, identified on signage outside Back to the Future: The Ride, *was named after Universal Studios' human-resources director.*

- **Kaner:** A student in Mister Arky's class at Hill Valley High School in 1952. She didn't like to contribute to class discussions [**BTF1-s1**].

- **Kareem:** One of several names that Verne Brown, having traveled back to before his birth, urged Emmett and Clara Brown to name him instead of Verne [**BFAN-21**].

  NOTE: Basketball star Kareem Abdul-Jabbar was popular during Verne's childhood.

- **Karen:** A business in Hill Valley, circa 1991. Emmett Brown recreated this shop in miniature for a board game that he created [**BFAN-6**].

  NOTE: The sign was obstructed, so it's possible there was more to the store's name.

- **Karloff, Boris:** A British actor best known for his portrayal of Frankenstein's Monster in Universal Pictures' *Frankenstein* (1931), *Bride of Frankenstein* (1935) and *Son of Frankenstein* (1939) [**REAL**].

  Zane Williams, a gangster and caricaturist at Irving "Kid" Tannen's speakeasy in 1931, was drawing Karloff when Marty McFly first visited the bar. *Frankenstein* was playing at a theater down the road at the time. Seeing that movie cemented Emmett Brown's lifelong passion for science [**TLTL-2**].

- **KCET**: A business in Los Angeles, California. In 1991, Emmett Brown read a help-wanted ad from KCET while searching for a job. The company was located at 4401 Sunset. The position listed was for a programmer/analyst [**BFAN-12**].

  NOTE: Given the company's name, KCET may have been a television station.

- **Keaton, Alex:** The author of the textbook *Keatonsian Economics*, which Marty McFly read while attending college [**BFCM-3**].

  NOTE: The title and author of this volume were an in-joke reference to Alex P. Keaton, a high school student with a passion for economics, from the 1980s TV series Family Ties, *portrayed by Michael J. Fox. This would indicate that both Fox and Keaton existed in the same reality—despite the fact that an excerpt of* Family Ties *was playing on a television screen when Marty visited Café 80's in* Back to the Future II.

- *Keatonsian Economics*: A textbook written by Alex Keaton. Marty McFly borrowed this volume from Hill Valley's local library in 1991, and returned it overdue [**BFCM-3**].

- **Keller, PFC:** A soldier at a U.S. government aboveground atomic bomb testing site in Atkins, Nevada. Emmett Brown and Marty McFly visited the base in 1952, in order to harness a bomb blast's nuclear energy to power a time machine and send Marty back to the future [**BTF1-s2**].

  NOTE: The nuclear test-site sequence was cut from the final version of BTTF1 (the setting of which was changed to 1955), though storyboards were included as a Blu-ray extra. The first two script drafts set the base in the fictional Nevada city of Atkins, while the third moved it to New Mexico.

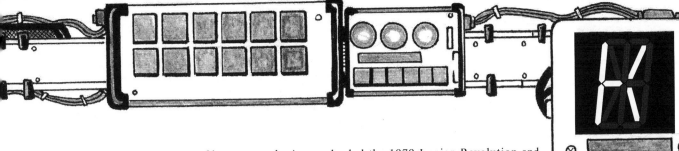

- **kelp:** A group of 30 genera of large seaweeds belonging to the brown algae family [**REAL**]. According to a *USA Today* report in 2015, pollution in the South Pacific caused an increase in kelp prices that year [**BTF2**].

- **Kelp:** A largely built, dim-witted, blue-haired athlete who attended college with Marty McFly and Jennifer Parker in 1991. When Jennifer agreed to tutor him, Marty became very jealous, mistaking their time together as romantic [**BFAN-4**].

   NOTE: Kelp may have also appeared in episode 14, "Mac the Black," as a similar-looking character picked Jennifer up in a sports car after she and Marty had a fight. That character, however, was not identified.

- **kelp tea:** A popular drink in 2015. Marty McFly Jr. enjoyed this beverage [**BTF2-d**].

- **Ken:** A fashion doll manufactured by Mattel, and introduced in 1961 as Barbie's boyfriend [**REAL**]. A Ken doll was among the items for sale at Blast From the Past, an antique and collectibles shop in 2015 Hill Valley [**BTF2**].

- **Kennedy, John Fitzgerald, President ("Jack"):** The 35th President of the United States, from 1961 to 1963 [**REAL**].
   John F. Kennedy Drive, a street in Hill Valley named in his memory, was located a block past Riverside Drive in 1985. Three decades prior, before Kennedy had distinguished himself in politics, it was known as Maple [**BTF1**].
   A bust of Kennedy was among the items for sale at Blast From the Past, an antique and collectibles shop in 2015 Hill Valley [**BTF2**].

- **Kenny:** A construction worker in Hill Valley, circa 1952. He and a co-worker, Benny, were assigned to demolish a skyscraper using dynamite. Emmett Brown, believing himself to be a superhero named Mega Brainman, tried to rescue the building's occupants, unaware it had previously been condemned and evacuated, and was caught in the explosion—which he somehow survived [**BFAN-24**].

- **Kentucky Red Eye:** A type of whiskey favored by Buford Tannen [**BTF3-s1**].

- **Khomeini, Ruhollah Musavi, Grand Ayatollah Sayyed:** An Iranian religious leader and politician who led the 1979 Iranian Revolution and overthrew Mohammad Reza Pahlavi, the Shah of Iran [**REAL**]. A Max Headroom-style video simulacrum of Khomeini greeted customers at the Café 80's, interrupting a simulacrum of Ronald Reagan to demand that visitors try the Hostage Special [**BTF2**].

   NOTE: This was an in-joke reference to a diplomatic crisis between Iran and the United States, from 1979 to 1981, in which 52 Americans were held hostage for 444 days by Islamist students and militants, backed by Khomeini, who took over the American Embassy in Tehran in support of the Iranian Revolution.

   In BTTF2's novelization, as well as in a combined script for both sequel films, titled Paradox, *the dish was called the Great Satan Special (referring to "Great Satan," a nickname for the United States among some Middle East countries). Onscreen, however, Khomeini urged visitors to try the "Hostage Special."*

- **Kick Me:** A phrase scrawled on a piece of paper that a schoolmate of George McFly taped to his back at Hill Valley High School in 1955, as a prank. Seeing George receiving kicks from other students, Emmett Brown speculated that George's future son, Marty, may have been adopted [**BTF1**].

- **Kid Jr.:** The name by which gangster Irving "Kid" Tannen referred to his handgun [**TLTL-2**].

- *Kids, The: Marty Junior and Marlene, Vol. 1-3:* A three-volume set of videobooks in the house of Marty and Jennifer McFly, circa 2015. When Jennifer's younger self from 1985 visited her future home, she saw these and other videobooks stored on a shelf [**BTF2-sx, BTF2-n**].

- **Kid's Ice Cream:** A front business owned by Irving "Kid" Tannen. In the event of a police raid of Tannen's speakeasy, El Kid, a panic button could be pushed by the bartender, Zane Williams, thereby hiding all liquor and gambling tables, and mechanically converting the place into an ice-cream parlor [**TLTL-2**].

- **Kidus:** An employee of the Crestview Service Center. One day, Kidus and three other automotive mechanics shared Bud Light beers while on break,

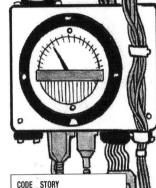

CODE	STORY
NIKE	*BTTF*-themed TV commercial: Nike
NTND	Nintendo *Back to the Future—The Ride* Mini-Game
PIZA	*BTTF*-themed TV commercial: Pizza Hut
PNBL	Data East *BTTF* pinball game
REAL	Real life
RIDE	Simulator: *Back to the Future—The Ride*
SCRM	2010 Scream Awards: *Back to the Future* 25th Anniversary Reunion (broadcast)
SCRT	2010 Scream Awards: *Back to the Future* 25th Anniversary Reunion (trailer)
SIMP	Simulator: *The Simpsons Ride*
SLOT	*Back to the Future Video Slots*
STLZ	Unused *BTTF* footage of Eric Stoltz as Marty McFly
STRY	*Back to the Future Storybook*
TEST	Screen tests: Crispin Glover, Lea Thompson and Tom Wilson
TLTL	Telltale Games' *Back to the Future—The Game*
TOPS	Topps' *Back to the Future II* trading-card set
TRIL	*BTTF: The Official Book of the Complete Movie Trilogy*
UNIV	Universal Studios Hollywood promotional video

SUFFIX	MEDIUM
-b	*BTTF2's* Biff Tannen Museum video (extended)
-c	Credit sequence to the animated series
-d	Film deleted scene
-n	Film novelization
-o	Film outtake
-p	1955 phone book from *BTTF1*
-v	Video game print materials or commentaries
-s1	Screenplay (draft one)
-s2	Screenplay (draft two)
-s3	Screenplay (draft three)
-s4	Screenplay (draft four)
-sp	Screenplay (production draft)
-sx	Screenplay (*Paradox*)

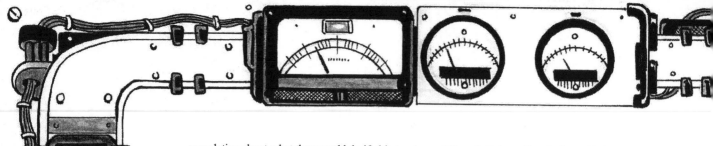

speculating about what they would do if able to time-travel. One, Ali, indicated he would invent fire and then copyright it, while Kidus said he would travel to the past and murder his father.

As they discussed the topic, Emmett Brown's DeLorean appeared on a nearby lift. Kidus suddenly vanished upon vowing patricide, having erased himself from history due to never having been born, and the DeLorean disappeared a moment later. Due to the temporal alteration, the others' knowledge of Kidus' existence was retroactively erased [**BUDL**].

- **Killer:** A name that Jules and Verne Brown considered for a baby Apatosaurus that Verne had found while visiting prehistoric times. Eventually, they settled on the ironic name Tiny [**BFAN-26**].

- **Killer Porsche:** A blue toy sports car used by Jules and Verne Brown to stage games of Turboliner Death-Race. Operated by Verne, the Killer Porsche raced the Diesel of Doom, a model train remote-controlled by Jules. While visiting England in 1367, the brothers modified the car to give their father, Emmett Brown, an advantage during a joust with Lord Biffingham [**BFAN-2**].

- **King City:** A city located east of Hill Valley, as indicated on a map in 2015 [**BTF3**].

- **kirgo:** A slang phrase used in 2015 meaning "crazy," as in "Are you kirgo? We could get our crags numped!" [**BTF2-sx, BTF2-n**].

- **Kirk Gibson Jr. Slugger 2000:** An adjustable baseball bat, painted red. The Slugger 2000 was a weapon of choice of thug Griff Tannen [**BTF2**].

    > ***NOTE:*** *Kirk Gibson was an outfielder for several Major League Baseball teams in the late 20th century. His son's name is Kirk Jr.*

- **Kit-Kat:** A manufacturer of classic feline-faced alarm clocks, with eyes that moved back and forth [**REAL**]. Emmett Brown had such a clock in his home, set to chime in synch with many others [**BTF1**].

- **Kitty Hawk:** A city in North Carolina, in which Wilbur and Orville Wright created the world's first successful airplane in 1903 [**REAL**]. Emmett Brown witnessed this historic event, having journeyed back to that year aboard his time-traveling DeLorean [**RIDE**].

- **Kiwanis International:** A worldwide coeducational service club [**REAL**] that operated a chapter in Hill Valley [**BTF1, BTF2**].

- **Kiwi:** An Australian-made brand of shoe polish [**REAL**]. While using Kiwi to shine Irving "Kid" Tannen's shoes, one of the gangster's underlings, Matches, became sloppy and spread the polish all over Kid's socks [**TLTL-1**].

- **KKHV:** A California radio station, circa 1955, that marketed itself as "the voice of Hill Valley" [**BTF2**].

- **KL-4253:** The telephone number of a prototype hands-free telephone model featured in the Phone Booth of the Future display at the 1931 Hill Valley Exposition [**TLTL-5**].

- **KL-4385:** The telephone number of Emmett Brown's family residence, circa 1931 [**TLTL-5**].

- **KL 5-438:** The telephone number of Lou's Café in 1955, according to the eatery's stationery [**BTF1**].

- **Klein, Calvin:** An American fashion designer, and the founder of Calvin Klein, Inc. [**REAL**]. As a teenager, Marty McFly wore Calvin Klein underwear. When Marty was struck by a car in 1955 belonging to his grandfather (Sam Baines), Marty's future mother (Lorraine Baines) noticed his underwear and assumed "Calvin Klein" to be his name. He continued to use the name throughout his stay in that era, claiming that people usually called him "Marty" rather than "Calvin" or "Cal" [**BTF1**].

- **Klein, Marty:** An alias used by Marty McFly when he performed at Hill Valley High School's 1955 student dance. He chose the name after his mother, Lorraine Baines, mistook the name "Calvin Klein" on his underwear as his own [**BTF1-s3**].

    > ***NOTE:*** *This name appeared in BTTF1's third-draft screenplay, in which Marvin Berry was called Marvin Moon. In that draft, the event was the Springtime in Paris Dance. Onscreen, Marty performed at the Enchantment Under the Sea Dance.*

- **Kline, Ark:** A Hollywood producer, circa 2015, who helped director Max Spielberg create *Jaws 19*, according to the film's poster [**BTF2**].

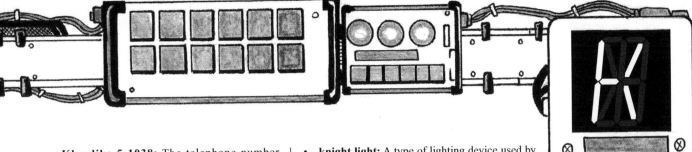

- **Klondike 5-1038:** The telephone number of Emmett Brown's family mansion in 1931 [**TLTL-1**].

- **Klondike 5-4385:** The telephone number of scientist Emmett Brown, circa 1955, at his home at 1640 Riverside Drive [**BTF1**].

  NOTE: In BTTF1*'s initial-draft screenplay, Brown lived at 788 West Spruce, with a phone number of Madison 3489.*

- **Klozoff, Oliver:** A name mentioned by Marty McFly as he tested out the Personal Phone Helmet in the House of Tomorrow exhibit at the 1931 Hill Valley Exposition. Assuming a false voice and the pseudonym Anthony, Marty dialed the nearby Phone Booth of the Future exhibit and asked for Oliver Klozoff. Sylvia "Trixie Trotter" Miskin, who answered the phone, was not amused by the joke [**TLTL-5**].

  NOTE: This practical joke played on the phonetic similarity between "Oliver Klozoff" and the phrase "all of her clothes off."

- **Klystron Beam Voltage Test Adjust:** A switch on Emmett Brown's giant guitar amplifier, and part of the device's Master control [**BTF1**].

  NOTE: A klystron—a specialized linear-beam vacuum tube—can be used as an amplifier at microwave and radio frequencies. Klystron amplifiers coherently amplify a reference signal so its output can be precisely controlled in amplitude, frequency and phase.

- **Klystron HV:** A toggle on Emmett Brown's giant guitar amplifier, and part of the device's Driver Adjust system [**BTF1**].

- **Klystron Test:** A setting on Emmett Brown's giant guitar amplifier, and part of the device's Variable Autotransformer, on a knob labeled "Type 200B / VARIAC / 115V 60~ 1A" [**BTF1**].

- **KM Avenue:** A road in Hill Valley. A pizzeria was located at the corner of 23rd Street and KM Avenue [**BFAN-22**].

  NOTE: This street's name was likely an in-joke reference to Ken Mitchroney, an animator who worked on the Back to the Future *cartoon series.*

- **knight light:** A type of lighting device used by Lord Biffingham, the Earl of Tannenshire, circa 1367. Before going to sleep at the end of each day, the tyrannical English nobleman turned on his knight light, which was shaped like a horse and armored knight [**BFHM**].

  NOTE: The lamp seemed to be electrically lit, but given the medieval setting in which he lived, it's possible it was actually candle-powered.

- **Koetter, C. ("Curly"):** An employee at the Institute of Future Technology, stationed in the East Wing [**RIDE**].

  NOTE: This individual was identified on signage outside Back to the Future: The Ride.

- **Konovalov, George:** An employee at the Institute of Future Technology, stationed in the West Wing [**RIDE**].

  NOTE: This individual, identified on signage outside Back to the Future: The Ride, *was named after a Universal Studios engineer.*

- **Kraft Foods:** An American food and beverage conglomerate, marketing such brands as Cadbury, Oscar Mayer, Nabisco, Maxwell House and others [**REAL**]. The McFly family often ate Kraft macaroni and cheese for dinner, much to Marty McFly's disgust [**BTF1-s4, BTF1-n**].

- **Krakatoa:** A volcanic island in the Sunda Strait, located between the Indonesian islands of Java and Sumatra. Krakatoa exploded in 1883, killing 40,000 inhabitants [**REAL**].

  Pursued by Emmett Brown, fraudulent scientist Walter Wisdom stole Doc's time-traveling DeLorean and fled to the year and site of that catastrophe, hoping to kill Doc and his family in the impending eruption. Only by donning Doc's Full-Body Oven Mits did the Browns survive the deadly lava [**BFAN-15**].

- **Krustyland:** A theme park owned by Krusty the Clown, built on the site of the former Institute of Future Technology (IFT). Professor John I.Q. Nerdelbaum Frink Jr., visiting the institute to see friend and colleague Emmett Brown, found it replaced by Krustyland.

  Curious as to why this change had occurred,

CODE	STORY
NIKE	*BTTF*-themed TV commercial: Nike
NTND	Nintendo *Back to the Future—The Ride* Mini-Game
PIZA	*BTTF*-themed TV commercial: Pizza Hut
PNBL	Data East *BTTF* pinball game
REAL	Real life
RIDE	Simulator: *Back to the Future—The Ride*
SCRM	2010 Scream Awards: *Back to the Future* 25th Anniversary Reunion (broadcast)
SCRT	2010 Scream Awards: *Back to the Future* 25th Anniversary Reunion (trailer)
SIMP	Simulator: *The Simpsons Ride*
SLOT	*Back to the Future Video Slots*
STLZ	Unused *BTTF* footage of Eric Stoltz as Marty McFly
STRY	*Back to the Future Storybook*
TEST	Screen tests: Crispin Glover, Lea Thompson and Tom Wilson
TLTL	Telltale Games' *Back to the Future—The Game*
TOPS	Topps' *Back to the Future II* trading-card set
TRIL	*BTTF: The Official Book of the Complete Movie Trilogy*
UNIV	Universal Studios Hollywood promotional video

SUFFIX	MEDIUM
-b	*BTTF2*'s Biff Tannen Museum video (extended)
-c	Credit sequence to the animated series
-d	Film deleted scene
-n	Film novelization
-o	Film outtake
-p	1955 phone book from *BTTF1*
-v	Video game print materials or commentaries
-s1	Screenplay (draft one)
-s2	Screenplay (draft two)
-s3	Screenplay (draft three)
-s4	Screenplay (draft four)
-sp	Screenplay (production draft)
-sx	Screenplay (*Paradox*)

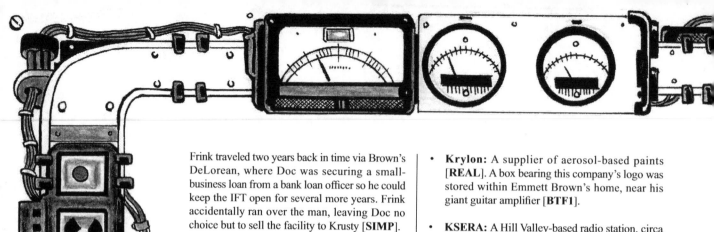

Frink traveled two years back in time via Brown's DeLorean, where Doc was securing a small-business loan from a bank loan officer so he could keep the IFT open for several more years. Frink accidentally ran over the man, leaving Doc no choice but to sell the facility to Krusty [**SIMP**].

> ***NOTE:*** *The theme park, from TV's* The Simpsons, *appeared in queue footage in* The Simpsons Ride, *as an in-joke reference to Universal Studios Florida's replacement of* Back to the Future: The Ride *with that attraction.*

- **Krusty the Clown:** A cynical, burnt-out television personality, born Herschel Shmoikel Pinchas Yerucham Krustofski. Krusty was the owner of the Krustyland theme park, which he built on the site of the former Institute of Future Technology (IFT), after Emmett Brown failed to secure a loan to keep the facility open [**SIMP**].

> ***NOTE:*** *This character, from TV's* The Simpsons, *appeared in queue footage in* The Simpsons Ride, *as an in-joke reference to Universal Studios Florida's replacement of* Back to the Future: The Ride *with that attraction.*

- **Krylon:** A supplier of aerosol-based paints [**REAL**]. A box bearing this company's logo was stored within Emmett Brown's home, near his giant guitar amplifier [**BTF1**].

- **KSERA:** A Hill Valley-based radio station, circa 2015, that played hits from the 1980s and '90s [**BTF2-s1**].

> ***NOTE:*** *The station's name had five call letters, indicating that by 2015, a fifth letter had been added to the naming convention for radio broadcasters.*

- **Kubsch, Christian:** An employee at the Institute of Future Technology, in charge of interdimensional studies [**RIDE**].

> ***NOTE:*** *This individual, identified on signage outside* Back to the Future: The Ride, *was named after an employee at Universal Studios, who worked on the ride as the production manager.*

- **Kurzweil, Larry, Ph.D.:** A project director at the Institute of Future Technology [**RIDE**].

> ***NOTE:*** *This individual, identified on signage outside* Back to the Future: The Ride, *was named after Universal Studios' president and chief operating officer.*

LIGHTNING

- **L-131:** A doorway at Hill Valley High School, circa 1955, that led to Gerald Strickland's office [**BTF2**].

- **L 894944210 B:** A serial number printed on "Biff Bucks" [**BTF2**].

    NOTE: *"Biff Buck" props in several denominations were created for use in* Back to the Future II, *all of which contained the same serial number.*

- **L9:** A button on a security keypad used to access the Institute of Future Technology's Anti-Gravitic Laboratory [**RIDE**].

- **La Bamba Tortilla Pie Platter Uno:** A menu item sold at Café 80's in 2015 [**BTF2**].

- **Lab Rats Gone Bad, The:** A trio of rodents owned by Walter Wisdom, the host of children's TV series *Mr. Wisdom* [**BFAN-15, BFAN-26**].

    The rodents, kept caged in the scientist's Big-Brain Bus, each had a different fur color: brown, light-blue and purple. Wisdom, a fraud who manipulated kids into buying spinoff merchandise by pretending to be a great scientist, used a pane of glass to distort the rats' image, making them appear mutated into foul-tempered giants [**BFAN-15**].

    Wisdom threatened to unleash the Lab Rats Gone Bad on Biff Tannen when it appeared that Biff had scammed him with a fake dinosaur [**BFAN-26**].

- **Ladies' Decency Society:** An organization in Hill Valley, circa 1931, of which Edna Strickland was a member. When Arthur McFly thwarted Edna's attempt to have Sylvia "Trixie Trotter" Miskin fired from her job at the Hill Valley Exposition, due to Trixie's Canadian citizenship, Edna threatened to bring the matter to the Ladies' Decency Society [**TLTL-5**].

CODE	STORY
NIKE	*BTTF*-themed TV commercial: Nike
NTND	Nintendo *Back to the Future—The Ride* Mini-Game
PIZA	*BTTF*-themed TV commercial: Pizza Hut
PNBL	Data East *BTTF* pinball game
REAL	Real life
RIDE	Simulator: *Back to the Future—The Ride*
SCRM	2010 Scream Awards: *Back to the Future 25th Anniversary Reunion* (broadcast)
SCRT	2010 Scream Awards: *Back to the Future 25th Anniversary Reunion* (trailer)
SIMP	Simulator: *The Simpsons Ride*
SLOT	*Back to the Future Video Slots*
STLZ	Unused *BTTF* footage of Eric Stoltz as Marty McFly
STRY	*Back to the Future Storybook*
TEST	Screen tests: Crispin Glover, Lea Thompson and Tom Wilson
TLTL	Telltale Games' *Back to the Future—The Game*
TOPS	Topps' *Back to the Future II* trading-card set
TRIL	*BTTF: The Official Book of the Complete Movie Trilogy*
UNIV	Universal Studios Hollywood promotional video

SUFFIX	MEDIUM
-b	*BTTF2*'s Biff Tannen Museum video (extended)
-c	Credit sequence to the animated series
-d	Film deleted scene
-n	Film novelization
-o	Film outtake
-p	1955 phone book from *BTTF1*
-v	Video game print materials or commentaries
-s1	Screenplay (draft one)
-s2	Screenplay (draft two)
-s3	Screenplay (draft three)
-s4	Screenplay (draft four)
-sp	Screenplay (production draft)
-sx	Screenplay (*Paradox*)

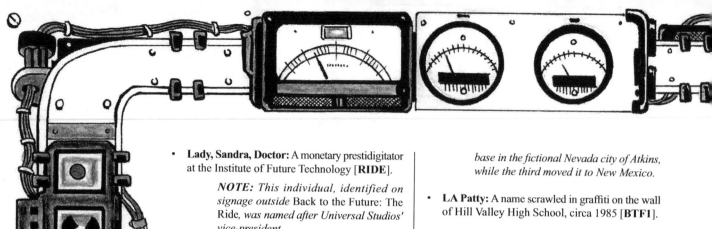

- **Lady, Sandra, Doctor:** A monetary prestidigitator at the Institute of Future Technology [**RIDE**].

  NOTE: This individual, identified on signage outside Back to the Future: The Ride, *was named after Universal Studios' vice-president.*

- **Laguna Hills**: A city in California's southern Orange County [**REAL**]. In 1991, Emmett Brown read a help-wanted ad for a company in this city while trying to find a job [**BFAN-12**].

  NOTE: The name of this company is unknown, as that portion of the ad was obstructed from view.

- **Lake, The:** A secluded body of water in or near Hill Valley. Marty McFly enjoyed taking his girlfriend, Jennifer Parker, here for romantic interludes beneath the stars [**BTF1**].

  NOTE: It's unknown if the lake had a proper name.

- **Lamont's House of Ermine:** A furrier located in Hill Valley. By 1931, Lamont's, hit hard by the Great Depression, closed for business [**TLTL-1**]. Lamont's later donated furs for use at a dinosaur diorama at the Hill Valley Exposition [**TLTL-4**].

  NOTE: The ermine (also called a short-tailed weasel, or stoat) is sometimes cultivated for its fur.

  It's unclear whether Lamont's donated the furs prior to going out of business, or resumed operation by the time of the expo.

- **Lancers Family Restaurant:** An eatery located near Emmett Brown's home in Hill Valley, circa 1985, that served food and cocktails [**BTF1**].

- **Land of Certain Obliteration:** *See* Pectoria

- **Lanza, Major:** A U.S. military officer at an aboveground atomic bomb testing site in Atkins, Nevada. Emmett Brown and Marty McFly visited his base in 1952, to harness a bomb blast's nuclear energy in order to send Marty back to the future [**BTF1-s1**].

  NOTE: The nuclear test-site sequence was cut from the final version of BTTF1 (the setting of which was changed to 1955), though storyboards were included as a Blu-ray extra. The first two script drafts set the

base in the fictional Nevada city of Atkins, while the third moved it to New Mexico.

- **LA Patty:** A name scrawled in graffiti on the wall of Hill Valley High School, circa 1985 [**BTF1**].

- **Lapinski, Betty:** The grandmother of Jennifer Parker, and wife of rookie policemen Daniel J. Parker—until Marty McFly inadvertently caused a series of events leading to Betty leaving Danny in 1931, thereby preventing Jen's birth. In the new timeline, Danny was demoted for losing both a witness he'd been guarding (Arthur McFly) and an arsonist he'd had in custody (Emmett Brown, disguised as drifter Carl Sagan).

  Danny attributed these failures to a futuristic "space-car" (Doc's DeLorean, driven by Marty) thwarting his efforts. This made Betty see Danny as a bad provider and a "head-case," and so she ended their relationship. To fix the damage, Marty convinced Danny to restore his reputation by arresting gangster Irving "Kid" Tannen. Betty came to respect and love him once again, and the two continued their courtship [**TLTL-2**].

  With the timeline restored, Betty and Danny had a son, Daniel Jr., who later fathered a daughter, Jennifer [**TLTL-3**].

- **Largo:** A name scrawled in graffiti on the wall of Hill Valley High School, circa 1985 [**BTF1**].

- **LaserDisc:** A home-video format popular in the 1980s and 1990s, and the first commercial optical disc-storage medium [**REAL**]. By 2015, old LaserDiscs were recycled by such companies as the P.K. Rata Recycling Center [**BTF2**].

- *Lassie*: A CBS television series that aired from 1954 to 1973, about a Rough Collie named Lassie and her human friends [**REAL**]. Marty McFly often watched reruns of this series as a child [**BTF3-n**].

- **Last Year Departed:** A gauge on the time circuits of a time-traveling DeLorean DMC-12 sports car designed by Emmett Brown. The gauge specified the month, day, year, hour and minute (as well as A.M. or P.M.) from which a time-traveler departed before arriving at his or her destination date, based on data entered on a keypad [**BTF1**].

- **Lathrop, Abraham:** An uncle of Emmett Brown, on whose ranch Emmett spent summers as a youth.

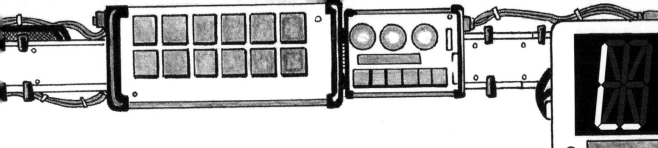

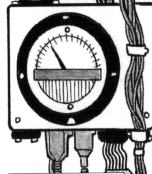

Abraham taught his nephew how to ride, shoot and rope, instilling in him a desire to be a cowboy, and preparing him for his time later spent in the Old West [**BTF3-sx**]. Abraham's sister, Sarah Lathrop, was Emmett's mother [**BTF3-s1**].

> *NOTE: Abraham was mentioned, sans surname, in the script* Paradox; *BTTF3's first-draft screenplay provided his last name of Lathrop.*
>
> *In the film's production-draft script, Doc indicated that he'd learned to ride and shoot on "Statler's ranch," not from Abraham.*

- **Lathrop, Sarah:** The mother of Emmett Brown [**BTF3-s1**], wife of Erhardt Brown [**TLTL-1**] and sister of Abraham Lathrop. Marty briefly met Sarah and her brother in 1885, when she was still a little girl. At the time, she had a rag doll named Emma [**BTF3-s1**].

- **lava lamp:** A decorative novelty item consisting of a glass vessel filled with clear liquid, in which blobs of colored wax rose and fell as their density changed due to heating from an incandescent light bulb [**REAL**].
  A lava lamp made in 1967 was among the items for sale at Blast From the Past, an antique and collectibles shop in 2015 Hill Valley [**BTF2**].

- ***Law:*** A book published in or before 1931, containing rules and guidelines governing citizens' behavior. As a young man, Emmett Brown had a copy of this book while working as a clerk at the Hill Valley Courthouse [**TLTL-1**].

- ***Law Journal:*** A multi-volume set of legal textbooks, circa 1931. As a young man working as a clerk at the Hill Valley Courthouse, Emmett Brown had a set of these books in his office [**TLTL-1, TLTL-5**].

- **Law Offices of Gale, Zemeckis, & Fine:** A group of lawyers operating in Hill Valley, circa 1931. Emmett Brown—who, at the time, worked as a clerk for his father, Judge Brown, at the Hill Valley Courthouse—sometimes dealt with the attorneys at this business [**TLTL-1**].

> *NOTE: This business was named after* Back to the Future *screenwriters Bob Gale and Robert Zemeckis, as well as the Three Stooges, which frequently used the*

names Howard, Howard and Fine (after Moe Howard, Curly Howard and Larry Fine). Gale and Zemeckis included several references to the Stooges in early drafts of BTTF1's screenplay (see Shemp entry).

- **Lawrence Building:** An edifice in Courthouse Square, circa 1985 [**BTF1**].

- **lawyer:** A person educated in a country's laws, and trained to serve as an attorney, counsel or solicitor [**REAL**]. By 2015, lawyers had been abolished from the U.S. legal system, making the justice process move much more swiftly [**BTF2**].

- **Lazy J Ranch:** An area of land in Hill Valley on which the Lazy J Riders raised grazing livestock in 1885. The ranch was among the most profitable in the area, until eventually falling on hard times. Photographs of the ranch were documented in the archives of the Hill Valley Historical Society [**BTF3**].

- **Lazy J Riders:** A group of ranchers who operated the successful Lazy J Ranch, circa 1885. Photographs of the Riders were stored among the Hill Valley Historical Society's archives. A dispute between the Lazy J Riders and Buford Tannen resulted in many ranchers dying during a shootout. At the inquest that followed, Tannen was aquitted since no witnesses could be found to testify against him. However, some accounts indicated that he'd just purchased a new set of Colt pistols, and that he was overheard to have claimed he "wanted to try them out" [**BTF3**].

- **LeBrock 2.0:** A computer program in Citizen Brown's dystopian timeline. LeBrock 2.0 provided anatomical constructs for use in multiple sciences [**TLTL-3**].

> *NOTE: This software's name paid homage to actress Kelly LeBrock, who portrayed an anatomically perfect woman created via computer in the film* Weird Science *(see* Weird Science *entry).*

- **Leech:** A teenage acquaintance of Marty McFly. Tall and thin, he had a skull tattoo on his right arm, and was the front man of the punk-rock band Leech and the Wooshbags. In Citizen Brown's dystopian timeline, Leech worked as a window cashier at a restaurant called SoupMo, and dated Jennifer Parker. He was allergic to dogs and disco.

CODE	STORY
NIKE	*BTTF*-themed TV commercial: Nike
NTND	Nintendo *Back to the Future—The Ride* Mini-Game
PIZA	*BTTF*-themed TV commercial: Pizza Hut
PNBL	Data East *BTTF* pinball game
REAL	Real life
RIDE	Simulator: *Back to the Future—The Ride*
SCRM	2010 Scream Awards: *Back to the Future 25th Anniversary Reunion* (broadcast)
SCRT	2010 Scream Awards: *Back to the Future 25th Anniversary Reunion* (trailer)
SIMP	Simulator: *The Simpsons Ride*
SLOT	*Back to the Future Video Slots*
STLZ	Unused *BTTF* footage of Eric Stoltz as Marty McFly
STRY	*Back to the Future Storybook*
TEST	Screen tests: Crispin Glover, Lea Thompson and Tom Wilson
TLTL	Telltale Games' *Back to the Future—The Game*
TOPS	Topps' *Back to the Future II* trading-card set
TRIL	*BTTF: The Official Book of the Complete Movie Trilogy*
UNIV	Universal Studios Hollywood promotional video

SUFFIX	MEDIUM
-b	*BTTF2's* Biff Tannen Museum video (extended)
-c	Credit sequence to the animated series
-d	Film deleted scene
-n	Film novelization
-o	Film outtake
-p	1955 phone book from *BTTF1*
-v	Video game print materials or commentaries
-s1	Screenplay (draft one)
-s2	Screenplay (draft two)
-s3	Screenplay (draft three)
-s4	Screenplay (draft four)
-sp	Screenplay (production draft)
-sx	Screenplay (*Paradox*)

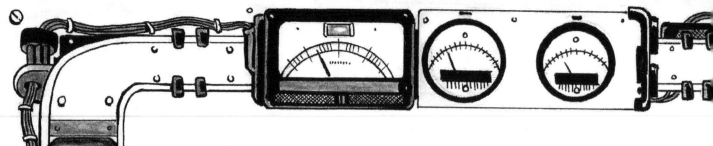

Marty, determined to win Jennifer away from Leech, challenged him to a guitar battle, in which the two dueled by playing complicated guitar riffs. Marty won when Leech lost his footing and fell into a dumpster, causing Jennifer to choose him over Leech [**TLTL-3**].

> *NOTE: Leech was originally intended to be Douglas J. Needles, Marty's high school nemesis from the sequel films, but when singer/actor Michael Peter "Flea" Balzary was unavailable to reprise his role as Needless, Telltale Games instead created a new, similar character named Leech.*
>
> *Marty's recognition and dislike of Leech in the dystopian timeline indicates that the two were rivals in both realities.*

- **Leech and the Wooshbags:** A teenage punk-rock band that performed in violation of the rules of Citizen Brown's oppressive utopia. In that timeline, Jennifer Parker was a fan of this group, and often spray-painted their name on public property [**TLTL-3**].

- *Legend of Gruno, The:* A video game in which a giant, one-eyed monster with twin antennas and orange fur rampaged through a city, besieged by helicopters. Verne Brown excelled at this particular game [**BFAN-1**].

- **Leo:** The owner of Super Mega Arcade World, located in Hill Valley, circa 1992. The nerdish, overweight businessman disliked bullies, and vainly tried to force Biff Tannen Jr. to stop bothering other children within his establishment [**BFAN-19**].

- **Leonardo da Vinci:** *See* da Vinci, Leonardo

- *Lepidoptera Martha*: A species of blue and purple butterfly discovered in 1850 by Daniel Clayton, which he named after his new bride, Martha O'Brien [**BFAN-13**].

- **Leromf:** A brand of Irish cream served at the El Kid speakeasy in 1931 [**TLTL-2**].

- **Lester:** A teenager who attended Hill Valley High School in 1955, and was often beaten up by Biff Tannen's gang since he was too scrawny to fight back [**BTF2-n**].

  When Marty McFly retrieved *Grays Sports*

Almanac from Biff Tannen—whom George McFly had knocked unconscious outside the Enchantment Under the Sea Dance—Lester mistook this action for pickpocketing and thought Marty had stolen Biff's wallet [**BTF2**].

After Biff awoke, Lester told him what had happened, hoping this would spare him further beatings for at least a few weeks [**BTF2-n**].

> *NOTE: This character, identified as "CPR Kid" in* BTTF2*'s closing credits, was named Lester in the novelization. Although the actor portraying Lester was featured only in* Back to the Future II, *the character had appeared (portrayed by an extra, sans dialog) during the same scene in the first movie, in which an identically clad student could be seen kneeling over Biff.*
>
> *Telltale Games'* BTTF *video game paid homage to Lester's line, "I think he took his wallet," by having a similar-looking man make the same accusation toward Marty in 1931.*

- **Lester:** A citizen of Hill Valley in Citizen Brown's dystopian timeline. A rebellious fellow, Lester privately commented that Brown could kiss his hairy rear end. George McFly spied on Lester's conversations for the government, via video monitors in his home [**TLTL-3**].

> *NOTE: It's unknown if this was meant to be the same Lester who'd accused Marty McFly of stealing Biff Tannen's wallet in 1955.*

- **Lester, Warren:** A neighbor of the McFly family, circa 1985. Warren, a piano tuner, had two young daughters. In Biffhorrific 1985, in which an African-American family inhabited the McFly home, Lester had no memory of the McFlys [**BTF2-s1**].

- **Lester Moon and the Midnighters:** *See* Marvin Berry and the Starlighters

- **Levi:** An old-timer who frequented Hill Valley's Palace Saloon and Hotel in 1885, along with Jeb, Zeke, Toothless, Eyepatch and Moustache [**BTF3-sp, BTF3-n**]. He had unkempt white hair, wore a brown derby hat and cackled when he laughed [**BTF3**].

Levi had a son who once returned from a trip to the east, wearing fancy clothing similar

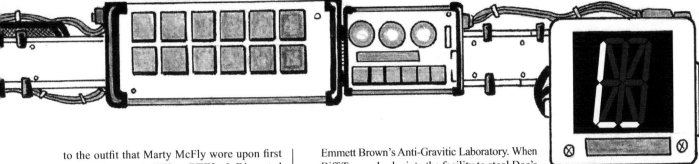

to the outfit that Marty McFly wore upon first arriving in 1885 [**BTF3-n, BTF3-o**]. Disgusted by his son's behavior, the oldster set fire to the lad [**BTF3-n**].

When Marty refused to fight Buford Tannen, Levi mocked his cowardice, telling him to go out and face the outlaw, as he had bet $20 in gold on the youth [**BTF3**].

> *NOTE: This character, unnamed onscreen, was identified as Levi in BTTF3's novelization and storyboards, as well as in Paradox, a combined script for both film sequels.*

- **Lewis:** An African-American man who lived in Marty McFly's former home in Lyon Estates, in Biffhorrific 1985. He and his wife, Louise, had two children, Loretta and Harold. Marty—unaware that time had changed, and that he didn't live there anymore—climbed into the window of what was once his bedroom, causing young Loretta to scream, and Lewis to furiously chase him out of the house with a baseball bat, mistaking Marty as one of Biff's enforcers, sent to bully them into selling their house [**BTF2**].

> *NOTE: The family was unnamed onscreen, though Loretta and Harold were identified in the end credits. BTTF2's novelization identified the father as Lewis, while the movie's first-draft script named the wife Louise.*

- **Lewis, Jerry:** An American actor, comedian, film producer and singer [**REAL**]. When Marty McFly tried to convince Emmett Brown, in 1955, that he was from the future, the scientist challenged him to name the president in 1985. Marty replied Ronald Reagan, but Brown scoffed at the notion, mockingly asking if Lewis was the vice-president [**BTF1**].

- **Lewis, Marty:** An alias that Emmett Brown gave to Marty McFly after the latter traveled back in time to 1952. According to the scientist's fictional backstory, Marty was Brown's second cousin on his mother's side [**BTF1-s1**].

- **Level 1:** A section of the Institute of Future Technology, containing numerous employee offices and labs [**RIDE**].

- **Level 2:** A section of the Institute of Future Technology. Sector 2 of this level contained

Emmett Brown's Anti-Gravitic Laboratory. When Biff Tannen broke into the facility to steal Doc's time-traveling DeLorean, the scientist checked in with several areas, including Level 2, to make sure they were secure [**RIDE**].

- **Level 3:** A section of the Institute of Future Technology, containing numerous employee offices and labs [**RIDE**].

- **Level 3:** A section of the parking lot outside the Hill Valley Bowl-o-rama [**BFCL-3**].

- **Liberace Fruit Salad:** A menu item sold at Café 80's in 2015 [**BTF2**].

- **Liberty Bell:** A famous symbol of American independence from Great Britain, located in Philadelphia, Pennsylvania [**REAL**].

The bell was cracked in 1752 when Emmett Brown collided with two gentlemen carrying it across a street as he was chasing his son Verne through the city [**BFAN-6**].

> *NOTE: The Liberty Bell is actually believed to have cracked upon its first striking after arriving in Philadelphia.*

- **Library, The:** An "infostore" located in Hill Valley, circa 2015, that marketed itself as "your complete information connection," and featured the works of various authors. Unlike 20th-century bookstores, The Library had only covers on display, with computer terminals behind them [**BTF2-s1**].

> *NOTE: In Back to the Future II's first-draft screenplay, Marty McFly purchased the almanac in this store rather than at Blast From the Past. In that script, the book was titled 2015 Sports Almanac: 50 Years of Sports Statistics 1965-2014.*

- **Libya:** A country in North Africa, bordering the Mediterranean Sea [**REAL**]. In 1985, Libyan nationalists stole a case of plutonium from the Pacific Nuclear Research Facility's vault, hiring scientist Emmett Brown to build a nuclear bomb for them [**BTF1**]. Members of this cell included its leader (codenamed Sam), a former fashion model called Uranda and others [**BTF1-n**].

Brown kept the plutonium for himself, providing the nationalists with used pinball-machine parts. Furious, the Libyans tracked

CODE	STORY
NIKE	*BTTF*-themed TV commercial: Nike
NTND	Nintendo *Back to the Future— The Ride* Mini-Game
PIZA	*BTTF*-themed TV commercial: Pizza Hut
PNBL	Data East *BTTF* pinball game
REAL	Real life
RIDE	Simulator: *Back to the Future—The Ride*
SCRM	2010 Scream Awards: *Back to the Future 25th Anniversary Reunion* (broadcast)
SCRT	2010 Scream Awards: *Back to the Future 25th Anniversary Reunion* (trailer)
SIMP	Simulator: *The Simpsons Ride*
SLOT	*Back to the Future* Video Slots
STLZ	Unused *BTTF* footage of Eric Stoltz as Marty McFly
STRY	*Back to the Future Storybook*
TEST	Screen tests: Crispin Glover, Lea Thompson and Tom Wilson
TLTL	Telltale Games' *Back to the Future—The Game*
TOPS	Topps' *Back to the Future II* trading-card set
TRIL	*BTTF: The Official Book of the Complete Movie Trilogy*
UNIV	Universal Studios Hollywood promotional video

SUFFIX	MEDIUM
-b	*BTTF2*'s Biff Tannen Museum video (extended)
-c	Credit sequence to the animated series
-d	Film deleted scene
-n	Film novelization
-o	Film outtake
-p	1955 phone book from *BTTF1*
-v	Video game print materials or commentaries
-s1	Screenplay (draft one)
-s2	Screenplay (draft two)
-s3	Screenplay (draft three)
-s4	Screenplay (draft four)
-sp	Screenplay (production draft)
-sx	Screenplay (*Paradox*)

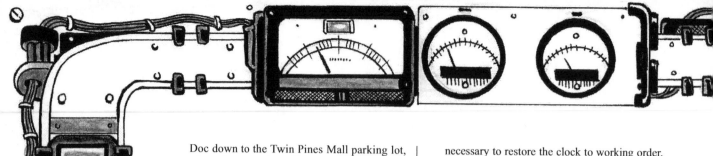

Doc down to the Twin Pines Mall parking lot, where they assassinated him and also tried to kill Marty McFly, who'd witnessed the murder. McFly evaded the Libyans in a time-traveling DeLorean, which propelled him back in time. The terrorists crashed their van into a Fox Photo one-hour film stand as the DeLorean vanished [**BTF1**], and were arrested minutes later by police dispatched to the scene [**BTF1-n**].

In Citizen Brown's dystopian timeline, Emmett Brown repaired the damaged DeLorean by once again entering into a "shady deal" with the Libyans, which (as in the original timeline) cost him his entire family fortune [**TLTL-4**].

> *NOTE: Adult Swim's animated series* Robot Chicken *featured a tongue-in-cheek video of Doc's initial meeting with the Libyans, in a sketch titled "Doc Brown's Plutonium." Doc (voiced by Christopher Lloyd) met with the terrorists, repeatedly assured them that he didn't need any plutonium for himself and wasn't making a time machine, and then provided them with a fully intact pinball machine instead of a bomb.*
>
> *The Web site Funny or Die presented another humorous take on the terrorists, in a short film from ETW Productions titled* Back to the Future: The Libyans, *told from the nationalists' point-of-view.*

- **LIFE:** *See* Game of Life, The (a.k.a. LIFE)

- **lightning:** An atmospheric electrical discharge accompanied by thunder [**REAL**].

    In 1752, Verne Brown altered history by tampering with Benjamin Franklin's lightning experiments, preventing him from ascertaining the nature of electricity, and thus plunging the future into darkness. However, Emmett Brown fixed the timestream by creating a second lightning storm for Franklin to study [**BFAN-6**].

    Emmett's life was endangered by lightning in 1931 when a storm dislodged a statue atop the Hill Valley Courthouse, nearly causing the budding scientist to fall to his death. However, Marty McFy, who was visiting that era to find his time-lost friend, saved Emmett's life [**TLTL-4**].

    In 1955, lightning struck the Hill Valley Courthouse, destroying the Clock Tower on its roof. Three decades later, the Hill Valley Preservation Society attempted to raise the funds

necessary to restore the clock to working order, by seeking donations on the street and handing out fliers to passersby. Marty McFly accepted one of the fliers, which detailed the exact date and time at which the lightning strike occurred. This foreknowledge proved invaluable when Marty was stranded in that year, as it enabled Emmett Brown to channel the lightning's 1.21 jigowatts of electricity into the DeLorean's Flux Capacitor, thereby sending Marty back to the future [**BTF1**].

Marty and Doc later returned to 1955 to prevent old Biff Tannen from changing the future by giving himself a copy of *Grays Sports Almanac*. This culminated in the DeLorean itself being struck by the same lightning storm, this time sending the vehicle and Doc back to 1885 [**BTF2**].

This created a short circuit, destroyed the car's flying circuits, damaged the time circuits and stranded the scientist in the Old West [**BTF3**]. Years later, Doc discovered, during a trip to 2025, that the lightning bolt had also created a temporal duplicate of the DeLorean, which was sent forward in time to that year [**TLTL-1**].

- **Li'l Fender:** One of three crash-test dummies, along with Fender and Bender, used in a safety video at the Institute of Future Technology's Anti-Gravitic Laboratory, to instruct Time-Travel Volunteers how to avoid being injured while operating Emmett Brown's Eight-Passenger DeLorean Time-Travel Vehicle. The dummies banged their heads, had limbs severed by closing doors and were strangulated by cameras caught in a safety restraint—and also broke rules regarding flash photography, eating and smoking—as a warning to those watching the video [**RIDE**].

- **Line 6:** A space on a Western Union receipt that Marty McFly signed in 1955 so he could receive a letter written 70 years earlier by Emmett Brown, during his time spent living in the Old West [**BTF2**].

- **Lions Club:** An international secular service organization formed to meet the needs of local and global communities [**REAL**]. The Lions Club operated a chapter in Hill Valley [**BTF1, BTF2**].

- **Liquid Nitrogen:** A type of fuel offered at Texaco's Hill Valley gas station, circa 2015, priced at $8.10 per gallon [**BTF2**].

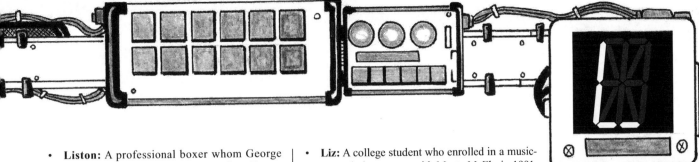

- **Liston:** A professional boxer whom George McFly bested in a 1966 match at Madison Square Garden, in a timeline in which George became a middleweight boxing champion [**BTF1-s1**].

  NOTE: Charles L. "Sonny" Liston became the World Heavyweight Champion in 1962, after knocking out Floyd Patterson during the first round of the match.

- **Lite Gin:** An idea proposed in 1927 by Chicago gangster Mugsy Tannen. The mobster forced pharmacist-in-training Jim McFly to work for him and his boss, Arnie "Eggs" Benedict, to create the beverage, which he hoped would have half the calories but all the taste of regular gin. McFly quit before inventing it, however [**BFCM-1**].

- **Lithium Mode:** A setting on home atmospheric controls in 2015 [**BTF2**].

  NOTE: Lithium compounds are a standard treatment for bipolar disorder and related diagnoses, such as schizoaffective disorder and cyclic major depression. This would imply that the Lithium Mode was used to calm an occupant's nerves.

- **Litter Bug:** A mobile trash-collection robot that roamed the streets of Hill Valley in 2015, providing a receptacle in which pedestrians could discard trash [**BTF2, PIZA**].

- **Little Sunshine:** Clara Clayton's nickname for the Copernicus lunar crater. She assigned the name to the Moon's geographical feature as a child while suffering from diphtheria, with only a telescope that her father had given to her to keep her occupied [**BTF3-n**].

- **liverdog:** A menu item at SoupMo, a restaurant in Citizen Brown's dystopian timeline. Liverdogs were made from peas, liver and soy cheese [**TLTL-3**].

  NOTE: In this reality, Hill Valley's citizens were all vegetarians, by law. Liver may have been exempt from this rule, or it may have been made from soy or some other non-meat product.

- **Livery & Feed Stable:** A business in Hill Valley, circa 1885 [**BTF3**]. Emmett Brown, stranded in that year, moved into the stable and opened a blacksmith shop [**BTF3-n**].

- **Liz:** A college student who enrolled in a music-appreciation course with Marty McFly in 1991. The pretty redhead consoled him when he scored a C- on a test [**BFAN-4**].

  The following year, the fickle and snobbish Liz invited Marty to attend the Country Club Dance with her, but later reneged on her invitation, choosing instead a rich young man named Milton Van Conrad III as her escort. Marty's interest in attending the dance nearly resulted in Jennifer Parker breaking up with him [**BFAN-25**].

- **Loans on Anything of Value:** A local shop in Hill Valley, located near the Cupids adult-books store, circa 1985 [**BTF1**].

- **lobo:** A slang term used by police in 2015 to refer to a person with a substance-abuse problem [**BTF2**].

  NOTE: Back to the Future II's first-draft screenplay spelled the term as "lobo," but the novelization and a combined script of both sequel films, titled Paradox*, hyphenated it as "lo-bo."*

- **Locomotive No. 131:** A passenger and freight steam locomotive for the Central Pacific Railroad that stopped at the Hill Valley Railroad Station, as well as at other stops leading up to the end of the line at San Francisco. The train normally cruised at a speed of 25 miles per hour (its top speed was 55), though engineer "Fearless Frank" Fargo was said to have managed to reach nearly 70 m.p.h. past Verde Junction.

  In 1885, Emmett Brown and Marty McFly hijacked the locomotive's engine, leaving the rest of the train and its crew behind, in order to push the damaged DeLorean up to 88 miles per hour, enabling them to achieve time travel and return to their own era. This involved using a trio of homemade Pres-to-Logs, timed to fire at different temperatures, giving the engine the necessary boost to achieve the desired speed.

  As the DeLorean returned Marty to the future, Doc stayed behind to save Clara Clayton's life. Locomotive No. 131, meanwhile, proceeded without a conductor, plummeting from an uncompleted bridge into the Shonash Ravine with a spectacular explosion [**BTF3**].

- **Logo:** A computer program in Citizen Brown's dystopian timeline. The software's name was

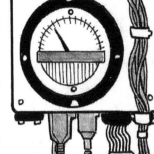

CODE	STORY
NIKE	*BTTF*-themed TV commercial: Nike
NTND	Nintendo *Back to the Future—The Ride* Mini-Game
PIZA	*BTTF*-themed TV commercial: Pizza Hut
PNBL	Data East *BTTF* pinball game
REAL	Real life
RIDE	Simulator: *Back to the Future—The Ride*
SCRM	2010 Scream Awards: *Back to the Future* 25th Anniversary Reunion (broadcast)
SCRT	2010 Scream Awards: *Back to the Future* 25th Anniversary Reunion (trailer)
SIMP	Simulator: *The Simpsons Ride*
SLOT	*Back to the Future Video Slots*
STLZ	Unused *BTTF* footage of Eric Stoltz as Marty McFly
STRY	*Back to the Future Storybook*
TEST	Screen tests: Crispin Glover, Lea Thompson and Tom Wilson
TLTL	Telltale Games' *Back to the Future—The Game*
TOPS	Topps' *Back to the Future II* trading-card set
TRIL	*BTTF: The Official Book of the Complete Movie Trilogy*
UNIV	Universal Studios Hollywood promotional video

SUFFIX	MEDIUM
-b	*BTTF2*'s Biff Tannen Museum video (extended)
-c	Credit sequence to the animated series
-d	Film deleted scene
-n	Film novelization
-o	Film outtake
-p	1955 phone book from *BTTF1*
-v	Video game print materials or commentaries
-s1	Screenplay (draft one)
-s2	Screenplay (draft two)
-s3	Screenplay (draft three)
-s4	Screenplay (draft four)
-sp	Screenplay (production draft)
-sx	Screenplay (*Paradox*)

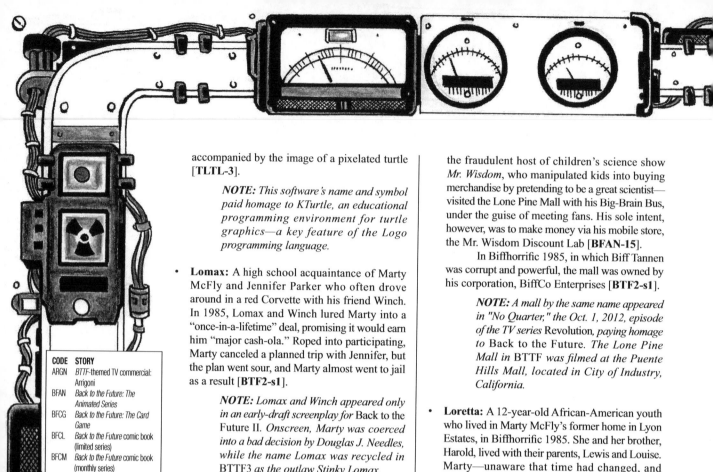

accompanied by the image of a pixelated turtle [**TLTL-3**].

> *NOTE: This software's name and symbol paid homage to KTurtle, an educational programming environment for turtle graphics—a key feature of the Logo programming language.*

- **Lomax:** A high school acquaintance of Marty McFly and Jennifer Parker who often drove around in a red Corvette with his friend Winch. In 1985, Lomax and Winch lured Marty into a "once-in-a-lifetime" deal, promising it would earn him "major cash-ola." Roped into participating, Marty canceled a planned trip with Jennifer, but the plan went sour, and Marty almost went to jail as a result [**BTF2-s1**].

> *NOTE: Lomax and Winch appeared only in an early-draft screenplay for* Back to the Future II. *Onscreen, Marty was coerced into a bad decision by Douglas J. Needles, while the name Lomax was recycled in BTTF3 as the outlaw Stinky Lomax.*

- **Lomax, Stinky:** An outlaw hanged in Haysville in 1885. Hill Valley's marshal, James Strickland, attended the hanging [**BTF3**].

> *NOTE: Strickland's attendance at the hanging might indicate an adversarial relationship between the marshal and Lomax.*

- **London:** The capital city of the United Kingdom, located in England [**REAL**]. In 2015, I-99's Hyperlane-Grid 4 contained an exit for flying cars that led to this city, as well as Phoenix, Boston and Hill Valley [**BTF2**].

- **Lone Pine:** A town located adjacent to Hill Valley, along U.S. Route 395 and among the foothills of the Sierra Nevada [**BTF3**].

- **Lone Pine Mall:** A shopping mall in Hill Valley, circa 1985, in an altered timeline in which Marty McFly ran over one of Otis Peabody's young pine trees in 1955; in the original timeline, the mall had been called Twin Pines. In the new timeline, as in the original, Emmett Brown conducted a test of his time-traveling DeLorean sports car at the mall's parking lot, with Marty McFly recording the experiment [**BFT1**].

In 1992, TV personality Walter Wisdom—the fraudulent host of children's science show *Mr. Wisdom*, who manipulated kids into buying merchandise by pretending to be a great scientist—visited the Lone Pine Mall with his Big-Brain Bus, under the guise of meeting fans. His sole intent, however, was to make money via his mobile store, the Mr. Wisdom Discount Lab [**BFAN-15**].

In Biffhorrific 1985, in which Biff Tannen was corrupt and powerful, the mall was owned by his corporation, BiffCo Enterprises [**BTF2-s1**].

> *NOTE: A mall by the same name appeared in "No Quarter," the Oct. 1, 2012, episode of the TV series* Revolution, *paying homage to* Back to the Future. *The Lone Pine Mall in BTTF was filmed at the Puente Hills Mall, located in City of Industry, California.*

- **Loretta:** A 12-year-old African-American youth who lived in Marty McFly's former home in Lyon Estates, in Biffhorrific 1985. She and her brother, Harold, lived with their parents, Lewis and Louise. Marty—unaware that time had changed, and that he thus didn't live there anymore—climbed into the window of what was once his bedroom, causing young Loretta to scream, and Lewis to furiously chase him out of the house with a baseball bat, mistaking Marty as one of Biff's enforcers, sent to bully them into selling their house [**BTF2**].

> *NOTE: The family was unnamed onscreen, though Loretta and Harold were identified in the end credits. BTTF2's novelization identified the father as Lewis, while the movie's first-draft script named the wife Louise.*

- **Los Angeles:** The most populated city in California, and the second most populous in the United States [**REAL**]. In 1985, as a group of teenagers visited the Greek Theatre, located in Los Angeles, to attend a Loverboy rock concert, a time-traveling DeLorean suddenly arrived outside the entrance. As the excited teens ran toward the vehicle, the occupant—clad in a radiation suit—switched the car's time circuits to bring him to the site of the 2010 Scream Awards [**SCRM**].

- **"Lost Fortnight":** The headline of a pamphlet given out by Edna Strickland at her street-corner Salvation Station, circa 1931, warning others

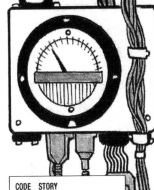

about the evils of alcohol. This particular handout told the true-life story of Johnny, who "woke up in a pile of his own sick, completely unable to remember the previous two weeks of his life" [**TLTL-2**].

- *Lost in Space*: A science fiction television series created by Irwin Allen, and broadcast on CBS from 1965 to 1968 [**REAL**]. As a youth, Ellen Baines often rushed through dinner so as not to miss any episodes [**BTF2-s1**].

- **Lotso' Nutty Choco Cake:** A type of candy bar. While visiting the year 3 million B.C., Jules Brown shared his Lotso' Nutty Choco Cake bar with a friendly pteranodon that he named Donny [**BFAN-3**].

- **Louie:** An individual murdered by Irving "Kid" Tannen sometime in or before 1931. Kid's bartender, Zane Williams, illustrated a caricature of Louie for the Wall of Honor at the gangster's speakeasy, El Kid [**TLTL-v**].

- **Louise:** An African-American woman who lived in Marty McFly's former home in Lyon Estates, in Biffhorrific 1985. She and her husband, Harold, had two children, Loretta and Harold. Marty—unaware that time had changed, and that he thus didn't live there anymore—climbed into the window of what was once his bedroom, causing young Loretta to scream, and Lewis to furiously chase him out of the house with a baseball bat, mistaking Marty as one of Biff's enforcers, sent to bully them into selling their house [**BTF2**].

     NOTE: The family was unnamed onscreen, though Loretta and Harold were identified in the end credits. BTTF2's novelization identified the father as Lewis, while the movie's first-draft script named the wife Louise.

- **Louis Watch Maker:** A business in Courthouse Square, circa 1955 [**BTF2**].

- **lounge lizards:** A nickname typically given to lounge musicians, as well as those who frequent nightclubs, seducing female patrons [**REAL**]. Emmett Brown used the term to describe the patrons of a nightclub in Dinocity, a time-altered Hill Valley inhabited by evolved dinosaurs [**BFAN-3**, **BFHM**].

- **Lou's Aerobic Fitness Center:** A gymnasium on Main Street in Courthouse Square, circa 1985, located on the site of the former Lou's Café, and named for café owner Lou Caruthers. While hitching skateboard rides to school on the back of passing vehicles, Marty McFly enjoyed waving at the attractive women exercising within [**BTF1**].

- **Lou's Café:** A diner in Courthouse Square, owned in the 1950s by Lou Caruthers, and located on the corner of Hill and Main. This popular teen hangout served malts, sundaes, burgers, coffee, sandwiches, soups and other food items. Future mayor Goldie Wilson worked here at that time as a busboy, but dreamed of making something of himself, and of cleaning up the town.

     Lorraine Baines and her friends, Babs and Betty, sometimes went to Lou's after school, as did Biff Tannen's gang. George McFly liked to eat breakfast here as well, until Biff bullied him into avoiding the place. It was here that Marty McFly first encountered his father as a teenager after being stranded in the past, and at which George later admitted his feelings for Lorraine.

     By 1985, a gymnasium called Lou's Aerobic Fitness Center was built on the site of the former café [**BTF1**].

     NOTE: In BTTF1's initial-draft screenplay, the establishment—called Wilson's Café—was owned by Dick Wilson in 1985, and by Dick's mother in 1955.

     In Back to the Future: The Musical, *a U.K. stage play produced in October 2012 by Mayhem Productions and Hertford Theatre, Lou's Café featured more prominently onstage than in the films.*

- **Loverboy:** A Canadian rock group popular in the 1980s, whose hit songs included "Turn Me Loose" and "Working for the Weekend" [**REAL**]. In 1985, as a group of teenagers attended a Loverboy concert at Los Angeles' Greek Theatre, a time-traveling DeLorean suddenly arrived outside the entrance. As the excited teens ran toward the vehicle, the occupant—clad in a radiation suit—switched the car's time circuits to bring him to the site of the 2010 Scream Awards [**SCRM**].

- **low-res:** A popular insult, circa 2015, as in "He's too low-res" [**BTF2**].

CODE	STORY
NIKE	*BTTF*-themed TV commercial: Nike
NTND	Nintendo *Back to the Future—The Ride* Mini-Game
PIZA	*BTTF*-themed TV commercial: Pizza Hut
PNBL	Data East *BTTF* pinball game
REAL	Real life
RIDE	Simulator: *Back to the Future—The Ride*
SCRM	2010 Scream Awards: *Back to the Future 25th Anniversary Reunion* (broadcast)
SCRT	2010 Scream Awards: *Back to the Future 25th Anniversary Reunion* (trailer)
SIMP	Simulator: *The Simpsons Ride*
SLOT	*Back to the Future Video Slots*
STLZ	Unused *BTTF* footage of Eric Stoltz as Marty McFly
STRY	*Back to the Future Storybook*
TEST	Screen tests: Crispin Glover, Lea Thompson and Tom Wilson
TLTL	Telltale Games' *Back to the Future—The Game*
TOPS	Topps' *Back to the Future II* trading-card set
TRIL	*BTTF: The Official Book of the Complete Movie Trilogy*
UNIV	Universal Studios Hollywood promotional video

SUFFIX	MEDIUM
-b	*BTTF2*'s Biff Tannen Museum video (extended)
-c	Credit sequence to the animated series
-d	Film deleted scene
-n	Film novelization
-o	Film outtake
-p	1955 phone book from *BTTF1*
-v	Video game print materials or commentaries
-s1	Screenplay (draft one)
-s2	Screenplay (draft two)
-s3	Screenplay (draft three)
-s4	Screenplay (draft four)
-sp	Screenplay (production draft)
-sx	Screenplay (*Paradox*)

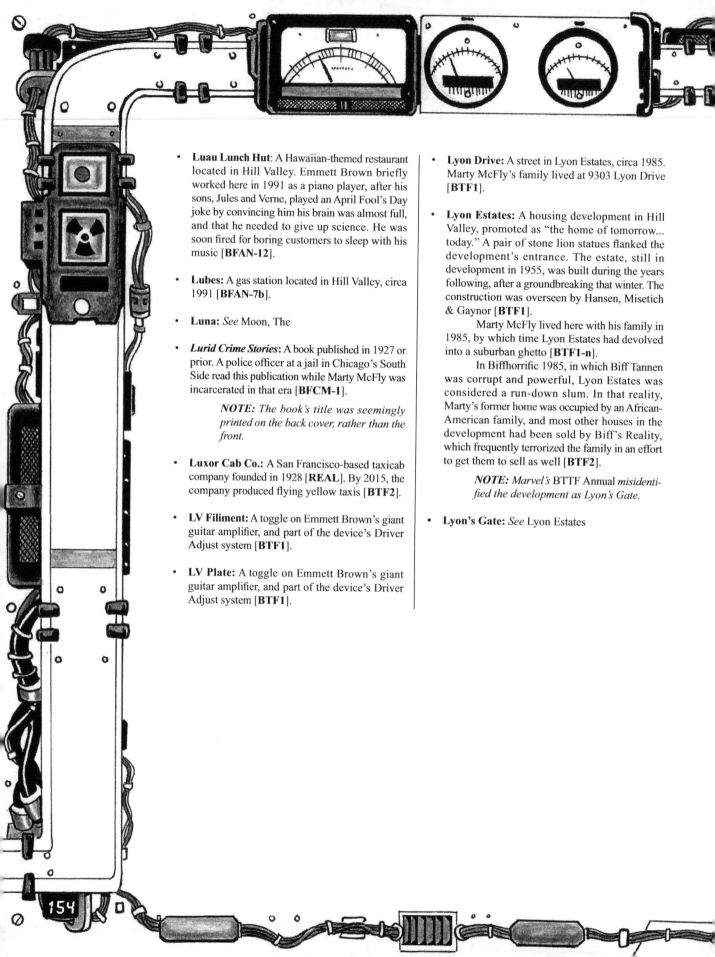

- **Luau Lunch Hut**: A Hawaiian-themed restaurant located in Hill Valley. Emmett Brown briefly worked here in 1991 as a piano player, after his sons, Jules and Verne, played an April Fool's Day joke by convincing him his brain was almost full, and that he needed to give up science. He was soon fired for boring customers to sleep with his music [**BFAN-12**].

- **Lubes**: A gas station located in Hill Valley, circa 1991 [**BFAN-7b**].

- **Luna**: *See* Moon, The

- ***Lurid Crime Stories***: A book published in 1927 or prior. A police officer at a jail in Chicago's South Side read this publication while Marty McFly was incarcerated in that era [**BFCM-1**].

  > ***NOTE**: The book's title was seemingly printed on the back cover, rather than the front.*

- **Luxor Cab Co.**: A San Francisco-based taxicab company founded in 1928 [**REAL**]. By 2015, the company produced flying yellow taxis [**BTF2**].

- **LV Filiment**: A toggle on Emmett Brown's giant guitar amplifier, and part of the device's Driver Adjust system [**BTF1**].

- **LV Plate**: A toggle on Emmett Brown's giant guitar amplifier, and part of the device's Driver Adjust system [**BTF1**].

- **Lyon Drive:** A street in Lyon Estates, circa 1985. Marty McFly's family lived at 9303 Lyon Drive [**BTF1**].

- **Lyon Estates:** A housing development in Hill Valley, promoted as "the home of tomorrow... today." A pair of stone lion statues flanked the development's entrance. The estate, still in development in 1955, was built during the years following, after a groundbreaking that winter. The construction was overseen by Hansen, Misetich & Gaynor [**BTF1**].

  Marty McFly lived here with his family in 1985, by which time Lyon Estates had devolved into a suburban ghetto [**BTF1-n**].

  In Biffhorrific 1985, in which Biff Tannen was corrupt and powerful, Lyon Estates was considered a run-down slum. In that reality, Marty's former home was occupied by an African-American family, and most other houses in the development had been sold by Biff's Reality, which frequently terrorized the family in an effort to get them to sell as well [**BTF2**].

  > ***NOTE**: Marvel's BTTF Annual misidentified the development as Lyon's Gate.*

- **Lyon's Gate:** *See* Lyon Estates

MCFLY, MARTY

(CENTER, WITH GEORGE, LORRAINE,
SEAMUS, WILLIAM AND MAGGIE)

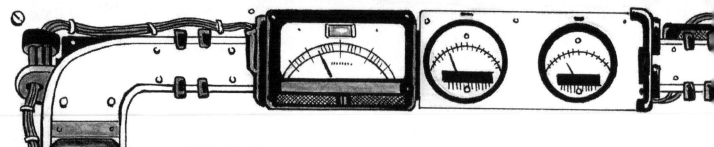

- **M-3D-TV:** A three-dimensional music television station, circa 1991. Upon seeing a holovision program in 2585, Verne Brown mistook the broadcast for M-3D-TV [**BFCL-1**].

  > *NOTE: This station's name was a derivation of MTV, a TV network initially geared toward the music industry.*

- **Ma:** An individual who received a cut of Irving "Kid" Tannen's illegal business, circa 1931 [**TLTL-1**].

  > *NOTE: It's unclear if "Ma" was just a nickname, or Kid's actual mother.*

- *Ma and Pa Kettle at Waikiki:* A 1955 comedy film directed by Lee Sholem [**REAL**]. The Pohatchee Drive-in Theater listed this movie on its marquee in 1955 [**BTF3**].

- **Mac, Captain ("Mac the Black"):** An infamous 17th-century pirate who operated in the Caribbean, with a hideout on Smilin' Skull Island. Considered the greatest pirate of all time—and an object of fantasy for many women of his era—he was tall, muscular and olive-skinned, with a goatee, an eye-patch and yellowing teeth.

  Marty McFly posed as Mac in 1697, hoping to woo a local woman named Maria Estrada, and unaware that Mac the Black was wanted by the government of Spain's King Charles II. This ruse resulted in Marty's being taken aboard Mac's ship as the pirates' leader, until the real Mac showed up.

  Marty was nearly executed for his actions, but Estrada—a special agent for the Spanish Armada, assigned to bring Mac to justice for stealing the fleet's flagship—freed Marty and arrested the pirate [**BFAN-14**].

- **Macintosh:** A line of personal computers introduced by Apple in 1984 [**REAL**]. A Macintosh PC was among the items for sale at Blast From the Past, an antique and collectibles shop in 2015 Hill Valley [**BTF2**].

- **MacPherson Instruments:** A business in San Diego, California, circa 1931. As a young man, Emmett Brown had a calendar advertising this company hanging in his office at the Hill Valley Courthouse [**TLTL-4**].

- **Mad Dog:** *See* Pit Bull

- **Madge:** A friend and classmate of Eileen Baines at Hill Valley High School, circa 1952 [**BTF1-s1**].

  > *NOTE: Madge appeared in early drafts of BTTF1's screenplay. Onscreen, Eileen was called Lorraine, and her friends were named Babs and Betty.*

- **Madison 3489:** *See* Klondike 5-4385

- **Mad Maximus:** A corpulent, powerful wrestler with the Small Town Professional Wrasslin organization. Despite his fearsome appearance, he liked to knit during downtime. Mad Maximus defeated Emmett "Brain Buster" Brown during the scientist's one and only wrestling match, in 1952 [**BFAN-24**].

- **Magic:** One of several names that Verne Brown, having traveled back to before his birth, urged Emmett and Clara Brown to name him instead of Verne [**BFAN-21**].

  > *NOTE: Basketball star Earvin "Magic" Johnson Jr. was very popular during Verne's childhood.*

- **mag-lev:** A transportation system utilizing magnetic levitation to suspend, guide and propel vehicles a few inches above a guideway surface, using magnets rather than such mechanical propulsion methods as wheels, axles and bearings [**REAL**].

  In 2015, Texaco's gas-station services included mag-lev adjustments [**BTF2**]. These devices only worked within six inches of the ground. Higher than that, the magnets ceased to function, causing the levitated object to drop [**BTF2-s1**].

- **mag-lev hover boots:** A type of fusion-powered footwear created by Emmett Brown at the Institute of Future Technology, for use with his Timeman personal time-travel suit [**RIDE**].

  > *NOTE: This footwear was described on signage at Universal Studios' Back to the Future: The Ride.*

- **Magnascope 4000:** A camera invented by Emmett Brown, with an extendable lens enabling a user to snap a photograph at extreme distances [**BFAN-15**].

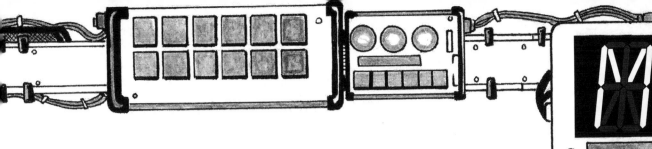

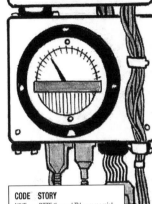

- **Magnavox Weekender:** A model of transistor AM radio [**REAL**]. A Weekender was among the items for sale at Blast From the Past, an antique and collectibles shop in 2015 Hill Valley [**BTF2**].

- **Magnetic Anti Gravity (MAG) Sneakers:** A style of self-lacing, LED-electroluminescent high-top footwear produced in 2015 by U.S. sportswear and equipment supplier Nike. Marty McFly wore Nike MAGs while he and Emmett Brown visited that era to save Marty's children from ruining their lives [**BTF2**].

    Emmett Brown later attempted to revisit 2015 to procure a pair of MAGs from a Nike retail store at the Lone Pine Mall. However, a problem with his DeLorean's time circuits caused him to arrive in 2011, before the self-lacing feature was incorporated [**NIKE**].

- **magneto-sandals:** A type of footwear invented by Emmett Brown, enabling the scientist to walk on walls and ceilings. Much to his wife's chagrin, the magneto-sandals left grease marks wherever he stepped [**BFAN-10**].

- **Magoo, Gertie:** A Puritan in Salem, Massachusetts, circa 1692. When she danced indiscreetly in public, the townsfolk deemed her and her cat to be witches, severely punishing them both. Marty McFly, while dancing to impress a Puritan named Mercy Tannen, drew similar suspicions from the townsfolk [**BFAN-4**].

- **MAIN BUS 1:** A button on an overhead console of Emmett Brown's DeLorean [**TLTL-5**].

- **MAIN BUS 2:** A button on an overhead console of Emmett Brown's DeLorean [**TLTL-5**].

- **Main Street—100:** A roadway in Hill Valley populated by numerous local shops, and intersecting Hill Street. Lou's Café was located on the corner of these two streets [**BTF1**].

- **Majestic Arms Inn:** A flophouse in Hill Valley for travelers seeking lodging and food, circa 1931. The Majestic advertised "Transients Welcome" [**TLTL-1**]. Emmett Brown hid from the police at this inn while on the run for burning down Irving "Kid" Tannen's speakeasy (a crime he didn't commit) [**TLTL-2**].

- **Major Dad:** An American sitcom that aired on CBS from 1989 to 1993, starring Gerald McRaney [**REAL**]. Verne Brown enjoyed this TV series, and thought the title character, Major John D. MacGillis, was a real person [**BFAN-15**].

- **mama meteorolgy:** An expression used by Emmett Brown to denote surprise, analogous to "mama mia" [**BFAN-5**].

- **"Man From Space, The":** An episode of *The Honeymooners,* a classic American situation comedy that aired on CBS from 1955 to 1956 [**REAL**].

    In 1955, Lorraine Baines' family watched the episode during its initial live broadcast. Marty McFly, while visiting that era, claimed to recognize it from reruns, which perplexed the Baines family, since it had never before been shown, and since they didn't know what a "rerun" was. Thirty years later, George McFly was also a fan of the series—particularly the episode "The Man From Space" [**BTF1**].

    > *NOTE: "The Man From Space" aired on Dec. 31, 1955, almost two months after Marty's arrival in that year. Moreover, reruns were not unknown in the 1950s.*

- **Manhattan Project:** A U.S.-led research and development program that resulted in the first atomic bomb, during World War II [**REAL**]. Emmett Brown was among the scientists who worked on this project during the 1940s [**GALE**].

    > *NOTE: This could explain why the Libyans hired Doc to build them an atomic bomb.*

- **Manitoba:** A Canadian province containing Winnipeg, its capital and largest city [**REAL**]. The discovery that Sylvia "Trixie Trotter" Miskin was from Manitoba disqualified her from working at the 1931 Hill Valley Exposition, as the expo's charter mandated that the hostess be a U.S. citizen [**TLTL-4**].

- **Mansfield, Jayne:** An American film, TV and theater actor, born Vera Jayne Palmer, and one of *Playboy* magazine's earliest Playmate models [**REAL**]. In Biffhorrific 1985, in which Biff Tannen was wealthy and corrupt, Biff was romantically linked with Mansfield and other starlets [**BTF2-b**].

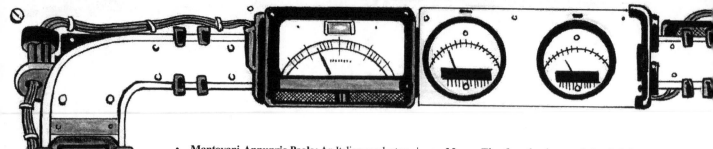

- **Mantovani, Annunzio Paolo:** An Italian conductor and light orchestra-styled entertainer [**REAL**]. Emmett Brown, not a fan of rock music, considered himself more of "a Mantovani man" [**BFAN-12**].

- **Maple:** A street in Hill Valley, circa 1955, located a block from Riverside Drive. By 1985, it was renamed John F. Kennedy Drive [**BTF1**].

- **Marble, Steven, Ph.D.:** A supervising scientist at the Institute of Future Technology's Anti-Gravitic Laboratory, security clearance SM1138, space-time coordinates 6-12-93-3. Marble's experiments included the development of a hoverbike utilizing a substance called Tandemonium to remain stable at speeds of up to 38 miles per hour [**RIDE**].

- **Mario Brothers, The:** A fictional charity that Marty McFly mentioned while meeting with Edna Strickland in 1931, after claiming to have donated time to several charities (which he hadn't actually done) [**TLTL-1**].

  > *NOTE: The Mario Brothers, Italian-American plumbers Mario and Luigi, have appeared in numerous video games produced by Nintendo since the 1980s.*

- **Mariposa:** A city located south of Hill Valley, as indicated on a map in 2015 [**BTF3**].

- **Mark Hopkins Hotel:** A hotel in San Francisco [**REAL**]. Marty McFly was conceived in this establishment, during the second anniversary of George and Lorraine McFly, who had previously spent their honeymoon there [**BTF2-s1**].

- **Marky:** One of several names that Verne Brown, having traveled back to before his birth, urged Emmett and Clara Brown to name him instead of Verne [**BFAN-21**].

  > *NOTE: Musician Mark Wahlberg—also known as Marky Mark—was very popular during Verne's childhood.*

- **Marquez, Bonnie:** An economic synergizer at the Institute of Future Technology [**RIDE**].

  > *NOTE: This individual, identified on signage outside* Back to the Future: The Ride, *was named after Universal Studios' marketing manager.*

- **Mars:** The fourth planet of the Sol System [**REAL**]. By the late 21st century, flights to this planet were commonplace, with Mars considered part of the Tri-Planet Area. In 2091, McFly Space Cruises launched the *MSC Marty*, the first passenger solar sailship to the red planet. Emmett Brown and Clara Clayton Brown were aboard the ship—which, due to sabotage perpetrated by Ziff Tannen, ended up stranded in space [**BFAN-9**].

- **Marshal:** A photographer in Hill Valley who, in 1952, snapped a picture of Emmett Brown purchasing the Cusimano Brothers Gearworks Factory from a man named Fredman, for $1.85 million [**BTF1-s2**].

- **Marshal:** The simple signage of Hill Valley's law-enforcement office during its Old West period. In 1885, the office was occupied by Marshal James Strickland [**BTF3**].

- **Marshall:** A professional runner who ran a three-minute mile in 2015, as reported by *USA Today* [**BTF2**].

- **Martha:** A co-worker of George McFly. George had hoped to invite her to a family barbecue in 1985, but was unable to convince his wife, Lorraine, that such a party would be a good idea [**TEST**].

- **Martians at the Beach:** A childhood game made up by Jules and Verne Brown to keep Emmett Brown from discovering a baby Apatosaurus that Verne had brought home from a trip to prehistoric times. The boys claimed to be playing Martians at the Beach, and that the dinosaur was their friend Elroy, painted green [**BFAN-26**].

  > *NOTE: Doc must have been extremely distracted, for the ruse worked.*

- **Marticus:** An alias employed by Marty McFly while visiting ancient Rome in 36 A.D. As Marticus, he battled Roman officer Bifficus Antanneny in a chariot race at the Circus Maximus. Marticus lost the race—purposely, in order to ensure the rise of Caligula and the fall of the Roman Empire [**BFAN-5**].

- **Martin, Nephew:** An alias used by Marty McFly in 1692 while he lived among the Puritans of Salem, Massachusetts. As Nephew Martin—a relative of

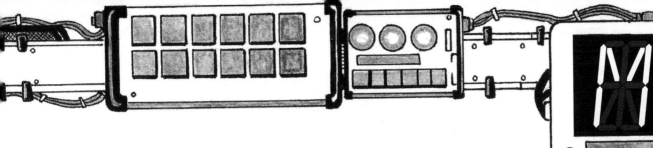

Emmett Brown, disguised as Goodman Brown—Marty was accused of witchcraft by Mercy Tannen after he spurned her affections.

The townsfolk thus subjected Marty to a ritual known as the Water Test, dropping him into a bay to determine his guilt; if he drowned, he would be declared innocent, but if he surfaced, he would be deemed a witch and be burned at the stake. Nephew Martin seemingly died during the test, but Marty avoided death, as Doc rescued him underwater using the DeLorean [**BFAN-4**].

- **Marty, MSC:** A huge, white-hulled passenger solar sailship operated by McFly Space Cruises, commanded by Captain Marta McFly and named after her great-grandfather, Marty McFly. The clear-domed luxury vessel launched its maiden voyage from the McFly Space Center in 2091.

  Emmett Brown and Clara Clayton Brown were aboard at the time, enjoying a second honeymoon. Employee Ziff Tannen, tired of hearing about the McFlys' many defeats of his ancestors, tried to sabotage the vessel. However, Jules and Verne Brown followed their parents into the future and towed the *Marty* to safety [**BFAN-9**].

- **MARTY 1:** The license plate of a Camaro Z28 that George and Lorraine McFly bought for their son, Marty, in a timeline in which they were happy and successful [**BTF1-s3**].

  NOTE: Onscreen, Marty had a Toyota SR5 4x4 truck, not a Camaro.

- **Marty and the Pinheads:** *See* Pinheads, The

- **Marty McFly impersonator:** A popular musical profession, circa 2091. Impersonators often wore Marty McFly facial masks and Elvis Presely-like jumpsuits, performing hit songs recorded by Marty during the late 20th and early 21st centuries [**BFAN-9**].

- **Marty McFly & the Pinheads:** *See* Pinheads, The

- **Marvin Berry and the Midnighters:** *See* Marvin Berry and the Starlighters

- **Marvin Berry and the Starlighters:** A musical group that performed at the Enchantment Under the Sea Dance in 1955. The Starlighters included Berry on guitar and lead vocals, Reginald on drums, and other musicians on piano, saxaphone and bass

fiddle [**BTF1**], including a member named Bob Jordan [**BTF1-n**].

After Berry injured his hand, Marty McFly—who needed the group to perform in order to ensure that his parents would kiss and fall in love—filled in on guitar, playing "Johnny B. Goode." Amazed at his first exposure to rock and roll, Marvin immediately called his cousin, Chuck Berry, who was seeking a new sound [**BTF1**].

> *NOTE: In the film's first-draft script, the band was called Lester Moon and the Midnighters, and Reginald was known as Sax. The second draft listed them as Marvin Berry and the Starlighters. By the third draft, this had changed to Marvin Moon and the Midnighters, which was changed back to Starlighters by the time of filming.*
>
> *In the fourth-draft screenplay, in which Emmett Brown was a socialite in 1955, the band was performing at a party at Doc's home when Marty first arrived.*
>
> *By introducing Chuck Berry to the song "Johnny B. Goode" three years before the tune was recorded, Marvin may have changed the course of history.*

- **Mary:** A name scrawled in graffiti on the entrance to Lyon Estates, circa 1985 [**BTF1**].

- **Mary Ann:** A friend of Sally Baines during their teen years. In 1967, Sally, Mary Ann and a third friend, Jeanne, went to see the film *To Sir, With Love* [**BTF2-s1**].

- **Mary Lou:** A relative of The Anderson Sisters, a female singing group that traveled with the United Service Organizations (USO) to help raise U.S. troop morale during World War II. Mary Lou had at least one child, and her branch of the Anderson clan was not considered attractive [**BFAN-17**].

- **Master:** A switch on Emmett Brown's giant guitar amplifier, labeled Klystron Beam Voltage Test Adjust [**BTF1**].

- **Master-Cook:** A wall-mounted food-preparation appliance for home use, circa 2015 [**BTF2**].

- **Match:** A member of Biff Tannen's gang in 1955, along with Joey ("Skinhead") and 3-D. Match—who had a tendency to chew on matchsticks—and his friends often trailed Biff, following his lead in

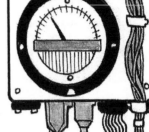

CODE	STORY
NIKE	*BTTF*-themed TV commercial: Nike
NTND	Nintendo *Back to the Future—The Ride* Mini-Game
PIZA	*BTTF*-themed TV commercial: Pizza Hut
PNBL	Data East *BTTF* pinball game
REAL	Real life
RIDE	Simulator: *Back to the Future—The Ride*
SCRM	2010 Scream Awards: *Back to the Future* 25th Anniversary Reunion (broadcast)
SCRT	2010 Scream Awards: *Back to the Future* 25th Anniversary Reunion (trailer)
SIMP	Simulator: *The Simpsons Ride*
SLOT	*Back to the Future* Video Slots
STLZ	Unused *BTTF* footage of Eric Stoltz as Marty McFly
STRY	*Back to the Future Storybook*
TEST	Screen tests: Crispin Glover, Lea Thompson and Tom Wilson
TLTL	Telltale Games' *Back to the Future—The Game*
TOPS	Topps' *Back to the Future II* trading-card set
TRIL	*BTTF: The Official Book of the Complete Movie Trilogy*
UNIV	Universal Studios Hollywood promotional video

SUFFIX	MEDIUM
-b	*BTTF2*'s Biff Tannen Museum video (extended)
-c	Credit sequence to the animated series
-d	Film deleted scene
-n	Film novelization
-o	Film outtake
-p	1955 phone book from *BTTF1*
-v	Video game print materials or commentaries
-s1	Screenplay (draft one)
-s2	Screenplay (draft two)
-s3	Screenplay (draft three)
-s4	Screenplay (draft four)
-sp	Screenplay (production draft)
-sx	Screenplay (*Paradox*)

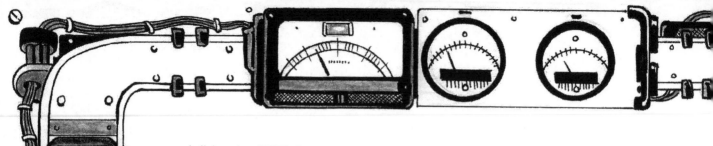

bullying others [**BTF1**, **BTF2**].

In Biffhorrific 1985, in which Biff Tannen was wealthy and corrupt, Match remained at Biff's side, along with Skinhead and 3-D, serving as Biff's major enforcers as he became Hill Valley's billionaire crime boss [**BTF2**].

> *NOTE: Though he was not named onscreen, this character's nickname appeared in BTTF1's credits, script and novelization. Marvel's BTTF Annual misidentified him as Matchstick.*

• **Matches:** A gangster who worked for Irving "Kid" Tannen in 1931. A loyal underling, Matches carried out any actions that Kid needed him to perform, such as shining shoes or causing harm to Kid's enemies [**TLTL-1**].

At Kid's speakeasy, El Kid, Matches served as a bouncer, admitting only those who uttered the correct string of passwords. Matches was arrested, along with his fellow mobsters, when policeman Danny Parker raided the speakeasy [**TLTL-2**].

> *NOTE: The names of Kid's lackeys in the Telltale Games video game corresponded to those of Biff Tannen's friends onscreen, possibly denoting familial relations. In Matches' case, his analog was Biff's friend Match.*

• *Match Made in Space, A*: A science fiction novel written by George McFly, published in an alternate version of 1985. The book, based on what he believed to have been a real-life extraterrestrial encounter in 1955, involved a young couple falling in love thanks to alien interference. The "alien" he'd met had actually been his time-traveling, son, Marty, who'd donned a radiation suit and posted as Darth Vader, of the planet Vulcan, in order to make sure that George married Lorraine Baines [**BTF1**].

The book, which earned George local praise as a "cultural treasure," was poised to end up a top-ten bestseller [**TLTL-v**]. A video miniseries based on the novel was also produced [**BTF2-s1**].

• **Matchstick:** *See* Match

• **Mathemagic Competition:** An academic contest held in Citizen Brown's dystopian timeline. In that reality, Marty McFly was very studious and competed in this event [**TLTL-3**].

• **Mattel:** A worldwide toy manufacturer [**REAL**]. While evading Griff Tannen's gang in 2015, Marty McFly appropriated a young girl's pink hoverboard, made by Mattel [**BTF2**].

• **Matthews, Tim:** A financial professional at the City Trust and Savings Bank who signed a check for $1,182,000 that was issued to Biff Tannen in 1958. The check covered Biff's first winnings in the Bifforrific timeline, after he began betting at the Valley Racing Association, using sporting-event results listed in *Grays Sports Almanac*. The check, #2634, was issued from the bank's main branch, located at the corner of Third and Main, and was drawn on account #1223 098 541 04290 327 486 [**BTF2**].

• **Maureen:** A heavyset employee of the Bob Brothers All-Star International Circus who managed the company's cotton-candy booth [**BFAN-18**].

• **Max:** One of several names that Verne Brown, having traveled back to before his birth, urged Emmett and Clara Brown to name him instead of Verne [**BFAN-21**].

> *NOTE: The Mad Max series of films, starring actor Mel Gibson, were very popular during Verne's childhood.*

• **Max Headroom:** *See* Headroom, Max

• **maxole:** A slang term, circa 2015, analogous to "asshole" [**BTF2-sx**].

• **Maxwell House:** A brand of coffee manufactured by Kraft Foods [**REAL**]. Marty McFly's family had a can of this coffee in their kitchen in 1985 [**BTF1**].

• **MB:** The monogram logo of Marvin Berry and the Starlighters, emblazoned on the band's bass drum [**BTF1**].

• **McCoy, Doctor:** A fictional scientist whom Marty McFly mentioned as a ruse in 1931, while trying to convince 17-year-old Emmett Brown to build a Rocket-Powered Drill so that he could use it to help Brown's older self escape from prison. Posing as a U.S. Patent Office representative, Marty threatened to award a patent to "Doctor McCoy" if Emmett failed to provide a fully functional model within a day [**TLTL-1**].

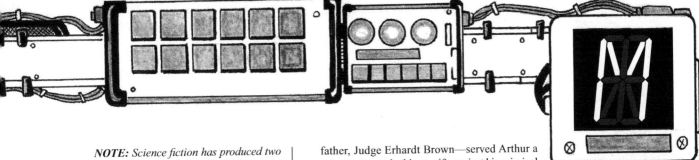

NOTE: *Science fiction has produced two iconic Doctor McCoys: Star Trek's Leonard McCoy and The X-Men's Hank "Beast" McCoy.*

- **McDermott's Canadian Whiskey:** A brand of alcohol served at the El Kid speakeasy in 1931 [**TLTL-2**].

- **McDonald, J.:** A citizen of Hill Valley who was listed on Arthur McFly's ledger at the 1931 Hill Valley Exposition [**TLTL-2**].

- **McDonald's:** A worldwide chain of fast-food hamburger restaurants [**REAL**]. After Emmett Brown inadvertently changed time so that dinosaurs never went extinct, a dinosaur-version of the company still existed in Hill Valley (then known as Dinocity), including its iconic golden-arches logo [**BFCM-2**, **BFHM**].

  Doc once recorded a short video at a McDonald's, describing several Happy Meal toys offered at that time [**MCDN**].

  In 2015, the restaurant chain utilized McWaiters to deliver food to customers' tables [**BTF2-s1**].

  NOTE: *In BTTF1's third-draft screenplay, David McFly worked at McDonald's rather than Burger King.*

- **McFarlane:** A citizen of Hill Valley in Biffhorrific 1985. Marty McFly saw this name while searching for his family's phone-book listing [**BTF2-s1**].

- **McFeeters:** A citizen of Hill Valley in Biffhorrific 1985. Marty McFly saw this name while searching for his family's phone-book listing [**BTF2-s1**].

- **McFly, Angus George Douglas:** *See* McFly, Seamus

- **McFly, Arthur ("Artie"):** The father of George McFly, and grandfather of Marty McFly. Arthur enlisted in World War I at age 16, was sent to France before the military found out his true age and was shipped home without ever firing a shot [**BTF1-n**].

  In 1931, Arthur worked as an accountant for gangster Irving "Kid" Tannen, who forced him to maintain the gang's books and kept him hidden at a safe house to prevent the police from finding him. That ended when 17-year-old Emmett Brown—working at the time as a law clerk for his father, Judge Erhardt Brown—served Arthur a subpoena to make him testify against his criminal employer [**TLTL-1**].

  Managing to avoid prison, Kid tried to murder Artie in retaliation, but the gangster's moll, Sylvia "Trixie Trotter" Miskin (whom Arthur had tutored, and who'd fallen in love with him) pleaded for his life. Kid let Arthur live, in return for Trixie not turning evidence of his tax evasion over to the government. Marty convinced Trixie that Tannen had reneged on the deal, however, in order to make her angry enough to betray Kid and testify. As Kid was escorted to jail, Trixie discovered that Artie was still alive and kissed him passionately, sparking a secret love affair between the two [**TLTL-2**].

  Portrayed by local newspapers as a hero for testifying against Kid Tannen, Arthur became a respected member of society, and was made the chief account and paymaster for the 1931 Hill Valley Exposition, in charge of finances, registration, hiring and firing. He helped Trixie obtain a job as the expo's hostess, but was later forced to fire her, according to the conference's rules, upon discovering that she was not a U.S. citizen [**TLTL-4**].

  To avoid having to terminate Trixie, Artie found a loophole in the regulations: He eloped with her, making her eligible for the job. Arthur, meanwhile, worked the door at the event, making sure the proceedings ran smoothly [**TLTL-5**].

  Arthur and Sylvia had a son, George, and lived in a house on Sycamore Street. At 17, George wanted to attend college and study writing or journalism, but Arthur talked him out of it, claiming college was difficult, that he would likely be rejected and that competing against other smart students would be an unnecessary aggravation. George accepted his father's defeatism, setting the course of his entire life, until Marty changed history by instilling in him greater confidence. George stood up to Artie and attended college, despite his father's misgivings, becoming very successful [**BTF1-n**].

  NOTE: *Arthur's fate is unknown, but since Marty barely remembered his grandfather from when he was a child, Artie may have passed away sometime during the 1970s.*

- **McFly, David R. ("Dave"):** The older brother of Marty and Linda McFly, and the son of George and Lorraine McFly. David worked at Burger King in 1985, and enjoyed watching *The Honeymooners*

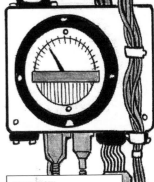

CODE	STORY
NIKE	*BTTF*-themed TV commercial: Nike
NTND	Nintendo *Back to the Future—The Ride* Mini-Game
PIZA	*BTTF*-themed TV commercial: Pizza Hut
PNBL	Data East *BTTF* pinball game
REAL	Real life
RIDE	Simulator: *Back to the Future—The Ride*
SCRM	2010 Scream Awards: *Back to the Future 25th Anniversary Reunion* (broadcast)
SCRT	2010 Scream Awards: *Back to the Future 25th Anniversary Reunion* (trailer)
SIMP	Simulator: *The Simpsons Ride*
SLOT	*Back to the Future Video Slots*
STLZ	Unused *BTTF* footage of Eric Stoltz as Marty McFly
STRY	*Back to the Future Storybook*
TEST	Screen tests: Crispin Glover, Lea Thompson and Tom Wilson
TLTL	Telltale Games' *Back to the Future—The Game*
TOPS	Topps' *Back to the Future II* trading-card set
TRIL	*BTTF: The Official Book of the Complete Movie Trilogy*
UNIV	Universal Studios Hollywood promotional video

SUFFIX	MEDIUM
-b	*BTTF2*'s Biff Tannen Museum video (extended)
-c	Credit sequence to the animated series
-d	Film deleted scene
-n	Film novelization
-o	Film outtake
-p	1955 phone book from *BTTF1*
-v	Video game print materials or commentaries
-s1	Screenplay (draft one)
-s2	Screenplay (draft two)
-s3	Screenplay (draft three)
-s4	Screenplay (draft four)
-sp	Screenplay (production draft)
-sx	Screenplay (*Paradox*)

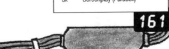

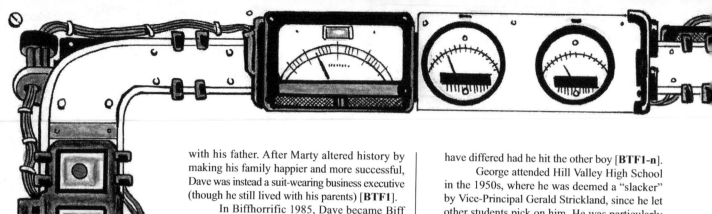

with his father. After Marty altered history by making his family happier and more successful, Dave was instead a suit-wearing business executive (though he still lived with his parents) [**BTF1**].

In Biffhorrific 1985, Dave became Biff Tannen's stepson after Biff murdered George and married Lorraine [**BTF2-d**]. A convicted criminal, Dave was sentenced to probation—a fact that Biff often used to his advantage, threatening to have his probation revoked if Lorraine ever left Biff [**BTF2**]. David ended up a homeless alcoholic in that reality, begging for handouts outside Biff Tannen's Pleasure Paradise [**BTF2-d**].

In Citizen Brown's dystopian timeline, Dave left Hill Valley to work for a big-city newspaper, losing touch with his family for long stretches of time [**TLTL-3**].

> *NOTE: In* BTTF1*'s second-draft screenplay, David was bearded and married, with two sons, ages four and six. In the third draft, he worked at McDonald's rather than Burger King. His middle initial appeared in* Back to the Future II*'s first-draft script.*
>
> *Dave's newspaper job was an in-joke reference to actor Marc McClure's casting as Jimmy Olsen in the* Superman *films and their spinoff,* Supergirl.

- **McFly, Doris ("Dor"):** *See* McFly, Marlene

- **McFly, Electra:** A descendant of Marty McFly in one possible timeline [**BFCG**].

- **McFly, George Douglas:** A nerdish, non-confident, thin-framed bookworm from Hill Valley, of Irish descent. He was a wimpy failure in some timelines, and a successful author in others. In all known timelines, George was the husband of Lorraine Baines, and the father of David, Linda and Martin [**BTF1**].

George grew up on Sycamore Street [**BTF1-n**], with his mother, Sylvia (*nee* Miskin) [**BTF1-s3, TLTL-5**], and father, Arthur [**BTF1-n**]. The great-grandson of Seamus and Maggie McFly, he was the grandson of William McFly (their son), the first McFly born in the United States [**BTF3**].

When George was 12 years old, a bully punched his friend, Billy Stockhausen, in the face. Furious, George wanted to strike Billy's tormentor, but lacked the courage to go through with it. From that day forward, he wondered how his life might

have differed had he hit the other boy [**BTF1-n**].

George attended Hill Valley High School in the 1950s, where he was deemed a "slacker" by Vice-Principal Gerald Strickland, since he let other students pick on him. He was particularly bullied by Biff Tannen (who continued to push him around on into adulthood), Biff's gang (thugs named Match, 3-D and Skinhead) and class clown Mark Dixon.

A wimpy introvert, George spent much of his time alone, watching *The Honeymooners* and *Science Fiction Theater*. He enjoyed reading sci-fi magazines, such as *Amazing Stories, Fantastic Story Magazine* and *Astounding Science Fiction* [**BTF1**], and was also fond of the works of Isaac Asimov [**TLTL-5**].

When Biff Tannen began tormenting him, George—who'd read Dale Carnegie's *How to Win Friends and Influence People*—tried being nice to him in an effort to defuse his hostility. Biff responded by rubbing a hero sandwich in his face. Thereafter, the youth retreated into introvertism and passivity, entirely unable to defend himself [**BTF1-n**].

George's shyness manifested in peeping on women undressing, rather than talking to them. On one occasion, he hid in a tree near Lorraine's house, spying on her naked form via binoculars. George slipped and fell out of the tree, and was struck by a car belonging to Lorraine's father, Sam Baines, who brought the injured youth into his home to recover. While taking care of him—and unaware of his peeping activities—Lorraine fell in love with him. The two shared their first kiss a week later, at the Enchantment Under the Sea Dance.

As a teen, George often penned science fiction stories, but never showed them to others since he greatly feared rejection [**BTF1**]. At age 17, he decided to attend college and study writing or journalism, though his father talked him out of it, claiming college was difficult, and that he would likely be rejected. This attitude of defeatism and self-doubt was instilled at an early age in George, who passed it along to his own children [**BTF1-n**].

George and Lorraine were married in 1966, and conceived Marty during their second anniversary, at the Mark Hopkins Hotel. The couple had stayed at the same hotel during their honeymoon, and had fond memories of the establishment [**BTF2-s1**].

By 1985, George worked in an office environment, with Biff Tannen as his abusive manager. Biff often made George write his reports,

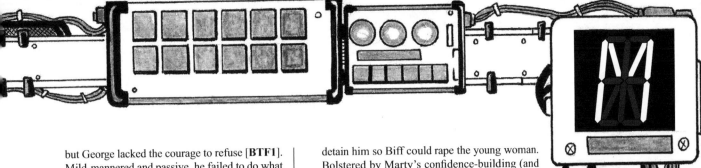

but George lacked the courage to refuse [**BTF1**]. Mild-mannered and passive, he failed to do what was necessary to climb the corporate ladder. An executive at his company, Mr. Callahan, promoted a worker named Jenkins over him, for example, simply because Jenkins played golf with the man [**BTF1-s2**]. One of his friends at that company was a co-worker named Martha [**TEST**].

George was often pushed around by his neighbor Howard [**BTF1-s4, BTF1-d, BTF1-n**], who spoke to him only when he needed something, or sought someone to berate [**BTF1-n**]. When Howard's daughter sold peanut brittle as a fundraiser for her sports team, the Cubs, Howard signed George up to buy a case, without asking permission. Uncomfortable with confrontation, George meekly agreed to the purchase, much to Marty's disgust [**BTF1-d, BTF1-s4**].

Married life with George was disappointing for Lorraine, due to his lack of confidence and drive. As such, she gained a great deal of weight and buried her misery in alcoholism. That changed when Marty altered history in 1955; after traveling back to that year in a time-machine built by Emmett Brown, he prevented George from being hit by Sam's car. Thus, Marty instead became the object of Lorraine's affections, causing Marty and his siblings to be slowly erased from future existence.

To fix his mistake, Marty (using the alias Calvin Klein) urged George to ask Lorraine out, hoping to re-spark their one-time romance. Though attracted to Lorraine, George refused to approach her. Marty, knowing of his fondness for science fiction, donned a radiation suit and hair dyer, and sneaked into George's bedroom, posing as an alien named Darth Vader, from the planet Vulcan. Placing a Sony Walkman headset near George's ears, Marty blasted a Van Halen cassette tape to scare him, then ordered him to ask Lorraine to the dance, threatening to melt his brain if he did not comply.

George did eventually ask her to the dance, but Lorraine was interested only in Marty, and instead asked *him* to accompany her. Marty used that to his advantage, staging an opportunity for George to "rescue" her from his lascivious advances at the dance. Though George was nervous, Marty reassured him that if he put his mind to it, he could accomplish anything.

George was delayed in arriving, and instead found Biff pawing Lorraine. Biff had removed Marty from the car, and had told his gang to detain him so Biff could rape the young woman. Bolstered by Marty's confidence-building (and possibly from having drank alcohol-spiked punch at the dance), George mustered the courage to knock Biff unconscious with a single punch, earning Lorraine's—and others'—respect. He accompanied her to the dance, and the two began dating, eventually marrying and having three children, as before [**BTF1**].

In 1967, George accepted a teaching fellowship in literature at Berkeley. This left Lorraine raising their young children, David (age 5) and Linda (age 2 ½) alone for a semester while he was away [**BTF2-s1**].

Upon returning to his own era from 1955, Marty discovered that his historical alterations in that year had made his family happier, healthier and more successful. In this new timeline, George and Lorraine were still in love, with Biff their humble employee [**BTF1**]. The couple had a uniformed maid named Bertha, and planned to move their family out of Hill Valley, to a nicer home [**BTF1-s3, BTF1-s4**].

George had become a successful author since punching Biff. The Darth Vader incident had provided the inspiration for his first novel, *A Match Made in Space* [**BTF1**], which had earned local praise as a "cultural treasure," and was poised to end up a top-ten bestseller [**TLTL-v**]. A video miniseries based on the novel was also produced [**BTF2-s1**]. As George proudly viewed the first printing of his novel, he offered his kids the same advice that Marty had given him 30 years prior: they could accomplish anything if they just put their minds to it [**BTF1**].

When Emmett Brown vanished in 1986, George oversaw a state-run auction of his belongings. Knowing of his son's friendship with the man, George made every effort to be sensitive to Doc's memory [**TLTL-1**].

In later years, George and Lorraine were still happily married, though disappointed that Marty's life had not turned out as he'd planned, due to his inability to walk away from a challenge. In 2015, George hurt his back on a golf course [**BTF2**], when a flying car fell from the sky and hit him. As a result, he wore an Ortho-lev—an orthopedic anti-gravity device that provided mobility while suspending him upside down—as his injury healed. Adding to his frustration, George was two under par when this incident had occurred [**BTF2-d**].

In one timeline, George became a middle-weight boxing champion after beating up Biff. In

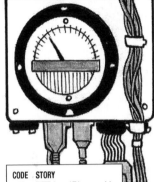

CODE	STORY
NIKE	*BTTF*-themed TV commercial: Nike
NTND	Nintendo *Back to the Future—The Ride* Mini-Game
PIZA	*BTTF*-themed TV commercial: Pizza Hut
PNBL	Data East *BTTF* pinball game
REAL	Real life
RIDE	Simulator: *Back to the Future—The Ride*
SCRM	2010 Scream Awards: *Back to the Future 25th Anniversary Reunion* (broadcast)
SCRT	2010 Scream Awards: *Back to the Future 25th Anniversary Reunion* (trailer)
SIMP	Simulator: *The Simpsons Ride*
SLOT	*Back to the Future Video Slots*
STLZ	Unused *BTTF* footage of Eric Stoltz as Marty McFly
STRY	*Back to the Future Storybook*
TEST	Screen tests: Crispin Glover, Lea Thompson and Tom Wilson
TLTL	Telltale Games' *Back to the Future—The Game*
TOPS	Topps' *Back to the Future II* trading-card set
TRIL	*BTTF: The Official Book of the Complete Movie Trilogy*
UNIV	Universal Studios Hollywood promotional video

SUFFIX	MEDIUM
-b	*BTTF2*'s Biff Tannen Museum video (extended)
-c	Credit sequence to the animated series
-d	Film deleted scene
-n	Film novelization
-o	Film outtake
-p	1955 phone book from *BTTF1*
-v	Video game print materials or commentaries
-s1	Screenplay (draft one)
-s2	Screenplay (draft two)
-s3	Screenplay (draft three)
-s4	Screenplay (draft four)
-sp	Screenplay (production draft)
-sx	Screenplay (*Paradox*)

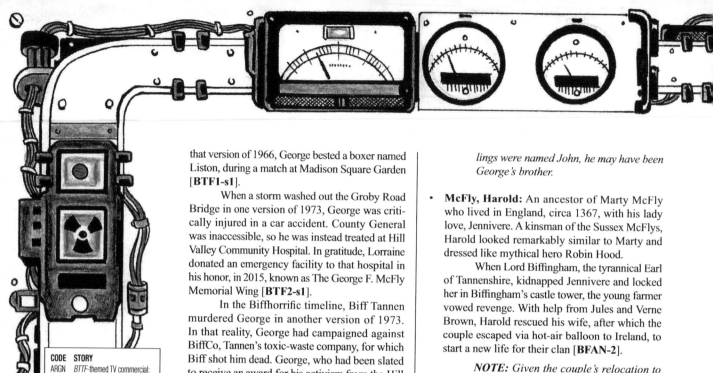

that version of 1966, George bested a boxer named Liston, during a match at Madison Square Garden [**BTF1-s1**].

When a storm washed out the Groby Road Bridge in one version of 1973, George was critically injured in a car accident. County General was inaccessible, so he was instead treated at Hill Valley Community Hospital. In gratitude, Lorraine donated an emergency facility to that hospital in his honor, in 2015, known as The George F. McFly Memorial Wing [**BTF2-s1**].

In the Biffhorrific timeline, Biff Tannen murdered George in another version of 1973. In that reality, George had campaigned against BiffCo, Tannen's toxic-waste company, for which Biff shot him dead. George, who had been slated to receive an award for his activism from the Hill Valley Community Center, was buried at Oak Park Cemetery. Biff married Lorraine, financially supporting the McFly children, but never treating them as his own family [**BTF2**].

In First Citizen Brown's dystopian timeline, George was loyal to the benevolent dictator, spying on others via video monitors within his home, and gathering candid documentary footage for Brown's promotional videos. This put him at odds with Lorraine, who disagreed with the government's oppressive laws, but George naïvely accepted whatever rules Citizen Brown and his wife, Edna Strickland, handed down.

After Edna sent a brainwashed Biff to beat him up and steal the videotapes, however, George recognized the system's corruption, and helped Marty and Jennifer Parker escape from the Citizen Plus Ward, in which they'd been incarcerated. He then attacked a security guard escorting Lorraine to the facility for reconditioning. After Marty prevented the creation of this dystopian timeline, George and Lorraine once again resumed wedded bliss [**TLTL-3**].

NOTE: George's middle initial was given as M in early drafts of BTTF1's screenplay, and as F in BTTF2's first-draft script, but his gravestone revealed his middle name to be Douglas.

BTTF1's first draft provided George and Lorraine with a robot butler named Sparky. In later drafts, this was changed to a human maid named Bertha.

Screentests filmed with Crisin Glover in character as George mentioned Marty's Uncle John. Since none of Lorraine's sib-

lings were named John, he may have been George's brother.

- **McFly, Harold:** An ancestor of Marty McFly who lived in England, circa 1367, with his lady love, Jennivere. A kinsman of the Sussex McFlys, Harold looked remarkably similar to Marty and dressed like mythical hero Robin Hood.

   When Lord Biffingham, the tyrannical Earl of Tannenshire, kidnapped Jennivere and locked her in Biffingham's castle tower, the young farmer vowed revenge. With help from Jules and Verne Brown, Harold rescued his wife, after which the couple escaped via hot-air balloon to Ireland, to start a new life for their clan [**BFAN-2**].

   NOTE: Given the couple's relocation to Ireland, it is likely they were direct ancestors of Seamus McFly.

- **McFly, Jennivere ("Jenny"):** The wife of Harold McFly and an ancestor of Marty McFly, circa 1367. A farmer from Sussex, England, she was kidnapped by Lord Biffingham, the tyrannical Earl of Tannenshire, who imprisoned her in his castle tower.

   Jennivere eventually escaped, thanks to help from Clara Clayton Brown, who'd also been captured by the trant. She and Harold then sailed away in a hot-air balloon, making their way to Ireland to begin anew [**BFAN-2**].

   NOTE: Given her name, as well as the cartoons' tendency to feature past analogs of the main characters, Jennivere could have been a medieval counterpart to Marty's girlfriend, Jennifer Parker. If so, that would make Marty and Jennifer related (consistent with the films' incestuous undertones).

- **McFly, Jim ("Bathtub Jim"):** A relative of Marty McFly who lived in Chicago's South Side, circa 1927, with his wife and baby. While visiting that era with Emmett Brown—to find a cure for cataracts for Doc's dog, Einstein—Marty was mistaken for Jim (due to their resemblance) by gangsters Mugsy Tannen and "Battleship" Potempkin.

   Although Jim wanted to attend pharmacy school, Mugsy forced him to work for their boss, Arnie "Eggs" Benedict, brewing liquor in a still, and striving to invent Lite Gin, which would have half the calories but all the taste of regular gin. Marty helped Jim leave the gang unharmed; once free, the ex-ganster moved his family to Hill Valley,

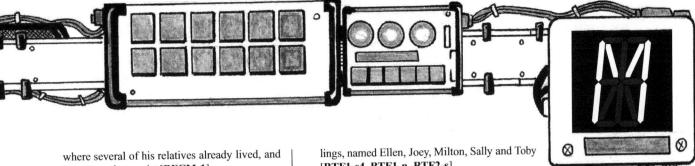

where several of his relatives already lived, and became a pharmacist [BFCM-1].

> NOTE: *Jim's history, forced to work for a Tannen gangster instead of living a respectable life, was similar to that of Marty's grandfather, Arthur McFly, as seen in the Telltale Games video game. Given that Artie was an adult in 1931, it would be impossible for him to have been Jim's child, thus negating the possibility that Jim was a direct ancestor of Marty's; more likely, he was an uncle or cousin.*

- **McFly, Jules:** A descendant of Marty McFly in one possible timeline [BFCG].

  > NOTE: *This character was apparently named after Jules Brown.*

- **McFly, Linda:** The middle child of George and Lorraine McFly. She had an older brother, David, and a younger brother, Martin. Overweight and awkward, Linda wore tacky clothing and glasses, and was frustrated at her inability to find a boyfriend.

  However, in an altered timeline in which Marty changed history by making their family happier and more successful, Linda grew up better supported financially, and thus shared her father's boosted confidence. In that reality, she had multiple boyfriends, including two young men named Greg and Craig [BTF1].

  In Biffhorrific 1985, Linda became Biff Tannen's stepdaughter, after Biff murdered George and married Lorraine. Linda was thus accustomed to having multiple credit cards at her disposal—a fact that Biff often used to his advantage, threatening to cancel those cards if Lorraine ever left Biff [BTF2].

  In Citizen Brown's dystopian timeline, Linda left Hill Valley to live at a women's boardinghouse, losing touch with her family for long stretches of time [TLTL-3].

  > NOTE: *Linda's boardinghouse relocation was an in-joke reference to late actor Wendie Jo Sperber's casting as Amy Cassidy on the television series* Bosom Buddies.

- **McFly, Lorraine Baines ("Lorry"):** The wife of George McFly, and the mother of David, Linda and Martin McFly. Lorraine, the daughter of Sam and Stella Baines [BTF1], had five younger siblings, named Ellen, Joey, Milton, Sally and Toby [BTF1-s4, BTF1-n, BTF2-s].

A once-beautiful woman, Lorraine became overweight and succumbed to alcoholism during middle age. She lived a boring, suburbanite existence in Hill Valley with her unassertive husband, waxing nostalgic about her youthful, more vibrant days in an effort to convince herself she was happy [BTF1].

In the 1950s, Lorraine attended Hill Valley High School. A typical teenager, she cheated on tests in high school [BTF1-d], smoked cigarettes, sneaked liquor from her mother's cabinet and liked to park in cars with boys she found attractive (though as a parent, she would later tell her children she did none of these things, hypocritically portraying herself as virtuous and conservative). In 1955, she could often be found hanging out at Lou's Café, gossiping with her best friends, Babs and Betty.

Classmate George McFly was secretly interested in her, but lacked the courage to make a move. Instead, he often spied on her undressing via binoculars, from a tree near the Baines home. George slipped one day and fell from the tree, and was struck by Sam Baines' car. Sam brought the injured youth into his home to recover. While taking care of him—and unaware of his peeping activities—Lorraine fell in love with the awkward teen. The two shared their first kiss a week later, at the Enchantment Under the Sea Dance [BTF1].

George and Lorraine were married in 1966, and conceived Marty during their second anniversary, at the Mark Hopkins Hotel. The couple had stayed at the same hotel during their honeymoon, and had fond memories of the establishment [BTF2-s1].

The couple's life together disappointed Lorraine, who was frustrated by George's lack of confidence and drive. That changed when Marty altered history, after traveling back to 1955 in Emmett Brown's time-traveling DeLorean. Preventing George from being hit by Sam's car, Marty (using the alias Calvin Klein) instead became the object of Lorraine's affections, causing Marty and his siblings to slowly be erased from future existence.

To fix this mistake, Marty urged George to ask Lorraine out, despite the other's complete lack of self-confidence. Lorraine was interested only in Marty, however. She wanted a man who was strong, who would stand up for her and protect her—qualities she saw in Marty, who'd twice saved her from Biff Tannen's lusty advances, but not in

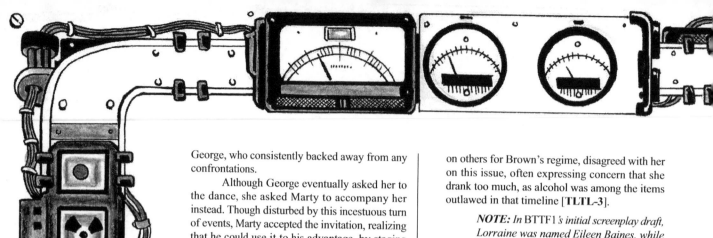

George, who consistently backed away from any confrontations.

Although George eventually asked her to the dance, she asked Marty to accompany her instead. Though disturbed by this incestuous turn of events, Marty accepted the invitation, realizing that he could use it to his advantage, by staging an opportunity for George to "rescue" her from his lascivious advances. George was delayed in arriving, however, and instead found Biff pawing Lorraine. Tannen had found Marty with Lorraine together in the car, and had told his gang to detain Marty so he could rape her.

Bolstered by Marty's advice, George mustered the courage to protect her, knocking Biff unconscious with a single punch, and earning Lorraine's admiration. Upon returning to his own era, Marty later learned that this turn of events had altered his family's history, by making them happier and more successful. In this new timeline, George and Lorraine were still in love in 1985, and Lorraine was thin and healthy, thanks to a regular routine of tennis with George, who was now a successful author [**BTF1**]. The couple had a uniformed maid named Bertha in this reality, and planned to soon leave Hill Valley for a nicer home [**BTF1-s3, BTF1-s4**].

In 1967, Lorraine opposed the Vietnam War, supporting the Hippie movement and its resistance to the government-imposed draft, and often attending rallies organized to protest the conflict. When Marty McFly (visiting that era disguised as a Hippie) was jailed for traveling without a draft card, Lorraine bailed him out, mistaking his actions for a public display of resistance [**BTF2-s1**].

In the Biffhorrific timeline, a corrupt and powerful Biff Tannen murdered George in 1973, after which Lorraine married Biff so as to have money to raise her children. Biff supported the McFlys financially, but made it clear that he didn't consider the children to be his family. He also paid for Lorraine to have multiple cosmetic surgeries to stay young-looking, including having her breasts enlarged to absurd proportions. Unhappy with her lot in life, but helpless to fix it, she once again drowned her sorrows in alcohol [**BTF2**]. Lorraine eventually grew tired of Biff's verbal abuse, and murdered him in 1996 using the same gun with which he'd killed George [**GALE**].

In First Citizen Brown's dystopian timeline, Lorrain resented the oppression enacted by benevolent dictator Emmett Brown and his wife, Edna Strickland. George, a loyal citizen who spied on others for Brown's regime, disagreed with her on this issue, often expressing concern that she drank too much, as alcohol was among the items outlawed in that timeline [**TLTL-3**].

> ***NOTE:*** *In* BTTF1*'s initial screenplay draft, Lorraine was named Eileen Baines, while the second draft changed her name to Mary Ellen ("Meg") Garber. Her nickname, Lorry, appeared in the film's novelization.*
>
> *The first draft provided Lorraine and George with a robot butler named Sparky. In later drafts, this was changed to a human maid named Bertha.*

- **McFly, Maggie:** The great-great-grandmother of Marty, Linda and David McFly, and the great-grandmother of George McFly. A no-nonsense Christian woman, kind but stern, she greatly resembled her future great-granddaughter-in-law, Lorraine Baines McFly [**BTF3**]. She and her husband, Seamus, originally hailed from Ballybowhill, a village in County Dublin, Ireland [**BTF3-n**].

  The couple relocated to the United States in 1881, in search of a better life, and to have land of their own [**BTF3-sp**]. Settling first in Virginia City, and later in Hill Valley, Maggie and Seamus purchased a farm and soon delivered the first American-born McFly, William Sean McFly.

  In 1885, Maggie tended to her time-traveling descendant, Marty, who was injured while evading a black bear. Realizing he was among his own family, Marty called himself Clint Eastwood. Though wary of Marty's anachronistic ways, and quick to express disapproval of his refusal to back down from a fight, Maggie came to respect him, particularly when he bested Buford Tannen without firing a shot.

  Eventually, Seamus and Maggie had at least four grandchildren: two boys and two girls [**BTF3**].

  > ***NOTE:*** *In a combined script for both film sequels, titled* Paradox*, Seamus was unmarried and flirted with a "bar girl" resembling Lorraine. Onscreen, however, Maggie—already his wife by the time of* Back to the Future III*—was very conservative and not the type to work at a saloon.*

- **McFly, Marlene:** The daughter of Marty and Jennifer McFly. She bore a striking resemblance to her father, enjoyed talking on the phone and was close with her grandmother, Lorraine McFly.

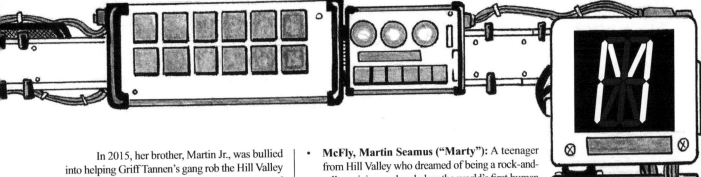

In 2015, her brother, Martin Jr., was bullied into helping Griff Tannen's gang rob the Hill Valley Payroll Substation, resulting in his being sentenced to 15 years at a state penitentiary. Marlene tried to break him out, but was also arrested and received a 20-year sentence. Their father, with help from Emmett Brown, altered time by preventing Marty Jr. from taking part in the theft. Griff's gang was instead imprisoned for a separate crime, and the McFly siblings both avoided jail time [**BTF2**].

In one possible timeline, Marlene became a musician like her father, eventually launching her own concert tour [**BFCG**].

> *NOTE: In* BTTF2's *first-draft screenplay, Marlene—acne-prone and 60 pounds over-weight—was called Doris McFly. The novelization, on the other hand, described her as athletic, in keeping with her onscreen appearance.*

- **McFly, Marta, Captain:** The great-granddaughter of Marty and Jennifer McFly. In 2091, she commanded the *MSC Marty*, a passenger solar sailship operated by McFly Space Cruises. She was very proud of her family's accomplishments [**BFAN-9**].

- **McFly, Martin:** The brother of Seamus McFly, and great-great-granduncle of Marta, David and Linda McFly. He often let others provoke him into fights, too concerned that people might call him a coward if he backed down from a challenge [**BTF3**].

  In 1881, this resulted in Martin's death, when a Virginia City saloon patron shoved a Bowie knife into his belly [**BTF3-sp**]. Thereafter, Seamus always avoided a fight, even if it meant looking cowardly to others [**BTF3**].

- **McFly, Martin ("Zipper"):** An alias used by Marty McFly while visiting Chicago's South Side, in 1927, with Emmett Brown to find a cure for cat-aracts for Doc's dog, Einstein. Doc gave Marty the moniker to prevent gangsters Mugsy Tannen, "Battleship" Potempkin and their boss, Arnie "Eggs" Benedict, from roughing him up.

  According to the ruse, Zipper McFly was a cousin of mobster "Bathtub Jim" McFly, and the head of one of the East Coast's largest organized crime families. Using his prestige as Zipper, Marty gained access to Benedict's still, eliciting Jim's help in brewing a cure for Einstein's illness [**BFCM-1**].

- **McFly, Martin Seamus ("Marty"):** A teenager from Hill Valley who dreamed of being a rock-and-roll musician, and ended up the world's first human time-traveler. Brave beyond his short stature, and slightly high-strung, Marty attended Hill Valley High School in 1985.

  During his high school years, Marty formed a rock band called The Pinheads, and had great dreams of making it big in the music industry. He often considered sending audition tapes to record labels, but lacked the confidence to do so. This self-doubt stemmed from his family life, as his passive father, George McFly, greatly feared rejection and confrontation.

  Marty's mother, Lorraine Baines McFly, was unhappy in her marriage to George, and showed her own defeatism by burying her depression in alcoholism. Like his older siblings, David and Linda, Marty followed in his parents' footsteps of self-made failure. His vice-principal, Gerald Strickland, thus deemed him a "slacker," frequently giving him detention.

  When Marty was eight years old, he accidentally set his family's living room on fire [**BTF1**]. Four years later, he injured himself while skateboarding down the steps of the Hill Valley Courthouse. This accident left a scar on his left knee [**TLTL-2**].

  One of Marty's closest friends was eccentric scientist Emmett "Doc" Brown, whom he met when he was 13 or 14 years old. Marty had heard people call Brown a dangerous crackpot and a lunatic, and was curious why this was so. Sneaking into Doc's laboratory, he was fascinated by the equipment he found within. Upon finding Marty in the lab, the scientist was delighted to learn that the boy thought he was cool, and accepted him for what he was. Since both were the black sheep in their respective environments, a close friendship formed. Doc gave Marty a part-time job, helping with experiments, tending to his lab and watching his dog, Einstein [**GALE**]. Brown, in turn, paid him 50 dollars per week, providing Marty with free beer and unlimited access to his vintage record collection [**BTF1-s4**].

  Marty was, in many ways, a typical teenager of the '80s. He adored his girlfriend, Jennifer Parker, and often visited Clayton Ravine with her so the two could make out in private [**BTF3-s1**]. Frequently late for school, he hitched skateboard rides on the backs of passing cars. He listened to the music of Eddie Van Halen, as well as Huey Lewis and the News [**BTF1**], and enjoyed hanging

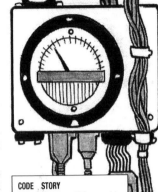

CODE	STORY
NIKE	*BTTF*-themed TV commercial: Nike
NTND	Nintendo *Back to the Future—The Ride* Mini-Game
PIZA	*BTTF*-themed TV commercial: Pizza Hut
PNBL	Data East *BTTF* pinball game
REAL	Real life
RIDE	Simulator: *Back to the Future—The Ride*
SCRM	2010 Scream Awards: *Back to the Future 25th Anniversary Reunion* (broadcast)
SCRT	2010 Scream Awards: *Back to the Future 25th Anniversary Reunion* (trailer)
SIMP	Simulator: *The Simpsons Ride*
SLOT	*Back to the Future Video Slots*
STLZ	Unused *BTTF* footage of Eric Stoltz as Marty McFly
STRY	*Back to the Future Storybook*
TEST	Screen tests: Crispin Glover, Lea Thompson and Tom Wilson
TLTL	Telltale Games' *Back to the Future—The Game*
TOPS	Topps' *Back to the Future II* trading-card set
TRIL	*BTTF: The Official Book of the Complete Movie Trilogy*
UNIV	Universal Studios Hollywood promotional video

SUFFIX	MEDIUM
-b	*BTTF2's* Biff Tannen Museum video (extended)
-c	Credit sequence to the animated series
-d	Film deleted scene
-n	Film novelization
-o	Film outtake
-p	1955 phone book from *BTTF1*
-v	Video game print materials or commentaries
-s1	Screenplay (draft one)
-s2	Screenplay (draft two)
-s3	Screenplay (draft three)
-s4	Screenplay (draft four)
-sp	Screenplay (production draft)
-sx	Screenplay (*Paradox*)

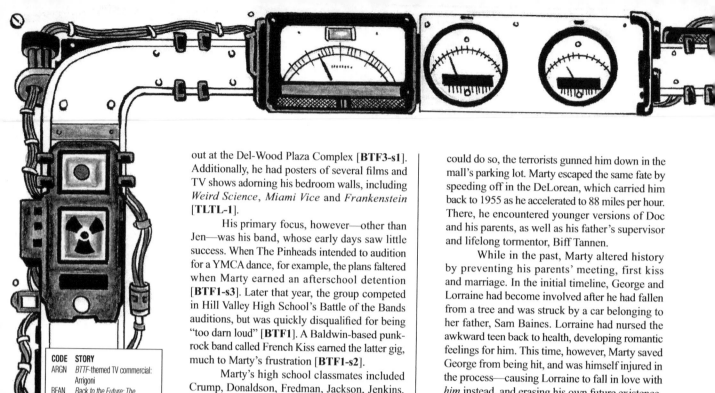

out at the Del-Wood Plaza Complex [**BTF3-s1**]. Additionally, he had posters of several films and TV shows adorning his bedroom walls, including *Weird Science*, *Miami Vice* and *Frankenstein* [**TLTL-1**].

His primary focus, however—other than Jen—was his band, whose early days saw little success. When The Pinheads intended to audition for a YMCA dance, for example, the plans faltered when Marty earned an afterschool detention [**BTF1-s3**]. Later that year, the group competed in Hill Valley High School's Battle of the Bands auditions, but was quickly disqualified for being "too darn loud" [**BTF1**]. A Baldwin-based punk-rock band called French Kiss earned the latter gig, much to Marty's frustration [**BTF1-s2**].

Marty's high school classmates included Crump, Donaldson, Fredman, Jackson, Jenkins, Newton, Stevenson, Weeze and Willis [**BTF1-s1, BTF1-s2, BTF1-s3**]; as well as Nick, a member of The Pinheads [**BTF1-s2**]; and rivals Douglas J. Needles [**BTF2**] and Leech [**TLTL-3**]. Two other students, Lomax and Winch, lured Marty into a "once-in-a-lifetime" deal, promising it would earn him "major cash-ola." Marty agreed to take part in the less-than-legal escapade, nearly ending up in jail as a result [**BTF2-s1**].

Among Marty's instructors at Hill Valley High School were Mister Arky, an embittered, pessimistic social-studies teacher [**BTF1-s1, BTF1-s2, BTF1-n**]; Mister Turkle, whose ill-informed advice (to play a Barry Mannilow tune) caused The Pinheads to flub an audition for the Springtime in Paris Dance [**BTF1-s2**]; and Mrs. Woods, who had little patience with Marty's tendency to violate school rules by playing his Walkman in class [**BTF1-s3**].

Throughout all of this, Marty's friendship with Doc Brown remained a constant. The night of the Battle of the Bands competition, Doc asked the teen to meet him at Twin Pines Mall, in order to help with one of his experiments. To his astonishment, Marty discovered that Doc had built a time machine—out of a DeLorean. The vehicle was powered by plutonium, which Brown had acquired by conning a group of Libyan nationalists who had hired him to build a nuclear bomb. Doc needed Marty to record Temporal Experiment Number One, in which Einstein was propelled one minute into the future, becoming the world's first time-traveler.

When that proved successful, the scientist prepared to test the vehicle himself, but before he could do so, the terrorists gunned him down in the mall's parking lot. Marty escaped the same fate by speeding off in the DeLorean, which carried him back to 1955 as he accelerated to 88 miles per hour. There, he encountered younger versions of Doc and his parents, as well as his father's supervisor and lifelong tormentor, Biff Tannen.

While in the past, Marty altered history by preventing his parents' meeting, first kiss and marriage. In the initial timeline, George and Lorraine had become involved after he had fallen from a tree and was struck by a car belonging to her father, Sam Baines. Lorraine had nursed the awkward teen back to health, developing romantic feelings for him. This time, however, Marty saved George from being hit, and was himself injured in the process—causing Lorraine to fall in love with *him* instead, and erasing his own future existence.

With help from 1955 Doc—who'd conceived of time travel that very day—Marty tried to repair the temporal damage by urging young George to ask Lorraine to the Enchantment Under the Sea Dance, as well as encouraging him to have more self-confidence. Lorraine was interested only in Marty, so he arranged for George to "rescue" her from his aggressive advances outside the dance. George missed his cue, arriving to find Biff attempting to rape her. Bolstered by Marty's confidence-building, George knocked Biff unconscious with a single punch, earning Lorraine's admiration.

During the dance, Marty performed with Marvin Berry and the Starlighters, after the group's guitarist, Marvin, injured his hand. Historically, George and Lorraine had shared their first kiss and fallen in love during the song "Earth Angel," and as Marty performed that song, history played out the same way in the new timeline. Marty also introduced Hill Valley's youth to rock and roll, by performing "Johnny B. Goode" three years before the tune would be recorded by Chuck Berry, Marvin's cousin.

With his family history repaired, Marty rushed to meet Doc, who had erected a system to harness lightning from an impending thunderstorm, in order to power the DeLorean's Flux Capacitor and send Marty back to the future. The youth wrote a letter informing his friend of the Libyans' actions, but Doc refused to read it, fearful of further changing history. After Marty and the car vanished, the scientist changed his mind and read the warning, enabling him to later survive the shooting by wearing a bullet-proof vest to the mall.

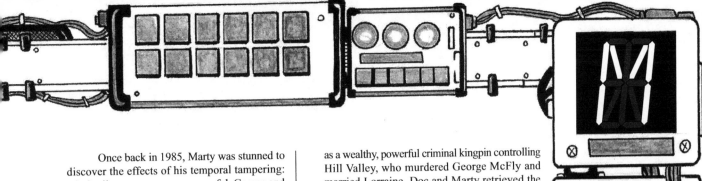

Once back in 1985, Marty was stunned to discover the effects of his temporal tampering: His family was now more successful, George and Lorraine were very much in love, Lorraine was healthier and happier, and George was a successful novelist, with Biff a humble automotive detailer working for the McFlys. What's more, Marty now had the car of his dreams: a Toyota SR5 4x4 truck [**BTF1**]. Inspired by his father's newfound confidence, Marty decided to send out an audition tape to R&G Records [**BTF1-s4**], but before he could do so, Doc returned from 2015, urging Marty to travel back with him to save his future children [**BTF1**].

In the future, Marty and Jennifer were married and living in Hilldale, but were unhappy [**BTF2**]. Marty, who'd shown an almost pathological aversion to being called "chicken," had been coerced into a drag race with Needles at age 17, causing him to collide with a Rolls-Royce and permanently injure his hand, thereby ending all hope of a musical career. What's more, the other vehicle's owner had sued Marty for damages. As a result, Marty had transformed, over the ensuing three decades, into a broken, sad failure [**BTF3**] who, instead of pursuing his music, worked a desk job at CusCo Industries, with Needles as his coworker. Even that ended when Needles coerced him into taking part in illegal activities, causing his boss, Ito T. Fujitsu, to fire him.

Meanwhile, Marty's son, Martin Jr., was being pressured to help Biff's grandson, Griff Tannen, rob the Hill Valley Payroll Substation. This resulted in Marty Jr. being arrested for the crime and receiving 15 years at a state penitentiary. Marty's daughter, Marlene, attempted to break her brother out of jail, but was also arrested, earning a 20-year sentence of her own. To prevent these events, Doc instructed Marty Sr. to pose as his son and refuse to help with the robbery.

The plan worked, but set off a string of events culminating in Biff (now an old man) stealing the DeLorean. Marty had purchased *Grays Sports Almanac: Complete Sports Statistics 1950-2000*, which listed the results of a half-century's worth of sporting events, in the hope of making money betting on the games described within. Doc had chastised him, annoyed that Marty would risk further contaminating the time stream, but old Biff, witnessing the exchange, stole the book and the car, then traveled back to 1955 to give his younger self the almanac.

In the resultant new timeline, Biff emerged as a wealthy, powerful criminal kingpin controlling Hill Valley, who murdered George McFly and married Lorraine. Doc and Marty retrieved the book from young Biff, thereby repairing the damage and restoring the McFlys' happiness. But moments later, the DeLorean was struck by lightning, sending the car and Doc back to 1885, and stranding Marty alone in the 1950s [**BTF2**].

While living in 1885, Doc forged a new career as a blacksmith, enjoying the wonders of the Old West—until he fixed a horseshoe for Buford "Mad Dog" Tannen. When the horse threw a shoe, the outlaw broke a bottle of whiskey and angrily shot the animal. Blaming Doc for the loss, Tannen demanded that he pay him $80, but the blacksmith refused, for which Buford shot him in the back.

Upon finding Doc's gravestone in 1955, Marty learned of his friend's fate and followed him back to the Old West to rescue him, under the alias Clint Eastwood. There, he befriended his ancestors, Seamus and Maggie McFly, who took care of him after he was injured fleeing from a black bear. Marty located Doc and urged him to return to the future. Though Doc enjoyed his frontier life, the looming threat of murder convinced him to accept Marty's suggestion.

The situation became more complicated when Doc became smitten with Hill Valley's new schoolteacher, Clara Clayton. In the original timeline, Clara's horse had been spooked by a snake, carrying her to her death over the side of the Shonash Ravine. This time, Emmett saved her life, preventing her from plummeting with the wagon. As the two enjoyed each other's company at the Hill Valley Festival, Buford tried to kill Doc, but Marty thwarted the attempt by throwing a Frisbie pie plate at Mad Dog's shooting hand. This earned Marty his own death threat, as the outlaw challenged him to a quick-draw, scheduled for later that week.

Seamus, a peaceful man, advised Marty to walk away from the fight, knowing that a duel with Tannen would likely get him killed. Marty accepted Buford's challenge, but later took Seamus' advice to heart, recreating a classic scene from Eastwood's film *A Fistful of Dollars,* by fashioning a bulletproof vest from an iron stove door. When Tannen shot Marty, the youth faked his own death, then stood and knocked the thug unconscious with the iron door. Buford and his gang were arrested, and Doc's fated death was avoided.

The two time-travelers prepared to return to their own era, using a stolen locomotive to push the

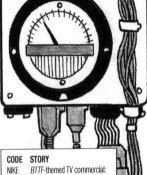

CODE	STORY
NIKE	*BTTF*-themed TV commercial: Nike
NTND	Nintendo *Back to the Future—The Ride* Mini-Game
PIZA	*BTTF*-themed TV commercial: Pizza Hut
PNBL	Data East *BTTF* pinball game
REAL	Real life
RIDE	Simulator: *Back to the Future—The Ride*
SCRM	2010 Scream Awards: *Back to the Future* 25th Anniversary Reunion (broadcast)
SCRT	2010 Scream Awards: *Back to the Future* 25th Anniversary Reunion (trailer)
SIMP	Simulator: *The Simpsons Ride*
SLOT	*Back to the Future Video Slots*
STLZ	Unused *BTTF* footage of Eric Stoltz as Marty McFly
STRY	*Back to the Future Storybook*
TEST	Screen tests: Crispin Glover, Lea Thompson and Tom Wilson
TLTL	Telltale Games' *Back to the Future—The Game*
TOPS	Topps' *Back to the Future II* trading-card set
TRIL	*BTTF: The Official Book of the Complete Movie Trilogy*
UNIV	Universal Studios Hollywood promotional video

SUFFIX	MEDIUM
-b	*BTTF2*'s Biff Tannen Museum video (extended)
-c	Credit sequence to the animated series
-d	Film deleted scene
-n	Film novelization
-o	Film outtake
-p	1955 phone book from *BTTF1*
-v	Video game print materials or commentaries
-s1	Screenplay (draft one)
-s2	Screenplay (draft two)
-s3	Screenplay (draft three)
-s4	Screenplay (draft four)
-sp	Screenplay (production draft)
-sx	Screenplay (*Paradox*)

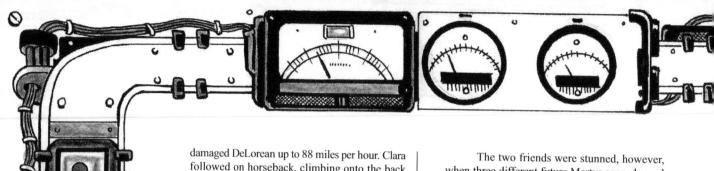

damaged DeLorean up to 88 miles per hour. Clara followed on horseback, climbing onto the back of the train. When she lost her footing and nearly fell under its wheels, Doc once again saved her from certain death, but missed the chance to join Marty in the process. As Marty and the DeLorean vanished into the future, the couple remained in the Old West, where they were eventually married and raised two sons, Jules and Verne. Moments after Marty arrived in 1985, another train struck the vehicle. Marty jumped to safety, but the time machine was completely demolished, making it impossible for him to retrieve his friend from the Old West [**BTF3**].

Over the next several years, while living in the 19th century, Doc converted a train engine car into a new time machine, which he christened the *Jules Verne Train* [**RIDE**]. Once the train was completed, he, Clara and the boys visited 1985 so they could pick up Einstein and say a proper goodbye to Marty [**BTF3**]. Eventually, the Browns relocated to the 20th century, and Marty embarked on many more time-traveling adventures with them. In so doing, they encountered a wide range of McFly, Parker and Tannen ancestors and descendants, in various periods of history [**BFAN-1 to BFAN-26, BFCM-1 to BFCM-4, BFCL-1 to BFCL-3**].

When Marty finished high school, Doc created for him, as a graduation gift, a photo album documenting the McFly family history. Unable to find much information about Marty's grandmother, Sylvia Miskin, he journeyed to 1931 to learn more about her life. Traveling under the alias Carl Sagan, the scientist was wrongly arrested for burning down gangster Irving "Kid" Tannen's speakeasy, El Kid, and failed to return to 1986.

Marty followed Doc back to 1931, where he accidentally caused the death of his own grandfather, Arthur McFly. In fixing that damage, he further contaminated the time stream with other blunders, such as erasing Jen's existence by breaking up her grandparents, Daniel Parker and Betty Lapinski, before they married and had kids. Although Marty restored both his and Jennifer's histories, he altered time yet again by causing Emmett Brown to fall in love with Edna Strickland. Smitten with the conservative Edna, Emmett abandoned his love of science and instead became Hill Valley's benevolent dictator—and, thus, never invented time travel. Faced with an ever-growing string of paradoxes, Marty eventually patched up his repeated temporal damages, then returned once more with Doc to their own period.

The two friends were stunned, however, when three different future Martys soon showed up simultaneously, seeking help regarding his great-grandchildren—each Marty from a different timeline, and each driving a different-colored DeLorean. As the three future Martys argued over whose existences should be erased, Doc and younger Marty jumped into their own car and avoided the squabble entirely [**TLTL-1 to TLTL-5**].

After high school, Marty and Jen attended Hill Valley College together [**BFAN-4, BFAN-12**]. Their relationship continued, though his irresponsibility and insecurities sometimes sabotaged their romance, such as when he expressed jealousy of her athletic friend, Kelp [**BFAN-4**], and when he showed romantic interest in another student, named Liz [**BFAN-25**].

His professors in college included "Old Buzzard" Babcock, who gave him a C- on a music-appreciation test, despite Marty having written an extra-credit report on the Bonedaddys' social significance [**BFAN-4**]. He proposed another extra-credit assignment, "Caesar: The Man, The Myth, The Salad," for his history class, and accompanied Doc to the year 36 A.D. as research, hoping to meet the Roman emperor firsthand [**BFAN-5**].

Marty continued to focus on his music throughout college, and (having avoided the Rolls-Royce accident) achieved some renown as a rock star. In 1991, The Pinheads performed on the steps of the Hill Valley Courthouse, introduced by concert promoter Ned the Fish [**BFAN-12**]. The band's first big hit, "Chapel O' Love" (a cover of the Dixie Cups' 1964 classic), was released in 1994, kicking off a string of successes. In 2015, the group released a greatest-hits album, *Fired Up*, which went platinum, topping the rock-and-roll charts [**BFCG**].

By 2091, Marty was well remembered for his music, with Marty McFly impersonators quite common in that era. One such impersonator, Jimmy, worked his routine aboard the *MSC Marty*, a passenger solar sailship operated by McFly Space Cruises. The vessel was commanded by Captain Marta McFly, and was named after Marty—her great-grandfather [**BFAN-9**].

> **NOTE:** *The above lexicon entry is, by necessity, not all-inclusive. Marty, as one of* Back to the Future's *primary protagonists, was involved in nearly all iterations of the mythos, and was usually the main focus. To include every detail of his adventures would*

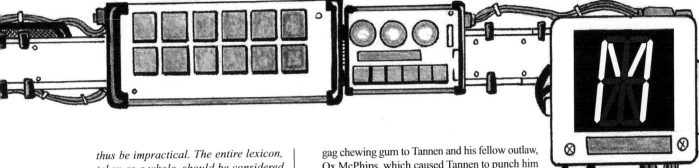

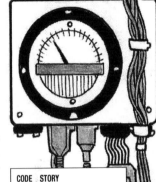

thus be impractical. The entire lexicon, taken as a whole, should be considered when examining Marty's life. In particular, his animated adventures are not described here in detail; to learn more about those tales, see Appendix I.

Eric Stoltz was originally cast in the role of Martin McFly. After being replaced by Michael J. Fox, Stoltz went on to portray a character named Martin in the film The Fly II. *The television series* Fringe *paid homage to this switch in 2010, featuring an alternate reality in which Stoltz did, in fact, star in* Back to the Future.

In BTTF2's first-draft screenplay, Marty's middle name was Hopkins (named after the Mark Hopkins Hotel, in San Francisco, where his parents conceived him). However, BTTF3 established his middle name as Seamus, after Seamus McFly.

For a full list of Marty's various aliases and known relatives, see Appendix III.

- **McFly, Martin Jr.:** The son of Marty and Jennifer McFly. He looked almost exactly like his father had looked at his age. Unlike Marty Sr., however, he spoke in a meek, frightened voice, particularly when bullied by Griff Tannen's gang.

    In 2015, Griff intimidated Martin into helping him rob the Hill Valley Payroll Substation, resulting in his being arrested for the crime and sentenced to 15 years at a state penitentiary. His sister, Marlene, attempted to break him out of jail, but was also arrested, receiving a 20-year sentence of her own.

    Hoping to prevent this from occurring, Emmett Brown brought Marty forward in time to pose as his own son and refuse Griff's scheme. This led to the thug's gang being incarcerated instead, with both McFly siblings avoiding arrest [**BTF2**].

    NOTE: *In BTTF2's first-draft screenplay, Marty Jr. was called Norman McFly, named after Jennifer's grandfather, Norman.*

- **McFly, Martin III ("Marty"):** A grandson of Marty and Jennifer McFly in one possible timeline [**BFCG**].

- **McFly, Marty ("Blackeye"):** An alias used by Marty McFly while infiltrating Thaddeus Tannen's gang in 1875. Known as a practical joker, he earned the nickname "Blackeye" after giving

gag chewing gum to Tannen and his fellow outlaw, Ox McPhips, which caused Tannen to punch him in the face [**BFAN-16**].

- **McFly, Mary Ellen:** *See* McFly, Lorraine Baines

- **McFly, Norman:** *See* McFly, Martin Jr.

- **McFly, Pee Wee:** An Irish ancestor of Marty McFly (his fifth cousin, thrice removed), and a Major League Baseball pitcher for the Boston Beeneaters. Jules Brown had a baseball card bearing his image, from an 1897 championship game—his last game before retiring, when he struck out during a crucial third playoff game, thereby costing his team the National League pennant.

    Hoping to change history, Marty went back in time to give Pee Wee one of Emmett Brown's inventions: a metal body framework connected to laser-tracking eyeglasses that would enable him to hit homeruns. After causing Pee Wee to be hit on the head with a baseball, however, Marty instead posed as his cousin (whom he resembled), using the device to win a game for the Beeneaters.

    This infuriated gangster Jimmy "Diamond Jim" Tannen, who'd paid Pee Wee to lose the game. Scared of Tannen, Pee Wee tried to leave town, but he eventually returned to win the next game, earning the Beeneaters the pennant [**BFAN-8**].

    NOTE: *"Boston Beeneaters" was the name by which the Atlanta Braves were known during that era. In 1897, the team won the league pennant against the Orioles.*

- **McFly, Seamus:** The great-great-grandfather of Marty, Linda and David McFly, and great-grandfather of George McFly [**BTF3**]. He and his wife, Maggie, originally hailed from Ballybowhill, a village in County Dublin, Ireland, before relocating to the United States in 1881 [**BTF3-sp, BTF3-n**].

    The couple settled first in Virginia City, where Seamus lost his brother, Martin, during a bar fight in which Martin was stabbed in the belly. In search of a new life, Seamus and Maggie purchased a farm in Hill Valley, where they soon delivered the first McFly born in America, William Sean McFly.

    Seamus—an optimistic and pacifistic Christian with red hair on his head and face—saved Marty's life in 1885 after finding him unconscious following an encounter with a black bear. He brought Marty to his home, where Maggie tended

CODE	STORY
NIKE	*BTTF*-themed TV commercial: Nike
NTND	Nintendo *Back to the Future—The Ride* Mini-Game
PIZA	*BTTF*-themed TV commercial: Pizza Hut
PNBL	Data East *BTTF* pinball game
REAL	Real life
RIDE	Simulator: *Back to the Future—The Ride*
SCRM	2010 Scream Awards: *Back to the Future 25th Anniversary Reunion* (broadcast)
SCRT	2010 Scream Awards: *Back to the Future 25th Anniversary Reunion* (trailer)
SIMP	Simulator: *The Simpsons Ride*
SLOT	*Back to the Future Video Slots*
STLZ	Unused *BTTF* footage of Eric Stoltz as Marty McFly
STRY	*Back to the Future Storybook*
TEST	Screen tests: Crispin Glover, Lea Thompson and Tom Wilson
TLTL	Telltale Games' *Back to the Future—The Game*
TOPS	Topps' *Back to the Future II* trading-card set
TRIL	*BTTF: The Official Book of the Complete Movie Trilogy*
UNIV	Universal Studios Hollywood promotional video

SUFFIX	MEDIUM
-b	*BTTF2*'s Biff Tannen Museum video (extended)
-c	Credit sequence to the animated series
-d	Film deleted scene
-n	Film novelization
-o	Film outtake
-p	1955 phone book from *BTTF1*
-v	Video game print materials or commentaries
-s1	Screenplay (draft one)
-s2	Screenplay (draft two)
-s3	Screenplay (draft three)
-s4	Screenplay (draft four)
-sp	Screenplay (production draft)
-sx	Screenplay (*Paradox*)

to his head wound. Marty, recognizing the couple as his kin, called himself Clint Eastwood so as not to arouse suspicions regarding his surname.

Despite Maggie's wariness of Marty's anachronistic ways, Seamus felt a bond with the youth and urged him to always avoid a fight, lest he face the same fate as Seamus' brother. His advice sunk in, and Marty, when forced to face Buford Tannen in a duel, found a way to survive without firing a shot [**BTF3**].

Seamus often taught his son that there was no sense in getting riled up about things over which one had no control—advice that Willie took to heart [**TLTL-5**]. Seamus and Maggie had at least four grandchildren: two boys and two girls [**BTF3**].

> *NOTE: In a combined script for both film sequels, titled* Paradox, *Seamus was unmarried and flirted with an unnamed "bar girl."* Back to the Future III*'s first-draft screenplay named him Angus George Douglas McFly.*

- **McFly, Sylvia ("Silvie," "Trixie Trotter"):** The mother of George McFly and husband of Arthur McFly, born Sylvia Miskin. In her later years, she had at least three grandchildren: Marty, David and Linda McFly [**TLTL-5**].

A chanteuse of the Prohibition era, Sylvia hailed from Manitoba, Canada, and was known as "the Songbird of the Sierras," "the Nightingale of the North," "the Floozy of the Foothills" and the "Winsome Wench of Winnpieg." As Trixie, she performed at gangster Irving "Kid" Tannen's speakeasy, El Kid, accompanied on piano by "Cue Ball" Donnely [**TLTL-2**]. In addition, she posed for a set of "artistic" nude postcards, which she quickly regretted [**TLTL-4**].

Sylvia kept her past (and even her name) a secret, claiming to be from Seattle. Journalist Edna Strickland suspected her of lying, however, since Edna's Washington sources had never heard of a "Trixie Trotter." She was romantically involved with Kid, though out of fear rather than love. Deep down, she knew Kid to be a creep, so she kept what she called an "insurance policy" to guarantee her own safety: Kid's ledgers, proving him guilty of tax evasion.

While dating Kid, Sylvia befriended Arthur McFly, an accountant working for the mobster against his will. Artie tutored her in etiquette, philosophy, accounting and other areas, seeing more in her than just a sexy lounge singer. She fell in love with the bookish McFly, and made a

deal with Kid after Artie testified against him in 1931: If he agreed not to hurt Arthur, she would withhold her evidence from the authorities.

Marty, visiting her era from the future, convinced Sylvia to betray Kid, claiming the mobster had killed Artie. Devastated by the loss, she presented the ledgers to policeman Danny Parker, who arrested the mobster and shut down the speakeasy. She later learned that Artie was still alive, and secretly began dating him [**TLTL-2**].

Following Kid's arrest, Arthur helped Sylvia become more respectable, by hiring her as the hostess of the 1931 Hill Valley Exposition, in the role of Techne, Muse of Progress. Unfortunately, the expo's charter stipulated that the hostess be a U.S. citizen. Once Edna discovered her nationality, Artie had no choice but to fire her. Furious, Sylvia got even, helping Marty break up Edna's relationship with Emmett Brown by pretending that the scientist had fathered a son with her, named Emmett Jr. [**TLTL-4**].

Luckily, Arthur found a loophole enabling Sylvia to retain her job—namely, he proposed to her. During the expo, she announced each on-stage presentation dressed as Techne, and later that night, she and Arthur eloped. Although Artie's father, William McFly, initially disapproved of their union, he soon saw beyond her disreputable past and gave the couple his blessing [**TLTL-5**].

> *NOTE: In Telltale Games' video game, Marty referred to his grandmother in the present tense, indicating she may have still been alive in 1986.*

- **McFly, William Sean ("Will," "Willie"):** The first McFly born in the United States, and the great-grandfather of Marty, David and Linda McFly, born to Irish immigrants Seamus and Maggie McFly in 1885. After traveling back to that year to prevent Emmett Brown from being killed by Buford Tannen, Marty stayed with Willie's parents and held his then-infant ancestor—who urinated on Marty.

As an adult, Willie married and had at least four children—two boys and two girls—with the family owning and operating a farm. A photo of his family, alongside Seamus and Maggie, was stored in the Hill Valley Historical Society's archives [**BTF3**].

In his later years, Willie worked for a business called Hill Valley Mercantile Deliveries. He disapproved of his son, Arthur, and was especially disappointed when Artie married Canadian lounge singer Sylvia "Trixie Trotter" Miskin. Once he got

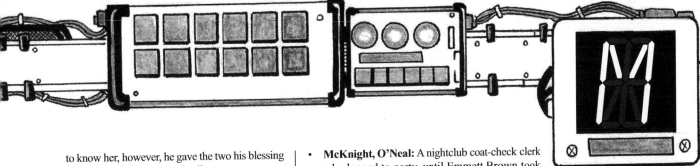

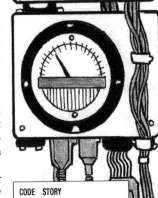

to know her, however, he gave the two his blessing and welcomed her to the family.

In an alternate timeline, in which Edna Strickland accidentally burnt down Hill Valley during its Old West period, the 1931 version of William McFly instead worked for Haysville Mercantile Deliveries. In that reality, Willie saved Marty's and Emmett Brown's lives when a half-crazed Edna tried to shoot them [**TLTL-5**].

- **McFly Museum of Aeronautics:** A museum at Hill Valley's McFly Space Center, circa 2091, named after Marty McFly. The facility was open to the public, and hosted school tours. A floating robot called Billy Spaceboy greeted visitors at the entrance [**BFAN-9**].

- *McFlys of Hill Valley, The:* An exhaustively detailed, hardbound history of Marty McFly's family, from the time of his great-great-grandfather, Seamus McFly, circa the 1800s, to Marty's immediate family, in 1986. Emmett Brown created the book for Marty as a high school graduation gift, based on traditional research, as well as firsthand accounts accrued via time travel.

While searching for information regarding Marty's paternal grandmother, Sylvia Miskin, Doc traveled back to 1931 to find her, inadvertently setting off a string of disastrous timeline alterations. These included his being imprisoned for arson, his marrying Edna Strickland, Hill Valley becoming a dystopian society under his oppressive rule, and Edna burning the city to the ground during the Old West period [**TLTL-5**].

- **McFly Space Center:** A Hill Valley-based facility owned by Marty McFly's descendants, circa 2091. The center, associated with McFly Space Cruises, contained the McFly Museum of Aeronautics. Parking cost $100 per hour, or $1,000 for a full day, and was overseen by a robot called Peter Park-It [**BFAN-9**].

- **McFly Space Cruises:** A Hill Valley business operated by Marty McFly's descendants, attached to the McFly Space Center and the McFly Museum of Aeronautics. In 2091, the firm launched the *MSC Marty*, the first passenger solar sailship to Mars [**BFAN-9**].

- **McHandy's Hardware Hutch:** A business located in Hill Valley, circa 1991. McHandy's sold batteries and other goods [**BFCM-4**].

- **McKnight, O'Neal:** A nightclub coat-check clerk who longed to party, until Emmett Brown took him to the year 2088 so that he could see what he was really meant to be. In that future, McKnight discovered his true potential as a club dancer and a ladies' man, while Doc took a turn spinning records in a D.J. booth [**CHEK**].

- **McPhips, Ox ("Blacklips"):** An outlaw in Thaddeus Tannen's gang, circa 1875, who was wanted for stagecoach robbery. Immensely large, but not overly bright, Ox was a skilled fighter, but also showed surprising manners and sensitivity for a ruffian.

Ox earned the nickname "Blacklips" after chewing a piece of gag gum that Marty McFly had given him, causing his lips to darken. Secretly in love with Tannen's sister, Hepzibah Tannen, Ox helped her deliver her brother to the police. He and Hep then gave up their life of crime, got married and opened an ice-cream shop together [**BFAN-16**].

- **McRibs:** A restaurant located in Hill Valley, circa 2585 [**BFCL-1**].

> *NOTE: Given the company's name and golden-arches logo design, McRibs was apparently a 26th-century derivation of fast-food chain McDonalds.*

- **McVey, Peggy Ann:** A teenager in Hill Valley who attended school with Martha Peabody in 1955. Martha was jealous of Peggy Ann's family, who owned a television—which Martha's old-fashioned father, Otis Peabody, refused to buy [**BTF1-n**].

- **McWaiters:** A service offered by McDonald's restaurants in 2015. Each table featured a touchpad menu for ordering, with pressure pads to scan a patron's thumbprint, after which a McWaiter would deliver food directly to that person's table [**BTF2-s1**].

- **Meadows, Mike:** A photographer working for the *Hill Valley Telegraph*. When Emmett Brown's mansion was destroyed in a fire, Meadows photographed firefighters battling the blaze [**BTF1**].

- **Meat Market:** A butcher shop in Hill Valley, circa 1885 [**BTF3**].

CODE	STORY
NIKE	*BTTF*-themed TV commercial: Nike
NTND	Nintendo *Back to the Future—The Ride* Mini-Game
PIZA	*BTTF*-themed TV commercial: Pizza Hut
PNBL	Data East *BTTF* pinball game
REAL	Real life
RIDE	Simulator: *Back to the Future—The Ride*
SCRM	2010 Scream Awards: *Back to the Future* 25th Anniversary Reunion (broadcast)
SCRT	2010 Scream Awards: *Back to the Future* 25th Anniversary Reunion (trailer)
SIMP	Simulator: *The Simpsons Ride*
SLOT	*Back to the Future* Video Slots
STLZ	Unused *BTTF* footage of Eric Stoltz as Marty McFly
STRY	*Back to the Future* Storybook
TEST	Screen tests: Crispin Glover, Lea Thompson and Tom Wilson
TLTL	Telltale Games' *Back to the Future—The Game*
TOPS	Topps' *Back to the Future II* trading-card set
TRIL	*BTTF: The Official Book of the Complete Movie Trilogy*
UNIV	Universal Studios Hollywood promotional video

SUFFIX	MEDIUM
-b	*BTTF2*'s Biff Tannen Museum video (extended)
-c	Credit sequence to the animated series
-d	Film deleted scene
-n	Film novelization
-o	Film outtake
-p	1955 phone book from *BTTF1*
-v	Video game print materials or commentaries
-s1	Screenplay (draft one)
-s2	Screenplay (draft two)
-s3	Screenplay (draft three)
-s4	Screenplay (draft four)
-sp	Screenplay (production draft)
-sx	Screenplay (*Paradox*)

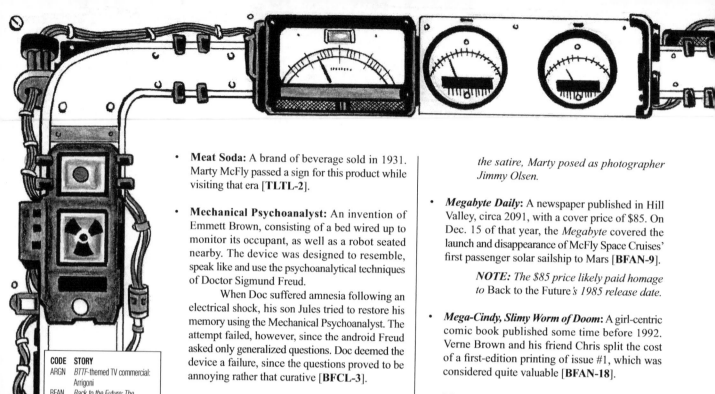

- **Meat Soda:** A brand of beverage sold in 1931. Marty McFly passed a sign for this product while visiting that era [**TLTL-2**].

- **Mechanical Psychoanalyst:** An invention of Emmett Brown, consisting of a bed wired up to monitor its occupant, as well as a robot seated nearby. The device was designed to resemble, speak like and use the psychoanalytical techniques of Doctor Sigmund Freud.

    When Doc suffered amnesia following an electrical shock, his son Jules tried to restore his memory using the Mechanical Psychoanalyst. The attempt failed, however, since the android Freud asked only generalized questions. Doc deemed the device a failure, since the questions proved to be annoying rather that curative [**BFCL-3**].

- **"Meet Me in St. Louis, Louis":** A popular song by Andrew B. Sterling and Kerry Mills, released in 1904 to celebrate the Louisiana Purchase Exposition [**REAL**].

    On June 29 of that year, Emmett and Clara Brown—having traveled back in time to attend the fair—recorded themselves singing "Meet Me in St. Louis, Louis" on an old-style recording device. Doc's sons, Jules and Verne, heard the recording while visiting the exposition in 1992 [**BFAN-25**].

- **Mega Brainman:** A superhero whom Emmett Brown briefly believed himself to be in 1952, after being hit on the head by a microphone during a wrestling match. His catch phrase was "Yoiks, and away!" As Mega Brainman, Doc considered himself a "friend to the friendless, champion to the championless, superhero to the superheroless." He wore a blue and red wrestling outfit and booster-boots, enabling him to run faster than moving vehicles and leap tall buildings, and claimed to have supersonic hearing and X-ray vision. A second knock on the skull cured Doc of this delusion [**BFAN-24**].

    NOTE: This alterego was a spoof of DC Comics' Superman, who dressed in the same colors; said "up, up and away" (in early incarnations of the character); and, in both the 1940s animated serials from Fleischer Studios and the 1950s TV series Adventures of Superman, *was said to be "faster than a speeding bullet, more powerful than a locomotive, able to leap tall buildings in a single bound." Furthering*

the satire, Marty posed as photographer Jimmy Olsen.

- *Megabyte Daily:* A newspaper published in Hill Valley, circa 2091, with a cover price of $85. On Dec. 15 of that year, the *Megabyte* covered the launch and disappearance of McFly Space Cruises' first passenger solar sailship to Mars [**BFAN-9**].

    NOTE: The $85 price likely paid homage to Back to the Future*'s 1985 release date.*

- *Mega-Cindy, Slimy Worm of Doom:* A girl-centric comic book published some time before 1992. Verne Brown and his friend Chris split the cost of a first-edition printing of issue #1, which was considered quite valuable [**BFAN-18**].

- **Mega Malt:** A beverage sold at the Mega Monster Mountain amusement park, at a price of $85 per cup [**BFAN-25**].

    NOTE: The $85 price likely paid homage to Back to the Future*'s 1985 release date.*

- **Megamaniac:** *See* Mega Musclemaniac

- **Mega Monster Mountain:** An exorbitantly priced amusement park in Hill Valley, featuring roller-coasters and other attractions. Emmett Brown took his family here in 1992, which cost $275 just to enter the park. Rides included the Brain Banger, the Chow Blower, the Ferris Wheel, the Gut Twister and the Spleen Splitter [**BFAN-25**].

- **Mega Muscleman:** A fictional superhero whose comic book exploits Verne Brown and his friends enjoyed reading. Able to fly, Mega Muscleman could jump over the Grand Canyon. Verne Brown's playmate and occasional bully, Jackson, liked to dress up as this character [**BFAN-24**].

- **Mega Muscleman Fan Club:** A club formed by Verne Brown's friends, emulating the exploits of comic book superhero Mega Muscleman. Those invited to join were dubbed Mega Musclemaniacs, after proving their heroism by swinging over Dead Man's Swamp [**BFAN-24**].

- **Mega Musclemaniac:** A title ("Megamaniac" for short) awarded to members of the Mega Muscleman Fan Club, following initiation [**BFAN-24**].

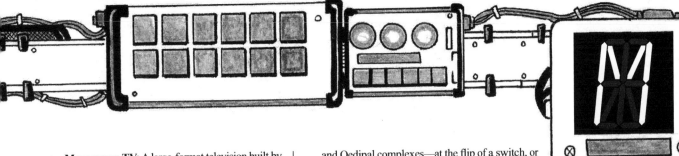

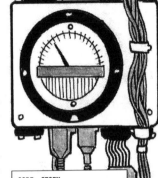

- **Megascreen TV:** A large-format television built by Emmett Brown, on which Doc enjoyed watching such classic science fiction films as *The War of the Worlds* [**BFAN-23**].

- **Mel**: A management-level employee of a business in Hill Valley. In 1991, Emmett Brown read a help-wanted ad for his firm while trying to find a job. Mel's company was located at 25 Carson [**BFAN-12**].

  > *NOTE: The name of Mel's company is unknown, as that portion of the ad was obstructed from view.*

- **Melvin:** An employee of Hill Valley's Records Office, circa 1931. When Arthur McFly secretly married Sylvia "Trixie Trotter" Miskin, Melvin told Artie's father, William McFly, about it [**TLTL-5**].

- **Memory Archive Recall Indexer and Enhancer (M.A.R.I.E.):** An invention of Emmett Brown, designed to enable a user to recall any memory, fact or information learned during that person's lifetime, by donning a large helmet wired to a computer. The helmet became very hot while in use, and the memory-recall process had a jarring effect on one's nervous system—and hairstyle. What's more, it only worked in reverse, making a user forget instead of remember.

  Walter Wisdom, Emmett's unscrupulous college roommate, stole the invention in 1992, intending to claim it as his own. Doc regained the device, however, discrediting Wisdom during a live television broadcast [**BFAN-15**].

- **Mendez, Lisa:** A metropolitan ambulation provision tech at the Institute of Future Technology [**RIDE**].

  > *NOTE: This individual's name appeared on signage outside* Back to the Future: The Ride.

- **Mental Alignment Meter (M.A.M.):** An invention of Emmett Brown in Citizen Brown's dystopian timeline, built in 1931 under the influence of Edna Strickland. The Mental Alignment Meter enabled Emmett to chart Mind Maps by reading and interpreting the subconscious desires of the human mind.

  Brown's goal in building the M.A.M. was to diagnose and cure mental disorders—from psychoses and neuroses to alcoholism, acrophobia and Oedipal complexes—at the flip of a switch, or to detect the truthfulness of a witness' courtroom testimony using a small, portable device. The design was the first step toward his transforming Hill Valley, with Edna's help, into an enlightened but repressed society in which no transgressions were tolerated [**TLTL-4**].

- **Mental Ward B:** A mental ward at Hill Valley Hospital. In the Biffhorrific timeline, Emmett Brown was declared legally insane and sentenced to this ward in 1983 [**BTF2**].

- *Merv Griffin Show, The*: An American television talk show that aired, on and off, from 1962 until 1986 [**REAL**]. Edna Strickland was a fan of this series, and had little patience for people who caused her to miss an episode [**TLTL-1**].

- **Mesquite Grilled Sushi Springsteen String Bean Pie:** A menu item sold at Café 80's in 2015 [**BTF2**].

- *Method of Reaching Extreme Altitudes, A*: A 1919 monograph written by inventor Robert Hutchings Goddard, considered a classic text of 20th-century rocket science [**REAL**]. In 1931, Emmett Brown researched this work while designing his Electrokinetic Levitator, based on his failed Rocket Car [**TLTL-5**].

- *Metropolis*: A ground-breaking 1927 silent film directed by Fritz Lang [**REAL**]. Verne Brown, as a child, had a poster of this movie hanging in his bedroom [**BFCL-1**].

- **M. Fennigot Millinery:** A store in 1885 Hill Valley that sold a variety of products, including Stetson hats and corsets from B.S. Gideon [**BTF3**].

- **Miami:** A city on the Atlantic coast of southeastern Florida [**REAL**]. In 2015, the Chicago Cubs won the World Series in five games against a Miami-based team [**BTF2**]. The latter team was the Miami Gators [**GALE**].

  > *NOTE: When* Back to the Future II *was released in 1989, there was no Major League Baseball team in Florida. In 1993, however, the Florida Marlins—later renamed the Miami Marlins—were formed. While the team is not called the Gators, it would nonetheless be possible for a Miami team to win in 2015.*

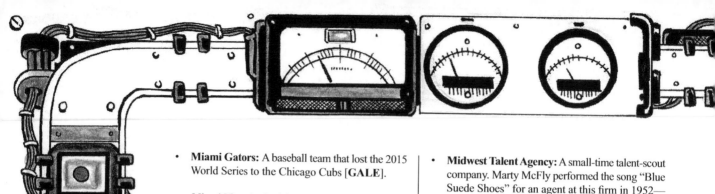

- **Miami Gators:** A baseball team that lost the 2015 World Series to the Chicago Cubs [**GALE**].

- *Miami Vice*: A television series that aired on NBC from 1984 to 1989, produced by Michael Mann, and starring Don Johnson and Philip Michael Thomas [**REAL**]. In 1986, Marty McFly had a poster from this TV show hanging in his bedroom [**TLTL-1**].

- **Mickey:** A generous uncle of Lorraine McFly who sent each of her children $50 on their birthdays. His wife, Doris, was a sick woman who was hospitalized in 1967 [**BTF2-s1**].

- **MICRD:** A label on a jar in the Hilldale home of Marty and Jennifer McFly in 2015 [**BTF2**].

- **Micro-C:** A type of digital format offered in 2015 as an alternative to printed books [**BTF2-s1**].

- **Microsoft Corp.:** A multinational provider of computer products and services [**REAL**].

   When Microsoft's senior vice-president, Robert L. Muglia, delivered a keynote address at Tech-Ed 2007 about his vision for the future, attendees tired of unrealized promises began pummeling him with vegetables. Therefore, Emmett Brown, using his time-traveling DeLorean, offered Muglia insights into Microsoft's past failures.

   The two men visited Acme.com in 2001 and 2003, where a nerdy IT worker, TechFly, faced technological setbacks due to faulty Microsoft software, and endured bullying from his manager, Mister Biff. As a result, history changed so that Muglia's keynote avoided the mistakes of Microsoft's past, while TechFly became more confident around Biff—who, in the new timeline, worked for him as a janitor [**MSFT**].

- **microstorage:** A process of shrinking vehicles and luggage down to a tiny size, utilized in the year 2091 by McFly Space Cruises to accommodate travelers aboard its passenger solar sailships, such as the *MSC Marty* [**BFAN-9**].

- **MICRV:** A label on a jar in the Hilldale home of Marty and Jennifer McFly in 2015 [**BTF2**].

- **Mid-Valley:** A section of Hill Valley, circa 2015, through which hover buses and express trams were available as public transportation [**BTF2**].

- **Midwest Talent Agency:** A small-time talent-scout company. Marty McFly performed the song "Blue Suede Shoes" for an agent at this firm in 1952—three years before it was first recorded—hoping to change history and gain fame as a musician. The agent was unimpressed, however, and threw Marty out of his office [**BTF1-s1**].

- **Mike:** A name scrawled in graffiti on the wall of Hill Valley High School, circa 1985 [**BTF1**].

- **Mikey:** A buck-toothed student at Hill Valley Elementary School who was sometimes bullied by Biff Tannen Jr. [**BFAN-26**].

- **Milk-Bone:** A brand of dog biscuit manufactured by the F. H. Bennett Biscuit Co. [**REAL**]. Emmett Brown sometimes purchased Milk-Bones for his dog, Einstein [**BTF1**].

- **Miller Brewing Co.:** An American brewer of alcoholic beer [**REAL**]. Marty McFly's family sometimes drank the company's Miller Lite product. Emmett Brown used the discarded cans from the McFlys' trash to fuel his DeLorean's Mr. Fusion Home Energy Reactor [**BTF1**].

   NOTE: *Miller brands appeared several other times throughout* BTTF1, *such as being advertised on delivery trucks.*

- **Milwaukee:** The largest city in the U.S. state of Wisconsin [**REAL**]. In 1926, while staying with his oddball Uncle Oliver, four-year-old Emmett Brown fell into a lake while fishing, and nearly drowned [**BFAN-11**].

- **Mind Map:** A recording of a person's mental patterns using a Mental Alignment Meter and a Mind Mapping Helmet [**TLTL-4**].

- **Mind Mapping Helmet:** A type of headgear invented by Emmett Brown in 1931, used to record a test subject's mental patterns for analysis by his Mental Alignment Meter (M.A.M.). The helmet could probe a person's brain by measuring fluctuations in skin conductance and electrical resistance on the surface of the parietal lobe.

   A subject was exposed to visual stimuli intended to provoke a series of positive, negative or indifferent responses, as indicated by a trio of lights, colored red, yellow and green. The recorded responses were relayed to a special typewriter known as a Mind Map Printer, which printed out

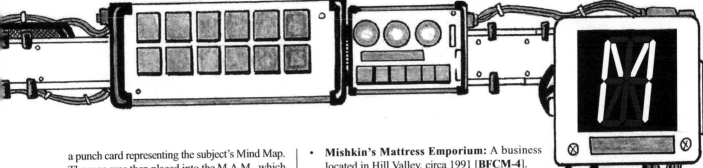

a punch card representing the subject's Mind Map. The map was then placed into the M.A.M., which deemed that individual either a model citizen, an honest Joe, a decent chap, a layabout, an inveterate liar, a hooligan or a degenerate criminal.

Privately, Doc knew the system to be a sham. Influenced by the manipulations of his girlfriend, Edna Strickland, he'd built it over a two-month period, adding several bells and whistles to a $5 potentiometer (a three-terminal resistor often used to control electrical devices, such as volume controls on audio equipment) to make it appear scientific. Though the machine could determine if a person liked or disliked what he or she was seeing, it could not actually sort criminals from model citizens—plus, about 90 percent of those scanned were branded as hooligans [**TLTL-4**].

> *NOTE: Similar devices created by Doc included the Brain-wave Analyzer, from BTTF1; the Brain Wave Analyzer, from the animated series; the Deep-Thought Mind-Reading Helmet, also seen in the cartoon; and the Deep-Thinking Mind-Reading Helmet, introduced in the Universal Studios ride.*

- **Mind Map Printer:** A printing mechanism invented by Emmett Brown in 1931 as part of his Mind Mapping Helmet. After Doc's Mental Alignment Meter (M.A.M.) probed a test subject's mind, this special typewriter printed a punch card pronouncing judgment on his or her mental state, ranging from model citizen to degenerate criminal [**TLTL-4**].

- **Mini-C:** A type of digital format offered in 2015 as an alternative to printed books [**BTF2-s1**].

- **Ministry of Tourism:** A government office located in Courthouse Square, in Citizen Brown's dystopian timeline [**TLTL-3**].

- **Mintz:** A university colleague of Emmett Brown in 1955. He, along with Dean Wooster and fellow colleague Cooper, requested that Doc take part in one of three projects: developing the Edsel automobile, creating a chemical-warfare compound (which would be called Agent Brown, in his honor) or helping to build the new Xerox company. Emmett, however, refused [**BTF3-s1**].

- **Mir Chicken Chernobyl Asparagus Tip O'Neil Goulash:** A menu item sold at Café 80's in 2015 [**BTF2**].

- **Mishkin's Mattress Emporium:** A business located in Hill Valley, circa 1991 [**BFCM-4**].

- **Miskin, Delores:** A woman whose image adorned a painting at Beauregard Tannen's Palace Saloon and Hotel, in 1876 Hill Valley [**TLTL-5**]. The book *Hill Valley Historical Society, 1865-1990* dubbed Miskin "the face that inspired a thousand barroom brawls" [**TLTL-v**].

> *NOTE: Presumably, Delores was an ancestor of Sylvia "Trixie Trotter" Miskin—and, thus, of Marty McFly.*

- **Miskin, Sylvia:** *See* McFly, Sylvia

- **Mission Control:** The main control center of McFly Space Cruises, circa 2091. Jules and Verne Brown visited this area while trying to prevent their parents from dying aboard the sabotaged passenger solar sailship *MSC Marty* [**BFAN-9**].

- **Miss Prettywhiskers:** Edna Strickland's housecat, circa 1986. The unfriendly feline was very particular—and threatening—about whom she allowed to handle her food [**TLTL-1**].

- **Mister Biff:** A heavyset IT manager at a firm called Acme.com, circa 2001. Biff often bullied a nerdy employee, named TechFly, forcing the latter to do his work for him despite a lack of effective software to handle assignments.

When Microsoft's senior vice-president, Robert L. Muglia, delivered a keynote address at Tech-Ed 2007 regarding his vision for the future, his rhetoric proved unpopular with attendees tired of unrealized promises. Emmett Brown, using his time-traveling DeLorean, thus provided Muglia with insights into Microsoft's past failures.

The two men visited Acme.com, where TechFly faced not only Biff's bullying, but also technological setbacks as a result of faulty Microsoft software. As a result, history changed so that Muglia's keynote avoided the mistakes of Microsoft's past, while TechFly became more confident around Biff—who, in the new timeline, worked for him at Microsoft as a janitor [**MSFT**].

- **MIT-0001:** The license plate number of a Mitsubishi Lancer sedan into which Emmett Brown's DeLorean mysteriously transformed during one particular time-travel experiment [**MITS**].

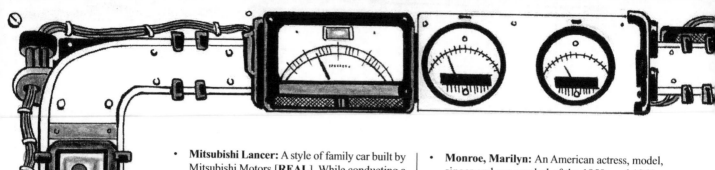

- **Mitsubishi Lancer:** A style of family car built by Mitsubishi Motors [**REAL**]. While conducting a time-travel experiment with Einstein at the Twin Pines Mall, Emmett Brown sent the DeLorean into the future, and was surprised when the vehicle returned as a Mitsubishi Lancer sedan. What's more, Einstein was now a robot. Intrigued, Doc took the new vehicle for a spin [**MITS**].

- **Model 1015:** A type of jukebox manufactured by Wurlitzer [**REAL**]. In 1955, Hill Valley restaurant Lou's Café had such a jukebox within its establishment [**BTF1**].

- **Model 25R:** A gauge on Emmett Brown's giant guitar amplifier, ranging in power level from 0 to 1.0, with an additional span labeled "Over Range" [**BTF1**].

- **Model UN:** A Hill Valley government program in Citizen Brown's dystopian timeline, with each member of the Model UN program representing a different country from around the world. In that reality, Marty McFly represented Djibouti, a nation in the Horn of Africa [**TLTL-3**].

- *Modern Discipline:* A book written in or around the 1930s, outlining how to maintain strict order. Gerald Strickland used this book as the basis of his policies while serving as the principal of Hill Valley High School [**BTF1-s3**].

- *Modern Inventions Monthly:* A magazine geared toward those dabbling in science and innovation. In 1931, this periodical published an article about the feasibility of creating a water engine. At the time, teenager Emmett Brown had a copy of this issue within his laboratory [**TLTL-1, TLTL-4**].

- **Moloney v. Tannen file:** A legal file that Emmett Brown handled while working for his father, Earhardt Brown, at the Hill Valley Courthouse in 1931 [**TLTL-v**].

  > *NOTE: Presumably, the case involved Irving "Kid" Tannen," given Emmett's role in having Kid imprisoned.*

- **money tree:** *See* Jules Brown Money-Tree

- *Monkey Business:* Biff Tannen's personal yacht in Biffhorrific 1985. Biff often entertained beautiful women on this boat [**BTF2-b**].

- **Monroe, Marilyn:** An American actress, model, singer and sex symbol of the 1950s and 1960s, born Norma Jeane Mortensen Baker [**REAL**]. In the Biffhorrific timeline, in which Biff Tannen was wealthy and corrupt, Biff was romantically linked with Monroe and other starlets [**BTF2-b**].

- **Monroe Avenue:** *See* Riverside Drive

- **Monster Mama:** A large-wheeled truck that competed in Hill Valley's Founder's Day Tractor-Pull Contest in 1992 [**BFAN-22**].

- **Monster Smash-up:** A type of truck that Verne Brown found "cool." As he and his brother, Jules, prepared a float for Hill Valley's Founder's Day celebration, Verne wished they were instead making one based on a Monster Smash-up truck [**BFAN-22**].

- **Monster Train Smash-Up:** A multi-level train set that Jules Brown's classmate, Jackson, wished he owned. When Jules invented a money-tree, providing the Brown family with instant wealth, Jackson non-subtly told Jules that anyone who bought him Monster Train Smash-Up would be his friend for life. An updated version of the playset included a fake flood [**BFAN-20**].

- **Monstrux ("The Demon Monstrux"):** A fictional villain in the video game *BraveLord and Monstrux*, said to be the "ruler of all that is evil." The demon's goal was to conquer the medieval kingdom of Pectoria, turn its citizens into zombie slaves and force them to eat Brussels sprouts.

  Monstrux had purple skin, a rotund body, a long tongue, green bat-like wings, thin arms and numerous tentacle-like legs. He oozed blue goo from his body, and could turn ordinary objects into his evil minions. When angered, Monstrux exposed his skeleton for intimidation. His arch-nemesis, BraveLord, was a brawny warrior who protected Pectoria.

  When a power surge at Super Mega Arcade World caused the two enemies to come to life, Monstrux made Biff Tannen his zombie and tried to take over the real world—where the demon enjoyed TV soap operas, snack foods and tabloid newspapers. Eventually, Verne managed to stop Monstrux, sending both the demon and BraveLord back to cyberspace [**BFAN-19**].

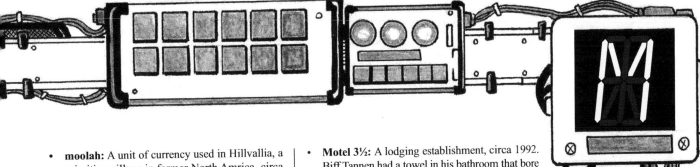

- **moolah:** A unit of currency used in Hillvallia, a primitive village in former North Amrica, circa 2,991,299,129,912,991 A.D. At Oxen's Gore Tavern & Bed 'N' Breakfast, a canteen of water cost 4 moolahs, plus 1 more as a container deposit [**BFCL-2**].

  > *NOTE: Many scientists believe Earth will cease to exist in approximately 7.6 billion years, with human life dying out within a billion years or so.*
  >
  > *The word "moolah" is a common slang term for money.*

- **Moon, Lester:** *See* Berry, Marvin

- **Moon, Marvin:** *See* Berry, Marvin

- **Moon, The:** Earth's only natural satellite (also called Luna), and the fifth largest moon in the Sol System [**REAL**]. Emmett Brown claimed to have visited the Moon, but his records of that adventure were misfiled, replaced with footage of Neil Armstrong's 1969 *Apollo 11* landing. Doc and his wife, Clara Clayton Brown, sometimes gazed at the Moon's Sea of Tranquility from a telescope at their home [**BFAN-9**].

- **Mopsy:** A word appearing on the side of a toy truck on sale at Fedgewick Toys, a London-based toy shop, in 1845 [**BFAN-10**].

- **Morgan, Sir Henry, Admiral:** A Welsh pirate and privateer who frequently raided Spanish settlements in the Caribbean during the 17th century [**REAL**]. In 1992, while using Morgan's reported ocean route to search for Jamaica aboard the S.S. *Clara*, Emmett Brown became stranded on an island in the Caribbean, where he was besieged by pirates [**BFAN-14**].

  > *NOTE: The outcome of this encounter, which occurred during a live-action segment of the animated series, is unrecorded.*

- **Morning Avenue:** A street in Hill Valley [**BFAN-20**].

- **Morrison, James ("Jim"):** The Institute of Future Technology's director of audiotronics [**RIDE**].

  > *NOTE: This individual, identified on signage outside* Back to the Future: The Ride, *was named after the lead singer of the rock group The Doors.*

- **Motel 3½:** A lodging establishment, circa 1992. Biff Tannen had a towel in his bathroom that bore the name of this motel [**BFCL-3**].

  > *NOTE: This business' name was based on that of the Motel 6 chain.*

- **Motel 6000:** A lodging establishment located in Hill Valley, circa 2585 [**BFCL-1**].

  > *NOTE: This business' name was based on that of the Motel 6 chain.*

- **Mother Nature:** The physical manifestation of nature's nurturing characteristics [**REAL**]. When Mother Nature became ill and was hospitalized in Anytown, Emmett Brown boarded his time-traveling DeLorean and discovered that the future would be grim if she could not be saved. After returning to the past, the scientist rushed to the hospital's emergency room, where he shared his foreknowledge with Mother Nature's physician, Douglas "Doogie" Howser [**ERTH**].

  > *NOTE: Howser, portrayed by Neil Patrick Harris, was the title character of* Doogie Howser, M.D., *an ABC television series that aired from 1989 to 1993. This unusual crossover occurred in a 1990 video from Time Warner, titled* The Earth Day Special, *in which celebrities—either in character or as themselves—came together to urge viewers to save the planet.*

- **Mothers Against War:** A speech delivered by Janis Steinberg at a Vietnam War protest rally, to which Lorraine McFly donated her time in 1967 [**BTF2-s1**].

- **Motors, General:** A fictional U.S. Army general. While serving as a soldier in Hill Valley, in 1944, Marty McFly escaped that era by claiming General Motors had ordered him to fix a car's engine [**BFAN-17**].

  > *NOTE: The officer's name was a play on that of automotive corporation General Motors—and the engine reference furthered the pun.*

- **Mountain Dew:** A soft drink produced by PepsiCo, Inc. [**REAL**]. The company's logo appeared on a baseball cap worn by the driver of a Jeep CJ-7 on which Marty McFly hitched a skateboard ride to school [**BTF1**].

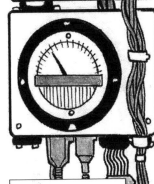

CODE	STORY
NIKE	*BTTF*-themed TV commercial: Nike
NTND	Nintendo *Back to the Future—The Ride* Mini-Game
PIZA	*BTTF*-themed TV commercial: Pizza Hut
PNBL	Data East *BTTF* pinball game
REAL	Real life
RIDE	Simulator: *Back to the Future—The Ride*
SCRM	2010 Scream Awards: *Back to the Future* 25th Anniversary Reunion (broadcast)
SCRT	2010 Scream Awards: *Back to the Future* 25th Anniversary Reunion (trailer)
SIMP	Simulator: *The Simpsons Ride*
SLOT	*Back to the Future Video Slots*
STLZ	Unused *BTTF* footage of Eric Stoltz as Marty McFly
STRY	*Back to the Future Storybook*
TEST	Screen tests: Crispin Glover, Lea Thompson and Tom Wilson
TLTL	Telltale Games' *Back to the Future—The Game*
TOPS	Topps' *Back to the Future II* trading-card set
TRIL	*BTTF: The Official Book of the Complete Movie Trilogy*
UNIV	Universal Studios Hollywood promotional video

SUFFIX	MEDIUM
-b	*BTTF2's* Biff Tannen Museum video (extended)
-c	Credit sequence to the animated series
-d	Film deleted scene
-n	Film novelization
-o	Film outtake
-p	1955 phone book from *BTTF1*
-v	Video game print materials or commentaries
-s1	Screenplay (draft one)
-s2	Screenplay (draft two)
-s3	Screenplay (draft three)
-s4	Screenplay (draft four)
-sp	Screenplay (production draft)
-sx	Screenplay (*Paradox*)

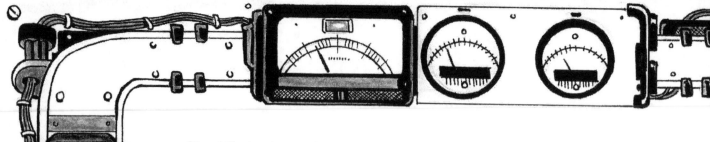

- **Mount Clayton:** A mountain in the Hill Valley area with an elevation of 2,761 feet. The Delgado Mine was located at its base, adjacent to Boot Hill Cemetary [**BTF3**].

  NOTE: Mount Clayton, indicated on Emmett Brown's map of the mine, may have been named after Clara Clayton. However, since he made the map before Clara arrived in Hill Valley and plummeted to her death in the Shonash Ravine, it's unclear why Hill Valley's citizens would have named the mountain after her, since they would not yet have known her.

- **Mouse, Mickey:** A cartoon character created in 1928 by Walt Disney [**REAL**]. Marty McFly's brother, Dave, had a t-shirt bearing Mickey Mouse's image [**BTF1**].

- ***Mouse in the Salon, The:*** A novel published sometimes in or before 1992 [**BFAN-14**].

  NOTE: A bouncer at The Roxy was reading this book while manning the theater's back-stage door.

- **Moustache:** An old-timer who frequented Hill Valley's Palace Saloon and Hotel in 1885, along with Jeb, Levi, Zeke, Toothless and Eyepatch. When Marty McFly considered backing out of a duel with Buford Tannen, Moustache branded Marty a coward [**BTF3-sx**].

  NOTE: The name "Moustache" appeared in BTTF3's production-draft screenplay. His birth name is unknown.

- **MPX125:** *See* Nemotech MPX125

- **Mr. Fusion Home Energy Center:** *See* Mr. Fusion Home Energy Reactor

- **Mr. Fusion Home Energy Reactor:** A 21st-century device used by Emmett Brown to power his time-traveling DeLorean after visiting the year 2015. The Mr. Fusion, when fitted to the back of the car, provided a clean power source, eliminating the need for plutonium. A user could simply drop garbage into the device, including fruit rinds, beer and aluminum cans, and the Mr. Fusion would convert it into energy [**BTF1**].

  The Mr. Fusion was manufactured by Fusion Industries [**BTF2**]. Doc also created a Super-Electromagnet powered by the Mr. Fusion [**BFAN-1**].

  NOTE: The device was known as the Westinghouse Fusion Energizer in BTTF1's revised fourth-draft screenplay, and the Mr. Fusion Home Energy Center in the movie's novelization. Although its name was a parody of the Mr. Coffee brand of coffee makers, the prop was constructed using a Krups coffee grinder.

- **Mr. Gin:** A device invented by Emmett Brown while visiting Chicago's South Side in 1927, to find a cure for cat-aracts for his dog, Einstein. With help from "Bathtub Jim" McFly, Doc created the Mr. Gin—which resembled a Mr. Coffee machine with a beaker for a coffee pot—and used it to brew a cure from juniper berries [**BFCM-1**].

  NOTE: Doc and Marty McFly traveled to 1927 to find a Prohibition Era still, in order to brew the medicine. Once there, Doc revealed he had a Mr. Gin for just that purpose. As such, it's unclear why the still was required.

- **Mr. Perfect All-Natural Steroids:** A business located in Courthouse Square, circa 2015 [**BTF2**].

- **Mr. Profusion:** An invention of Emmett Brown, conceived at the Institute of Future Technology, and offering safe, efficient fusion power for the home [**RIDE**].

  NOTE: This device was described on signage at Universal Studios' Back to the Future: The Ride.

- **Mrs. Bruer & Sons Bakery:** A business listed in the 1955 Hill Valley phone book [**BTF1-p**].

- ***Mr. Wisdom:*** A science-based children's TV series, circa 1992 [**BFAN-15, BFAN-26**]. Biff Tannen Jr. enjoyed watching this series on Channel 92 [**BFAN-26**].

  The show was hosted by Walter Wisdom, a fraud who manipulated kids into buying overpriced spinoff merchandise by pretending to be a great scientist. Verne Brown greatly enjoyed this show as well, and was overjoyed when Wisdom and his Big-Brain Bus visited the Lone Pine Mall in 1992, to meet fans and sell products in his Mr. Wisdom Discount Lab. The youth soon learned, however, that his idol was a con man [**BFAN-15**].

  NOTE: Wisdom and his TV series paid homage to Donald Jeffrey Herbert Kemske,

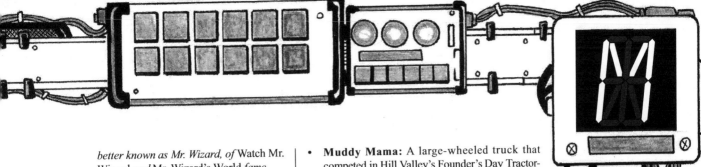

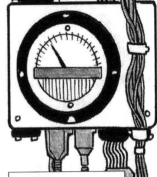

better known as Mr. Wizard, of Watch Mr. Wizard *and* Mr. Wizard's World *fame.*

- **Mr. Wisdom Cappuccino:** A product marketed by television personality Walter Wisdom to merchandise his TV science series, *Mr. Wisdom*. The cappuccino maker, which sported glasses and a bushy mustache to resemble the scientist, was one of many products sold at the Mr. Wisdom Discount Lab, a mobile retail center set up at malls visited by his Big-Brain Bus [**BFAN-15**].

- **Mr. Wisdom Chemistry Set:** A product marketed by television personality Walter Wisdom to merchandise his TV science series, *Mr. Wisdom*. The chemistry set was one of many products sold at the Mr. Wisdom Discount Lab, a mobile retail center set up at malls visited by his Big-Brain Bus [**BFAN-15**].

- **Mr. Wisdom Discount Lab:** A mobile retail center used by Walter Wisdom, the host of *Mr. Wisdom*, to merchandise his popular children's science TV series. The Discount Lab, set up at malls visited by the celebrity's Big-Brain Bus, sold a variety of over-priced official Mr. Wisdom products, including hats, cappuccino makers, chemistry sets, wall pennants, backpacks, hamster cages and Big-Brain Bus wind-up toys [**BFAN-15**].

- *Mr. Wisdom's Live Super-Duper Dinosaur Special:* A 1992 episode of children's television series *Mr. Wisdom*, in which host Walter Wisdom planned to unveil Tiny, Verne Brown's pet Apatosaurus. Wisdom had purchased Tiny from Biff Tannen (who'd stolen the dinosaur for him), renaming the animal Dinosaurus Humongous. The show was a bust, as Verne rescued Tiny before showtime, replacing it with a fake-looking substitute, and thereby publicly humiliating Wisdom and Biff [**BFAN-26**].

- *MSC Jennifer:* See *Jennifer, MSC*

- *MSC Marty:* See *Marty, MSC*

- **MSP:** A brand or product name printed on the side of a box stored at the Sisters of Mercy Soup Kitchen during its time as a front business for Irving "Kid" Tannen's speakeasy [**TLTL-1**].

- **Mt. Clayton:** See *Mount Clayton*

- **Muddy Mama:** A large-wheeled truck that competed in Hill Valley's Founder's Day Tractor-Pull Contest in 1992 [**BFAN-22**].

- **Muglia, Robert L., Senior Vice-President ("Bob"):** A Microsoft executive, circa 2007 [**REAL**].

    When Muglia delivered a keynote address at Tech-Ed 2007 regarding his vision for the future, attendees tired of unrealized promises began pummeling him with vegetables. Emmett Brown, using his time-traveling DeLorean, provided Muglia with insights into Microsoft's past failures.

    The two men visited Acme.com in 2001 and 2003, where a nerdy IT worker named TechFly faced technological setbacks as a result of faulty Microsoft software, and endured bullying from his manager, Mister Biff. As a result, history changed so that Muglia's keynote avoided the mistakes of Microsoft's past, while TechFly became more confident around Biff—who, in the new timeline, worked for him as a janitor [**MSFT**].

- **Muldoon, Vera, Officer:** An undercover police officer, badge number 91, who infiltrated the operations of gangster Jimmy "Diamond Jim" Tannen in 1897. Posing as Jimmy's girlfriend, she collected evidence to arrest him for his many crimes [**BFAN-8**].

- **Mulholland Drive**: A street in Woodland Hills, California [**REAL**]. While trying to find a job in 1991, Emmett Brown read a help-wanted ad for a company located at 23251 Mulholland Drive [**BFAN-12**].

- **multi-motif leaf tree:** A variety of tree synthetically designed by Jules Brown, containing striped and polka-dotted leaves, as well as pink hearts, yellow moons and green clovers. Jules' goal in designing it: to create leaves resembling cheap upholstery. The potted tree took weeks to cultivate, and was very sensitive; when Verne Brown yelled loudly next to it, in fact, all of its leaves fell off. This led to Jules instead engineering a synthetic money-tree [**BFAN-20**].

    ***NOTE:** The mention of hearts, moons and clovers referred to commercials for General Mills' Lucky Charms breakfast cereal.*

- **Mundania:** A small empire in North America, circa 2,991,299,129,912,991 A.D., located in the former southeastern United States, including Florida [**BFCL-2**].

> *NOTE: Many scientists believe Earth will cease to exist in approximately 7.6 billion years, with human life dying out within a billion years or so.*

- **Murdock:** A thug operating in London, circa 1845, who forced street urchins to work for him as pickpockets, and who shared a hideout with a fellow ruffian named Wilkins. Murdock had yellow teeth, spectacles, and thick red facial hair and eyebrows.

  When Emmett Brown's family visited that era, an urchin named Reginald picked Jules Brown's pocket, stealing a watch fob once owned by Clara's Grandpa Clayton, containing the keys to Doc's DeLorean. In order to get it back, Jules and his brother, Vern, began working for Murdock as pickpockets. Thanks to Doc's intervention, however, Murdock and Wilkins were eventually captured by police [**BFAN-10**].

  > *NOTE: Murdock was modeled after the character of Fagin, from Charles Dickens' 1838 novel,* Oliver Twist.

- **Murphy, Jim:** An employee at the Institute of Future Technology, stationed in the West Wing [**RIDE**].

  > *NOTE: This individual was identified on signage outside* Back to the Future: The Ride.

- **Murphy, Mrs.:** An acquaintance of baseball player Pee Wee McFly, sometime in or before 1897. A fellow acquaintance, Tommy-Boy, was said to have thrown Pee Wee's overalls in her chowder [**BFAN-8**].

- **Murray:** Emmett Brown's stock broker, circa 1955. After witnessing the time-traveling DeLorean that his future self would create 30 years later, the scientist—believing the car to be typical of vehicles from 1985—called Murray and told him to heavily invest in stainless steel, under the assumption that all automobiles would be made from this material in the future [**BTF1-s4**].

- **Music Appreciation:** A college course attended by Marty McFly in 1991, taught by an instructor called "Old Buzzard" Babcock. Marty scored a C- on a test, despite writing an extra-credit report on the social significance of the Bonedaddys [**BFAN-4**].

- **Music Pavilion:** A kiosk at the 1904 St. Louis World Exposition, in which visitors could record themselves singing. Emmett and Clara Brown, having traveled back in time to attend the fair, recorded themselves singing "Meet Me in St. Louis, Louis" at this booth. By 1992, the stand had been replaced by a shop simply called "CD," which played recordings from prior expositions—including that of Doc and Clara [**BFAN-25**].

- **Mussenden, Felix, Ph.D.:** An employee at the Institute of Future Technology, stationed in the East Wing [**RIDE**].

  > *NOTE: This individual, identified on signage outside* Back to the Future: The Ride, *was named after the former president of Universal Studios' Orlando theme-park operations.*

- *Mustang:* A magazine published by Patterson Publishing, covering Ford's various Mustang automobiles [**REAL**]. In Biffhorrific 1985, Biff had issues of this publication in his penthouse suite, in a rack on his bar [**BTF2**].

- **Mutant Alien Two-Headed Elvis:** A creature reported in a 1991 issue of a tabloid magazine, the *Enquisitor* [**BFCM-4**].

  > *NOTE: Given that the* Enquisitor *was based on* The National Enquirer, *which has a reputation for fabricated stories, it's unlikely that the Mutant Alien Two-Headed Elvis—probably named after Elvis Presley—existed.*

- **"My Melancholy Baby":** A popular foxtrot ballad written by Ernie Burnett, with lyrics by George A. Norton, published in 1912 [**REAL**].

  This song was among "Cue Ball" Donnely's piano sheet music (published by Joe Morris Music Co.) at the El Kid speakeasy in 1931, which he played for the bar's patrons, accompanied by singer Sylvia "Trixie Trotter" Miskin. This particular tune often put Officer Danny Parker in a melancholy mood [**TLTL-2**].

- *My Success Secrets:* A book that Marty McFly read while attending college [**BFCM-3**].

  > *NOTE: The title of this work paid homage to the 1987 film* The Secret of My Success, *starring Michael J. Fox.*

NEEDLES, DOUGLAS

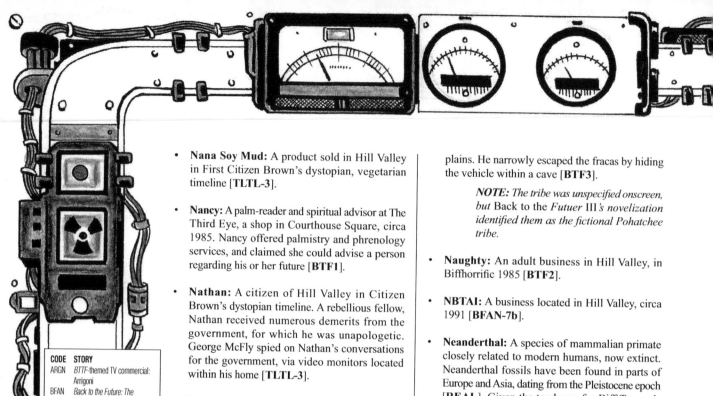

- **Nana Soy Mud:** A product sold in Hill Valley in First Citizen Brown's dystopian, vegetarian timeline [**TLTL-3**].

- **Nancy:** A palm-reader and spiritual advisor at The Third Eye, a shop in Courthouse Square, circa 1985. Nancy offered palmistry and phrenology services, and claimed she could advise a person regarding his or her future [**BTF1**].

- **Nathan:** A citizen of Hill Valley in Citizen Brown's dystopian timeline. A rebellious fellow, Nathan received numerous demerits from the government, for which he was unapologetic. George McFly spied on Nathan's conversations for the government, via video monitors located within his home [**TLTL-3**].

- **National Aeronautics and Space Administration (NASA):** An agency of the U.S. government's executive branch. NASA was responsible for the nation's civilian space program, as well as aerospace and aeronautics research [**REAL**].

  The Hill Valley Space Center and Air-Sickness Clinic housed a NASA facility as part of its Discovery Program. In 1992, Emmett Brown visited this center to be suited up for a trip to outer space, in order to help a local cable company overhaul its communications satellite. In return, he received free cable service, including premium channels [**BFAN-15**].

- **National Grange of the Order of Patrons of Husbandry:** A fraternal organization for American farmers that encouraged farm families to band together for their common economic and political well-being [**REAL**]. The organization operated a chapter in Hill Valley [**BTF1**].

- ***National Lampoon's Animal House:*** A 1978 American comedy film directed by John Landis [**REAL**]. A VHS copy of this film was among the items for sale at Blast From the Past, an antique and collectibles shop in 2015 Hill Valley [**BTF2**].

- **Native Americans:** The indigenous peoples of North America within the boundaries of the United States, comprising numerous tribes and ethnic groups [**REAL**].

  After traveling back to 1885 in the DeLorean, Marty McFly found himself caught in the middle of a dispute between a U.S. Cavalry battalion and a tribe of Native Americans across the plains. He narrowly escaped the fracas by hiding the vehicle within a cave [**BTF3**].

  > ***NOTE:*** *The tribe was unspecified onscreen, but* Back to the Futuer III*'s novelization identified them as the fictional Pohatchee tribe.*

- **Naughty:** An adult business in Hill Valley, in Biffhorrific 1985 [**BTF2**].

- **NBTAI:** A business located in Hill Valley, circa 1991 [**BFAN-7b**].

- **Neanderthal:** A species of mammalian primate closely related to modern humans, now extinct. Neanderthal fossils have been found in parts of Europe and Asia, dating from the Pleistocene epoch [**REAL**]. Given the tendency for Biff Tannen's ancestors and descendants to be abusive and rude, Emmett Brown suspected the presence of rogue Neanderthal genes in the family line's DNA [**TLTL-2**].

- **neatloaf:** A vegetarian menu item sold at SoupMo—a restaurant in First Citizen Brown's dystopian, vegetarian timeline—made with textured wheat protein [**TLTL-3**].

- **Ned ("Ned the Fish"):** A concert promoter who spoke with a typical cheesy disk-jockey voice. In 1991, he introduced Marty McFly's rock band, The Pinheads, for a performance on the steps of the Hill Valley Courthouse [**BFAN-12**].

  > ***NOTE:*** *Onscreen, in the animated episode "Retired," Ned had dark skin; he dressed in fancy suits, wore large white eyeglass frames, was adorned with a gold tooth and kept his purple hair in a flat-top cut. In the episode's comic adaptation, however, he was Caucasian, wore jeans and a t-shirt, and had an orange, spiked Mohawk.*

- **Needleman:** A citizen of Hill Valley, circa 1931. Needleman was among those whose brains Emmett Brown scanned to create a Mind Map for the exhibition of his Mental Alignment Meter at the 1931 Hill Valley Exposition. His results branded him as a "hooligan" [**TLTL-4**].

- **Needles, Amy:** The daughter of Douglas J. and Laura Anne Needles, born in 1995. She had a sister named Roberta [**BTF2**].

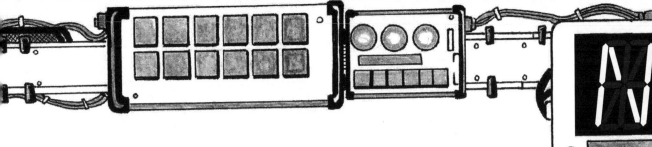

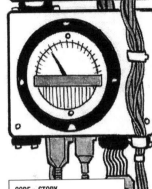

- **Needles, Darlene:** A relative of Douglas J. Needles in one possible version of 2015 [**BFCG**].

- **Needles, Douglas J.:** A sneering, gap-toothed classmate of Marty McFly and Jennifer Parker. He had a punk-rock haircut and enjoyed racing his car against other drivers.

  In 1985, Needles' gang challenged Marty to a race, calling him a chicken when Marty declined. Unable to accept such a slur, Marty gave in, and was thus involved in a car accident moments later, when he collided with a Rolls-Royce. This effectively ruined Marty's future, as his guitar hand was mangled during the collision, causing him to give up his musical aspirations. The other driver sued him for damages [**BTF3**].

  In 2015, Needles was Marty's co-worker at CusCo Industries, in charge of the firm's systems operations. As an adult, he was a fan of basketball, jogging, slamball and tennis; liked to drink scotch and beer; and lacked political affiliations. He had a wife, Lauren Anne, and two daughters, Roberta and Amy.

  An unscrupulous, manipulative individual, Needles caused Marty to be fired from CusCo in 2015, after pressuring him into undertaking an illegal business practice, knowing that Marty's family faced financial problems. Though reluctant, Marty relented when Needles again called him a chicken—and was summarily terminated by their boss, Ito T. Fujitsu, who was monitoring the conversation [**BTF2**]. Marty suspected that Needles, his long-time rival, may have set him up to take the fall [**BTF2-n**].

  Armed with foreknowledge of these events, Marty instead ducked out of the car race in 1985, resulting in his not hitting the Rolls-Royce and dooming himself to a miserable office job with no hope of a music career [**BTF3**].

  In Citizen Brown's dystopian timeline, Lorraine McFly was assigned to polish a public statue when Needles' mother, originally assigned the task, ate bad tofu, making her sick [**TLTL-3**].

  NOTE: In an early draft of Back to the Future II*'s screenplay, Needles was named Harrison, and was trying to cajole Marty into taking part in a scheme called "the 902 deal." In another draft, two youths named Lomax and Winch tried to coerce Marty into entering a bad investment deal, nearly resulting in his ending up in prison. These individuals were replaced with Needles by the time of filming—a suitable name, given his tendency to needle Marty into making bad decisions throughout his life.*

  Needles' onscreen gang comprised a trio of unnamed characters portrayed by actors who had each previously played a different Tannen cronie: Skinhead, from Biff's gang in BTTF1; Data, from Griff's gang in BTTF2; and Stubble, from Buford's gang in BTTF3.

  In 2011, Needles was slated to return in Telltale Games' BTTF video game, but when singer/actor Michael Peter "Flea" Balzary was unavailable to reprise his role, the company instead created a new, similar character named Leech.

- **Needles, Frankie:** An ancestor of Douglas Needles. In 1931, journalist Edna Strickland witnessed him crashing his car into a fire hydrant [**TLTL-2**].

- **Needles, Lauren Anne:** The wife of Douglas J. Needles, and the mother of Roberta and Amy Needles, circa 2015 [**BTF2**].

- **Needles, Roberta:** The daughter of Douglas J. and Laura Anne Needles, born in 1992. She had a sister named Amy [**BTF2**].

- **Nemotech FXD:** A make and model of computer disk drive sold in Citizen Brown's dystopian timeline [**TLTL-3**].

- **Nemotech MPX125:** A make and model of computer keyboard sold in Citizen Brown's dystopian timeline [**TLTL-3**].

- **Nerdy Names Anonymous:** A fictional company that Marty McFly and Verne Brown pretended to represent while visiting author Jules Verne in the late 1800s. Young Verne, hating his first name, hoped that by convincing the novelist to rename himself something less geeky-sounding by 20th-century standards, the youth would benefit (since his parents had named him after the writer) [**BFAN-21**].

- **Ness, Eliot:** An agent of the U.S. Bureau of Prohibition who famously led a team of law-enforcement agents nicknamed "The Untouchables" [**REAL**]. While Marty McFly was incarcerated in a 1927 jail in Chicago's South Side,

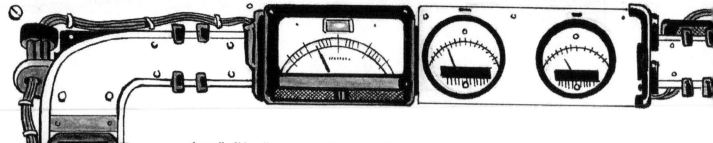

the wall of his cell contained graffiti stating "Eliot Ness is a fink" [**BFCM-1**].

- **Nevada:** The seventh largest state of the United States [**REAL**].

  In the 1950s, the U.S. government performed aboveground atomic bomb testing in the Nevada city of Atkins. Emmett Brown and Marty McFly visited the Atkins base in 1952, hoping to harness a bomb blast's nuclear energy in order to power Doc's time machine and send Marty back to the future [**BTF1-s1**].

  Decades later, Doc conducted experiments to locate water in Nevada's desert, footage of which he included in his Science Journal. An attempt to use a divining rod during these tests brought him to Hoover Dam, where he accidentally caused a power outage while attempting to fill his canteen from a water spout [**BFAN-22**].

  NOTE: The test-site sequence was cut from the final version of BTTF1 (the setting of which was changed to 1955), though storyboards were included as a Blu-ray extra. The first two script drafts set the base in the fictional city of Atkins, while the third moved it to New Mexico.

- **Nevada City:** The county seat of Nevada County, California [**REAL**]. Beauregard B. Tannen acquired a large sum of money in this city in or before 1876, enabling him to relocate to Hill Valley and build the Palace Saloon and Hotel [**TLTL-5**].

- **New Deal Used Cars:** An automotive dealership, the logo of which appeared on the key ring of Emmett Brown's flying DeLorean [**TLTL-2**].

- **New Horizon Unison:** A brand of alcohol served at the El Kid speakeasy in 1931 [**TLTL-2**].

- **New Mexico:** *See* Atkins

- **newsstand robot:** A type of automaton designed to operate kiosks selling newspapers and magazines. In 2015, Marty McFly encounterd a newsstand robot called Bernie, from whom he tried to purchase a copy of *Grays Sports Almanac*. His poor credit rating, however, prevented Marty from paying via thumbprint [**BTF2-s2**].

- **Newton:** Emmett Brown's dog in 1967, named after scientist Sir Isaac Newton [**BTF2-s1**].

- **Newton:** A friend of Marty McFly at Hill Valley High School, circa 1985. He sometimes tried to borrow money from Marty [**BTF1-s1**].

- **Newton:** A horse belonging to Emmett Brown in 1885, during his time as a blacksmith in Hill Valley's Old West. The horse was named after scientist Sir Isaac Newton [**BTF3-sp, BTF3-n**].

- **Newton, Isaac:** An employee at the Institute of Future Technology [**RIDE**].

  NOTE: This individual, identified on signage outside Back to the Future: The Ride, was named after the famous physicist, mathematician and astronomer.

- **Newton, Isaac, Sir:** An English mathematician, astronomer and physicist who described universal gravitation and the three laws of motion [**REAL**]. Emmett Brown kept a portrait of the scientist on his fireplace mantle [**BTF1**].

- **New World Tattoos:** A tattoo parlor in the Caribbean, circa 1697. This shop, run by an obese man with a bald head and a thick mustache, advertised that it could "do Mother in eight languages." Verne Brown, determined to get an earring despite his mother's refusal, visited this business clad as a buccaneer, but was thrown out by the proprietor, who followed a strict "no earrings for muchachos" credo [**BFAN-14**].

- *New Yorker, The:* An American magazine published by Condé Nast, containing news coverage, essays, cartoons and fiction, among other content [**REAL**]. Zane Williams, a mobster in Irving "Kid" Tannen's gang, secretly wished he could quit crime and become a caricaturist for *The New Yorker* [**TLTL-2**].

- **Nick:** A friend and schoolmate of Marty McFly at Hill Valley High School, and a member of Marty's band, The Pinheads [**BTF1-s2**].

- **Nicks Cantina—The Road to Ruin:** A bar in Hill Valley, circa 1885 [**BTF3**].

- **Nielesky, John, Professor:** An employee at the Institute of Future Technology [**RIDE**].

  NOTE: This individual, identified on signage outside Back to the Future: The Ride, was named after Universal Studios' director of compliance.

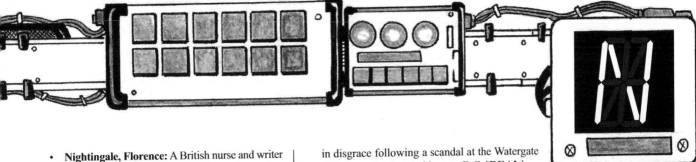

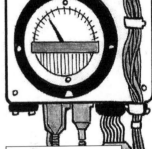

- **Nightingale, Florence:** A British nurse and writer who believed she was doing God's work by tending to wounded soldiers during the Crimean War [**REAL**]. Emmett and Clara Brown considered naming their second-born child after her if it turned out to be a girl—which was not the case, as they had a boy, whom they named Verne [**BFAN-21**].

- **Nightingale of the North:** *See* McFly, Sylvia

- **"Night Train":** A blues instrumental tune, first recorded in 1951 by Jimmy Forrest [**REAL**]. Marvin Berry and the Starlighters performed this song at the Enchantment Under the Sea Dance in 1955. George McFly danced to the tune while awaiting his cue to come to Lorraine Baines' rescue in the school parking lot [**BTF1**].

- **Nike:** A U.S. sportswear and equipment supplier [**REAL**]. In 1985, Marty McFly owned a pair of sneakers produced by this manufacturer [**BTF1**].

  By 2015, the company offered high-top sneakers with power laces, known as Nike MAG (**M**agnetic **A**nti **G**ravity) shoes. Martin McFly Jr. wore such shoes, so Emmett Brown procured a pair for his father, Marty McFly Sr., to wear while posing as his lookalike son. He also gave Marty clothing appropriate to that year, stored in a black gym bag emblazoned with a Nike Footwear logo [**BTF2**].

  Doc Brown later attempted to revisit 2015 to procure a pair of self-lacing, LED-electroluminescent sneakers from a Nike retail store at the Lone Pine Mall. A problem with his DeLorean's time circuits, however, caused him to arrive in 2011, before the self-lacing feature was incorporated [**NIKE**].

- **Ninth System of the Andromeda Galaxy:** *See* Andromeda Galaxy

- **Nippoco:** *See* Texaco

- **Nitty, Frank:** A person who, in 1926, carved his initials into a police desk at a jail in Chicago's South Side [**BFCM-1**].

  > *NOTE: This individual's name was a play on Frank "The Enforcer" Nitti, one of Al Capone's top lieutenants who went on to lead the Chicago underworld.*

- **Nixon, Richard Milhous:** The 37th President of the United States, from 1969 to 1974. Nixon resigned in disgrace following a scandal at the Watergate office complex in Washington, D.C. [**REAL**].

  In the Biffhorrific timeline, Nixon was still president in the 1980s, when he sought a fifth term in office. In that reality, the Vietnam War was still being fought, though Nixon vowed to end the conflict by 1985 [**BTF2**].

  Emmett Brown traveled back in time to meet Nixon and attended one of his public speeches, alongside the president's advisors. Knowing of the man's future crimes, Brown had to resist the temptation to alter history [**RIDE**].

  > *NOTE: The United States has a two-term limit on the presidency. Thus, Biff Tannen's altered timeline not only prevented Nixon's disgrace, but also somehow removed presidential term limits.*

- **NO. 1 ELEC:** A button on an overhead console of Emmett Brown's DeLorean [**TLTL-5**].

- **No. 131:** *See* Locomotive No. 131

- **NO. 2 ELEC:** A button on an overhead console of Emmett Brown's DeLorean [**TLTL-5**].

- **No Future:** A slogan on the leather jackets of several female gang members who, in the Biffhorrific timeline, hung out at Biff Tannen's Pleasure Paradise [**BTF2-d**].

- **Nogura, Chester ("Whitey"):** A member of Griff Tannen's gang, along with Leslie "Spike" O'Malley and Rafe "Data" Unger. Whitey—an 18-year-old of Asian descent—was a loyal follower of Griff, often helping him bully others.

  In 2015, Griff's gang manipulated Martin McFly Jr. into helping them rob the Hill Valley Payroll Substation, leaving Marty to take the blame (and jail time) when he was caught in the act. Emmett Brown, hoping to prevent this from occurring, brought Marty Sr. into the future to take his son's place, instructing Marty to refuse to take part in the theft.

  The gang engaged Marty in a hoverboard chase through Courthouse Square, with Whitey and his friends hooked onto Griff's Pit Bull board. Thus, when Griff crashed into the side of a manmade lake, all four youths were propelled through the courthouse's windows, and were instead the ones arrested [**BTF2**].

  > *NOTE: Nogura was not named onscreen,*

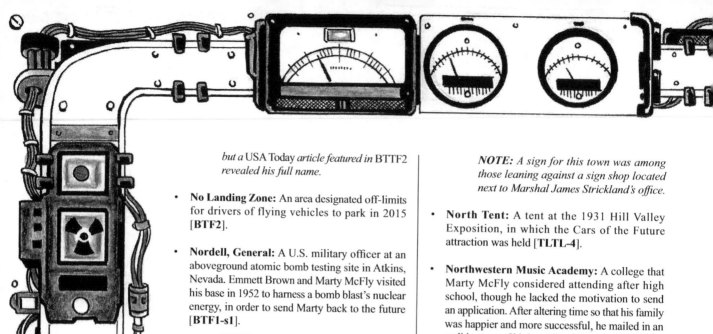

but a USA Today *article featured in* BTTF2 *revealed his full name.*

- **No Landing Zone:** An area designated off-limits for drivers of flying vehicles to park in 2015 [**BTF2**].

- **Nordell, General:** A U.S. military officer at an aboveground atomic bomb testing site in Atkins, Nevada. Emmett Brown and Marty McFly visited his base in 1952 to harness a bomb blast's nuclear energy, in order to send Marty back to the future [**BTF1-s1**].

    NOTE: Nordell's rank was listed as colonel in BTTF1*'s initial two screenplay drafts, but was changed to general as of draft three.*

    The nuclear test-site sequence was cut from the final version of the movie (the setting of which was changed to 1955), though storyboards were included as a Blu-ray extra. The first two script drafts set the base in the fictional Nevada city of Atkins, while the third moved it to New Mexico.

- **Noriega Fried Peas Gorbachev Satan Special:** A menu item sold at Café 80's in 2015 [**BTF2**].

- **Norman:** A grandfather of Jennifer Parker [**BTF2-s1**].

    NOTE: Since Jennifer's paternal grandfather was named Daniel Parker, Norman was likely her mother's father. His last name is unknown.

- ***Northern Exposure***: An American television series set in Alaska that aired on CBS from 1990 to 1995 [**REAL**]. Clara, Jules and Verne Brown were great fans of this show—so much so that when Emmett Brown caused a city-wide brown-out, Clara rigged up the family TV to a workout bicycle, so that she and the boys would not have to miss an episode [**BFAN-22**].

- **North Gate:** An entranceway to Hill Valley's gated community in Citizen Brown's dystopian timeline. In this reality, visitors to the city were required to enter via this gate [**TLTL-3**].

- **North Park:** A town near Hill Valley, circa 1885. Its mayor was J.M. Ennis [**BTF3**].

NOTE: A sign for this town was among those leaning against a sign shop located next to Marshal James Strickland's office.

- **North Tent:** A tent at the 1931 Hill Valley Exposition, in which the Cars of the Future attraction was held [**TLTL-4**].

- **Northwestern Music Academy:** A college that Marty McFly considered attending after high school, though he lacked the motivation to send an application. After altering time so that his family was happier and more successful, he mailed in an audition tape of his band, The Pinheads [**BTF1-s4**].

    NOTE: In BTTF1*'s fourth-draft screenplay, Marty was preparing the tape to accompany an application to Northwestern Music Academy. This was changed to R&G Records in a revised fourth-draft.*

- **North Wing:** A section of the Institute of Future Technology, containing numerous offices and laboratories [**RIDE**].

- **Norwood, Theresa, Ph.D.:** An amusement system facilitator at the Institute of Future Technology [**RIDE**].

    NOTE: This individual, identified on signage outside Back to the Future: The Ride, *was named after a Universal Studios employee.*

- **Nostalgia International:** An entertainment company that sponsored 3-D holographic concerts in 2015, featuring classic performers of the past, such as Huey Lewis and the News [**BTF2-s1**].

- **notdog:** A vegetarian menu item sold at SoupMo, a restaurant in Citizen Brown's dystopian timeline [**TLTL-3**].

- **No Tech Knowhow:** A model of hoverboard sold in 2015. Rafe "Data" Unger owned such a board [**BTF2**].

- **NOTIME:** *See* OUTATIME

- **Nouveau Riche:** A hair style offered at The Combformist, a Hill Valley business in Citizen Brown's dystopian timeline [**TLTL-v**].

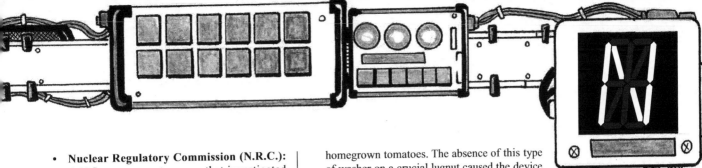

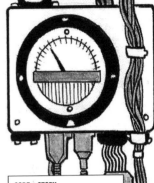

- **Nuclear Regulatory Commission (N.R.C.):** A U.S. government agency that investigated Emmett Brown's theft of plutonium to power his time machine. N.R.C. agents Reese and Foley approached Marty McFly to learn about the scientist's activities [**BTF1-s1**].

- **Nueves Ala Charo Hostage Special, Bread and Water:** A menu item sold at Café 80's in 2015 [**BTF2**].

- **Number 19:** A locomotive of the Central Pacific Railroad, circa 1885. After breaking up with Emmett Brown, Clara Clayton boarded this train for a one-way trip to Sacramento, planning to put Emmett and Hill Valley behind her.

  While on the train, however, Clara overheard a salesman telling a friend about a heartbroken man he'd met at the Palace Saloon and Hotel. Realizing he was talking about Emmett, she stopped the train and ran back to town to find him [**BTF3-sp**].

- **Number 2 washer:** A component of Emmett Brown's invention for automatically canning homegrown tomatoes. The absence of this type of washer on a crucial lugnut caused the device to fail to work properly, instead making it propel the fruits across his kitchen at a high speed [**BFAN-14**].

- **nump:** A slang term in 2015, analogous to the word "fuck," and used to express anger or frustration. Examples of usage: 1) "Are you kirgo? We could get our crags numped!" 2) "She could make no sense at all out of those numping regulations." 3) "Nump off!" 4) "Nump!" [**BTF2-sx, BTF2-n**].

- **Nye, William Sanford ("Bill," "The Science Guy):** An American science educator, comedian and mechanical engineer, as well as the one-time host of Disney's *Bill Nye the Science Guy* television program [**REAL**].

  A colleague of Emmett Brown, Bill Nye helped his fellow academic create a Video Encyclopedia database for students, in which Nye demonstrated various science experiments. Brown provided an accompanying narration [**BFAN-1 to BFAN-26**].

CODE	STORY
NIKE	*BTTF*-themed TV commercial: Nike
NTND	Nintendo *Back to the Future—The Ride* Mini-Game
PIZA	*BTTF*-themed TV commercial: Pizza Hut
PNBL	Data East *BTTF* pinball game
REAL	Real life
RIDE	Simulator: *Back to the Future—The Ride*
SCRM	2010 Scream Awards: *Back to the Future* 25th Anniversary Reunion (broadcast)
SCRT	2010 Scream Awards: *Back to the Future* 25th Anniversary Reunion (trailer)
SIMP	Simulator: *The Simpsons Ride*
SLOT	*Back to the Future Video Slots*
STLZ	Unused *BTTF* footage of Eric Stoltz as Marty McFly
STRY	*Back to the Future Storybook*
TEST	Screen tests: Crispin Glover, Lea Thompson and Tom Wilson
TLTL	Telltale Games' *Back to the Future—The Game*
TOPS	Topps' *Back to the Future II* trading-card set
TRIL	*BTTF: The Official Book of the Complete Movie Trilogy*
UNIV	Universal Studios Hollywood promotional video

SUFFIX	MEDIUM
-b	*BTTF2*'s Biff Tannen Museum video (extended)
-c	Credit sequence to the animated series
-d	Film deleted scene
-n	Film novelization
-o	Film outtake
-p	1955 phone book from *BTTF1*
-v	Video game print materials or commentaries
-s1	Screenplay (draft one)
-s2	Screenplay (draft two)
-s3	Screenplay (draft three)
-s4	Screenplay (draft four)
-sp	Screenplay (production draft)
-sx	Screenplay (*Paradox*)

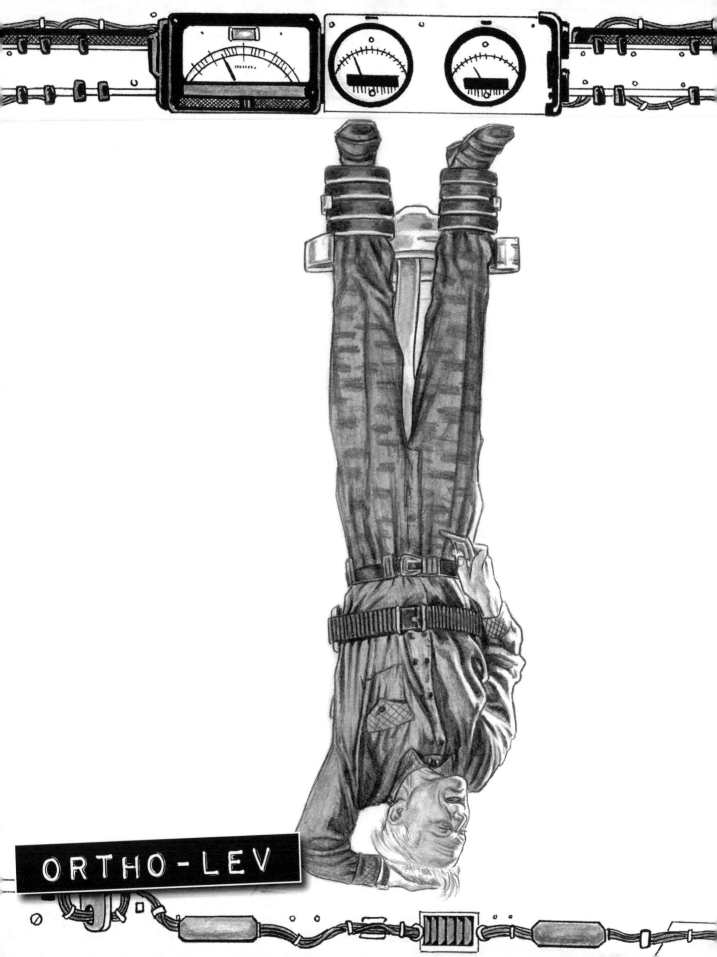

ORTHO-LEV

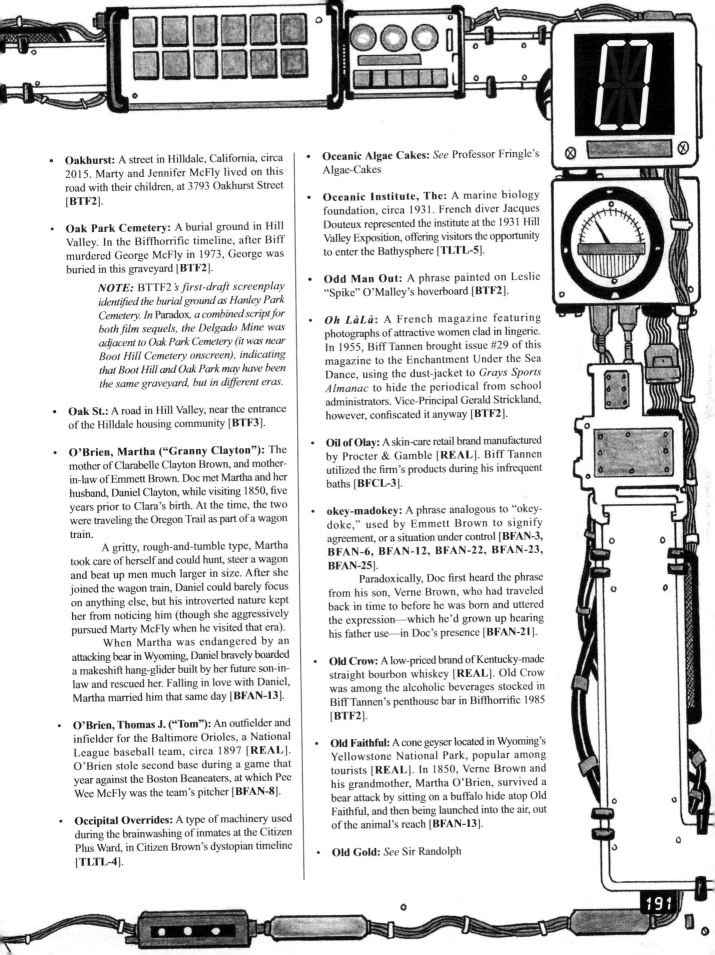

- **Oakhurst:** A street in Hilldale, California, circa 2015. Marty and Jennifer McFly lived on this road with their children, at 3793 Oakhurst Street [**BTF2**].

- **Oak Park Cemetery:** A burial ground in Hill Valley. In the Biffhorrific timeline, after Biff murdered George McFly in 1973, George was buried in this graveyard [**BTF2**].

  > *NOTE: BTTF2's first-draft screenplay identified the burial ground as Hanley Park Cemetery. In* Paradox, *a combined script for both film sequels, the Delgado Mine was adjacent to Oak Park Cemetery (it was near Boot Hill Cemetery onscreen), indicating that Boot Hill and Oak Park may have been the same graveyard, but in different eras.*

- **Oak St.:** A road in Hill Valley, near the entrance of the Hilldale housing community [**BTF3**].

- **O'Brien, Martha ("Granny Clayton"):** The mother of Clarabelle Clayton Brown, and mother-in-law of Emmett Brown. Doc met Martha and her husband, Daniel Clayton, while visiting 1850, five years prior to Clara's birth. At the time, the two were traveling the Oregon Trail as part of a wagon train.

  A gritty, rough-and-tumble type, Martha took care of herself and could hunt, steer a wagon and beat up men much larger in size. After she joined the wagon train, Daniel could barely focus on anything else, but his introverted nature kept her from noticing him (though she aggressively pursued Marty McFly when he visited that era).

  When Martha was endangered by an attacking bear in Wyoming, Daniel bravely boarded a makeshift hang-glider built by her future son-in-law and rescued her. Falling in love with Daniel, Martha married him that same day [**BFAN-13**].

- **O'Brien, Thomas J. ("Tom"):** An outfielder and infielder for the Baltimore Orioles, a National League baseball team, circa 1897 [**REAL**]. O'Brien stole second base during a game that year against the Boston Beaneaters, at which Pee Wee McFly was the team's pitcher [**BFAN-8**].

- **Occipital Overrides:** A type of machinery used during the brainwashing of inmates at the Citizen Plus Ward, in Citizen Brown's dystopian timeline [**TLTL-4**].

- **Oceanic Algae Cakes:** *See* Professor Fringle's Algae-Cakes

- **Oceanic Institute, The:** A marine biology foundation, circa 1931. French diver Jacques Douteux represented the institute at the 1931 Hill Valley Exposition, offering visitors the opportunity to enter the Bathysphere [**TLTL-5**].

- **Odd Man Out:** A phrase painted on Leslie "Spike" O'Malley's hoverboard [**BTF2**].

- *Oh LàLà:* A French magazine featuring photographs of attractive women clad in lingerie. In 1955, Biff Tannen brought issue #29 of this magazine to the Enchantment Under the Sea Dance, using the dust-jacket to *Grays Sports Almanac* to hide the periodical from school administrators. Vice-Principal Gerald Strickland, however, confiscated it anyway [**BTF2**].

- **Oil of Olay:** A skin-care retail brand manufactured by Procter & Gamble [**REAL**]. Biff Tannen utilized the firm's products during his infrequent baths [**BFCL-3**].

- **okey-madokey:** A phrase analogous to "okey-doke," used by Emmett Brown to signify agreement, or a situation under control [**BFAN-3, BFAN-6, BFAN-12, BFAN-22, BFAN-23, BFAN-25**].

  Paradoxically, Doc first heard the phrase from his son, Verne Brown, who had traveled back in time to before he was born and uttered the expression—which he'd grown up hearing his father use—in Doc's presence [**BFAN-21**].

- **Old Crow:** A low-priced brand of Kentucky-made straight bourbon whiskey [**REAL**]. Old Crow was among the alcoholic beverages stocked in Biff Tannen's penthouse bar in Biffhorrific 1985 [**BTF2**].

- **Old Faithful:** A cone geyser located in Wyoming's Yellowstone National Park, popular among tourists [**REAL**]. In 1850, Verne Brown and his grandmother, Martha O'Brien, survived a bear attack by sitting on a buffalo hide atop Old Faithful, and then being launched into the air, out of the animal's reach [**BFAN-13**].

- **Old Gold:** *See* Sir Randolph

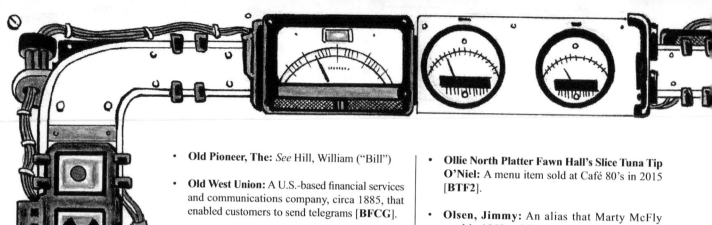

- **Old Pioneer, The:** *See* Hill, William ("Bill")

- **Old West Union:** A U.S.-based financial services and communications company, circa 1885, that enabled customers to send telegrams [**BFCG**].

    NOTE: This company's name was based on that of Western Union.

- **Olfactory Slider:** A section of the control panel used to recondition inmates' minds at the Citizen Plus Ward, in Citizen Brown's dystopian timeline. This slider controlled the Aroma Tanks of the Scent Dispenser, an apparatus that dispelled various substances into the air, in order to influence a person's reactions to stimuli.

    Marty McFly, posing as a security guard at the facility, manipulated this control while trying to help Emmett Brown escape the complex. In so doing, he inadvertently caused his friend a great deal of discomfort [**TLTL-4**].

- **Oliver, Uncle ("Oddball"):** A compassionate but eccentric uncle of Emmett Brown, of German descent. In 1926, Doc spent a span of time living at Oliver's home in Milwaukee, Wisconsin. During that period, Oliver had legal guardianship over young Emmett, and could make decisions for him.

    While at Oliver's home, Emmett fell into a lake while fishing, nearly drowning in the process. Surrounded by various types of fish, he panicked, thereafter suffering a deep-seated fear of fishing. History changed, however, when Doc's sons, Jules and Verne, altered the timeline to prevent their father from developing such a phobia.

    In this new history, Doc enjoyed a brief career as Daredevil Emmett Brown, a Hollywood stunt actor and marketing sensation, with Uncle Oliver serving as his manager. When Emmett nearly died during a stunt for D.W. Tannen's film *Raging Death Doom*, Oliver ended his nephew's acting career to keep him safe [**BFAN-11**].

    NOTE: Oliver's last name is undetermined, as he signed his name "Oddball Uncle Oliver" on Emmett's contract. Given his heavy German accent, it's possible he was a von Braun (the family's original last name), rather than Brown.

    This episode indicated Doc to have been four years old in 1926. However, in the Telltale Games video game, set in 1931, the scientist was 17 years old.

- **Ollie North Platter Fawn Hall's Slice Tuna Tip O'Niel:** A menu item sold at Café 80's in 2015 [**BTF2**].

- **Olsen, Jimmy:** An alias that Marty McFly used in 1952, while protecting the identity of Mega Brainman, Emmett Brown's superhero alterego during that era. As Olsen, Marty posed as a photographer and Mega Brainman's friend [**BFAN-24**].

    NOTE: In the DC Comics universe, Superman's pal, Jimmy Olsen, was a photojournalist for the Daily Planet.

- **Olympia:** A brand of beverage. In 1986, Marty McFly used discarded Olympia cans to power the DeLorean's Mr. Fusion so he could travel back to 1931 and rescue Emmett Brown from prison [**TLTL-1**].

- **O'Malley, Leslie ("Spike"):** A member of Griff Tannen's gang, along with Chester "Whitey" Nogura and Rafe "Data" Unger. Spike, an attractive but vicious 18-year-old punk-rocker with blonde hair and sharp nails, was a loyal follower of Griff, often helping him bully others.

    In 2015, Griff's gang manipulated Martin McFly Jr. into helping them rob the Hill Valley Payroll Substation, leaving Marty to take the blame (and jail time) when he was caught in the act. Emmett Brown, hoping to prevent this from occurring, brought Marty Sr. into the future to take his son's place, instructing Marty to refuse to take part in the theft.

    The gang engaged Marty in a hoverboard chase through Courthouse Square, with Spike and her friends hooked onto Griff's Pit Bull board. Thus, when Griff crashed into the side of a manmade lake, all four youths were propelled through the courthouse's windows, and were instead the ones arrested [**BTF2**].

    NOTE: O'Malley was not named onscreen, but a USA Today article featured in BTTF2 revealed her full name.

- **O'Malley & Sons:** A barber shop located in Hill Valley, circa 1931 [**TLTL-1**].

    NOTE: This business may have been owned by one of Leslie O'Malley's ancestors.

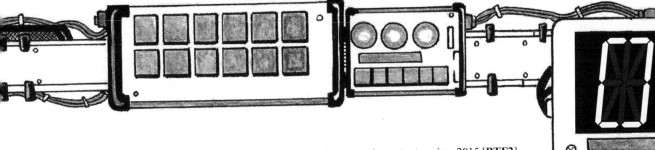

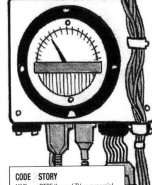

- **Omega-1 Priority Alert:** A protocol used in Citizen Brown's dystopian timeline to warn Hill Valley's citizens of potentially disruptive nonconformists [**TLTL-4**].

- **On Robots:** A book written by science fiction author Harlan Ellison. Verne Brown referenced this work while writing a school essay on the subject of robotics [**BFCL-1**].

  > **NOTE:** *No book by this name was written by Ellison in the real world.*

- **Optics Slider:** A section of the control panel used to recondition inmates' minds at the Citizen Plus Ward, in Citizen Brown's dystopian timeline. Pushing this slider forced a subject to endure disturbing visual images. Marty McFly, posing as a security guard, manipulated this control while trying to help Emmett Brown escape the complex; in so doing, he inadvertently caused his friend a great deal of discomfort [**TLTL-4**].

- **Optimist International:** A service-club organization founded to foster caring, hope and a positive vision in children [**REAL**]. The organization operated a chapter in Hill Valley [**BTF1**].

- **Orgy American Style:** A 1973 X-rated film directed by Carlos Tobalina, and starring Sharon Kelly [**REAL**]. Hill Valley's Essex Theater showed this movie in 1985 [**BTF1**].

  > **NOTE:** *This film's title satirized* Love, American Style, *a comedy anthology TV series that aired on ABC from 1969 to 1974. By coincidence, the cast included actor George "Buck" Flower, who portrayed Red the bum in the first two* Back to the Future *films.*

- **Orpheum Theater:** A theater in Hill Valley, located near the home of Emmett Brown, circa 1985 [**BTF1-s1**].

- **Orson and Tillich, Attorneys at Law:** A law office in Hill Valley, circa 1955 [**BTF1**].

  > **NOTE:** *When Marty visited 1955 in the second movie, this business was called Jacobson & Field, Attorneys at Law. Why the firm changed names during the span of that week is unknown.*

- **Ortegua:** A sports star, circa 2015 [**BTF2**].

  > **NOTE:** *The sport in which he competed was unspecified, but his photo appeared in an issue of* USA Today *alongside blurbs related to articles about slamball and baseball.*

- **Ortho-lev:** An anti-gravity belt used to provide mobility to those with back injuries, which could be set to carry an individual either face-down or –up [**BTF2**]. In 2015, George McFly wore an Ortho-lev device after a flying vehicle ran him over on a golf course [**BTF2-d**].

  > **NOTE:** *The device was un-named onscreen, but the designation "Ortho-lev" appeared on a diagram among the special features of* Back to the Future II*'s Blu-ray release, and was also printed on the contraption itself.*

- **Orwell, George:** An English journalist and novelist known for his books *Animal Farm* and *1984* (a.k.a. *Nineteen Eighty-Four*). The latter novel concered a society called Oceania, ruled by an oligarchical dictatorship known as the Party, which used pervasive government surveillance and public mind control to keep the masses in line [**REAL**]. In Citizen Brown's timeline, Edna Strickland used the same tactics described by Orwell to subjugate Hill Valley's citizens [**TLTL-3, TLTL-4**].

- **Orxs:** An ice cream shop located in Boston, Massachusetts, circa 1897. Its street address was 112 [**BFAN-8**].

  > **NOTE:** *Since part of the store's sign was not visible, there may have been additional, unseen letters at the start of its name.*

- **Oscillator Gigathruster:** A component of the Static Accumulator—an invention of Emmett Brown, built in 1931 to generate a static charge, thereby enabling cars to fly [**TLTL-v**].

- **ouch-a-ma-gouch-a:** An expression used by Emmett Brown to denote pain [**BFAN-1, BFAN-5, BFAN-11, BFAN-14, BFAN-20, BFAN-24**]

  > **NOTE:** *Variations included "ouch-a-ma-groucho-o," used by Verne Brown to describe Benjamin Franklin's perpetual bad mood in 1752, and "ouch-a-ma-geisha," uttered by Doc while he and his family hid from a mob by dressing in Japanese geisha garb.*

CODE	STORY
NIKE	*BTTF*-themed TV commercial: Nike
NTND	Nintendo *Back to the Future—The Ride* Mini-Game
PIZA	*BTTF*-themed TV commercial: Pizza Hut
PNBL	Data East *BTTF* pinball game
REAL	Real life
RIDE	Simulator: *Back to the Future—The Ride*
SCRM	2010 Scream Awards: *Back to the Future* 25th Anniversary Reunion (broadcast)
SCRT	2010 Scream Awards: *Back to the Future* 25th Anniversary Reunion (trailer)
SIMP	Simulator: *The Simpsons Ride*
SLOT	*Back to the Future* Video Slots
STLZ	Unused *BTTF* footage of Eric Stoltz as Marty McFly
STRY	*Back to the Future Storybook*
TEST	Screen tests: Crispin Glover, Lea Thompson and Tom Wilson
TLTL	Telltale Games' *Back to the Future—The Game*
TOPS	Topps' *Back to the Future II* trading-card set
TRIL	*BTTF: The Official Book of the Complete Movie Trilogy*
UNIV	Universal Studios Hollywood promotional video

SUFFIX	MEDIUM
-b	*BTTF2*'s Biff Tannen Museum video (extended)
-c	Credit sequence to the animated series
-d	Film deleted scene
-n	Film novelization
-o	Film outtake
-p	1955 phone book from *BTTF1*
-v	Video game print materials or commentaries
-s1	Screenplay (draft one)
-s2	Screenplay (draft two)
-s3	Screenplay (draft three)
-s4	Screenplay (draft four)
-sp	Screenplay (production draft)
-sx	Screenplay (*Paradox*)

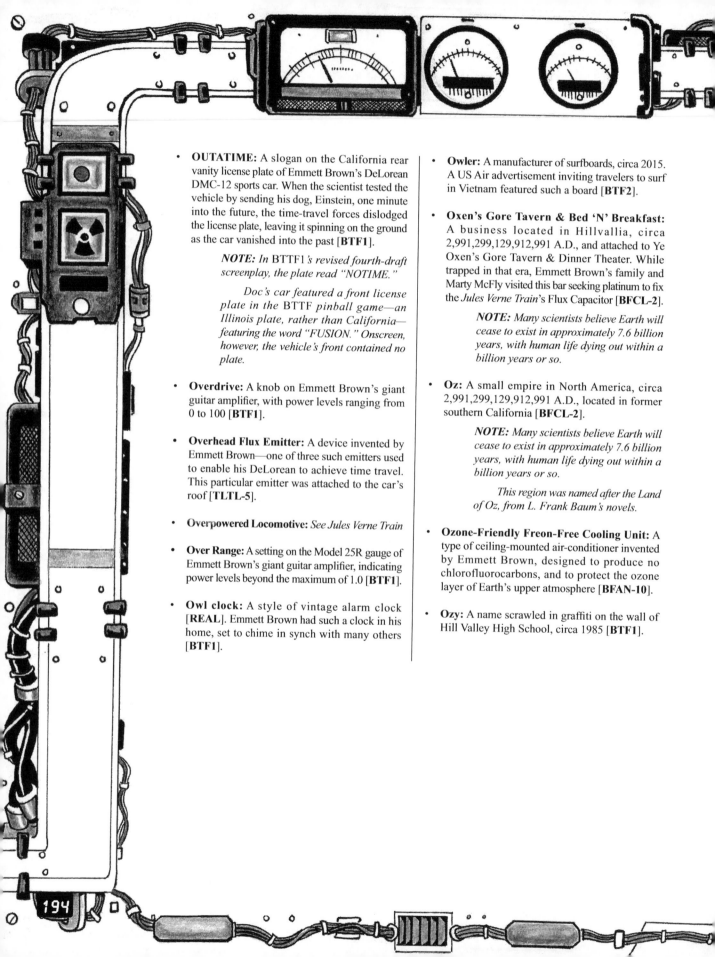

- **OUTATIME:** A slogan on the California rear vanity license plate of Emmett Brown's DeLorean DMC-12 sports car. When the scientist tested the vehicle by sending his dog, Einstein, one minute into the future, the time-travel forces dislodged the license plate, leaving it spinning on the ground as the car vanished into the past [**BTF1**].

    NOTE: In BTTF1's revised fourth-draft screenplay, the plate read "NOTIME."

    Doc's car featured a front license plate in the BTTF pinball game—an Illinois plate, rather than California—featuring the word "FUSION." Onscreen, however, the vehicle's front contained no plate.

- **Overdrive:** A knob on Emmett Brown's giant guitar amplifier, with power levels ranging from 0 to 100 [**BTF1**].

- **Overhead Flux Emitter:** A device invented by Emmett Brown—one of three such emitters used to enable his DeLorean to achieve time travel. This particular emitter was attached to the car's roof [**TLTL-5**].

- **Overpowered Locomotive:** *See Jules Verne Train*

- **Over Range:** A setting on the Model 25R gauge of Emmett Brown's giant guitar amplifier, indicating power levels beyond the maximum of 1.0 [**BTF1**].

- **Owl clock:** A style of vintage alarm clock [**REAL**]. Emmett Brown had such a clock in his home, set to chime in synch with many others [**BTF1**].

- **Owler:** A manufacturer of surfboards, circa 2015. A US Air advertisement inviting travelers to surf in Vietnam featured such a board [**BTF2**].

- **Oxen's Gore Tavern & Bed 'N' Breakfast:** A business located in Hillvallia, circa 2,991,299,129,912,991 A.D., and attached to Ye Oxen's Gore Tavern & Dinner Theater. While trapped in that era, Emmett Brown's family and Marty McFly visited this bar seeking platinum to fix the *Jules Verne Train*'s Flux Capacitor [**BFCL-2**].

    NOTE: Many scientists believe Earth will cease to exist in approximately 7.6 billion years, with human life dying out within a billion years or so.

- **Oz:** A small empire in North America, circa 2,991,299,129,912,991 A.D., located in former southern California [**BFCL-2**].

    NOTE: Many scientists believe Earth will cease to exist in approximately 7.6 billion years, with human life dying out within a billion years or so.

    This region was named after the Land of Oz, from L. Frank Baum's novels.

- **Ozone-Friendly Freon-Free Cooling Unit:** A type of ceiling-mounted air-conditioner invented by Emmett Brown, designed to produce no chlorofluorocarbons, and to protect the ozone layer of Earth's upper atmosphere [**BFAN-10**].

- **Ozy:** A name scrawled in graffiti on the wall of Hill Valley High School, circa 1985 [**BTF1**].

PARKER, JENNIFER

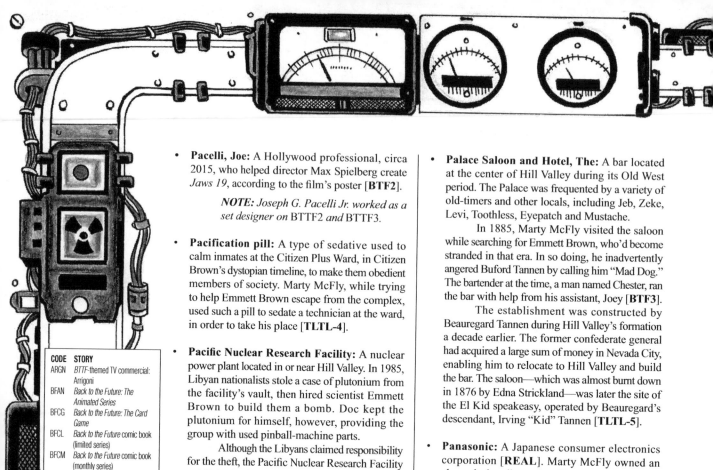

- **Pacelli, Joe:** A Hollywood professional, circa 2015, who helped director Max Spielberg create *Jaws 19*, according to the film's poster [**BTF2**].

  > **NOTE:** *Joseph G. Pacelli Jr. worked as a set designer on BTTF2 and BTTF3.*

- **Pacification pill:** A type of sedative used to calm inmates at the Citizen Plus Ward, in Citizen Brown's dystopian timeline, to make them obedient members of society. Marty McFly, while trying to help Emmett Brown escape from the complex, used such a pill to sedate a technician at the ward, in order to take his place [**TLTL-4**].

- **Pacific Nuclear Research Facility:** A nuclear power plant located in or near Hill Valley. In 1985, Libyan nationalists stole a case of plutonium from the facility's vault, then hired scientist Emmett Brown to build them a bomb. Doc kept the plutonium for himself, however, providing the group with used pinball-machine parts.

  Although the Libyans claimed responsibility for the theft, the Pacific Nuclear Research Facility publicly denied that it occurred, blaming the incident on a clerical error. The FBI looked into the matter, offering no comment to the press [**BTF1**].

  > **NOTE:** *In early drafts of BTTF1's screenplay, the plutonium came from the San Onofre Nuclear Power Plant.*

- **Packard Clipper:** A style of car produced in the 1950s [**REAL**]. In 1955, Emmett Brown owned a cream-colored Packard, license plate 8N 39742. Marty McFly borrowed this car to take Lorraine Baines to the Enchantment Under the Sea Dance [**BTF1**].

- **Page, Pattie:** A traditional pop-music singer of the 1950s [**REAL**]. In 1955, Roy's Records displayed her album *In the Land of Hi-Fi* within its front window [**BTF1**].

- **Pakk:** A business located in Boston, Massachusetts, circa 1897. Its street address was 444 [**BFAN-8**].

  > **NOTE:** *The store's sign was difficult to read; as such, this spelling might not be entirely accurate.*

- **Palace of Electricity:** An exhibit at the 1904 St. Louis World Exposition. Emmett and Clara Brown intended to visit this attraction while attending the fair, but were distracted by the unexpected arrival of Doc's time-traveling locomotive [**BFAN-25**].

- **Palace Saloon and Hotel, The:** A bar located at the center of Hill Valley during its Old West period. The Palace was frequented by a variety of old-timers and other locals, including Jeb, Zeke, Levi, Toothless, Eyepatch and Mustache.

  In 1885, Marty McFly visited the saloon while searching for Emmett Brown, who'd become stranded in that era. In so doing, he inadvertently angered Buford Tannen by calling him "Mad Dog." The bartender at the time, a man named Chester, ran the bar with help from his assistant, Joey [**BTF3**].

  The establishment was constructed by Beauregard Tannen during Hill Valley's formation a decade earlier. The former confederate general had acquired a large sum of money in Nevada City, enabling him to relocate to Hill Valley and build the bar. The saloon—which was almost burnt down in 1876 by Edna Strickland—was later the site of the El Kid speakeasy, operated by Beauregard's descendant, Irving "Kid" Tannen [**TLTL-5**].

- **Panasonic:** A Japanese consumer electronics corporation [**REAL**]. Marty McFly owned an alarm clock-radio produced by Panasonic [**BTF1**].

- **pan-dimensional field generator:** The control mechanism for Emmett Brown's Extradimensional Storage Closet, a room within his lab that was larger on the inside than outside, since it contained access to multiple dimensions. When an electrical surge shorted out the device, a cascading catastrophe threatened to collapse Earth into a black hole, but Doc averted the crisis by using his DeLorean to restore the closet's proper configuration [**BFCL-3**].

- **"Papa Loves Mambo":** A song recorded by Perry Como in 1954 [**REAL**]. Biff Tannen listened to this tune on the radio while driving to the Enchantment Under the Sea Dance in 1955 [**BTF2**].

- **PA Plate:** A toggle on Emmett Brown's giant guitar amplifier, and part of the device's Driver Adjust system [**BTF1**].

- **PA Plate Voltage Adjust:** A switch on Emmett Brown's giant guitar amplifier, and part of the device's variable autotransformer [**BTF1**].

- **Paradise:** A small empire in North America, circa 2,991,299,129,912,991 A.D., located in former Alaska [**BFCL-2**].

  > **NOTE:** *Many scientists believe Earth will cease to exist in approximately 7.6 billion*

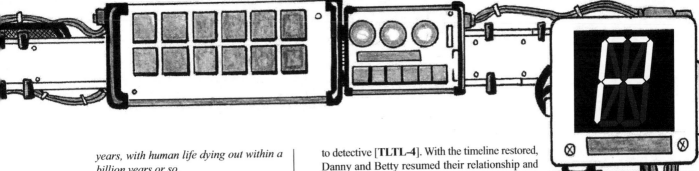

years, with human life dying out within a billion years or so.

- **Pardieu, Joseph:** A voluntary assistance humanitarian at the Institute of Future Technology [**RIDE**].

    > *NOTE: This individual, identified on signage outside* Back to the Future: The Ride, *was named after a Universal Studios employee.*

- **Paris:** France's capital and largest city, containing the Eiffel Tower [**REAL**]. Emmett Brown recorded a portion of his Science Journal while he and Clara were visiting the tower as tourists. A century earlier, their son Verne had visited the same city with Marty McFly while searching for the boy's namesake, author Jules Verne [**BFAN-21**].

- **Parker, Betty:** *See* Lapinski, Betty

- **Parker, Daniel J., Officer/Detective ("Danny," "Danny Boy"):** The paternal grandfather of Jennifer Parker, and husband of Betty Lapinski. A rookie policeman in Hill Valley, Danny made a name for himself in 1931 by arresting gangster Irving "Kid" Tannen—until Marty McFly and Emmett Brown inadvertently altered history.

    Parker had been assigned to guard Marty's future grandfather, Arthur McFly, a government witness against Tannen. When Marty and Doc helped Artie leave town to avoid Kid's wrath, Parker was punished for losing track of his witness. Parker also failed to arrest Doc—known in that era as suspected arsonist Carl Sagan—when Marty rescued him in the flying DeLorean. What's more, he blamed these failures on the arrival of a flying "space car" out of *Buck Rogers*.

    Discredited and demoted after reporting these events, Parker was sent to see a psychiatrist. He developed a drinking problem in the resultant new timeline, spending much of his time at Tannen's speakeasy, El Kid, and was crushed when Betty ended their relationship, deeming him a bad provider and a "head-case." His life in ruins, and no longer considered a good cop, Parker began accepting bribes from Tannen.

    To restore the timeline and thus ensure Jennifer's existence, Marty got to know Parker, bolstering his confidence enough that the officer decided to arrest Tannen and shut down the speakeasy. In so doing, the fallen cop regained his lost honor [**TLTL-2**] and earned a promotion to detective [**TLTL-4**]. With the timeline restored, Danny and Betty resumed their relationship and ultimately wed. In time, the couple had a son, Daniel Jr., who eventually got married and fathered Jennifer [**TLTL-3**].

    Parker's "tainted" past left him at the mercy of Edna Strickland, who threatened to use her influence with the police chief to have him expelled from the force unless he did her bidding. During the 1931 Hill Valley Exposition, she monopolized his time, distracting him from his role as the host of the Future of Law Enforcement exhibit. Edna told Parker to arrest Marty—whom she realized was trying to alter her history—but the detective stopped catering to her wishes [**TLTL-5**].

    > *NOTE: In the Telltale Games video game, Jennifer's paternal grandfather was named Daniel Parker, but in the animated series, he was called Peter Parker. This discrepancy has not been reconciled.*

- **Parker, Daniel Jr. ("Danny"):** The father of Jennifer Parker, and son of Daniel J. Parker and Betty Lapinski [**TLTL-2, TLTL-3**]. In 1985, he gave Jennifer a ride home after Marty McFly failed to win the Battle of the Bands audition [**BTF1**].

    Danny Jr. initially worked as a shoe salesman, until time was altered so that Hill Valley was a dystopian society run by First Citizen Brown. In that reality's 1986, the mustached Parker became a police officer, like his father, enforcing Brown's strict, repressive laws under Doc's rule, and guarding the city's mayoral office [**TLTL-3**].

    > *NOTE: Jennifer's father briefly appeared in* BTTF1, *unnamed, but had no lines.*

- **Parker, Genevieve ("Gen"):** The great-great-grandmother of Jennifer Parker, with whom she shared a strong family resemblance. Genevieve and her husband, Wendel, operated the Parker BTQ Ranch in the late 1800s.

    In 1875, Thaddeus Tannen tied Gen to a set of railroad tracks in order to force Wendel to sign over the deed to their ranch. However, Marty McFly infiltrated the outlaw's gang and thwarted their plans, then freed Gen and helped the ranchers retain their property [**BFAN-16**].

- **Parker, Jennifer Jane ("Jen"):** A beautiful young woman who dated Marty McFly while attending Hill Valley High School in the 1980s [**BTF1, BTF2, BTF3**].

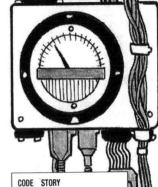

CODE	STORY
NIKE	*BTTF*-themed TV commercial: Nike
NTND	Nintendo *Back to the Future—The Ride* Mini-Game
PIZA	*BTTF*-themed TV commercial: Pizza Hut
PNBL	Data East *BTTF* pinball game
REAL	Real life
RIDE	Simulator: *Back to the Future—The Ride*
SCRM	2010 Scream Awards: *Back to the Future 25th Anniversary Reunion* (broadcast)
SCRT	2010 Scream Awards: *Back to the Future 25th Anniversary Reunion* (trailer)
SIMP	Simulator: *The Simpsons Ride*
SLOT	*Back to the Future Video Slots*
STLZ	Unused *BTTF* footage of Eric Stoltz as Marty McFly
STRY	*Back to the Future Storybook*
TEST	Screen tests: Crispin Glover, Lea Thompson and Tom Wilson
TLTL	Telltale Games' *Back to the Future—The Game*
TOPS	Topps' *Back to the Future II* trading-card set
TRIL	*BTTF: The Official Book of the Complete Movie Trilogy*
UNIV	Universal Studios Hollywood promotional video

SUFFIX	MEDIUM
-b	*BTTF2's* Biff Tannen Museum video (extended)
-c	Credit sequence to the animated series
-d	Film deleted scene
-n	Film novelization
-o	Film outtake
-p	1955 phone book from *BTTF1*
-v	Video game print materials or commentaries
-s1	Screenplay (draft one)
-s2	Screenplay (draft two)
-s3	Screenplay (draft three)
-s4	Screenplay (draft four)
-sp	Screenplay (production draft)
-sx	Screenplay (*Paradox*)

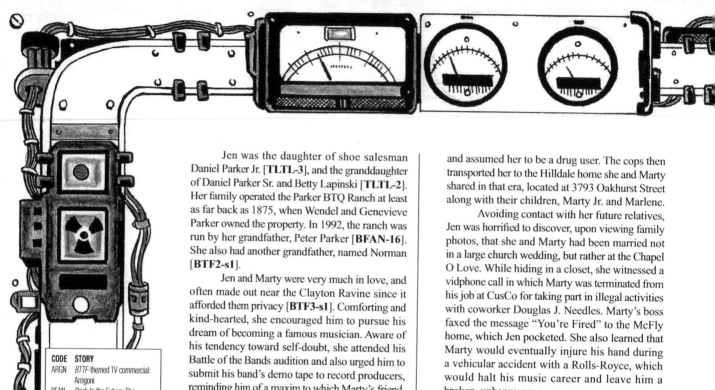

Jen was the daughter of shoe salesman Daniel Parker Jr. [**TLTL-3**], and the granddaughter of Daniel Parker Sr. and Betty Lapinski [**TLTL-2**]. Her family operated the Parker BTQ Ranch at least as far back as 1875, when Wendel and Genevieve Parker owned the property. In 1992, the ranch was run by her grandfather, Peter Parker [**BFAN-16**]. She also had another grandfather, named Norman [**BTF2-s1**].

Jen and Marty were very much in love, and often made out near the Clayton Ravine since it afforded them privacy [**BTF3-s1**]. Comforting and kind-hearted, she encouraged him to pursue his dream of becoming a famous musician. Aware of his tendency toward self-doubt, she attended his Battle of the Bands audition and also urged him to submit his band's demo tape to record producers, reminding him of a maxim to which Marty's friend, Emmett Brown, ascribed: that he could accomplish anything if he put his mind to it [**BTF1**].

In 1985, the couple planned a weekend camping trip at the Lake, out under the stars. Knowing how his mother, Lorraine McFly, felt about teenage romance, Marty lied about his plans, claiming he would be camping with male friends. Lorraine expressed dislike for Jen due to her frequently calling Marty on the telephone, but after he altered history by making his parents happier, healthier people, his mom's opinion of Jen became much more positive.

Jennifer's grandmother was still alive in 1985, and her family sometimes visited the woman on weekends. Before one such visit—following Marty's failure at the Battle of the Bands competition—Jen cheered him up by writing down her grandma's phone number (555-4823) on a "Save the Clock Tower" flyer and signing the note, "I love you." This gesture endeared her to Marty even more [**BTF1**].

After Marty visited 1955 in Doc's DeLorean, Jen accompanied him and Doc on a trip to 2015, as the scientist reported that their future children, Marty Jr. and Marlene, were in danger of being sent to prison, thanks to a robbery plotted by Griff Tannen. Doc had intended to bring only Marty into the future, but since Jen was with him at the time, he brought her along as well. To minimize the risk of temporal contamination, Doc used a Sleep-Inducing Alpha-Rhythm Generator to render her unconscious for the duration of their mission. He and Marty left her asleep in an alleyway while attending to the future McFlys, but a pair of police officers, Reese and Foley, found her sleeping form

and assumed her to be a drug user. The cops then transported her to the Hilldale home she and Marty shared in that era, located at 3793 Oakhurst Street along with their children, Marty Jr. and Marlene.

Avoiding contact with her future relatives, Jen was horrified to discover, upon viewing family photos, that she and Marty had been married not in a large church wedding, but rather at the Chapel O Love. While hiding in a closet, she witnessed a vidphone call in which Marty was terminated from his job at CusCo for taking part in illegal activities with coworker Douglas J. Needles. Marty's boss faxed the message "You're Fired" to the McFly home, which Jen pocketed. She also learned that Marty would eventually injure his hand during a vehicular accident with a Rolls-Royce, which would halt his music career and leave him a broken, unhappy man.

Jennifer tried to sneak out of the house, but as she opened the front door, her older self arrived, each fainting in shock. Marty and Doc removed her from the house before any further contamination could take place, and left her on the porch of the Parker family home, hoping that when she awoke, she'd chalk the entire experience up to a bad dream [**BTF2**].

As she slept, Marty spent a week in 1885, rescuing Doc from being stranded in the Old West. Upon returning, he found Jen still asleep where he'd left her, and awoke her with a kiss. Initially, she believed she'd been dreaming. But upon seeing a sign for Hilldale, witnessing a near-accident involving Marty, Needles and a Rolls-Royce (which Marty, warned of his grim future, now avoided), and finding the CusCo fax, she realized it had all actually occurred.

Marty told Jen the full truth and brought her to view the final resting place of the DeLorean, which had been destroyed during a collision with a locomotive. Moments later, Doc returned from the past with his wife and sons, telling Marty and Jennifer that the future was not yet written until they made it happen [**BTF3**].

After high school, Jen and Marty attended Hill Valley College [**BFAN-4, BFAN-12**], and she dyed her hair blonde [**BFAN-2**]. Their relationship continued, but his irresponsibility and lack of confidence sometimes sabotaged their romance, as he showed interest in another girl named Liz [**BFAN-25**], and expressed jealousy of her athletic friend, Kelp [**BFAN-4**].

In 1991, Marty and Jennifer enjoyed a date to the Puttputt Miniature Golf course, which

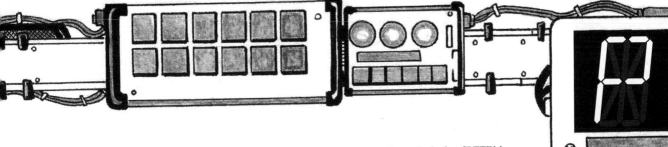

offered elaborate setups at each hole, including a laughing witch, a windmill, a dinosaur scene, firefighters dousing a blaze, an erupting volcano and more. Marty's wild putting caused her to be doused with water and simulated lava, which amused him more than it did her [**BFAN-25**].

Jen was fond of Walk DMC. When the music group played a sold-out concert at the Roxy theater in 1992, Marty tried to get her tickets to the show, but was unable to procure them [**BFAN-14**]. Her favorite snacks included Triple Cheesey-Cheese Pizza [**BFAN-25**].

During a trip to 1931, Marty inadvertently changed history so that Jen was never born, by preventing Daniel Parker and Betty Lapinski from marrying and having children. Realizing his mistake, Marty worked to get the couple back together, thus ensuring his girlfriend's future existence [**TLTL-2**].

In Citizen Brown's dystopian timeline, Jennifer was a nonconformist punk rocker who was sentenced to community service for vandalism, cleaning up trash near the city's South Gate. Her crime: spraying graffiti on public property. Jen was a fan of a rock group called Baby Fist, and owned a t-shirt emblazoned with the band's emblem. She briefly dated Marty in this timeline as well, but was turned off by his clean-cut, studious image and nerdy reputation. Instead, she dated Leech, the front man of punk band Leech and the Wooshbags [**TLTL-3**].

Determined to win back Jennifer's love (despite his plan to restore the prior timeline, which would automatically reunite them as a couple), Marty challenged Leech to the Ring of Rock, in order to prove himself a better guitarist. Seeing Marty cutting loose on the guitar made Jen fall for him again, and she kissed him passionately. When she was subjected to the Citizen Plus Program and reconditioned as a model citizen, Marty broke through her brainwashing by piping loud rock music into her cell, then helped her to escape the facility [**TLTL-4**].

In one possible timeline, Marty and Jennifer had a grandson named Martin McFly III [**BFCG**]. They also had a great-great-granddaughter, Marta McFly, who commanded the *MSC Marty* in 2091. A similar vessel, the *MSC Jennifer*—the first model of passenger solar sailship built by McFly Space Cruises—was named in her honor. After being decommissioned, the *Jennifer* was maintained at Hill Valley's McFly Museum of Aeronautics [**BFAN-9**].

NOTE: In early drafts of BTTF1's screenplay, Jennifer was named Suzy Parker, and was seeing a psychiatrist. Her middle name was revealed in BTTF2.

Jennifer may have been a cheerleader in high school. In BTTF2, a white and maroon school jacket with a megaphone emblem was visible in her closet, bearing the name "Jennifer."

A children's storybook based on the first film claimed that her planned camping trip with Marty was their first official date, but that seems highly unlikely, given the nature of the date, the comfortable affection the two shared and their use of the phrase "I love you."

In the Telltale Games video game, Jennifer's paternal grandfather was named Daniel Parker, but in the animated series, he was called Peter Parker. This discrepancy has not been reconciled. Given the existence of Daniel and Peter as paternal grandfathers, it's likely that Norman was her maternal granddad. No mention has ever been made of Jen's mother.

For a full list of Jen's known relatives, see Appendix III.

- **Parker, Peter ("Grandpa Parker"):** The paternal grandfather of Jennifer Parker, and the proprietor of the Parker BTQ Ranch. In 1992, Biff Tannen tried to wrest control of the ranch from Peter, after finding a century-old deed signed over to his ancestor, Thaddeus Tannen, by Peter's forebearer, Wendel Parker.

To prevent this from occurring, Marty McFly traveled back to 1875 and gave Wendel a pen filled with disappearing ink. This rendered the deed invalid, once Wendel's signature vanished, thereby ensuring that the Parkers would be able to keep their land [**BFAN-16**].

NOTE: This character's name pad homage to Peter Parker, also known as Marvel Comics' Spider-Man.

In the animated series, Jennifer's paternal grandfather was named Peter Parker, but in the Telltale Games video game, he was called Daniel Parker. This discrepancy has not been reconciled.

- **Parker, Suzy:** *See* Parker, Jennifer

CODE	STORY
NIKE	*BTTF*-themed TV commercial: Nike
NTND	Nintendo *Back to the Future—The Ride* Mini-Game
PIZA	*BTTF*-themed TV commercial: Pizza Hut
PNBL	Data East *BTTF* pinball game
REAL	Real life
RIDE	Simulator: *Back to the Future—The Ride*
SCRM	2010 Scream Awards: *Back to the Future 25th Anniversary Reunion* (broadcast)
SCRT	2010 Scream Awards: *Back to the Future 25th Anniversary Reunion* (trailer)
SIMP	Simulator: *The Simpsons Ride*
SLOT	*Back to the Future Video Slots*
STLZ	Unused *BTTF* footage of Eric Stoltz as Marty McFly
STRY	*Back to the Future Storybook*
TEST	Screen tests: Crispin Glover, Lea Thompson and Tom Wilson
TLTL	Telltale Games' *Back to the Future—The Game*
TOPS	Topps' *Back to the Future II* trading-card set
TRIL	*BTTF: The Official Book of the Complete Movie Trilogy*
UNIV	Universal Studios Hollywood promotional video

SUFFIX	MEDIUM
-b	*BTTF2's* Biff Tannen Museum video (extended)
-c	Credit sequence to the animated series
-d	Film deleted scene
-n	Film novelization
-o	Film outtake
-p	1955 phone book from *BTTF1*
-v	Video game print materials or commentaries
-s1	Screenplay (draft one)
-s2	Screenplay (draft two)
-s3	Screenplay (draft three)
-s4	Screenplay (draft four)
-sp	Screenplay (production draft)
-sx	Screenplay (*Paradox*)

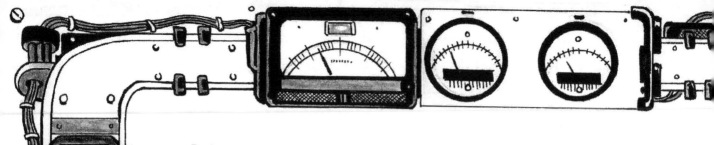

- **Parker, Wendel ("Wen"):** The great-great-grandfather of Jennifer Parker. Wendel and his wife, Genevieve, operated the Parker BTQ Ranch in the late 1800s. In 1875, Thaddeus Tannen tried to force the Parkers to sign over the deed to their ranch, by tying Gen to a set of train tracks while Wendel was helpless to rescue her.

  Marty McFly freed Genevieve, however, and helped the ranchers keep their property, by giving Wendel a pen filled with disappearing ink. His signature eventually vanished, thus nullifying the deed [**BFAN-16**].

- **Parker BTQ Ranch:** A boutique ranch in Hill Valley, owned by the family of Jennifer Parker. In 1992, Biff Tannen unearthed a deed indicating that Jennifer's grandparents, Wendel and Genevieve Parker, had signed the ranch over to his ancestor, Thaddeus Tannen, in 1875.

  Biff tried to turn the property into a toxic waste dump and miniature golf course, but Marty McFly traveled back in time, infiltrated Thaddeus' gang and helped the ranchers keep their property [**BFAN-16**].

- **Parkerville:** A town located near Hill Valley [**BTF1-s2**].

  > *NOTE: It's unknown if the town was named after one of Jennifer Parker's ancestors.*

- ***Parlormaid's Predicament, The:*** A play in which Sylvia "Trixie Trotter" Miskin performed, sometime in or before 1931. Trixie used a scene from this play as the basis of a scheme to help Marty McFly break up Emmett Brown's relationship with Edna Strickland, in which she claimed to be Emmett's lover and the mother of his illegitimate child, Emmett Jr. [**TLTL-4**].

- **passenger solar sailship:** A type of clear-domed luxury space vehicle used to ferry travelers off Earth. The sailship was powered by booster rockets and large solar sails that acted like a mirror, reflecting sunlight to propel the craft through space.

  In 2091, McFly Space Cruises launched the first Mars-bound passenger solar sailship, the *MSC Marty*, which was reported lost in space after Ziff Tannen sabotaged it. Emmett and Clara Brown were among its passengers at the time. Jules and Verne Brown rescued their parents by towing the *Marty* back to base, using the *MSC Jennifer*—the first model of passenger solar sailship ever produced [**BFAN-9**].

- **Patrini Shoes:** A retail store that sold footwear [**REAL**]. Patrini operated a Hill Valley location in 1985, across the street from the Twin Pines Mall [**BTF1**].

- **Paul:** An individual who died in or before 1967. A member of Lorraine McFly's anti-war protest group that year wore an armband in his honor, bearing the slogan "Paul R.I.P." [**BTF2-s1**].

  > *NOTE: Given the era, and that the group was protesting the Vietnam War, it's likely Paul died during that conflict.*

- **Pay Up:** A slogan on the Café 80's menu in 2015, alongside a thumbprint-activated payment device [**BTF2**].

- **PDA Law:** *See* Statute 476-D

- **Peabody, Dingus:** A grizzled citizen of Hill Valley, circa 1885, and an ancestor of Otis Peabody. Dingus was missing several teeth, and was friendly with Emmett Brown during the latter's stint in that era as a blacksmith.

  Fond of pine trees, Dingus sought Emmett's permission to plant a few in the dirt behind Doc's shop. The scientist agreed, asking Dingus to pick up Clara Clayton at the Hill Valley Railroad Station for him. Dingus immediately lost the address, however, leaving Doc to handle the task himself [**BTF3-sp**].

  > *NOTE: Since Dingus Peabody and Farmer Peabody appeared in different drafts of* Back to the Future III*'s screenplay, it's possible they were intended to be the same character.*

- **Peabody, Eli:** *See* Peabody, Otis

- **Peabody, Elsie ("Ma"):** The wife of farmer Otis Peabody. The couple married in 1938, and had two children, Martha and Sherman [**BTF1-n**].

  In 1955, Otis and Elsie were awakened during the night by a commotion in their barn, caused by the arrival of Marty McFly—whom they mistook as an alien upon seeing Marty's futuristic radiation suit and DeLorean. When Elsie fainted in fright, Sherman—who often read horror and science fiction tales—convinced his father that the "alien" had killed her and turned her into a mind-controlled "space zombie," without free will [**BTF1-s3**].

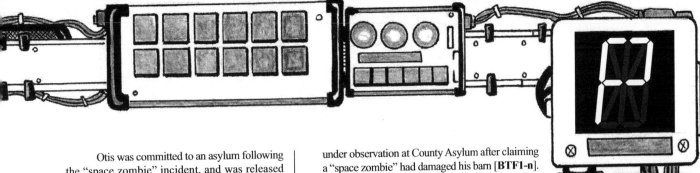

Otis was committed to an asylum following the "space zombie" incident, and was released in 1967—only to once again see the DeLorean as Emmett Brown flew the vehicle past the Peabodys' car. Otis was summarily re-admitted to the sanitarium, along with Elsie, who this time witnessed the UFO sighting as well [**BTF2-s1**].

> *NOTE: This character, unnamed onscreen, was dubbed Elsie in BTTF1's novelization. In BTTF2's first-draft screenplay, she was called Maybelle.*

- **Peabody, Farmer:** A citizen of Hill Valley, circa the 1880s. Emmett Brown, while serving as the town's blacksmith, repaired the man's damaged wagon [**BTF3-sx**].

> *NOTE: Since Farmer Peabody and Dingus Peabody appeared in different drafts of BTTF3's screenplay, it's unknown whether they were meant to be the same individual.*

- **Peabody, Martha:** The daughter of farmers Otis and Elsie Peabody. She had a younger brother named Sherman [**BTF1-n**].

> *NOTE: This character, unnamed onscreen, was identified as Martha in BTTF1's novelization. The screenplays described her as being buxom and beautiful, a reference to popular off-color jokes about farmers' daughters.*

- **Peabody, Maybelle:** *See* Peabody, Elsie

- **Peabody, Otis ("Old Man Peabody," "Pa"):** A farmer who owned a large patch of Hill Valley land in the 1950s. Peabody had two young pine trees that he planned to breed—a notion deemed "crazy" by some, including Emmett Brown [**BTF1**]. Otis had a wife, Elsie, and two children, Martha and Sherman. The couple wed in 1938 [**BTF1-n**].

In 1955, Marty McFly, propelled into the past in a time-traveling DeLorean, crashed into the Peabodys' barn in the middle of the night. The family investigated, discovering Marty in a radiation suit. A fan of horror and science fiction comics, Sherman panicked his family by convincing them an alien spacecraft was in their midst, and that Marty was a "space zombie." Marty tried to apologize, but drove away in haste when Otis opened fire, thereby killing one of the farmer's pine trees [**BTF1**]. A local newspaper covered the incident, noting that Peabody was

under observation at County Asylum after claiming a "space zombie" had damaged his barn [**BTF1-n**].

Released from the sanitarium in 1967, Otis returned to his farm on the advice of his psychiatrist, to prove to himself that flying saucers did not exist. Upon arriving, however, he saw the DeLorean flying overhead and suffered a relapse, then was re-admitted to the asylum—along with Elsie, who this time saw the "spacecraft" as well. After again being released, Otis discovered the DeLorean's discarded door. Finally able to prove the experience occurred, he earned renown as a UFO expert and wrote a book on the subject, titled *Trash Dumps of the Gods*. By 1975, Peabody (age 75) offered lectures on alien spaceships, using the car part as evidence of alien life [**BTF2-s1**].

By the 1980s, Peabody's land was the site of a shopping center called the Twin Pines Mall, in honor of his prized trees. After Marty altered time by destroying one of the saplings, however, the mall was instead christened the Lone Pine Mall [**BTF1**].

> *NOTE: This character, named Otis in BTTF1's credits, was mis-identified as "Eli Peabody" in a trivia track included on the movie's Blu-ray release.*

> *A deleted scene near the end of* Back to the Future II *would have featured Peabody seeing Doc and the DeLorean flying out from behind the Lyon Estates billboard, and firing on the car in panic. This sequence was included on the movie's Blu-ray release, in storyboard form.*

- **Peabody, Sherman:** The young son of Hill Valley farmers Otis and Elsie Peabody [**BTF1-n**]. The child had a fondness for comic books, such as *Tales from Space*, and thus mistook radiation-suited Marty McFly as an alien invader—and the DeLorean as a spaceship—when Marty crashed the vehicle into the family's barn in 1955 [**BTF1**].

> *NOTE: This character, identified in BTTF1's credits and script, was named after Sherman, a young assistant to time traveler Mr. Peabody on* The Rocky and Bullwinkle Show. *Writers Bob Gale and Robert Zemeckis were both fans of this cartoon series.*

- **Peabody Farm:** A produce company, circa 1931. As a young man, Emmett Brown had an apple crate from this farm in his laboratory [**TLTL-4**].

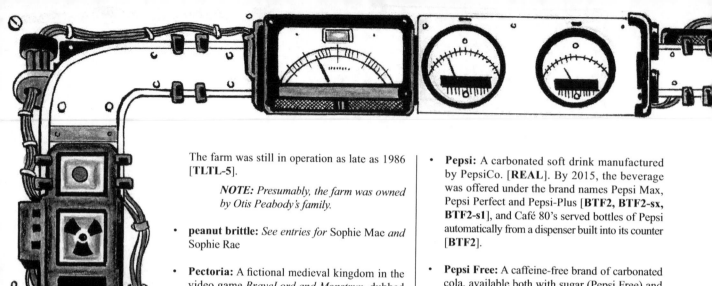

The farm was still in operation as late as 1986 [**TLTL-5**].

> *NOTE: Presumably, the farm was owned by Otis Peabody's family.*

- **peanut brittle:** *See entries for* Sophie Mae *and* Sophie Rae

- **Pectoria:** A fictional medieval kingdom in the video game *BraveLord and Monstrux*, dubbed the Land of Certain Obliteration. Known for its citizens' strength and bravery, Pectoria was protected from the demon Monstrux by a brawny warrior, BraveLord [**BFAN-19**].

> *NOTE: The name "Pectoria" was a play on "pectoral," referring to BraveLord's massive chest muscles.*

- **Pedestrian Speed Way:** A 26th-century mode of travel that carried non-vehicle-based travelers across long distances at high speeds, with exits at numerous cities, including Hill Valley [**BFCL-1**].

- **Pedro:** A name scrawled in graffiti on the entrance to Lyon Estates, circa 1985 [**BTF1**].

- **Peitsch, Jeff:** An employee at the Institute of Future Technology, stationed in the East Wing [**RIDE**].

> *NOTE: This individual was identified on signage outside* Back to the Future: The Ride.

- **Pellenon, Gattaca:** The author of *Caesar*, a book published in ancient Rome sometime in or before 36 A.D. While traversing an underground cataombs in that era with escaped slave Judah Ben-Hur, Jules and Verne Brown came across the skeleton of a person who'd apparently died reading this book [**BFAN-5**].

> *NOTE: "Pelle non," in Italian, translates as "no skin" (a pun, since the corpse was skinless). The term "Gattaca," in science, refers to the four nucleotides of deoxyribonucleic acid (DNA): guanine (G), adenine (A), thymine (T) and cytosine (C).*

- **Pep Rally:** An event held at Hill Valley High School, circa 1955, to encourage support for the school's sports teams. The rally was held on a Friday at 3:00 P.M., in the boys' gymnasium, a week before the Enchantment Under the Sea Dance [**BTF1**].

- **Pepsi:** A carbonated soft drink manufactured by PepsiCo. [**REAL**]. By 2015, the beverage was offered under the brand names Pepsi Max, Pepsi Perfect and Pepsi-Plus [**BTF2, BTF2-sx, BTF2-s1**], and Café 80's served bottles of Pepsi automatically from a dispenser built into its counter [**BTF2**].

- **Pepsi Free:** A caffeine-free brand of carbonated cola, available both with sugar (Pepsi Free) and without (Diet Pepsi Free) [**REAL**].

  In 1985, the McFly family drank the soda by the can. Marty McFly tried to order a Pepsi Free at Lou's Café in 1955, but since the brand had yet to be introduced, proprietor Lou Caruthers mistook his order as a request for a soda free of charge, and replied that if Marty wanted a Pepsi, he'd have to pay for it [**BTF1**].

> *NOTE: Pepsi products have appeared throughout the* Back to the Future *saga, though the film's initial draft referenced Coca-Cola. See also the entry for Fepsi.*

- **Pepsi Max:** A brand of Pepsi sold in 2015 [**BTF2**].

- **Pepsi Perfect:** A brand of Pepsi sold in 2015, in tall, curved plastic bottles with large blue caps [**BTF2, RIDE**]. Marty McFly Jr. was fond of this beverage [**BTF2**].

- **Pepsi-Plus:** A brand of vitamin-enriched Pepsi sold in 2015 [**BTF2-sx, BTF2-s1**].

- **Pepson:** A manufacturer of dot-matrix printers in Citizen Brown's dystopian timeline [**TLTL-3**].

> *NOTE: The company's name referred to printer maker Epson.*

- **Percent Power:** A gauge on the time circuits of Emmett Brown's DeLorean [**BTF1**].

- **Permacel:** An industrial adhesive-tape manufacturing firm [**REAL**]. A box bearing this company's logo was located in Emmett Brown's home, near his giant guitar amplifier [**BTF1**].

- **Permacell:** A brand of 12-volt car battery used to power flying cars, circa 2015. Upon visiting that era, Emmett Brown installed a Permacell battery in his DeLorean, enabling the vehicle to achieve flight [**TLTL-3**].

> *NOTE: Batteries branded as Permacell*

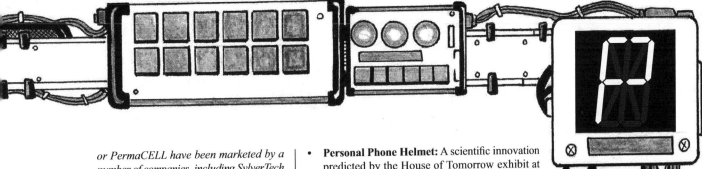

or PermaCELL have been marketed by a number of companies, including SylverTech and Trak Auto Corp., but there appears to be no connection to the model of battery that Doc used.

- **Perpa-Hoop:** *See* Perpetual-Motion Hula Hoop

- **Perpetual Motion Foot-Massage Unit:** An invention of Emmett Brown, consisting of an elaborate machine on which a person could hang upside down and receive automated foot care that felt ticklish and uncomfortable. Doc used the contraption in an attempt to cure Marty McFly's athlete's foot fungus [**BFAN-7a**].

- **Perpetual-Motion Hula Hoop:** An invention of Emmett Brown, created while the scientist attended the American College of Technological Science & Difficult Math. This innovation, also called a Perpa-Hoop, utilized a battery and internal gyros to eliminate stress and injuries caused by what he saw as a "wacky fad."

  Doc built the device to submit to the Inter-Collegiate Science Invent-Off, but his roommate, Walter Wisdom, stole the idea as his own. This landed Wisdom a lucrative contract with Glunko Toys, created a new nationwide craze and resulted in Wisdom attaining his own TV series, titled *Mr. Wisdom* [**BFAN-15**].

- **Perrier:** A brand of naturally carbonated mineral water, bottled in France [**REAL**]. A case of Perrier was among the items for sale at Blast From the Past, an antique and collectibles shop in 2015 Hill Valley [**BTF2**].

- **Perry, Luke:** One of several names that Marty McFly and Verne Brown urged Jules Verne to adopt, since Verne (who'd been named in the novelist's honor) hated the name Verne [**BFAN-21**].

  NOTE: *Actor Luke Perry starred on the television series* Beverly Hills, 90210, *which aired during Verne's childhood.*

- **Perry, O.P.:** A citizen of Hill Valley who was listed on Arthur McFly's ledger at the 1931 Hill Valley Exposition [**TLTL-2**].

- **Personality Rebuild:** A technique used by Edna Strickland, in Citizen Brown's dystopian timeline, to program a subject's mind using a combination of complex machinery and brainwashing [**TLTL-4**].

- **Personal Phone Helmet:** A scientific innovation predicted by the House of Tomorrow exhibit at the 1931 Hill Valley Exposition. According to a narrated recording played at the exhibit, future homes would contain voice-activated Personal Phone Helmets enabling private telephone conversations [**TLTL-5**].

  NOTE: *In essence, the device was a 1930s analog to a modern-day Bluetooth headset.*

- **Personal Tunneling Devices:** An idea that Emmett Brown considered demonstrating at the 1931 Hill Valley Exposition, but ultimately rejected in favor of other innovations [**TLTL-v**].

- **Peter Park-It:** A polite model of droid, resembling a human butler that oversaw the parking facilities at Hill Valley's McFly Space Center, circa 2091. Peter Park-It shrank each parked vehicle down to a tiny size, using a vacuum-like appendage, in a process known as microstorage [**BFAN-9**].

  NOTE: *This droid's name was a pun on that of Peter Parker, better known as Marvel Comics' Spider-Man—and also the name of Jennifer Parker's grandfather.*

- **Petersen, Mart:** An automobile mechanic in Hill Valley, circa 1955, who serviced the family car of Otis and Elsie Peabody [**BTF1-n**].

- **Petrucci, Melvin:** One of several names that Emmett Brown guessed while trying to telepathically determine Marty McFly's identity in 1955, using his Brain-wave Analyzer [**BTF1-n**].

- **Phelps, Officer:** A police officer in Hill Valley, who tried to pull over Emmett Brown's DeLorean when Doc's family was speeding while tracking Jules Brown's stolen money-tree. The sports car easily out-ran the motorcycle cop, but Doc later turned himself in, feeling guilty. Verne Brown hoped Phelps would not recall that he'd littered the man's yard with toilet paper the previous summer [**BFAN-20**].

- **Philco:** A manufacturer of numerous products, including radios, televisions and household appliances [**REAL**].

  In 1952, in order to send Marty McFly back to his own era, Emmett Brown sneaked into an atomic bomb testing site in Atkins, Nevada, to use the bomb's nuclear energy to power a time machine. His plan involved modifying the top of

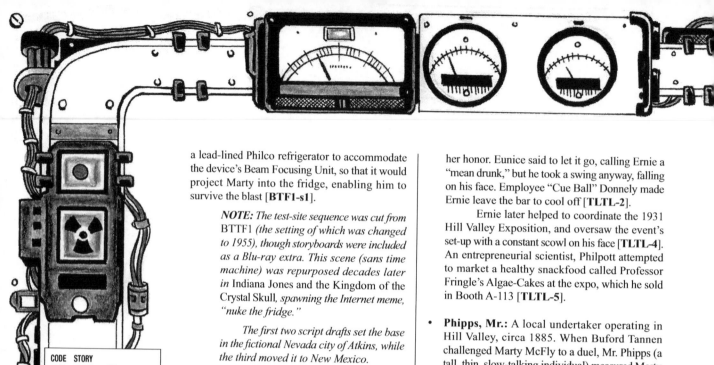

a lead-lined Philco refrigerator to accommodate the device's Beam Focusing Unit, so that it would project Marty into the fridge, enabling him to survive the blast [**BTF1-s1**].

> *NOTE: The test-site sequence was cut from BTTF1 (the setting of which was changed to 1955), though storyboards were included as a Blu-ray extra. This scene (sans time machine) was repurposed decades later in* Indiana Jones and the Kingdom of the Crystal Skull, *spawning the Internet meme, "nuke the fridge."*
>
> *The first two script drafts set the base in the fictional Nevada city of Atkins, while the third moved it to New Mexico.*

- **Philips, Dan ("Engineer Dan"):** The heavyset, red-goateed owner of the Engineer Dan Hobby Hut, located in Hill Valley. The toyshop owner had a daughter named Franny—on whom Jules Brown had a crush—and operated his store clad in a train engineer's outfit. Upon learning that Jules had invented a money-tree, Dan extended first-class store credit to the youth [**BFAN-20**].

- **Philips, Franny:** A classmate of Jules Brown at Hill Valley Elementary School, on whom Jules had a strong crush [**BFAN-20, BFAN-26**].

  The short, redheaded girl—whose father, Dan Philips, owned the Engineer Dan Hobby Hut—often laughed at other students' taunting of Jules. When he created a money-tree (a synthetic plant containing leaves resembling U.S. paper currency), she pretended to like him.

  The money-tree proved useless as a source of legal tender, as the money leaves soon shriveled, but by then, Franny realized that she genuinely liked Jules. She thus remained his girlfriend even after he no longer had wealth [**BFAN-20**].

- **Phillips, Mrs.:** A teacher at Dan Quayle Elementary School. In 2091, she took her fifth-grade class to visit Hill Valley's McFly Museum of Aeronautics [**BFAN-9**].

- **Philpott, Ernest ("Ernie"):** A middle-aged citizen of Hill Valley, circa 1931, who sometimes patronized the El Kid speakeasy. He had a pencil-thin mustache, glasses and a shrill voice.

  When Marty McFly entered El Kid, Ernie drunkenly assumed Marty was staring at his girlfriend, Eunice, and threatened to fight for

her honor. Eunice said to let it go, calling Ernie a "mean drunk," but he took a swing anyway, falling on his face. Employee "Cue Ball" Donnely made Ernie leave the bar to cool off [**TLTL-2**].

Ernie later helped to coordinate the 1931 Hill Valley Exposition, and oversaw the event's set-up with a constant scowl on his face [**TLTL-4**]. An entrepreneurial scientist, Philpott attempted to market a healthy snackfood called Professor Fringle's Algae-Cakes at the expo, which he sold in Booth A-113 [**TLTL-5**].

- **Phipps, Mr.:** A local undertaker operating in Hill Valley, circa 1885. When Buford Tannen challenged Marty McFly to a duel, Mr. Phipps (a tall, thin, slow-talking individual) measured Marty for a new suit—and for a coffin, given the odds against his surviving the fight [**BTF3-n**].

  Phipps loved Hill Valley, which he considered beautiful. He marveled at the town's technology, such as the railroad, and found it amusing when foreigners were awed by amenities he took for granted—the town's barber shop, for instance. Although he disliked Buford and hoped Marshall James Strickland would bring the outlaw down, Phipps did acknowledge that Tannen brought him much business [**BTFA**].

  > *NOTE: This character appeared unnamed in BTTF3, but was identified as Mr. Phipps in the movie's novelization.*

- **Phoenix:** The capital city of Arizona [**REAL**]. In 2015, I-99's Hyperlane-Grid 4 contained an exit for flying cars that led to this city, as well as to Boston, London and Hill Valley [**BTF2**].

- **phone book:** A listing of telephone subscribers within a particular geographical area [**REAL**]. In 1955, Marty McFly visited Lou's Café while searching for Emmett Brown's address. Spotting a phone booth, he opened the local telephone directory, turned to the B section and located Doc's entry, then tore out the page to carry away with him, much to the annoyance of proprietor Lou Caruthers [**BTF1**].

  > *NOTE: Due to the sheer volume of names and street addresses listed in the fictional phone book (which covered a pair of two-page spreads), it would be impractical to incorporate all of that information into this lexicon. A scan of the actual torn-out prop page used in the film, containing the Brown listings, appears in Appendix V.*

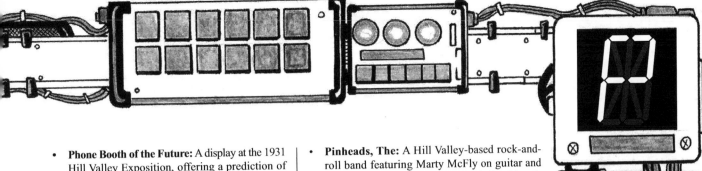

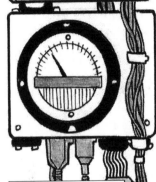

- **Phone Booth of the Future:** A display at the 1931 Hill Valley Exposition, offering a prediction of how communication technologies would function decades into the future. The booth, made with unbreakable, soundproof glass provided by a company called Atlas, had an automatically closing door and a hands-free setup, enabling users to "enjoy a sandwich or a cigarette while chatting with friends in perfect privacy" [**TLTL-5**].

- **Photo-Electric Chemical Power Converter:** An invention of Emmett Brown, designed to efficiently convert radiation into electrical energy. The scientist developed the device from 1949 to 1985, but achieved little success until Marty McFly poured Coca-Cola into it, causing it to work brilliantly [**BTF1-s1**].

  > **NOTE:** *This device, mentioned in* BTTF1*'s initial screenplay draft, became the Flux Capacitor in later drafts.*

- **Pickford, Mary ("Scary Mary"):** An alias used by Edna Strickland after she stole Emmett Brown's DeLorean and traveled back to 1876. As Pickford, Edna felt at home in that era, but saw Beauregard Tannen's Palace Saloon and Hotel as a blight on Hill Valley society, and thus decided to burn it down—but in so doing, she inadvertently torched the entire city. For 55 years, Edna/Mary remained Hill Valley's sole remaining inhabitant, living in a decrepit home and going slowly insane while blocking out the memory of her guilt [**TLTL-5**].

  > **NOTE:** *The real-world Mary Pickford, dubbed "America's Sweetheart" (despite being Canadian), was among the most popular stars of the silent film era. The actress co-founded United Artists and was one of the original founders of the Academy of Motion Picture Arts and Sciences. She starred in 236 films from 1908 to 1935.*

- **Picture Radio:** A display at the 1931 Hill Valley Exposition, offering a prediction of how entertainment would develop in the future. The Picture Radio, as its name suggested, resembled a radio of that era, but with a small video screen in the middle [**TLTL-5**].

  > **NOTE:** *In essence, the device was a 1930s analog to a television.*

- **Pine City Stage:** A stagecoach robbed by Buford Tannen's gang in 1885 [**BTF3**].

- **Pineheads, The:** A Hill Valley-based rock-and-roll band featuring Marty McFly on guitar and lead vocals [**BTF1**], and others, including Marty's friend Nick [**BTF1-s2**]. Marty performed with The Pinheads during his high school years [**BTF1**], throughout college [**BFAN**] and until at least 2015 [**BFCG**].

  In 1985, The Pinheads auditioned for Hill Valley High School's Battle of the Bands contest, but were quickly disqualified for being "too darn loud" [**BTF1**]. Instead, a Baldwin-based punk-rock band called French Kiss earned the gig [**BTF1-s2**].

  That same year, The Pinheads intended to audition for a YMCA dance, but these plans faltered when Marty earned an afterschool detention with his high school vice-principal, Gerald Strickland [**BTF1-s3**].

  While visiting 1931, Marty mused that a park gazebo in Courthouse Square would have been a great place to perform, if it still existed in his era [**TLTL-2**]. In 1991, the band performed a concert on the steps of the Hill Valley Courthouse, where they were introduced by concert promoter Ned the Fish [**BFAN-12**].

  The band's first big hit, "Chapel O' Love" (a cover of the Dixie Cups' 1964 classic "Chapel of Love"), was released in 1994, kicking off a string of successes. In 2015, the group released a greatest-hits album, *Fired Up*, which went platinum, topping the rock-and-roll charts [**BFCG**].

  > **NOTE:** *In the first* Back to the Future *film, Marty called his band The Pinheads. The animated series referred to the group as Marty McFly & the Pinheads, while* Back to the Future—The Card Game *called them Marty and the Pinheads.*
  >
  > *In the animated series, the band looked completely different than they did on film. This could indicate membership changed, or that the animators simply were inconsistent.*
  >
  > *The Pinheads' blonde guitarist was portrayed by Paul Hanson, Michael J. Fox's guitar coach.*

- **Pioneer Boulevard:** A street in Artesia, California. A business known as ACI was located at 17100 Pioneer Boulevard, in Suite 320 [**BFAN-12**].

- **Pismo Beach:** A beach city in southern San Luis Obispo County, California [**REAL**]. Emmett Brown and a girlfriend, Jill Wooster, once enjoyed a romantic interlude at this location [**BTF3-s1**].

CODE	STORY
NIKE	*BTTF*-themed TV commercial: Nike
NTND	Nintendo *Back to the Future—The Ride* Mini-Game
PIZA	*BTTF*-themed TV commercial: Pizza Hut
PNBL	Data East *BTTF* pinball game
REAL	Real life
RIDE	Simulator: *Back to the Future—The Ride*
SCRM	2010 Scream Awards: *Back to the Future 25th Anniversary Reunion* (broadcast)
SCRT	2010 Scream Awards: *Back to the Future 25th Anniversary Reunion* (trailer)
SIMP	Simulator: *The Simpsons Ride*
SLOT	*Back to the Future Video Slots*
STLZ	Unused *BTTF* footage of Eric Stoltz as Marty McFly
STRY	*Back to the Future Storybook*
TEST	Screen tests: Crispin Glover, Lea Thompson and Tom Wilson
TLTL	Telltale Games' *Back to the Future—The Game*
TOPS	Topps' *Back to the Future II* trading-card set
TRIL	*BTTF: The Official Book of the Complete Movie Trilogy*
UNIV	Universal Studios Hollywood promotional video

SUFFIX	MEDIUM
-b	*BTTF2*'s Biff Tannen Museum video (extended)
-c	Credit sequence to the animated series
-d	Film deleted scene
-n	Film novelization
-o	Film outtake
-p	1955 phone book from *BTTF1*
-v	Video game print materials or commentaries
-s1	Screenplay (draft one)
-s2	Screenplay (draft two)
-s3	Screenplay (draft three)
-s4	Screenplay (draft four)
-sp	Screenplay (production draft)
-sx	Screenplay (*Paradox*)

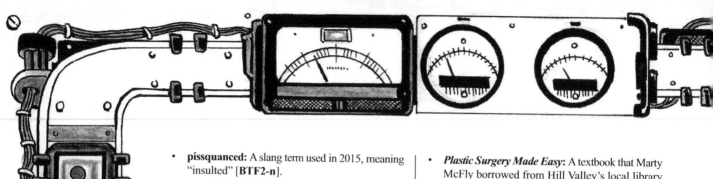

- **pissquanced:** A slang term used in 2015, meaning "insulted" [**BTF2-n**].

- **Pita Banana Peel Sweet Madonna Springsteen:** A menu item sold at Café 80's in 2015 [**BTF2**].

- **Pit Bull:** A model of high-powered hoverboard sold in 2015, capable of hovering over water. Griff Tannen owned such a board, which came with ropes enabling his gang—Chester "Whitey" Nogura, Leslie "Spike" O'Malley and Rafe "Data" Unger—to be pulled along on their own hoverboards [**BTF2**].

  NOTE: Early names given to the board during production included Mad Dog and Screwboard.

- **Pix Video Rental:** A business located in Hill Valley, circa 1991 [**BFAN-7b**].

- **Pizza Go:** A restaurant located in Hill Valley, circa 2015 [**RIDE**].

- **Pizza Hut:** An American restaurant chain and international franchise offering several styles of pizza, along with various side dishes [**REAL**].

  A Pizza Hut branch operated in Courthouse Square, circa 2015. The company also sold rehydrated pizza, enabling a 15-inch pie to be stored within a foil-wrapped package only a few inches in diameter. Rehydrated pizzas—available with a variety of toppings, including pepperoni and green peppers—could be cooked in only two seconds in a Hydrator unit, and could serve a family of eight. The pizza's packaging warned shoppers not to consume the product unless fully rehydrated [**BTF2**].

  Two hungry young men from 1989, exploring 2015 aboard a time-traveling DeLorean, discovered that the Domino's restaurant chain had been transformed into a hardware store known as Domino's Hardware. Therefore, they instead dined at Pizza Hut [**PIZA**].

- **P.K. Rata Recycling Center:** A facility in Hill Valley, circa 2015, at which plastic materials, such as old LaserDiscs and silicone, were recycled [**BTF2**].

- **Placerville:** A city in El Dorado County, California [**REAL**]. When Placerville's police department employed a team of bloodhounds, Officer Daniel Parker tried to convince his boss to do the same in Hill Valley, but the chief refused [**TLTL-2**].

- ***Plastic Surgery Made Easy:*** A textbook that Marty McFly borrowed from Hill Valley's local library in 1991—and returned overdue [**BFCM-3**].

- **plasto-plaster:** A plastic-based substance used for molding purposes. After traveling 3,000 years into Egypt's past, Emmett Brown and his son, Verne, angered the ancient Egyptians by placing a large fake nose, mustache and eyeglasses—which Verne had constructed from plasto-plaster—on the statue's face [**BFAN-4**].

- ***Playboy:*** A men's magazine founded by Hugh Hefner, featuring photographs of nude women, along with articles and short stories [**REAL**]. Upon discovering an issue of *Playboy* in his older self's suitcase in 1955, Emmett Brown decided that the future looked "a whole lot better" [**BTF1-d**].

- **Pleistocene Epoch**: A period of time spanning from approximately 2.6 million to 12,000 years ago [**REAL**]. Emmett Brown, after falling victim to his sons' April Fool's Day prank to make him think he'd used up his brain power, traveled to this era to be free of science and thereby conserve his remaining intelligence. Bored with the simple minds of Cro-Magnon humans, however, he soon returned to his own timeframe [**BFAN-12**].

- **Plumbot:** A type of plumbing robot utilized by the human citizens of Robot City, a domed station in the Asteroid Belt of Earth's solar system, circa 2585 [**BFCL-1**].

- **plutonium:** A radioactive chemical element with symbol Pu and atomic number 94, used during the production of weapons or reactor fuel [**REAL**].

  In 1985, Libyan nationalists stole a case of plutonium from the Pacific Nuclear Research Facility, and then hired Emmett Brown to build a bomb for them. The scientist kept the substance for himself, however, providing the terrorists with a case full of used pinball-machine parts, so that he could use the plutonium to power his time-traveling DeLorean [**BTF1**].

  Doc once invented a laptop-style computer notebook that proved too unstable to use, since it was powered by plutonium instead of a standard battery [**GARB**].

- **Plutonium Chamber:** A gauge on the time circuits of Emmett Brown's DeLorean that monitored the amount of ionizing radiation given off by the

CODE	STORY
ARGN	*BTTF*-themed TV commercial: Arrigoni
BFAN	*Back to the Future: The Animated Series*
BFCG	*Back to the Future: The Card Game*
BFCL	*Back to the Future* comic book (limited series)
BFCM	*Back to the Future* comic book (monthly series)
BFHM	*BTTF*-themed McDonald's Happy Meal boxes
BTFA	*Back to the Future Annual* (Marvel Comics)
BTF1	Film: *Back to the Future*
BTF2	Film: *Back to the Future Part II*
BTF3	Film: *Back to the Future Part III*
BUDL	*BTTF*-themed TV commercial: Bud Light
CHEK	*BTTF*-themed music video: O'Neal McKnight, "Check Your Coat"
CHIC	Photographs hanging in the Doc Brown's Chicken restaurant at Universal Studios
CITY	*BTTF*-themed music video: Owl City, "Deer in the Headlights"
CLUB	*Back to the Future* Fan Club Magazine
DCTV	*BTTF*-themed TV commercial: DirecTV
ERTH	*The Earth Day Special*
GALE	Interviews and commentaries: Bob Gale and/or Robert Zemeckis
GARB	*BTTF*-themed TV commercials for Garbarino
HUEY	*BTTF*-themed music video: Huey Lewis and the News, "The Power of Love"
LIMO	*BTTF*-themed music video: The Limousines, "The Future"
MCDN	*BTTF*-themed TV commercial: McDonald's
MITS	*BTTF*-themed TV commercial: Mitsubishi Lancer
MSFT	*BTTF*-themed TV commercial: Microsoft

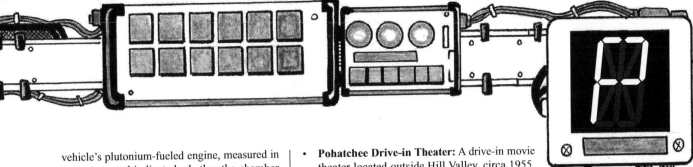

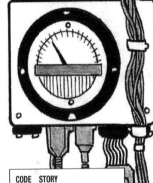

vehicle's plutonium-fueled engine, measured in roentgens, and indicated whether the chamber was empty or fueled [**BTF1**].

- **plutonium spitwads:** A late 21st-century equivalent of chewing gum. The McFly Museum of Aeronautics urged visiting children not to chew plutonium spitwads within its facilities [**BFAN-9**].

- **Plymouth Reliant:** A model of "K-car"—a series of compact-to-midsize vehicles designed to carry six adults on two bench seats—manufactured by Chrysler Corp. [**REAL**].
  George McFly owned a 1979 Reliant, license plate number BTD629, which was damaged during a car accident in 1985, when George's supervisor, Biff Tannen, borrowed and crashed it while drinking beer. Biff refused to pay for the damage, claiming it was George's fault since the vehicle supposedly had a blind spot [**BTF1-n**].

- **Pocari Sweat:** A popular Japanese soft drink and sports drink, manufactured by Otsuka Pharmaceutical Co. [**REAL**]. In 2015, Marty and Jennifer McFly had pouches of this beverage in their kitchen [**BTF2**].

- **pocket binoculars:** A 21st-century viewing device providing binocular vision when viewing distant objects, consisting of a flat plastic card with two eyeholes. Emmett Brown used a set of pocket binoculars to scout out Courthouse Square after bringing Marty McFly to the year 2015 to save his future children [**BTF2-n**].

- **Poetry for Speech:** A speech delivered by Jo Potosi at a Vietnam War protest rally to which Lorraine McFly donated her time in 1967 [**BTF2-s1**].

- **Pohatchee:** A Native American tribe, circa 1885, living in what would later be Hill Valley, California. The Pohatchee had an adversarial relationship with local settlers, and often ended up in skirmishes with them, particularly in the 1880s [**BTF3-n**].
  Moments after traveling back to 1885, Marty McFly encountered a group of horse-mounted Pohatchee warriors being chased across the plains by the U.S. Cavalry. The tribe fired on the DeLorean, rupturing its fuel line, and leaving the vehicle without gasoline. Marty narrowly survived, by hiding the car within a cave [**BTF3-sp, BTF3-n**].

- **Pohatchee Drive-in Theater:** A drive-in movie theater located outside Hill Valley, circa 1955, decorated with a Native American motif. The theater featured a booth housing the Pohatchee Snackbar, as well as a Western memorabilia shop called Braves.
  Emmett Brown chose the drive-in's parking lot for Marty McFly to use to travel back to 1885, since there were no trees in either period at that location, and because its remoteness would reduce the risk of being seen. Before time-traveling, Marty obtained supposedly authentic cowboy garb from the Braves shop—but upon arriving in the Old West, he soon realized how anachronistic he looked [**BTF3**].

  NOTE: In Back to the Future III*'s first-draft screenplay, Marty departed from the Indian Rocks State Park, rather than from the drive-in.*

- **Pohatchee Snackbar:** A food stand at the Pohatchee Drive-in Theater, circa 1955 [**BTF3**].

- **Polla:** A business located in Hill Valley, circa 1944 [**BFAN-17**].

- **Pollers Pass:** An area of Hill Valley, circa 1885, as indicated on a map hanging at the Hill Valley Railroad Station [**BTF3**].

- **Pollo de Pope John Paul II Princess Di Spud Cake:** A menu item sold at Café 80's in 2015 [**BTF2**].

- **Polo Shirt Thursday:** A mandate of Hill Valley's dress code in Citizen Brown's dystopian timeline. On this day each week, citizens were required to wear identical khaki pants and orange polo shirts, as per Civic Ordinance 9-Triple-E [**TLTL-3**].

- **Pontiac:** An automobile brand established by General Motors in 1926 [**REAL**]. A Pontiac branch operated in Courthouse Square, circa 2015, offering sales and hover-conversion services [**BTF2**].

- **Pop:** A beverage advertised on a billboard during the 1897 National League pennant game between the Baltimore Orioles and the Boston Beaneaters [**BFAN-8**].

- **Popov:** A brand of vodka produced by Diageo North America [**REAL**]. In 1985, Lorraine McFly

CODE	STORY
NIKE	BTTF-themed TV commercial: Nike
NTND	Nintendo Back to the Future—The Ride Mini-Game
PIZA	BTTF-themed TV commercial: Pizza Hut
PNBL	Data East BTTF pinball game
REAL	Real life
RIDE	Simulator: Back to the Future—The Ride
SCRM	2010 Scream Awards: Back to the Future 25th Anniversary Reunion (broadcast)
SCRT	2010 Scream Awards: Back to the Future 25th Anniversary Reunion (trailer)
SIMP	Simulator: The Simpsons Ride
SLOT	Back to the Future Video Slots
STLZ	Unused BTTF footage of Eric Stoltz as Marty McFly
STRY	Back to the Future Storybook
TEST	Screen tests: Crispin Glover, Lea Thompson and Tom Wilson
TLTL	Telltale Games' Back to the Future—The Game
TOPS	Topps' Back to the Future II trading-card set
TRIL	BTTF: The Official Book of the Complete Movie Trilogy
UNIV	Universal Studios Hollywood promotional video

SUFFIX	MEDIUM
-b	BTTF2's Biff Tannen Museum video (extended)
-c	Credit sequence to the animated series
-d	Film deleted scene
-n	Film novelization
-o	Film outtake
-p	1955 phone book from BTTF1
-v	Video game print materials or commentaries
-s1	Screenplay (draft one)
-s2	Screenplay (draft two)
-s3	Screenplay (draft three)
-s4	Screenplay (draft four)
-sp	Screenplay (production draft)
-sx	Screenplay (Paradox)

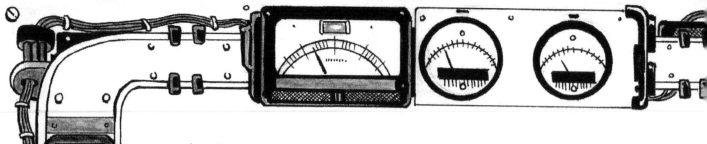

showed signs of alcoholism, frequently filling her glass with this beverage [**BTF1**].

- **Popular Mechanics**: An American magazine published by Hearst Corp. [**REAL**]. Emmett Brown sometimes consulted *Popular Mechanics* in the event that his inventions malfunctioned [**BFCM-1**].

- **Porche, Curtis, Professor**: The merriment facilitator of the Institute of Future Technology [**RIDE**].

    NOTE: *This individual, identified on signage outside* Back to the Future: The Ride, *was named after an employee at Universal Studios.*

- **pork, bacon and ham sandwich dipped in hog fat**: A type of sandwich that Hepzibah Tannen prepared for Marty McFly during a picnic lunch to celebrate their arranged engagement in 1875. Marty declined the pig-meat meal, causing her to cry [**BFAN-16**].

- **Porsche**: A German brand of luxury automobiles [**REAL**]. As a teenager, Marty McFly owned a silver jacket bearing the company's logo [**BTF1-s1**].

    In 2152, two men in a time-traveling DeLorean journeyed back in time to 2011. Crashing head-on into a Porsche upon arrival, they were thrown through a windshield and onto a dirt road, their bodies smashed. During their final moments before death, the men had an out-of-body experience in which they dreamed of numerous other people dying under horrible circumstances [**LIMO**].

    NOTE: *The men had a yellow case in the DeLorean's trunk that was identical to the plutonium crate seen in BTTF1, but without a radiation symbol.*

- **Portable Thumb Unit**: A technology used in 2015 to identify individuals at the press of a thumb, for the purpose of automatic, electronic payments [**BTF2-n**].

- **Port Flux Emitter**: A device invented by Emmett Brown—one of three such emitters used to enable his DeLorean to achieve time travel. This particular emitter was attached to the hood on the vehicle's front driver's side [**TLTL-5**].

- **Portrait of Luke Perry**: An illustration of author Jules Verne, drawn by Verne Brown, in the hope of convincing the novelist to rename himself "Luke Perry" so that young Verne would no longer be named "Verne" in the novelist's honor [**BFAN-21**].

    NOTE: *Actor Luke Perry starred on the television series* Beverly Hills, 90210, *which was very popular during Verne's childhood.*

- **Positronic Brain Surgery Made Easy**: A book written by science fiction author Isaac Asimov. Verne Brown referenced this work while writing a school essay on the subject of robotics [**BFCL-1**].

    NOTE: *No book by this name was written by Asimov in the real world.*

- **positronic brain units**: A type of robotic brain component manufactured by Asterobotics, circa 2585 [**BFCL-1**].

    NOTE: *The term "positronic brain" was coined by science fiction author Isaac Asimov in his* Robot *novels, and was later featured in the* Doctor Who *and* Star Trek *franchises, in regard to the Daleks and Data, respectively.*

- **post-historic**: A term coined by Emmett Brown to describe Hill Valley, after he and his sons, Jules and Verne, inadvertently prevented the extinction of the dinosaurs, thereby changing history so that dinosaurs replaced mankind as Earth's dominant animal lifeform [**BFAN-3**].

    NOTE: *The term was a play on the word "prehistoric."*

- **Potato Krunchos**: A brand of potato chips that Emmett Brown enjoyed [**BFCM-4**].

- **Potempkin ("Battleship")**: An abnormally tall, knuckle-dragging gangster operating in Chicago's South Side, circa 1927. He said little, but was very strong. Battleship worked with fellow mobster Mugsy Tannen under crime boss Arnie "Eggs" Benedict. After being arrested in that era, Marty McFly and Emmett Brown were temporarily incarcerated along with Potempkin and Tannen. [**BFCM-1**].

    NOTE: *This character was named after the Russian pre-dreadnought battleship* Potempkin *(spelled differently), famed for*

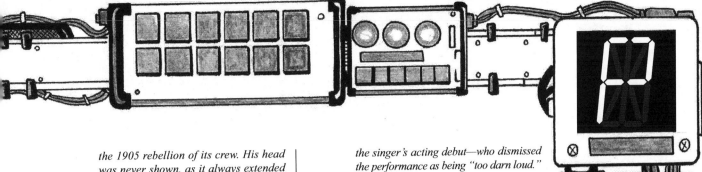

the 1905 rebellion of its crew. His head was never shown, as it always extended beyond the comic book panel's top border.

- **Poticar, Grace:** A mercantile systems technician at the Institute of Future Technology [**RIDE**].

  NOTE: This individual, identified on signage outside Back to the Future: The Ride, *was named after a Universal Studios employee.*

- **Potosi, Jo:** A speaker who presented at a Vietnam War protest rally to which Lorraine McFly donated her time in 1967. Her speech was titled "Poetry for Peace" [**BTF2-s1**].

- **Powell, Thomas:** An employee at the Institute of Future Technology, in charge of monetary unit redistribution [**RIDE**].

  NOTE: This individual, identified on signage outside Back to the Future: The Ride, *was named after Universal Studios' finance manager.*

- **power laces:** An innovation of the Nike footwear company, circa 2015. Nike's high-top sneakers that year were equipped with power laces, enabling them to self-seal [**BTF2**].

- **"Power of Love, The":** A song recorded by Huey Lewis and the News in 1985 [**REAL**]. Marty McFly's band, The Pinheads, auditioned with this tune at Hill Valley High School's Battle of the Bands competition, but failed to impress the judges [**BTF1**].

  That year, Huey Lewis and the News performed the song at a nightclub called Uncle Charlie's. While Emmett Brown attended the concert, a young couple fascinated with his time-traveling DeLorean took the vehicle for a joyride [**HUEY**].

  After being fired from his job at CusCo in 2015, Marty consoled himself by performing "The Power of Love" on his guitar. However, a hand injury suffered three decades prior prevented him from playing it well [**BTF2**].

  NOTE: "The Power of Love" was included on Back to the Future's *soundtrack, and Christopher Lloyd appeared as Doc in the song's music video. One Battle of the Bands judge was portrayed by Lewis himself—in*

the singer's acting debut—who dismissed the performance as being "too darn loud."

- **Power—Watts:** A tuning gauge on Emmett Brown's giant guitar amplifier, designated Type 157 [**BTF1**].

- **Pratt Hotel:** A business located in Chicago's South Side, circa 1927 [**BFCM-1**].

- **Prayer for Peace, A:** A speech delivered by Guru Ahm Dali Raj at a Vietnam War protest rally to which Lorraine McFly donated her time in 1967 [**BTF2-s1**].

- **Present Time:** A gauge on the time circuits of Emmett Brown's DeLorean that specified the vehicle's current month, day, year, hour and minute (as well as A.M. or P.M.), based on information entered on a keypad [**BTF1**].

- *President's Album, The*: A picture disc bearing the face of former U.S. President Ronald Reagan [**REAL**]. *The President's Album* was among the items for sale at Blast From the Past, an antique and collectibles shop in 2015 Hill Valley [**BTF2**].

- **Pres-to-Logs:** An artificial wood-burning stove fuel used to recycle sawdust [**REAL**]. In order to increase Locomotive No. 131's speed to 88 miles per hour and enable the damaged DeLorean to achieve time-travel in 1885, Emmett Brown utilized a trio of homemade Pres-to-Logs, using compressed wood with anthracite dust chemically treated to burn harder and longer, which he normally used in his blacksmith forge so he wouldn't have to stoke it. The logs were color-coded (green, yellow and red) and numbered 1 to 3, and were each designed to ignite sequentially in order to make the fire burn hotter, kick up the boiler pressure and make the train move faster [**BTF3**].

- *Price Is Right, The*: A television game show franchise originally produced by Mark Goodson and Bill Todman, most notably hosted by Bob Barker [**REAL**].

  George McFly, in an effort to raise his family's morale, suggested that he, his wife and children try out for a game show, such as *The Price is Right*. However, his son Marty recommended *Family Feud*, since that would enable the entire family, including his uncle John, to take part [**TEST**].

CODE	STORY
NIKE	*BTTF*-themed TV commercial: Nike
NTND	Nintendo *Back to the Future—The Ride* Mini-Game
PIZA	*BTTF*-themed TV commercial: Pizza Hut
PNBL	Data East *BTTF* pinball game
REAL	Real life
RIDE	Simulator: *Back to the Future—The Ride*
SCRM	2010 Scream Awards: *Back to the Future 25th Anniversary Reunion* (broadcast)
SCRT	2010 Scream Awards: *Back to the Future 25th Anniversary Reunion* (trailer)
SIMP	Simulator: *The Simpsons Ride*
SLOT	*Back to the Future Video Slots*
STLZ	Unused *BTTF* footage of Eric Stoltz as Marty McFly
STRY	*Back to the Future Storybook*
TEST	Screen tests: Crispin Glover, Lea Thompson and Tom Wilson
TLTL	Telltale Games' *Back to the Future—The Game*
TOPS	Topps' *Back to the Future II* trading-card set
TRIL	*BTTF: The Official Book of the Complete Movie Trilogy*
UNIV	Universal Studios Hollywood promotional video

SUFFIX	MEDIUM
-b	*BTTF2's* Biff Tannen Museum video (extended)
-c	Credit sequence to the animated series
-d	Film deleted scene
-n	Film novelization
-o	Film outtake
-p	1955 phone book from *BTTF1*
-v	Video game print materials or commentaries
-s1	Screenplay (draft one)
-s2	Screenplay (draft two)
-s3	Screenplay (draft three)
-s4	Screenplay (draft four)
-sp	Screenplay (production draft)
-sx	Screenplay (*Paradox*)

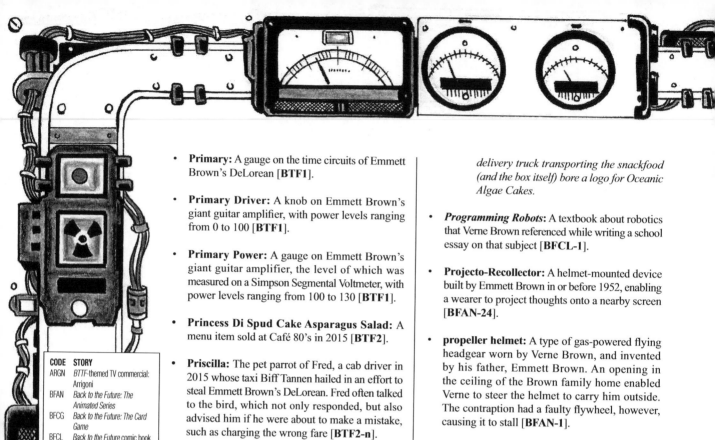

- **Primary:** A gauge on the time circuits of Emmett Brown's DeLorean [**BTF1**].

- **Primary Driver:** A knob on Emmett Brown's giant guitar amplifier, with power levels ranging from 0 to 100 [**BTF1**].

- **Primary Power:** A gauge on Emmett Brown's giant guitar amplifier, the level of which was measured on a Simpson Segmental Voltmeter, with power levels ranging from 100 to 130 [**BTF1**].

- **Princess Di Spud Cake Asparagus Salad:** A menu item sold at Café 80's in 2015 [**BTF2**].

- **Priscilla:** The pet parrot of Fred, a cab driver in 2015 whose taxi Biff Tannen hailed in an effort to steal Emmett Brown's DeLorean. Fred often talked to the bird, which not only responded, but also advised him if he were about to make a mistake, such as charging the wrong fare [**BTF2-n**].

- **Privacy Act:** A law in Hill Valley, circa 2015, preventing anyone, including police officers, to use a citizen's thumb-activated identipad to access another individual's home without permission [**BTF2-sx, BTF2-n**].

- **Professor Fringle's Algae-Cakes:** A healthy, algae-based snackfood product sold in 1931. "Cue Ball" Donnely ate a case of the cakes while loading them onto a truck for the 1931 Hill Valley Exposition, which turned the former gangster's teeth green [**TLTL-4**].

    The treats were created by scientist and entrepreneur Ernest Philpott, who marketed them at the expo as being a "miracle food from the swamps." Algae-cakes, containing vitamins A through J, were made from pond scum, sweetened with corn syrup and held together in solid clumps by gum arabic (a natural gum made of hardened sap).

    Although most people found the cakes unpalatable, Edna Strickland found them quite tasty. Later in life, she would use a substance of similar taste and color to induce stomach discomfort in subjects undergoing Citizen Plus reconditioning [**TLTL-5**].

    NOTE: *Although the video game's subtitles and Marty's dialog gave the product's name as **Doctor** Frinkle's Algae Cakes, Philpott's banner at the expo referred to them as **Professor** Fringle's Algae-Cakes, while a*

delivery truck transporting the snackfood (and the box itself) bore a logo for Oceanic Algae Cakes.

- ***Programming Robots:*** A textbook about robotics that Verne Brown referenced while writing a school essay on that subject [**BFCL-1**].

- **Projecto-Recollector:** A helmet-mounted device built by Emmett Brown in or before 1952, enabling a wearer to project thoughts onto a nearby screen [**BFAN-24**].

- **propeller helmet:** A type of gas-powered flying headgear worn by Verne Brown, and invented by his father, Emmett Brown. An opening in the ceiling of the Brown family home enabled Verne to steer the helmet to carry him outside. The contraption had a faulty flywheel, however, causing it to stall [**BFAN-1**].

- **proprietary ultrasonic subatomic molecular redistributor:** A type of cyclotron—a particle accelerator used to speed up charged particles utilizing a high-frequency, alternating voltage—created in 1991 by Emmett Brown, resembling a fancy vacuum cleaner. Using the device's cyclotronic core, the molecular redistributor stimulated atomic particles, enabling it to pull molecules apart, thus disintegrating an object. The machine also worked in reverse, rematerializing disintegrated objects.

    The scientist's goal in creating the proprietary ultrasonic subatomic molecular redistributor was to eliminate garbage dumps and landfills. He nearly wiped out mankind's existence, however, when he destroyed a meteor in 3 million B.C., inadvertently preventing the extinction of dinosaurs [**BFAN-3**].

- **Protein Flakes:** A substance that Emmett Brown fed to tuber bacteria in 1931, in order to generate the nitrogen necessary to catalyze a chemical reaction enabling him to convert alcohol to rocket fuel [**TLTL-1**].

- **Psuedonymia:** The capital city of Apocrypha, the largest empire of former North America, circa 2,991,299,129,912,991 A.D. [**BFCL-2**].

    NOTE: *Many scientists believe Earth will cease to exist in approximately 7.6 billion years, with human life dying out within a billion years or so.*

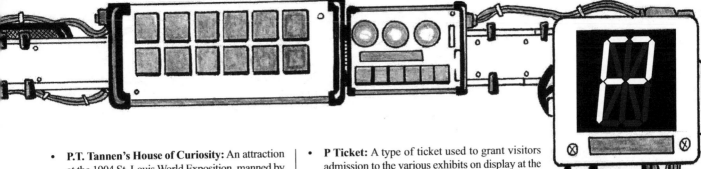

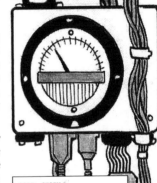

- **P.T. Tannen's House of Curiosity:** An attraction at the 1904 St. Louis World Exposition, manned by P.T. Tannen and his assistant, Clyde. The exhibit featured Marty McFly sporting ever-changing hairstyles, due to the malfunction of Emmett Brown's Haircut Omatic [**BFAN-25**].

- **P.T. Tannen's Villains Through History in Wax:** A wax-museum exhibit at the 1904 St. Louis World Exposition, run by P.T. Tannen and his assistant, Clyde. The exhibit contained the likenesses of infamous historical persons, including Attila the Hun, Ivan the Terrible and Bob the Nasty (the latter represented P.T.'s uncle, Bob Tannen).

  Unable to draw in visitors, P.T. paid passersby a nickel to attend, but soon grew tired of doing so. Upon seeing Marty McFly—who'd traveled back in time to find Emmett Brown after Doc's Haircut Omatic caused Marty to sport ever-changing hairstyles—P.T. realized people would pay to see such a freak, and kidnapped Marty as part of his next attraction, P.T. Tannen's House of Curiosity [**BFAN-25**].

- **pteranodon:** A pterosaur (flying reptile) from North America's Late Cretaceous period [**REAL**]. Emmett, Jules and Verne Brown befriended a pteranodon after journeying 3 million years into the past. The creature, which Verne nicknamed "Donny," had purple skin, green tailfeathers and tufts, and a smiling, yellow, red-banded beak, and could keep up with the DeLorean as it reached a velocity of 88 miles per hour. After the Browns returned to their own era, Verne noticed a small bird similar in appearance to Donny, an indication that pteranodons may have survived extinction [**BFAN-3**].

  NOTE: *The Cretaceous period ended 65.5 million years ago, making it highly unlikely that any pteranodons would remain by 3 million B.C.*

  It should be noted that pteranodons were not actually dinosaurs, despite Jules and Verne identifying Donny as such, but rather pterosaurs.

- **P Ticket:** A type of ticket used to grant visitors admission to the various exhibits on display at the 1931 Hill Valley Exposition [**TLTL-5**].

- **Public Enemy, The:** A 1931 film starring James Cagney, about a thug's rise up through the American criminal underworld during the Prohibition era [**REAL**]. Emmett Brown saw this movie as a youth, at Hill Valley's Town Theater, and fondly recalled Cagney's line, "Why you dirty rat." [**TLTL-4**].

  NOTE: *"Why you dirty rat," frequently misattributed to Cagney, was never spoken by the actor in* The Public Enemy*, or in any other film. His actual line was "'Why, that dirty, no-good, yellow-bellied stool.'"*

- **Puddin':** A name that Jules and Verne Brown considered for a baby Apatosaurus that Verne had found while visiting prehistoric times. Eventually, they settled on the ironic name Tiny [**BFAN-26**].

- **Pulse:** An enclosed motorcycle, or "autocycle," with two main wheels and two outrigger wheels, one on each side of the vehicle, produced by the Owosso Motor Car Co. [**REAL**]. Flying Pulses were commonly used in 2015 [**BTF2**].

- **Puttputt Miniature Golf:** A mini-golf course in Hill Valley with elaborate setups at each hole, including a laughing witch, a windmill, a dinosaur scene, firefighters dousing a blaze, an erupting volcano and more. When Marty McFly brought Jennifer Parker here for a day of fun, his wild putting caused her to be doused with water and simulated lava, which amused him more than it did her [**BFAN-25**].

  NOTE: *In the real world, the name Putt-Putt (with a hyphen) is a trademark of American minigolf franchise company Putt-Putt Fun Centers.*

QUARTER

- **Q23-A6-1:** A hover-bus route, circa 2015, that passed through Hilldale and Afton [**BTF2**].

- **Quadrant 1:** An area within the Institute of Future Technology's Anti-Gravitic Laboratory. When Biff Tannen broke into the facility to steal Emmett Brown's DeLorean, the scientist checked in with several areas, including Quadrant 1, to make sure they were secure [**RIDE**].

- **Quality Chewing Tobacco:** A smokeless tobacco product sold at Otis Peabody's farm in 1955, to be

quarters and other coins were rarely utilized. Instead, electronic payments were commonplace, using portable thumb units and similar devices [**BTF3**].

In 1985, Marty McFly donated a quarter to the Hill Valley Preservation Society's Save the Clock Tower fund, after a woman on the street thrust a donation cup in his face and handed him a flier detailing the date and time at which a lightning strike damaged the clock in 1955. This foreknowledge later proved invaluable after he was stranded in that year, enabling Emmett Brown to channel the lightning's 1.21 jigowatts of electricity into the DeLorean's Flux Capacitor and send Marty back to the future [**BTF1**].

> *NOTE: Marty's act of donating money made it possible for him later to return to his own era. As such, the first film's ending—and, thus, the events of the sequels, cartoons and video games—are entirely dependent on the exchange of a single quarter.*

- **Queen Diana:** A monarch who visited the United States in 2015, as reported by *USA Today* [**BTF2**].

> *NOTE: This likely referred to Lady Diana Spencer, who, at the time of* Back to the Future II*'s release, was the Princess of Wales and—until her divorce from Prince Charles Mountbatten-Windsor—England's future queen. In the real world, Diana died in 1997—an event the filmmakers could not have predicted—negating her ascension to the British throne.*

- **Queen of Apocrypha:** The leader of Apocrypha, the largest empire of former North America, circa 2,991,299,129,912,991 A.D. The beautiful, blonde monarch offered Tannen the Barbarian great riches if he stole for her the Ruby Begonia. He, in turn, elicited help from Marty McFly and Emmett Brown in finding the valuable jewel, in return for his assistance in freeing Doc's family from the queen's guards. When the trio delivered the ruby, however, they found the Browns well cared for, as the monarch and Clara had struck up a friendship, with Clara teaching her how to crochet [**BFCL-2**].

> *NOTE: Many scientists believe Earth will cease to exist in approximately 7.6 billion years, with human life dying out within a billion years or so.*

- ***Quiet Man, The:*** *See* Cattle Queen of Montana

placed between a person's cheek and gums, and then chewed. Peabody's barn featured a large sign advertising this product's availability [**BTF1**].

- **quarter:** A U.S. coin worth 25 cents, or one-fourth of a dollar, introduced in 1796 [**REAL**]. By 2015,

CODE	STORY
NIKE	*BTTF*-themed TV commercial: Nike
NTND	Nintendo *Back to the Future—The Ride* Mini-Game
PIZA	*BTTF*-themed TV commercial: Pizza Hut
PNBL	Data East *BTTF* pinball game
REAL	Real life
RIDE	Simulator: *Back to the Future—The Ride*
SCRM	2010 Scream Awards: *Back to the Future* 25th Anniversary Reunion (broadcast)
SCRT	2010 Scream Awards: *Back to the Future* 25th Anniversary Reunion (trailer)
SIMP	Simulator: *The Simpsons Ride*
SLOT	*Back to the Future* Video Slots
STLZ	Unused *BTTF* footage of Eric Stoltz as Marty McFly
STRY	*Back to the Future Storybook*
TEST	Screen tests: Crispin Glover, Lea Thompson and Tom Wilson
TLTL	Telltale Games' *Back to the Future—The Game*
TOPS	Topps' *Back to the Future II* trading-card set
TRIL	*BTTF: The Official Book of the Complete Movie Trilogy*
UNIV	Universal Studios Hollywood promotional video

SUFFIX	MEDIUM
-b	*BTTF2*'s Biff Tannen Museum video (extended)
-c	Credit sequence to the animated series
-d	Film deleted scene
-n	Film novelization
-o	Film outtake
-p	1955 phone book from *BTTF1*
-v	Video game print materials or commentaries
-s1	Screenplay (draft one)
-s2	Screenplay (draft two)
-s3	Screenplay (draft three)
-s4	Screenplay (draft four)
-sp	Screenplay (production draft)
-sx	Screenplay (*Paradox*)

RADIATION SUIT

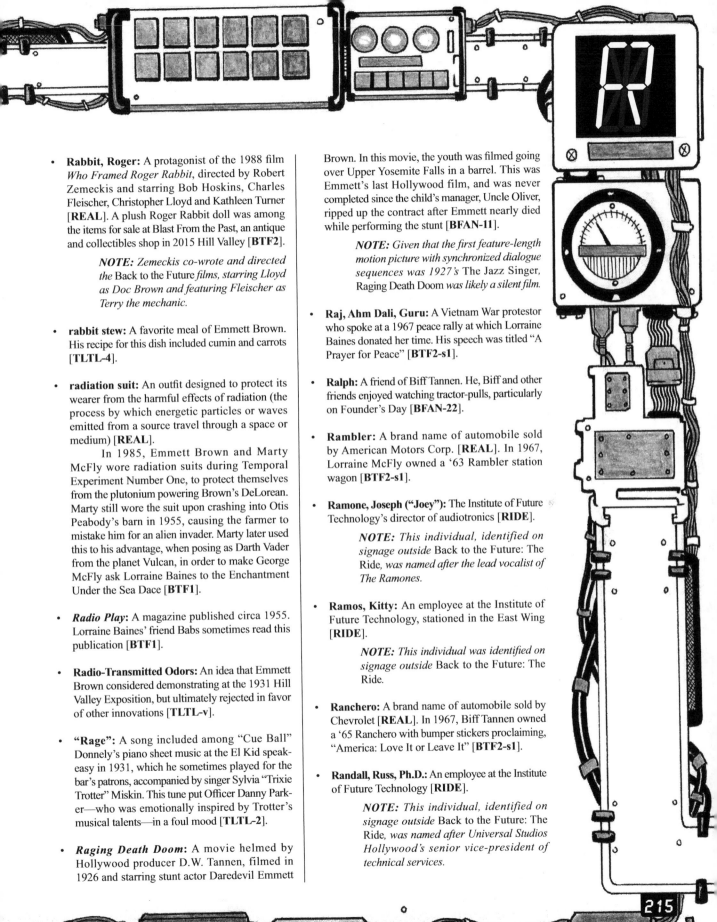

- **Rabbit, Roger:** A protagonist of the 1988 film *Who Framed Roger Rabbit*, directed by Robert Zemeckis and starring Bob Hoskins, Charles Fleischer, Christopher Lloyd and Kathleen Turner [**REAL**]. A plush Roger Rabbit doll was among the items for sale at Blast From the Past, an antique and collectibles shop in 2015 Hill Valley [**BTF2**].

  NOTE: Zemeckis co-wrote and directed the Back to the Future *films, starring Lloyd as Doc Brown and featuring Fleischer as Terry the mechanic.*

- **rabbit stew:** A favorite meal of Emmett Brown. His recipe for this dish included cumin and carrots [**TLTL-4**].

- **radiation suit:** An outfit designed to protect its wearer from the harmful effects of radiation (the process by which energetic particles or waves emitted from a source travel through a space or medium) [**REAL**].

  In 1985, Emmett Brown and Marty McFly wore radiation suits during Temporal Experiment Number One, to protect themselves from the plutonium powering Brown's DeLorean. Marty still wore the suit upon crashing into Otis Peabody's barn in 1955, causing the farmer to mistake him for an alien invader. Marty later used this to his advantage, when posing as Darth Vader from the planet Vulcan, in order to make George McFly ask Lorraine Baines to the Enchantment Under the Sea Dace [**BTF1**].

- *Radio Play*: A magazine published circa 1955. Lorraine Baines' friend Babs sometimes read this publication [**BTF1**].

- **Radio-Transmitted Odors:** An idea that Emmett Brown considered demonstrating at the 1931 Hill Valley Exposition, but ultimately rejected in favor of other innovations [**TLTL-v**].

- **"Rage":** A song included among "Cue Ball" Donnelly's piano sheet music at the El Kid speakeasy in 1931, which he sometimes played for the bar's patrons, accompanied by singer Sylvia "Trixie Trotter" Miskin. This tune put Officer Danny Parker—who was emotionally inspired by Trotter's musical talents—in a foul mood [**TLTL-2**].

- *Raging Death Doom*: A movie helmed by Hollywood producer D.W. Tannen, filmed in 1926 and starring stunt actor Daredevil Emmett

Brown. In this movie, the youth was filmed going over Upper Yosemite Falls in a barrel. This was Emmett's last Hollywood film, and was never completed since the child's manager, Uncle Oliver, ripped up the contract after Emmett nearly died while performing the stunt [**BFAN-11**].

  NOTE: Given that the first feature-length motion picture with synchronized dialogue sequences was 1927's The Jazz Singer, Raging Death Doom *was likely a silent film.*

- **Raj, Ahm Dali, Guru:** A Vietnam War protestor who spoke at a 1967 peace rally at which Lorraine Baines donated her time. His speech was titled "A Prayer for Peace" [**BTF2-s1**].

- **Ralph:** A friend of Biff Tannen. He, Biff and other friends enjoyed watching tractor-pulls, particularly on Founder's Day [**BFAN-22**].

- **Rambler:** A brand name of automobile sold by American Motors Corp. [**REAL**]. In 1967, Lorraine McFly owned a '63 Rambler station wagon [**BTF2-s1**].

- **Ramone, Joseph ("Joey"):** The Institute of Future Technology's director of audiotronics [**RIDE**].

  NOTE: This individual, identified on signage outside Back to the Future: The Ride, *was named after the lead vocalist of The Ramones.*

- **Ramos, Kitty:** An employee at the Institute of Future Technology, stationed in the East Wing [**RIDE**].

  NOTE: This individual was identified on signage outside Back to the Future: The Ride.

- **Ranchero:** A brand name of automobile sold by Chevrolet [**REAL**]. In 1967, Biff Tannen owned a '65 Ranchero with bumper stickers proclaiming, "America: Love It or Leave It" [**BTF2-s1**].

- **Randall, Russ, Ph.D.:** An employee at the Institute of Future Technology [**RIDE**].

  NOTE: This individual, identified on signage outside Back to the Future: The Ride, *was named after Universal Studios Hollywood's senior vice-president of technical services.*

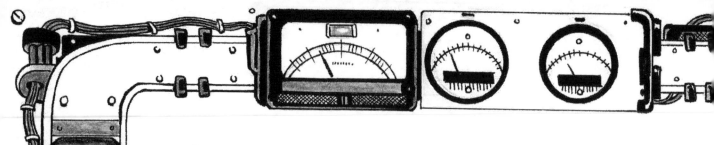

- **Raphael:** One of several names that Marty McFly and Verne Brown urged Jules Verne to adopt, since Verne (who'd been named in the novelist's honor) hated the name Verne [**BFAN-21**].

  NOTE: Raphael was one of the Teenage Mutant Ninja Turtles, who was named after Raffaello Sanzio da Urbino, an Italian architect and painter of the High Renaissance period. The turtles' first animated TV series was very popular during Verne's childhood.

- **Raven clock:** A popular style of alarm clock bearing the image of a large-bodied bird with black plumage [**REAL**]. Emmett Brown had such a clock in his home, set to chime in synch with many others [**BTF1**].

- **Reagan, Ronald Wilson, President:** A film and television actor who became the 40th president of the United States, from 1981 to 1989 [**REAL**].

  When Marty McFly visited Emmett Brown in 1955, and claimed to be from the future, the scientist challenged him to name the president in 1985. Marty replied Ronald Reagan, but Brown scoffed, asking if the vice-president, First Lady and secretary of the treasury were Jerry Lewis, Jane Wyman and Jack Benny, respectively [**BTF1**].

  A Max Headroom-style video simulacrum of Reagan greeted customers at the Café 80's, reading various menu items but sometimes interrupted by a recreation of Ayatollah Khomeini [**BTF2**].

  NOTE: Ronald Reagan was offered the role of Mayor Hubert in BTTF3, but turned it down.

- **Reagan Scramble Salad:** A menu item sold at Café 80's in 2015, named after the U.S. president [**BTF2**].

- **Reames, John:** An employee at the Institute of Future Technology [**RIDE**].

  NOTE: This individual's name appeared on signage outside Back to the Future: The Ride.

- **rear display:** A 21st-century innovation enabling a flying vehicle's driver to view behind the car by looking through a par of silver eyewear, rather than having to turn to see a mirror or glance over one's shoulder [**BTF2**].

- **Rebecca Anne:** A person buried at the Boot Hill Cemetery, near the entrance of the abandoned Delgado Mine. She died in 1892 at age 5 months [**BTF3**].

  NOTE: Rebecca Anne's surname was not included on the gravestone.

- **Rebecca's Donuts:** An eatery in Hill Valley, circa 1991, that advertised donuts for 50 cents apiece [**BFCM-4**].

- **Recording Plant:** A scientific innovation for police personnel, presented at the 1931 Hill Valley Exposition by Detective Daniel Parker, as part of the Future of Law Enforcement exhibit. The potted plant contained a button that, when pressed, could discreetly record nearby sounds, thereby helping officers to spy on criminals' conversations [**TLTL-5**].

  NOTE: In essence, the device was a 1930s analog to modern-day police recording devices.

- **Records Office:** A department of Hill Valley's local government, circa 1931 [**TLTL-5**].

- **Red:** A red-haired teenager who attended high school with George McFly, Lorraine Baines and Biff Tannen. In 1955, while stranded in the past, Marty McFly interrupted a romantic interlude between Red and his girlfriend, when he tripped over the necking couple while running through a park wearing a radiation suit. Furious, Red pummeled Marty, angry that his neighborhood was going to hell [**BTF1-s3**].

  Over the next three decades, Red became homeless. After Marty returned to 1985, he again disturbed Red as the bum slept on an outdoor bench in that same park. This time, Red muttered his disgust at "crazy drunk drivers" [**BTF1**].

  In the Biffhorrific timeline, Marty once more bumped into Red—still homeless—outside Biff Tannen's Pleasure Paradise in 1985. This time, Red called the youth a "crazy, drunk pedestrian" [**BTF2**].

  NOTE: Some Web sites have misidentified Red the bum as being the 1980s version of Frank "Red" Thomas, Hill Valley's mayor in 1955. However, a campaign-van photo of Thomas featured set decorator Hal Gausman, while the vagrant was played by George "Buck" Flower. Adding to the

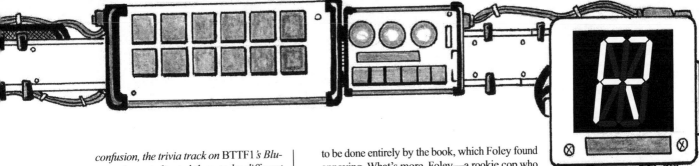

confusion, the trivia track on BTTF1's Blu-ray release indicated them to be different characters, while that same Blu-ray also showed a side-by-side comparison, implying the two Reds were the same man.

The movie's Blu-ray subtitles, meanwhile, identified this character as "Fred." Some fans have claimed that Marty called the bum "Brett," but the film's third-draft screenplay specified his name as being Red. Since that script featured Red as a young man in the '50s, it would not be feasible for him to have been Thomas, who was an adult politician at the time. The bum would be far too young in 1985 to have been the mayor's visible age 30 years prior—by the '80s, Thomas would have been a very old man.

It's possible that Red may have been Thomas' son, thus explaining their shared nickname. However, there is no evidence to confirm or deny such a relationship.

- **Red Ryder Cowboy Carbine:** A BB gun manufactured by Daisy Outdoor Products, introduced in 1938 and popularized by the film *A Christmas Story* [**REAL**]. An advertisement for this product appeared on the back of the comic book *Tales From Space #8* [**BTF1**].

- **Reese, Agent:** A special agent with the Nuclear Regulatory Commission (N.R.C.) who investigated Emmett Brown's theft of plutonium in 1985, with his partner, Agent Foley [**BTF1-s1**].

    > **NOTE:** *As a running joke, Bob Gale and Robert Zemeckis have included police officers and agents named Reese and Foley in many scripts throughout their careers.*

- **Reese, Officer:** A member of the Hill Valley Police force, circa 2015, who patrolled the streets with her partner, Officer Foley, forming Unit N11-11. When Emmett Brown left Jennifer Parker asleep in an alleyway, Foley and Reese found her unconscious and assumed her to be a drug user. Mistaking Jennifer for her older self—and assuming she'd received rejuvenation therapy to retain her youth—the duo delivered Jen to the home she and Marty shared in that era [**BTF2**].
    Reese and Foley rarely agreed about anything, partly due to Reese's fanaticism regarding rules and regulations—everything had

to be done entirely by the book, which Foley found annoying. What's more, Foley—a rookie cop who often empathized with those in poorer areas, like Hilldale—felt that Reese had lost her humanity after years spent on the job [**BTF2-n**].

- **Reese, Officer:** A Hill Valley beat cop in 1967 who greatly disliked the Hippie movement, complaining that he couldn't tell the men from the women [**BTF2-s1**].

- ***Reference Quarterly (RQ):*** A magazine for library professionals [**REAL**]. After altering the past by making his father more assertive, Marty McFly had a copy of this periodical in his bedroom [**BTF1, TLTL-1**].

    > **NOTE:** *It's unclear why Marty would have such a magazine in his possession, unless he was planning, in the altered timeline, to become a librarian.*

- ***Reflexology:*** A book in the personal library of Emmett Brown, circa 1992 [**BFAN-17**].

    > **NOTE:** *Reflexology is an alternative medicine involving the application of pressure to a person's hands, feet or ears, sans oils or lotions.*

- **Reginald:** The drummer of Marvin Berry and the Starlighters, a musical group that performed at the Enchantment Under the Sea Dance in 1955 [**BTF1**]. He had a tendency to lock the group's car keys in the trunk of the band's Cadillac, much to Berry's frustration [**BTF1-n**].

    > **NOTE:** *Berry spoke Reginald's name while Marty McFly was locked in the car's trunk, and BTTF1's subtitles also identified him by that name. In the movie's first-draft script, Reginald was called Sax, with the name "Reginald" held by another character, Reginald Washington.*

- **Reginald ("Reg," "Reggie"):** An orphaned street urchin in London who, in 1845, frequented the Hogshead Tavern and worked as a pickpocket for an unscrupulous thug named Murdock. When Emmett Brown's family visited Reg's era, the youth picked Jules Brown's pocket, stealing a watch fob once owned by Jules' great-grandfather, which contained the keys to Doc's DeLorean.
    In order to retrieve the watch, Jules and his brother Verne worked alongside Reginald as

CODE	STORY
NIKE	*BTTF*-themed TV commercial: Nike
NTND	Nintendo *Back to the Future—The Ride* Mini-Game
PIZA	*BTTF*-themed TV commercial: Pizza Hut
PNBL	Data East *BTTF* pinball game
REAL	Real life
RIDE	Simulator: *Back to the Future—The Ride*
SCRM	2010 Scream Awards: *Back to the Future 25th Anniversary Reunion* (broadcast)
SCRT	2010 Scream Awards: *Back to the Future 25th Anniversary Reunion* (trailer)
SIMP	Simulator: *The Simpsons Ride*
SLOT	*Back to the Future Video Slots*
STLZ	Unused *BTTF* footage of Eric Stoltz as Marty McFly
STRY	*Back to the Future Storybook*
TEST	Screen tests: Crispin Glover, Lea Thompson and Tom Wilson
TLTL	Telltale Games' *Back to the Future—The Game*
TOPS	Topps' *Back to the Future II* trading-card set
TRIL	*BTTF: The Official Book of the Complete Movie Trilogy*
UNIV	Universal Studios Hollywood promotional video

SUFFIX	MEDIUM
-b	*BTTF2*'s Biff Tannen Museum video (extended)
-c	Credit sequence to the animated series
-d	Film deleted scene
-n	Film novelization
-o	Film outtake
-p	1955 phone book from *BTTF1*
-v	Video game print materials or commentaries
-s1	Screenplay (draft one)
-s2	Screenplay (draft two)
-s3	Screenplay (draft three)
-s4	Screenplay (draft four)
-sp	Screenplay (production draft)
-sx	Screenplay (*Paradox*)

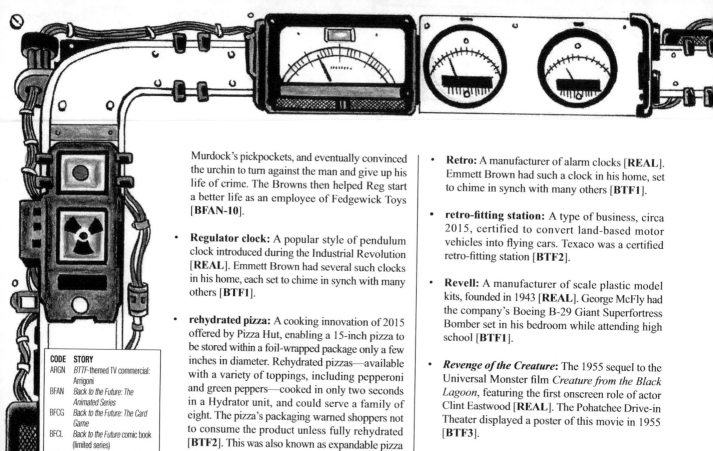

Murdock's pickpockets, and eventually convinced the urchin to turn against the man and give up his life of crime. The Browns then helped Reg start a better life as an employee of Fedgewick Toys [**BFAN-10**].

- **Regulator clock:** A popular style of pendulum clock introduced during the Industrial Revolution [**REAL**]. Emmett Brown had several such clocks in his home, each set to chime in synch with many others [**BTF1**].

- **rehydrated pizza:** A cooking innovation of 2015 offered by Pizza Hut, enabling a 15-inch pizza to be stored within a foil-wrapped package only a few inches in diameter. Rehydrated pizzas—available with a variety of toppings, including pepperoni and green peppers—cooked in only two seconds in a Hydrator unit, and could serve a family of eight. The pizza's packaging warned shoppers not to consume the product unless fully rehydrated [**BTF2**]. This was also known as expandable pizza [**BTF2-n**].

- **Rejuvenation Clinic:** A type of business popular in 2015, at which customers could restore their lost youth. Emmett Brown visited such a clinic, receiving an All-Natural Overhaul consisting of skin-wrinkle removal, hair repair, blood changing and the replacement of his spleen and colon, thereby adding 30 or 40 years to his life [**BTF2**].

- **Reno:** The county seat of Washoe County, Nevada [**REAL**]. Arthur McFly and Sylvia "Trixie Trotter" Miskin were wed in this city in 1931 [**TLTL-5**].

- **Research Lab, The:** A facility in a society of intelligent dinosaurs that evolved after Emmett Brown inadvertently prevented the dinosaurs' extinction [**BFAN-3**]. The lab was located in or near Dinocity, that reality's version of Hill Valley [**BFHM**].

  When a pair of dinosaur police officers noticed Brown and his family in the flying DeLorean, one cop, an Allosaurus called Officer Tannnen, decided to sell the car to the Research Lab. The other officer protested, knowing its strange occupants (Doc's family) would be dissected. Eventually, the Browns escaped this fate [**BFAN-3**].

- **Reset:** A switch used to reboot the time circuits of a device built by Emmett Brown to turn a DeLorean DMC-12 sports car into a time machine [**BTF1**].

- **Retro:** A manufacturer of alarm clocks [**REAL**]. Emmett Brown had such a clock in his home, set to chime in synch with many others [**BTF1**].

- **retro-fitting station:** A type of business, circa 2015, certified to convert land-based motor vehicles into flying cars. Texaco was a certified retro-fitting station [**BTF2**].

- **Revell:** A manufacturer of scale plastic model kits, founded in 1943 [**REAL**]. George McFly had the company's Boeing B-29 Giant Superfortress Bomber set in his bedroom while attending high school [**BTF1**].

- *Revenge of the Creature*: The 1955 sequel to the Universal Monster film *Creature from the Black Lagoon*, featuring the first onscreen role of actor Clint Eastwood [**REAL**]. The Pohatchee Drive-in Theater displayed a poster of this movie in 1955 [**BTF3**].

- **R&G Records:** A record label to which Marty McFly planned to send an audition tape for his high school rock band, The Pinheads. Initially, Marty lacked the courage to mail it out, but after altering time so that his family was more successful and motivated, he decided to take a chance and send it [**BTF1-s4**].

  > ***NOTE:*** *In BTTF1's fourth-draft screenplay, Marty was preparing the tape to accompany an application to Northwestern Music Academy, which was changed to R&G Records in a revised fourth-draft script.*
  >
  > *The results of this audition are unknown, though he was attending college during the animated series, set six years after the trilogy's "present-day" scenes, which may indicate that the audition was unsuccessful.*
  >
  > *Back to the Future—The Card Game revealed that The Pinheads did enjoy success as a musical group, which may or may not have been with R&G Records.*

- **Richey, Dave:** An employee at the Institute of Future Technology, stationed in the West Wing [**RIDE**].

  > ***NOTE:*** *This individual was identified on signage outside* Back to the Future: The Ride.

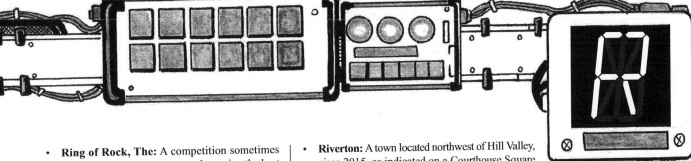

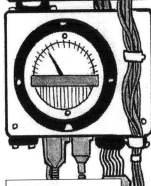

- **Ring of Rock, The:** A competition sometimes staged by Hill Valley teens to determine the best guitarist. In Citizen Brown's dystopian timeline, Marty McFly challenged Jennifer Parker's boyfriend, Leech, to the Ring of Rock, hoping to gain Jennifer's love. The battle was fierce, ending only when Leech fell into a dumpster, making Marty the winner—both of the contest, and of Jen's affections [**TLTL-3**].

- **Rising Sun:** A model of hoverboard sold in 2015. Chester "Whitey" Nogura owned such a board [**BTF2**].

- **Rivera, Julio:** A temporary inhabitant affiliator at the Institute of Future Technology [**RIDE**].

    > *NOTE: This individual, identified on signage outside* Back to the Future: The Ride, *was named after a Universal Studios employee.*

- **Riverburg Big Dudes:** A baseball team that sometimes competed against the Hill Valley Dreamers—and often won, given the Dreamers' inability to score [**BFAN-25**].

- **"River Pirates, The":** A comic book story featuring fictional crime reporter Joe Condon, published in *Headline Comics* #67, in September/October 1954 [**BTF1**].

- **River Road Tunnel:** A tunnel in Hill Valley leading from the suburban section of town to Hill Valley High School. Marty McFly passed through this tunnel while hiding in Biff Tannen's car in 1955, in order to retrieve *Grays Sports Almanac* from him, and later returned to the tunnel during a second attempt. The second time, Marty rode alongside Biff's car on a hoverboard, and was nearly killed in the process [**BTF2**].

    > *NOTE:* Back to the Future II*'s novelization called this Deacon's Hill Tunnel, but the name River Road Tunnel was used onscreen.*

- **Riverside Drive:** A street in Hill Valley, circa 1955, located a block past Maple (or John F. Kennedy Drive, as Maple would later be renamed). Emmett Brown lived on this road, at number 1640 [**BTF1**].

    > *NOTE: In the initial draft of* BTTF1*'s screenplay, the scientists lived at 2980 Monroe Avenue.*

- **Riverton:** A town located northwest of Hill Valley, circa 2015, as indicated on a Courthouse Square map [**BTF2**].

- **R. Nelson Photographic Art Studio:** A Hill Valley-based photography business, circa 1885, that offered ambrotypes (photographs creating a positive image on a sheet of glass via the wet-plate collodion process), frames, scenery images, lifesize photos and "Indian portraits." A photographer for this studio took pictures at the Hill Valley Festival, including a shot of Marty McFly and Emmett Brown standing in front of the new Clock Tower. By 1985, this photo was stored in the Hill Valley Historical Society's archives [**BTF3**].

- **"Robbie":** The first short story of science fiction author Isaac Asimov to deal with robotics, published in 1939 [**REAL**]. Verne Brown referenced this tale while writing a school essay on that subject [**BFCL-1**].

- **Robert:** A wild rattlesnake cared for by Windjammer Diefendorfer, circa 1888. The kindly old man sometimes bathed Robert, despite the danger involved. Marty McFly assisted in the snake's bath while visiting Diefendorfer's home [**BFAN-21**].

- **Robinson's:** A department-store chain founded in 1881, which was acquired by May Department Stores Co. in 1986, and rebranded as Macy's in 2005 [**REAL**]. A Robinson's store was located outside Hill Valley's Twin Pines Mall in 1985, a year before the acquisition [**BTF1**].

    > *NOTE: In Telltale Games'* BTTF *video game, Marty McFly had a dream in which the store was called Rubarbison's.*

- **Robinson, E.:** A name printed on the doorbell of a small apartment used by gangster Irving "Kid" Tannen to hide Arthur McFly from the police in 1931 [**TLTL-1**].

- **Robogriddle:** An invention of Jules Brown that utilized five robotic arms to automatically produce flapjacks at high speed, from batter-pouring to table service [**BFAN-16**].

- **Robot:** A multi-volume series of books published by Time Life, detailing the robotics industry. Verne Brown referenced this series while writing a school essay on that subject [**BFCL-1**].

CODE	STORY
NIKE	*BTTF*-themed TV commercial: Nike
NTND	Nintendo *Back to the Future—The Ride* Mini-Game
PIZA	*BTTF*-themed TV commercial: Pizza Hut
PNBL	Data East *BTTF* pinball game
REAL	Real life
RIDE	Simulator: *Back to the Future—The Ride*
SCRM	2010 Scream Awards: *Back to the Future 25th Anniversary Reunion* (broadcast)
SCRT	2010 Scream Awards: *Back to the Future 25th Anniversary Reunion* (trailer)
SIMP	Simulator: *The Simpsons Ride*
SLOT	*Back to the Future Video Slots*
STLZ	Unused *BTTF* footage of Eric Stoltz as Marty McFly
STRY	*Back to the Future Storybook*
TEST	Screen tests: Crispin Glover, Lea Thompson and Tom Wilson
TLTL	Telltale Games' *Back to the Future—The Game*
TOPS	Topps' *Back to the Future II* trading-card set
TRIL	*BTTF: The Official Book of the Complete Movie Trilogy*
UNIV	Universal Studios Hollywood promotional video

SUFFIX	MEDIUM
-b	*BTTF2*'s Biff Tannen Museum video (extended)
-c	Credit sequence to the animated series
-d	Film deleted scene
-n	Film novelization
-o	Film outtake
-p	1955 phone book from *BTTF1*
-v	Video game print materials or commentaries
-s1	Screenplay (draft one)
-s2	Screenplay (draft two)
-s3	Screenplay (draft three)
-s4	Screenplay (draft four)
-sp	Screenplay (production draft)
-sx	Screenplay (*Paradox*)

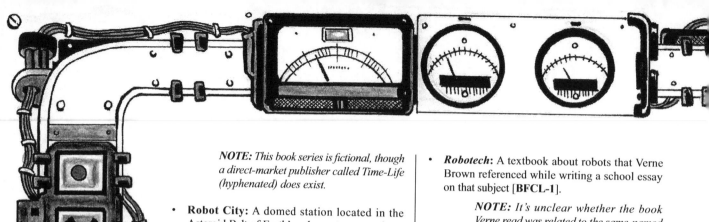

NOTE: This book series is fictional, though a direct-market publisher called Time-Life (hyphenated) does exist.

- **Robot City:** A domed station located in the Asteroid Belt of Earth's solar system, on a large rock between the orbits of Mars and Jupiter. When Verne Brown showed an interest in robotics, his father, Emmett Brown, took their family on a journey to the year 2585, to visit Robot City so that Verne could see the technology in action.

   Upon arrival, the Browns discovered a robotic revolution in progress against the local political leader, Governor Tannen, and the lazy human citizens who oppressed the machines. Sympathizing with the robots' plight, Verne convinced them to stop attacking humanity and helped them overcome slavery by reprogramming them to ignore any human commands they deemed unworthy of following.

   Following the rebellion, the robots vowed to make Tannen and other humans exercise more and eat better, and to spend less time watching holovision [**BFCL-1**].

   NOTE: The android and robotic citizens of Robot City included a number of iconic characters from science fiction TV series and films, including Mecha-Kong (King Kong Escapes), R2-D2 (Star Wars), Twiki (Buck Rogers in the 25th Century), Robby (Forbidden Planet), Gort (The Day the Earth Stood Still) and Woody Allen's robotic household butler (Sleeper), as well as a drone similar to Silent Running's Dewey, Huey and Louie models.

- **Robot History:** A textbook about robots that Verne Brown referenced while writing a school essay on that subject [**BFCL-1**].

- **Robot Recycling Center:** A facility in Robot City, a domed community located in the Asteroid Belt of Earth's solar system, circa 2585. All robots deemed too old or out of style were sent to the center to destroy themselves in a large crushing mechanism [**BFCL-1**].

- **Robot Visions:** A 1990 collection of short stories written by science fiction author Isaac Asimov [**REAL**]. Verne Brown referenced this work while writing a school essay on the subject of robotics [**BFCL-1**].

- **Robotech:** A textbook about robots that Verne Brown referenced while writing a school essay on that subject [**BFCL-1**].

   NOTE: It's unclear whether the book Verne read was related to the same-named Japanese anime series.

- **Robotic:** A textbook about robots that Verne Brown referenced while writing a school essay on that subject [**BFCL-1**].

- **Robotic Dictionary:** A textbook about robots that Verne Brown referenced while writing a school essay on that subject [**BFCL-1**].

- **Robotics:** A textbook about robots that Verne Brown referenced while writing a school essay on that subject [**BFCL-1**].

- **"Robots":** An essay about robotics, written by Verne Brown in 1991. Although the child did not generally receive good grades in school, he scored an A- on this paper, to the disbelief of his family, thanks to his keen interest in the subject [**BFCL-1**].

- **Robots: Fact & Fiction:** A textbook about robotics that Verne Brown referenced while writing a school essay on that subject [**BFCL-1**].

- **Robots in Films:** A textbook about robotics that Verne Brown referenced while writing a school essay on that subject [**BFCL-1**].

- **Rochester:** A U.S. city in which the Small Town Professional Wrasslin organization was headquartered [**BFAN-24**].

   NOTE: It's unknown in which particular Rochester the facility was located, as there are several within the United States.

- **ROCK:** A tattoo on the arm of Marty's rival, Leech, in Citizen Brown's dystopian timeline. The tattoo featured the word "ROCK," stylized over a skull with an eight-ball on its forehead [**TLTL-3**].

- **Rocket Car:** A flying vehicle invented by Emmett Brown. The scientist built a prototype of the device in 1931, at age 17, intending to unveil it at that year's Hill Valley Exposition. Emmett tested the contraption in Courthouse Square, with the help of his future dog, Einstein, who'd been left behind after Marty McFly and Emmett's older self had returned to their own era.

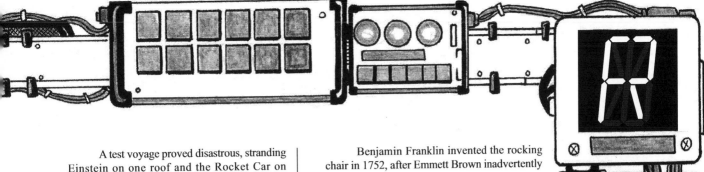

A test voyage proved disastrous, stranding Einstein on one roof and the Rocket Car on another, so Brown abandoned the invention for many years [**TLTL-2**]. Ultimately, he deemed the vessel's rocket propulsion system too unreliable, and abandoned this line of research [**TLTL-4**].

> *NOTE: BTTF1's initial screenplay draft indicated Doc had designed a flying car called an Aero-Mobile. It's unknown whether these were intended to be the same invention, or whether he was responsible for the use of flying vehicles by 2015.*

- **Rocket Jet:** *See* Rocket-Powered Drill

- **Rocket-Powered Drill:** An invention of Emmett Brown, which he created at age 17 after reading Jules Verne's *Journey to the Center of the Earth* [**TLTL-1**]. Other names for the device included Jet-drill [**TLTL-2**] and Rocket Jet [**TLTL-v**].

    Emmett applied for a patent for the Rocket-Powered Drill, but never heard back from the U.S. Patent Office, and thus abandoned the project until 1931, when his time-traveling older self was arrested and learned that he'd soon be killed by gangsters. The elder scientist sent Marty McFly to procure the device from his younger analog, so that he could break out of jail and escape his grim fate.

    Posing as a Patent Office representative, Marty visited the youth, saying he needed to see the drill to evaluate it before he could award a patent. Though excited, Emmett lamented that he lacked the necessary fuel: 190-proof grain alcohol, difficult to obtain during Prohibition. Marty helped the teen obtain the hooch from gangster Irving "Kid" Tannen's speakeasy, then used the Rocket-Powered Drill to break the older Doc Brown from prison. Young Emmett was crestfallen to discover that he would not receive a patent, as promised [**TLTL-1**].

- **Rocket-Powered Skates:** A type of footwear worn by Jules Brown, and invented by his father, Emmett Brown. The skates propelled Jules at high speeds, sometimes resulting in his crashing through the doors of his family's home [**BFAN-1**].

- **rocking chair:** A type of seat utilizing a curved band of wood attached to the bottom of each leg, enabling an occupant to soothingly rock back and forth by shifting weight or pushing lightly with his or her feet [**REAL**].

Benjamin Franklin invented the rocking chair in 1752, after Emmett Brown inadvertently wrecked the man's home, causing a chair to land on two curved barrel boards. Finding the rocking motion pleasing, Franklin considered several names, including the to-and-fro chair, the back-and-forth chair and the rocking seat. He hit upon the final nomenclature after a rock fell on his head [**BFAN-6**].

> *NOTE: Historically, Franklin has often been credited with inventing the rocking chair, though this has never been definitively proven.*

- **rocking seat:** *See* rocking chair

- **Rogers, Roy:** An American singer and cowboy actor, born Leonard Franklin Slye. Rogers was a star of more than 100 movies [**REAL**].

    Emmett Brown watched Roy Rogers' films as a youth, sitting in Saturday matinees. Thus, when choosing clothing for Marty McFly to wear in 1885, Doc picked out an outfit that matched what he'd seen onscreen—but that was wildly out of fashion for the Old West, thus making Marty a laughing-stock [**BTF3-n**].

- **Roller Board:** *See* skateboard

- **Rolling Stones, The:** A British rock-and-roll band formed in the 1960s, considered one of the most commercially and critically successful groups in music history [**REAL**]. The Stones' music, like all rock-and-roll, was deemed illegal by Edna Strickland in Citizen Brown's dystopian timeline [**TLTL-3**].

- **Rolls-Royce:** A British manufacturer of luxury automobiles [**REAL**].

    Marty McFly was involved in a traffic accident with a Rolls-Royce in 1985 after being called a chicken, injuring his hand and destroying his chance at having a musical career [**BTF2**]. Forewarned that his life would be ruined in this manner, Marty opted out of a race with Douglas J. Needles, thereby avoiding the collision with the Rolls-Royce and changing his fate for the better [**BTF3**].

    Irving "Kid" Tannen owned a Rolls-Royce in an alternate timeline in which he and his sons, Biff, Riff and Cliff, formed the notorious Tannen Gang. Its license plate read TANNEN1 [**TLTL-2**].

CODE	STORY
NIKE	*BTTF*-themed TV commercial: Nike
NTND	Nintendo *Back to the Future—The Ride* Mini-Game
PIZA	*BTTF*-themed TV commercial: Pizza Hut
PNBL	Data East *BTTF* pinball game
REAL	Real life
RIDE	Simulator: *Back to the Future—The Ride*
SCRM	2010 Scream Awards: *Back to the Future* 25th Anniversary Reunion (broadcast)
SCRT	2010 Scream Awards: *Back to the Future* 25th Anniversary Reunion (trailer)
SIMP	Simulator: *The Simpsons Ride*
SLOT	*Back to the Future Video Slots*
STLZ	Unused *BTTF* footage of Eric Stoltz as Marty McFly
STRY	*Back to the Future Storybook*
TEST	Screen tests: Crispin Glover, Lea Thompson and Tom Wilson
TLTL	Telltale Games' *Back to the Future—The Game*
TOPS	Topps' *Back to the Future II* trading-card set
TRIL	*BTTF: The Official Book of the Complete Movie Trilogy*
UNIV	Universal Studios Hollywood promotional video

SUFFIX	MEDIUM
-b	*BTTF2*'s Biff Tannen Museum video (extended)
-c	Credit sequence to the animated series
-d	Film deleted scene
-n	Film novelization
-o	Film outtake
-p	1955 phone book from *BTTF1*
-v	Video game print materials or commentaries
-s1	Screenplay (draft one)
-s2	Screenplay (draft two)
-s3	Screenplay (draft three)
-s4	Screenplay (draft four)
-sp	Screenplay (production draft)
-sx	Screenplay (*Paradox*)

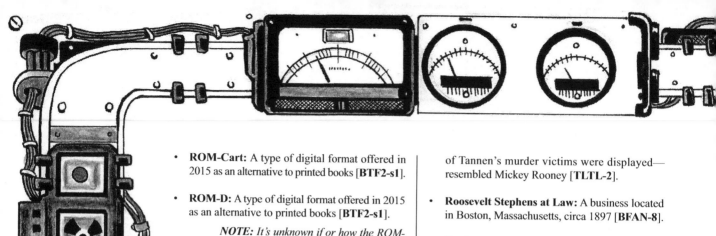

- **ROM-Cart:** A type of digital format offered in 2015 as an alternative to printed books [**BTF2-s1**].

- **ROM-D:** A type of digital format offered in 2015 as an alternative to printed books [**BTF2-s1**].

  > *NOTE: It's unknown if or how the ROM-Cart and ROM-D formats differed.*

- **Rome:** A city in Italy, and the heart of the ancient Roman Empire [**REAL**].

  Emmett Brown visited Rome in the year 36 A.D., accompanied by Marty McFly (using the alias Marticus), to research the city's arcades and update his records of that period. Jules and Verne Brown, confusing the term "arcades" as referring to video games, followed them back in time. The brothers helped to free a slave named Judah Ben-Hur from captivity, while Marty accidentally offended a Roman officer, Bifficus Antanneny, by spilling food on the man's tunic.

  The soldier challenged Marty to a chariot race at the Circus Maximus. Realizing Bifficus had to win for the rise of Caligula and the fall of the Empire to occur as recorded (his power was vital in Caligula becoming emperor), Doc advised Marty to lose the race. When the emperor allowed Antanneny, the victor, to decide Marty's fate, the officer asked that he be fed to the lions. Marty and the Browns, however, escaped in Doc's DeLorean [**BFAN-5**].

  > *NOTE: The emperor was not named onscreen. Historically, the Empire's leader in that year—and Caligula's predecessor—was Tiberius Julius Caesar Augustus.*

- **Ronco Aroma Amplifier:** An invention of Emmett Brown, consisting of a funnel connected to an electronic box, and a hose running out the other side and attaching to a user's nose. The amplifier enabled a wearer—such as Doc's dog, Einstein—to track a person based on scent [**BTF2-s1**].

  > *NOTE: Ronco, founded in 1964 by Ron Popeil, manufactures and sells a wide range of products, including kitchen devices. It's unknown whether Doc sold the device to the company.*

- **Rooney, Mickey:** An American actor and entertainer of film, stage and television [**REAL**]. Lounge singer Sylvia "Trixie Trotter" Miskin noted that a caricature of Marty McFly—drawn by Zane Williams for the Wall of Honor at Irving "Kid" Tannen's speakeasy, on which portraits

of Tannen's murder victims were displayed—resembled Mickey Rooney [**TLTL-2**].

- **Roosevelt Stephens at Law:** A business located in Boston, Massachusetts, circa 1897 [**BFAN-8**].

- **Roris von Hinklehofen's Flying Circus:** A stunt-pilot troop that operated in Milwaukee, Wisconsin, circa 1926. As a child, Emmett Brown inadvertently performed a stunt-flying routine at this circus during the filming of a movie, after the line of his fishing pole snagged a passing stunt plane. As a result, the youth was hired by Hollywood talent scout Harvey Wannamaker, who transformed him into child star and marketing sensation Daredevil Emmett Brown [**BFAN-11**].

- **Rosenfield, Steve:** An employee at the Institute of Future Technology, stationed in the West Wing [**RIDE**].

  > *NOTE: This individual, identified on signage outside* Back to the Future: The Ride*, was named after the construction manager of Universal Studios' amusement-park ride.*

- **Rosie:** The beautiful older sister of Dorothy, Verne Brown's dance instructor. She had long, fiery red hair, which drew the unwanted attentions of Sergeant Frank Tannen, a dim-witted U.S. soldier. While visiting 1944 with Marty McFly, Verne met Rosie's younger self as she and Dorothy tended to Hill Valley's Victory Garden [**BFAN-17**].

- **Ross:** A business located cross the street from Hill Valley's Twin Pines Mall, circa 1985 [**BTF1**].

- **Ross, General:** A ranking military officer whose name Emmett Brown forged in order to access an atomic bomb test site in Atkins, Nevada, in 1952, so he could use radiation from a nuclear blast to send Marty McFly back to the future [**BTF1-s2**].

- **Ross Dress for Less:** A store at the Twin Pines Mall, circa 1985 [**BTF1**].

- **Rossie, Matt:** An employee at the Institute of Future Technology, in charge of constructivist determination [**RIDE**].

  > *NOTE: This individual's name appeared on signage outside* Back to the Future: The Ride*.*

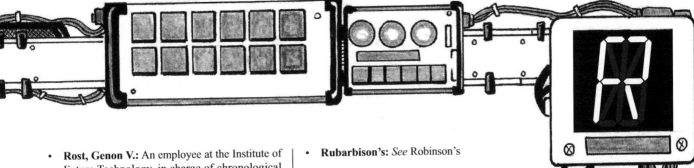

- **Rost, Genon V.:** An employee at the Institute of Future Technology, in charge of chronological inevitabilities [**RIDE**].

  NOTE: This individual, identified on signage outside Back to the Future: The Ride, *was named after employee Genon Murray, who worked on the project team that built Universal Studios.*

- **Rotary International:** A global service-club organization [**REAL**] that operated a chapter in Hill Valley [**BTF1**].

- **Route 295:** *See* U.S. Route 295

- **Route 395:** *See* U.S. Route 395

- **Route 8:** *See* U.S. Route 8

- **Roxy, The:** A theater located in Hill Valley [**BFAN-9, BFAN-12, BFAN-14**]. In 1992, popular band Walk DMC played a sold-out concert at this venue. Marty McFly tried, but failed, to get tickets to this show for his girlfriend, Jennifer Parker [**BFAN-14**]. The theater was still in operation in 2585 [**BFCL-1**].

  NOTE: Issue #4 of Harvey Comics' monthly BTTF *comic book called this theater the Roxy Cinegog, which was once a popular theater in Victoria, British Columbia, Canada.*

- **Roy:** A soldier in the Union Army, circa 1864, who fought in the American Civil War under General Ulysses S. Clayton. His younger cousin, Jimmy, was a drummer-boy for the Confederate forces of General Beauregard Tannen. Roy was stocky and bald, with a missing tooth, a thick Boston accent and deep forehead creases [**BFAN-1**].

- **Roy's Records:** A record store located in Courthouse Square, circa 1955 [**BTF1**].

- *RQ:* See Reference Quarterly (RQ)

- ***Rubáiyát of Omar Khayyám, The:*** The title of a book containing the works of Persian poet Omar Khayyám, as translated by Edward FitzGerald [**REAL**]. In 1955, Lorraine Baines was holding this book when Marty McFly introduced her to George McFly in the hallway of Hill Valley High School [**BTF1**].

- **Rubarbison's:** *See* Robinson's

- **Rubinstein, Norman:** One of several professionals who helped to compile material for *Grays Sports Almanac: Complete Sports Statistics 1950-2000* [**BTF2**].

  NOTE: This individual was named on the book's title page.

- **Ruby Begonia, The:** A priceless, flower-shaped jewel carved from an enormous gemstone, set in a platinum base. The jewel was thought to be protected by wizardry. In 2,991,299,129,912,991 A.D., the queen of Apocrypha promised Tannen the Barbarian great riches if he stole it for her from the Enchanted Tower.

  Believing Marty McFly and Emmett Brown to be sorcerers, Tannen agreed to help free Doc's captured family from the queen, in return for their assistance in bypassing the enchantment spell. Although the ruby was guarded by a giant green serpent, the theft was successful [**BFCL-2**].

  NOTE: Many scientists believe Earth will cease to exist in approximately 7.6 billion years, with human life dying out within a billion years or so.

- **Rumore, Christina:** An employee at the Institute of Future Technology, assigned as the facility's frivolity generator [**RIDE**].

  NOTE: This individual, identified on signage outside Back to the Future: The Ride, *was named after a performer at Universal Studios Hollywood and Universal Studios Florida.*

- *R.U.R.:* A 1921 play by Czech writer Karel Čapek, noted for first coining the term "robot" [**REAL**]. Verne Brown referenced this work while writing a school essay on the subject of robotics [**BFCL-1**].

- **Rusy:** A business located in Hill Valley, circa 1991 [**BFAN-12**].

- **Ruth, George Herman Jr. ("Babe"):** An American Major League baseball player for the Boston Red Sox, the New York Yankees and the Boston Braves [**REAL**]. Emmett Brown considered Ruth the greatest player who ever lived [**BFAN-1**].

- **Ruth's Frock Shop:** A business in Courthouse Square, circa 1955. By 1985, this store was replaced with Goodwill Industries [**BTF1, BTF-2**].

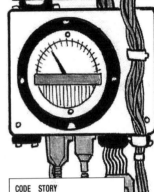

STRICKLAND, GERALD

(CENTER, WITH JAMES AND EDNA)

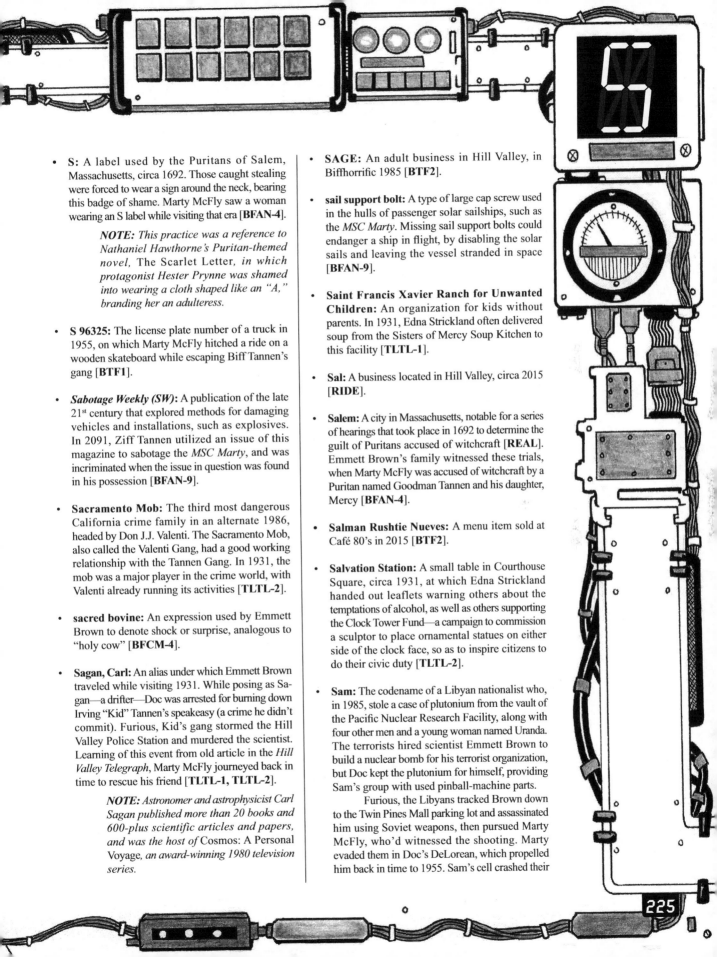

- **S:** A label used by the Puritans of Salem, Massachusetts, circa 1692. Those caught stealing were forced to wear a sign around the neck, bearing this badge of shame. Marty McFly saw a woman wearing an S label while visiting that era [**BFAN-4**].

    > **NOTE:** *This practice was a reference to Nathaniel Hawthorne's Puritan-themed novel,* The Scarlet Letter, *in which protagonist Hester Prynne was shamed into wearing a cloth shaped like an "A," branding her an adulteress.*

- **S 96325:** The license plate number of a truck in 1955, on which Marty McFly hitched a ride on a wooden skateboard while escaping Biff Tannen's gang [**BTF1**].

- ***Sabotage Weekly (SW):*** A publication of the late 21st century that explored methods for damaging vehicles and installations, such as explosives. In 2091, Ziff Tannen utilized an issue of this magazine to sabotage the *MSC Marty*, and was incriminated when the issue in question was found in his possession [**BFAN-9**].

- **Sacramento Mob:** The third most dangerous California crime family in an alternate 1986, headed by Don J.J. Valenti. The Sacramento Mob, also called the Valenti Gang, had a good working relationship with the Tannen Gang. In 1931, the mob was a major player in the crime world, with Valenti already running its activities [**TLTL-2**].

- **sacred bovine:** An expression used by Emmett Brown to denote shock or surprise, analogous to "holy cow" [**BFCM-4**].

- **Sagan, Carl:** An alias under which Emmett Brown traveled while visiting 1931. While posing as Sagan—a drifter—Doc was arrested for burning down Irving "Kid" Tannen's speakeasy (a crime he didn't commit). Furious, Kid's gang stormed the Hill Valley Police Station and murdered the scientist. Learning of this event from old article in the *Hill Valley Telegraph*, Marty McFly journeyed back in time to rescue his friend [**TLTL-1, TLTL-2**].

    > **NOTE:** *Astronomer and astrophysicist Carl Sagan published more than 20 books and 600-plus scientific articles and papers, and was the host of* Cosmos: A Personal Voyage, *an award-winning 1980 television series.*

- **SAGE:** An adult business in Hill Valley, in Biffhorrific 1985 [**BTF2**].

- **sail support bolt:** A type of large cap screw used in the hulls of passenger solar sailships, such as the *MSC Marty*. Missing sail support bolts could endanger a ship in flight, by disabling the solar sails and leaving the vessel stranded in space [**BFAN-9**].

- **Saint Francis Xavier Ranch for Unwanted Children:** An organization for kids without parents. In 1931, Edna Strickland often delivered soup from the Sisters of Mercy Soup Kitchen to this facility [**TLTL-1**].

- **Sal:** A business located in Hill Valley, circa 2015 [**RIDE**].

- **Salem:** A city in Massachusetts, notable for a series of hearings that took place in 1692 to determine the guilt of Puritans accused of witchcraft [**REAL**]. Emmett Brown's family witnessed these trials, when Marty McFly was accused of witchcraft by a Puritan named Goodman Tannen and his daughter, Mercy [**BFAN-4**].

- **Salman Rushtie Nueves:** A menu item sold at Café 80's in 2015 [**BTF2**].

- **Salvation Station:** A small table in Courthouse Square, circa 1931, at which Edna Strickland handed out leaflets warning others about the temptations of alcohol, as well as others supporting the Clock Tower Fund—a campaign to commission a sculptor to place ornamental statues on either side of the clock face, so as to inspire citizens to do their civic duty [**TLTL-2**].

- **Sam:** The codename of a Libyan nationalist who, in 1985, stole a case of plutonium from the vault of the Pacific Nuclear Research Facility, along with four other men and a young woman named Uranda. The terrorists hired scientist Emmett Brown to build a nuclear bomb for his terrorist organization, but Doc kept the plutonium for himself, providing Sam's group with used pinball-machine parts.

    Furious, the Libyans tracked Brown down to the Twin Pines Mall parking lot and assassinated him using Soviet weapons, then pursued Marty McFly, who'd witnessed the shooting. Marty evaded them in Doc's DeLorean, which propelled him back in time to 1955. Sam's cell crashed their

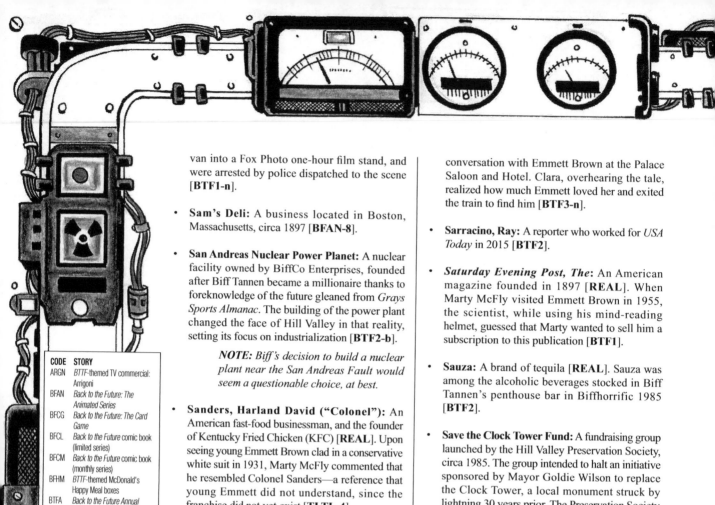

van into a Fox Photo one-hour film stand, and were arrested by police dispatched to the scene [**BTF1-n**].

- **Sam's Deli:** A business located in Boston, Massachusetts, circa 1897 [**BFAN-8**].

- **San Andreas Nuclear Power Planet:** A nuclear facility owned by BiffCo Enterprises, founded after Biff Tannen became a millionaire thanks to foreknowledge of the future gleaned from *Grays Sports Almanac*. The building of the power plant changed the face of Hill Valley in that reality, setting its focus on industrialization [**BTF2-b**].

  > *NOTE: Biff's decision to build a nuclear plant near the San Andreas Fault would seem a questionable choice, at best.*

- **Sanders, Harland David ("Colonel"):** An American fast-food businessman, and the founder of Kentucky Fried Chicken (KFC) [**REAL**]. Upon seeing young Emmett Brown clad in a conservative white suit in 1931, Marty McFly commented that he resembled Colonel Sanders—a reference that young Emmett did not understand, since the franchise did not yet exist [**TLTL-4**].

- **San Diego:** The second largest city in California, and the eighth largest in the United States [**REAL**]. In 1931, MacPherson Instruments was located in San Diego [**TLTL-4**].

- **San Diego Padres:** A California-based Major League baseball team [**REAL**]. The Padres were Marty McFly's favorite team [**BTF1-n**].

- **San Fernando Valley:** An urbanized valley in the Los Angeles metropolitan area of southern California [**REAL**]. In 1991, a business called THOR was headquartered here [**BFAN-12**].

- **San Onofre Nuclear Power Plant:** *See* Pacific Nuclear Research Facility

- **San Quentin State Prison:** A California Department of Corrections and Rehabilitation state prison for men, located in San Quentin, California [**REAL**]. Irving "Kid" Tannen was sentenced to a life sentence at this facility in 1932 [**TLTL-1**].

- **Sara:** One of two names (along with Cara) that a barbed-wire salesman mistook for Clara Clayton's in 1885, while telling a fellow traveler about his

conversation with Emmett Brown at the Palace Saloon and Hotel. Clara, overhearing the tale, realized how much Emmett loved her and exited the train to find him [**BTF3-n**].

- **Sarracino, Ray:** A reporter who worked for *USA Today* in 2015 [**BTF2**].

- ***Saturday Evening Post, The:*** An American magazine founded in 1897 [**REAL**]. When Marty McFly visited Emmett Brown in 1955, the scientist, while using his mind-reading helmet, guessed that Marty wanted to sell him a subscription to this publication [**BTF1**].

- **Sauza:** A brand of tequila [**REAL**]. Sauza was among the alcoholic beverages stocked in Biff Tannen's penthouse bar in Biffhorrific 1985 [**BTF2**].

- **Save the Clock Tower Fund:** A fundraising group launched by the Hill Valley Preservation Society, circa 1985. The group intended to halt an initiative sponsored by Mayor Goldie Wilson to replace the Clock Tower, a local monument struck by lightning 30 years prior. The Preservation Society believed that the clock's damaged nature should be maintained for posterity [**BTF1**].

  In 1931, a similar grass-roots campaign, known as the Clock Tower Fund, had been created by Edna Strickland to commission a sculptor to place ornamental gargoyle statues on either side of the clock face, in order to inspire citizens to do their civic duty [**TLTL-2**]. In 2015, an elderly citizen named Terry took part in another such campaign, to raise the support needed to preserve the tower as an historic landmark [**BTF2**].

- **Savoy:** A movie theater in Hill Valley, circa 1944 [**BFAN-17**].

  > *NOTE: An actual theater known as the Savoy is located in London, England.*

- **sawdust dog food:** A type of pet chow served by one of Emmett Brown's inventions, the Canine Cafeteria. Although it was made from sawdust, dogs happily ate it [**RIDE**].

- **sawdust pancakes:** A food product produced by one of Emmett Brown's inventions, the Automated Flapjack Maker. The recipe failed to thrill those who tried the pancakes, resulting in the contraption's failure to catch on [**RIDE**].

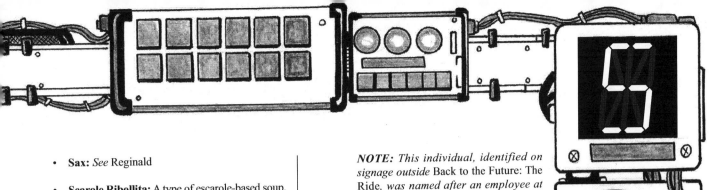

- **Sax:** *See* Reginald

- **Scarole Ribollita:** A type of escarole-based soup. "Cue Ball" Donnely, a member of Irving "Kid" Tannen's gang in 1931, followed a "secret recipe" to make the soup for the mob's front business at the Sisters of Mercy Soup Kitchen—namely, using cabbage instead of escarole. Despite Donnely's determination to make the soup tasty by adding various spices, the concoction was barely edible [**TLTL-1**].

    In Citizen Brown's dystopian timeline, the SoupMo restaurant served this same soup 50 years later [**TLTL-3**].

- **Scat Hovercraft:** A type of motor vehicle used in 2015, utilizing hover technology and surrounded at the bottom by a black plastic skirt [**BTF2, TOPS**].

- **Scenery Channel:** A 21st-century scenescreen channel that broadcast beautiful outdoor views, 24 hours a day, circa 2015. The Scenery Channel created the illusion of pleasant scenery outside a home's window, regardless of the surroundings. Marty and Jennifer McFly utilized this channel to beautify the view at their home, but the device was broken, resulting in images interrupted by static [**BTF2**].

- **scenescreen:** A 21st-century innovation that projected images onto a house's windows, enabling a homeowner to control the view outside. Subscribing to the Scenery Channel provided a variety of scenescreen settings [**BTF2**].

- **Scent Dispenser:** A type of equipment used in Citizen Brown's dystopian timeline, as part of the Personality Rebuild process utilized in Citizen Plus Program reconditioning. The Scent Dispenser dispelled various substances into the air from a trio of Aroma Tanks, in order to influence a person's reactions to stimuli [**TLTL-4**].

- **Schlander, Susan:** A retail technician at the Institute of Future Technology [**RIDE**].

    NOTE: This individual, identified on signage outside Back to the Future: The Ride, *was named after Universal Studios Hollywood's administration manager.*

- **Schmidt, James, Doctor:** An employee at the Institute of Future Technology [**RIDE**].

    NOTE: This individual, identified on signage outside Back to the Future: The Ride, *was named after an employee at Universal Studios.*

- **Schneider, Chuck:** An employee at the Institute of Future Technology, stationed in the West Wing [**RIDE**].

    NOTE: This individual was identified on signage outside Back to the Future: The Ride.

- **Schwinn Bicycle Shop:** A business in Courthouse Square, circa 1955 [**BTF2**].

- *Science*: A book in the personal library of Emmett Brown, circa 1992 [**BFAN-17**].

- *Science Fiction Theater*: An American sci-fi anthology television series that aired from 1955 to 1957 [**REAL**]. George McFly considered *Science Fiction Theater* his favorite TV show while attending high school [**BTF1**].

- **Science Journal:** A series of broadcasts recorded by Emmett Brown to educate students about various facets of science [**BFAN-10**]. These recordings, created with help from a television producer named B.G. [**BFAN-23**], were often accompanied by appended Video Encyclopedia files featuring scientist Bill Nye [**BFAN-1 to BFAN-26**].

    The Science Journal provided ongoing audio-visual scientific documentation [**BFAN-8**], and was filmed using a camera optics device known as an auto-iris [**BFAN-4**]. Doc sometimes broadcast these entries from the past, via sub-ether transmission linkup [**BFAN-3**].

    NOTE: See the Video Encyclopedia entry on page 273 for more information.

- **scientists of the future:** A term used by Emmett Brown, referring to students who viewed files in his Video Encyclopedia database [**BFAN-1 to BFAN-26**].

    NOTE: It's unclear whether Doc actually broadcast his videos to students in the future, or if he simply meant that they would one day grow up to become scientists thanks to his teachings.

- **Scissors Lock:** A type of wrestling move favored by Verne Brown. When he tried it on Tiny—his

CODE	STORY
NIKE	*BTTF*-themed TV commercial: Nike
NTND	Nintendo *Back to the Future—The Ride* Mini-Game
PIZA	*BTTF*-themed TV commercial: Pizza Hut
PNBL	Data East *BTTF* pinball game
REAL	Real life
RIDE	Simulator: *Back to the Future—The Ride*
SCRM	2010 Scream Awards: *Back to the Future 25th Anniversary Reunion* (broadcast)
SCRT	2010 Scream Awards: *Back to the Future 25th Anniversary Reunion* (trailer)
SIMP	Simulator: *The Simpsons Ride*
SLOT	*Back to the Future Video Slots*
STLZ	Unused *BTTF* footage of Eric Stoltz as Marty McFly
STRY	*Back to the Future Storybook*
TEST	Screen tests: Crispin Glover, Lea Thompson and Tom Wilson
TLTL	Telltale Games' *Back to the Future—The Game*
TOPS	Topps' *Back to the Future II* trading-card set
TRIL	*BTTF: The Official Book of the Complete Movie Trilogy*
UNIV	Universal Studios Hollywood promotional video

SUFFIX	MEDIUM
-b	*BTTF2*'s Biff Tannen Museum video (extended)
-c	Credit sequence to the animated series
-d	Film deleted scene
-n	Film novelization
-o	Film outtake
-p	1955 phone book from *BTTF1*
-v	Video game print materials or commentaries
-s1	Screenplay (draft one)
-s2	Screenplay (draft two)
-s3	Screenplay (draft three)
-s4	Screenplay (draft four)
-sp	Screenplay (production draft)
-sx	Screenplay (*Paradox*)

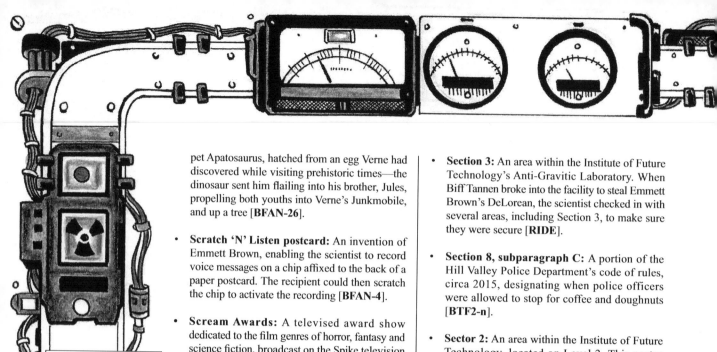

pet Apatosaurus, hatched from an egg Verne had discovered while visiting prehistoric times—the dinosaur sent him flailing into his brother, Jules, propelling both youths into Verne's Junkmobile, and up a tree [**BFAN-26**].

- **Scratch 'N' Listen postcard:** An invention of Emmett Brown, enabling the scientist to record voice messages on a chip affixed to the back of a paper postcard. The recipient could then scratch the chip to activate the recording [**BFAN-4**].

- **Scream Awards:** A televised award show dedicated to the film genres of horror, fantasy and science fiction, broadcast on the Spike television station from 2006 until 2011 [**REAL**].

  In 1985, as a group of teenagers attended a Loverboy concert at Los Angeles' Greek Theatre, a time-traveling DeLorean suddenly arrived outside the entrance. As the excited teens ran toward the vehicle, the occupant—clad in a radiation suit—switched the car's time circuits to bring him to the site of the 2010 Scream Awards [**SCRM**].

  Marty McFly attended the 2010 show, using the DeLorean to get there. A female passerby asked where he was headed, and after telling her, Marty offered her a "lift" [**SCRT**].

  NOTE: It's unknown who the woman was, or whether she accompanied Marty to the Scream Awards.

- **Screwboard:** *See* Pit Bull

- **scrotes:** A slang term popular in 2015, meaning "testicles" or "scrotum," and used to denote courage (as in "you got no scrotes") [**BTF2**].

- **Sea of Tranquility (a.k.a. Mare Tranquillitatis):** A large, dark, basaltic plain within the Tranquillitatis basin of Earth's moon [**REAL**]. Emmett Brown and his wife, Clara Clayton Brown, sometimes gazed at the Sea of Tranquility through a telescope on the roof of their home in Hill Valley [**BFAN-9**].

- **Second Street:** A road that ran through Hill Valley, intersecting Main Street at Courthouse Square [**BTF1**].

- **Second Street Gunsmith Shop:** A firearms dealer located on Second Street, in Hill Valley, circa 1885. Buford Tannen posed for a photograph in front of this shop after killing several men [**BTF3**].

- **Section 3:** An area within the Institute of Future Technology's Anti-Gravitic Laboratory. When Biff Tannen broke into the facility to steal Emmett Brown's DeLorean, the scientist checked in with several areas, including Section 3, to make sure they were secure [**RIDE**].

- **Section 8, subparagraph C:** A portion of the Hill Valley Police Department's code of rules, circa 2015, designating when police officers were allowed to stop for coffee and doughnuts [**BTF2-n**].

- **Sector 2:** An area within the Institute of Future Technology, located on Level 2. This sector contained Emmett Brown's Anti-Gravitic Laboratory [**RIDE**].

- **Sector L:** A section of Hill Valley in Citizen Brown's dystopian timeline. The McFly family lived in this particular sector, along with other "common" folk. A duty roster, posted each week, indicated citizens' assigned cleaning tasks, thereby keeping Hill Valley pristine [**TLTL-3**].

- **Sector X:** A section of Hill Valley in Citizen Brown's dystopian timeline, to which unfortunate families considered "hopeless cases" were assigned to live [**TLTL-3**].

- **Seeburg Select-O-Matic:** A vintage style of jukebox [**REAL**]. Emmett Brown had such a jukebox in his home in 1985 [**BTF1**].

- **Seen and Not Heard:** A game played by Puritan children in Salem, Massachusetts, circa 1692. This diversion involved a contest to see who could stand still and silent for the longest time. While stranded in that era, Jules Brown learned how to play from local Puritan kids, and considered himself a natural, given his understanding of the laws of inertia. His brother, Verne, did not find the game as interesting as he did [**BFAN-4**].

- **Seiko:** A Japanese watch manufacturer [**REAL**]. Scientist Emmett Brown used a pair of Seiko stopwatches to measure the passage of time, both aboard his time-traveling DeLorean and in real time, during Temporal Experiment Number One [**BTF1**].

- **Selee, Frank Gibson:** The manager of the Boston Beaneaters, circa 1897 [**REAL**]. A short, stout

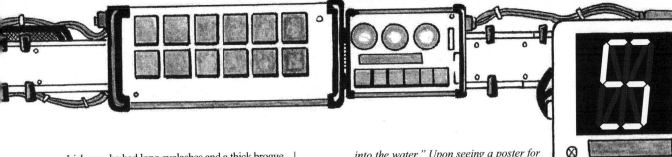

Irishman, he had long eyelashes and a thick brogue [**BFAN-8**].

> *NOTE: In the real world, Selee actually managed the team that year. The real Selee, however, did not resemble his animated counterpart.*

• **Self-Cleaning Windows:** An idea that Emmett Brown considered demonstrating at the 1931 Hill Valley Exposition, but ultimately rejected in favor of other innovations [**TLTL-v**].

• **Self-Watering Onion-Potatoes:** A type of hybrid vegetable created by Emmett Brown. The onions made the potatoes' eyes water [**BFAN-20**].

• **Service Station:** A roadside business along a highway outside Hill Valley, circa 1931. Marty McFly passed this station while trying to help Emmett Brown escape from a police vehicle stolen by Irving "Kid" Tannen, who planned to murder the scientist [**TLTL-1**].

• **Seventh Dimension, The:** A Euclidean construct for a hypothetical seventh dimension of space. A power surge in Emmett Brown's Extradimensional Storage Closet sent the Brown family, as well as Marty McFly, on a trip through the Seventh Dimension, causing them to jump around randomly in time and space. Only when they began thinking in seven dimensions could they control their destination [**BFCL-3**].

• **SFY:** A phrase scrawled in graffiti on the entrance to Lyon Estates, circa 1985 [**BTF1**]. This same word appeared on the Lyon Estates entrance in the Biffhorrific timeline [**BTF2**].

• **Shady Acres Rest Home:** A mental-health facility in Hill Valley. In 1931, Edna Strickland often delivered soup from the Sisters of Mercy Soup Kitchen to this facility [**TLTL-1**].

> *NOTE: Shady Acres is a common setting in television shows and films.*

• **Shark:** A motion picture shown at Hill Valley's Essex Theater in 1931, starring Cooper Jackson and Claire Stephens. Its tagline: "You will never bathe in the ocean again" [**TLTL-1**].

> *NOTE: This film paid homage to the tagline of Stephen Spielberg's* Jaws, *"Just when you thought it was safe to go back*

into the water." Upon seeing a poster for this movie, Marty McFly commented that the shark looked real—an homage to his noting, in Back to the Future III, *that the shark in* Jaws 19 *looked fake.*

• **Sharp, Bill:** A disk jockey at a radio station broadcast in Hill Valley, circa 1985. His repertoire included music by Eddie Fisher and Patti Page [**BTF1-n**].

• **Shatner, William Alan:** A Canadian-born actor and author, famous for his roles on *Star Trek*, *T.J. Hooker* and *Boston Legal* [**REAL**]. Mistaking Emmett Brown for an extraterrestrial in 1992, Biff Tannen threatened to call the police, the U.S. Air Force and William Shatner [**BFAN-23**].

• **Sheepish Schoolboy:** A hair style offered at The Combformist, a Hill Valley business in Citizen Brown's dystopian timeline [**TLTL-v**].

• **Sheldon, Ben, P.E.:** An employee at the Institute of Future Technology [**RIDE**].

> *NOTE: This individual, identified on signage outside* Back to the Future: The Ride, *was named after the senior vice-president of engineering at Universal Studios' Islands of Adventure.*

• **Sheldon, Sidney:** An American television show writer and novelist [**REAL**]. Emmett Brown read one of his books in 1991, while avoiding activities that might use up his brain power [**BFCM-4**].

• **Shemp:** The simian pet of Emmett Brown, circa 1982 [**BTF1-s1, BTF1-s2**].

> *NOTE: Shemp—named after Samuel Horwitz "Shemp" Howard, a member of The Three Stooges comedy team—appeared in* BTTF1*'s early-draft screenplays. In draft one, he was a Capuchin (or "organ-grinder monkey"), while draft two changed his species to chimpanzee. Onscreen, Doc's pet was a dog named Einstein.*

• **Sherwin-Williams Co.:** An American business in the general building-materials industry, focused on the manufacture, distribution and sale of paints, coatings and related products [**REAL**]. The company operated a shop in Courthouse Square, circa 1985 [**BTF1**].

CODE	STORY
NIKE	*BTTF*-themed TV commercial: Nike
NTND	Nintendo *Back to the Future—The Ride* Mini-Game
PIZA	*BTTF*-themed TV commercial: Pizza Hut
PNBL	Data East *BTTF* pinball game
REAL	Real life
RIDE	Simulator: *Back to the Future—The Ride*
SCRM	2010 Scream Awards: *Back to the Future* 25th Anniversary Reunion (broadcast)
SCRT	2010 Scream Awards: *Back to the Future* 25th Anniversary Reunion (trailer)
SIMP	Simulator: *The Simpsons Ride*
SLOT	*Back to the Future Video Slots*
STLZ	Unused *BTTF* footage of Eric Stoltz as Marty McFly
STRY	*Back to the Future Storybook*
TEST	Screen tests: Crispin Glover, Lea Thompson and Tom Wilson
TLTL	Telltale Games' *Back to the Future—The Game*
TOPS	Topps' *Back to the Future II* trading-card set
TRIL	*BTTF: The Official Book of the Complete Movie Trilogy*
UNIV	Universal Studios Hollywood promotional video

SUFFIX	MEDIUM
-b	*BTTF2*'s Biff Tannen Museum video (extended)
-c	Credit sequence to the animated series
-d	Film deleted scene
-n	Film novelization
-o	Film outtake
-p	1955 phone book from *BTTF1*
-v	Video game print materials or commentaries
-s1	Screenplay (draft one)
-s2	Screenplay (draft two)
-s3	Screenplay (draft three)
-s4	Screenplay (draft four)
-sp	Screenplay (production draft)
-sx	Screenplay (*Paradox*)

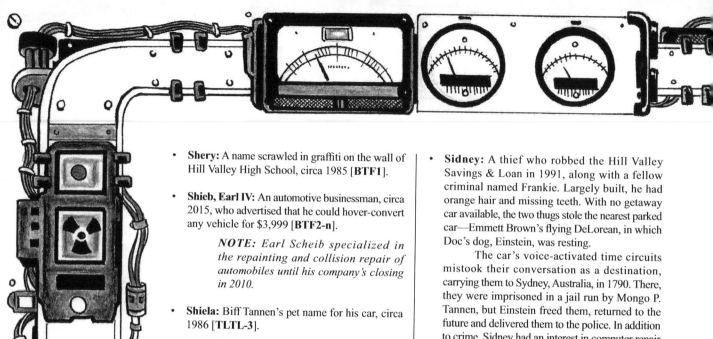

- **Shery:** A name scrawled in graffiti on the wall of Hill Valley High School, circa 1985 [**BTF1**].

- **Shieb, Earl IV:** An automotive businessman, circa 2015, who advertised that he could hover-convert any vehicle for $3,999 [**BTF2-n**].

    NOTE: Earl Scheib specialized in the repainting and collision repair of automobiles until his company's closing in 2010.

- **Shiela:** Biff Tannen's pet name for his car, circa 1986 [**TLTL-3**].

- **Shonash Ravine:** A landform in Hill Valley, so named by the area's Native American population. The Shonash Ravine was renamed Clayton Ravine following Clara Clayton's death in one possible timeline, and Eastwood Ravine following the disappearance of Clint Eastwood (Marty McFly's alias in 1885) in another. A bridge was constructed over the ravine by the Central Pacific Railroad, which was completed in the summer of 1886 [**BTF3**].

    NOTE: Paradox, a combined screenplay for both sequel films, dubbed this landform Carson Ravine.

- **Shops:** A shopping plaza in Hill Valley. Marty McFly sometimes rode his hoverboard past this complex [**BFAN-c**].

    NOTE: It's unclear if this plaza, featured in the opening credits of the animated series, was intended to be the Lone Pine Mall. The sign above its entrance read simply "Shops."

- **shred that:** A dismissive phrase popular among teenagers, circa 2015, analogous to "forget that" or "screw that" [**BTF2-sx, BTF2-n**].

- **Shrew, The:** A gangster murdered by Irving "Kid" Tannen, sometime in or before 1931. Following the man's death, Kid's bartender, Zane Williams, drew a caricature for his speakeasy's Wall of Honor, with the caption "The Shrew. Didn't burrow deep enough" [**TLTL-2**].

- **SHUTOFF:** A button on an overhead console of Emmett Brown's DeLorean [**TLTL-5**].

- **Sidney:** A thief who robbed the Hill Valley Savings & Loan in 1991, along with a fellow criminal named Frankie. Largely built, he had orange hair and missing teeth. With no getaway car available, the two thugs stole the nearest parked car—Emmett Brown's flying DeLorean, in which Doc's dog, Einstein, was resting.

    The car's voice-activated time circuits mistook their conversation as a destination, carrying them to Sydney, Australia, in 1790. There, they were imprisoned in a jail run by Mongo P. Tannen, but Einstein freed them, returned to the future and delivered them to the police. In addition to crime, Sidney had an interest in computer repair technology, having seen broadcasts about it on late-night television [**BFAN-7b**].

- **Sierra Nevada:** A mountain range in the U.S. states of California and Nevada [**REAL**]. Hill Valley was located at the base of Sierra Nevada, according to a map of the city [**BTF3**].

- **Sight Sound and Mind:** A business in Courthouse Square, circa 2015 [**BTF2**].

- **Signs:** A sign-making shop in Hill Valley, circa 1885, located next to Marshal James Strickland's office [**BTF3**].

- **Silver, Long John:** A pirate acquainted with Mac the Black, circa 1697. His signature was tattooed on Mac's chest [**BFAN-14**].

    NOTE: Long John Silver was a fictional antagonist in Robert Louis Stevenson's novel Treasure Island.

- **Silver City:** A U.S. city in which Clara Clayton was widowed sometime in or before 1885 [**BTF3-s1**].

    NOTE: It's unclear in which Silver City this occurred, as there are several within the United States.

- **simian business:** An expression used by Emmett Brown to describe the trouble his children got into when unsupervised, analogous to "monkey business" [**BFAN-9**].

- **Simon, B.:** A contact person at a company listed in a 1991 help-wanted ad that Emmett Brown read while trying to find a job. The business was located at 23251 Mulholland Drive, in Woodland

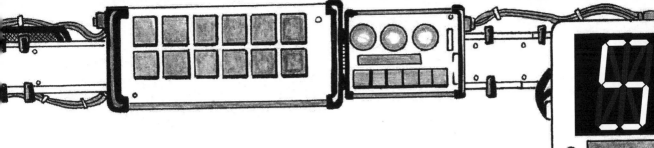

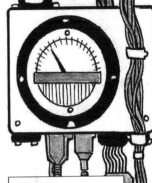

Hills, California, 91365. The position was for a programming analyst [**BFAN-12**].

- **Simple Orange:** A biodegradable cleaning product [**REAL**]. In Citizen Brown's dystopian timeline, Lorraine McFly used Simple Orange to clean a statue of Citizen Brown [**TLTL-3**].

- **Simpson, Bart:** One of several names that Marty McFly and Verne Brown urged Jules Verne to adopt, since Verne (who'd been named in the novelist's honor) hated the name Verne [**BFAN-21**].

  > *NOTE: Bart Simpson is a character on the animated series* The Simpsons, *which was very popular during Verne's childhood. Back to the Future has crossed over with that series, as Emmett Brown appeared in Universal Studios'* The Simpsons Ride, *in queue footage explaining the replacement of BTTF: The Ride with that attraction.*
  >
  > *The video featured Doc interacting with The Simpsons' Krusty the Clown and Professor John I.Q. Nerdelbaum Frink. In addition, actor Dan Castellaneta (the voice of Homer Simpson) portrayed Doc in the BTTF animated series.*

- **Simpson Segmental Voltmeter:** A gauge on Emmett Brown's giant guitar amplifier, used to measure the system's Primary Power level, from 100 to 130 [**BTF1**].

- **Simulex:** A business in Courthouse Square, circa 2015 [**BTF2**].

- **Sir Randolph:** A brand of cigarettes manufactured in 1955. While dining with his mother's family in that year, Marty McFly saw a commercial in which a surgeon promoted the Sir Randolph brand, claiming its tobacco flavor soothed his nerves and improved his circulation after a long day spent performing lung operations [**BTF1-d**].

  > *NOTE: This fake commercial, starring John McCook, was produced for* Back to the Future *but was cut before the film's release, though it did appear in the novelization. The deleted scene was announced as being included on the movie's initial DVD release, but was later removed. Fans discovered the file on the disc, however, and have made it available online.*

*In the film's third-draft screenplay, the commercial was for Old Gold cigarettes, though this was changed to Sir Randolph by draft four. The novelization named the brand Sir **Walter** Randolph, which did not match the physician's dialog, either in the screenplay or onscreen.*

- **Sir Walter Randolph:** *See* Sir Randolph

- **"Sister Christian":** A power ballad recorded in 1984 by hard-rock band Night Ranger [**REAL**]. Upon meeting singer Trixie Trotter in 1931, Marty McFly asked if she knew this song, to which she responded, "I don't do religious tunes" [**TLTL-2**].

  > *NOTE: It would have been impossible for Trixie to know this song, given the era.*

- **Sisters of Mercy Soup Kitchen:** An establishment in Hill Valley that offered free soup to the hungry, and also promised salvation. Edna Strickland made soup deliveries from this soup kitchen to the Hill Valley Orphanage, the Saint Francis Xavier Ranch for Unwanted Children, the Foggy Mountain Home for the Incurably Insane, the Shady Acres Rest Home and others. In 1931, mobster Irving "Kid" Tannen took over the soup kitchen as a front organization for his gang's Prohibition-era speakeasy [**TLTL-1**].

- **"Sixteen Tons":** A popular tune recorded by Tennessee Ernie Ford [**REAL**]. In 1955, Roy's Records, located in Courthouse Square, sold recordings of this tune [**BTF1**].

- **Six-Wheel Van:** A model of Freeway Flyer, circa 2015 [**BTF2**].

  > *NOTE: This name appeared in production materials included on BTTF2's Blu-ray release.*

- **S.J.:** The initials of a person who carved his or her initials into a police desk at a jail in Chicago's South Side, sometime in or before 1927 [**BFCM-1**].

- **skateboard:** A specially constructed plywood board with a polyurethane coating and four small wheels, used for the extreme sport of skateboarding [**REAL**].

  Marty McFly utilized a skateboard to get from one place to another in Hill Valley, sometimes "skitching" rides on the backs of passing vehicles.

CODE	STORY
NIKE	*BTTF*-themed TV commercial: Nike
NTND	Nintendo *Back to the Future—The Ride* Mini-Game
PIZA	*BTTF*-themed TV commercial: Pizza Hut
PNBL	Data East *BTTF* pinball game
REAL	Real life
RIDE	Simulator: *Back to the Future—The Ride*
SCRM	2010 Scream Awards: *Back to the Future* 25th Anniversary Reunion (broadcast)
SCRT	2010 Scream Awards: *Back to the Future* 25th Anniversary Reunion (trailer)
SIMP	Simulator: *The Simpsons Ride*
SLOT	*Back to the Future Video Slots*
STLZ	Unused *BTTF* footage of Eric Stoltz as Marty McFly
STRY	*Back to the Future Storybook*
TEST	Screen tests: Crispin Glover, Lea Thompson and Tom Wilson
TLTL	Telltale Games' *Back to the Future—The Game*
TOPS	Topps' *Back to the Future II* trading-card set
TRIL	*BTTF: The Official Book of the Complete Movie Trilogy*
UNIV	Universal Studios Hollywood promotional video

SUFFIX	MEDIUM
-b	*BTTF2's* Biff Tannen Museum video (extended)
-c	Credit sequence to the animated series
-d	Film deleted scene
-n	Film novelization
-o	Film outtake
-p	1955 phone book from *BTTF1*
-v	Video game print materials or commentaries
-s1	Screenplay (draft one)
-s2	Screenplay (draft two)
-s3	Screenplay (draft three)
-s4	Screenplay (draft four)
-sp	Screenplay (production draft)
-sx	Screenplay (*Paradox*)

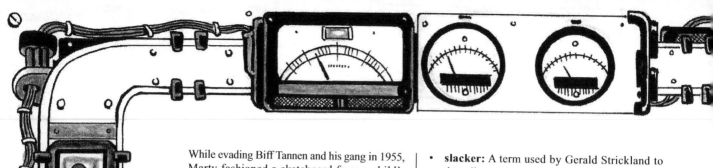

While evading Biff Tannen and his gang in 1955, Marty fashioned a skateboard from a child's wooden-crate scooter, to the amazement of all who witnessed him riding it [**BTF1**].

One of Biff's gang members, 3-D, decided to steal the idea and market it as a Roller Board [**BTF1-s4**].

> *NOTE: It's unknown whether 3-D changed history by stealing the skateboard design.*
>
> *BTTF1's fourth-draft screenplay established that the skateboard Marty used onscreen was not his own, but rather belonged to his friend, Weeze.*
>
> *After several children in Australia were injured while mimicking Marty's skateboard habits, Michael J. Fox filmed a public-service announcement warning of the dangers of skitching.*

- **Skin:** A pornographic movie deemed illegal in Citizen Brown's dystopian timeline. Confiscated VHS copies of *Skin* were discarded in Decycling Bins and stored in an underground control room by Edna Strickland [**TLTL-3**].

- **Skinhead:** *See* Joey ("Skinhead")

- **Skulls:** A gang that frequented Biff Tannen's Pleasure Paradise in Biffhorrific 1985. Members of the Skulls dressed all in black, with leather jackets or vests bearing a triple-skull logo [**BTF2-d**].

- **skuzball:** An insult used in 2015 [**BTF2**].

- **Skyramp 35:** A Hill Valley roadway entrance for flying vehicles, circa 2015 [**RIDE**].

- **Skyway 35:** A road leading into Hill Valley, circa 2015, intended for flying vehicles. Skyway 35, running underneath a sign welcoming visitors to the city, had four hover lanes and a 20-foot maximum height, with no hovering allowed [**RIDE**].

- **Skyway Condition:** A real-time monitor mounted in Courthouse Square, circa 2015, advising flying car operators regarding the skyway's driving conditions, as well as ozone and humidity levels, and local driving laws [**BTF2**].

- **skyway flier:** Another name for a flying car, in use circa 2015 [**BTF2**].

- **slacker:** A term used by Gerald Strickland to describe students at Hill Valley High School who misbehaved or showed a lack of ambition. Strickland considered both George and Marty McFly to be slackers [**BTF1, BTF2**].

- **slamball:** A type of sport popular in 2015. *USA Today* covered the slamball playoffs in October of that year, held in Denver, Colorado [**BTF2**]. The antigravity sport involved players trying to smack each other with a ball while wearing "grip shoes" and running around spherical courts, on walls and upside-down [**BTF2-s2**].

  > *NOTE: In an early-draft script for* Back to the Future II, *Griff Tannen's gang chased Marty McFly into a slamball court, where Marty's Nike grip-shoes enabled him to run up curved walls and escape.*

- **Slappy:** A name scrawled in graffiti on the entrance to Lyon Estates in Biffhorrific 1985, in which the housing development was a slum. This individual was romantically involved with someone named Frog [**BTF2**].

- **Sleep-Inducing Alpha-Rhythm Generator:** A device used in 2015 to instantly put a person to sleep. When Jennifer Parker asked too many questions about her future, Emmett Brown utilized the generator to render her unconscious. He later used it on Marty McFly Jr. as well, to keep him unconscious while Marty Sr. took his place [**BTF2**].

- **Sleeping Beauty:** A classic fairytale involving a beautiful princess enchanted by an evil spell, and a handsome prince who saved her from eternal slumber [**BFAN-26**]. In 1991, Hill Valley Elementary School's Drama Club performed a play based on this story. Verne Brown dreaded having to appear in it, for fear that he'd have to kiss fellow student Beatrice Spalding [**BFAN-26**].

- **Slice:** A menu item sold at Café 80's in 2015 [**BTF2**].

  > *NOTE: Given the joking nature of the menu's other entries, it's unclear whether "Slice" referred to the real-world lemon-line-favored soft drink of the same name.*

- **Slip:** A popular brand of soft drink, circa 2015 [**BTF2**].

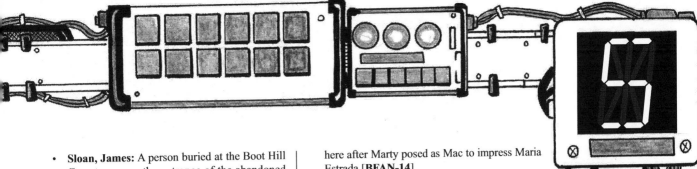

- **Sloan, James:** A person buried at the Boot Hill Cemetery, near the entrance of the abandoned Delgado Mine, along with family members Sarah Sloan and Thomas Sloan [**BTF3**].

- **Sloan, Sarah:** A person buried at the Boot Hill Cemetery, near the entrance of the abandoned Delgado Mine, along with family members Thomas Sloan and James Sloan [**BTF3**].

- **Sloan, Thomas:** A person buried at the Boot Hill Cemetery, near the entrance of the abandoned Delgado Mine, along with family members Sarah Sloan and James Sloan [**BTF3**].

- **Slurpee:** A flavored frozen drink sold by 7-Eleven [**REAL**]. The beverage was still popular in 2015. When Marty McFly returned a "borrowed" pink hoverboard to its rightful owner, the young girl's friend was drinking a Slurpee [**BTF2**].

- **SM1138:** The security clearance of Steven Marble, Ph.D., at the Institute of Future Technology's Anti-Gravitic Laboratory [**RIDE**].

  > **NOTE:** *This clearance code paid homage to THX 1138, a 1971 science fiction film directed by George Lucas.*

- **Small Town Professional Wrasslin:** A Rochester-based wrestling organization, circa 1952. Emmett Brown had a brief career as a fighter with this organization that year, known as "Brain Buster" Brown. However, the scientist was quickly defeated during his only match, against a much larger man called Mad Maximus [**BFAN-24**].

- **Smegma SxP:** A phrase scrawled in graffiti on the wall of Hill Valley High School, circa 1985 [**BTF1**].

  > **NOTE:** *Smegma—a combination of moisture, skin oils and exfoliated epithelial cells—is produced by the genitalia of male and female mammals, and acts as a lubricant during sexual intercourse.*

- **Smiley:** A name scrawled in graffiti on the wall of Hill Valley High School, circa 1985 [**BTF1**].

- **Smilin' Skull Island:** The Caribbean hideout of pirate Captain Mac the Black, circa 1697, so named due to the presence of a large, skull-shaped cliff. Marty McFly and Verne Brown ended up

here after Marty posed as Mac to impress Maria Estrada [**BFAN-14**].

- **Smirnoff, Yakov:** A Ukrainian-born comedian whose routines employed irony and wordplay to contrast life in the United States with that in the Communist-led Soviet Union [**REAL**]. In order to stop Marty McFly from altering history, First Citizen Brown—an alternate-reality Emmett Brown—claimed that Marty was a Russian named anarchist Yakov Smirnoff, bent on sowing chaos and destruction [**TLTL-5**].

- **Smith:** An FBI agent who, along with fellow agent Jones, investigated Jules Brown's money-tree to determine if the youth was the kingpin of an international counterfeiting racket. Smith had a fondness for cream soda, crullers and the comic strip *Garfield* [**BFAN-20**].

  > **NOTE:** *It is a common motif in fiction for pairs of characters to be named Smith and Jones, particularly with regard to government agents. This convention was utilized in The Matrix, as well as in promotional materials for the Men in Black films and in numerous other fictional series.*

- **Smith, Steve:** An employee at the Institute of Future Technology, stationed in the West Wing [**RIDE**].

  > **NOTE:** *This individual, identified on signage outside Back to the Future: The Ride, was named after a Universal Studios employee.*

- **Smith & Wesson Model 60:** A 5-shot snubnosed revolver chambered in either .38 Special or .357 Magnum calibers [**REAL**]. In the Biffhorrific timeline, Biff Tannen used such a weapon to murder George McFly, and later tried to kill Marty McFly with it as well, which he saw as "poetic justice" [**BTF2**].

- ***Smut Video***: A pornographic movie deemed illegal in Citizen Brown's dystopian timeline. Confiscated VHS copies of *Smut Video* were discarded in Decycling Bins and stored in an underground control room by Edna Strickland [**TLTL-3**].

- **Snovell, Burleigh:** A person buried at the Boot Hill Cemetery, near the entrance of the abandoned Delgado Mine [**BTF3**].

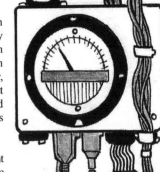

CODE	STORY
NIKE	*BTTF*-themed TV commercial: Nike
NTND	Nintendo *Back to the Future—The Ride* Mini-Game
PIZA	*BTTF*-themed TV commercial: Pizza Hut
PNBL	Data East *BTTF* pinball game
REAL	Real life
RIDE	Simulator: *Back to the Future—The Ride*
SCRM	2010 Scream Awards: *Back to the Future 25th Anniversary Reunion* (broadcast)
SCRT	2010 Scream Awards: *Back to the Future 25th Anniversary Reunion* (trailer)
SIMP	Simulator: *The Simpsons Ride*
SLOT	*Back to the Future* Video Slots
STLZ	Unused *BTTF* footage of Eric Stoltz as Marty McFly
STRY	*Back to the Future Storybook*
TEST	Screen tests: Crispin Glover, Lea Thompson and Tom Wilson
TLTL	Telltale Games' *Back to the Future—The Game*
TOPS	Topps' *Back to the Future II* trading-card set
TRIL	*BTTF: The Official Book of the Complete Movie Trilogy*
UNIV	Universal Studios Hollywood promotional video

SUFFIX	MEDIUM
-b	*BTTF2's* Biff Tannen Museum video (extended)
-c	Credit sequence to the animated series
-d	Film deleted scene
-n	Film novelization
-o	Film outtake
-p	1955 phone book from *BTTF1*
-v	Video game print materials or commentaries
-s1	Screenplay (draft one)
-s2	Screenplay (draft two)
-s3	Screenplay (draft three)
-s4	Screenplay (draft four)
-sp	Screenplay (production draft)
-sx	Screenplay (*Paradox*)

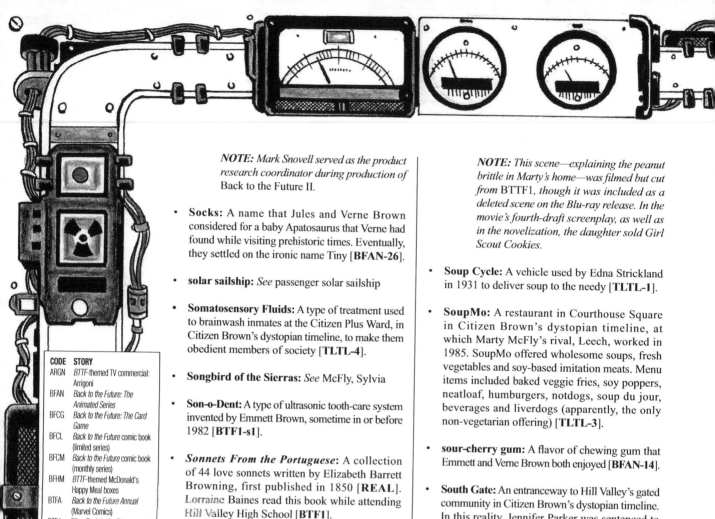

NOTE: Mark Snovell served as the product research coordinator during production of Back to the Future II.

- **Socks:** A name that Jules and Verne Brown considered for a baby Apatosaurus that Verne had found while visiting prehistoric times. Eventually, they settled on the ironic name Tiny [**BFAN-26**].

- **solar sailship:** *See* passenger solar sailship

- **Somatosensory Fluids:** A type of treatment used to brainwash inmates at the Citizen Plus Ward, in Citizen Brown's dystopian timeline, to make them obedient members of society [**TLTL-4**].

- **Songbird of the Sierras:** *See* McFly, Sylvia

- **Son-o-Dent:** A type of ultrasonic tooth-care system invented by Emmett Brown, sometime in or before 1982 [**BTF1-s1**].

- ***Sonnets From the Portuguese:*** A collection of 44 love sonnets written by Elizabeth Barrett Browning, first published in 1850 [**REAL**]. Lorraine Baines read this book while attending Hill Valley High School [**BTF1**].

- **Sonskoid, Paul:** A Hollywood producer, circa 2015, who helped director Max Spielberg create *Jaws 19*, according to the film's poster [**BTF2**].

- **Sony:** *See* Walkman

- **Sophia Rae:** A brand of peanut brittle enjoyed by George McFly in Citizen Brown's dystopian timeline [**TLTL-3**].

  > *NOTE: The confection's name was based on that of Sophie Mae, the brand of brittle that George consumed in* BTTF1.

- **Sophie Mae:** A brand of peanut brittle (a confection consisting of flat, broken, nut-embedded pieces of hard sugar candy) [**REAL**]. In Citizen Brown's dystopian timeline, a similarly named brand, Sophia Rae, was produced [**TLTL-3**].
  Marty McFly's family had a large supply of peanut brittle in their home [**BTF1**]. This had been sold to them by a pushy neighbor named Howard, who pressured George McFly into buying an entire case from his daughter, to help with a fundraiser for her baseball team, the Cubs [**BTF1-d, BTF1-s4**].

NOTE: This scene—explaining the peanut brittle in Marty's home—was filmed but cut from BTTF1, though it was included as a deleted scene on the Blu-ray release. In the movie's fourth-draft screenplay, as well as in the novelization, the daughter sold Girl Scout Cookies.

- **Soup Cycle:** A vehicle used by Edna Strickland in 1931 to deliver soup to the needy [**TLTL-1**].

- **SoupMo:** A restaurant in Courthouse Square in Citizen Brown's dystopian timeline, at which Marty McFly's rival, Leech, worked in 1985. SoupMo offered wholesome soups, fresh vegetables and soy-based imitation meats. Menu items included baked veggie fries, soy poppers, neatloaf, humburgers, notdogs, soup du jour, beverages and liverdogs (apparently, the only non-vegetarian offering) [**TLTL-3**].

- **sour-cherry gum:** A flavor of chewing gum that Emmett and Verne Brown both enjoyed [**BFAN-14**].

- **South Gate:** An entranceway to Hill Valley's gated community in Citizen Brown's dystopian timeline. In this reality, Jennifer Parker was sentenced to community service for vandalism, and was made to clean up trash near this gate [**TLTL-3**].

- **South Kelsey:** A street in Hill Valley. In 1944, Emmett Brown lived in an apartment on this road, located above a gas station. His address was 1191 South Kelsey, apartment 3B [**BFAN-17**].

- **South Pacific:** The southern portion of the Pacific Ocean, containing a number of islands [**REAL**]. According to a *USA Today* report, pollution in the South Pacific caused an increase in kelp prices in 2015 [**BTF2**].

- **South Wing:** A section of the Institute of Future Technology, containing numerous offices and laboratories [**RIDE**].

- **soy-dog:** A vegetarian menu item at SoupMo, a restaurant in Citizen Brown's dystopian timeline [**TLTL-3**].

- **Spacers:** A professional football team in a league known as IFL, circa 2015 [**BTF2-n**].

  > *NOTE: It's unknown what the acronym "IFL" stood for, though it was may have*

been short for *"International Football League,"* given that *"NFL"* is short for *"National Football League."*

- **space zombies:** Fictional undead creatures featured in "Space Zombies From Pluto," a story published in 1954 in *Tales from Space* issue #8 [**BTF1**]. Otis Peabody thought his wife, Elsie, was a space zombie reanimated from the dead after she fainted upon seeing an "alien" (Marty McFly in a radiaition suit) in her barn [**BTF1-s4**]. Otis later told others that his barn had been damaged by a space zombie, resulting in his being sent to County Asylum [**BTF1-n**].

    NOTE: See also zombies.

- **"Space Zombies From Mars":** *See* "Space Zombies From Pluto"

- **"Space Zombies From Pluto":** A science fiction tale published in *Tales from Space* issue #8, a comic book printed in August 1954. Sherman Peabody, having read that story, mistook Emmett Brown's DeLorean for a spacecraft, causing his father, Otis, to shoot at Marty McFly—who, clad in a 1980s radiation suit, resembled an alien invader [**BTF1**]. When Otis' wife, Elsie, fainted at the site of the "alien," the Peabodys believed she'd been killed and reanimated as a zombie [**BTF1-s4**].

    NOTE: Though styled after classic sci-fi and horror comics of the 1950s, Tales from Space was not a real-world publication. However, the prop comic has since appeared in other fictional series, including Heroes *and* 3rd Rock from the Sun.

    This comic first appeared in the third-draft screenplay for the film, though the story and magazine were titled "Space Zombies From Mars" and Weird Science, respectively.

- **Spalding, Beatrice:** A classmate of Verne Brown at Hill Valley Elementary School, who starred in the Drama Club's production of *Sleeping Beauty* in 1992. Verne feared being forced to join the cast, worried that he might have to kiss Beatrice [**BFAN-26**].

- **Sparky:** A robot servant owned by Marty McFly's family in an alternate version of 1982, based on the design of Emmett Brown's Mechanical Home Butler [**BTF1-s1**].

- **Special Soup:** A code word used by Irving "Kid" Tannen's gang in 1931, during the Prohibition era, to refer to alcohol, which the mob secretly served in the cellar of their front business, the Sisters of Mercy Soup Kitchen [**TLTL-1**].

- **Spectra 2000:** A model of color television, circa 1985 [**REAL**]. Emmett Brown had a Spectra 2000 TV in his home, set to automatically activate at specified times [**BTF1**].

- **Sphinx:** *See* Great Sphinx of Giza

- **Spider Car:** A model of automobile sold in 2015, also known as the Spinner [**BTF2, TOPS**].

    NOTE: This type of vehicle first appeared in the film Blade Runner.

- **Spielberg, Max:** A film director whose works included *Jaws 19* [**BTF2**].

    NOTE: Max Spielberg is the real-life son of filmmaker Steven Spielberg, who directed the original Jaws.

- **Spike:** *See* O'Malley, Leslie ("Spike")

- **Spina, Chuck:** An employee at the Institute of Future Technology, in charge of visual prestidigitation [**RIDE**].

    NOTE: This individual, identified on signage outside Back to the Future: The Ride, *was named after a Universal Studios design manager.*

- **Spinner:** A model of automobile sold in 2015, also known as the Spider Car [**BTF2, TOPS**].

    NOTE: This type of vehicle first appeared in the film Blade Runner.

- **Spleen Splitter, The:** A ride at the Mega Monster Mountain amusement park, known for making riders vomit. Verne and Jules Brown were fond of this attraction, though Verne was expelled for repeatedly vomiting on other customers. Jules estimated that he and his brother could ride the Spleen Splitter 38.5 times over a span of two hours [**BFAN-25**].

- **Sports:** A 1983 album by Huey Lewis and the News [**REAL**]. Marty McFly had a poster for this album hanging in his bedroom in 1985 [**BTF1**].

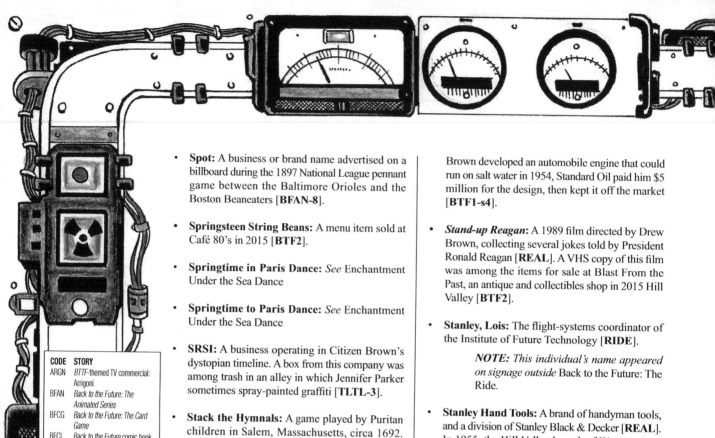

- **Spot:** A business or brand name advertised on a billboard during the 1897 National League pennant game between the Baltimore Orioles and the Boston Beaneaters [**BFAN-8**].

- **Springsteen String Beans:** A menu item sold at Café 80's in 2015 [**BTF2**].

- **Springtime in Paris Dance:** *See* Enchantment Under the Sea Dance

- **Springtime to Paris Dance:** *See* Enchantment Under the Sea Dance

- **SRSI:** A business operating in Citizen Brown's dystopian timeline. A box from this company was among trash in an alley in which Jennifer Parker sometimes spray-painted graffiti [**TLTL-3**].

- **Stack the Hymnals:** A game played by Puritan children in Salem, Massachusetts, circa 1692. While stranded in that era, Jules and Verne Brown learned how to play from local Puritan kids. Verne found the game boring, while Jules reveled in using simple geometric logic to repeatedly win [**BFAN-4**].

- *Stag*: A pornographic movie deemed illegal in Citizen Brown's dystopian timeline. Confiscated VHS copies of *Stag* were discarded in Decycling Bins and stored within an underground control room by Edna Strickland [**TLTL-3**].

- **Stair NO3AB P1:** A stairwell leading from the penthouse apartment to the rooftop of Biff Tannen's Pleasure Paradise, in Biffhorrific 1985. Marty ran up these stairs while fleeing Biff and his henchmen [**BTF2**].

- **"Stairway to Heaven":** A 1971 release by English rock band Led Zeppelin [**REAL**]. Upon meeting singer Sylvia "Trixie Trotter" Miskin in 1931, Marty McFly asked if she knew this song, to which she responded, "You want hymns, go to a church" [**TLTL-2**].

  > ***NOTE:*** *It would have been impossible for Trixie to know this song, given the era.*

- **Standard-C:** A type of digital format offered in 2015 as an alternative to printed books [**BTF2-s1**].

- **Standard Oil:** An American oil firm co-founded by John D. Rockefeller [**REAL**]. When Emmett Brown developed an automobile engine that could run on salt water in 1954, Standard Oil paid him $5 million for the design, then kept it off the market [**BTF1-s4**].

- ***Stand-up Reagan***: A 1989 film directed by Drew Brown, collecting several jokes told by President Ronald Reagan [**REAL**]. A VHS copy of this film was among the items for sale at Blast From the Past, an antique and collectibles shop in 2015 Hill Valley [**BTF2**].

- **Stanley, Lois:** The flight-systems coordinator of the Institute of Future Technology [**RIDE**].

  > ***NOTE:*** *This individual's name appeared on signage outside* Back to the Future: The Ride.

- **Stanley Hand Tools:** A brand of handyman tools, and a division of Stanley Black & Decker [**REAL**]. In 1955, the Hill Valley branch of Western Auto Stores sold such products [**BTF1**].

- **Star:** A business located in Hill Valley, circa 2015 [**RIDE**].

- **Starbase Zero:** A video arcade in Hill Valley. In 1986, Edna Strickland lived in an apartment above this business [**TLTL-1**]. In an alternate reality, the Tannen Gang (Irving "Kid" Tannen and his sons, Biff, Cliff and Riff) robbed the arcade [**TLTL-2**].

- **Starboard Flux Emitter:** A device invented by Emmett Brown—one of three such emitters used to enable his DeLorean to achieve time travel. This particular emitter was attached to the hood on the vehicle's front passenger's side [**TLTL-5**].

- **Starcar:** An automobile model sold in 2015 [**BTF2**].

  > ***NOTE:*** *This type of car first appeared in the film* The Last Starfighter.

- **State Line Gas:** A desert gas station, circa 1952, bordering Nevada and Utah. Emmett Brown and Marty McFly stopped here to fuel the scientist's car while traveling to a nuclear test site in Atkins, Nevada [**BTF1-s1**].

  > ***NOTE:*** *This business, which appeared in* BTTF1*'s initial-draft screenplay, was changed to Atomic Gas by the third draft.*

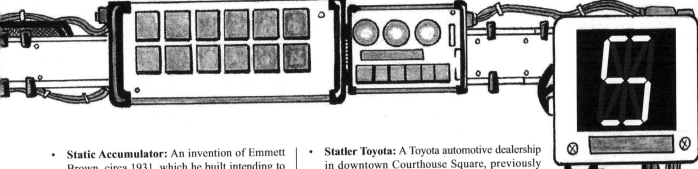

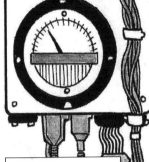

- **Static Accumulator:** An invention of Emmett Brown, circa 1931, which he built intending to unveil it at the 1931 Hill Valley Exposition. A glowing coil able to hover, it generated a static charge. Once activated, it became difficult to grab [**TLTL-5**]. The device included a part called an Oscillator Gigathruster, which was attached above a stainless-steel casing [**TLTL-v**].

- **Static-o-Matic Electric Hair Chair:** An invention of Emmett Brown enabling barbers to harness 200,000 volts of static electricity to make human hair stand on end, thereby making it easier to cut [**RIDE**].

- **Statler:** A rancher for whom Emmett Brown worked during summers as a youth. Statler taught young Emmett how to ride, shoot and rope, instilling in him a desire to be a cowboy, and preparing him for his time spent in the Old West as an adult [**BTF3-sp**]. When Statler sold the ranch and went into the used-car business, Emmett realized there wasn't much future in being a cowpuncher [**BTF3-n**].

  NOTE: In a combined screenplay for both film sequels, titled Paradox, *Doc said he'd learned to ride and shoot on his Uncle Abraham's farm.*

- **Statler, Joe ("Honest Joe"):** A businessman who sold, bought and traded horses in Hill Valley, circa 1885, with a business called Honest Joe Statler's Fine Horses. Statler also rented buckboards, including one used by Clara Clayton following her arrival in Hill Valley. The wagon was destroyed, however, when the horses became spooked and ran out of control, causing it to plummet into the Shonash Ravine [**BTF3**].

- **Statler DeSoto:** An automotive dealership that sponsored the Cars of the Future attraction at the 1931 Hill Valley Exposition [**TLTL-4**].

  NOTE: The Statler family would continue to operate dealerships in Hill Valley for the next several decades, as illustrated below.

- **Statler Motors Studebaker:** A Studebaker automotive dealership in Courthouse Square, circa 1955. Its name was changed to Statler Toyota sometime before 1985 [**BTF1**].

  NOTE: An advertisement printed in a 1955 newspaper indicated the store to be located on Hubbard Avenue.

- **Statler Toyota:** A Toyota automotive dealership in downtown Courthouse Square, previously known as Statler Motors Studebaker. In 1985, the firm conducted an inventory of that year's model Toyotas, offering a sale on its remaining stock of the vehicles. Marty McFly long wished he could own a 4x4 pickup truck sold at Statler Toyota [**BTF1**].

  NOTE: In early drafts of BTTF1*'s screenplay, this business was a Chevrolet dealership.*

- **Statute 357-K:** A legal mandate in Citizen Brown's dystopian timeline, strictly prohibiting Hill Valley's inhabitants from owning a dog—due to Edna Strickland's severe dislike for canines [**TLTL-3**].

- **Statute 476-D:** A legal mandate in Citizen Brown's dystopian timeline, also known as the PDA Law, prohibiting all public displays of affection—specifically, open-mouth kissing involving tongues [**TLTL-3**].

- **staycation:** A marketing term used by Stemmles' Staycations, a Hill Valley business in Citizen Brown's dystopian timeline [**TLTL-3**].

  NOTE: Given Hill Valley's isolationist nature in that timeline, the term likely referred to time off enjoyed within the city's limits.

- **Stay Sober Society (S.S.S.):** An organization in Hill Valley, circa 1931, that encouraged abstinence from alcohol, in an effort to "turn hopeless drunken bums into *former* hopeless drunken bums." Its slogan: "Listen to your mothers—stay sober!" Among its founding members was Edna Strickland. The group met at the Sisters of Mercy Soup Kitchen, until gangster Irving "Kid" Tannen purchased that facility and revoked access [**TLTL-1**].

- **STBY 1:** A button on an overhead console of Emmett Brown's DeLorean [**TLTL-5**].

- **STBY 2:** A button on an overhead console of Emmett Brown's DeLorean [**TLTL-5**].

- **STBY 3:** A button on an overhead console of Emmett Brown's DeLorean [**TLTL-5**].

CODE	STORY
NIKE	*BTTF*-themed TV commercial: Nike
NTND	Nintendo *Back to the Future—The Ride* Mini-Game
PIZA	*BTTF*-themed TV commercial: Pizza Hut
PNBL	Data East *BTTF* pinball game
REAL	Real life
RIDE	Simulator: *Back to the Future—The Ride*
SCRM	2010 Scream Awards: *Back to the Future* 25th Anniversary Reunion (broadcast)
SCRT	2010 Scream Awards: *Back to the Future* 25th Anniversary Reunion (trailer)
SIMP	Simulator: *The Simpsons Ride*
SLOT	*Back to the Future* Video Slots
STLZ	Unused *BTTF* footage of Eric Stoltz as Marty McFly
STRY	*Back to the Future* Storybook
TEST	Screen tests: Crispin Glover, Lea Thompson and Tom Wilson
TLTL	Telltale Games' *Back to the Future—The Game*
TOPS	Topps' *Back to the Future II* trading-card set
TRIL	*BTTF: The Official Book of the Complete Movie Trilogy*
UNIV	Universal Studios Hollywood promotional video

SUFFIX	MEDIUM
-b	*BTTF2*'s Biff Tannen Museum video (extended)
-c	Credit sequence to the animated series
-d	Film deleted scene
-n	Film novelization
-o	Film outtake
-p	1955 phone book from *BTTF1*
-v	Video game print materials or commentaries
-s1	Screenplay (draft one)
-s2	Screenplay (draft two)
-s3	Screenplay (draft three)
-s4	Screenplay (draft four)
-sp	Screenplay (production draft)
-sx	Screenplay (*Paradox*)

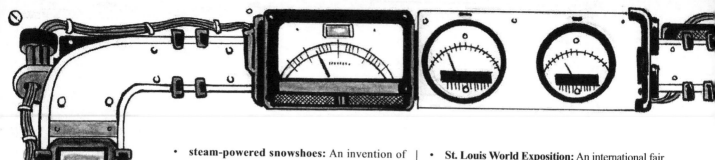

- **steam-powered snowshoes:** An invention of Emmett Brown, created in or before 1888, while he and his wife, Clara, lived in that era. The shoes were not entirely effective, as the steam sometimes condensed, causing an ice storm around a wearer's ankles [**BFAN-21**].

- **Steel:** A brand of alcohol served at the El Kid speakeasy in 1931 [**TLTL-2**].

- **Steinberg, Janis:** An organizer of a Vietnam War protest rally to which Lorraine McFly donated her time in 1967. Her speech was titled "Mothers Against War" [**BTF2-s1**].

- **Stemmles' Staycations:** A business in Courthouse Square in Citizen Brown's dystopian timeline [**TLTL-3**].

  ***NOTE:** This company was named after Telltale Games designer Mike Stemmle.*

- **Stephanie:** A young girl in Hill Valley who enjoyed baseball, circa 1991. When Verne Brown and other boys refused to let her play the sport with them, she retaliated by activating a lawn sprinkler system, dousing them. Soon thereafter, Verne learned not to discriminate based on gender, after befriending another girl named Christine [**BFAN-18**].

- **Stephen's Hat Shop:** A business in Boston, Massachusetts, circa 1897 [**BFAN-8**].

- **Stephens, Claire:** An actor who starred in the motion picture *Shark* in 1931, alongside costar Cooper Jackson [**TLTL-1**].

- **Stetson:** A brand of hat manufactured by John B. Stetson Co., founded in 1865 [**REAL**]. In 1885, a Hill Valley business known as M. Fennigot Millinery sold Stetson merchandise [**BTF3-n**].

- **Stevens, Mister:** A customer who purchased a toy from Fedgewick Toys, a London-based toy shop, in 1845 [**BFAN-10**].

  ***NOTE:** This name appeared on a gift-box tag, labeled "Sold to Mr. Stevens."*

- **Stevenson:** A schoolmate of Marty McFly at Hill Valley High School, circa 1985. When he violated Gerald Strickland's "No Walkman" policy, the vice-principal gave him detention and crushed the player in a woodworking vice [**BTF1-n**].

- **St. Louis World Exposition:** An international fair held in St. Louis, Missouri, in 1904 [**REAL**]. On June 29 of that year, Emmett and Clara Brown recorded themselves singing "Meet Me in St. Louis, Louis" on an old-style recording device. Doc's sons, Jules and Verne, heard the recording while visiting the exposition in 1992 [**BFAN-25**].

  ***NOTE:** In 1904, the Louisiana Purchase Exposition (or Saint Louis World's Fair) was held in the real world. Doc claimed that hot dogs, iced tea and ice cream cones were first introduced there, but although this was true for ice cream cones, hot dogs were sold as early as 1880, while iced tea existed even earlier.*

- **Stockhausen, Billy:** A childhood friend of George McFly, when George was 12 years old. When another student punched Billy in the face, George nearly struck the bully, but failed to go through with it, out of fear. George often wondered how his life might have been different had he actually hit the other boy, recognizing that his inaction in that moment had set him on a course of failure, defeatism and non-confrontationalism.

  In one timeline, George's memories of this event helped him muster the courage to punch Biff Tannen and stop him from raping Lorraine Baines in 1955. This set in motion a new future, in which he was more confident and successful [**BTF1-n**].

- **Stockmann:** A Finnish retail trade firm [**REAL**]. A box bearing this company's logo was stored in Emmett Brown's home in 1985, near his giant guitar amplifier [**BTF1**].

- **Stonehenge:** A prehistoric monument composed of earthworks surrounding large standing stones, located in England's Wiltshire County, the origin of which has long been debated by archeologists [**REAL**].

  Emmett Brown took his family to this structure during a trip to 1367—and found that even then, the locals debated its function [**BFAN-2**]. After Doc visited this site, a photo commemorating the occasion was displayed at Doc Brown's Chicken [**CHIC**].

- ***Street Cars and Where to Get Them:*** The title of a flyer hanging on the wall of Emmett Brown's laboratory in 1931 [**TLTL-4**].

  ***NOTE:** An actual map of Los Angeles,*

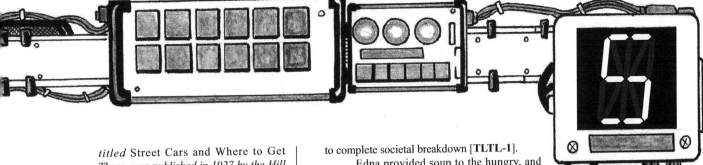

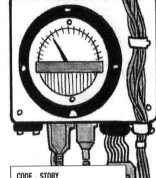

titled Street Cars and Where to Get Them, *was published in 1927 by the Hill Publishing Co.*

- **Strickland, Blackout Warden:** A U.S. Army officer stationed in Hill Valley, where he was assigned to enforce a mandatory blackout during World War II. Bald and powerfully built, he took discipline and curfew seriously, and had a very suspicious nature. Marty McFly and Verne Brown encountered the warden while visiting that era to track down a set of blueprints. Strickland was not pleased at their lack of discipline [**BFAN-17**].

  > ***NOTE:*** *Given the warden's hairless head, adherence to discipline and use of the phrase "slackers," it's possible that he was intended to be Gerald Strickland, from the films.*

- **Strickland, Clay:** A descendant of Gerald Strickland, circa 2015, in one possible timeline [**BFCG**].

- **Strickland, Dean:** An authority figure at a college attended by Marty McFly. Marty was worried that Strickland would expel him if he flunked his Civil War exam [**BFAN-1**].

- **Strickland, Edna ("Mary Pickford," "Scary Mary"):** The older sister of Gerald Strickland. An etiquette columnist for the *Hill Valley Telegraph* and the *Hill Valley Herald*, Edna also wrote for *Cat Lover's Quarterly*, and proudly displayed a trio of editorial trophies awarded by that magazine [**TLTL-1**]. Her parents were Roger and Irene Strickland, and she also had an older brother named Robert [**TLTL-v**].

  By 1986, Edna lived alone in an apartment above the Starbase Zero arcade, yelling at passersby via a bullhorn—especially skateboarders, whom she deemed hooligans. A curmudgeonly spinster, she was obsessed with watching *The Merv Griffin Show*, as well as maintaining her collection of old *Telegraph* issues. Like her brother, she often called people—particularly McFlys—"slackers." She vehemently hated dogs, but adored cats, and had a pet feline named Miss Prettywhiskers.

  As a young woman in 1931, Edna had been beautiful and spirited, with her own etiquette column, titled "Ask Edna." This doubled as a pro-temperance soapbox, showing her bias against liquor, organized crime and debauchery, as she believed the consumption of alcohol would lead

to complete societal breakdown [**TLTL-1**].

Edna provided soup to the hungry, and operated a small table in Courthouse Square that she called Salvation Station. There, she handed out leaflets warning about the temptations of alcohol—along with others supporting the Clock Tower Fund, a campaign to commission a sculptor to place ornamental statues on either side of the clock face, to inspire citizens to do their civic duty. Secretly, Edna was also an arsonist who burned down several speakeasies, including one belonging to gangster Irving "Kid" Tannen.

Marty McFly inadvertently changed history by causing a chain of events that led to Edna falling in love with 17-year-old Emmett Brown. This prevented Emmett from seeing the film *Frankenstein*—which had originally cemented his passion for science—and thus altered the timeline by setting him on a different path [**TLTL-2**].

As a result, Emmett instead devoted himself to turning Hill Valley into a pristine, self-sustaining, walled, dystopian society with strict rules of propriety—the United States' first fully incorporated gated city. In this reality, by 1986, he became First Citizen Brown, Hill Valley's benevolent dictator, with Edna by his side. Together, the couple promoted civil and social engineering, using Hill Valley as a prototype for tomorrow's cities.

Edna and Emmett mandated that citizens live as vegetarians and wear ID badges, and also implemented strict dress codes—such as Polo Shirt Thursday and Hawaiian Shirt Friday. Many items and concepts were illegalized, including weapons, alcohol, cigarettes, cigars, bubblegum, dogs, Circus Peanuts, science fiction, skateboards, rock-and-roll, *Dungeons and Dragons*, pinball games, novelty items (such as X-ray specs, joy buzzers and trick gum), pornography, public displays of affection and more.

Although Emmett intended only good in forming this society, he was merely a pawn manipulated by Edna, whose single-minded obsession with curtailing vice and subversion perverted his ideals. Thanks to Marty, Citizen Brown came to realize his mistake—but before they could fix the timeline, Edna subjected her husband to hypnotic re-conditioning [**TLTL-3**].

Marty helped Citizen Brown escape from Edna, and the two men returned to 1931 to repair history, by breaking up young Emmett's relationship before Edna could pervert his inventions. While there, they learned that the teen

CODE	STORY
NIKE	*BTTF*-themed TV commercial: Nike
NTND	Nintendo *Back to the Future—The Ride* Mini-Game
PIZA	*BTTF*-themed TV commercial: Pizza Hut
PNBL	Data East *BTTF* pinball game
REAL	Real life
RIDE	Simulator: *Back to the Future—The Ride*
SCRM	2010 Scream Awards: *Back to the Future* 25th Anniversary Reunion (broadcast)
SCRT	2010 Scream Awards: *Back to the Future* 25th Anniversary Reunion (trailer)
SIMP	Simulator: *The Simpsons Ride*
SLOT	*Back to the Future* Video Slots
STLZ	Unused *BTTF* footage of Eric Stoltz as Marty McFly
STRY	*Back to the Future* Storybook
TEST	Screen tests: Crispin Glover, Lea Thompson and Tom Wilson
TLTL	Telltale Games' *Back to the Future—The Game*
TOPS	Topps' *Back to the Future II* trading-card set
TRIL	*BTTF: The Official Book of the Complete Movie Trilogy*
UNIV	Universal Studios Hollywood promotional video

SUFFIX	MEDIUM
-b	*BTTF2*'s Biff Tannen Museum video (extended)
-c	Credit sequence to the animated series
-d	Film deleted scene
-n	Film novelization
-o	Film outtake
-p	1955 phone book from *BTTF1*
-v	Video game print materials or commentaries
-s1	Screenplay (draft one)
-s2	Screenplay (draft two)
-s3	Screenplay (draft three)
-s4	Screenplay (draft four)
-sp	Screenplay (production draft)
-sx	Screenplay (*Paradox*)

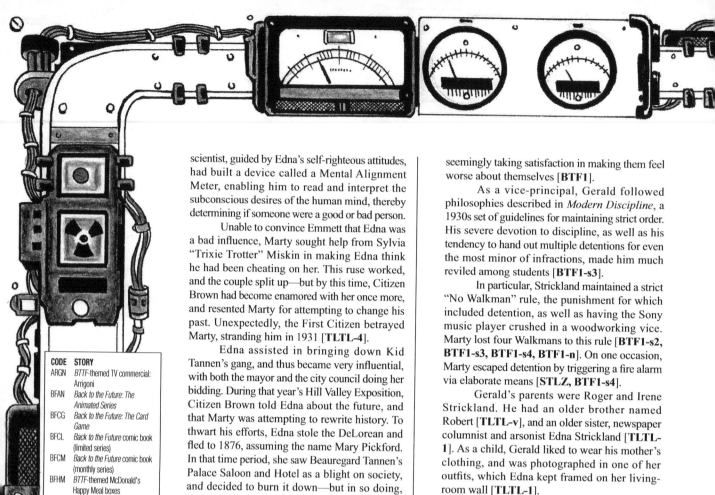

scientist, guided by Edna's self-righteous attitudes, had built a device called a Mental Alignment Meter, enabling him to read and interpret the subconscious desires of the human mind, thereby determining if someone were a good or bad person.

Unable to convince Emmett that Edna was a bad influence, Marty sought help from Sylvia "Trixie Trotter" Miskin in making Edna think he had been cheating on her. This ruse worked, and the couple split up—but by this time, Citizen Brown had become enamored with her once more, and resented Marty for attempting to change his past. Unexpectedly, the First Citizen betrayed Marty, stranding him in 1931 [**TLTL-4**].

Edna assisted in bringing down Kid Tannen's gang, and thus became very influential, with both the mayor and the city council doing her bidding. During that year's Hill Valley Exposition, Citizen Brown told Edna about the future, and that Marty was attempting to rewrite history. To thwart his efforts, Edna stole the DeLorean and fled to 1876, assuming the name Mary Pickford. In that time period, she saw Beauregard Tannen's Palace Saloon and Hotel as a blight on society, and decided to burn it down—but in so doing, she inadvertently torched all of Hill Valley. In the resultant new timeline, Edna spent the next 55 years crazy with guilt, earning the nickname "Scary Mary."

After Marty and Doc repaired Edna's time tamperings, the arsonist was sent to prison for her crimes. While incarcerated, she ironically fell in love with Kid. The two married following their release, enjoying a happy, quiet life together— one in which she not only loved dogs, but even watched Emmett's dog, Einstein, from time to time [**TLTL-5**]. The book *Hill Valley Historical Society, 1865-1990* dubbed Edna a "fiery temperance crusader and all-around busybody," though after her prison sentence, she was a much kinder person [**TLTL-v**].

• **Strickland, Gerald, Vice-Principal ("Gerry," "Old Man," "S.S. Strickland"):** An administrator at Hill Valley High School from at least 1955 (when George McFly and Lorraine Baines attended the school) until as late as 1985 (when Marty McFly and Jennifer Parker were students there).

Short, solidly built and completely bald for much of his adult life—making him look the same age at both ends of his career—Strickland ridiculed students who misbehaved or showed a lack of ambition, calling them "slackers" and

seemingly taking satisfaction in making them feel worse about themselves [**BTF1**].

As a vice-principal, Gerald followed philosophies described in *Modern Discipline*, a 1930s set of guidelines for maintaining strict order. His severe devotion to discipline, as well as his tendency to hand out multiple detentions for even the most minor of infractions, made him much reviled among students [**BTF1-s3**].

In particular, Strickland maintained a strict "No Walkman" rule, the punishment for which included detention, as well as having the Sony music player crushed in a woodworking vice. Marty lost four Walkmans to this rule [**BTF1-s2, BTF1-s3, BTF1-s4, BTF1-n**]. On one occasion, Marty escaped detention by triggering a fire alarm via elaborate means [**STLZ, BTF1-s4**].

Gerald's parents were Roger and Irene Strickland. He had an older brother named Robert [**TLTL-v**], and an older sister, newspaper columnist and arsonist Edna Strickland [**TLTL-1**]. As a child, Gerald liked to wear his mother's clothing, and was photographed in one of her outfits, which Edna kept framed on her living-room wall [**TLTL-1**].

In the Biffhorrific timeline, after the high school was burned down in 1979, Gerald became a gun-toting and facially scarred paranoic [**BTF2**]. No longer a school administrator, he now worked as a uniformed security guard at Biff Tannen's Pleasure Paradise [**BTF2-s1**].

In that reality, Strickland nearly shot Marty, believing the youth was stealing newspapers from his porch. As Marty ran away in panic, Strickland entered a shootout with local gang members, his outlook grim [**BTF2**].

> *NOTE: Strickland's first name, Gerald, appeared in BTTF1's novelization, as well as in Telltale Games'* Back to the Future: The Game. *His office door in* Back to the Future II, *however, called him "S.S. Strickland," as did the first movie's Blu-ray Setups and Payoffs track. Supplemental packaging included with the game gave him the childhood nickname of "Gerry," reinforcing "Gerald" as his name—but also called him Stanford S. Strickland, in keeping with the door sign. His title of vice-principal was mentioned in the first two novelizations, as well as in the video game.*
>
> *For a full list of Strickland's known relatives, see Appendix III.*

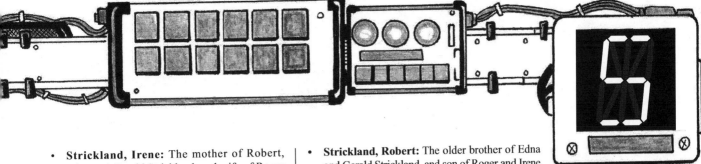

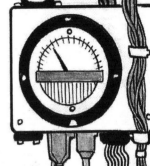

- **Strickland, Irene:** The mother of Robert, Edna and Gerald Strickland, and wife of Roger Strickland. The family was considered Hill Valley's "first family during the gaslight era" [**TLTL-v**].

- **Strickland, James, Marshal:** The highest-ranking law-enforcement agent in Hill Valley from 1869 [**TLTL-5**] until his death in 1885 [**BTF3**]. He had at least three grandchildren: Gerald, Edna and Robert Strickland [**BTFA, TLTL-1, TLTL-v**].

    Marshal Strickland had long hair and a drooping mustache and wore a black coat and hat. He strongly valued discipline and encouraged his young son to do so as well. The lawman greatly disliked Buford "Mad Dog" Tannen and his gang, and looked forward to one day seeing the outlaws hanged [**BTF3**].

    That day never came, however, as Tannen killed him first, in 1885, shortly after that year's Hill Valley Festival. Encountering Strickland and his son in the woods, Buford warned the officer to stay out of his way while he murdered Emmett Brown and Marty McFly. Strickland complied for the sake of his son's safety, but Mad Dog still shot him in the back, leaving the man to die in the child's arms. The son vowed to live by his father's code of discipline, and to make sure every Strickland did so as well, for generations to come [**BTF3-d, BTF3-n, TLTL-1, BTFA**].

    A century later, the book *Hill Valley Historical Society, 1865-1990* dubbed Strickland "the man who brought order to a lawless territory" [**TLTL-v**]. His legacy lived on, as his grandchildren took his philosophy, which they called the Strickland Code, to heart [**BTF1, TLTL-1**].

    NOTE: *The name of Strickland's son is unknown, but Marvel's* BTTF Annual *specifically identified the boy as Gerald Strickland's father.*

- **Strickland, Ricky:** A relative of Edna and Gerald Strickland. The pimpled teen had blonde hair and red glasses [**TLTL-v**].

    NOTE: *This character, created for the Telltale Games video game, was not utilized in the final game. However, an illustration of Ricky appeared in supplemental materials included with the game's packaging, with no additional information provided.*

- **Strickland, Robert:** The older brother of Edna and Gerald Strickland, and son of Roger and Irene Strickland [**TLTL-v**].

- **Strickland, Roger:** The father of Robert, Edna and Gerald Strickland, and husband of Irene Strickland. The family was considered Hill Valley's "first family during the gaslight era" [**TLTL-v**].

- **Strickland, S.S.:** *See* Strickland, Gerald

- **Strickland, Stanford S.:** *See* Strickland, Gerald

- **Strickland, Vice-Principal:** A school administrator at Verne Brown's elementary school, circa 1991. Like other Stricklands, he had little use for the McFly family, believing they just took up space [**BFAN-9**].

    Verne sometimes pulled pranks on the man, such as giving him worm-filled apples on April Fool's Day, causing him to become sick [**BFAN-12**]. Verne's brother, Jules, also pulled stunts, such as putting itching power in Strickland's shorts [**BFCM-4**].

    NOTE: *It's unclear whether this character was intended to be Gerald Strickland or a separate individual.*

- **Strickland Code, The:** The personal motto of Marshal James Strickland, circa 1885: "Don't give an inch, and maintain discipline at all times" [**BTF3-n**]. This philosophy was later shared by the marshal's ancestors, Gerald Strickland [**BTF1, BTF2**] and Edna Strickland [**TLTL-1 to TLTL-5**].

- **Strickland College:** A university in Citizen Brown's dystopian timeline, named after Brown's wife, Edna Strickland. In that reality, Marty McFly earned a full-ride scholarship to the college [**TLTL-3**].

- **Stubble:** A member of Buford Tannen's gang in 1885. He had blonde hair and facial stubble, and seemed to be a good deal smarter than Buford [**BTF3-s1, BTF3-sx**].

    NOTE: *This character, unnamed onscreen, was identified in* Back to the Future III*'s screenplays. Actor Christopher Wynne, who played Stubble, also portrayed a member of Douglas J. Needles' gang, possibly a clue that the two were related.*

CODE	STORY
NIKE	*BTTF*-themed TV commercial: Nike
NTND	Nintendo *Back to the Future—The Ride* Mini-Game
PIZA	*BTTF*-themed TV commercial: Pizza Hut
PNBL	Data East *BTTF* pinball game
REAL	Real life
RIDE	Simulator: *Back to the Future—The Ride*
SCRM	2010 Scream Awards: *Back to the Future* 25th Anniversary Reunion (broadcast)
SCRT	2010 Scream Awards: *Back to the Future* 25th Anniversary Reunion (trailer)
SIMP	Simulator: *The Simpsons Ride*
SLOT	*Back to the Future* Video Slots
STLZ	Unused *BTTF* footage of Eric Stoltz as Marty McFly
STRY	*Back to the Future Storybook*
TEST	Screen tests: Crispin Glover, Lea Thompson and Tom Wilson
TLTL	Telltale Games' *Back to the Future—The Game*
TOPS	Topps' *Back to the Future II* trading-card set
TRIL	*BTTF: The Official Book of the Complete Movie Trilogy*
UNIV	Universal Studios Hollywood promotional video

SUFFIX	MEDIUM
-b	*BTTF2*'s Biff Tannen Museum video (extended)
-c	Credit sequence to the animated series
-d	Film deleted scene
-n	Film novelization
-o	Film outtake
-p	1955 phone book from *BTTF1*
-v	Video game print materials or commentaries
-s1	Screenplay (draft one)
-s2	Screenplay (draft two)
-s3	Screenplay (draft three)
-s4	Screenplay (draft four)
-sp	Screenplay (production draft)
-sx	Screenplay (*Paradox*)

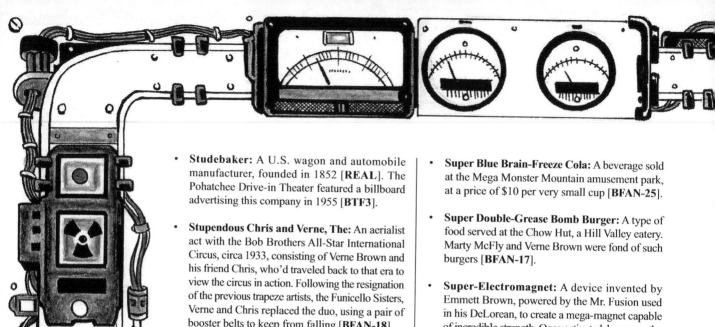

- **Studebaker:** A U.S. wagon and automobile manufacturer, founded in 1852 [**REAL**]. The Pohatchee Drive-in Theater featured a billboard advertising this company in 1955 [**BTF3**].

- **Stupendous Chris and Verne, The:** An aerialist act with the Bob Brothers All-Star International Circus, circa 1933, consisting of Verne Brown and his friend Chris, who'd traveled back to that era to view the circus in action. Following the resignation of the previous trapeze artists, the Funicello Sisters, Verne and Chris replaced the duo, using a pair of booster belts to keep from falling [**BFAN-18**].

- **Sub-ether Time-Tracking Scanner:** A device aboard Emmett Brown's Eight-Passenger DeLorean Time-Travel Vehicle, enabling occupants to track other cars' temporal movements [**RIDE**].

- **Sub-ether Tracking System:** A computer program installed at the Institute of Future Technology's Anti-Gravitic Laboratory, used to confirm space-time coordinates [**RIDE**].

- **Sub-ether Transmission Linkup:** A faster-than-light method of communicating information via hovercam, used by the Institute of Future Technology to broadcast messages into the past or future [**RIDE**]. Emmett Brown utilized this technology to transmit educational recordings from various eras, including 3 million B.C. [**BFAN-3**].

- **Suc-o-Matic:** A self-propelled, energy-saving vacuum cleaner invented by Emmett Brown, and powered by the very dust it picked up. Doc developed this device at the Institute of Future Technology [**RIDE**].

- **Sue's Diner**: A restaurant located in Hill Valley, circa 1991 [**BFAN-12**].

- **sugar-frosted nut and sweet raisin-apple-treat mix:** Verne Brown's favorite after-school snack [**BFAN-26**].

- **Sunset**: A street in Los Angeles, California. KCET was located at 4401 Sunset [**BFAN-12**].

- **Sunshine Diner:** A roadside eatery along a highway outside Hill Valley, circa 1931. Marty McFly passed this restaurant while trying to help Emmett Brown escape from a police vehicle stolen by Irving "Kid" Tannen, who planned to murder the scientist [**TLTL-1**].

- **Super Blue Brain-Freeze Cola:** A beverage sold at the Mega Monster Mountain amusement park, at a price of $10 per very small cup [**BFAN-25**].

- **Super Double-Grease Bomb Burger:** A type of food served at the Chow Hut, a Hill Valley eatery. Marty McFly and Verne Brown were fond of such burgers [**BFAN-17**].

- **Super-Electromagnet:** A device invented by Emmett Brown, powered by the Mr. Fusion used in his DeLorean, to create a mega-magnet capable of incredible strength. Once activated, however, the device began attracting every steel object within its immediate vicinity—including the camera Doc used to record the experiment, which crashed into the Super-Electromagnet, damaging both it and the camera [**BFAN-1**].

- **Super-Growth Mondo-Corn:** A strain of corn genetically engineered by Emmett and Clara Brown, so named for its massive size—a single ear nearly filled Doc's garage workshop. In order to pop the corn's enormous kernels, the scientist also invented the room-sized ELB Quick-o-Popper [**BFAN-21**].

- **Super Inflatable "Tit":** A breast-enhancement product offered by Bottoms Up, a plastic-surgery franchise, circa 2015, "for that last-minute adjustment" [**BTF2**].

- **Super Large Deluxe Gigantor Pizza**: A specialty dish on the menu of Tony's Pizza, a restaurant located in Hill Valley [**BFAN-12**].

- **Super Mega Arcade World:** A video arcade in Hill Valley, owned by a man named Leo. Verne Brown spent much time at this establishment during his youth, playing such games as *BraveLord and Monstrux*.

  When a power surge at Super Mega Arcade World caused that game's title characters to come to life, the demon Monstrux possessed the building, causing tentacles resembling castle towers to sprout from its roof, and a great maw to appear on its storefront. Eventually, Verne defeated Monstrux, then sent the demon and BraveLord back to cyberspace, restoring the building's appearance [**BFAN-19**].

- **Super-Splash Water World:** A water park in or near Hill Valley, circa 1991. Verne Brown was particularly fond of this attraction [**BFAN-2, BFAN-11**].

- **Super-Sudsy Soap:** A concentrated, lemon-scented cleaning solution invented by Emmett Brown. Doc used two drops to wash his ELB Hot-Diggity Dogger—which proved to be one drop too many, as the second drop caused a river of soap suds to spew from his workshop and into the family's home and yard [**BFAN-22**].

- **Super Unleaded Plus:** A type of fuel offered at Texaco's Hill Valley gas station, circa 2015, priced at $8.99 per gallon [**BTF2**].

- **Super-Winnelumbago:** A model of motor home. Biff Tannen purchased a custom-built, extra-deluxe Super-Winnelumbago at the Hill Valley Livery Vehicle Hut, containing two television sets [**BFAN-20**].

  NOTE: The vehicle's name was a play on "Winnebago" (a popular recreational vehicle produced by Winnebago Industries) and "lumbago" (a common musculoskeletal disorder involving lower back pain).

- **Super X-Tra Fusion Plus:** A type of fuel offered at Texaco's Hill Valley gas station, circa 2015, priced at $7.62 per gallon [**BTF2**].

- **Supreme Klingon, The:** A fictional extraterrestrial leader mentioned during Marty McFly's ruse to pose as Darth Vader, from the planet Vulcan, in order to convince George McFly to ask Lorraine Baines to the Enchantment Under the Sea Dance [**BTF1-d**].

  NOTE: The Supreme Klingon—named after Star Trek*'s Klingon Empire—was not mentioned in the filmed version of the scene, but was added in the novelization.*

- **suspended animation kennel:** A type of business in 2015, at which individuals could leave pets for extended periods of time. Emmett Brown left Einstein in the care of such a kennel when he returned to 1985 to retrieve Marty McFly, in order to save Marty's children from going to prison [**BTF2**].

- **Sussex McFlys, The:** A branch of the McFly clan from Sussex, England, circa 1367. Among the Sussex McFlys were Harold and Jennivere McFly [**BFAN-2**].

- **Sweetie-pi-r-squared:** An affectionate nickname that Emmett Brown sometimes used when addressing his wife, Clara [**BFAN-8**].

- **Sweet Madonna Liberace Fruit:** A menu item sold at Café 80's in 2015 [**BTF2**].

- **Swiss Terrorists:** A resistance organization operating in 2015. According to a *USA Today* report, the CIA considered the threat posed by the terrorists to be genuine [**BTF2**].

  NOTE: The existence of Swiss terrorists was an ironic joke, as the Swiss Confederation has a long history of armed neutrality, has not been in a state of war internationally since 1815 and is frequently involved in peace-building processes.

- **Switzerland:** A landlocked European country consisting of 26 cantons (member-states), bordered by Austria, France, Germany, Italy and Liechtenstein [**REAL**]. In Biffhorrific 1985, Biff Tannen—now Marty McFly's step-father, after murdering George McFly—sent Marty away to a boarding school in Switzerland [**BTF2**].

- **Sybor:** A word scrawled in graffiti on the entrance to Lyon Estates in Biffhorrific 1985, in which the housing development was a slum [**BTF2**].

- **Sycamore Street:** A road in Hill Valley, located near 2nd, and lined with houses built during the 1920s and '30s. George McFly grew up in a home on this street [**BTF1-n**].

- **Sydney:** A city in Australia and the state capital of New South Wales [**REAL**]. Sydney was the site of HM Prison, a penal facility run in 1790 by warden Mongo P. Tannen. Two thugs from the future, Frankie and Sidney, spent time at this prison after stealing Emmett Brown's DeLorean, which brought them into Sydney's past after its voice-activated time circuits mistook their conversation as a destination [**BFAN-7b**].

  NOTE: Presumably, "HM" stood for "His Majesty's."

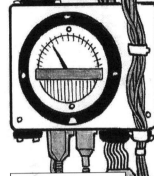

CODE	STORY
NIKE	*BTTF*-themed TV commercial: Nike
NTND	Nintendo *Back to the Future—The Ride* Mini-Game
PIZA	*BTTF*-themed TV commercial: Pizza Hut
PNBL	Data East *BTTF* pinball game
REAL	Real life
RIDE	Simulator: *Back to the Future—The Ride*
SCRM	2010 Scream Awards: *Back to the Future 25th Anniversary Reunion* (broadcast)
SCRT	2010 Scream Awards: *Back to the Future 25th Anniversary Reunion* (trailer)
SIMP	Simulator: *The Simpsons Ride*
SLOT	*Back to the Future Video Slots*
STLZ	Unused *BTTF* footage of Eric Stoltz as Marty McFly
STRY	*Back to the Future Storybook*
TEST	Screen tests: Crispin Glover, Lea Thompson and Tom Wilson
TLTL	Telltale Games' *Back to the Future—The Game*
TOPS	Topps' *Back to the Future II* trading-card set
TRIL	*BTTF: The Official Book of the Complete Movie Trilogy*
UNIV	Universal Studios Hollywood promotional video

SUFFIX	MEDIUM
-b	*BTTF2*'s Biff Tannen Museum video (extended)
-c	Credit sequence to the animated series
-d	Film deleted scene
-n	Film novelization
-o	Film outtake
-p	1955 phone book from *BTTF1*
-v	Video game print materials or commentaries
-s1	Screenplay (draft one)
-s2	Screenplay (draft two)
-s3	Screenplay (draft three)
-s4	Screenplay (draft four)
-sp	Screenplay (production draft)
-sx	Screenplay (*Paradox*)

TANNEN, BIFF

(CENTER, WITH BUFORD, IRVING AND GRIFF)

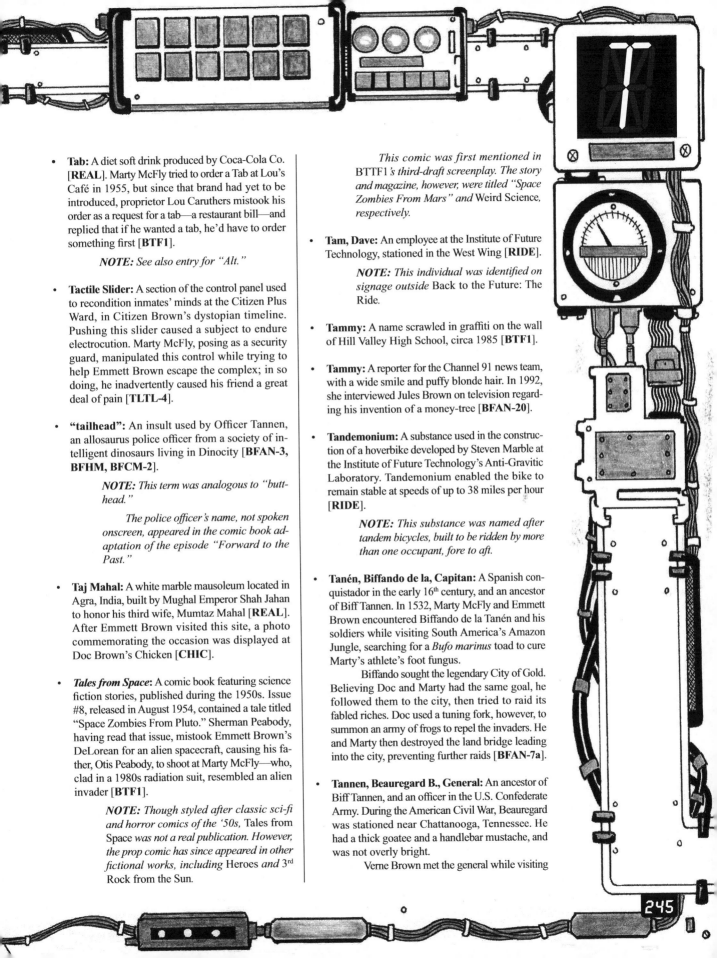

- **Tab:** A diet soft drink produced by Coca-Cola Co. [**REAL**]. Marty McFly tried to order a Tab at Lou's Café in 1955, but since that brand had yet to be introduced, proprietor Lou Caruthers mistook his order as a request for a tab—a restaurant bill—and replied that if he wanted a tab, he'd have to order something first [**BTF1**].

     NOTE: See also entry for "Alt."

- **Tactile Slider:** A section of the control panel used to recondition inmates' minds at the Citizen Plus Ward, in Citizen Brown's dystopian timeline. Pushing this slider caused a subject to endure electrocution. Marty McFly, posing as a security guard, manipulated this control while trying to help Emmett Brown escape the complex; in so doing, he inadvertently caused his friend a great deal of pain [**TLTL-4**].

- **"tailhead":** An insult used by Officer Tannen, an allosaurus police officer from a society of intelligent dinosaurs living in Dinocity [**BFAN-3, BFHM, BFCM-2**].

     NOTE: This term was analogous to "butt-head."

     The police officer's name, not spoken onscreen, appeared in the comic book adaptation of the episode "Forward to the Past."

- **Taj Mahal:** A white marble mausoleum located in Agra, India, built by Mughal Emperor Shah Jahan to honor his third wife, Mumtaz Mahal [**REAL**]. After Emmett Brown visited this site, a photo commemorating the occasion was displayed at Doc Brown's Chicken [**CHIC**].

- *Tales from Space*: A comic book featuring science fiction stories, published during the 1950s. Issue #8, released in August 1954, contained a tale titled "Space Zombies From Pluto." Sherman Peabody, having read that issue, mistook Emmett Brown's DeLorean for an alien spacecraft, causing his father, Otis Peabody, to shoot at Marty McFly—who, clad in a 1980s radiation suit, resembled an alien invader [**BTF1**].

     NOTE: Though styled after classic sci-fi and horror comics of the '50s, Tales from Space *was not a real publication. However, the prop comic has since appeared in other fictional works, including* Heroes *and* 3rd Rock from the Sun.

This comic was first mentioned in BTTF1's third-draft screenplay. The story and magazine, however, were titled "Space Zombies From Mars" and Weird Science, *respectively.*

- **Tam, Dave:** An employee at the Institute of Future Technology, stationed in the West Wing [**RIDE**].

     NOTE: This individual was identified on signage outside Back to the Future: The Ride.

- **Tammy:** A name scrawled in graffiti on the wall of Hill Valley High School, circa 1985 [**BTF1**].

- **Tammy:** A reporter for the Channel 91 news team, with a wide smile and puffy blonde hair. In 1992, she interviewed Jules Brown on television regarding his invention of a money-tree [**BFAN-20**].

- **Tandemonium:** A substance used in the construction of a hoverbike developed by Steven Marble at the Institute of Future Technology's Anti-Gravitic Laboratory. Tandemonium enabled the bike to remain stable at speeds of up to 38 miles per hour [**RIDE**].

     NOTE: This substance was named after tandem bicycles, built to be ridden by more than one occupant, fore to aft.

- **Tanén, Biffando de la, Capitan:** A Spanish conquistador in the early 16th century, and an ancestor of Biff Tannen. In 1532, Marty McFly and Emmett Brown encountered Biffando de la Tanén and his soldiers while visiting South America's Amazon Jungle, searching for a *Bufo marinus* toad to cure Marty's athlete's foot fungus.

     Biffando sought the legendary City of Gold. Believing Doc and Marty had the same goal, he followed them to the city, then tried to raid its fabled riches. Doc used a tuning fork, however, to summon an army of frogs to repel the invaders. He and Marty then destroyed the land bridge leading into the city, preventing further raids [**BFAN-7a**].

- **Tannen, Beauregard B., General:** An ancestor of Biff Tannen, and an officer in the U.S. Confederate Army. During the American Civil War, Beauregard was stationed near Chattanooga, Tennessee. He had a thick goatee and a handlebar mustache, and was not overly bright.

     Verne Brown met the general while visiting

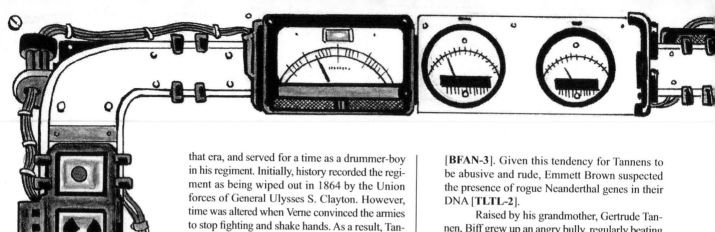

that era, and served for a time as a drummer-boy in his regiment. Initially, history recorded the regiment as being wiped out in 1864 by the Union forces of General Ulysses S. Clayton. However, time was altered when Verne convinced the armies to stop fighting and shake hands. As a result, Tannen's soldiers never fought a single battle, and thus survived the war [**BFAN-1**].

Sometime before 1875, Beauregard relocated to Hill Valley as a civilian. Acting like a swaggering bigshot and throwing money around, he purchased a plot of land and built the Palace Saloon and Hotel. Edna Strickland, deeming the bar a blight on Hill Valley, tried to burn it to the ground, but Marty McFly thwarted her plans [**TLTL-5**].

The book *Hill Valley Historical Society, 1865-1990* noted that after Marshal James Strickland brought order to a formerly lawless Hill Valley, Beauregard Tannen "tipped the balance back toward 'lawless'" [**TLTL-v**]. His image was among the visual stimuli used by Emmett Brown to evoke reactions from test subjects using his Mental Alignment Meter [**TLTL-4**].

NOTE: Beauregard's middle initial, B., was revealed in Telltale Games' video game.

- **Tannen, Biff Howard:** A largely built, dim-witted and violent thug in Hill Valley, who bullied and abused others throughout his life to get whatever he wanted [**BTF1**]. The son of gangster Irving "Kid" Tannen [**TLTL-1**], Biff had two brothers, named Cliff and Riff [**TLTL-2**]. He bathed infrequently, using Oil of Olay, baby shampoo and Doggy Dip for Fleas and Ticks; played with a rubber duck in the tub; and had a tattoo of a heart on his left thigh [**BFCL-3**].

Biff was born in 1938. His mother had been impregnated the previous year, when Kid escaped from San Quentin State Prison for three hours [**TLTL-1**]. Biff called people "buttheads" and frequently misspoke when using slang phrases, such as "make like a tree and get out of here" for "make like a tree and leave" [**BTF1**], and "hasta la bye-bye" for "hasta la vista" [**RIDE**].

Biff Tannen descended from a long line of bullying, corrupt Tannens [**BTF2, BTF3, BFAN-1 to BFAN-26, BFCM-1 to BFCM-4, BFCL-1 to BFCL-3, TLTL-1 to TLTL-5**]. Marty McFly dubbed these individuals "Biffsters," astounded at how frequently they shared his physical characteristics and personality traits [**BFAN-4**]. In one timeline, Marty even encountered a dinosaur with Tannen characteristics

[**BFAN-3**]. Given this tendency for Tannens to be abusive and rude, Emmett Brown suspected the presence of rogue Neanderthal genes in their DNA [**TLTL-2**].

Raised by his grandmother, Gertrude Tannen, Biff grew up an angry bully, regularly beating up other children, no matter how young [**BTF2**]. A student at Hill Valley High School, he was often in trouble with Vice-Principal Gerald Strickland, who had little patience for his antics. Biff was openly attracted to classmate Lorraine Baines, frequently harassing her and vowing that he would one day make her his girl. Lorraine had no interest in him, but Biff was unwilling to take no for an answer [**BTF1**].

Biff drove a Ford Super Deluxe, of which he was extremely fond [**BTF1**], and named it Shiela [**TLTL-3**]. Only Biff could start the vehicle—not even his mechanic, Terry [**BTF2**]. He and his gang—Match, 3-D and Joey ("Skinhead")—frequently terrorized others, stealing money from the helpless and manhandling young women [**BTF1**]. One frequent victim was Lester, a youth too scrawny to fight back [**BTF2-n**].

George McFly was also vulnerable to Biff's taunting. Tannen often intimidated George, as well as forcing him to do Biff's homework. This pattern continued three decades later, when Biff—as George's work supervisor—forced George to write reports for him, just as he had in high school. On one occasion, in 1985, Biff forced George to lend him his car (despite owning his own), which he then drove while intoxicated, causing an accident, the damage from which he refused to pay for. This infuriated Marty, who wished his father would stand up for himself. George, however, lacked the self-confidence to confront his lifelong tormentor.

That year, Brown built a time machine out of a DeLorean sports car. While helping Doc test the contraption, Marty ended up stranded in 1955, after fleeing from a group of Libyan nationalists, from whom Doc had stolen plutonium to power the vehicle. While spending a week in the past, Marty worked hard to bolster George's self-confidence so that he would ask Lorraine to the Enchantment Under the Sea Dance, in order to repair a timeline fracture caused by Lorraine falling for Marty instead of his father.

Marty hated seeing how Tannen treated both of his parents during their teen years, and felt a strong need to protect them. He repeatedly humiliated Biff in public, first tripping him at Lou's Café as he bullied George, and then causing him to

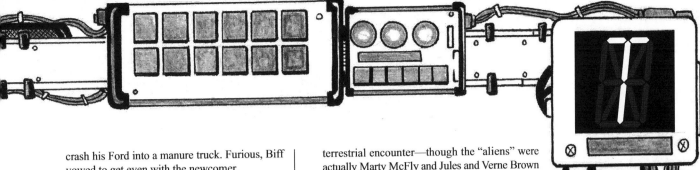

crash his Ford into a manure truck. Furious, Biff vowed to get even with the newcomer.

On the night of the dance, Biff found the opportunity to do so. Hauling Marty out of a car, he told his gang to take him away while Biff stayed in the vehicle with Lorraine. Minutes later, George found Biff trying to rape her in the high school parking lot and, though terrified, he refused to back down. McFly's newfound confidence made him willing to stand up to Biff, and he defended her honor, knocking the would-be sex offender unconscious with a single punch. This earned him Lorraine's admiration, as well as the respect of his fellow students, who were excited to see the bully get what had long been coming to him.

This incident drastically changed both men's lives, making George more successful, while humbling Biff in the process. When Marty returned to his own era, the former bully was now the smiley proprietor of Biff's Automotive Detailing. Though still a conniver who tried to avoid hard work, the docile and obsequious Biff feared and respected George, humbly backing down whenever confronted [**BTF1**].

When a team of time-travel scientists from the Institute of Future Technology visited 1955, young Biff stowed away as the group returned to 1991. Infiltrating the institute's Anti-Gravitic Laboratory, he stole Doc's DeLorean and attempted to alter history, locking the scientist within his lab. Unable to pursue the thief, Doc dispatched a team of Time-Travel Volunteers aboard his Eight-Passenger DeLorean Time-Travel Vehicle. Tannen evaded the other car as it chased him to 2015 and back to prehistoric times.

Narrowly evading a Tyrannosaurus rex, Biff found himself in imminent danger from an underground lava spring. The Time-Travel Volunteers rescued him in time, bumping the stolen car while accelerating to 88 miles per hour. This transported both vehicles back to the institute, where Biff was detained and then returned to his own era [**RIDE**].

Biff graduated high school late, repeating his senior year. This, he claimed, was done on purpose, as a favor to help out the school's football team [**BTF2-b**].

In 1967, Tannen was staunchly in favor of the Vietnam War, and had a pet German Shepherd named Chopper. During that era, he owned a '65 Ranchero with bumper stickers proudly proclaiming "America: Love It or Leave It" [**BTF2-s1**].

That same year, during the arrival of Comet Kahooey, he had what he believed to be an extra-terrestrial encounter—though the "aliens" were actually Marty McFly and Jules and Verne Brown in disguise. Biff told others about this experience, gaining a reputation as an expert on aliens. He later wrote an autobiography detailing the encounter, titled *Aliens Who I Have Known & Loved*, which he sold at a roadside stand called Biff's Alien Souvenirs. When the comet returned in 1992, Biff panicked, inciting mass hysteria by convincing folks that it heralded the arrival of invaders from the stars—and that Emmett Brown was one of them (since Biff had mistaken Doc's Flying Observatory for a spacecraft) [**BFAN-23**].

As he grew older, Biff became a weak failure, like George McFly had once been, with even his grandson, Griff, pushing him around. But in 2015, upon discovering the existence of Doc's time machine, he decided to use the invention to improve his life. Stealing the vehicle, Biff brought a copy of *Grays Sports Almanac: Complete Sports Statistics 1950-2000* back to 1955, where he delivered it to his younger self. The book listed the results of a half-century's worth of sporting events, which young Biff used to earn billions of dollars betting on the games described within [**BTF2**]. He made his first millions on his 21st birthday, betting on horse races at the Valley Racing Association [**BTF2-b**].

In the resultant "Biffhorrific" timeline, Biff emerged as a powerful criminal kingpin who controlled Hill Valley, with Match, 3-D and Skinhead serving as his loyal enforcers. In that reality, Biff murdered George McFly in 1973. He later married Lorraine, though she never loved him and only agreed to the joining in order to have the money to care for her fatherless children. Biff supported the McFly kids financially, but made it clear that he didn't consider them his family. He also paid for Lorraine to have multiple cosmetic surgeries to stay young-looking, including having her breasts greatly enlarged. Unhappy with her lot in life, and with her manufactured physique, she once again drowned her sorrows in alcohol [**BTF2**].

Obscenely wealthy, Tannen founded BiffCo Enterprises, which included such holdings as the San Andreas Nuclear Power Plant, Biff's Pleasure Palace, Biff's Realty, the Biff Tannen Museum, BiffCoToxic Waste Disposal and more. He used his power to legalize casino gambling in California [**BTF2-b**], and to have his son, Biff Jr., named the state's governor [**BTF2-s2**]. U.S. presidential term limits were repealed in this reality, enabling Richard Nixon to retain the office until at least

CODE	STORY
NIKE	*BTTF*-themed TV commercial: Nike
NTND	Nintendo *Back to the Future—The Ride* Mini-Game
PIZA	*BTTF*-themed TV commercial: Pizza Hut
PNBL	Data East *BTTF* pinball game
REAL	Real life
RIDE	Simulator: *Back to the Future—The Ride*
SCRM	2010 Scream Awards: *Back to the Future* 25th Anniversary Reunion (broadcast)
SCRT	2010 Scream Awards: *Back to the Future* 25th Anniversary Reunion (trailer)
SIMP	Simulator: *The Simpsons Ride*
SLOT	*Back to the Future* Video Slots
STLZ	Unused *BTTF* footage of Eric Stoltz as Marty McFly
STRY	*Back to the Future* Storybook
TEST	Screen tests: Crispin Glover, Lea Thompson and Tom Wilson
TLTL	Telltale Games' *Back to the Future—The Game*
TOPS	Topps' *Back to the Future II* trading-card set
TRIL	*BTTF: The Official Book of the Complete Movie Trilogy*
UNIV	Universal Studios Hollywood promotional video

SUFFIX	MEDIUM
-b	*BTTF2*'s Biff Tannen Museum video (extended)
-c	Credit sequence to the animated series
-d	Film deleted scene
-n	Film novelization
-o	Film outtake
-p	1955 phone book from *BTTF1*
-v	Video game print materials or commentaries
-s1	Screenplay (draft one)
-s2	Screenplay (draft two)
-s3	Screenplay (draft three)
-s4	Screenplay (draft four)
-sp	Screenplay (production draft)
-sx	Screenplay (*Paradox*)

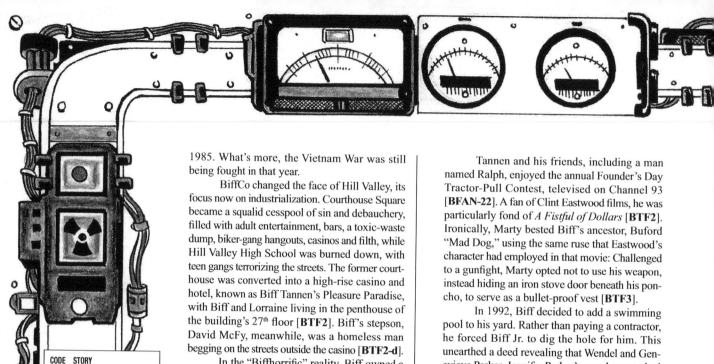

1985. What's more, the Vietnam War was still being fought in that year.

BiffCo changed the face of Hill Valley, its focus now on industrialization. Courthouse Square became a squalid cesspool of sin and debauchery, filled with adult entertainment, bars, a toxic-waste dump, biker-gang hangouts, casinos and filth, while Hill Valley High School was burned down, with teen gangs terrorizing the streets. The former courthouse was converted into a high-rise casino and hotel, known as Biff Tannen's Pleasure Paradise, with Biff and Lorraine living in the penthouse of the building's 27th floor [**BTF2**]. Biff's stepson, David McFy, meanwhile, was a homeless man begging on the streets outside the casino [**BTF2-d**].

In the "Biffhorrific" reality, Biff owned a yacht called the *Monkey Business*, as well as a massive gated mansion known as Tannen Manor, and had a number of prominent friends, including teamster boss Jimmy Hoffa. Moreover, his wealth afforded Tannen the luxury of dating beautiful Hollywood starlets, including Jayne Mansfield and Marilyn Monroe [**BTF2-b**].

Discovering what Biff had done to alter history, Marty and Doc retrieved the almanac from the past, though Biff nearly murdered Marty using the same gun that had once killed his father. This restored the city to its prior state, eliminating Biff's wealth and influence [**BTF2**].

During the 1990s, Biff once again manifested his former cockiness, corruption and laziness, launching a slew of schemes to get rich quick. After watching a TV news report about Jules Brown's invention of a money-tree, Biff stole the plant, intending to use it to attain instant wealth. Ecstatic with greed, he and Biff Jr. ordered a custom-built, extra-deluxe Super-Winnelumbago from the Hill Valley Livery Vehicle Hut—which Biff then had to pay for himself once the money-tree's leaves shriveled, making it useless as a source of legal tender [**BFAN-20**].

When children's TV host Walter Wisdom offered a $50,000 reward to anyone who brought a live dinosaur or Bigfoot to his studio, Biff thought of his uncle, Tim Tannen, whose face, head and chest were excessively hairy. Biff considered trying to pass Tim off as a Bigfoot and swindle Wisdom out of the money. Instead he kidnapped Verne Brown's pet Apatosaurus, Tiny, and delivered the creature to the studio. Verne rescued Tiny before showtime, replacing him with a fake-looking substitute, and thus publicly humiliating Wisdom and Biff [**BFAN-26**].

Tannen and his friends, including a man named Ralph, enjoyed the annual Founder's Day Tractor-Pull Contest, televised on Channel 93 [**BFAN-22**]. A fan of Clint Eastwood films, he was particularly fond of *A Fistful of Dollars* [**BTF2**]. Ironically, Marty bested Biff's ancestor, Buford "Mad Dog," using the same ruse that Eastwood's character had employed in that movie: Challenged to a gunfight, Marty opted not to use his weapon, instead hiding an iron stove door beneath his poncho, to serve as a bullet-proof vest [**BTF3**].

In 1992, Biff decided to add a swimming pool to his yard. Rather than paying a contractor, he forced Biff Jr. to dig the hole for him. This unearthed a deed revealing that Wendel and Genevieve Parker, Jennifer Parker's grandparents, had signed over the Parker BTQ Ranch to his ancestor, Thaddeus Tannen, in 1875. Biff tried to turn the property into a toxic-waste dump and miniature golf course, but Marty traveled back in time to help the ranchers keep their property, arranging for Wendel to sign the deed in disappearing ink. By Biff's era, the deed thus appeared unsigned, and was deemed invalid [**BFAN-16**].

In addition to Biff Jr., Biff also had a daughter, Tiffany Tannen [**TLTL-1, BFCG**]. Tiff dressed in typical punk-rock fashion, her hair dyed several colors [**TLTL-v**].

In an alternate timeline in which Kid Tannen did not spend his life in prison, Kid and his three sons terrorized Hill Valley, calling themselves the Tannen Gang. With their father running the show, the Tannen brothers badly beat George after the Enchantment Under the Sea Dance, leaving him paralyzed in a wheelchair, and ran his kids out of town. Marty averted this version of history, however, by returning to 1931 to make sure Kid ended up behind bars [**TLTL-2**].

In so doing, Marty inadvertently spawned a new timeline—one in which Hill Valley evolved into a dystopian society, ruled by Emmett Brown, now known as First Citizen Brown. Biff, a lifelong delinquent, was subjected to the Citizen Plus Program, a government re-education initiative enacted by Edna Strickland, encouraging the wayward to become better citizens. Hypnotherapy tamed his negative urges, rendering obedience automatic by making it impossible for him to break any rules without feeling physically ill. Due to this brainwashing, Biff became meek and obedient, fearful of the consequences if he resisted.

Biff received a digital watch that performed various functions, including emitting a signal in-

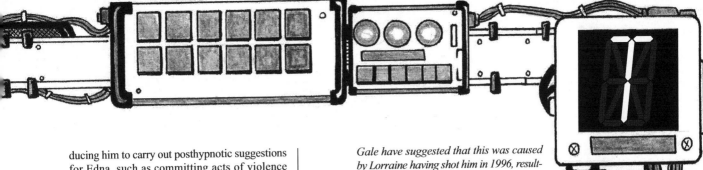

ducing him to carry out posthypnotic suggestions for Edna, such as committing acts of violence against those she deemed dangerous. Realizing this to be the case, Marty—looking to create a diversion—broke through Biff's reconditioning, causing him to grow violent. As a result, the former bully was incarcerated at the Citizen Plus Ward [**TLTL-3, TLTL-4**].

Marty and Doc eventually eliminated this timeline. But in so doing, they created yet another reality, in which Edna and Kid fell in love in prison, and later married, thereby making Edna Strickland Biff's stepmother [**TLTL-5**].

NOTE: Robert Zemeckis and Bob Gale named Biff after Ned Tanen, a former production chief at Universal, with whom the filmmakers clashed during pre-production of BTTF1.

In the initial draft of that film's screenplay, Biff was a security officer with a young daughter. Years later, Looney Labs' BTTF card game and Telltale Games' BTTF video game named her Tiffany "Tiff" Tannen.

An inscription on Biff's cane in BTTF2 indicated his middle initial to be H, but his full middle name, Howard, was unknown until Episode 3 of the video game. A separate character by the name of Howard appeared in an early draft of BTTF1, along with a daughter who may have been a prototype for Tiff Tannen.

Back to the Future: The Ride claimed Biff graduated high school in 1955, but since he was still attending the school in November of that year, during the first two films, the earliest he could have graduated would have been 1956.

The name "Biffhorrific" was coined by the film crew while BTTF2 was being produced. Other monikers for that alternate Hill Valley included "Hell Valley" (scrawled on the city's greeting sign), "Biff City" (mentioned in the movie's first-draft screenplay) and "Tannen Valley" (in the second-draft script).

After returning from 1955, old Biff was seen clutching his chest in pain, then was gone by the time Marty and Doc returned to the DeLorean. A deleted scene revealed that this was due to his having vanished, as though erased from history. Zemeckis and

Gale have suggested that this was caused by Lorraine having shot him in 1996, resulting in his no longer existing by 2015.

The identity of Biff Jr.'s and Tiffany's mother(s) is unknown, as are the name and whereabouts of Biff's own mom. Moreover, it's unclear whether Cliff and Riff existed in the original timeline, or only in the alternate timeline in which Kid had not gone to prison. In BTTF2, Biff and his grandmother appeared to live alone.

For a full list of known Biffsters, see Appendix III.

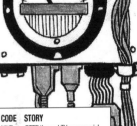

- **Tannen, Biff Jr. ("Junior"):** One of Biff Tannen's children, circa 1992 [**BFAN-16, BFAN-19, BFAN-20, BFAN-21, BFAN-22, BFAN-26**]. Obese and unkempt, Biff Jr. appeared unhappy with his life, particularly when his father forced him to perform manual labor, such as digging a swimming pool in their back yard [**BFAN-16**].

  Like his father, Biff Jr. bullied others to get what he wanted. This annoyed Leo, the owner of Super Mega Arcade World, who had no tolerance for young Biff's tendency to cut in line and abuse the equipment and other patrons [**BFAN-19**]. Biff sometimes teamed up with a classmate named Jackson to bully Verne Brown, calling him "Verne the Worm" and other taunts. The dim-witted Biff Jr. usually resorted to simply repeating Jackson's insults, word for word, as though they were his own [**BFAN-21**].

  A fan of television cartoons, the youth was frustrated at Biff Sr.'s tendency to monopolize the Tannen family's only television [**BFAN-20**]. Among his favorite TV series were *Mr. Wisdom* and the *He-Boy Gladiator Show* [**BFAN-26**].

  In the Biffhoriffic version of 1985, Biff Jr. was the governor of California, thanks to the influence of his powerful father. By 2015, he was a businessman who owned several franchises, including Café 80's [**BTF2-s2**].

  NOTE: Given that Biff Jr. would have been a young child in 1985, it's unclear how he could have been California's governor, even with his corrupt father's backing.

- **Tannen, Bob ("Bob the Nasty"):** An ancestor of Biff Tannen who was immortalized in P.T. Tannen's *Villains Through History* in Wax, a wax-museum exhibit at the 1904 St. Louis World Exposition, manned by Bob's nephew, P.T. Tannen. Bob, ac-

CODE	STORY
NIKE	*BTTF*-themed TV commercial: Nike
NTND	Nintendo *Back to the Future—The Ride* Mini-Game
PIZA	*BTTF*-themed TV commercial: Pizza Hut
PNBL	Data East *BTTF* pinball game
REAL	Real life
RIDE	Simulator: *Back to the Future—The Ride*
SCRM	2010 Scream Awards: *Back to the Future* 25th Anniversary Reunion (broadcast)
SCRT	2010 Scream Awards: *Back to the Future* 25th Anniversary Reunion (trailer)
SIMP	Simulator: *The Simpsons Ride*
SLOT	*Back to the Future Video Slots*
STLZ	Unused *BTTF* footage of Eric Stoltz as Marty McFly
STRY	*Back to the Future Storybook*
TEST	Screen tests: Crispin Glover, Lea Thompson and Tom Wilson
TLTL	Telltale Games' *Back to the Future—The Game*
TOPS	Topps' *Back to the Future II* trading-card set
TRIL	*BTTF: The Official Book of the Complete Movie Trilogy*
UNIV	Universal Studios Hollywood promotional video

SUFFIX	MEDIUM
-b	*BTTF2*'s Biff Tannen Museum video (extended)
-c	Credit sequence to the animated series
-d	Film deleted scene
-n	Film novelization
-o	Film outtake
-p	1955 phone book from *BTTF1*
-v	Video game print materials or commentaries
-s1	Screenplay (draft one)
-s2	Screenplay (draft two)
-s3	Screenplay (draft three)
-s4	Screenplay (draft four)
-sp	Screenplay (production draft)
-sx	Screenplay (*Paradox*)

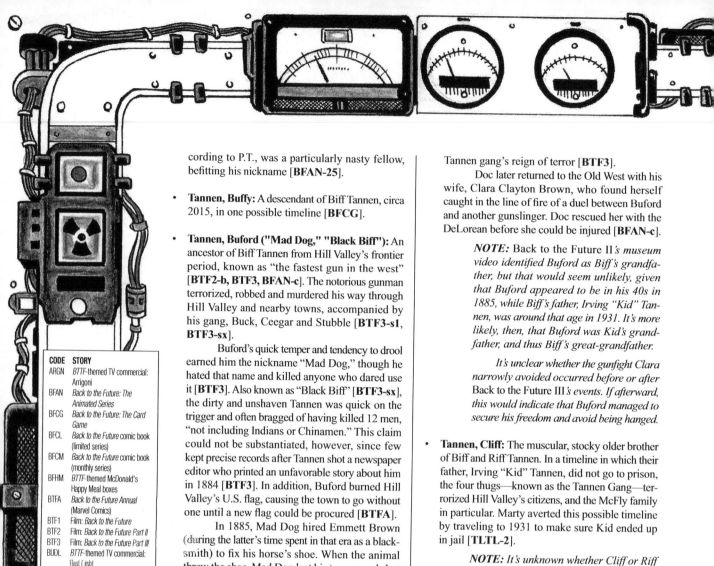

cording to P.T., was a particularly nasty fellow, befitting his nickname [**BFAN-25**].

- **Tannen, Buffy:** A descendant of Biff Tannen, circa 2015, in one possible timeline [**BFCG**].

- **Tannen, Buford ("Mad Dog," "Black Biff"):** An ancestor of Biff Tannen from Hill Valley's frontier period, known as "the fastest gun in the west" [**BTF2-b, BTF3, BFAN-c**]. The notorious gunman terrorized, robbed and murdered his way through Hill Valley and nearby towns, accompanied by his gang, Buck, Ceegar and Stubble [**BTF3-s1, BTF3-sx**].

  Buford's quick temper and tendency to drool earned him the nickname "Mad Dog," though he hated that name and killed anyone who dared use it [**BTF3**]. Also known as "Black Biff" [**BTF3-sx**], the dirty and unshaven Tannen was quick on the trigger and often bragged of having killed 12 men, "not including Indians or Chinamen." This claim could not be substantiated, however, since few kept precise records after Tannen shot a newspaper editor who printed an unfavorable story about him in 1884 [**BTF3**]. In addition, Buford burned Hill Valley's U.S. flag, causing the town to go without one until a new flag could be procured [**BTFA**].

  In 1885, Mad Dog hired Emmett Brown (during the latter's time spent in that era as a blacksmith) to fix his horse's shoe. When the animal threw the shoe, Mad Dog lost his temper and shot it, breaking a bottle of his favorite liquor in the process. Furious, he demanded that Doc pay him the $80 he lost on the horse and booze. When Brown refused, Tannen tried to kill him at the Hill Valley Festival. Marty McFly (traveling under the alias Clint Eastwood) intervened, hitting Buford with a Frisbie pie plate, and earning his own death-mark in the process. Marshal James Strickland forced Tannen and his gang to leave the city, but they returned the following Monday, intent on killing both Marty and Doc [**BTF3**]. Tannen shot Strickland in the process, in view of the man's son [**BTF3-d**].

  When Marty tried to back out of a duel, Buford threatened to kill him in cold blood. Marty outsmarted the thug, hiding an oven door underneath his pancho to protect himself, just as Clint Eastwood's character had done in the film *A Fistful of Dollars*. His hand busted, Tannen was no match for Marty, who punched him in the face, causing him to land in a manure cart. Strickland's deputy arrested Buford and his cronies, thus ending the

Tannen gang's reign of terror [**BTF3**].

  Doc later returned to the Old West with his wife, Clara Clayton Brown, who found herself caught in the line of fire of a duel between Buford and another gunslinger. Doc rescued her with the DeLorean before she could be injured [**BFAN-c**].

  > *NOTE: Back to the Future II's museum video identified Buford as Biff's grandfather, but that would seem unlikely, given that Buford appeared to be in his 40s in 1885, while Biff's father, Irving "Kid" Tannen, was around that age in 1931. It's more likely, then, that Buford was Kid's grandfather, and thus Biff's great-grandfather.*
  >
  > *It's unclear whether the gunfight Clara narrowly avoided occurred before or after Back to the Future III's events. If afterward, this would indicate that Buford managed to secure his freedom and avoid being hanged.*

- **Tannen, Cliff:** The muscular, stocky older brother of Biff and Riff Tannen. In a timeline in which their father, Irving "Kid" Tannen, did not go to prison, the four thugs—known as the Tannen Gang—terrorized Hill Valley's citizens, and the McFly family in particular. Marty averted this possible timeline by traveling to 1931 to make sure Kid ended up in jail [**TLTL-2**].

  > *NOTE: It's unknown whether Cliff or Riff existed in the original timeline, as little is known about Biff's immediate family.*

- **Tannen, D.W.:** A cheesy, unscrupulous Hollywood movie director and producer of the 1920s, and an ancestor of Biff Tannen. D.W. was fond of calling actors "Sweetheart," and frequently fired people for annoying or offending him. His films included *Aaaargh! My Leg!* and *Raging Death Doom*.

  In 1926, child stunt actor Daredevil Emmett Brown performed a scene for the goateed filmmaker that involved the youth going over Upper Yosemite Falls in a barrel. Concerned only with fame and money, D.W. cared little whether or not young Emmett was injured or killed during the stunt [**BFAN-11**].

  > *NOTE: D.W. Tannen may have been the son of P.T. Tannen, an unscrupulous amusement-park barner of the early 1900s, given Verne's exchange with P.T. in which the youth told him that movies would be the next big industry.*

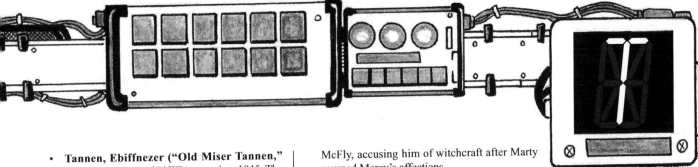

- **Tannen, Ebiffnezer ("Old Miser Tannen," "Eb"):** A relative of Biff Tannen, circa 1845. The miserly landlord had great wealth and political power, enabling him to control the police.

    The ruthless Tannen owned the building housing Fedgewick Toys, and was strict about the rent always being paid on time. When shop owner Fedgewick was an hour late in making one payment, Ebiffnezer foreclosed on the store and sent Fedgewick and his wife to Debtor's Prison, along with Clara Clayton Brown, who was in the shop at the time as a customer.

    In order to help Clara and the Fedgewicks, Marty McFly posed as the Ghost of Christmas and frightened Tannen into freeing the inmates and clearing their debts, by showing him a 3-D film of a Godzilla-like monster destroying a town, and claiming that would be the man's fate. Tannen made an effort to be joyous and generous—until seeing Marty in normal attire and realizing he'd been duped [**BFAN-10**].

    > **NOTE:** *Ebiffnezer Tannen was named after Ebenezer Scrooge, the main character of Charles Dickens' 1843 novel,* A Christmas Carol.

- **Tannen, Frank, Sergeant:** A soldier in the U.S. military, circa 1944, who was stationed in Hill Valley during World War II. The dim-witted Tannen, an ancestor of Biff Tannen, often made unwanted sexual advances on a woman named Rosie.

    Tannen had a tendency to use German phrases in his speech, which he hastily corrected to their English equivalents. When Marty McFly inadvertently joined the U.S. Army while visiting that era, Tannen served as his drill sergeant [**BFAN-17**].

    > **NOTE:** *Frank's tendency to slip into German may indicate the man to have been a spy for the Nazis.*

- **Tannen, Gertrude:** Biff Tannen's grandmother, who raised Biff in his youth. An unpleasant woman, she had a loud, shrill voice. In 1955, she and Biff lived in a house in Hill Valley that was in need of repairs and repainting [**BTF2**].

- **Tannen, Goodman:** An ancestor of Biff Tannen who lived in Salem, Massachusetts, circa 1692. While stranded in that era, Emmett Brown served as a trash collector for the Puritan and his daughter, Mercy. Tannen took an immediate dislike to Marty

McFly, accusing him of witchcraft after Marty spurned Mercy's affections.

    As a result, local townsfolk dropped Marty into a bay to determine his guilt, as per the Water Test; if he drowned, he would be declared innocent, but if he surfaced, he would be deemed a witch and be burned at the stake. When Doc rescued Marty underwater in his DeLorean, Tannen reacted in fury, inadvertently propelling himself into a pile of pig manure [**BFAN-4**].

- **Tannen, Governor:** A descendant of Biff Tannen who, in 2585, was the political leader of Robot City, a domed community located in the Asteroid Belt of Earth's solar system. The self-serving governor oppressed and enslaved the city's robotic and android servants, leaving them no choice but to stage an uprising against humanity (which, thanks to Marty McFly and the family of Emmett Brown, was ultimately averted).

    Like many lazy humans of his era, Tannen spent most of his time reclining, with an android servant programmed to slap people around—and call them "buttheads"—for him. After the rebellion ended, the robots vowed to make Tannen and other humans exercise more and eat better, and to spend less time watching holovision [**BFCL-1**].

    > **NOTE:** *The governor's android servant was drawn to resemble Woody Allen's robotic household butler from* Sleeper.

- **Tannen, Griff:** The cybernetically enhanced and psychologically unstable grandson of Biff Tannen. A tall, muscular, sociopathic 19-year-old, Griff had bionic implants that gave him improved strength and reflexes. Griff terrorized Hill Valley in the early 21st century, along with his gang: Chester "Whitey" Nogura, Leslie "Spike" O'Malley and Rafe "Data" Unger.

    In 2015, Griff bullied Martin McFly Jr. into helping his gang rob the Hill Valley Payroll Substation. The thug's plan was to let McFly get caught, so that he would take the blame and jail time for the crime. To prevent this from occurring, Emmett Brown brought Marty Sr. into the future to take his son's place, instructing Marty to refuse to help Griff.

    Furious, the delinquents chased Marty on hoverboards through Courthouse Square, with Griff's gang hooked onto his Pit Bull board as the cyborg attempted to pummel Marty with a baseball bat. When Griff crashed into the side of a manmade lake, he and his friends were propelled

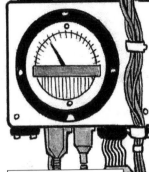

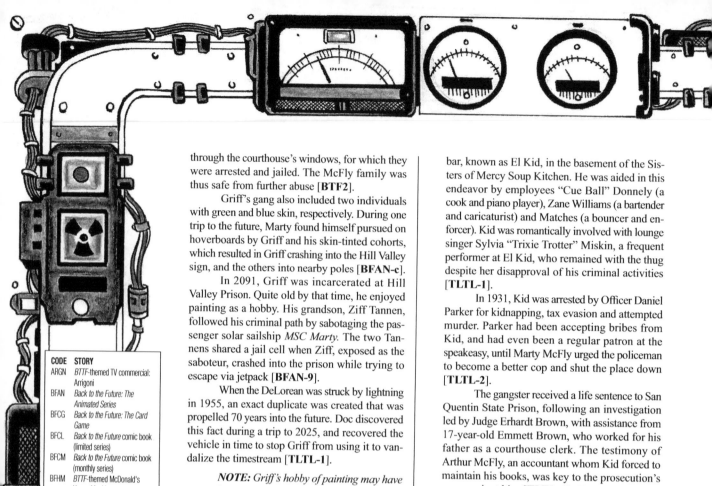

through the courthouse's windows, for which they were arrested and jailed. The McFly family was thus safe from further abuse [**BTF2**].

Griff's gang also included two individuals with green and blue skin, respectively. During one trip to the future, Marty found himself pursued on hoverboards by Griff and his skin-tinted cohorts, which resulted in Griff crashing into the Hill Valley sign, and the others into nearby poles [**BFAN-c**].

In 2091, Griff was incarcerated at Hill Valley Prison. Quite old by that time, he enjoyed painting as a hobby. His grandson, Ziff Tannen, followed his criminal path by sabotaging the passenger solar sailship *MSC Marty*. The two Tannens shared a jail cell when Ziff, exposed as the saboteur, crashed into the prison while trying to escape via jetpack [**BFAN-9**].

When the DeLorean was struck by lightning in 1955, an exact duplicate was created that was propelled 70 years into the future. Doc discovered this fact during a trip to 2025, and recovered the vehicle in time to stop Griff from using it to vandalize the timestream [**TLTL-1**].

> ***NOTE:** Griff's hobby of painting may have been a reference to actor Thomas F. Wilson's second career as a painter.*

• **Tannen, Hepzibah ("Hep"):** The great-great-grandaunt of Biff Tannen, and the sister of outlaw Thaddeus Tannen. Marty McFly met her in 1875 while working to prevent Thaddeus from stealing the family ranch of his girlfriend, Jennifer Parker.

The largely built and unusually tall woman, who lived in a rundown shack and aided in her brother's criminal activities, formed an immediate attraction to Marty. Thaddeus thus took him into his gang and gave his blessing for Marty and Hepzibah to wed—despite Marty's protests.

After Marty ended their relationship, Thaddeus' fellow outlaw, Ox McPhips, revealed that he was secretly in love with her. Returning his affections, she turned her brother over to the police, after which Hep and Ox gave up their life of crime, got married and opened an ice-cream shop [**BFAN-16**].

• **Tannen, Irving ("Kid"):** A gangster in Hill Valley during the Great Depression, and the father of three sons: Cliff, Biff and Riff Tannen [**TLTL-1, TLTL-2**]. Kid operated an illegal speakeasy in Hill Valley during Prohibition, which was burned down in 1931 by arsonist Edna Strickland [**TLTL-5**].

Undaunted, the mobster opened a second bar, known as El Kid, in the basement of the Sisters of Mercy Soup Kitchen. He was aided in this endeavor by employees "Cue Ball" Donnely (a cook and piano player), Zane Williams (a bartender and caricaturist) and Matches (a bouncer and enforcer). Kid was romantically involved with lounge singer Sylvia "Trixie Trotter" Miskin, a frequent performer at El Kid, who remained with the thug despite her disapproval of his criminal activities [**TLTL-1**].

In 1931, Kid was arrested by Officer Daniel Parker for kidnapping, tax evasion and attempted murder. Parker had been accepting bribes from Kid, and had even been a regular patron at the speakeasy, until Marty McFly urged the policeman to become a better cop and shut the place down [**TLTL-2**].

The gangster received a life sentence to San Quentin State Prison, following an investigation led by Judge Erhardt Brown, with assistance from 17-year-old Emmett Brown, who worked for his father as a courthouse clerk. The testimony of Arthur McFly, an accountant whom Kid forced to maintain his books, was key to the prosecution's case against him [**TLTL-1**]. Emmett was later granted permission to chart a Mind Map of Kid's brain patterns, for use during an exhibition of his Mental Alignment Meter at the 1931 Hill Valley Exposition [**TLTL-4**].

Kid and Edna were imprisoned together. Despite Edna having burned down his speakeasy, the two fell in love and were eventually married upon finishing their prison sentences. Once free, the elderly couple built a normal, happy life together and, by 1986, were on friendly terms with both Emmett and Marty, unaware of the roles the two time-travelers had played in putting them behind bars in the first place [**TLTL-5**].

In an alternate timeline, Kid Tannen and his sons formed a deadly crime family known as the Tannen Gang, ruthlessly terrorizing Hill Valley's citizens. Once Marty restored history, however, Kid was imprisoned before this could occur [**TLTL-2**].

> ***NOTE:** It's unknown whether Cliff or Riff existed in the original timeline, as little is known about Biff's immediate family. The identity of their mother is unknown.*

• **Tannen, Jimmy ("Diamond Jim"):** An ancestor of Biff Tannen who, in 1897, forced baseball pitcher Pee Wee McFly to throw the final National League championship game, causing his team, the Boston Beeneaters, to lose the pennant to the Baltimore

---

CODE	STORY
ARGN	*BTTF*-themed TV commercial: Arrigoni
BFAN	*Back to the Future: The Animated Series*
BFCG	*Back to the Future: The Card Game*
BFCL	*Back to the Future* comic book (limited series)
BFCM	*Back to the Future* comic book (monthly series)
BFHM	*BTTF*-themed McDonald's Happy Meal boxes
BTFA	*Back to the Future Annual* (Marvel Comics)
BTF1	Film: *Back to the Future*
BTF2	Film: *Back to the Future Part II*
BTF3	Film: *Back to the Future Part III*
BUDL	*BTTF*-themed TV commercial: Bud Light
CHEK	*BTTF*-themed music video: O'Neal McKnight, "Check Your Coat"
CHIC	Photographs hanging in the Doc Brown's Chicken restaurant at Universal Studios
CITY	*BTTF*-themed music video: Owl City, "Deer in the Headlights"
CLUB	*Back to the Future Fan Club Magazine*
DCTV	*BTTF*-themed TV commercial: DirecTV
ERTH	*The Earth Day Special*
GALE	Interviews and commentaries: Bob Gale and/or Robert Zemeckis
GARB	*BTTF*-themed TV commercials for Garbarino
HUEY	*BTTF*-themed music video: Huey Lewis and the News, "The Power of Love"
LIMO	*BTTF*-themed music video: The Limousines, "The Future"
MCDN	*BTTF*-themed TV commercial: McDonald's
MITS	*BTTF*-themed TV commercial: Mitsubishi Lancer
MSFT	*BTTF*-themed TV commercial: Microsoft

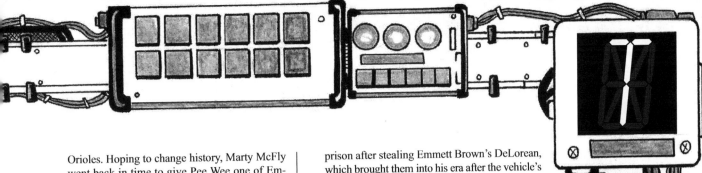

Orioles. Hoping to change history, Marty McFly went back in time to give Pee Wee one of Emmett Brown's inventions: a metal body framework connected to laser-tracking eyeglasses that would enable him to hit homeruns.

After inadvertently causing Pee Wee to be hit on the head with a baseball, Marty posed as his cousin and used the device to win a game for the Beaneaters, infuriating Diamond Jim. Before Tannen could hurt Pee Wee, however, the gangster's girlfriend, Vera Muldoon—who was really an undercover police officer collecting evidence against Tannen—arrested him for his illegal activities [**BFAN-8**].

- **Tannen, Mac ("Old Mac"):** An ancestor of Biff Tannen who owned a patch of farmland in 1933, known as the Tannen Farm. Old Mac Tannen was an overweight bumpkin with a great fondness for pigs, particularly his pet Cleopatra, whom he treated as though a member of his family.

  Tannen rented out a portion of his farmland to the Bob Brothers All-Star International Circus and the Hill Valley Fairgrounds. Hoping to foreclose on the property and take over the circus, the pig farmer greatly increased the rent, but backed off when circus owners Robert and Bob Brothers raised the money they owed him [**BFAN-18**].

  NOTE: "Old Mac Tannen" was a play on the song "Old MacDonald Had a Farm"—a pun furthered by the farmer singing the tune's "EIEIO" refrain during the episode.

- **Tannen, Mercy:** An ancestor of Biff Tannen who lived in Salem, Massachusetts, circa 1692. Although a Puritan, the attractive redhead (the daughter of Goodman Tannen) was aggressive and direct with men to whom she was attracted.

  When Marty McFly spurned Mercy's affections (out of fear of her father), she falsely accused him of making improper advances and practicing witchcraft. Marty was thus subjected to the Water Test and seemingly died in the process (in reality, Emmett Brown saved him from drowning), causing Mercy to regret her actions [**BFAN-4**].

- **Tannen, Mongo P.:** An ancestor of Biff Tannen who oversaw HM Prison, located in Sydney, Australia, in the late 18th century. The cruel warden forced inmates to perform hard labor, and often gloated over their incarceration.

  In 1790, two thugs from the future, named Frankie and Sidney, spent time at Mongo Tannen's prison after stealing Emmett Brown's DeLorean, which brought them into his era after the vehicle's voice-activated time circuits mistook their conversation as a destination [**BFAN-7b**].

  NOTE: Presumably, "HM" stood for "His Majesty's."

- **Tannen, Mugsy:** An ancestor of Biff Tannen who operated as a gangster in Chicago's South Side, circa 1927, under crime boss Arnie "Eggs" Benedict. Marty McFly and Emmett Brown encountered Tannen and fellow mobster, "Battleship" Potempkin, while incarcerated with them in that era.

  Mugsy mistook Marty for "Bathtub Jim" McFly, Marty's similar-looking ancestor, who was forced to work for their boss. Although Jim wanted to be a pharmacist, Tannen forced him to serve the mob so he could create a liquor called Lite Gin, which would have half the calories but all the taste of regular gin.

  Marty posed as Jim's cousin, kingpin "Zipper" McFly, to gain access to the gang's still so he and Doc could find a cure for cat-aracts for Doc's dog, Einstein. When Mugsy realized "Zipper" didn't exist, Eggs tried to kill the two time travelers, but they simulated a police shootout electronically, convincing the gangsters they were for real. To punish Tannen for his "mistake," Benedict told Potempkin to rough him up a bit [**BFCM-1**].

- **Tannen, Officer:** An orange-skinned allosaurus police officer from an alternate timeline created when Emmett, Jules and Verne Brown inadvertently prevented the mass extinction of all dinosaurs, enabling the creatures to evolve and replace mankind as Earth's dominant animal lifeform. Upon returning to their own era, the Browns discovered that Hill Valley was now a dinosaur metropolis known as Dinocity.

  Among its citizens was Officer Tannen, who somehow bore an uncanny resemblance to Biff Tannen. The cop tried to capture the Browns' DeLorean, intending to sell it to a research lab for dissection, but instead ended up with a badly stretched-out tongue when the vehicle broke free of his bite [**BFAN-3, BFCM-2, BFHM**].

  NOTE: This character, unnamed onscreen, was called Officer Tannen in the comic book adaptation of the episode "Forward to the Past." The onscreen credits of that episode referred to him simply as "Tannensaurus."

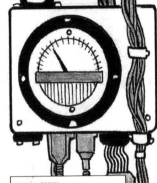

CODE	STORY
NIKE	*BTTF*-themed TV commercial: Nike
NTND	Nintendo *Back to the Future—The Ride* Mini-Game
PIZA	*BTTF*-themed TV commercial: Pizza Hut
PNBL	Data East *BTTF* pinball game
REAL	Real life
RIDE	Simulator: *Back to the Future—The Ride*
SCRM	2010 Scream Awards: *Back to the Future 25th Anniversary Reunion* (broadcast)
SCRT	2010 Scream Awards: *Back to the Future 25th Anniversary Reunion* (trailer)
SIMP	Simulator: *The Simpsons Ride*
SLOT	*Back to the Future Video Slots*
STLZ	Unused *BTTF* footage of Eric Stoltz as Marty McFly
STRY	*Back to the Future Storybook*
TEST	Screen tests: Crispin Glover, Lea Thompson and Tom Wilson
TLTL	Telltale Games' *Back to the Future—The Game*
TOPS	Topps' *Back to the Future II* trading-card set
TRIL	*BTTF: The Official Book of the Complete Movie Trilogy*
UNIV	Universal Studios Hollywood promotional video

SUFFIX	MEDIUM
-b	*BTTF2*'s Biff Tannen Museum video (extended)
-c	Credit sequence to the animated series
-d	Film deleted scene
-n	Film novelization
-o	Film outtake
-p	1955 phone book from *BTTF1*
-v	Video game print materials or commentaries
-s1	Screenplay (draft one)
-s2	Screenplay (draft two)
-s3	Screenplay (draft three)
-s4	Screenplay (draft four)
-sp	Screenplay (production draft)
-sx	Screenplay (*Paradox*)

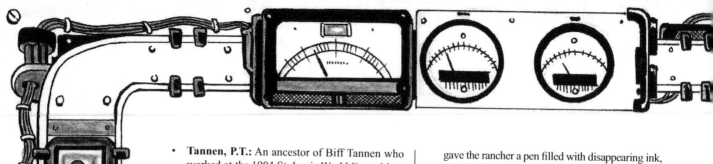

- **Tannen, P.T.:** An ancestor of Biff Tannen who worked at the 1904 St. Louis World Exposition, manning an exhibit called P.T. Tannen's Villains Through History in Wax, along with his assistant, Clyde. Unable to draw in visitors, P.T. began paying passersby a nickel to attend his attraction, which he soon grew tired of doing.

  P.T. was amazed upon seeing Marty McFly, who'd traveled back in time to find Emmett Brown after Doc's invention, the Haircut Omatic, caused Marty's hairstyle to constantly change. P.T. realized people would pay to see such a bizarre sight, and thus changed the booth's name to P.T. Tannen's House of Curiosity. He then kidnaped and caged Marty, forcing him to work as a fair exhibit [**BFAN-25**].

  > *NOTE: P.T. Tannen may have been the father of D.W. Tannen, an unscrupulous Hollywood director of the 1920s, given Verne's exchange with P.T. in which the youth told him that movies would be the next big industry.*

- **Tannen, Riff:** The younger brother of Biff and Cliff Tannen. Thinner than his brothers, Riff had a Fu Manchu mustache and wore his long, reddish hair in a hairband.

  In a timeline in which their father, Irving "Kid" Tannen, did not go to prison, the four thugs—known as the Tannen Gang—terrorized Hill Valley's citizens, and the McFly family in particular. Marty averted this possible timeline by traveling to 1931 to make sure Kid ended up in jail [**TLTL-2**].

  > *NOTE: It's unknown whether Riff or Cliff existed in the original timeline, as little is known about Biff's immediate family.*

- **Tannen, Thaddeus ("Thaddy," "Blacktooth"):** The great-great-granduncle of Biff Tannen. A known train robber, wanted dead or alive, he led an outlaw gang that included Ox McPhips. Thaddeus earned his nickname, "Blacktooth," after chewing a piece of gag gum, causing his teeth to darken.

  In 1875, Thaddy tried to take control of the Parker BTQ Ranch, by tying Genevieve Parker to a set of train tracks and forcing her husband, Wendel, to sign over the property's deed. This enabled Biff Tannen, in 1992, to lay claim to the ranch upon unearthing the long-buried deed.

  To thwart the Tannens' plans, Marty McFly traveled back in time, infiltrated the outlaws and gave the rancher a pen filled with disappearing ink, causing his signature to vanish, and rendering the deed invalid. Thaddeus was ultimately arrested for his crimes after his sister, Hepzibah Tannen, turned him in to the police [**BFAN-16**].

- **Tannen, Tiffany ("Tiff"):** The daughter of Biff Tannen [**TLTL-1, BFCG**] and sister of Biff Tannen Jr. [**BFAN-16**]. She dressed in typical punk-rock fashion, with her hair dyed several colors [**TLTL-v**].

  A teen hoodlum, Tiffany often stole cars' hubcaps. After witnessing her do so in 1986, Edna Strickland warned Tiff to stop or she'd call her father [**TLTL-1**].

  > *NOTE: This character, intended to appear in the Telltale Games video game, was not utilized in the final game. However, an illustration of Tiff appeared in supplemental materials included with the game's packaging. Tiff's punk look, reminiscent of singer Cyndi Lauper, was instead used for an alternate-universe version of Jennifer Parker.*

- **Tannen, Tim:** An uncle of Biff Tannen who had an excessively hairy face, head and chest—so much so that Biff considered trying to pass him off as a Bigfoot in order to swindle TV personality Walter Wisdom out of $50,000 [**BFAN-26**].

- **Tannen, "Wild Bill":** A thief, bully and kidnapper, and an ancestor of Biff Tannen. Bug-infested, dirty, scraggly-haired and malodorous, Wild Bill hated being called old (though he didn't mind being labeled as smelly). He was missing several teeth, and rode a broken-down burro that wore an eye-patch and a ragged hat.

  In 1850, while harassing a passing wagon train, Tannen abducted pioneer Martha O'Brien, intending to make her his mate. The rough-and-tumble Martha beat him up, however, and escaped [**BFAN-13**].

- **Tannen, Ziff:** The grandson of Griff Tannen, and the great-great-grandson of Biff Tannen. In 2091, Ziff worked as a maintenance worker for McFly Space Cruises.

  The rotund mechanic, tired of hearing how the McFly family had frequently defeated his ancestors, sabotaged the maiden voyage of the passenger solar sailship *MSC Marty,* by removing a critical sail support bolt from the hull, damaging the solar sail and leaving the ship stranded in space.

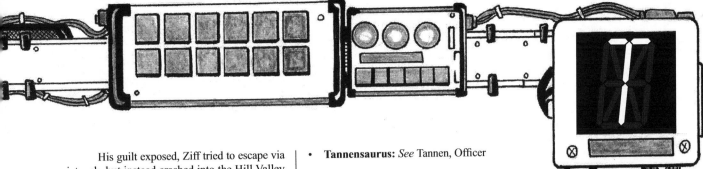

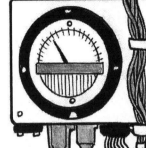

His guilt exposed, Ziff tried to escape via jetpack, but instead crashed into the Hill Valley Prison—landing in the same cell occupied by Griff Tannen. The two Tannens then shared a cell together at the facility [**BFAN-9**].

- **TANNEN1:** The license plate number of a Rolls-Royce owned by mobster Kid Tannen, in a timeline in which he and his sons, Biff, Riff and Cliff, formed the notorious Tannen Gang [**TLTL-2**].

- **Tannen Farm:** An area of land in Hill Valley, circa 1933, owned by farmer Mac Tannen. A sign on the property warned passersby to "keep out unless you're a pig." A portion of the farm was rented out to the Bob Brothers All-Star International Circus and the Hill Valley Fairgrounds [**BFAN-18**].

- **Tannen Gang:** The fifth most dangerous crime family in California, in a timeline in which Irving "Kid" Tannen never went to prison. The gang consisted of Kid and his three sons: Biff, Cliff and Riff.

    The violent brothers wore Adods running suits and liked to beat people up with baseball bats and other blunt objects. Among their victims were George and Lorraine McFly, whom they spent decades terrorizing, as retribution for Biff's humiliation at the Enchantment Under the Sea Dance in 1955.

    In that reality, the Tannens badly beat George, paralyzing him and relegating him to a wheelchair, and also ran his and Lorraine's children out of town. Marty averted this timeline, however, by traveling back to 1931 to make sure Kid ended up in jail. With the original timeline restored, the Tannen Gang ceased to exist [**TLTL-2**].

- **Tannen Manor:** A massive gated mansion owned by billionaire Biff Tannen in the Biffhorrific timeline [**BTF2-b**].

- **Tannenosaurus:** A term coined by Marty McFly at the 1931 Hill Valley Exposition, as he viewed a diorama of Hill Valley's ancient past containing model dinosaurs. Marty, knowing his propensity for encountering ancestors of Biff Tannen throughout history, idly wondered if the creature would be called a Tannenosaurus [**TLTL-4**].

    NOTE: A Tannen-esque dinosaur police officer did appear in the animated series, but was not identified as a Tannenosaurus; see entries on Dinocity and Officer Tannen.

- **Tannensaurus:** *See* Tannen, Officer

- **Tannenshire:** A medieval town in England, circa 1367, ruled by a cruel tyrant named Lord Biffingham, the Earl of Tannenshire [**BFAN-2**].

    NOTE: Tannenshire was apparently near Stonehenge, located in southern England, in County Wiltshire.

- **Tannen the Barbarbain:** A hugely muscled warrior, circa 2,991,299,129,912,991 A.D., who wore a loincloth and a scabbard, and carried a massive sword. When Emmett Brown's family and Marty McFly were trapped in his far distant future, Tannen—a self-described thief, reaver and despoiler, and a descendant of Biff Tannen—protected them from locals who feared their superior technology as sorcery.

    When Doc's family was captured by the queen of Apocrypha, the barbarian (who'd witnessed the arrival of their train, and thus believed Marty and Doc capable of magic) helped free them in return for the time travelers' assistance in stealing the Ruby Begonia for the queen, who promised him great riches if he found it for her [**BFCL-2**].

    NOTE: Many scientists believe Earth will cease to exist in approximately 7.6 billion years, with human life dying out within a billion years or so.

    Tannen was drawn to resemble actor Arnold Schwarzenegger's cinematic depiction of Robert E. Howard's iconic Conan character, in the films Conan the Barbarian *and* Conan the Destroyer.

- **Tannen Valley:** Hill Valley's name in an alternate 1985 in which Biff Tannen was a corrupt and powerful criminal kingpin [**BTF2-s2**].

    NOTE: Back to the Future: The Official Book of the Complete Movie Trilogy *dubbed this darker Hill Valley as "Biffhorrific." Another moniker, "Hell Valley," was scrawled on the city's greeting sign in the film, while the film's first-draft screenplay called it "Biff City."*

- **Tannen Wing:** A section of the Debtor's Prison, a correctional facility in London, England, in which people unable to pay their debts were incarcerated. This wing was used to house those whose businesses were foreclosed by miserly landlord

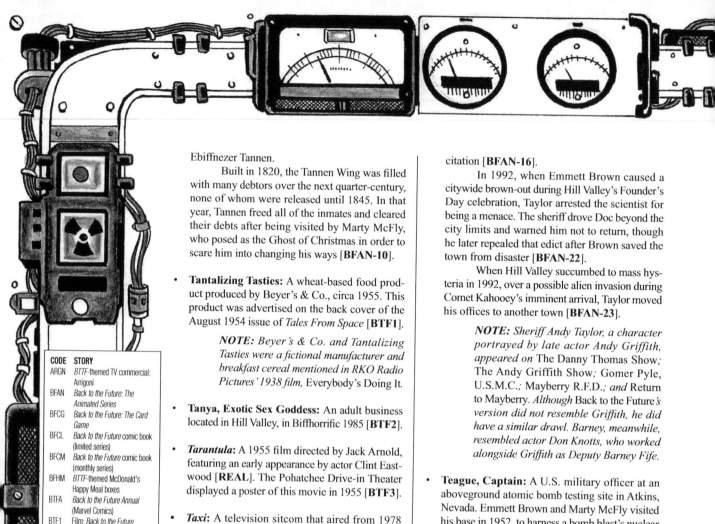

Ebiffnezer Tannen.

Built in 1820, the Tannen Wing was filled with many debtors over the next quarter-century, none of whom were released until 1845. In that year, Tannen freed all of the inmates and cleared their debts after being visited by Marty McFly, who posed as the Ghost of Christmas in order to scare him into changing his ways [**BFAN-10**].

- **Tantalizing Tasties:** A wheat-based food product produced by Beyer's & Co., circa 1955. This product was advertised on the back cover of the August 1954 issue of *Tales From Space* [**BTF1**].

  NOTE: Beyer's & Co. and Tantalizing Tasties were a fictional manufacturer and breakfast cereal mentioned in RKO Radio Pictures' 1938 film, Everybody's Doing It.

- **Tanya, Exotic Sex Goddess:** An adult business located in Hill Valley, in Biffhorrific 1985 [**BTF2**].

- ***Tarantula:*** A 1955 film directed by Jack Arnold, featuring an early appearance by actor Clint Eastwood [**REAL**]. The Pohatchee Drive-in Theater displayed a poster of this movie in 1955 [**BTF3**].

- ***Taxi:*** A television sitcom that aired from 1978 to 1983, first on ABC and later on NBC, starring Christopher Lloyd and other actors [**REAL**]. In 2015, the Café 80's played an excerpt from an episode of this series on one of its many video monitors [**BTF2**].

  NOTE: This was an in-joke reference to the fact that Lloyd (Doc Brown) also portrayed Reverend Jim Ignatowski on Taxi.

- **Taxi O'bot:** A robotic taxicab business operating in Robot City, a domed station in the Asteroid Belt of Earth's solar system, circa 2585 [**BFCL-1**].

- **Taylor, Andy, Sheriff:** A law-enforcement official in California's Hill County, circa 1992, with a large mustache, bushy eyebrows and a southern drawl. His headquarters were located in Hill Valley [**BFAN-16, BFAN-22, BFAN-23**], and his deputy was named Barney [**BFAN-22**].

  When Biff Tannen found a deed naming his family as the owners of the Parker BTQ Ranch, Andy accompanied Biff to evict the family from the land. After Marty changed history, however—by causing it to appear unsigned, thereby invalidating the deed—the sheriff instead issued Biff a citation [**BFAN-16**].

  In 1992, when Emmett Brown caused a citywide brown-out during Hill Valley's Founder's Day celebration, Taylor arrested the scientist for being a menace. The sheriff drove Doc beyond the city limits and warned him not to return, though he later repealed that edict after Brown saved the town from disaster [**BFAN-22**].

  When Hill Valley succumbed to mass hysteria in 1992, over a possible alien invasion during Comet Kahooey's imminent arrival, Taylor moved his offices to another town [**BFAN-23**].

  NOTE: Sheriff Andy Taylor, a character portrayed by late actor Andy Griffith, appeared on The Danny Thomas Show; The Andy Griffith Show; Gomer Pyle, U.S.M.C.; Mayberry R.F.D.; *and* Return to Mayberry. *Although* Back to the Future's *version did not resemble Griffith, he did have a similar drawl. Barney, meanwhile, resembled actor Don Knotts, who worked alongside Griffith as Deputy Barney Fife.*

- **Teague, Captain:** A U.S. military officer at an aboveground atomic bomb testing site in Atkins, Nevada. Emmett Brown and Marty McFly visited his base in 1952, to harness a bomb blast's nuclear energy in order to send Marty back to the future [**BTF1-s1**].

  NOTE: The nuclear test-site sequence was cut from the final version of BTTF1 (the setting of which was changed to 1955), though storyboards were included as a Blu-ray extra. The first two script drafts set the base in the fictional Nevada city of Atkins, while the third moved it to New Mexico.

- **Tech-Ed 2007:** A trade event held in Orlando, Florida, in June 2007, at which Microsoft's senior vice-president, Robert L. Muglia, provided a keynote address about his vision for the future. When attendees tired of unrealized promises began pummeling him with vegetables, Emmett Brown, using his time-traveling DeLorean, offered Muglia insights into Microsoft's past failures so he could improve his speech [**MSFT**].

- **TechFly:** A nerdy, insecure IT worker at a company called Acme.com, circa 2001, whose manager, Mister Biff, often bullied him into doing his work for him, despite a lack of effective software to handle assignments. TechFly suffered numerous

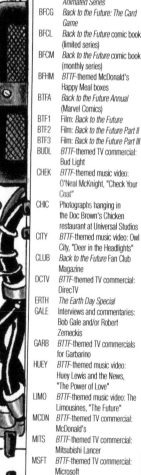

CODE	STORY
ARGN	*BTTF*-themed TV commercial: Arrigoni
BFAN	*Back to the Future: The Animated Series*
BFCG	*Back to the Future: The Card Game*
BFCL	*Back to the Future comic book (limited series)*
BFCM	*Back to the Future comic book (monthly series)*
BFHM	*BTTF*-themed McDonald's Happy Meal boxes
BTFA	*Back to the Future Annual (Marvel Comics)*
BTF1	Film: *Back to the Future*
BTF2	Film: *Back to the Future Part II*
BTF3	Film: *Back to the Future Part III*
BUDL	*BTTF*-themed TV commercial: Bud Light
CHEK	*BTTF*-themed music video: O'Neal McKnight, "Check Your Coat"
CHIC	Photographs hanging in the Doc Brown's Chicken restaurant at Universal Studios
CITY	*BTTF*-themed music video: Owl City, "Deer in the Headlights"
CLUB	*Back to the Future Fan Club Magazine*
DCTV	*BTTF*-themed TV commercial: DirecTV
ERTH	*The Earth Day Special*
GALE	Interviews and commentaries: Bob Gale and/or Robert Zemeckis
GARB	*BTTF*-themed TV commercials for Garbarino
HUEY	*BTTF*-themed music video: Huey Lewis and the News, "The Power of Love"
LIMO	*BTTF*-themed music video: The Limousines, "The Future"
MCDN	*BTTF*-themed TV commercial: McDonald's
MITS	*BTTF*-themed TV commercial: Mitsubishi Lancer
MSFT	*BTTF*-themed TV commercial: Microsoft

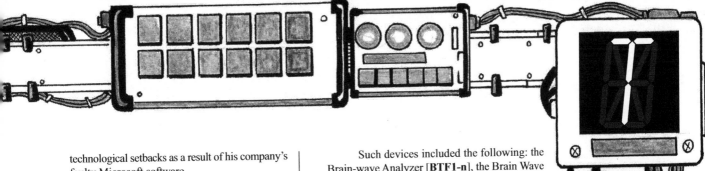

technological setbacks as a result of his company's faulty Microsoft software.

When Microsoft's senior vice-president, Robert L. Muglia, provided a keynote address at Tech-Ed 2007 about his vision for the future, his rhetoric proved unpopular with attendees tired of unrealized promises. Emmett Brown provided Muglia with insights into Microsoft's failures, by taking him into the past to view TechFly's dilemma.

As a result of their time-traveling, history changed so that Muglia's keynote speech avoided his firm's past mistakes. What's more, TechFly became more confident around Biff—who, in the new timeline, worked for him as a janitor at Microsoft [**MSFT**].

- **Techne, Muse of Progress:** A persona portrayed by Sylvia "Trixie Trotter" Miskin at the 1931 Hill Valley Exposition. In costume as Techne—a fictional goddess who inspired men and women to make great discoveries—Trixie stood outside Hill Valley High School and welcomed visitors prior to the expo [**TLTL-4**]. She later served as the emcee, introducing scientists offering stage presentations at the event, and bestowing the Golden Sundial on the winning contestant [**TLTL-5**].

  Because the expo's charter stipulated that the hostess be a U.S. citizen, Trixie—a Canadian—was terminated when Edna Strickland (who disapproved of her liberal lifestyle and blatant sex appeal) revealed her nationality [**TLTL-4**]. However, Arthur McFly found a loophole allowing her to retain her job, by marrying her [**TLTL-5**].

  NOTE: "Techne," in Greek, is a philosophical term referring to the accomplishment of a goal or objective in a craft or the arts.

- **Teflon:** A brand name of Polytetrafluoroethylene (PTFE), a synthetic fluoropolymer used in numerous applications, such as a non-stick cookware coating [**REAL**]. In Citizen Brown's dystopian timeline, the city's walls were coated with Teflon, making them easy to clean and causing graffiti paint to quickly streak [**TLTL-3**].

- **TEL 25:** The license plate of a car in Hill Valley, circa 1992 [**BFAN-26**].

- **telepathy:** The ability to transmit and receive a person's thoughts. Emmett Brown built a number of inventions to enable telepathy, mind-reading and/or mind control, to varying degrees of success.

Such devices included the following: the Brain-wave Analyzer [**BTF1-n**], the Brain Wave Analyzer [**BFAN-12**], the Deep-Thought Mind-Reading Helmet [**BFAN-1**], the Deep-Thinking Mind-Reading Helmet [**RIDE**], the Thought-inducing Auto-pacer [**BFAN-1**], the Memory Archive Recall Indexer and Enhancer (M.A.R.I.E.) [**BFAN-15**], the Flashback-o-Matic [**BFAN-17**], the Projecto-Recollector [**BFAN-24**] the ELB Pediatric Policer [**BFAN-26**], and the Mind Mapping Helmet [**TLTL-4**].

> *NOTE: For more information about these innovations, see Appendix II, as well as the individual lexicon entries for each invention.*

- **Telescope Hat:** An invention of Emmett Brown consisting of an over-sized, helmet-mounted telescope, built to view the arrival of Comet Kahooey [**BFAN-23**].

- **Telltale Daddy:** A racehorse that competed in 1931. Telltale Daddy was among several horses mentioned during a radio broadcast as Marty McFly and Emmett Brown attempted to steal liquor from Irving "Kid" Tannen's speakeasy [**TLTL-1**].

> *NOTE: This horse was an in-joke reference to Telltale Games, the company that produced the BTTF video game.*

- **Temporal Body Scan:** A type of testing conducted at the Institute of Future Technology, for the purpose of monitoring visitors entering the facility [**RIDE**].

- **temporal displacement:** Emmett Brown's scientific term for time travel [**BTF1**].

- **Temporal Dynamics Model 580:** A project undertaken by Emmett Brown sometime in or before 1985 at the University of California, Berkeley, involving capacitor discharge. Doc's research was conducted during his development of a working time machine [**TLTL-1**].

- **Temporal Experiment Number 1:** A test conducted by scientist Emmett Brown to determine if his time machine—converted from a DeLorean DMC-12 sports car—would work. The experiment, sending Brown's dog, Einstein, one minute into the future, proved successful, thus making the pooch the world's first time-traveler [**BTF1**].

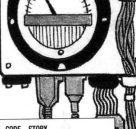

CODE	STORY
NIKE	*BTTF*-themed TV commercial: Nike
NTND	Nintendo *Back to the Future—The Ride* Mini-Game
PIZA	*BTTF*-themed TV commercial: Pizza Hut
PNBL	Data East *BTTF* pinball game
REAL	Real life
RIDE	Simulator: *Back to the Future—The Ride*
SCRM	2010 Scream Awards: *Back to the Future 25th Anniversary Reunion* (broadcast)
SCRT	2010 Scream Awards: *Back to the Future 25th Anniversary Reunion* (trailer)
SIMP	Simulator: *The Simpsons Ride*
SLOT	*Back to the Future Video Slots*
STLZ	Unused *BTTF* footage of Eric Stoltz as Marty McFly
STRY	*Back to the Future Storybook*
TEST	Screen tests: Crispin Glover, Lea Thompson and Tom Wilson
TLTL	Telltale Games' *Back to the Future—The Game*
TOPS	Topps' *Back to the Future II* trading-card set
TRIL	*BTTF: The Official Book of the Complete Movie Trilogy*
UNIV	Universal Studios Hollywood promotional video

SUFFIX	MEDIUM
-b	*BTTF2*'s Biff Tannen Museum video (extended)
-c	Credit sequence to the animated series
-d	Film deleted scene
-n	Film novelization
-o	Film outtake
-p	1955 phone book from *BTTF1*
-v	Video game print materials or commentaries
-s1	Screenplay (draft one)
-s2	Screenplay (draft two)
-s3	Screenplay (draft three)
-s4	Screenplay (draft four)
-sp	Screenplay (production draft)
-sx	Screenplay (*Paradox*)

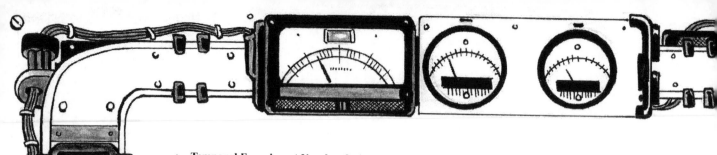

- **Temporal Experiment Number 2:** A test conducted by Emmett Brown, following a successful time-travel experiment involving Einstein, in which the scientist intended to propel himself 25 years into the future, in order to view mankind's progress. This test was cut short, however, when Libyan terrorists—whom Brown had conned out of plutonium for his time machine—arrived on the scene and murdered him [**BTF1-s3**].

- **Temporal Field Capacitor (T.F.C.):** *See* Flux Capacitor

- **Tennis Club:** An organization in Hill Valley, circa 1952, advertised on a billboard atop the Hill Valley Bank [**BFAN-24**].

- **Tenorio, Rogelio:** The operational services arbiter of the Institute of Future Technology [**RIDE**].

  > *NOTE: This individual's name appeared on signage outside* Back to the Future: The Ride.

- **Terminator, The:** A four-barrel shotgun built by Emmett Brown in 1885. The weapon was loaded with double-aught buck, nails, broken glass and shiny new dimes, making it exceedingly deadly [**BTF3-sx, BTF3-sp**]. According to Doc, the weapon could "shoot the fleas off a dog's back at 500 yards" [**BTF3**].

  > *NOTE: Doc apparently named the weapon after James Cameron's 1984 science fiction film* The Terminator, *starring Arnold Schwarzenegger and Linda Hamilton.*

- **Terry:** A car mechanic at Western Auto Stores who fixed Biff Tannen's car in 1955 after it collided with a manure truck while chasing Marty McFly. Biff refused to pay the bill, however, deeming it excessive [**BTF2**].

  For decades, Terry continued to resent Biff's refusal, and often reminded him of this fact. Annoyed, Biff accused Terry of living in the past [**BTF2-d**].

  In 2015, Marty encountered an elderly Terry as the latter raised funds to preserve the Clock Tower as an historic landmark. Terry commented that he wished he could go back in time and bet on the Chicago Cubs (who'd won that year's World Series), inspiring Marty to purchase *Grays Sports Almanac* and do the same [**BTF2**].

- **Terry:** A young boy who enjoyed a 25-cent dinosaur ride outside a local supermarket in Hill Valley. Terry failed to recognize the difference between the fake dinosaur and Tiny, Verne Brown's pet Apatosaurus [**BFAN-26**].

- **Terry Lumber Co.:** A business located near Emmett Brown's home in Hill Valley, circa 1985 [**BTF1**].

- **Tesla, Nicola:** An employee at the Institute of Future Technology, stationed in the East Wing [**RIDE**].

  > *NOTE: This individual, identified on signage outside* Back to the Future: The Ride, *was named after the famous inventor and engineer.*

- **Texaco:** An American gas-station chain [**REAL**]. A Texaco station operated in Courthouse Square, near the corner of Main Street and Hill Street. Marty regularly passed this station while skateboarding to high school. After traveling back to 1955, he found a more old-fashioned version of the business already in operation [**BTF1**].

  In 2015, the station sold Havoline oil and offered robotic automotive fueling, as well as aerodynamic kits, mag-lev adjustments and retro-fitting services. The station featured several types of fuel, including regular unleaded gasoline, Fusion Gold, Super X-Tra Fusion Plus, Liquid Nitrogen and Super Unleaded Plus [**BTF2**].

  > *NOTE: Early during the production of* Back to the Future II, *the intention was to replace Texaco in 2015 with a Japanese company called Nippoco.*

- **TFC Drive Circuits:** A component of a system built by Emmett Brown to turn a DeLorean DMC-12 sports car into a time machine [**BTF1**].

- **Theremin Booth:** *See* Continuuophone

- **Thermae:** A Roman bath house, circa 36 A.D. While visiting ancient Rome, Jules and Verne Brown found themselves in trouble after causing a disturbance in the Thermae. The baths consisted of a calidarium (a hot room in which visitors sweated out impurities) and a frigidarium (a chilly facility used to stimulate circulation). Inside the Thermae, the boys befriended a slave named Judah Ben-Hur, whom they freed from captivity [**BFAN-5**].

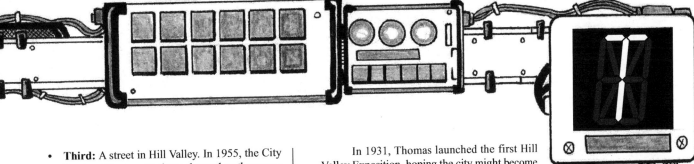

- **Third:** A street in Hill Valley. In 1955, the City Trust and Savings Bank was located on the corner of this road and Main [**BTF2**].

- **Third Eye, The:** A palm-reading shop in Courthouse Square, featuring a spiritual advisor named Nancy who offered palmistry and phrenology services [**BTF1**].

- **Thomas, Frank, Mayor ("Red"):** An elected politician in Hill Valley, circa 1955, when he launched a re-election platform under the campaign slogans "Progress Is His Middle Name" and "Honesty, Decency, Integrity." Decades later, Mayor Goldie Wilson would run for re-election using a similar platform [**BTF1**].

    Already known as "Red" as early as 1931, Thomas was among those whose brains Emmett Brown scanned to create a Mind Map for the exhibition of his Mental Alignment Meter at that year's Hill Valley Exposition [**TLTL-4**].

    NOTE: Thomas' first name appeared in BTTF1's fourth-draft screenplay; his nickname, "Red," was mentioned in his campaign slogan. Some Web sites have identified the bum in 1985, also called Red, as the former mayor. However, a photo of Thomas on a campaign van featured set decorator Hal Gausman, while the vagrant was played by George "Buck" Flower.

    Confusing the issue, the trivia track on the film's Blu-ray release indicated them to be different characters, while that same Blu-ray also showed a side-by-side comparison, implying the two Reds were the same man.

    Since the third-draft screenplay featured additional scenes involving Red as a young man in 1955, it would not be feasible for him to be Red Thomas, who was an adult politician at the time. What's more, the bum in 1985 would be far too young to have been the mayor's visible age 30 years prior.

- **Thomas, Jack, Mayor ("Gentleman Jack," "Good Time Mayor"):** The mayor of Hill Valley in 1931. A heavyset man, he had greased black hair and a handlebar mustache [**TLTL-1**]. Journalist Edna Strickland, while keeping an eye out for story ideas one night, spotted Thomas trying to slink out of Irving "Kid" Tannen's speakeasy [**TLTL-2**].

In 1931, Thomas launched the first Hill Valley Exposition, hoping the city might become a magnet for big investors in the technology sector. The venture folded after only three years, after an influenza exhibit leaked into the concession stand [**TLTL-4**].

    NOTE: Thomas—who may have been an ancestor of Frank "Red" Thomas, the city's mayor in 1955—strongly resembled Jackie Gleason's Ralph Kramden character from The Honeymooners. This may have been an intentional in-joke, given Kramden's recurring appearance in the first Back to the Future film.

- **Thomas, Red, Mayor:** *See* Thomas Frank, Mayor ("Red")

- **Thomas, Richard:** A signature printed on so-called "Biff Bucks" [**BTF2**].

    NOTE: It's unknown if Richard Thomas was related to Frank and Jack Thomas.

- **THOR:** A business located in San Fernando Valley, California [**REAL**]. In 1991, Emmett Brown read a help-wanted ad for this company while searching for a job. The contact person was Steve Garfield, at telephone number 818-710-1800 [**BFAN-12**].

- **Thought-inducing Auto-pacer:** A contraption invented by Emmett Brown to help a person focus on a problem at hand. A set of gears and a conveyor belt enabled a user to walk in place, while footage of various structures, such as the Giza pyramids, the Leaning Tower of Pisa, the Eiffel Tower, the Golden Gate Bridge and the Parthenon, scrawled by on a screen. Doc did not always find the Auto-pacer useful [**BFAN-1**].

- **three-dimensional holographic projector:** A device invented by Emmett Brown, enabling him to project a 3-D hologram of an object or a person to a second location. Doc's sons, Jules and Verne, liked to play with the contraption—much to his frustration, since he designed it not as a toy, but as a home-security device, to deceive burglars into believing the Browns were home when the house was empty [**BFAN-5**].

    NOTE: A McDonald's Happy Meal box themed after the animated series called the device a hologram projector.

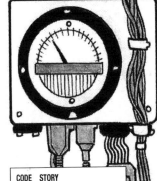

CODE	STORY
NIKE	*BTTF*-themed TV commercial: Nike
NTND	Nintendo *Back to the Future—The Ride* Mini-Game
PIZA	*BTTF*-themed TV commercial: Pizza Hut
PNBL	Data East *BTTF* pinball game
REAL	Real life
RIDE	Simulator: *Back to the Future—The Ride*
SCRM	2010 Scream Awards: *Back to the Future* 25th Anniversary Reunion (broadcast)
SCRT	2010 Scream Awards: *Back to the Future* 25th Anniversary Reunion (trailer)
SIMP	Simulator: *The Simpsons Ride*
SLOT	*Back to the Future* Video Slots
STLZ	Unused *BTTF* footage of Eric Stoltz as Marty McFly
STRY	*Back to the Future Storybook*
TEST	Screen tests: Crispin Glover, Lea Thompson and Tom Wilson
TLTL	Telltale Games' *Back to the Future—The Game*
TOPS	Topps' *Back to the Future II* trading-card set
TRIL	*BTTF: The Official Book of the Complete Movie Trilogy*
UNIV	Universal Studios Hollywood promotional video

SUFFIX	MEDIUM
-b	*BTTF2's* Biff Tannen Museum video (extended)
-c	Credit sequence to the animated series
-d	Film deleted scene
-n	Film novelization
-o	Film outtake
-p	1955 phone book from *BTTF1*
-v	Video game print materials or commentaries
-s1	Screenplay (draft one)
-s2	Screenplay (draft two)
-s3	Screenplay (draft three)
-s4	Screenplay (draft four)
-sp	Screenplay (production draft)
-sx	Screenplay (*Paradox*)

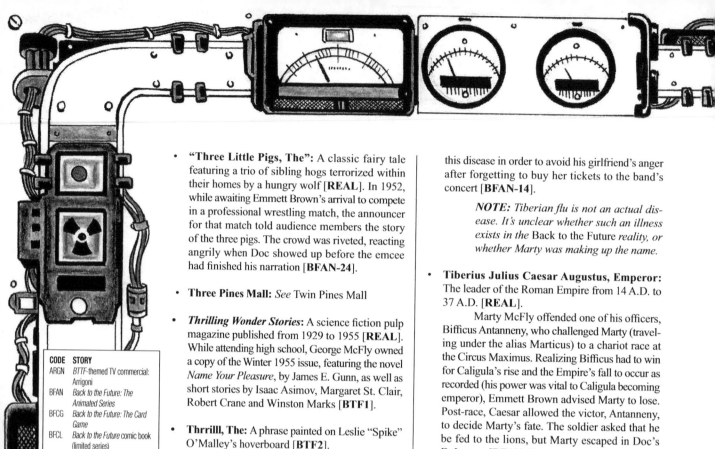

- **"Three Little Pigs, The":** A classic fairy tale featuring a trio of sibling hogs terrorized within their homes by a hungry wolf [**REAL**]. In 1952, while awaiting Emmett Brown's arrival to compete in a professional wrestling match, the announcer for that match told audience members the story of the three pigs. The crowd was riveted, reacting angrily when Doc showed up before the emcee had finished his narration [**BFAN-24**].

- **Three Pines Mall:** *See* Twin Pines Mall

- ***Thrilling Wonder Stories:*** A science fiction pulp magazine published from 1929 to 1955 [**REAL**]. While attending high school, George McFly owned a copy of the Winter 1955 issue, featuring the novel *Name Your Pleasure*, by James E. Gunn, as well as short stories by Isaac Asimov, Margaret St. Clair, Robert Crane and Winston Marks [**BTF1**].

- **Thrrilll, The:** A phrase painted on Leslie "Spike" O'Malley's hoverboard [**BTF2**].

  > *NOTE: The misspelling of "thrill" is consistent with what was seen onscreen, and is not a typo.*

- **Thru-Haul:** An interdimensional large-item auxiliary transport vehicle created by Emmett Brown at the Institute of Future Technology, "for time travelers on the move." The device, model THV-4483/EX, could be attached to the back of Doc's eight-passenger DeLorean, for the purpose of hauling belongings [**RIDE**].

  > *NOTE: This device was described on signage at Universal Studios' Back to the Future: The Ride.*

- **thumb bandits:** A group of outlaws who, as reported by *USA Today*, went on strike in 2015 following an amputation [**BTF2**].

  > *NOTE: The details of this strike, as well as the nature of the so-called thumb bandits, are unknown.*

- **thumb plate:** *See* identipad

- **THV-4483/EX:** The model number of Emmett Brown's Thru-Haul interdimensional large-item auxiliary transport vehicle [**RIDE**].

- **Tiberian flu:** A strain of influenza virus. Marty McFly claimed the members of Walk DMC had

this disease in order to avoid his girlfriend's anger after forgetting to buy her tickets to the band's concert [**BFAN-14**].

  > *NOTE: Tiberian flu is not an actual disease. It's unclear whether such an illness exists in the* Back to the Future *reality, or whether Marty was making up the name.*

- **Tiberius Julius Caesar Augustus, Emperor:** The leader of the Roman Empire from 14 A.D. to 37 A.D. [**REAL**].

  Marty McFly offended one of his officers, Bifficus Antanneny, who challenged Marty (traveling under the alias Marticus) to a chariot race at the Circus Maximus. Realizing Bifficus had to win for Caligula's rise and the Empire's fall to occur as recorded (his power was vital to Caligula becoming emperor), Emmett Brown advised Marty to lose. Post-race, Caesar allowed the victor, Antanneny, to decide Marty's fate. The soldier asked that he be fed to the lions, but Marty escaped in Doc's DeLorean [**BFAN-5**].

  > *NOTE: The emperor was not named onscreen, though historically, the Empire's leader in that year—and Caligula's predecessor—was Tiberius Julius Caesar Augustus (who, in busts of his likeness, did not appear rotund, as he was in the cartoon).*

- **"Time Bomb Town":** A song recorded by Lindsay Buckingham in 1985 [**BTF1**]. This tune was playing on Marty McFly's alarm clock-radio when Emmett Brown called to remind him to meet the scientist at the Twin Pines Mall [**BTF1**].

- **Time Car:** *See* DeLorean DMC-12

- **time circuit:** A component of a system built by Emmett Brown to turn a DeLorean DMC-12 sports car into a time machine. Pulling a lever on the time circuits activated the device, illuminating three gauges, labeled "Destination Time," "Present Time" and "Last Year Departed." The vehicle's operator could then specify the month, day, year, hour and minute (as well as A.M. or P.M.) for each trip through time [**BTF1**].

- **time-circuit control microchip:** A component of Emmett Brown's flying DeLorean, enabling the vehicle to travel into the past or future. When this microchip was shorted out by a lightning strike in 1955, the resultant surge stranded the scientist 70

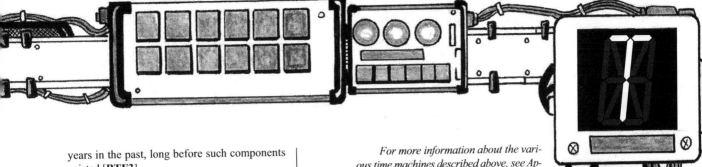

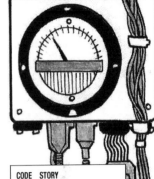

years in the past, long before such components existed [**BTF3**].

- **Time Life:** A publishing house that produced a multi-volume series of books under the title *Robot*, in or before 1991. Verne Brown referenced this series while writing a school essay on robotics [**BFCL-1**].

  > *NOTE: This series is fictional, though a direct-market publisher called Time-Life (hyphenated) does exist.*

- **time machine:** A device enabling an individual to visit other periods of history. Emmett Brown built several time machines in the course of his lifetime.

  Brown first conceived of the idea on Nov. 5, 1955—when, while standing on a wet toilet to hang a clock, he fell and struck his head on a sink. Upon awakening, he experienced a revelation of the Flux Capacitor, which he spent the next three decades and his family's fortune trying to invent.

  In 1985, Doc completed his work on the time machine, which he built using a DeLorean DMC-12 sports car. Although the device's time circuits were electrical in nature, a nuclear reaction was required to generate the 1.21 jigowatts of electricity necessary to power the Flux Capacitor, and thus make time travel possible. To that end, Brown fueled the vehicle with plutonium [**BTF1**].

  Brown later created other time machines as well, including a flying locomotive called the *Jules Verne Train* [**BTF3, RIDE**]; the Eight-Passenger DeLorean Time Travel Vehicle [**RIDE**]; a foldable DeLorean with the capacity to fit the entire Brown family, as well as audio-activated time circuits [**BFAN-1**]; a miniature time-traveling mail truck [**BFAN-4**]; the Timespan [**RIDE**]; and the Timeman personal time-travel suit [**RIDE**].

  In addition, an exact duplicate of the original DeLorean time machine was created when the vehicle was struck by lightning in 1955. Doc discovered the duplicated car while visiting the future [**TLTL-5**].

  > *NOTE: Doc's time machine was originally conceived as being made from a refrigerator, but Robert Zemeckis and Steven Spielberg changed it to a car, fearing that children might emulate the film by climbing into a fridge and suffocating. The filmmakers eventually chose a DeLorean to pay homage to the gull-wing doors of Klaatu's spaceship in The Day the Earth Stood Still.*

  For more information about the various time machines described above, see Appendix II, as well as the individual lexicon entries for each invention.

- **Time Machine Science Contest:** A televised competition in 1992 between Emmett Brown and Walter Wisdom, intended to determine which scientist had actually created the time-traveling DeLorean (which Wisdom had stolen from Doc, intending to market it on TV for $999,995). Doc publicly discredited his rival during the contest, regaining possession of his invention [**BFAN-15**].

  > *NOTE: This would indicate that as of 1992, the existence of Doc's time machine was common knowledge, explaining a number of TV commercials (for Pizza Hut, Microsoft and Arrigoni) and music videos (by Huey Lewis and the News, as well as O'Neal McKnight) in which others have been seen traveling in the vehicle, with or without Doc. It might also explain why the Institute of Future Technology could invite Time Travel Volunteers to use the eight-passenger DeLorean to explore history.*

- **Timeman:** A personal time-travel suit with fusion-powered maglev hover boots, created by Emmett Brown at the Institute of Future Technology [**RIDE**].

  > *NOTE: This suit was described on signage at Universal Studios' Back to the Future: The Ride.*

- **Time Police:** A law-enforcement agency in an alternate version of Hill Valley [**TLTL-v**].

  > *NOTE: This discarded concept for the Telltale Games video game was briefly discussed in the game's commentary track.*

- **Times Box Z-016 LA**: A newspaper help-wanted ad that Emmett Brown read in 1991 while trying to find a job [**BFAN-12**].

- **Timespan:** An invention of Emmett Brown, conceived at the Institute of Future Technology, and involving holographic place/time projection [**RIDE**].

  > *NOTE: This device was described on signage at Universal Studios' Back to the Future: The Ride.*

CODE	STORY
NIKE	*BTTF*-themed TV commercial: Nike
NTND	Nintendo *Back to the Future—The Ride* Mini-Game
PIZA	*BTTF*-themed TV commercial: Pizza Hut
PNBL	Data East *BTTF* pinball game
REAL	Real life
RIDE	Simulator: *Back to the Future—The Ride*
SCRM	2010 Scream Awards: *Back to the Future 25th Anniversary Reunion* (broadcast)
SCRT	2010 Scream Awards: *Back to the Future 25th Anniversary Reunion* (trailer)
SIMP	Simulator: *The Simpsons Ride*
SLOT	*Back to the Future Video Slots*
STLZ	Unused *BTTF* footage of Eric Stoltz as Marty McFly
STRY	*Back to the Future Storybook*
TEST	Screen tests: Crispin Glover, Lea Thompson and Tom Wilson
TLTL	Telltale Games' *Back to the Future—The Game*
TOPS	Topps' *Back to the Future II* trading-card set
TRIL	*BTTF: The Official Book of the Complete Movie Trilogy*
UNIV	Universal Studios Hollywood promotional video

SUFFIX	MEDIUM
-b	*BTTF2*'s Biff Tannen Museum video (extended)
-c	Credit sequence to the animated series
-d	Film deleted scene
-n	Film novelization
-o	Film outtake
-p	1955 phone book from *BTTF1*
-v	Video game print materials or commentaries
-s1	Screenplay (draft one)
-s2	Screenplay (draft two)
-s3	Screenplay (draft three)
-s4	Screenplay (draft four)
-sp	Screenplay (production draft)
-sx	Screenplay (*Paradox*)

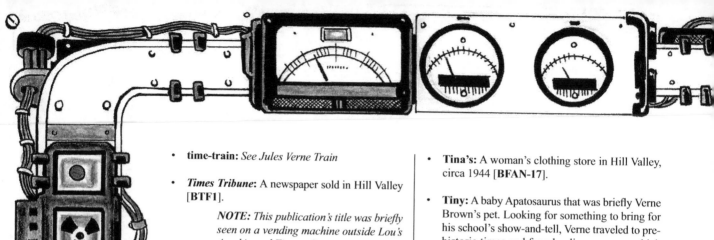

- **time-train:** *See Jules Verne Train*

- ***Times Tribune:*** A newspaper sold in Hill Valley [**BTF1**].

    > **NOTE:** *This publication's title was briefly seen on a vending machine outside Lou's Aerobic and Fitness Center.*

- **time-traveling locomotive:** *See Jules Verne Train*

- **time-traveling mail truck:** A miniature time machine built by Emmett Brown while he and his family were trapped in Salem, Massachusetts, in 1692. The device was built from a toy mail truck and a Flux Capacitor cannibalized from the *Jules Verne Train*. Doc used the device to deliver a call for help to Marty McFly in 1991 [**BFAN-4**].

    > **NOTE:** *Given the lack of such toy vehicles in 1692, it presumably belonged to one of Doc's sons.*

- **Time-Travel Volunteers:** A designation assigned to those signing up to travel through time aboard Emmett Brown's Eight-Passenger DeLorean Time-Travel Vehicle, as part of research conducted at the Institute of Future Technology's Anti-Gravitic Laboratory. After stowing away with a science team studying 1955, Biff Tannen infiltrated the facility in 1991 and stole Doc's earlier-model DeLorean. Trapped within his lab, Doc dispatched a team of Time-Travel Volunteers to pursue Biff aboard the eight-occupant vehicle.

    Biff evaded the other car as it chased him to 2015 and back to prehistoric times. Narrowly evading a Tyrannosaurus rex, Biff found himself in imminent danger from an underground lava spring. The volunteers rescued him, bumping the stolen car while accelerating to 88 miles per hour, which brought both cars back to the institute [**RIDE**].

    > **NOTE:** *The term "Time-Travel Volunteers" referred to those attending Universal Studios' Back to the Future: The Ride attraction—in other words, the park's customers.*

- ***Times, The:*** A daily national newspaper published in London, England, launched in 1785 [**REAL**]. In 1845, forced to work as a pickpocket for a thug named Murdock, Verne Brown tried to rob a man reading an issue of *The Times* bearing the headline "Pickpocket Menace." Verne, unaccustomed to thievery, fell into the man's coat pocket [**BFAN-10**].

- **Tina's:** A woman's clothing store in Hill Valley, circa 1944 [**BFAN-17**].

- **Tiny:** A baby Apatosaurus that was briefly Verne Brown's pet. Looking for something to bring for his school's show-and-tell, Verne traveled to prehistoric times and found a dinosaur egg, which hatched shortly after he returned to his own era. The creature's growth rate was affected by Earth's present-day atmospheric conditions, causing it to change color and grow larger in sudden spurts.

    Verne and his brother considered a number of names, such as Elroy, Bootsie, Puddin', Socks and Killer. Eventually, they settled on the ironic name Tiny. When the dinosaur escaped their property, Biff Tannen captured the animal and tried to sell it to TV personality Walter Wisdom, in response to a public offer of $50,000 for a live dinosaur.

    Wisdom turned Tiny into a ratings-grabbing event, marketed as *Mr. Wisdom's Live Super-Duper Dinosaur Special*, and renamed the creature Dinosaurus Humongous. However, Verne and Jules rescued the dinosaur, replacing it with a fake-looking substitute, and thereby publicly humiliating both Biff and Wisdom. Verne then returned Tiny to the past, using a special Utility Box Car connected to the time-traveling locomotive [**BFAN-26**].

- **Tiny's:** A business located in Hill Valley, circa 2015 [**RIDE**].

- **T.L. Livingston, Cabinet Maker:** A business located in Hill Valley, circa 1885 [**BTF3**].

- **to-and-fro chair:** *See rocking chair*

- **Tokyo:** The capital city of Japan [**REAL**]. In 2015, as reported by *USA Today*, Tokyo's stocks averaged a one-point increase [**BTF2**].

- **Toma:** A popular beverage, circa 1992 [**BFAN-20**].

- **Tommy:** A classmate of Verne Brown at Hill Valley Elementary School in 1991 [**BFAN-13**].

    > **NOTE:** *One of his drawings was hanging up in Verne's classroom.*

- **Tommy ("Tommy-Boy"):** An acquaintance of baseball player Pee Wee McFly, sometime in or before 1897. He was said to have thrown Pee Wee's overalls in the chowder of a woman called Mrs. Murphy [**BFAN-8**].

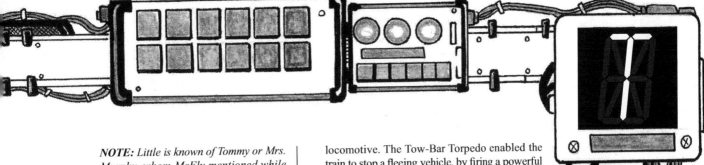

NOTE: Little is known of Tommy or Mrs. Murphy, whom McFly mentioned while delirious after being hit on the head with a baseball.

- **Tommy's Palm Reading**: A business located in Hill Valley, circa 1991 [**BFAN-12**].

- **Tom's Diner:** A business located in Boston, Massachusetts, circa 1897 [**BFAN-8**].

- **Tony:** A model of robot that collected visitors' tickets at the entrance of Hill Valley's McFly Space Center, circa 2091. The polite droid somewhat resembled a human doorman, with epaulets worn on its metal shoulders [**BFAN-9**].

- **Tony's Pizza**: A pizzeria located in Hill Valley as early as 1952 [**BFAN-24**], and in operation until at least 1991 [**BFAN-12, BFCM-4**].

  Emmett Brown briefly worked here as a pizza chef after his sons, Jules and Verne, played an April Fool's Day joke by convincing him his brain was almost full, and that he needed to give up science. He was soon fired for using too much yeast, causing the restaurant to fill up with pizza dough. Among its available pizza sizes was the Super Large Deluxe Gigantor Pizza [**BFAN-12**].

  Toppings offered included anchovies, mushrooms, olives, ham, beef, chives, grapes, onions, tomatoes, leeks, kiwi fruit, truffles, butterscotch, peanuts, chocolate, Red Hots, Oreos, sprouts, coffee beans, corn nuts, M&Ms, extra mozzarella, artichokes and escargot [**BFCM-4**].

- **Toothless:** An old-timer who frequented Hill Valley's Palace Saloon and Hotel in 1885, along with Jeb, Levi, Zeke, Eyepatch and Moustache. He had long, straggly hair, a bushy beard and no teeth. When Marty McFly considered backing out of a duel with Buford Tannen, Toothless and Eyepatch branded Marty a coward [**BTF3-sx**].

  NOTE: The name "Toothless" appeared in BTTF3's production-draft screenplay. His birth name is unknown.

- ***To Sir, With Love:*** A 1967 British film starring Sidney Poitier [**REAL**]. Sally Baines went to see the movie that year with her friends, Jeanne and Mary Ann [**BTF2-s1**].

- **Tow-Bar Torpedo:** An innovation of Emmett Brown, built into the front of his time-traveling locomotive. The Tow-Bar Torpedo enabled the train to stop a fleeing vehicle, by firing a powerful towing cable at it [**BFAN-15**].

- **Townley, Jason K.:** The Institute of Future Technology's supervisor of visual imaging [**RIDE**].

  NOTE: This individual, identified on signage outside Back to the Future: The Ride, *was named after an employee at Universal Studios who worked on* The Simpsons Ride.

- **Town Theater:** A movie theater located in Hill Valley. In 1931, the Town Theater showed *Frankenstein*, a Universal Pictures horror film starring Boris Karloff. Seeing this movie as a youth instilled in Emmett Brown a lifelong love for science [**TLTL-1**]. In 1955, the theater showed *The Atomic Kid*, starring Mickey Rooney (released a year prior) [**BTF1, BTF2**].

  Sometime during the next three decades, the theater was torn down and replaced by the Assembly of Christ church [**BTF1**]. Marty McFly demolished the building in 1985 upon crashing the DeLorean through its front wall [**BTF2**].

  In Citizen Brown's dystopian timeline, Edna Strickland ordered the Town Theater torn down in 1971, as she was convinced that movies were corrupting the younger generation [**TLTL-4**].

- **Toxic Waste Reclamation Plant:** A Hill Valley business in Biffhorrific 1985 [**BTF2**].

- **Toyota SR5 4x4:** A model of pickup truck manufactured by Toyota Motor Corp. [**REAL**]. Statler Toyota, a dealership in Hill Valley, sold this style of vehicle in 1985. Marty McFly long wished he could own such a truck—which he did, after altering the future by making his father, George, more confident and successful [**BTF1**].

  NOTE: An advertisement printed in a 1955 newspaper indicated the store to be located on Hubbard Avenue. In BTTF1's third- and fourth-draft screenplays, the car was a Camaro Z28, while the revised fourth draft changed it to a Toyota Supra.

- **Toyota Supra:** See Toyota SR5 4x4

- **Toys "R" Us:** An international toy-store chain [**REAL**]. Emmett Brown's garage apartment in Hill Valley was located next to a Toys "R" Us location [**BTF1**].

CODE	STORY
NIKE	*BTTF*-themed TV commercial: Nike
NTND	Nintendo *Back to the Future—The Ride* Mini-Game
PIZA	*BTTF*-themed TV commercial: Pizza Hut
PNBL	Data East *BTTF* pinball game
REAL	Real life
RIDE	Simulator: *Back to the Future—The Ride*
SCRM	2010 Scream Awards: *Back to the Future* 25th Anniversary Reunion (broadcast)
SCRT	2010 Scream Awards: *Back to the Future* 25th Anniversary Reunion (trailer)
SIMP	Simulator: *The Simpsons Ride*
SLOT	*Back to the Future Video Slots*
STLZ	Unused *BTTF* footage of Eric Stoltz as Marty McFly
STRY	*Back to the Future Storybook*
TEST	Screen tests: Crispin Glover, Lea Thompson and Tom Wilson
TLTL	Telltale Games' *Back to the Future—The Game*
TOPS	Topps' *Back to the Future II* trading-card set
TRIL	*BTTF: The Official Book of the Complete Movie Trilogy*
UNIV	Universal Studios Hollywood promotional video

SUFFIX	MEDIUM
-b	*BTTF2*'s Biff Tannen Museum video (extended)
-c	Credit sequence to the animated series
-d	Film deleted scene
-n	Film novelization
-o	Film outtake
-p	1955 phone book from *BTTF1*
-v	Video game print materials or commentaries
-s1	Screenplay (draft one)
-s2	Screenplay (draft two)
-s3	Screenplay (draft three)
-s4	Screenplay (draft four)
-sp	Screenplay (production draft)
-sx	Screenplay (*Paradox*)

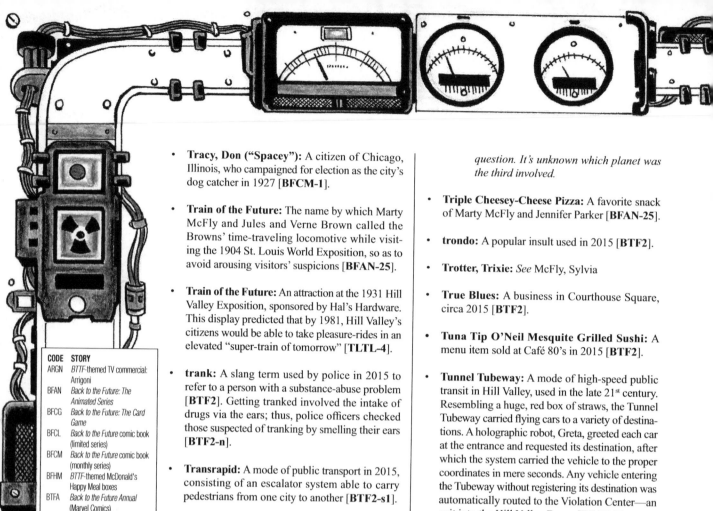

- **Tracy, Don ("Spacey"):** A citizen of Chicago, Illinois, who campaigned for election as the city's dog catcher in 1927 [**BFCM-1**].

- **Train of the Future:** The name by which Marty McFly and Jules and Verne Brown called the Browns' time-traveling locomotive while visiting the 1904 St. Louis World Exposition, so as to avoid arousing visitors' suspicions [**BFAN-25**].

- **Train of the Future:** An attraction at the 1931 Hill Valley Exposition, sponsored by Hal's Hardware. This display predicted that by 1981, Hill Valley's citizens would be able to take pleasure-rides in an elevated "super-train of tomorrow" [**TLTL-4**].

- **trank:** A slang term used by police in 2015 to refer to a person with a substance-abuse problem [**BTF2**]. Getting tranked involved the intake of drugs via the ears; thus, police officers checked those suspected of tranking by smelling their ears [**BTF2-n**].

- **Transrapid:** A mode of public transport in 2015, consisting of an escalator system able to carry pedestrians from one city to another [**BTF2-s1**].

- **Tranz X Playmates:** A phrase scrawled in graffiti on the wall of Hill Valley High School, circa 1985, along with the slogan "We Jam" [**BTF1**].

  NOTE: *This may indicate Tranz X Playmates to have been a music group.*

- ***Trash Dumps of the Gods:*** A book about extraterrestrials, written sometime between 1967 and 1985 by Otis Peabody, detailing the farmer's multiple encounters with a UFO (in actuality, Emmett Brown's flying DeLorean from the future) [**BTF2-s1**].

- **Treharne, Georgia:** An employee at the Institute of Future Technology, in charge of visual prestidigitation [**RIDE**].

  NOTE: *This individual, identified on signage outside* Back to the Future: The Ride, *was named after Universal Studios' manager of administrative services.*

- **Tri-Planet Area:** A region of Earth's solar system, thus defined sometime in or before 2091 [**BFAN-9**].

  NOTE: *Two of the planets were likely Earth and Mars, given the plot of the episode in*

question. It's unknown which planet was the third involved.

- **Triple Cheesey-Cheese Pizza:** A favorite snack of Marty McFly and Jennifer Parker [**BFAN-25**].

- **trondo:** A popular insult used in 2015 [**BTF2**].

- **Trotter, Trixie:** *See* McFly, Sylvia

- **True Blues:** A business in Courthouse Square, circa 2015 [**BTF2**].

- **Tuna Tip O'Neil Mesquite Grilled Sushi:** A menu item sold at Café 80's in 2015 [**BTF2**].

- **Tunnel Tubeway:** A mode of high-speed public transit in Hill Valley, used in the late 21st century. Resembling a huge, red box of straws, the Tunnel Tubeway carried flying cars to a variety of destinations. A holographic robot, Greta, greeted each car at the entrance and requested its destination, after which the system carried the vehicle to the proper coordinates in mere seconds. Any vehicle entering the Tubeway without registering its destination was automatically routed to the Violation Center—an exit into the Hill Valley Dump [**BFAN-9**].

- **Turboliner Death-Race:** A game that Jules and Verne Brown sometimes played as children at their Hill Valley home. The game involved an elaborate set-up of model train tracks on which a diesel-powered toy train (the Diesel of Doom, operated by Jules) raced a toy sports car (the Killer Porsche, remote-controlled by Verne) [**BFAN-2**].

- **Turkle, Mister:** A teacher at Hill Valley High School. Following his advice to choose a mainstream song, Marty McFly's rock band, The Pinheads, auditioned for the Springtime in Paris Dance by playing a tune by Barry Manilow, causing them to lose the gig to a punk-rock group called French Kiss [**BTF1-s2**].

- **Turtle Wax:** A manufacturer of automotive appearance products [**REAL**]. A billboard for this company's products was erected outside Lou's Café in 1955 [**BTF1**].

- **tuum de gluteus maximus:** An insult used by Bifficus Antanneny to describe Marty McFly during the latter's visit to ancient Rome, circa 36 A.D. [**BFAN-5**].

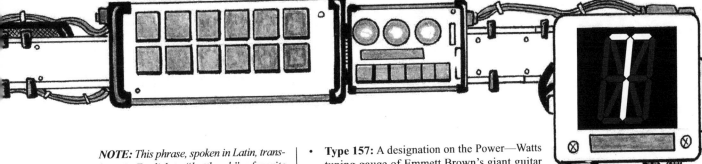

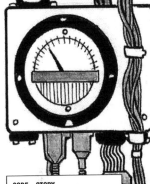

NOTE: *This phrase, spoken in Latin, translates in English to "butthead," a favorite catchphrase of Antanneny's descendant, Biff Tannen.*

- **TV Trash:** A periodical that Emmett Brown read while avoiding activities that might use up his brain power [**BFCM-4**].]

    NOTE: *The magazine's name and logo were based on those of* TV Guide, *making it likely that the magazine provided television listings.*

- **TWA:** *See* US Air

- **Twain, Mark:** *See* Clemens, Samuel Langhorne ("Mark Twain")

- ***Twenty Thousand Leagues Under the Sea***: A science fiction novel by French writer Jules Verne, published in 1870 [**BTF3**]. At age 11, Emmett Brown read this book, inspiring him to devote his life to science [**BTF3**].

- **Twin Pines Mall:** A shopping mall in Hill Valley. In 1985, Emmett Brown conducted a test of his time-traveling DeLorean in the mall's parking lot after closing time, with Marty McFly recording the experiment.

    The mall was named after a pair of pine trees at the lot's entrance, cultivated by farmer Otis Peabody, on whose land—the former Twin Pines Ranch—the shopping center was built. When McFly altered history by running over one of the pines in 1955, the mall was then named the Lone Pine Mall [**BTF1**].

    NOTE: *The Twin Pines Mall was filmed at the Puente Hills Mall, located in City of Industry, California. The mall was absent from the film's first two screenplay drafts; it debuted in the third draft, but was called Three Pines Mall.*

- **Twin Pines Ranch:** A vast area of farmland owned by Otis Peabody in 1955, and named after the pair of pine-tree saplings he planned to cultivate. Peabody lived on the ranch with his wife, Elsie, and two children, Martha and Sherman [**BTF1**].

- **Type 157:** A designation on the Power—Watts tuning gauge of Emmett Brown's giant guitar amplifier [**BTF1**].

- **Type 200B / VARIAC / 115V 60~ 1A:** A knob on Emmett Brown's giant guitar amplifier, and part of the device's variable autotransformer, with a maximum setting of 140. At 50, the knob was marked "Klystron Test" [**BTF1**].

- **Tyrannosaurus rex:** A genus of theropod dinosaur that inhabited western North America during the upper Cretaceous Period [**REAL**]. In 1931, a model of a Tyrannosaurus rex was featured at the Hill Valley Exposition, in a diorama about the city's ancient past. Marty McFly jokingly wondered if the creature was called a Tannenosaurus [**TLTL-4**].

    Emmett, Jules and Verne Brown were nearly eaten by such a beast while visiting that era, but a friendly Pteranodon, which Verne named Donny, helped them escape [**BFAN-3**]. During a second voyage to the Cretaceous, the Browns encountered another Tyrannosaurus rex, upon landing the DeLorean on its head. As the car accelerated for time travel, the resulting flames ignited the dinosaur's tail [**BFAN-c**].

    A group of Time-Travel Volunteers were almost consumed by a Tyrannosaurus while pursuing Biff Tannen, who'd stolen one of Doc's DeLorean time machines in 1991. The dinosaur swallowed the volunteers' car—an Eight-Passenger DeLorean Time Travel Vehicle—but both vehicles managed to escape unscathed [**RIDE**].

    NOTE: *Marty's "Tannenosaurus" joke referred to Officer Tannen, a police dinosaur resembling Biff Tannen who appeared in the BTTF animated series.*

- **Tyrrell Real Estate Broker:** A business in Hill Valley, circa 1885 [**BTF3**].

    NOTE: *A sign for this business was among those leaning against a sign shop located next to Marshal James Strickland's office.*

CODE	STORY
NIKE	*BTTF*-themed TV commercial: Nike
NTND	Nintendo *Back to the Future—The Ride* Mini-Game
PIZA	*BTTF*-themed TV commercial: Pizza Hut
PNBL	Data East *BTTF* pinball game
REAL	Real life
RIDE	Simulator: *Back to the Future—The Ride*
SCRM	2010 Scream Awards: *Back to the Future 25th Anniversary Reunion* (broadcast)
SCRT	2010 Scream Awards: *Back to the Future 25th Anniversary Reunion* (trailer)
SIMP	Simulator: *The Simpsons Ride*
SLOT	*Back to the Future Video Slots*
STLZ	Unused *BTTF* footage of Eric Stoltz as Marty McFly
STRY	*Back to the Future Storybook*
TEST	Screen tests: Crispin Glover, Lea Thompson and Tom Wilson
TLTL	Telltale Games' *Back to the Future—The Game*
TOPS	Topps' *Back to the Future II* trading-card set
TRIL	*BTTF: The Official Book of the Complete Movie Trilogy*
UNIV	Universal Studios Hollywood promotional video

SUFFIX	MEDIUM
-b	*BTTF2*'s Biff Tannen Museum video (extended)
-c	Credit sequence to the animated series
-d	Film deleted scene
-n	Film novelization
-o	Film outtake
-p	1955 phone book from *BTTF1*
-v	Video game print materials or commentaries
-s1	Screenplay (draft one)
-s2	Screenplay (draft two)
-s3	Screenplay (draft three)
-s4	Screenplay (draft four)
-sp	Screenplay (production draft)
-sx	Screenplay (*Paradox*)

UNGER, DATA

(CENTER, WITH SPIKE O'MALLEY
AND WHITEY NOGURA)

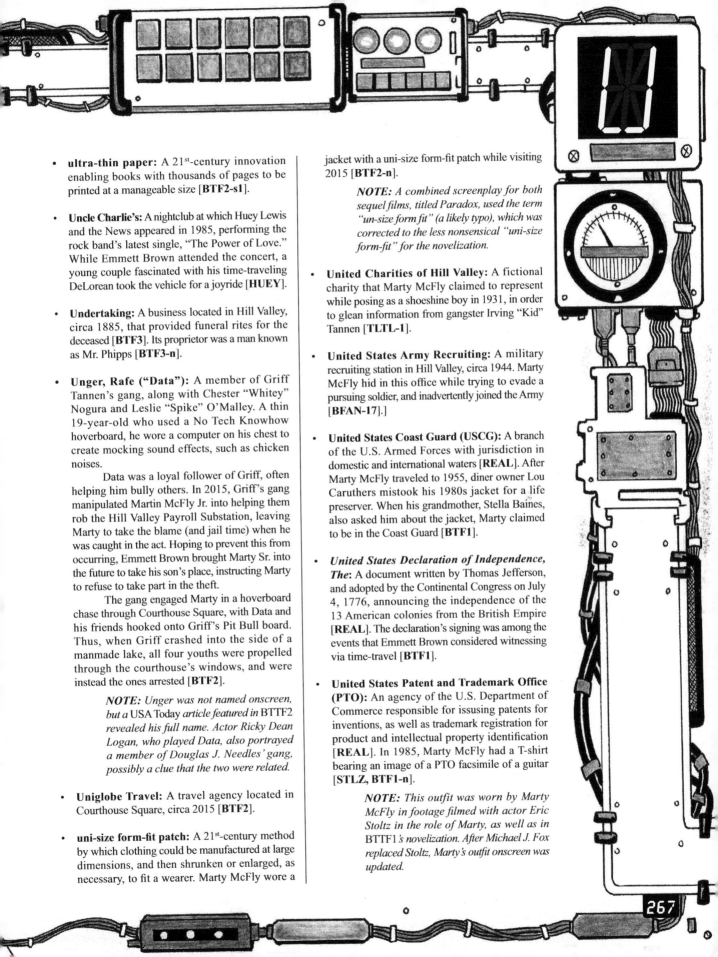

- **ultra-thin paper:** A 21st-century innovation enabling books with thousands of pages to be printed at a manageable size [**BTF2-s1**].

- **Uncle Charlie's:** A nightclub at which Huey Lewis and the News appeared in 1985, performing the rock band's latest single, "The Power of Love." While Emmett Brown attended the concert, a young couple fascinated with his time-traveling DeLorean took the vehicle for a joyride [**HUEY**].

- **Undertaking:** A business located in Hill Valley, circa 1885, that provided funeral rites for the deceased [**BTF3**]. Its proprietor was a man known as Mr. Phipps [**BTF3-n**].

- **Unger, Rafe ("Data"):** A member of Griff Tannen's gang, along with Chester "Whitey" Nogura and Leslie "Spike" O'Malley. A thin 19-year-old who used a No Tech Knowhow hoverboard, he wore a computer on his chest to create mocking sound effects, such as chicken noises.

  Data was a loyal follower of Griff, often helping him bully others. In 2015, Griff's gang manipulated Martin McFly Jr. into helping them rob the Hill Valley Payroll Substation, leaving Marty to take the blame (and jail time) when he was caught in the act. Hoping to prevent this from occurring, Emmett Brown brought Marty Sr. into the future to take his son's place, instructing Marty to refuse to take part in the theft.

  The gang engaged Marty in a hoverboard chase through Courthouse Square, with Data and his friends hooked onto Griff's Pit Bull board. Thus, when Griff crashed into the side of a manmade lake, all four youths were propelled through the courthouse's windows, and were instead the ones arrested [**BTF2**].

  > *NOTE: Unger was not named onscreen, but a USA Today article featured in BTTF2 revealed his full name. Actor Ricky Dean Logan, who played Data, also portrayed a member of Douglas J. Needles' gang, possibly a clue that the two were related.*

- **Uniglobe Travel:** A travel agency located in Courthouse Square, circa 2015 [**BTF2**].

- **uni-size form-fit patch:** A 21st-century method by which clothing could be manufactured at large dimensions, and then shrunken or enlarged, as necessary, to fit a wearer. Marty McFly wore a jacket with a uni-size form-fit patch while visiting 2015 [**BTF2-n**].

  > *NOTE: A combined screenplay for both sequel films, titled Paradox, used the term "un-size form fit" (a likely typo), which was corrected to the less nonsensical "uni-size form-fit" for the novelization.*

- **United Charities of Hill Valley:** A fictional charity that Marty McFly claimed to represent while posing as a shoeshine boy in 1931, in order to glean information from gangster Irving "Kid" Tannen [**TLTL-1**].

- **United States Army Recruiting:** A military recruiting station in Hill Valley, circa 1944. Marty McFly hid in this office while trying to evade a pursuing soldier, and inadvertently joined the Army [**BFAN-17**].]

- **United States Coast Guard (USCG):** A branch of the U.S. Armed Forces with jurisdiction in domestic and international waters [**REAL**]. After Marty McFly traveled to 1955, diner owner Lou Caruthers mistook his 1980s jacket for a life preserver. When his grandmother, Stella Baines, also asked him about the jacket, Marty claimed to be in the Coast Guard [**BTF1**].

- ***United States Declaration of Independence, The***: A document written by Thomas Jefferson, and adopted by the Continental Congress on July 4, 1776, announcing the independence of the 13 American colonies from the British Empire [**REAL**]. The declaration's signing was among the events that Emmett Brown considered witnessing via time-travel [**BTF1**].

- **United States Patent and Trademark Office (PTO):** An agency of the U.S. Department of Commerce responsible for issuing patents for inventions, as well as trademark registration for product and intellectual property identification [**REAL**]. In 1985, Marty McFly had a T-shirt bearing an image of a PTO facsimile of a guitar [**STLZ, BTF1-n**].

  > *NOTE: This outfit was worn by Marty McFly in footage filmed with actor Eric Stoltz in the role of Marty, as well as in BTTF1's novelization. After Michael J. Fox replaced Stoltz, Marty's outfit onscreen was updated.*

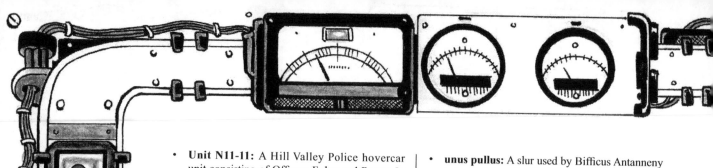

- **Unit N11-11:** A Hill Valley Police hovercar unit consisting of Officers Foley and Reese. In 2015, this team found teenage Jennifer Parker unconscious in an alleyway and delivered her to the home that Jennifer and Marty McFly shared in that era [**BTF2**].

- **universal linguistics translator:** An invention of Emmett Brown, built into the grill of his DeLorean, capable of translating any language—including that of evolved dinosaurs [**BFAN-3, BFAN-5**]. A smaller version could fit in a person's ear [**BFAN-7a**].

- **Universal Positronics:** A business located in Hill Valley, circa 2585 [**BFCL-1**].

- **Universal Studios Florida:** An amusement park located in Orlando, Florida, built around the film and television entertainment industry [**REAL**].

    In 1988, the company asked Emmett Brown to travel back to 1990, to assist in documenting the planned theme park. Jumping two years into the future, Doc videotaped the park, interacting with characters and components of numerous attractions, including Lassie, *Ghostbusters'* Stay Puft Marshmallow Man, *Psycho's* Norma Bates, the great-white shark from *Jaws*, Jessica Fletcher from *Murder, She Wrote*, E.T., King Kong, Fred Flintstone and more. While there, Doc saw every attraction except for *Back to the Future: The Ride*, which he lacked the time to visit before returning to his own era [**UNIV**].

    NOTE: This promotional video, featuring Christopher Lloyd as Doc Brown, metafictionally works the Back to the Future *franchise into its own history. (See also entries on* Back to the Future, *Christopher Lloyd and Michael J. Fox.)*

- **University of California (UC), Berkeley:** A public research university [**REAL**]. Emmett Brown conducted research with its physics department in the area of capacitor discharge, as part of a project known as Temporal Dynamics Model 580 [**TLTL-1**].

- **Uniview:** An invention of Jules Brown, consisting of a helmet and lenses connected to a long tube, enabling a wearer to watch television without annoying others [**BFAN-11**].

- **unus pullus:** A slur used by Bifficus Antanneny to insult Marty McFly in 36 A.D. Upon realizing that the Latin phrase translated into English as "chicken," Marty accepted Antanneny's challenge to a chariot race at the Circus Maximus [**BFAN-5**].

    NOTE: In the films, Marty had an almost pathological aversion to being called "chicken," which nearly ruined his music career.

- **unvelked:** A slang term used in 2015 to indicate that the Velcro fastener of a person's footwear was loose, as in "Your shoe's unvelked" [**BTF2**].

- **Upper Yosemite Falls:** A powerful series of waterfalls in North America, located in Yosemite National Park, in California's Sierra Nevada mountain range [**REAL**]. In 1926, Hollywood stunt actor Daredevil Emmett Brown filmed a scene here for *Raging Death Doom*, a movie produced by D.W. Tannen, in which the youth traveled over the falls in a barrel [**BFAN-11**].

- **Upson, Barry:** An employee at the Institute of Future Technology, stationed in the West Wing [**RIDE**].

    NOTE: This individual, identified on signage outside Back to the Future: The Ride, *was named after an executive in charge of the concept, facility design, construction and operation of the original Univeral Studios Tour in Hollywood.*

- **Uranda:** A 25-year-old ex-fashion model from Damascus, Syria, who joined a group of Libyan nationalists in the early 1980s. She resented that her terrorist group was not perceived as ruthless enough, and enjoyed shooting people to disprove that perception.

    In 1985, Uranda's group stole a case of plutonium from the Pacific Nuclear Research Facility's vault, for use in building a nuclear bomb. Her leader, Sam, hired Emmett Brown to build the bomb, but the scientist kept the plutonium for himself, giving them a shiny case of used pinball-machine parts.

    Furious, the Libyans tracked him down to the Twin Pines Mall parking lot, intent on assassinating him using Soviet weapons. Uranda was among those in the van that found him. The Libyans then chased Marty McFly, who had witnessed the murder.

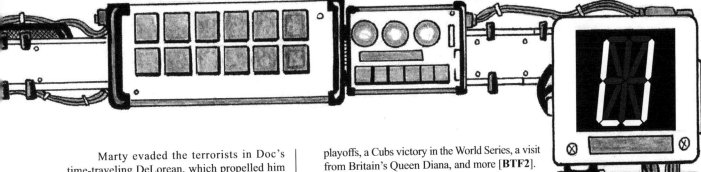

Marty evaded the terrorists in Doc's time-traveling DeLorean, which propelled him back in time to 1955. As he vanished, the van crashed into a Fox Photo one-hour film stand, and Uranda's group was arrested by police alerted to the commotion [**BTF1-n**].

- *USA Hooray*: A newspaper that interviewed Jules Brown in 1992 regarding his invention of a money-tree, for a story titled "Brown Turns Greenback Tree Into Gold" [**BFAN-20**].

  NOTE: The periodical's name was based on that of USA Today.

- **US Air:** A major airline based in Tempe, Arizona [**REAL**]. In 2015, US Air offered flights to Vietnam for surfers [**BTF2**].

  NOTE: In BTTF2*'s first-draft screenplay, as well as in a combined script for both sequel films, titled* Paradox, *the airline was identified as TWA, not US Air.*

- **U.S. Army Recruiting Office:** A military branch in Hill Valley, circa 1955, that sought to recruit new soldiers for the U.S. Army. The office was located on the second floor, above Jacobson & Field, Attorneys at Law [**BTF2**].

- *USA Today*: A national American daily newspaper, published by the Gannett Co. [**REAL**]. By 2015, the publication had a readership of 3 billion, and a cover price of $6.00. That year, the paper covered the arrest of Martin McFly Jr., following a robbery of the Hill Valley Payroll Substation. After Emmett Brown changed time to prevent this from occurring, the headline switched to the arrest of Griff Tannen, Chester "Whitey" Nogura, Leslie "Spike" O'Malley and Rafe "Data" Unger.

  Other articles that day covered research suggesting cholesterol as a cancer cure, an organization formed by auto rebels, slamball

playoffs, a Cubs victory in the World Series, a visit from Britain's Queen Diana, and more [**BTF2**].

- **U.S. Capitol:** The headquarters of the U.S. Congress, located in Washington, D.C. [**REAL**]. After Emmett Brown visited this site, a photo commemorating the occasion was displayed at Doc Brown's Chicken [**CHIC**].

- **U.S. Cavalry:** A mounted force of the United States Army from the late 18th to early 20th centuries [**REAL**]. After traveling back to 1885, Marty McFly found himself in the middle of a dispute between a Cavalry battalion and a tribe of Native Americans, which he narrowly escaped by hiding the DeLorean within a cave [**BTF3**].

  NOTE: The tribe was unspecified onscreen, but BTTF3*'s novelization identified it as the fictional Pohatchee.*

- **Usher's:** A brand of whiskey [**REAL**]. Usher's was among the alcoholic beverages stocked in Biff Tannen's penthouse bar in Biffhorrific 1985 [**BTF2**].

- **U.S. Route 295:** A road that passed through Hill Valley. Courthouse Square was located at the junction of 295 East and U.S. Route 395 West [**BTF1-n**].

- **U.S. Route 395:** A road that passed through Hill Valley, where it merged with U.S. Route 8. Courthouse Square was located at the junction of 395 West and U.S. Route 295 East [**BTF1**].

- **U.S. Route 8:** A road that passed through Hill Valley, where it merged with U.S. Route 395 at Courthouse Square [**BTF1**].

- **Utility Box Car:** A detachable train car for Emmett Brown's time-traveling locomotive, large enough to carry a young Apatosaurus [**BFAN-26**].

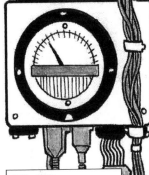

CODE	STORY
NIKE	*BTTF*-themed TV commercial: Nike
NTND	Nintendo *Back to the Future—The Ride* Mini-Game
PIZA	*BTTF*-themed TV commercial: Pizza Hut
PNBL	Data East *BTTF* pinball game
REAL	Real life
RIDE	Simulator: *Back to the Future—The Ride*
SCRM	2010 Scream Awards: *Back to the Future* 25th Anniversary Reunion (broadcast)
SCRT	2010 Scream Awards: *Back to the Future* 25th Anniversary Reunion (trailer)
SIMP	Simulator: *The Simpsons Ride*
SLOT	*Back to the Future Video Slots*
STLZ	Unused *BTTF* footage of Eric Stoltz as Marty McFly
STRY	*Back to the Future Storybook*
TEST	Screen tests: Crispin Glover, Lea Thompson and Tom Wilson
TLTL	Telltale Games' *Back to the Future—The Game*
TOPS	Topps' *Back to the Future II* trading-card set
TRIL	*BTTF: The Official Book of the Complete Movie Trilogy*
UNIV	Universal Studios Hollywood promotional video

SUFFIX	MEDIUM
-b	*BTTF2's* Biff Tannen Museum video (extended)
-c	Credit sequence to the animated series
-d	Film deleted scene
-n	Film novelization
-o	Film outtake
-p	1955 phone book from *BTTF1*
-v	Video game print materials or commentaries
-s1	Screenplay (draft one)
-s2	Screenplay (draft two)
-s3	Screenplay (draft three)
-s4	Screenplay (draft four)
-sp	Screenplay (production draft)
-sx	Screenplay (*Paradox*)

VOLKSWAGEN

- **V8:** A button on a security keypad used to access the Institute of Future Technology's Anti-Gravitic Laboratory [**RIDE**].

- **Vader, Darth:** A villain in Lucasfilm's *Star Wars* film franchise, and the father of Luke Skywalker and Leia Organa. According to the film series, Vader was once known as Anakin Skywalker, before turning to the Dark Side of the Force [**REAL**].

  In 1955, Marty McFly—while working to convince George McFly to ask Lorraine Baines to the Enchantment Under the Sea Dance—posed as Darth Vader, from the planet Vulcan, and threatened to melt George's brain if he didn't ask her out [**BTF1**].

  As Vader, Marty claimed he had a spaceship called the *Battlestar Galactica*, as well as a weapon known as a heat ray (in actuality, a Conair hairdryer), and that he reported to the Supreme Klingon [**BTF1-n, BTF1-d**].

NOTE: In BTTF1's third-draft screenplay, Marty visited Biff Tannen, not George (since Lorraine had agreed to be Biff's date), and ordered Biff to cancel the date and leave town. Marty used a similar ruse on Biff in the animated series, when he and Verne Brown posed as aliens during the arrival of Comet Kahooey.

Marty would appear, like his father, to have some knowledge of popular science fiction, given his combination of elements from the Star Trek, Star Wars and Battlestar Galactica mythologies.

- **Valenti, J.J., Don:** The godfather of the Sacramento Mob, a California crime family in an alternate 1986, also known as the Valenti Gang. Valenti sent a gun-shaped cigarette lighter to Biff Tannen, as a gift from his crime family to Biff's, the Tannen Gang. Marty McFly used the fake gun, after traveling back to 1931, to convince gangster

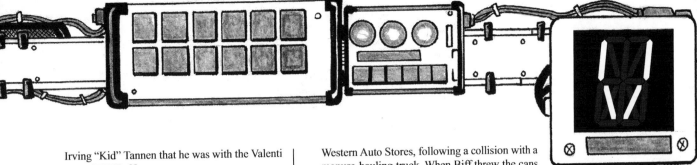

Irving "Kid" Tannen that he was with the Valenti Gang [**TLTL-2**].

> *NOTE: A commentary track for the Telltale Games video game noted that this character's name was an in-joke reference to pro-copyright lobbyist Jack Joseph Valenti, a former president of the Motion Picture Association of America who created the MPAA film-rating system.*

- **Valenti Gang:** A crime family in Prohibition era Hill Valley, also called the Sacramento Mob. Marty McFly posed as a member of this gang while visiting the El Kid speakeasy in 1931, to avoid arousing suspicion from mobster Irving "Kid" Tannen [**TLTL-2**].

- **Valley Central Railway:** A railroad company that operated a train line through Hill Valley in 1985. Upon returning from a century prior, Marty McFly barely managed to exit the time-traveling DeLorean before a yellow Valley Central Railway locomotive ran into the vehicle, completely demolishing it [**BTF3**].

- **Valley Racing Association:** An organization in Hill Valley that paid Biff Tannen his first millions of gambling winnings, after he won a number of horse-racing events on his 21st birthday. This seeming great luck was due to Biff's foreknowledge of the future, gleaned from information contained in *Grays Sports Almanac* [**BTF2-b**].

- **Valley Video:** A residence in Hill Valley, erected in February 1932 upon the site of a speakeasy that burned down under mysterious circumstances. Biff Tannen often rented adult videos from this establishment [**TLTL-1**].

- **Valterra:** A brand of skateboard popular in 1985 [**REAL**]. Marty McFly used a Valterra skateboard to travel around Hill Valley, "skitching" rides on passing cars [**BTF1**].

> *NOTE: BTTF1's fourth-draft screenplay established that the skateboard Marty used onscreen was not his own, but rather belonged to his friend Weeze.*

- **Valvoline:** A U.S. producer of motor oil, circa 1955 [**REAL**]. Biff Tannen purchased a case of Valvoline that year after having his car fixed by

Western Auto Stores, following a collision with a manure-hauling truck. When Biff threw the cans in the back seat, they landed on the groin of Marty McFly, who was hiding on the floor [**BTF2**].

- **Van Conrad, Milton III:** A rich young man in Hill Valley who attended a Country Club Dance in 1992 as the escort of Liz, a snobby fellow student of Marty McFly. Liz had initially invited Marty, before spurning him for the wealthier Milton [**BFAN-25**].

- **Van Halen, Edward Lodewijk ("Eddie"):** A Dutch-American musician, and co-founder and lead guitarist of the hard-rock band Van Halen [**REAL**].

    In 1955, while working to convince George McFly to ask Lorraine Baines to the Enchantment Under the Sea Dance, Marty McFly posed as an alien called Darth Vader, threatening to melt George's brain if he didn't ask her out. To add to the effect, Marty played a loud cassette of Eddie Van Halen's tune "Donut City" [**BTF1**].

> *NOTE: "Donut City" was recorded for the soundtrack of The Wild Life, a film starring Lea Thompson (Lorraine) and Eric Stoltz (who was initially cast as Marty).*

- **Van Horn Dance Studio:** A business located in Chicago's South Side, circa 1927 [**BFCM-1**].

- **Variable Autotransformer:** A panel on Emmett Brown's giant guitar amplifier [**BTF1**].

- **Vector 12:** The direction and magnitude at which Emmett Brown's flying DeLorean was traveling when it arrived in 2015, nearly causing a midair collision [**BTF2-sx**].

- **Velcro:** The brand name of a fabric hook-and-loop fastener patented in 1955 [**REAL**]. That year, while trying to send Marty McFly back to the future, Emmett Brown used a pair of future-made Velcro shoes to prevent an electrical wire from falling from the Hill Valley Courthouse clock [**BTF1**].

> *NOTE: Since Velcro was not commercially available in 1955, it's likely that Doc found the shoes in his future self's suitcase.*

- **velked:** A slang term used in 2015, referring to the Velcro fastener of a person's footwear being

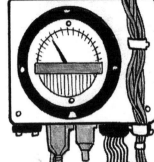

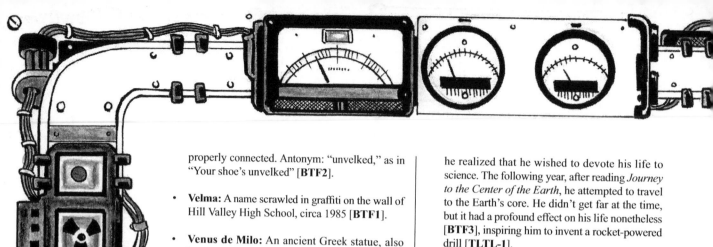

properly connected. Antonym: "unvelked," as in "Your shoe's unvelked" [**BTF2**].

- **Velma:** A name scrawled in graffiti on the wall of Hill Valley High School, circa 1985 [**BTF1**].

- **Venus de Milo:** An ancient Greek statue, also known as Aphrodite of Milos. The Venus is generally believed to depict Greek goddess Aphrodite [**REAL**].

    While visiting ancient Rome, circa 36 A.D., Jules and Verne Brown inadvertently broke off the statue's arms while its sculptor was still creating it. Though at first angered, the artist was pleased upon seeing how the statue looked without arms [**BFAN-5**].

    NOTE: The Venus de Milo is believed to have been sculpted between 130 and 100 B.C.—more than a century before the Browns witnessed its creation in the animated series.

- **Verde Junction:** A railroad-track location along Hill Valley's train line, circa 1885. Engineer "Fearless Frank" Fargo was reputed to have successfully managed to reach 70 miles per hour using a steam-powered locomotive out past Verde Junction [**BTF3**].

- **Verne, Jules:** An employee at the Institute of Future Technology [**RIDE**].

    NOTE: This individual, identified on signage outside Back to the Future: The Ride, *was named after the famous French science fiction author.*

- **Verne, Jules Gabriel:** A French author who predicted air, space and underwater travel long before the invention of air vehicles, submarines or spacecraft. His works included *A Journey to the Center of the Earth, Twenty Thousand Leagues Under the Sea* and *Around the World in Eighty Days* [**REAL**].

    Emmett Brown and Clara Clayton were both great fans of the author's work [**BTF3**]. Doc, in fact, owned a multi-volume hardbound collection of his writings, titled *Jules Verne, Collected Works, Vol. 1 to Vol. IV* [**TLTL-1**]. Doc's ex-girlfriend, Jill Wooster, was also a fan of Verne's books [**BTF3-s1**].

    At age 11, Doc read Jules Verne's *Twenty Thousand Leagues Under the Sea*, at which point he realized that he wished to devote his life to science. The following year, after reading *Journey to the Center of the Earth*, he attempted to travel to the Earth's core. He didn't get far at the time, but it had a profound effect on his life nonetheless [**BTF3**], inspiring him to invent a rocket-powered drill [**TLTL-1**].

    To honor the author, Emmett and Clara named their sons Jules and Verne, and Doc also dubbed his time-traveling locomotive the *Jules Verne Train* [**BTF3, RIDE**]. Verne hated his name, however, and asked Marty McFly to travel back in time with him, to rename the author so that Verne's identity would be changed as well. Among their suggested alternates were Bill, James Bond, Charles Dickens, Frank, Hammer, Luke Perry, Raphael, Bart Simpson, Dr. Seuss and Mark Twain. The attempt failed, and both Vernes retained their original names [**BFAN-21**].

- **Veronica:** An acquaintance of baseball player Pee Wee McFly, sometime in or before 1897 [**BFAN-8**].

    NOTE: Little is known of Veronica, whom McFly mentioned while delirious after being hit on the head with a baseball.

- **Verreaux, E.S.:** A Hollywood professional, circa 2015, who helped director Max Spielberg create *Jaws 19*, according to the film's poster [**BTF2**].

    NOTE: Ed Verreaux worked as an assistant art director on BTTF2 *and* BTTF3.

- **Versateller:** An automatic teller machine (ATM) used by Bank of America, enabling customers to deposit and withdraw money during off-hours [**REAL**]. In 2015, the Bank of America located in Courthouse Square included a Versateller [**BTF2**].

- **Veterinarian Pet Hospital:** A medical facility in Hill Valley, to which Emmett Brown sometimes took his dog, Einstein, in the event of illness or injury [**BFAN-26**].

- **Victory Garden:** An outdoor garden in Hill Valley's Courthouse Square, circa 1944, maintained by two young sisters named Rosie and Dorothy [**BFAN-17**].

- **vid-book:** *See* videobook

- **videobook:** A 21st-century innovation used to store family memories, similar to a photo album,

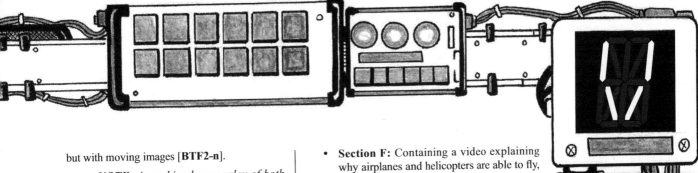

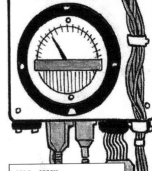

but with moving images [**BTF2-n**].

> **NOTE:** *A combined screenplay of both film sequels, titled* Paradox *called it a "vidbook." In* BTTF2*'s novelization, however, it was changed to "videobook."*

- **Video Encyclopedia:** A database used by Emmett Brown to educate students regarding various aspects of science, with help from fellow scientist Bill Nye [**BFAN-1 to BFAN-26**] and a television producer known as B.G. [**BFAN-23**]. In each video file, or "section," of the encyclopedia—named for a letter of the English alphabet—Nye demonstrated a different type of experiment, with Brown narrating [**BFAN-1 to BFAN-26**].

These videos, appended to entries in Doc's Science Journal [**BFAN-10**], provided ongoing audio-visual scientific documentation [**BFAN-8**], and were filmed using a camera optics device known as an auto-iris [**BFAN-4**]. Doc sometimes broadcast them from the past, via sub-ether transmission linkup [**BFAN-3**].

Among the entries in the Video Encyclopedia were:

- **Section C:** Containing videos illustrating the scientific principle of cloud formation, using a clear plastic cylinder capped at both ends, a tube connected to a rubber stopper, a small air pump, a lit match and water [**BFAN-12**]; explaining center of mass via two demonstrations—one utilizing two forks, a potato, a toothpick, a coffee cup and a glass of water, and another involving a man and a woman attempting to lift a chair while leaning their foreheads against a wall [**BFAN-17**]; and showing how to make a homemade ice-cream cone from butter, egg whites, powdered sugar, salt, vanilla and sifted flour, molded around a template created using thin cardboard, a dinner plate, a geometric compass, a pencil, a pair of scissors and a stapler [**BFAN-25**].
- **Section D:** Containing a video outlining the scientific principle of drag (air resistance), using a parachute break on the back of a toy car [**BFAN-5**].
- **Section E:** Containing videos showing how to create an electromagnet using a screwdriver, insulated wire and two batteries [**BFAN-1**]; and explaining how to use the property of inertia to distinguish raw and cooked eggs without cracking them open, simply by spinning them (since raw eggs stop turning more quickly) [**BFAN-26**].

- **Section F:** Containing a video explaining why airplanes and helicopters are able to fly, and showing how to make a toy helicopter out of a file folder, a pencil, tape and scissors [**BFAN-24**].
- **Section G:** Containing videos discussing the history of Sir Isaac Newton, and illustrating the scientific principle of gravity, by simultaneously dropping an apple and a bowling ball [**BFAN-11**]; and explaining the mechanics of geysers, using a heat source, a beaker of boiling water and an upside-down funnel [**BFAN-13**].
- **Section H:** Containing videos exploring the principles of balloon aeronautics by showing how to construct a hot-air balloon from a plastic bag, adhesive tape and a blow dryer [**BFAN-2**]; and describing how to create a homemade cannon, utilizing an empty soda bottle, a half-cup of water, a half-cup of vinegar, a teaspoon of baking soda, paper towel, a cork and ribbons [**BFAN-14**].
- **Section I:** Containing a video showing how to create invisible ink using a lemon, a knife, a cotton swab, a small bowl, a piece of paper and a heated iron [**BFAN-16**].
- **Section L:** Containing videos outlining how to build a lemon battery, using three lemons, copper tubing, aluminum foil, cardboard pieces, electrical wiring and a battery-operated digital clock [**BFAN-3**]; and illustrating how to make a long-distance communications device, utilizing two plastic drinking cups, a small nail and approximately fifty feet of kite string [**BFAN-19**].
- **Section O:** Containing videos discussing why the Earth orbits the sun, defining the principles of gravity, inertia, and centripetal and centrifugal forces, and showing how to build a model of a space satellite, using a baseball, tape, a toilet-paper tube, string, modeling clay and a small bag [**BFAN-15**]; and describing how to create an optical illusion known as persistence of vision, either with two identical cardboard squares, a pencil and tape, or by using a marker, a t-shirt and a swivel chair [**BFAN-23**].
- **Section P:** Containing videos explaining how a pendulum works, and illustrating the difference between potential and kinetic energy, using a bowling ball suspended from a cord [**BFAN-10**]; and discussing the concept of pressure by showing how to create a hovercraft

CODE	STORY
NIKE	*BTTF*-themed TV commercial: Nike
NTND	Nintendo *Back to the Future— The Ride* Mini-Game
PIZA	*BTTF*-themed TV commercial: Pizza Hut
PNBL	Data East *BTTF* pinball game
REAL	Real life
RIDE	Simulator: *Back to the Future—The Ride*
SCRM	2010 Scream Awards: *Back to the Future* 25th Anniversary Reunion (broadcast)
SCRT	2010 Scream Awards: *Back to the Future* 25th Anniversary Reunion (trailer)
SIMP	Simulator: *The Simpsons Ride*
SLOT	*Back to the Future Video Slots*
STLZ	Unused *BTTF* footage of Eric Stoltz as Marty McFly
STRY	*Back to the Future Storybook*
TEST	Screen tests: Crispin Glover, Lea Thompson and Tom Wilson
TLTL	Telltale Games' *Back to the Future—The Game*
TOPS	Topps' *Back to the Future II* trading-card set
TRIL	*BTTF: The Official Book of the Complete Movie Trilogy*
UNIV	Universal Studios Hollywood promotional video

SUFFIX	MEDIUM
-b	*BTTF2*'s Biff Tannen Museum video (extended)
-c	Credit sequence to the animated series
-d	Film deleted scene
-n	Film novelization
-o	Film outtake
-p	1955 phone book from *BTTF1*
-v	Video game print materials or commentaries
-s1	Screenplay (draft one)
-s2	Screenplay (draft two)
-s3	Screenplay (draft three)
-s4	Screenplay (draft four)
-sp	Screenplay (production draft)
-sx	Screenplay (*Paradox*)

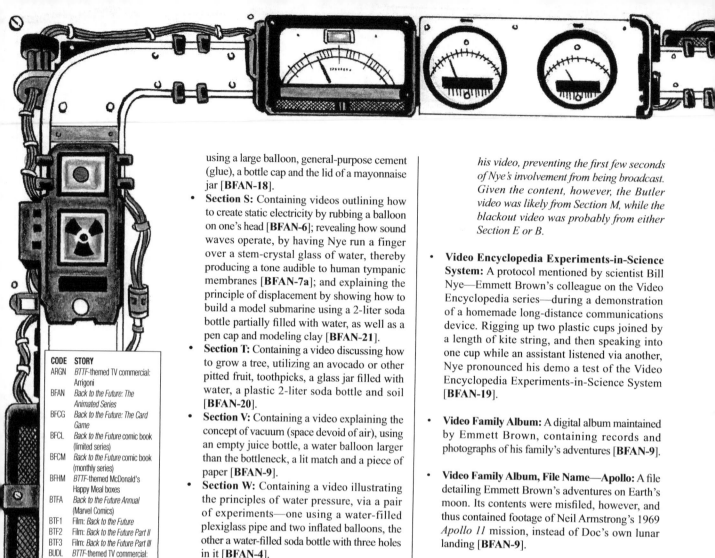

using a large balloon, general-purpose cement (glue), a bottle cap and the lid of a mayonnaise jar [**BFAN-18**].

- **Section S:** Containing videos outlining how to create static electricity by rubbing a balloon on one's head [**BFAN-6**]; revealing how sound waves operate, by having Nye run a finger over a stem-crystal glass of water, thereby producing a tone audible to human tympanic membranes [**BFAN-7a**]; and explaining the principle of displacement by showing how to build a model submarine using a 2-liter soda bottle partially filled with water, as well as a pen cap and modeling clay [**BFAN-21**].

- **Section T:** Containing a video discussing how to grow a tree, utilizing an avocado or other pitted fruit, toothpicks, a glass jar filled with water, a plastic 2-liter soda bottle and soil [**BFAN-20**].

- **Section V:** Containing a video explaining the concept of vacuum (space devoid of air), using an empty juice bottle, a water balloon larger than the bottleneck, a lit match and a piece of paper [**BFAN-9**].

- **Section W:** Containing a video illustrating the principles of water pressure, via a pair of experiments—one using a water-filled plexiglass pipe and two inflated balloons, the other a water-filled soda bottle with three holes in it [**BFAN-4**].

- **Section [*unknown*]:** Containing a video explaining the Magnus effect and the physics of throwing a curveball, with help from Los Angeles Dodgers centerfielder Brett Butler [**BFAN-8**].

- **Section [*unknown*]:** Containing a video exploring how to make an emergency candle during a blackout, using heavy string, a metal nut or washer, a small dish or ashtray, a few ounces of vegetable oil and a matchbook [**BFAN-22**].

> *NOTE: Each episode of the animated series concluded with Doc showing a Video Encyclopedia entry pertaining to that episode's subject matter. Every video contained footage of Bill Nye except for the one in episode #8, which featured Brett Butler.*
>
> *The Butler segment did not specify a section letter, and neither did that in episode #22, in which Doc caused a power failure at Hoover Dam while transmitting his video, preventing the first few seconds of Nye's involvement from being broadcast. Given the content, however, the Butler video was likely from Section M, while the blackout video was probably from either Section E or B.*

- **Video Encyclopedia Experiments-in-Science System:** A protocol mentioned by scientist Bill Nye—Emmett Brown's colleague on the Video Encyclopedia series—during a demonstration of a homemade long-distance communications device. Rigging up two plastic cups joined by a length of kite string, and then speaking into one cup while an assistant listened via another, Nye pronounced his demo a test of the Video Encyclopedia Experiments-in-Science System [**BFAN-19**].

- **Video Family Album:** A digital album maintained by Emmett Brown, containing records and photographs of his family's adventures [**BFAN-9**].

- **Video Family Album, File Name—Apollo:** A file detailing Emmett Brown's adventures on Earth's moon. Its contents were misfiled, however, and thus contained footage of Neil Armstrong's 1969 *Apollo 11* mission, instead of Doc's own lunar landing [**BFAN-9**].

- **video game consoles:** Interactive entertainment computers or customized computer systems designed to produce a video signal for use with a television, a monitor or some other display device [**REAL**]. As a youth in 1986, Verne Brown had a number of consoles built in the 21st century, which he attained using his father's time machine. These included wireless headsets—long before they were commercially available [**TLTL-5**].

- **VideoMovie:** A cassette-tape home-video camera manufactured by JVC [**REAL**]. Emmett Brown owned a VideoMovie camera, with which Marty McFly recorded Temporal Experiment Number One. Marty later utilized the device to convince the scientist's younger self that he was from the future [**BTF1**].

- **Video Slots:** A slot machine designed for casino gambling, for which Emmett Brown recorded a number of brief, humorous videos, encouraging users to bet money in the hope of winning a jackpot [**SLOT**].

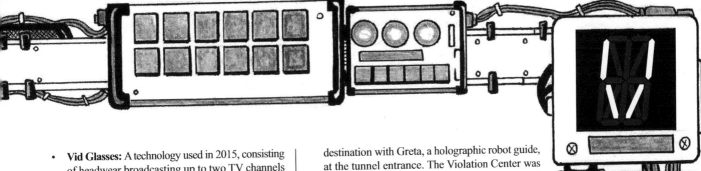

- **Vid Glasses:** A technology used in 2015, consisting of headwear broadcasting up to two TV channels to a wearer's eyes. Similar headgear allowed for phone service [**BTF2**].

    NOTE: The glasses, unnamed in BTTF2, were designated "Vid Glasses" on production sketches included on the film's Blu-ray release.

- **vidmemo:** A type of communication technology used by office workers in 2015. Douglas J. Needles typically had a long row of vidmemos awaiting his attention in his office at CusCo. [**BTF2-n**].

- **vidphone:** A 21st-century telephony innovation consisting of a large, wall-mounted screen enabling individuals to communicate over distances via video and audio. Marty and Jennifer McFly had a vidphone in their den in 2015, which doubled as a television capable of simultaneously showing multiple channels [**BTF2-n**].

    NOTE: In essence, the writers of Back to the Future II accurately predicted not only wall-mounted large-screen televisions, but also voice-over-Internet-Protocol (VoIP) services and instant-messaging clients, such as Skype and ooVoo, as well as the integration of computers, phone service and television.

- **Vietnam:** The easternmost country on the Indochina Peninsula in Southeast Asia [**REAL**]. In 2015, US Air offered flights to Vietnam for surfers [**BTF2**].

- **Vietnam War:** A Cold War-era military conflict fought in Vietnam, Cambodia and Laos, from 1955 to 1975 [**REAL**]. In 1967, Lorraine McFly donated much of her time to rallies protesting the war, out of concern that her brother might be drafted to fight in the conflict. Her father, Sam Baines, disagreed, considering the war a worthy effort [**BTF2-s1**].

    In Biffhorrific 1985, U.S. President Richard Nixon—still in office at the time—vowed to end the Vietnam War, which was still being fought [**BTF2**].

- **Violation Center:** An area of Hill Valley, designated for vehicles entering the Tunnel Tubeway—a mode of high-speed public transit, used circa 2091—without first registering their destination with Greta, a holographic robot guide, at the tunnel entrance. The Violation Center was merely an exit tube into the Hill Valley Dump [**BFAN-9**].

- **Virginia City:** The county seat of Storey County, Nevada [**REAL**]. Martin McFly, the brother of Seamus McFly, was killed at a saloon in this city when he refused to back down from a fight and ended up with a Bowie knife in his belly as a result [**BTF3**].

- ***Virtuous Husband, The***: A 1931 comedy starring Jean Arthur and Elliot Nugent [**REAL**]. In a timeline in which Emmett Brown married Edna Strickland, the couple's first date was to see *The Virtuous Husband*. Since Brown had originally watched *Frankenstein* on that night, the course of his entire life changed, leading to an altered reality in which instead of pursuing science, he became Hill Valley's benevolent dictator, known as First Citizen Brown [**TLTL-3**].

- **Visitor's Day:** An event sponsored by the Hill Valley Fire Department in November 1955. The HVFD posted fliers around town, inviting citizens to attend [**BTF2**].

- **Volkswagen:** An international automobile manufacturer [**REAL**]. In 1985, a group of Libyan nationalists hired scientist Emmett Brown to build them a bomb, but he instead stole the plutonium for himself, providing them with used pinball-machine parts. Furious, the terrorists tracked him down in a blue Volkswagen Station Wagon [**BTF1**].

- **Volume Slider:** A section of the control panel used to recondition inmates' minds at the Citizen Plus Ward, in Citizen Brown's dystopian timeline. Pushing this slider forced a subject to endure very loud noises. Marty McFly, posing as a security guard, manipulated this control while trying to help Emmett Brown escape the complex; in so doing, he inadvertently caused his friend a great deal of discomfort [**TLTL-4**].

- **Vol. XVII, No. 32:** An edition of a Hill Valley newspaper stored in the archives of the city's library in 1955. After discovering his own gravestone in Boot Hill Cemetery, Emmett Brown accessed this and other records about Buford Tannen, recorded as having killed Doc in 1885 [**BTF3**].

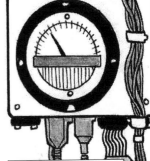

CODE	STORY
NIKE	*BTTF*-themed TV commercial: Nike
NTND	Nintendo *Back to the Future—The Ride* Mini-Game
PIZA	*BTTF*-themed TV commercial: Pizza Hut
PNBL	Data East *BTTF* pinball game
REAL	Real life
RIDE	Simulator: *Back to the Future—The Ride*
SCRM	2010 Scream Awards: *Back to the Future* 25th Anniversary Reunion (broadcast)
SCRT	2010 Scream Awards: *Back to the Future* 25th Anniversary Reunion (trailer)
SIMP	Simulator: *The Simpsons Ride*
SLOT	*Back to the Future Video Slots*
STLZ	Unused *BTTF* footage of Eric Stoltz as Marty McFly
STRY	*Back to the Future Storybook*
TEST	Screen tests: Crispin Glover, Lea Thompson and Tom Wilson
TLTL	Telltale Games' *Back to the Future—The Game*
TOPS	Topps' *Back to the Future II* trading-card set
TRIL	*BTTF: The Official Book of the Complete Movie Trilogy*
UNIV	Universal Studios Hollywood promotional video

SUFFIX	MEDIUM
-b	*BTTF2*'s Biff Tannen Museum video (extended)
-c	Credit sequence to the animated series
-d	Film deleted scene
-n	Film novelization
-o	Film outtake
-p	1955 phone book from *BTTF1*
-v	Video game print materials or commentaries
-s1	Screenplay (draft one)
-s2	Screenplay (draft two)
-s3	Screenplay (draft three)
-s4	Screenplay (draft four)
-sp	Screenplay (production draft)
-sx	Screenplay (*Paradox*)

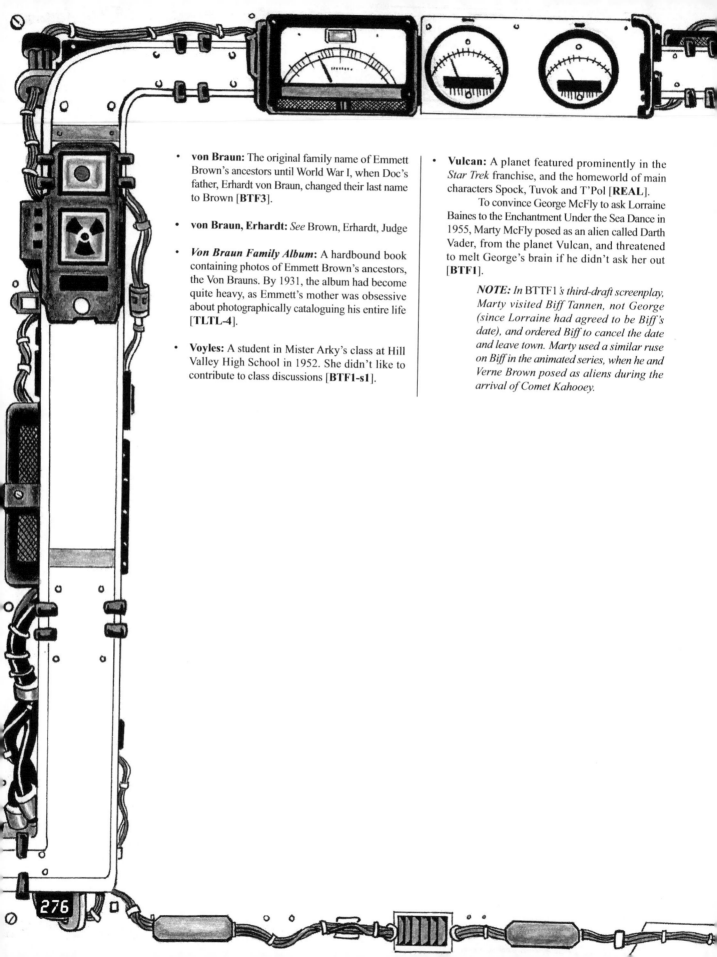

- **von Braun:** The original family name of Emmett Brown's ancestors until World War I, when Doc's father, Erhardt von Braun, changed their last name to Brown [**BTF3**].

- **von Braun, Erhardt:** *See* Brown, Erhardt, Judge

- ***Von Braun Family Album:*** A hardbound book containing photos of Emmett Brown's ancestors, the Von Brauns. By 1931, the album had become quite heavy, as Emmett's mother was obsessive about photographically cataloguing his entire life [**TLTL-4**].

- **Voyles:** A student in Mister Arky's class at Hill Valley High School in 1952. She didn't like to contribute to class discussions [**BTF1-s1**].

- **Vulcan:** A planet featured prominently in the *Star Trek* franchise, and the homeworld of main characters Spock, Tuvok and T'Pol [**REAL**].

    To convince George McFly to ask Lorraine Baines to the Enchantment Under the Sea Dance in 1955, Marty McFly posed as an alien called Darth Vader, from the planet Vulcan, and threatened to melt George's brain if he didn't ask her out [**BTF1**].

    NOTE: *In* BTTF1*'s third-draft screenplay, Marty visited Biff Tannen, not George (since Lorraine had agreed to be Biff's date), and ordered Biff to cancel the date and leave town. Marty used a similar ruse on Biff in the animated series, when he and Verne Brown posed as aliens during the arrival of Comet Kahooey.*

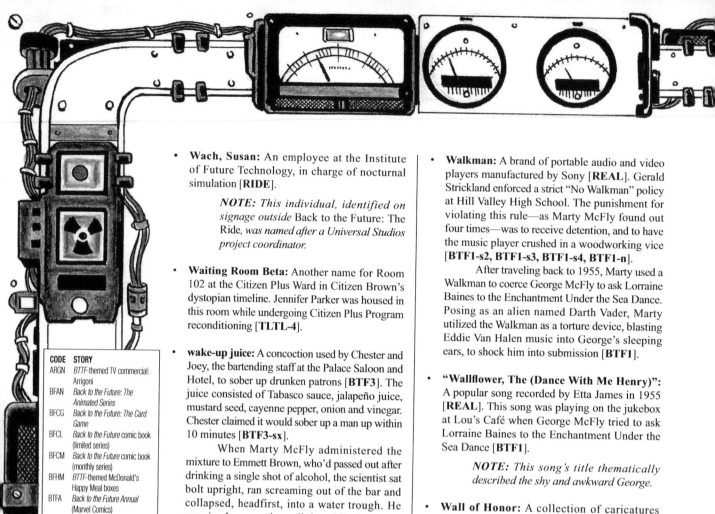

- **Wach, Susan:** An employee at the Institute of Future Technology, in charge of nocturnal simulation [**RIDE**].

    NOTE: This individual, identified on signage outside Back to the Future: The Ride, *was named after a Universal Studios project coordinator.*

- **Waiting Room Beta:** Another name for Room 102 at the Citizen Plus Ward in Citizen Brown's dystopian timeline. Jennifer Parker was housed in this room while undergoing Citizen Plus Program reconditioning [**TLTL-4**].

- **wake-up juice:** A concoction used by Chester and Joey, the bartending staff at the Palace Saloon and Hotel, to sober up drunken patrons [**BTF3**]. The juice consisted of Tabasco sauce, jalapeño juice, mustard seed, cayenne pepper, onion and vinegar. Chester claimed it would sober up a man up within 10 minutes [**BTF3-sx**].

    When Marty McFly administered the mixture to Emmett Brown, who'd passed out after drinking a single shot of alcohol, the scientist sat bolt upright, ran screaming out of the bar and collapsed, headfirst, into a water trough. He remained unconscious all the while, however, which Chester attributed to a "reflex action" [**BTF3**].

- **Wales, Alvis:** An employee at the Institute of Future Technology, stationed in the East Wing [**RIDE**].

    NOTE: This individual was identified on signage outside Back to the Future: The Ride.

- **Walk DMC:** A musical group that played a sold-out performance at Hill Valley's Roxy theater in 1992. Marty McFly promised to buy Jennifer Parker tickets to that concert, knowing that she was a fan of the band, but forgot to do so [**BFAN-14**].

    NOTE: The group's name was based on that of 1980s hip-hop group Run—D.M.C.

- **Walker, Nelson:** An animated system facilitator at the Institute of Future Technology [**RIDE**].

    NOTE: This individual, identified on signage outside Back to the Future: The Ride, *was named after a Universal Studios employee.*

- **Walkman:** A brand of portable audio and video players manufactured by Sony [**REAL**]. Gerald Strickland enforced a strict "No Walkman" policy at Hill Valley High School. The punishment for violating this rule—as Marty McFly found out four times—was to receive detention, and to have the music player crushed in a woodworking vice [**BTF1-s2, BTF1-s3, BTF1-s4, BTF1-n**].

    After traveling back to 1955, Marty used a Walkman to coerce George McFly to ask Lorraine Baines to the Enchantment Under the Sea Dance. Posing as an alien named Darth Vader, Marty utilized the Walkman as a torture device, blasting Eddie Van Halen music into George's sleeping ears, to shock him into submission [**BTF1**].

- **"Wallflower, The (Dance With Me Henry)":** A popular song recorded by Etta James in 1955 [**REAL**]. This song was playing on the jukebox at Lou's Café when George McFly tried to ask Lorraine Baines to the Enchantment Under the Sea Dance [**BTF1**].

    NOTE: This song's title thematically described the shy and awkward George.

- **Wall of Honor:** A collection of caricatures adorning the wall of Irving "Kid" Tannen's speakeasy, El Kid, honoring those killed by the gangster. The portraits were all drawn by Kid's bartender, Zane Williams [**TLTL-2**].

    NOTE: A commentary track for the Telltale Games video game noted that the caricatures were actually based on members of the Telltale staff.

- **Wally's World of Wonderment:** A business located in Hill Valley, owned by Wally Wonderment, that sold overpriced science- and space-based toys. Jules and Verne Brown tried to purchase a telescope at this store to witness the arrival of Comet Kahooey, but the price tag was out of their range [**BFAN-23**].

- **Wannamaker, Harvey:** A famous Hollywood talent scout who made a silent-film star out of young Emmett Brown in 1926, after watching footage of the youth hanging from the back of a stunt plane by the line of a fishing pole. Wannamaker marketed "Daredevil Emmett" as a child icon, with his name and likeness adorning such products as comics, soda, soup, nuts, trading cards, record albums and more [**BFAN-11**].

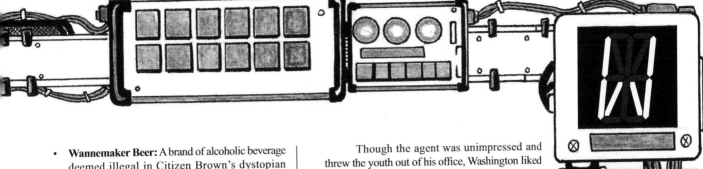

- **Wannemaker Beer:** A brand of alcoholic beverage deemed illegal in Citizen Brown's dystopian timeline. Confiscated cases of the contraband beer were discarded in Decycling Bins and stored in an underground control room by Edna Strickland [**TLTL-3**].

- **War as Racism:** A speech delivered by Muhammed Goldie Wilson at a Vietnam War protest rally to which Lorraine McFly donated her time in 1967 [**BTF2-s1**].

- **Ward, Bob:** An employee at the Institute of Future Technology, stationed in the West Wing [**RIDE**].

  NOTE: This individual, identified on signage outside Back to the Future: The Ride, *was named after a co-founder and key executive of Universal Studios' creative think-tank.*

- **Warnke, John:** A Hollywood professional, circa 2015, who helped director Max Spielberg create *Jaws 19*, according to the film's poster [**BTF2**].

  NOTE: John Warnke worked as an assistant art director on BTTF3.

- *War of the Worlds, The:* A 1953 science fiction film produced by George Pal and directed by Byron Haskin [**REAL**].
  Verne Brown had a poster of this movie hanging in his bedroom when he was a child [**BFCL-1**]. His father, Emmett Brown, also enjoyed this film, which he watched on his Mega-Screen TV [**BFAN-23**].

- **War Zone:** A Hill Valley business in Biffhorrific 1985 [**TOPS**].

- **Washington, Felicia:** An employee at the Institute of Future Technology, in charge of nutritional services [**RIDE**].

  NOTE: This individual's name appeared on signage outside Back to the Future: The Ride.

- **Washington, Reginald:** An African-American band manager, born in 1930. In 1952, he overheard Marty playing the song "Blue Suede Shoes" at the Midwest Talent Agency. At the time, Marty was trying to change history and gain fame as a musician by performing the song three years before it was first recorded.

Though the agent was unimpressed and threw the youth out of his office, Washington liked what he heard and asked Marty to play it again for a New York record executive. The opportunity never arose, however, as Marty returned to his own era before meeting with the exec [**BTF1-s1**].

- **"Washington Post, The":** A patriotic march composed in 1889 by John Philip Sousa [**REAL**]. Goldie Wilson used the music to accompany his 1985 mayoral re-election campaign [**BTF1**].

- **water engine:** A positive-displacement engine driven by water pressure, often resembling a steam engine [**REAL**]. This innovation was discussed in a 1931 issue of *Modern Inventions Monthly* magazine. As a teenager, Emmett Brown had a copy of this issue in his laboratory [**TLTL-1**].

- **waterproof tennis shoes:** An invention of Emmett Brown, created using a pair of high-top sneakers, a can of lard and electric current. This idea proved to be a failure, as it resulted in deep-fried (and un-wearable) footwear. Undaunted, Doc considered marketing the concept to the fast-food industry [**BFAN-11**].

- **Water Test:** A method sometimes used by the Puritans of Salem, Massachusetts, to determine the guilt or innocence of a person accused of witchcraft. The accused was bound and tossed into a bay, while townsfolk waited to see if he or she rose to the surface—if so, that individual was deemed a witch and burnt at the stake, but if the accused drowned, he or she was seen as having been innocent [**REAL**].
  Marty McFly faced the Water Test in 1692, when Mercy Tannen accused him of witchcraft for spurning her affections. Marty only narrowly avoided death, thanks to Doc rescuing him underwater in his DeLorean [**BFAN-4**].

- **Weather Channel:** A U.S. cable and satellite television network that broadcast up-to-the-minute weather forecasts and news 24 hours a day [**REAL**]. Martin McFly Jr. sometimes watched this channel, simultaneous with other stations [**BTF2**].

- *Wedding—Jennifer & Marty:* A videobook in the house of Marty and Jennifer McFly, circa 2015. When Jennifer's younger self from 1985 visited her future home, she saw this and other videobooks stored on a shelf [**BTF2-sx**].

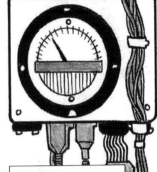

CODE	STORY
NIKE	*BTTF*-themed TV commercial: Nike
NTND	Nintendo *Back to the Future—The Ride* Mini-Game
PIZA	*BTTF*-themed TV commercial: Pizza Hut
PNBL	Data East *BTTF* pinball game
REAL	Real life
RIDE	Simulator: *Back to the Future—The Ride*
SCRM	2010 Scream Awards: *Back to the Future* 25th Anniversary Reunion (broadcast)
SCRT	2010 Scream Awards: *Back to the Future* 25th Anniversary Reunion (trailer)
SIMP	Simulator: *The Simpsons Ride*
SLOT	*Back to the Future Video Slots*
STLZ	Unused *BTTF* footage of Eric Stoltz as Marty McFly
STRY	*Back to the Future Storybook*
TEST	Screen tests: Crispin Glover, Lea Thompson and Tom Wilson
TLTL	Telltale Games' *Back to the Future—The Game*
TOPS	Topps' *Back to the Future II* trading-card set
TRIL	*BTTF: The Official Book of the Complete Movie Trilogy*
UNIV	Universal Studios Hollywood promotional video

SUFFIX	MEDIUM
-b	*BTTF2*'s Biff Tannen Museum video (extended)
-c	Credit sequence to the animated series
-d	Film deleted scene
-n	Film novelization
-o	Film outtake
-p	1955 phone book from *BTTF1*
-v	Video game print materials or commentaries
-s1	Screenplay (draft one)
-s2	Screenplay (draft two)
-s3	Screenplay (draft three)
-s4	Screenplay (draft four)
-sp	Screenplay (production draft)
-sx	Screenplay (*Paradox*)

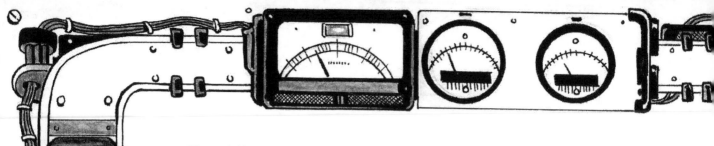

- **Weeze:** A thin-faced schoolmate of Marty McFly at Hill Valley High School, circa 1985 [**BTF1-n**]. He often carried a skateboard around with him at school, which Marty sometimes borrowed [**BTF1-s4**].

  > *NOTE: Weeze's brief scene in BTTF1's fourth-draft screenplay indicated that the skateboard Marty used onscreen was not his own, but rather his friend's.*

- *Weird Science*: A 1985 teen comedy film written and directed by John Hughes, and starring Kelly LeBrock, Anthony Michael Hall and Ilan Mitchell-Smith [**REAL**]. In 1986, Marty McFly had a poster from this movie hanging in his bedroom [**TLTL-1**].

  > *NOTE: The Hill Valley Courthouse façade was re-used in the film* Weird Science.
  >
  > *In BTTF1's third-draft screenplay, the comic book* Tales From Space *was titled* Weird Science.

- **Wells Fargo & Co.:** A multinational financial services company with operations worldwide [**REAL**]. In 1885, Wells Fargo maintained a branch in Hill Valley [**BTF3**].

- **Wentworth, Evan Jr.:** One of several names that Emmett Brown guessed while trying to telepathically determine Marty McFly's identity in 1955, using his Brain-wave Analyzer [**BTF1-n**].

- **Western Auto Stores:** A retail chain specializing in automobile parts and accessories, which claimed to be the "world's leading auto accessory stores" [**REAL**]. The company operated a store in Courthouse Square, circa 1955 [**BTF1**].

  > *NOTE: In Telltale Games' BTTF video game, the store was called Eastern Auto Stores.*

- **Western Union:** A U.S. provider of financial services and communications, such as money orders and (until 2006) telegrams [**REAL**].

  After being trapped in 1885, Emmett Brown sent a Western Union telegram to Marty McFly, with orders not to deliver it until a specified date and time in 1955. The Western Union staff was intrigued, taking bets on whether or not anyone would be there to receive it. To the deliveryman's surprise, Marty was there to sign for Doc's message, which explained how to retrieve the DeLorean and return to his own era [**BTF2**].

Marty instead visited 1885, intent on rescuing Doc from the past. There, he found himself near Western Union's telegraph office [**BTF3**].

- **Westinghouse Fusion Energizer:** *See* Mr. Fusion Home Energy Reactor

- **West Spruce:** *See* Riverside Drive

- **West Wing:** A section of the Institute of Future Technology, containing numerous offices and laboratories [**RIDE**].

- **Wet Buger:** A business in Hill Valley, circa 2015 [**NTND**].

  > *NOTE: This company was advertised on a billboard in the* Back to the Future: The Ride *mini-game. The name may have been an accidental misspelling of "Wet Burger."*

- **"We the People":** The slogan of Hill Valley High School. The phrase appeared on the wall of the school's gymnasium [**BTF1**].

  > *NOTE: "We the People"—the first three words of the Preamble to the United States Constitution—was visible above the stage during the Battle of the Bands auditions.*

- **Weyland, R.:** A neighbor of Edna Strickland, circa 1986 [**TLTL-1**].

- **Which Came First Experiment:** A research project conducted by Jules Brown in the summer of 1991, to determine whether the egg preceded the chicken, or vice versa. The extreme summer heat, however, caused the egg to hard-boil and the chicken to become lethargic, thoroughly botching the results [**BFAN-10**].

- **"Whisper in My Ear (The Secret Song)":** A song included among "Cue Ball" Donnely's piano sheet music at the El Kid speakeasy in 1931, which he sometimes played for the bar's patrons, accompanied by singer Sylvia "Trixie Trotter" Miskin. This tune put Officer Danny Parker—who was emotionally inspired by Trotter's musical talents—in the mood to wallow in his misery, causing him to discuss his problems with anyone who would listen [**TLTL-2**].

- **Whitcomb, Bill, P.E.:** An employee at the Institute of Future Technology [**RIDE**].

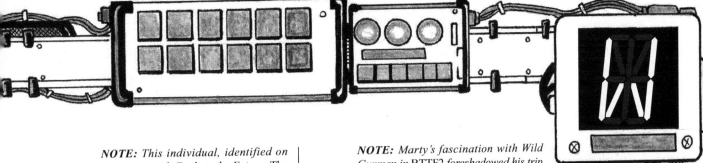

NOTE: This individual, identified on signage outside Back to the Future: The Ride, was named after a sound and video technician at Universal Studios.

- *White Trash Cooking:* A book displayed on the window sill of Marty and Jennifer McFly's kitchen, circa 2015 [**BTF2**].

- **Whitey:** *See* Nogura, Chester ("Whitey")

- **Whopper:** A type of hamburger sandwich sold by global fast-food restaurant chain Burger King [**REAL**]. Emmett Brown's home was littered with several Whopper wrappers, due to his home being located next-door to a Burger King location [**BTF1**].

  NOTE: See also entry for "WOPR."

- **Wilbur:** An elderly citizen of Hill Valley, circa 1955. When Marty McFly was stranded in that year, Wilbur and his wife, terrified by the futuristic radiation suit Marty wore, refused to stop and help him [**BTF1**].

- **Wilcox, Corporal:** A soldier of the Confederate Army, circa 1864, in the regiment of General Beauregard Tannen. He had a long thick mustache, and only two teeth on his bottom jaw. Wilcox arrested Marty McFly and Einstein (Emmett Brown's dog) as they searched for Doc's son Verne, mistaking them for Yankee deserters [**BFAN-1**].

- **Wild Gunman:** A light-gun shooter game introduced by Nintendo in 1974 [**REAL**].

  Marty McFly was an expert at Wild Gunman, and prided himself at his ability to shoot fast and score high. In 2015, upon seeing the game at the Café 80's, he tried to impress two young boys by showing off his prowess—only to be humiliated when one boy deemed it a game for babies, since it required the use of a player's hands [**BTF2**].

  Marty's experience playing Wild Gunman proved helpful when he visited 1885, enabling him to expertly shoot down several moving targets at the Hill Valley Festival [**BTF3**]. Elmer H. Johnson, a salesman for Colt's Patent Firearms Manufacturing Co., was so impressed by Marty's shooting that he gave him a free Colt Peacemaker for use during his duel with Buford Tannen [**BTF3-sp, BTF3-n**].

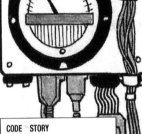

NOTE: Marty's fascination with Wild Gunman in BTTF2 foreshadowed his trip back to the Old West and showdown with Tannen in BTTF3.

In a combined script of both film sequels, titled Paradox, *the video game was called* Gunfighter.

- **wild juice:** A type of narcotic popular in 2015. Those who used wild juice were said to be "floating" [**BTF2-s1**].

- **Wild Will:** A name scrawled in graffiti on the wall of Hill Valley High School, circa 1985 [**BTF1**].

- **Wilkins:** A corpulent, unkempt London citizen who, in 1845, shared a hideout with a fellow thug named Murdock. Wilkins frequented the Hogshead Tavern and had a surly mutt called Crusher; both he and the dog wore eye-patches.

  When Jules and Vern Brown became lost in that year, Emmett Brown paid Wilkins to help him find his sons, unaware the man's partner in crime had already kidnapped them. Thanks to Doc's intervention, Murdock and Wilkins were arrested and brought to justice [**BFAN-10**].

- **Williams, Chris:** An employee at the Institute of Future Technology, in charge of extravaganza development [**RIDE**].

  NOTE: This individual, identified on signage outside Back to the Future: The Ride, *was named after an art director at Universal Studios.*

- **Williams, Zane:** A gangster who worked for Irving "Kid" Tannen in 1931. He had great artistic talent, and painted posters to be hung on the walls of Tannen's speakeasy, El Kid. Zane served as Kid's bartender and caricaturist, sketching portraits of the mobster's murder victims, which he hung on the bar's Wall of Honor.

  Secretly, Zane wished he could leave his life of crime behind and become a professional cartoonist for *The New Yorker*. Instead, he was arrested, along with his fellow criminals, when policeman Danny Parker raided the speakeasy [**TLTL-2**].

  NOTE: This character was named after actor Billy Zane, who played Biff Tannen's friend Match in the first two BTTF films. His last name, Williams, was revealed in

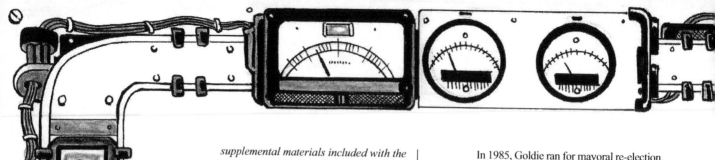

supplemental materials included with the packaging to the Telltale Games video game.

- **Willis:** A schoolmate of Marty McFly at Hill Valley High School, circa 1985. He and Marty sometimes endured detention together, under Vice-Principal Gerald Strickland. During one such detention, Strickland mocked him for indicating on his homework that the capitol of Oklahoma was New York City [**BTF1-s3**].

- **Wilshire**: A street in Los Angeles, California. IG Systems was located at 3345 Wilshire #501 [**BFAN-12**].

- **Wilson, Clara:** A descendant of Goldie Wilson, circa 2015, in one possible timeline [**BFCG**].

  NOTE: This character may have been named after Clara Clayton Brown.

- **Wilson, Dick ("Dickie"):** The proprietor of Wilson's Café, a diner in Hill Valley, circa 1985. He took over the establishment from his mother, who ran the place in the 1950s when Dickie was a child [**BTF1-s1**].

  NOTE: Onscreen, the establishment was known as Lou's Café, and was owned by Lou Caruthers.

- **Wilson, Goldie (Muhammed), Mayor:** The mayor of Hill Valley in 1985. Goldie, an African-American man, sported a single gold tooth and wore his hair in an Afro cut.

  As a teenager in 1955, Goldie showed great ambition, vowing to one day make a name for himself despite his skin color. Marty McFly encountered young Goldie working as a busboy at Lou's Café, and inspired him by mentioning that he'd one day be mayor. Goldie's boss, Lou Caruthers, scoffed at the notion [**BTF1**].

  By the late 1960s, Goldie—now calling himself Muhammed Wilson—worked to put himself through law school, and served as a public defender, facing derision from many of Hill Valley's white citizens. In 1967, he represented Marty (traveling under the guise of a Hippie from that era) when the latter was arrested for violating the Selective Service Act by not having a draft card [**BTF2-s1**].

  In 1985, Goldie ran for mayoral re-election. That same year, he sponsored an initiative to replace the Clock Tower in Courthouse Square, which had been struck by lightning in 1955, during the same week in which he'd met Marty. This initiative was protested by the Hill Valley Preservation Society's Save the Clock Tower Fund [**BTF1**].

  Goldie's son, Goldie Wilson Jr., followed in his footsteps as Hill Valley's mayor in 2015, while his grandson, Goldie Wilson III, founded Wilson Conversion Systems [**BTF3**]. His family also founded Goldie Wilson, Inc., which rented billboard space in Hill Valley, including on a wall outside the Blast From the Past antique store [**RIDE**].

  NOTE: Wilson's full name appeared in BTTF2's first-draft script.

- **Wilson, Goldie Jr., Mayor:** The municipal leader of Hill Valley, circa 2015. The son of previous mayor Goldie Wilson, he had a son, Goldie Wilson III, who ran Wilson Conversion Systems. In October 2015, Goldie Jr. ran for mayoral re-election [**BTF2**].

- **Wilson, Goldie III:** The grandson of Goldie Wilson and son of Goldie Wilson Jr. He greatly resembled his forebearers, but chose not to follow in their shoes, opting to become a businessman instead of a politician. In 2015, Goldie ran Wilson Conversion Systems, and advertised his business via holographic commercials in Courthouse Square [**BTF2**].

- **Wilson Conversion Systems:** A business in 2015 Hill Valley with 29 locations, run by Goldie Wilson III. The company advertised that it could hover-convert any road car into a skyway flier for only $39,999.95 [**BTF2**].

- **Wilson's Café:** A diner in Hill Valley, circa 1985. Marty McFly sometimes ate breakfast at this restaurant, and was on first-name terms with its proprietor, Dick Wilson, who inherited it from his mother [**BTF1-s1**].

  NOTE: Onscreen, the establishment was known as Lou's Café, and was owned by Lou Caruthers.

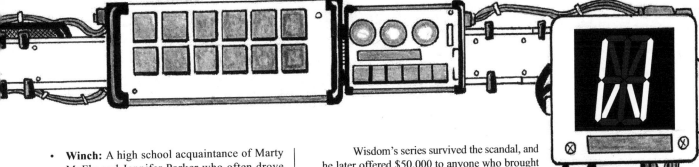

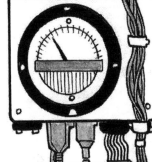

- **Winch:** A high school acquaintance of Marty McFly and Jennifer Parker who often drove around in a red Corvette with his friend, Lomax. In 1985, Winch and Lomax lured Marty into a "once-in-a-lifetime" deal, promising it would earn him "major cash-ola." Roped into participating, Marty canceled a planned trip with Jennifer, but the plan went sour, and Marty almost went to jail as a result [**BTF2-s1**].

  NOTE: Lomax and Winch appeared only in an early-draft screenplay for BTTF2. Onscreen, Marty was coerced into a bad decision by Douglas J. Needles.

- **Winged Goddess, The:** A statue packed in a crate in which Marty McFy hid in 1931, in order to sneak into Irving "Kid" Tannen's speakeasy and rescue his grandfather, Arthur McFly. Upon opening the crate, Marty inadvertently shattered the statue [**TLTL-2**].

- **Winsome Wench of Winnipeg, The:** *See* McFly, Sylvia

- **Wisdom, Walter ("Walt," "Mr. Wisdom"):** The unscrupulous host of *Mr. Wisdom*, a children's science television series on Channel 92 [**BFAN-15, BFAN-26**].

  Wisdom had a bald head and a yellow-toothed overbite, and wore eyeglasses, a green graduation outfit, and a thick fake mustache and bushy eyebrows. A con man pretending to be a great scientist, he manipulated kids into buying overpriced merchandise whenever he drove his popular Big-Brain Bus to local malls.

  Verne Brown enjoyed his TV series, but his brother, Jules, considered the man a phony—as did Emmett Brown, stemming from their college days. While attending the American College of Technological Science & Difficult Math, Wisdom had been Doc's roommate and fraternity brother. When Doc invented the Perpetual-Motion Hula Hoop, intending to submit it to the Inter-Collegiate Science Invent-Off, Wisdom stole the idea, earning a lucrative contract with Glunko Toys and his own television show.

  At Hill Valley's Lone Pine Mall in 1992, Wisdom met Verne and accompanied him back to Doc's lab. Once there, he stole several more of Doc's inventions—including the DeLorean, which he tried to sell on TV for $999,995—but Doc publicly discredited the thief during a live broadcast, regaining his stolen items [**BFAN-15**].

Wisdom's series survived the scandal, and he later offered $50,000 to anyone who brought a live alien, dinosaur or Bigfoot to his studio. To cash in, Biff Tannen captured Tiny, Verne Brown's pet Apatosaurus, and presented it to the TV host.

Wisdom renamed the animal Dinosaurus Humongous, planning to unveil it on the *Mr. Wisdom's Live Super-Duper Dinosaur Special*. Verne and Jules rescued their pet, however, and replaced it with a fake-looking substitute, publicly humiliating both Biff and Wisdom [**BFAN-26**].

  NOTE: This character and his TV series paid homage to scientist Donald Jeffrey Herbert "Mr. Wizard" Kemske, of Watch Mr. Wizard *and* Mr. Wizard's World *fame. The motif of a wizard putting on one face in public but another in private also played on the "man behind the curtain" device of L. Frank Baum's Oz books.*

  Wisdom may have been conceived as a relative of Biff Tannen, as he sounded much like Thomas F. Wilson (who portrayed Biff's numerous cartoon ancestors and descendants) and had the typical Tannen yellow eyes and teeth.

- **Winnick, Terry:** A senior inventive officer at the Institute of Future Technology [**RIDE**].

  NOTE: This individual, identified on signage outside Back to the Future: The Ride, *was named after Terry A. Winnick, the ride's producer.*

- **Wizard:** A word scrawled in graffiti on the wall of Hill Valley High School, circa 1985 [**BTF1**].

- **Wiz-Kids:** A nickname by which TV personality Walter Wisdom referred to the children in his television viewing audience at *Mr. Wisdom* [**BFAN-26**].

- **W.J. Chang:** A business located in Hill Valley, circa 1885 [**BTF3**].

- **Wood, Sharyn, Dr.:** The contingencies comptroller of the Institute of Future Technology [**RIDE**].

  NOTE: This individual's name appeared on signage outside Back to the Future: The Ride.

CODE	STORY
NIKE	*BTTF*-themed TV commercial: Nike
NTND	Nintendo *Back to the Future— The Ride* Mini-Game
PIZA	*BTTF*-themed TV commercial: Pizza Hut
PNBL	Data East *BTTF* pinball game
REAL	Real life
RIDE	Simulator: *Back to the Future—The Ride*
SCRM	2010 Scream Awards: *Back to the Future* 25th Anniversary Reunion (broadcast)
SCRT	2010 Scream Awards: *Back to the Future* 25th Anniversary Reunion (trailer)
SIMP	Simulator: *The Simpsons Ride*
SLOT	*Back to the Future* Video Slots
STLZ	Unused *BTTF* footage of Eric Stoltz as Marty McFly
STRY	*Back to the Future* Storybook
TEST	Screen tests: Crispin Glover, Lea Thompson and Tom Wilson
TLTL	Telltale Games' *Back to the Future—The Game*
TOPS	Topps' *Back to the Future II* trading-card set
TRIL	*BTTF: The Official Book of the Complete Movie Trilogy*
UNIV	Universal Studios Hollywood promotional video

SUFFIX	MEDIUM
-b	*BTTF2*'s Biff Tannen Museum video (extended)
-c	Credit sequence to the animated series
-d	Film deleted scene
-n	Film novelization
-o	Film outtake
-p	1955 phone book from *BTTF1*
-v	Video game print materials or commentaries
-s1	Screenplay (draft one)
-s2	Screenplay (draft two)
-s3	Screenplay (draft three)
-s4	Screenplay (draft four)
-sp	Screenplay (production draft)
-sx	Screenplay (*Paradox*)

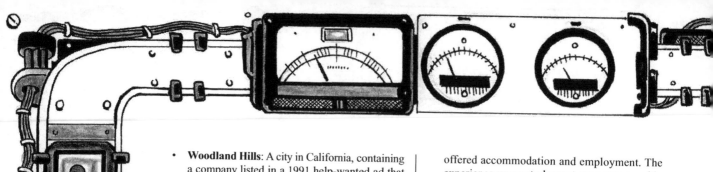

- **Woodland Hills**: A city in California, containing a company listed in a 1991 help-wanted ad that Emmett Brown read while trying to find a job. The business was located at 23251 Mulholland Drive, in Woodland Hills, California [**BFAN-12**].

- **Woodman Road:** A road running through Hill Valley, circa 1985. The Del-Wood Plaza Complex was located at the corner of Delgado Highway and Woodman Road [**BTF3-s1**].

- **Woods, Mrs.:** One of Marty McFly's teachers at Hill Valley High School. The 45-year-old woman had little patience with Marty's tendency to violate school rules by playing his Walkman in class [**BTF1-s3**].

  > NOTE: *Woods appeared in* BTTF1*'s third-draft screenplay, replacing Mr. Arky from the prior two drafts.*

- **Woodward, Ron:** A student at Hill Valley High School who ran for senior class president in 1955, under the platform, "The Right Man for the Job" [**BTF1**].

  > NOTE: *Ronald T. Woodward, the key grip for* Back to the Future, *was responsible for lighting and rigging the movie's sets.*

- **Wooster, Dean:** Emmett Brown's boss in 1955, at a local college known as Hill Valley University [**BTF2-s1, BTF3-s1**]. Doc briefly dated his daughter, Jill.

  Wooster and his colleagues, Cooper and Mintz, requested that Doc, as a member of their staff, agree to take part in one of three projects: developing the Edsel automobile, creating a chemical-warfare compound (to be called Agent Brown in his honor) or helping to build the new Xerox company. When Doc declined, the dean threatened to put an end to his relationship with Jill [**BTF3-s1**].

- **Wooster, Jill:** A girlfriend of Emmett Brown, circa 1955, with whom he shared a romantic interlude in Pismo Beach, California. Jill, the daughter of Dean Wooster (his boss at the time), enjoyed the works of Jules Verne. This relationship became strained after Doc refused to help with any of her father's pet projects [**BTF3-s1**].

- **Workhouse:** A facility in 1845 London at which juveniles unable to support themselves were offered accommodation and employment. The experience was not pleasant, so a street urchin named Reginald chose to pick pockets for a thug named Murdock, rather than live at the Workhouse. Marty McFly, posing as the Ghost of Christmas, brought Ebiffnezer Scrooge here to show him children working on Christmas Eve [**BFAN-10**].

- **World O' Transponders:** A business located in the Hill Valley Courthouse Mall, an underground shopping center beneath the Hill Valley Courthouse, circa 2015 [**BTF2-n**].

- *World Tomorrow*: A newspaper published in the early 21st century, and sold in Hill Valley. In one timeline, *World Tomorrow* reported on the arrest and imprisonment of Marty McFly Jr. in 2015 [**BFCG**].

  > NOTE: *This publication's name was based on that of* USA Today.

- **Wonderment, Wally ("Mister Wonderment"):** The proprietor of Wally's World of Wonderment, a science store located in Hill Valley, California, circa 1991. A small man with glasses and Hippie clothing, Wally sold overpriced science- and space-based toys, and was willing to cheat a customer in order to make money.

  After Biff Tannen broke an expensive telescope in his shop, Wonderment offered to sell him the "Galaxy Viewfinder-500," which he described as a "magical and sophisticated apparatus," for only $10. Although it was actually just an empty shoebox with a hole poked in either end, Biff naïvely decided to buy two [**BFAN-23**].

- **WOPR:** A computer program sold in Citizen Brown's dystopian timeline [**TLTL-3**].

  > NOTE: *This software's name, pronounced "Whopper," paid homage to the military supercomputer featured in the films* WarGames *and* WarGames: The Dead Code*—and may have also referenced the many Whopper wrappers seen in Doc's home in* BTTF1.
  > *See also entry for "Whopper."*

- **Wright Brothers:** A pair of brother inventors, Wilbur and Orville Wright, credited with creating the world's first successful airplane in 1903, and with making the first controlled, powered and sustained heavier-than-air human flight, which

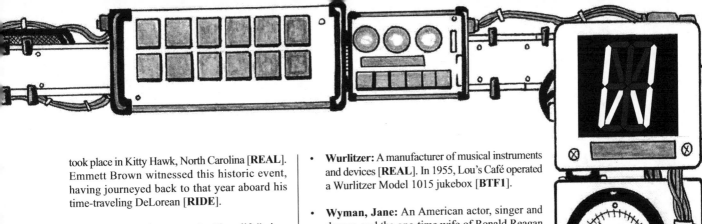

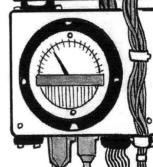

took place in Kitty Hawk, North Carolina [**REAL**]. Emmett Brown witnessed this historic event, having journeyed back to that year aboard his time-traveling DeLorean [**RIDE**].

- **wrinkle job:** A slang term for "face-lift," circa 2015 [**BTF2-s1**].

- **Write-o-Matic:** An invention of Emmett Brown, consisting of a pen and a wire-attached suction cup [**BTF1-s1**].

- **WRM EMIT:** A button on an overhead console of Emmett Brown's DeLorean [**TLTL-5**].

- **Wurlitzer:** A manufacturer of musical instruments and devices [**REAL**]. In 1955, Lou's Café operated a Wurlitzer Model 1015 jukebox [**BTF1**].

- **Wyman, Jane:** An American actor, singer and dancer, and the one-time wife of Ronald Reagan [**REAL**]. When Marty McFly tried to convince Emmett Brown, in 1955, that he was from the future, the scientist challenged him to name the president in 1985. Marty replied Ronald Reagan, but Brown scoffed at the notion, mockingly asking if Wyman was the First Lady [**BTF1**].

- **X:11:** A code used to trigger graduates of the Citizen Plus Program, a brainwashing technique used in Citizen Brown's dystopian timeline to keep Hill Valley's populace subservient to the benevolent dictator. Once the X:11 code was transmitted via a special wristwatch, Citizen Plus graduates were compelled to perform violent acts on behalf of Edna Strickland, such as beating up enemies of the state [**TLTL-3**].

- **X5:** A button on a security keypad used to access the Institute of Future Technology's Anti-Gravitic Laboratory [**RIDE**].

- **Xerox Corp.:** A document-management corporation providing color and black-and-white printers, photocopiers, digital-production printing presses and other products [**REAL**].

    In 1952, a colleague of Emmett Brown named Charles tried to convince him to become a major stockholder and employee of the fledgling Xerox Corp. Convinced that the firm had no future, since few would know how to pronounce its name—he initially mispronounced it "X-rox"—Brown turned down the offer [**BTF1-s1**].

    In 1955, Doc's university boss, Dean Wooster, along with two colleagues, Cooper and Mintz, urged him to take part in the Xerox project, but he refused [**BTF3-s1**].

    NOTE: Charles was likely Charles Peter McColough, one of Xerox's co-founders.

- **XXX:** An identifier used by the pornography industry to denote particularly explicit X-rated adult films [**REAL**]. Hill Valley's adult theater, the Essex, showed a classic XXX film in 1985 titled *Orgy American Style* [**BTF1**].

    In Biffhorrific 1985, Courthouse Square was filled with other adult businesses, in addition to the Essex. In that reality, the sidewalk outside the graffiti-covered theater was a popular hangout for local hoods and the homeless [**BTF2**].

    NOTE: Actor George "Buck" Flower, who portrayed Red the bum in the first two Back to the Future *films, also appeared in* Orgy American Style.

- **XYA 1:** The license plate number of a car owned by gangsters in 1931. Marty McFly nearly crashed the DeLorean into this vehicle upon arriving in that year. At that moment, the thugs were involved in a shootout with the Hill Valley Police. The DeLorean's sudden arrival between the vehicles nearly caused a deadly pile-up [**TLTL-1**].

CODE	STORY
NIKE	*BTTF*-themed TV commercial: Nike
NTND	Nintendo *Back to the Future—The Ride* Mini-Game
PIZA	*BTTF*-themed TV commercial: Pizza Hut
PNBL	Data East *BTTF* pinball game
REAL	Real life
RIDE	Simulator: *Back to the Future—The Ride*
SCRM	2010 Scream Awards: *Back to the Future* 25th Anniversary Reunion (broadcast)
SCRT	2010 Scream Awards: *Back to the Future* 25th Anniversary Reunion (trailer)
SIMP	Simulator: *The Simpsons Ride*
SLOT	*Back to the Future* Video Slots
STLZ	Unused *BTTF* footage of Eric Stoltz as Marty McFly
STRY	*Back to the Future* Storybook
TEST	Screen tests: Crispin Glover, Lea Thompson and Tom Wilson
TLTL	Telltale Games' *Back to the Future—The Game*
TOPS	Topps' *Back to the Future II* trading-card set
TRIL	*BTTF: The Official Book of the Complete Movie Trilogy*
UNIV	Universal Studios Hollywood promotional video

SUFFIX	MEDIUM
-b	*BTTF2*'s Biff Tannen Museum video (extended)
-c	Credit sequence to the animated series
-d	Film deleted scene
-n	Film novelization
-o	Film outtake
-p	1955 phone book from *BTTF1*
-v	Video game print materials or commentaries
-s1	Screenplay (draft one)
-s2	Screenplay (draft two)
-s3	Screenplay (draft three)
-s4	Screenplay (draft four)
-sp	Screenplay (production draft)
-sx	Screenplay (*Paradox*)

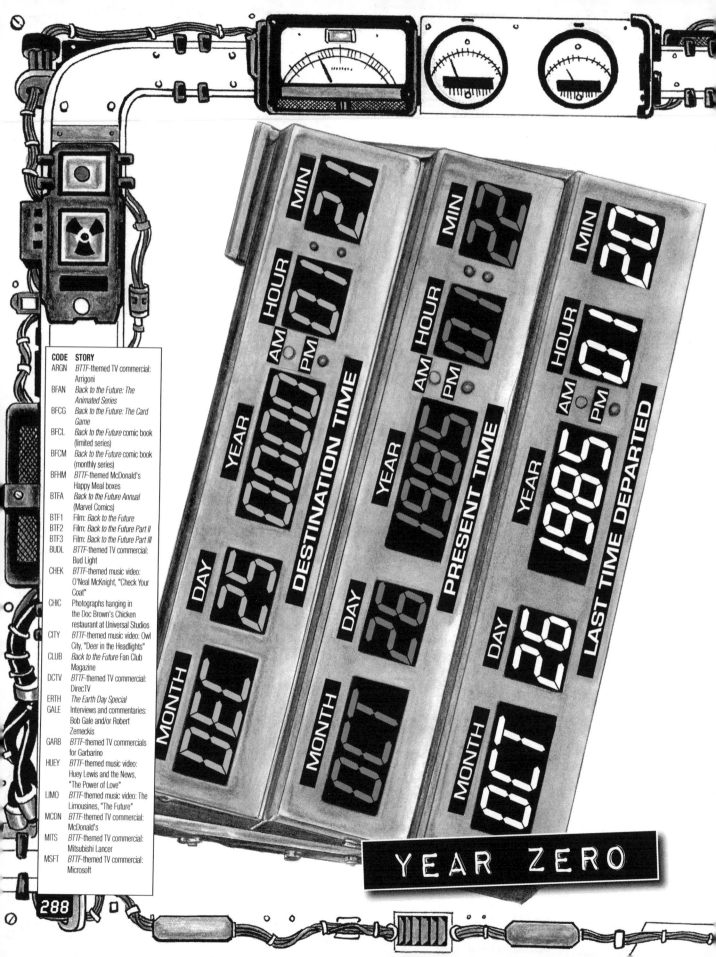

YEAR ZERO

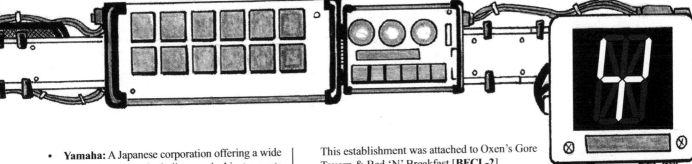

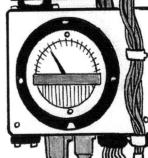

- **Yamaha:** A Japanese corporation offering a wide range of products, including musical instruments and motorcycles [**REAL**]. The drummer of Marty McFly's high school rock band, The Pinheads, played a Yamaha drum set [**BTF1**].

- **Yankees:** A professional baseball team based in The Bronx, New York [**REAL**]. According to a *USA Today* report, the Yankees had a bad season in 2015, which the team's manager attributed to a bad start and inclement weather [**BTF2**].

- **Year Zero:** A name often ascribed to a year nonexistent on either the Julian or Gregorian calendars, in which 1 BC is immediately followed by 1 AD, with no year "0" occurring between those calendar years [**REAL**].

  While preparing to embark on his maiden voyage aboard his time-traveling DeLorean, Emmett Brown considered visiting Dec. 25, 0000, perhaps to witness the birth of Jesus Christ [**BTF1**].

  > *NOTE: Since "Year Zero" is nonexistent, it's unknown when Doc would have ended up had he attempted to travel to 0000. Buddhist and Hindu calendars do contain a zero year, but this was clearly not the system used for the DeLorean's time circuits.*
  >
  > *Moreover, the year of Jesus' birth is generally considered to have occurred a few years BC, and not in December—so even if there were a "Year Zero," Doc would have missed Jesus' birth by entering such a destination time.*

- **Yellowstone National Park:** A U.S. national park located in Wyoming, known for its many geothermal features, including the geyser Old Faithful [**REAL**]. In 1850, Verne Brown and his grandmother, Martha O'Brien, survived a bear attack by sitting on a buffalo hide atop Old Faithful, which launched them into the air and out of the animal's reach [**BFAN-13**].

- **Ye Oxen's Gore Tavern & Dinner Theater:** A business located in Hillvallia, circa 2,991,299,129,912,991 A.D. While trapped in that distant future, Emmett Brown's family and Marty McFly visited this bar looking to find platinum, in order to fix the *Jules Verne Train*'s Flux Capacitor.

This establishment was attached to Oxen's Gore Tavern & Bed 'N' Breakfast [**BFCL-2**].

> *NOTE: Many scientists believe Earth will cease to exist in approximately 7.6 billion years, with human life dying out within a billion years or so.*

- **Yesterday's Soup:** A daily special offered at the Sisters of Mercy Soup Kitchen, circa 1931 [**TLTL-1**].

- **Young Men's Christian Association (YMCA):** A federated organization comprising local and national organizations fostering Christian goals [**REAL**]. The organization operated a chapter in Hill Valley, circa 1985 [**BTF1**].

  Marty McFly's rock band, The Pinheads, intended to audition for a YMCA dance that year. However, these plans faltered when Marty earned an afterschool detention with his high school vice-principal, Gerald Strickland [**BTF1-s3**].

- **"You Should Care":** An upbeat, inspirational song written by Edna Strickland sometime in or before 1931, which she sang to passersby while playing an accordion. The song preached against the vice of drinking alcohol, urging people to care about its effects. Marty McFly considered the song catchy, but Edna's singing voice bad.

  Lounge singer Sylvia "Trixie Trotter" Miskin sang a song with a similar tune, titled "I Don't Care," at the El Kid speakeasy, accompanied by "Cue Ball" Donnely on piano. As Trixie performed, Marty noticed that Danny Parker—a depressed, corrupt policeman who regretted lacking the courage to arrest gangster Irving "Kid" Tannen—was emotionally affected by the mood of her music.

  To that end, Marty switched Trixie's lyrics sheet with that of "You Should Care," thereby inspiring Parker to care about his life again, resulting in his restoring his honor by shutting down the speakeasy [**TLTL-2**].

- ***Yuk:*** A monster magazine that Verne Brown enjoyed reading [**BFAN-26**].

- **yumping:** A slang term in 2015, used as an insult—as in, "You yumping-looking punk" [**BTF2-d**].

ZEKE

(CENTER, WITH LEVI AND JEB)

- **Z:** A label used by the Puritans of Salem, Massachusetts, circa 1692. Those caught sleeping in church were forced to wear a sign around the neck, bearing this badge of shame. Marty McFly saw a man wearing such a label while visiting that era [**BFAN-4**].

  NOTE: *This practice was a reference to Nathaniel Hawthorne's Puritan-themed novel,* The Scarlet Letter, *in which protagonist Hester Prynne was shamed into wearing a cloth shaped like an "A,"* branding her an adulteress. In this case, the letter "Z" presumably referred to "Zzz," an onomatopoeia commonly used to symbolize snoring.

- **Z28:** *See* Toyota SR5 4x4

- **Zales Jewelers:** A North American specialty jewelry retailer [**REAL**]. In 1985, the company operated a shop at Hill Valley's Twin Pines Mall. That year, Marty McFly and Jennifer Parker passed

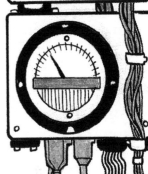

telling him to go out and face the outlaw, as he'd bet $30 in gold against the youth [**BTF3**].

> NOTE: *This character, unnamed onscreen, was identified as Zeke in* BTTF3*'s novelization and storyboards, as well as in* Paradox, *a combined script for both film sequels.*

- **Zemeckis, Robert ("Robbin"):** A gangster operating in Chicago's South Side, circa 1927. A wanted poster for this individual hung in a jail in which Marty McFly was briefly incarcerated. The poster indicated a reward was being offered for the criminal's capture [**BFCM-1**].

> NOTE: *This character was named after Robert Zemeckis, who directed the* Back to the Future *trilogy.*

- **Zemeckis-Gale Diagram:** *See* Gale-Zemeckis Diagram

- **ziphead:** A slang term used by the Hill Valley Police in 2015 to refer to a person with a substance-abuse problem [**BTF2**].

- **zombies:** Fictional undead creatures with a craving for consuming live human flesh, and frequently used in horror fiction [**REAL**]. An issue of the *Hill Valley Telegraph* contained the front-page headline, "Local Shopkeeper Robbed By Zombies" [**TLTL-1**].

> NOTE: *See also space zombies.*

- **Zone 4:** An area within the Institute of Future Technology's Anti-Gravitic Laboratory. When Biff Tannen broke into the facility to steal Emmett Brown's DeLorean, the scientist checked in with several areas, including Zone 4, to make sure they were secure. Biff had already infiltrated this zone, however, preventing workers in this section from responding to Doc's hail [**RIDE**].

- **Zoo, The:** A facility used by a society of intelligent dinosaurs that evolved after Emmett Brown inadvertently prevented the dinosaurs' extinction. When a pair of dinosaur police officers noticed Doc's DeLorean, one cop mistook it for a metallic egg and suggested bringing it to the Zoo so it could hatch. His partner, an Allosaurus called Officer Tannen, fought him for the object, intending to sell it to a research lab for dissection [**BFAN-3**]. The zoo was located in or near Dinocity, that reality's version of Hill Valley [**BFHM**].

a sign for the store, near the table of the Save the Clock Tower Fund campaign [**BTF1**].

- **Zane:** *See* Williams, Zane

- **Zeke:** An old-timer who frequented Hill Valley's Palace Saloon and Hotel in 1885, along with Jeb, Levi, Toothless, Eyepatch and Moustache [**BTF3-sp, BTF3-n**].

> Zeke had a white beard and mustache, and wore a tall, dark hat. When Marty refused to fight Buford Tannon, Zeke mocked his cowardice,

CODE	STORY
NIKE	*BTTF*-themed TV commercial: Nike
NTND	Nintendo *Back to the Future—The Ride* Mini-Game
PIZA	*BTTF*-themed TV commercial: Pizza Hut
PNBL	Data East *BTTF* pinball game
REAL	Real life
RIDE	Simulator: *Back to the Future—The Ride*
SCRM	2010 Scream Awards: *Back to the Future* 25th Anniversary Reunion (broadcast)
SCRT	2010 Scream Awards: *Back to the Future* 25th Anniversary Reunion (trailer)
SIMP	Simulator: *The Simpsons Ride*
SLOT	*Back to the Future Video Slots*
STLZ	Unused *BTTF* footage of Eric Stoltz as Marty McFly
STRY	*Back to the Future Storybook*
TEST	Screen tests: Crispin Glover, Lea Thompson and Tom Wilson
TLTL	Telltale Games' *Back to the Future—The Game*
TOPS	Topps' *Back to the Future II* trading-card set
TRIL	*BTTF: The Official Book of the Complete Movie Trilogy*
UNIV	Universal Studios Hollywood promotional video

SUFFIX MEDIUM

-b	*BTTF2*'s Biff Tannen Museum video (extended)
-c	Credit sequence to the animated series
-d	Film deleted scene
-n	Film novelization
-o	Film outtake
-p	1955 phone book from *BTTF1*
-v	Video game print materials or commentaries
-s1	Screenplay (draft one)
-s2	Screenplay (draft two)
-s3	Screenplay (draft three)
-s4	Screenplay (draft four)
-sp	Screenplay (production draft)
-sx	Screenplay (*Paradox*)

APPENDIX I ◄▬▬

Back to the Future Episode Guide

"Last night, Darth Vader came down from planet Vulcan and told me that if I didn't take Lorraine out, he'd melt my brain!"

—**George McFly**

The following guide details the many stories comprising the *Back to the Future* mythos, including the films, cartoons, comics, games, simulator rides and more.

Several older *BTTF*-themed video games, which were merely film re-hashes and did not add new in-universe information, are not represented in this book aside from their inclusion in the cover gallery in Appendix IV. These include games produced for a variety of console and computer platforms, such as Nintendo Entertainment System, Sega Genesis, LJN, Amiga and Super Famicon.

Also not covered, for the same reason: *Back to the Future: The Pinball* (Data East Pinball), *Back to the Future Pachinko* (Cross Media International), *Back to the Future: Blitz Through Time* (a Facebook application modeled after *Bejeweled*) and *Back to the Future Video Slots* (International Game Technology).

KEY:

A = interior artist
C = cover artist
D = director
W = writer
N = novelist

Theatrical Films
(Universal Pictures and Amblin Entertainment)

Back to the Future
Release date: July 3, 1985. W: Bob Gale and Robert Zemeckis. D: Robert Zemeckis. N: George Gipe.
LEXICON CODE: BTF1

In 1985, high school student Marty McFly learns that his friend, Emmett "Doc" Brown, has built a time machine from a DeLorean. Libyan terrorists, whom Doc defrauded in order to obtain plutonium to fuel the car's Flux Capacitor, murder the eccentric scientist before he can explore the past. Marty escapes the same fate in the DeLorean, and ends up in 1955, where he encounters his parents (George McFly and Lorraine Baines) as teens, inadvertently preventing them from falling in love, and thereby erasing his own existence. Marty and Doc must undo the damage by making sure George and Lorraine kiss at a school dance. In so doing, Marty builds up nerdy George's confidence, causing him to stand up to the school bully—his future boss—Biff Tannen. Upon returning to his own era, Marty discovers that his temporal tampering has made his family more successful, and that Doc (forewarned about the Libyans by a note from Marty) has taken precautions

to prevent his own demise. Doc visits the future, but soon returns to retrieve Marty and his girlfriend, Jennifer Parker, claiming their future children are in danger.

Back to the Future Part II
Release date: Nov. 22, 1989. W: Bob Gale and Robert Zemeckis. D: Robert Zemeckis. N: Craig Shaw Gardner.
LEXICON CODE: BTF2

In the year 2015, Doc tells Marty that his son, Martin Jr., will be goaded into taking part in a heist by Griff Tannen, Biff's grandson, and be sentenced to prison. Marty poses as his son and prevents him from taking part in the heist. He then purchases a copy of *Grays Sports Almanac*, featuring 50 years' worth of sports statistics, hoping to place bets in the past and become wealthy. Doc discovers and discards the almanac, but an elderly Biff, who has realized their identities, steals the book, takes the DeLorean into the past and gives the almanac to his younger self in 1955. Thus, when Marty returns to 1985, he finds a much darker version of Hill Valley, in which Biff—now a powerful and corrupt political figure—has killed his father and married his mother. Marty returns to the same day in

1955 that he'd previously visited, retrieves the almanac and restores the time stream. However, a lightning storm causes Doc and the DeLorean to vanish, stranding Marty in the 1950s. Moments later, a Western Union delivery man arrives with a letter from the scientist, dated 1885, telling him where to find the DeLorean, hidden for 70 years in a cave.

Back to the Future Part III
Release date: May 25, 1990. W: Bob Gale and Robert Zemeckis. D: Robert Zemeckis. N: Craig Shaw Gardner.
LEXICON CODE: BTF3

In 1885, Marty finds Doc living as a blacksmith in the Old West, and gets to know his own ancestors, Seamus and Maggie McFly. Posing as Clint Eastwood, Marty helps fix the DeLorean—the gas line of which was damaged during travel—for a return to the 1980s. However, outlaw Buford "Mad Dog" Tannen (one of Biff's ancestors) claims that Doc owes him money, and announces his intention to kill him. Marty comes to Doc's defense and is challenged to a duel, taking a cue from the real Clint Eastwood in devising a clever cheat to avoid dying during the gunfight. In the meantime,

Doc falls in love with schoolteacher Clara Clayton—who had been historically fated to die falling into a ravine, but whose life they have now saved. Though he cares deeply for her, Doc decides to end the relationship, fearful of tampering with history. However, as he and Marty prepare to return to the future, using a modified locomotive to push the DeLorean up to time-travel speed, Clara follows them and again nearly dies. Saving her life once more, Doc stays behind with Clara as Marty returns to 1985 and is reunited with Jennifer. There, the youth watches in horror as the DeLorean is struck by a modern train and destroyed. Later, a time-traveling locomotive arrives, carrying Doc, Clara and their two sons, Jules and Verne, who have come to bid farewell and retrieve Doc's dog, Einstein. The future, he tells Marty and Jennifer, is not written until they write it.

Simulator Rides
(Universal Studios)

Back to the Future: The Ride
Release date: May 2, 1991. W: Peyton Reed and Bob Gale. D: David De Vos and Douglas Trumbull.
LEXICON CODE: RIDE

Doc Brown founds the Institute of Future Technology, which specializes in creating futuristic inventions, including an eight-passenger DeLorean time machine. As Doc and a group of time-travel volunteers test the new vehicle, Biff Tannen stows away in one team's time machine and travels from 1955 to 1991. Biff infiltrates the institute and steals the DeLorean, traveling to 2015 and into the distant past before finally being apprehended by the time-travel volunteers and returned to his own era.

The Simpsons Ride
Release year: 2008. D: Mike B. Anderson and John Rice.
LEXICON CODE: SIMP

Professor John Nerdelbaum Frink Jr. visits the Institute of Future Technology to see friend and colleague Doc Brown, but finds it replaced by the Krustyland theme park. Curious, he travels two years back in time via a DeLorean, where Doc is securing a small-business loan from a bank-loan officer, Mr. Friedman, so he can keep the IFT open for years to come. Frink accidentally runs over the man, forcing Doc to sell the facility to Krusty the Clown—hence, ironically, the reason Frink found it replaced by Krustyland in the first place.

> *NOTE: The ride's queue featured video footage of Christopher Lloyd as Doc Brown, intended as an in-joke reference to Universal Studios Florida's replacement of* Back to the Future: The Ride *with* The Simpsons Ride.

Animated Series
(CBS)

BACK TO THE FUTURE, SEASON 1

Episode 1: "Brothers"
Airdate: Sept. 7, 1991. W: John Loy and John Ludin. D: John Hays and Phil Robinson.
LEXICON CODE: BFAN-1

It is 1991, and Doc, Clara and their sons have returned from the past and moved to a farm in Hill Valley. Verne runs away from home, taking the DeLorean back to 1864, where he becomes a drummer boy for the Confederate Army during the American Civil War, under General Beauregard Tannen. Jules, meanwhile, ends up in the Union Army, serving under the boys' great-uncle, General Ulysses S. Clayton. Battle is thwarted when both sides, touched at seeing the brothers embrace on the battlefield, shake hands and make peace.

Episode 2: "A Family Vacation"
Airdate: Sept. 14, 1991. W: Wayne Kaatz and John Loy. D: John Hays.
LEXICON CODE: BFAN-2

When the Brown family grows too dependent on technology, Doc takes them to medieval times—England, in 1367—to prove mankind can get by without electricity. Clara is kidnapped by the evil Lord Biffingham, Doc is thrown into the tyrant's dungeon, and Jules and Verne meet their ancestors, Harold and Jennivere McFly. As Doc and Biffingham joust, Clara builds a hot-air balloon and saves her family.

Episode 3: "Forward to the Past"
Airdate: Sept. 21, 1991. W: Earl Kress. D: Phil Robinson.
LEXICON CODE: BFAN-3

Doc Brown travels with his sons 3 million years into the past to test his latest invention: a disintegration device. A Tyrannosaurus Rex tries to eat the family, but a friendly Pteranodon, whom Verne nicknames Donny, helps them escape. When they spot a meteor plummeting toward Earth, Doc uses the device to destroy it, thereby preventing the extinction of the dinosaurs and halting human evolution. Upon returning to the future, they find a society inhabited by intelligent dinosaurs and realize they must un-do what they did in the past in order to put time right.

> *NOTE: This episode was adapted in issue #2 of the Harvey Comics series.*

Episode 4: "Witchcraft"
Airdate: Sept. 28, 1991. W: Mary Jo Ludin. D: John Hays.
LEXICON CODE: BFAN-4

Marty McFly and the Brown family travel back in time to 1692, the era of the infamous witch trials of Salem, Massachusetts. There, Marty earns the enmity of a citizen named Goodman Tannen, which worsens when Marty tries to woo Tannen's daughter, Mercy. Marty is accused of witchcraft and subjected to the Puritans' Water Test, but Doc rescues him underwater with the DeLorean, and the time-travelers return to 1991.

Episode 5: "Roman Holiday" (a.k.a. "Swing Low, Sweet Chariot Race")
Airdate: Oct. 5, 1991. W: Mark Klastorin, Michael Klastorin and John Ludin. D: Phil Robinson.
LEXICON CODE: BFAN-5

When Doc and Marty visit ancient Rome, Jules and Verne stow away in the DeLorean, having mistaken the term "arcade" as referring to video games. Marty insults Bifficus Antanneny and must face him in a chariot race, but lets the soldier lose, knowing that this must happen for Caligula to become the next Emperor, leading to the fall of the Roman Empire. Doc, meanwhile, is mistaken for a rebellious slave and is then sentenced to be fed to lions. However, he uses a holographic device to escape. The boys befriend slave Judah Ben-Hur, helping him gain his freedom.

> *NOTE: This episode was adapted in issue #3 of the Harvey Comics series.*

Episode 6: "Go Fly a Kite"
Airdate: Oct. 12, 1991. W: Randy Gale, Michael Zimbalist, John Loy and John Ludin. D: John Hays.
LEXICON CODE: BFAN-6

Believing himself to be Benjamin Franklin's son, Verne steals the DeLorean and travels to 1752, in Philadelphia, to find his real "father." In so doing, he interrupts Franklin's kite-flying experiments, altering history by preventing him from discovering the nature of electricity. Following Verne back in time on his time-traveling locomotive, Doc meets his idol face-to-face, inspires the invention of the rocking chair, cracks the Liberty Bell and reassures Verne that they're really related. The Browns then restore history by creating another lightning storm for Franklin to study.

Episode 7a: "Time Waits for No Frog"
Airdate: Oct. 19, 1991. W: Cliff MacGillivray, John Loy and John Ludin. D: Phil Robinson.
LEXICON CODE: BFAN-7a

To cure Marty's athlete's foot fungus, Doc and Marty visit the Amazon jungle of South America, in 1532, to procure an extinct toad species—*Bufo marinus*—that emits an acid from its skin. In so doing, they encounter Spanish conquistador Biffando de la Tanén, who is searching for the legendary City of Gold. The mission is a success, and the time-travelers bring back several toads to their own era, in order to repopulate the species.

> *NOTE: This episode was split up into two mini-episodes, "Time Waits for No Frog" and "Einstein's Adventure."*

Episode 7b: "Einstein's Adventure"
Airdate: Oct. 19. W: Alex Herschlag. D: Phil Robinson.
LEXICON CODE: BFAN-7b

With Doc stopping at the Hill Valley Hardware Store, Einstein falls asleep in the back of the DeLorean. As the dog snoozes, two bank robbers, known as Sidney and Frankie, steal the car and inadvertently ac-tivate the vehicle's time circuits, causing it to carry them back to 1790, in Sydney, Australia. The crooks spend time in an Australian prison run by Mongo P. Tannen, until Einstein frees them, returns to the future and delivers the duo to the police.

Episode 8: "Batter Up"
Airdate: Oct. 26, 1991. W: Mark Hoffmeier, John Loy and John Ludin. D: John Hays.
LEXICON CODE: BFAN-8

Marty visits 1897 to help his ancestor, Pee Wee McFly—a pitcher for the Boston Beaneaters—win the National League pennant, by giving him one of Doc's inventions that will help him pitch well and hit homeruns. Marty poses as Pee Wee after causing him to be injured, earns a win for the Beaneaters, and infuriates gangster Jimmy "Diamond Jim" Tannen, who had strong-armed Pee Wee into throwing the game. Pee Wee wins the pennant, and Tannen is arrested by his girlfriend, Vera Muldoon, who turns out to be an undercover police officer infiltrating his criminal organization.

Episode 9: "Solar Sailors"
Airdate: Nov. 2, 1991. W: Earl Kress, John Luy and John Ludin. D: Phil Robinson.
LEXICON CODE: BFAN-9

To celebrate his parents' anniversary, Jules gives Doc and Clara tickets on a space cruise to Mars in the year 2091. The couple visits the future board the *MSC Jennifer*, a passenger solar sailship captained by Marty McFly's great-granddaughter, Marta McFly. When Griff Tannen's grandson, Ziff Tannen, sabotages the vessel to avenge his ancestors' many defeats at the hands of McFlys, Jules and Verne journey forward in time to save their parents. Ziff is imprisoned for his crimes—in the same cell as Griff—and the Browns return safely to their own era.

Episode 10: "Dickens of a Christmas"
Airdate: Nov. 9, 1991. W: Rick Cunningham, John Luy and John Ludin. D: John Hays.
LEXICON CODE: BFAN-10

Marty and the Brown family visit London, in 1845, to celebrate Christmas a la Charles Dickens. Doc entrusts a pocket watch containing his DeLorean key to Jules, but a pickpocket named Reginald steals it. While trying to retrieve it, the boys are captured by Murdock, the same thug for whom Reg works, and are made to serve as pickpockets. Clara, meanwhile, is incarcerated for striking Ebiffnezer Tannen, a wealthy miser with a history of foreclosing on local businesses and sending the shop owners to Debtor's Prison. In order to frighten Tannen into changing his ways, Marty disguises himself as the Ghost of Christmas.

Episode 11: "Gone Fishin'"
Airdate: Nov. 16, 1991. W: Wayne Kaatz and John Ludin. D: Phil Robinson.
LEXICON CODE: BFAN-11

Jules and Verne, hoping to get their father to take them to the Hill Valley Father and Son Big Mouth Bass Off despite his fear of fishing, visit 1926 to alter history by preventing Doc from developing such a phobia. In so doing, they trigger events leading to his becoming a Hollywood icon—four-year-old movie stunt actor Daredevil Emmett Brown. Hired by D.W. Tannen to star in a film called *Raging Death Doom*, Emmett nearly dies plunging over Upper Yosemite Falls in a barrel. This scares the boy's guardian, Uncle Oliver, who rips up his contract, ending the future scientist's brief acting career. History is restored—but without Doc being afraid of fishing.

Episode 12: "Retired"
Airdate: Nov. 23, 1991. W: Peyton Reed, Mark Gowen, John Ludin and John Luy. D: John Hays.
LEXICON CODE: BFAN-12

Jules and Verne perpetrate a series of April Fool's Day pranks on their father, including sabotaging his Brain Wave Analyzer to make him think his brain is nearly full to capacity. In a panic, Doc retires from science and pursues a series of jobs in which he won't need to think (such as parking cars and preparing pizzas), then travels back to the Cro-Magnon period to avoid science entirely. When Marty borrows an invention to create special effects at his band's concert, but instead nearly destroys Hill Valley with catastrophic storms, the boys confess their prank, and Doc uses his know-how to stem the danger.

> *NOTE: This episode was adapted in issue #4 of the Harvey Comics series.*

Episode 13: "Clara's Folks"
Airdate: Nov. 30, 1991. W: John Loy and Mary Jo Ludin. D: Phil Robinson.
LEXICON CODE: BFAN-13

Marty visits 1850 Wyoming with Jules and Verne, where they meet Clara's as-yet-unmarried parents, Daniel Clayton and Martha O'Brien, pioneers on the Oregon Trail. When Martha shows romantic interest in Marty, he and the boys arrange for her to instead fall in love with Daniel, but "Wild

Bill" Tannen kidnaps Martha for himself. She escapes, but is then stalked by a bear. Daniel and Doc—who'd come back in time after Clara had begun vanishing due to the boys' tampering—rescue Martha. She and Daniel fall in love and are wed that same day, thus restoring history.

BACK TO THE FUTURE, SEASON 2

Episode 14: "Mac the Black"
Airdate: Sept. 5, 1992. W: John Loy and John Ludin. D: John Hays.
LEXICON CODE: BFAN-14

Verne Brown decides to get an earring, but his parents refuse to let him, so he steals the DeLorean and visits the Caribbean with Marty, circa 1697. Marty pretends to be pirate Mac the Black in order to impress a woman, but his lie backfires when the pirate's crew brings him aboard ship, expecting him to serve as their captain. The real Mac the Black arrives and threatens to kill the two stowaways, but the Spanish Armada attacks, intent on bringing Mac to justice for stealing the fleet's flagship. In the chaos, Marty and Verne escape. Returning to the future, Marty must face Jennifer Parker, to whom he'd previously lied about concert tickets he'd forgotten to buy for her.

Episode 15: "Put on Your Thinking Caps, Kids! It's Time for Mr. Wisdom!"
Airdate: Sept. 12, 1992. W: Wayne Kaatz. D: John Hays.
LEXICON CODE: BFAN-15

Children's TV personality Mr. Wisdom visits the Lone Pine Mall to sell merchandise to fans, and Verne convinces Marty to take him to meet his idol. They invite Wisdom back to Doc's lab, unaware that he and Doc were college roommates, and that Wisdom became famous after stealing one of his inventions. Wisdom once again steals Doc's latest innovations—including the time-traveling DeLorean—and tries to kill the Brown family by stranding them in the Krakatoa volcano just before its 1883 eruption. The time-travelers escape, after which Doc and Wisdom compete on television to determine who really invented the time machine.

Episode 16: "A Friend in Deed"
Airdate: Sept. 19, 1992. W: Sean Derek, John Loy and John Ludin. D: John Hays.
LEXICON CODE: BFAN-16

Biff Tannen tries to steal the family ranch of Jennifer Parker, using a century-old deed signed over to his ancestor, Thaddeus Tannen. To prevent this from happening, Marty travels back to 1875 with Jules and Verne, where Marty infiltrates Thaddeus' gang and is forced to become engaged to the outlaw's sister, Hepzibah Tannen. By providing Jennfer's ancestor, Wendel Parker, with a pen filled with invisible ink, Marty ensures that the deed will appear to be unsigned in the future—and thus be rendered invalid.

Episode 17: "Marty McFly PFC"
Airdate: Sept. 26, 1992. W: Mary Jo Ludin. D: John Hays.
LEXICON CODE: BFAN-17

When Verne has trouble with his dance lessons, Doc reveals that he had once created blueprints for a pair of dance shoes that could help him improve his steps, but that they'd been lost years prior. Verne and Marty, therefore, travel back to 1944, hoping to retrieve the missing document. In the process, Verne befriends a younger version of his elderly instructor, and ultimately wins a dance contest as her partner. Marty, meanwhile, inadvertently joins the U.S. Army, serving under Sergeant Frank Tannen.

Episode 18: "Verne's New Friend"
Airdate: Oct. 3, 1992. W: Mary Jo Ludin. D: John Hays.
LEXICON CODE: BFAN-18

After refusing to let two girls play baseball with him and his friends, Verne befriends another child named Chris—a girl who has chosen to hide her gender. Traveling back to 1933 to watch an old-time circus performance, the two friends help circus owners Bob and Robert Brothers avoid losing their business to landlord Mac Tannen, by serving as trapeze aerialists and rejuvenating audience interest. Verne is initially upset upon learning Chris' true identity but comes to realize that he should never discriminate based on gender.

Episode 19: "Bravelord and the Demon Monstrux"
Airdate: Oct. 10, 1992. W: Wayne Kaatz. D: John Hays.
LEXICON CODE: BFAN-19

Addicted to the video game *BraveLord and Monstrux*, Verne begins neglecting his chores. When his parents ban him from visiting the arcade, Jules and Marty help him bypass this rule by rigging up a contraption to electronically transfer the game to Verne's bedroom TV. However, a power surge brings the game's characters to life, allowing Monstrux to make Biff Tannen his slave and attempt to conquer the world. Doc, meanwhile, is transported into the game, and Clara must keep her husband alive via the joystick. Ultimately, Verne and Jules defeat Monstrux, send BraveLord and the demon back to cyberspace, and restore Doc to reality.

Episode 20: "The Money Tree"
Airdate: Oct. 17, 1992. W: Earl Kress. D: John Hays.
LEXICON CODE: BFAN-20

Tired of being an outcast with other kids, Jules Brown grows a money-tree, making him popular and wealthy—but as this brings his family fame and notoriety, they soon succumb to greed. When a television news program runs Jules' story, the FBI investigates the Browns for possible criminal activity, and Biff Tannen steals the plant for his own use. Once the tree's money leaves shrivel, however, Jules' popularity fades and he soon goes back to being ostracized by other children—except for a girl named Franny Philips, on whom Jules has a crush.

Episode 21: "A Verne by Any Other Name"
Airdate: Oct. 24, 1992. W: Earl Kress. D: John Hays.
LEXICON CODE: BFAN-21

Tired of being teased about his unusual name, Verne Brown asks Marty McFly to travel back with him to 1800s France, in the hope of convincing author Jules Verne—after whom the youth was named—to rename himself. When the novelist refuses to comply, they make their way to Doc's and Clara's home in 1888, mere days before Verne's birth, to suggest alternative names. Instead, Verne becomes the source of his own name, as the couple name the baby after him.

Episode 22: "Hill Valley Brown-Out"
Airdate: Oct. 31, 1992. W: Wayne Kaatz. D: John Hays.
LEXICON CODE: BFAN-22

Doc enrages his family and the Hill Valley townspeople after causing a power outage in Hill Valley during the planning of the annual Founder's Day celebration. The scientist tries to fix the problem by building a generator able to provide unlimited free power, but this causes all electrical devices to run amuck—including those not even plugged in. Biff Tannen leads an angry mob to run the Browns out of town, nearly destroying Hill Valley while trying to fix the device himself. After Doc alleviates the danger by cutting power once more, the citizens of Hill Valley realize they can still enjoy Founder's Day as the pioneers did—without electricity.

Episode 23: "My Pop's a Alien"
Airdate: Nov. 7, 1992. W: Mark Hoffmeier and Mary Jo Ludin. D: John Hays.
LEXICON CODE: BFAN-23

Biff panics as Comet Kahooey passes Earth, causing him to recall an extraterrestrial encounter he experienced when the comet last arrived, in 1967. Finding what he believes to be a spacecraft—but is really a flying vehicle that Doc built to view the comet—Biff incites mass hysteria, convincing people that the scientist is an alien. Marty travels back to 1967 with Jules and Verne to ascertain if Biff's claims are true, and there meets a younger version of Doc. While in the past, they pose as aliens and change history by scaring Biff into keeping his encounter a secret.

> *NOTE: The episode title's non-grammatical nature ("a alien" instead of "an alien") is how it appeared onscreen, as it was supposed to sound like something Verne would say.*

Episode 24: "Super Doc"
Airdate: Nov. 14, 1992. W: Wayne Kaatz. D: John Hays.
LEXICON CODE: BFAN-24

Verne is pressured by his friend Jackson to swing over Dead Man's Swamp, but is afraid to do so. Upon learning that Doc almost became a professional wrestler in 1952, he travels back in time to convince his father to go through with the match, in the hope that it would make Verne cooler in other boys' eyes. The younger Emmett reluctantly agrees to fight, but is struck on the head by a microphone and becomes convinced that he is a superhero called Mega Brainman. After Doc is cured of the delusion, Verne returns to the future and faces Jackson, refusing to give in to peer pressure. Mocking him, Jackson jumps in his place—but makes a fool of himself by crashing into the swamp.

Episode "25: St. Louis Blues"
Airdate: Nov. 21, 1992. W: Mark Valenti. D: John Hays.
LEXICON CODE: BFAN-25

After using Doc's new (and unperfected) hairstyling device so he can go on a date with his friend Liz, Marty begins experiencing frequent and spontaneous style changes. Marty learns that Doc and Clara have traveled back in time to witness the 1904 World's Fair, and follows them back, hoping the scientist can fix the problem—only to be captured by P.T. Tannen and forced to serve as a sideshow exhibit at the fair.

Episode 26: "Verne Hatches an Egg"
Airdate: Nov. 28, 1992. W: Mark Klastorn, Michael Klastorn, John Loy and John Ludin. D: John Hays.
LEXICON CODE: BFAN-26

Hoping to find something interesting for show-and-tell at school, Verne visits a prehistoric era and brings back a dinosaur egg. The egg soon hatches, making Verne the parent to a baby Apatosaurus, which he names Tiny. Noticing the animal in his yard, Biff Tannen captures Tiny and sells it to unscrupulous TV personality Walter Wisdom. Verne and his family manage to rescue the dinosaur, then return to the past to bring Tiny back to its native environment.

Comic Books
(Harvey Comics)

NOTE: The bi-monthly comics were numbered #1-4 (ongoing) and #1-3 (miniseries). Ongoing issues #2-4 adapted TV episodes #2, #3 and #12, respectively, while ongoing #1 and miniseries #1-3 contained original stories. The debut issue was printed with preview and retail variant covers.

BACK TO THE FUTURE MONTHLY SERIES

Issue 1: "The Gang's All Here"
Cover date: November 1991. W: Dwayne McDuffie. A: Nelson Dewey and Ken Selig. C: Gil Kane.
LEXICON CODE: BFCM-1

When Einstein comes down with cataracts (a canine disease making him see everyone and everything as cats), Doc and Marty travel back to 1927 Chicago to find a Prohibition Era liquor still with which to brew a cure. In the process, they pose as mobsters in order to infiltrate the gang of Arine "Eggs" Benedict, whose members include Mugsy Tannen and "Bathtub Jim" McFly.

Issue 2: "Forward to the Past"
Cover date: January 1992. Adapted by: Dwayne McDuffie. A: Nelson Dewey. C: Gil Kane.
LEXICON CODE: BFCM-2

> *NOTE: This issue adapted the plot of animated episode #2, with some minor new bits added.*

Issue 3: "Roman Holiday"
Cover date: March 1992. Adapted by: Dwayne McDuffie. A: Nelson Dewey. C: Gil Kane.
LEXICON CODE: BFCM-3

> *NOTE: This issue adapted the plot of animated episode #3, with some minor new bits added.*

Issue 4: "Retired"
Cover date: June 1992. Adapted by: Dwayne McDuffie. A: Nelson Dewey. C: Gil Kane.
LEXICON CODE: BFCM-4

> *NOTE: This issue adapted the plot of animated episode #12, with some minor new bits added.*

BACK TO THE FUTURE LIMITED MINISERIES

Issue 1: "Forward to the Future"
Cover date: October 1992. W: Dwayne McDuffie. A: Nelson Dewey. C: Nelson Dewey.

LEXICON CODE: BFCL-1

Doc's family and Marty travel to 2585, to visit Robot City, a domed station in the Asteroid Belt at which hundreds of robots cater to humanity's needs. Arriving amidst a robotic revolution against Governor Tannen and the droids' lazy human masters, the Browns convince the automata to halt hostilities and help the humans become healthier and less dependent on technology. Suddenly, an electric shock from the train's Flux Capacitor leaves Doc with amnesia.

Issue 2: "The Jewel in the Tower"
Cover date: November 1992. W: Dwayne McDuffie. A: Nelson Dewey. C: Nelson Dewey.
LEXICON CODE: BFCL-2

Jules tries to fix the damaged Flux Capacitor, but the train carries Marty and the Browns almost 3 quadrillion years into the future, to find civilization replaced with primitive villages. Setting out to find platinum for the Flux Capacitor, they encounter Tannen the Barbarian, who elicits their help in stealing the Ruby Begonia for the Queen of Apocrypha. In the matriarch's castle, Jules finds the required platinum, and the Browns leave the distant future behind.

Issue 3: "The Great Indoors"
Cover date: January 1993. W: Dwayne McDuffie. A: Nelson Dewey. C: Nelson Dewey.
LEXICON CODE: BFCL-3

Verne uses Doc's Extradimensional Storage Closet—a room offering access to multiple dimensions of time and space—in the hope of delivering a sufficient electrical shock to restore his father's lost memory, but the resultant power surge turns the closet inside out, damaging the fabric of the space-time continuum. This causes the Brown family and Marty to randomly jump around in time and space, and threatens to collapse the entire planet into a black hole. Luckily, Doc regains his memories and averts the crisis.

Commercials Featuring
Back to the Future Elements

Pizza Hut
Release year: 1989
LEXICON CODE: PIZA

Two young men from 1989 travel to the year 2015 aboard a time-traveling DeLorean to explore Hill Valley's future. They discover that the former Domino's pizza restaurant chain has been transformed into a hardware store, now known as Domino's Hardware, so they dine at Pizza Hut instead.
> *NOTE: This commercial featured sets from* Back to the Future II, *as well as the DeLorean.*

McDonalds
Release year: 1992
LEXICON CODE: MCDN

Doc Brown records a short video at a McDonald's restaurant in 1992, describing several Happy Meal toys offered at that time.
> *NOTE: This commercial featured Dan Castellaneta reprising his animated-series role as Doc Brown.*

DirecTV
Release year: 2007
LEXICON CODE: DCTV

After sending Marty McFly back to the future in 1955, Doc Brown realizes he forgot to tell Marty to sign up for DirecTV HD instead of cable once he gets home.
> *NOTE: This commercial featured Christopher Lloyd reprising his role as Doc Brown, both in vintage footage from BTTF1, as well as new shots designed to look as though part of that same film.*

Microsoft
Release year: 2007
LEXICON CODE: MSFT

Robert L. Muglia, Microsoft's senior vice-president, provides a keynote address at Tech-Ed 2007 about his vision for the future, but attendees tired of unrealized promises pummel him with vegetables. Therefore, Doc Brown, using his time-traveling DeLorean, offers Muglia insights into Microsoft's past failures. The two men visit Acme.com in 2001 and 2003, where a nerdy IT worker named TechFly faces technological setbacks due to faulty Microsoft software, and endures bullying from his manager, Mister Biff. As a result, history changes so that Muglia's keynote avoids the mistakes of Microsoft's past, while TechFly becomes more confident around Biff—who, in the new timeline, works for him as a janitor. Doc appears on stage with Muglia at Tech-Ed, promising to keep an eye to make sure he avoids any more missteps.
> *NOTE: This commercial featured Christopher Lloyd reprising his role as Doc Brown.*

Garbarino
Release year: 2011
LEXICON CODE: GARB

Doc Brown travels to the years 2011 and visits Garbarino, an Argentinian electronics store, where he is astonished to view all of the modern technology—such as flatscreen TVs and cell phones—available for sale.
> *NOTE: This series of commercials from Argentina featured Christopher Lloyd reprising his role as Doc Brown.*

Nike
Release year: 2011
LEXICON CODE: NIKE

Doc Brown travels into the future to procure a pair of self-lacing sneakers from a Nike star at the Lone Pine Mall. A problem with his DeLorean's time circuits, however, results in his arriving not in 2015, but rather in 2011, by which time the self-lacing feature is not yet incorporated.
> *NOTE: This commercial featured Christopher Lloyd as Doc Brown, as well as* Saturday Night Live's *Bill Hader, basketball star Kevin Durant, Nike designer Tinker Hatfield and* Back to the Future *actor Donald Fullilove (Mayor Goldie Wilson), promoting the unveiling of Nike Mags—sneakers designed to resemble the futuristic self-sealing shoes worn by Marty McFly in* Back to the Future II. *An auction of 1,500 pairs of the sneakers raised money for the Michael J. Fox Foundation for Parkinson's Research.*

Bud Light: "Time Machine"
Release year: 2012
LEXICON CODE: BUDL

Four auto mechanics share Bud Light beers while on break, speculating about what they would do if able to travel through time. One says he would travel to the past and murder his own father, then immediately vanishes, erased from existence due to never having been born. Doc Brown's DeLorean time machine, meanwhile, sits on a nearby lift, awaiting service. Due to the temporal alteration, the others soon forget their missing friend ever existed.

NOTE: *This commercial, dubbed "Time Machine" on a preview recording, was slated to air during Super Bowl XLVI, featuring Doc's DeLorean time machine, but no actors from the films. It was ultimately unaired during the game due to a problem obtaining music rights, but was posted online. The DeLorean used in the commercial was very inaccurately converted.*

Mitsubishi Lancer
Release year: 2012
LEXICON CODE: MITS

While conducting a time-travel experiment with Einstein at the Twin Pines Mall, Doc Brown sends the DeLorean into the future, and is stunned when the vehicle returns as an entirely different vehicle—a Mitsubishi Lancer sedan. What's more, Einstein is now a robot. Intrigued, Doc takes the new car for a spin.

NOTE: *This Brazilian commercial featured Christopher Lloyd reprising his role as Doc Brown.*

Arrigoni
Release year: Unknown
LEXICON CODE: ARGN

A pair of Italian teenagers, upon visiting the future in a time-traveling DeLorean, are amazed not by the futuristic marvels awaiting them, but by an Arrigoni vending machine, at which they stock up on snacks and drinks before returning to the past.

NOTE: *This Italian commercial featured a DeLorean customized to resemble the* Back to the Future *vehicle.*

Music Videos Featuring
Back to the Future Elements

Huey Lewis and the News: "The Power of Love"
Release year: 1985
LEXICON CODE: HUEY

While Doc Brown attends a Huey Lewis concert at a nightclub called Uncle Charlie's, a young couple fascinated with his DeLorean takes the time-traveling vehicle for a joyride.

NOTE: *This music video, promoting BTTF1, featured Christopher Lloyd as Doc Brown.*

O'Neal McKnight: "Check Your Coat"
Release year: 2008
LEXICON CODE: CHEK

Doc Brown takes O'Neal McKnight—a nightclub coat-check clerk who longs to party—to the year 2088 so that he can see what he's really meant to be. In that future,

McKnight discovers his true potential as a club dancer and a ladies' man, while Doc takes a turn spinning records in a D.J. booth.

NOTE: *This music video featured Christopher Lloyd as Doc Brown.*

The Limousines: "The Future"
Release year: 2012
LEXICON CODE: LIMO

Two men in a time-traveling DeLorean journey back in time from 2152 to 2011. Crashing head-on into a Porsche upon arrival, they are thrown through a windshield and onto the road, their bodies smashed. During their final moments before death, the two share an out-of-body experience in which they dream of people dying in various grisly ways.

NOTE: *This music video featured Doc's DeLorean time machine, but no actors from the films.*

Owl City: "Deer in the Headlights"
Release year: 2012
LEXICON CODE: CITY

A man on a skateboard encounters a time-traveling DeLorean out on a road, which opens its gull-wing driver's-side door, inviting him to take it for a ride. While driving, he experiences several unusual visions involving deer, whales, jellyfish, farm animals, dinosaurs and more. Stopping at a convenience store for coffee, his mind continues to see the deer, as well as a beautiful young woman who isn't really there. He returns to his car, which eventually reaches 88 miles per hour, propelling him to the year 2015, where he nearly runs over an individual wearing a spacesuit.

NOTE: *This rather surreal music video featured Doc's DeLorean time machine, but no actors from the films.*

Other Videos Featuring
Back to the Future Elements

Screen Tests
Release year: N/A
LEXICON CODE: TEST

George McFly tries to be more assertive with his wife, Lorraine, and his boss, Biff Tannen. His passive nature, however, sabotages his efforts, allowing them to walk all over him.

NOTE: *This rare footage of Crispin Glover, Lea Thompson and Thomas F. Wilson, from pre-*

production on the first Back to the Future *film, surfaced on YouTube in 2010, containing amusing scenes not included in the movie, set within the McFly household and outdoors.*

Eric Stoltz Footage
Release year: N/A
LEXICON CODE: STLZ

While helping Emmett Brown test his time-traveling DeLorean, Marty McFly

finds himself transported back to 1955, where he must make sure his parents fall in love, and avoid being beaten up by school bully Biff Tannen.

NOTE: *Stoltz was originally cast for the first film as Marty McFly, until being replaced by Michael J. Fox once the producers realized he wasn't right for the role. All scenes filmed with Stoltz had to be re-shot, and Marty's wardrobe was changed. One notable exception was the Twin Pines Mall* sequence, in which Marty drove the DeLorean to evade the Libyans; since Stoltz's face was not visible in the long shots, those were retained for the final film. Most of the remaining footage is not publicly available, though some stills have been released, and a few clips, sans sound, were included in a Blu-ray documentary titled "In the Beginning." The television series Fringe *paid homage to this switch in 2010, by featuring an alternate reality in which Stoltz starred in the film. Coincidentally, Stoltz went on to portray a character named Martin in the film* The Fly II.

Universal Studios Promotional Film
Release year: 1988
LEXICON CODE: UNIV

Doc Brown travels via DeLorean to 1990, to assist Universal Pictures' corporate executives in documenting Universal Studios planned theme park in Orlando, Florida. Doc videotapes how the park will appear, interacting with characters and components of numerous attractions, including Lassie, *Ghostbusters'* Stay Puft Marshmallow Man, *Psycho's* Norma Bates, the great-white shark from *Jaws*, Jessica Fletcher from *Murder, She Wrote*, E.T., King Kong, Fred Flintstone and more. Ultimately, Doc sees every attraction except for *Back to the Future: The Ride*, which he lacks the time to visit before returning to his own era.
> **NOTE:** *This metafictional video featured Christopher Lloyd reprising his role as Doc Brown.*

The Earth Day Special (Time Warner)
Release year: 1990
LEXICON CODE: ERTH

Mother Nature, a maternal personification of nature's nurturing characteristics, falls ill and is rushed to a hospital in Anytown, USA. Concerned, Doc Brown boards his time-traveling DeLorean and discovers that the future will be grim if she can not be saved. Returning to the past, the scientist rushes to the hospital's emergency room to share his foreknowledge with Mother Nature's physician, Dr. Douglas "Doogie" Howser.
> **NOTE:** *This TV movie was created to educate viewers about the importance of saving the planet Earth from ecological damage, and featured Christopher Lloyd as Emmett Brown. In addition to Doc, the special also included characters from multiple television shows and movies of that era, such as* The Cosby Show, E.T.: The Extra-Terrestrial, The Fresh Prince of Bel-Air, Ghostbusters, The Golden Girls, Looney Tunes, Married With Children, Murphy Brown, Saturday Night Live, Doogie Howser, M.D. *and many others. Only the portions pertaining to the* Back to the Future *mythos are covered in this lexicon.*

Scream Awards: **Back to the Future 25th Anniversary Reunion (trailer)**
Release year: 2010
LEXICON CODE: SCRT

As Marty McFly prepares to drive the DeLorean to the 2010 Scream Awards, a woman passerby asks where he's headed. After telling her his destination, Marty offers the woman a "lift."
> **NOTE:** *This trailer for the Scream Awards, starring Michael J. Fox as Marty, paid homage to the original trailer for the first BTTF film, faithfully recreating it shot for shot.*

Scream Awards: **Back to the Future 25th Anniversary Reunion (broadcast)**
Release year: 2010
LEXICON CODE: SCRM

In 1985, as a group of teenagers visit Los Angeles' Greek Theatre to attend a Loverboy rock concert, the DeLorean arrives outside the entrance. As the excited teens run toward the vehicle, the occupant—clad in a radiation suit—switches the car's time circuits to bring him to the site of the 2010 Scream Awards.
> **NOTE:** *This footage, filmed to introduce the awards show, segued to actor David Spade emerging from a DeLorean onstage. The program—dedicated to the horror, fantasy and science fiction film genres, and which aired on Spike on Oct. 19—honored Michael J. Fox and Christopher Lloyd for their work in the BTTF trilogy.*

Games

Back to the Future: The Ride Mini-Game
Release year: 2001
LEXICON CODE: NTND

Biff Tannen steals a time-traveling DeLorean and escapes into various historical eras, pursued by another driver (a young girl with pigtails, flying a second DeLorean) dispatched to bring back Biff and the stolen car.
> **NOTE:** *This mini-game—a simplified re-telling of Universal Studios'* Back to the Future: The Ride *attraction—was included in the* Universal Studios Theme Parks Adventure *video game, created by Kemco for the Nintendo Game-Cube. The game featured Woody Woodpecker urging players to catch Biff.*

Back to the Future: The Card Game
Release year: 2010. Game designers: Andrew Looney, Looney Labs.
LEXICON CODE: BFCG

Ten individuals—Verne Brown, Marty McFly III, Jules McFly, Electra McFly, Marlin Berry, Clara Wilson, Buffy Tannen, Tiffany Tannen, Clay Strickland and Darlene Needles—set out to preserve their own existence by bringing about specific linchpin events in the history of Hill Valley, California, that others have altered or prevented. These individuals must ensure that their changes become permanent by stopping Doc Brown from inventing time travel in the first place, thus halting others' attempts to change time further— and, paradoxically, nullifying their own temporal tampering in the process.

Back to the Future: The Game— Episode One: It's About Time
Release year: 2010. W: Michael Stemmle and Andy Hartzell. D: Dennis Lenart. Designers: Michael Stemmle, Andy Hartzell, Dave Grossman and Jonathan Straw.
LEXICON CODE: TLTL-1

When Doc vanishes for nearly a year, Marty investigates and discovers that the scientist was murdered in 1931 after being arrested for burning down the speakeasy of gangster Irving "Kid" Tannen—Biff's father. Hoping to rescue his friend, Marty follows him back in time and tries to stage a jailbreak. To accomplish this task, Marty must enlist the help of Doc's 17-year-old self, whose Rocket-Powered Drill he needs to blast through the wall of Doc's jail cell. Marty also encounters his grandfather,

Arthur McFly, as well as Edna Strickland, a holier-than-thou newspaper columnist favoring Prohibition and working to help feed the needy.

> **NOTE:** *This serialized series of adventure video games was produced for the PC, Mac, iPad, Playstation 3 and Nintendo Wii platforms. All five episodes were sold separately, and were later packaged together as a Collector's Edition.*

Back to the Future: The Game—Episode Two: Get Tannen!
Release year: 2011. W: Michael Stemmle and Andy Hartzell. D: Peter Tsaykel. Designers: Michael Stemmle, Andy Hartzell and Jonathan Straw.
LEXICON CODE: TLTL-2

Realizing they inadvertently altered history in Episode One by allowing Kid Tannen to avoid imprisonment and thus form a crime family with Biff and two other sons, Cliff and Riff, Marty and Doc must return to 1931 so that Marty can convince lounge singer Trixie Trotter to turn damning evidence over to the authorities that could put Kid away for life. In so doing, they must also repair additional damage they caused, by preventing Officer Danny Parker from losing his career and his fiancée, thereby negating the birth of Marty's girlfriend, Jennifer Parker.

Back to the Future: The Game—Episode Three: Citizen Brown
Release year: 2011. W: Jonathan Straw, Michael Stemmle and Andy Hartzell. D: Eric Parsons. Designers: Jonathan Straw and Andy Hartzell.
LEXICON CODE: TLTL-3

Marty discovers that his time in 1931 altered history again, so that instead of pursuing a career in science, Doc married Edna Strickland. Together, the couple turned Hill Valley into a dystopian society, with Doc installed as leader First Citizen Brown. Since then, Edna has perverted Doc's vision of a perfect society, outlawing everything from alcohol and pornography to science fiction, rock music and Circus Peanuts, and using police intimidation to keep the disenchanted in line. In this timeline, Jennifer is a punk-rocker vandal, Lorraine is an alcoholic, George spies on his neighbors for the government, and Biff is a brainwashed do-gooder. Eventually, Marty convinces Brown that time has been corrupted, and together the two set out to restore Hill Valley's proper history.

Back to the Future: The Game—Episode Four: Double Visions
Release year: 2011. W: Michael Stemmle and Andy Hartzell. D: Dave Grossman. Designers: Michael Stemmle and Andy Hartzell.
LEXICON CODE: TLTL-4

Citizen Brown and Marty return to 1931, where they discover that Edna Strickland has perverted young Emmett's scientific genius by having him create technology to socially condition Hill Valley's citizens. Marty hopes to end Emmett's and Edna's budding romance and inspire the younger Brown to regain his interest in science, but the First Citizen, still in love with Edna, feels guilt-ridden over ruining her life and abandons their cause.

Back to the Future: The Game—Episode Five: OUTATIME
Release year: 2011. W: Michael Stemmle and Andy Hartzell. D: Dennis Lenart. Designers: Michael Stemmle and Andy Hartzell.
LEXICON CODE: TLTL-5

At the 1931 Hill Valley Exposition, Marty vows to make Emmett's presentation a success, but Edna Strickland and First Citizen Brown work to thwart his efforts. Marty succeeds in restoring Doc's passion for science, but Edna steals the DeLorean and travels back to the Old West, where she inadvertently burns the city to the ground and goes insane out of extreme guilt. After Hill Valley vanishes around them, replaced with miles of undeveloped land, Marty and Doc must figure out how Edna altered history and un-do the damage.

Additional Resources

The following sources were also researched during this lexicon's compilation:

- *Back to the Future: The Official Book of the Complete Movie Trilogy* (Hamlyn Publishing Company, 1990, written by Michael Klastorin and Sally Hibbin)
- *Back to the Future: The Story* (Berkley Books, 1985, adapted by Robert Loren Fleming)
- *Back to the Future Annual* (Marvel Comics, 1990, written by David Bishop, Randall D. Larson and John Freeman, edited by John Freeman)
- *Back to the Future Adventure Game Books* (Nabisco, 1985, six booklets included in Shreddies cereal, England only)
- *BFI Film Classics: Back to the Future* (British Film Institute, 2010, written by Anderew Shail and Robin Stoate)
- *Back to the Future II Photo Book* (published only in Japan)
- *The Worlds of Back to the Future: Critical Essays on the Films* (McFarland, 2010, edited by Sorcha Ni Fhlainn)
- *Back to the Future Fan Club Magazine* (four issues, 1989-1990, Fan Clubs Inc., edited by John S. Davis, published by Dan Madsen)
- *BTTF Souvenir Magazine* (published by Ira Friedman, 1985)

- *Back to the Future* Happy Meals (four boxes, McDonalds, 1991)
- *Back to the Future II* trading-card set (Topps, 1989)
- *The Secrets of the Back to the Future Trilogy* (VHS, 1991)
- The Official *Back to the Future* News Source (bttf.com)
- Futurepedia (backtothefuture.wikia.com)
- *BTTF: The Board Game* (1990, Movie Licensing Games)
- "The Other Marty McFly?" (*Starlog* #108, July 1986)
- The Studio Tour (www.thestudiotour.com/ush/attractions/backtothefuture.shtml)
- KristenSheley.com (www.kristensheley.com/bttf)
- Doc Brown's Chicken (restaurant, Universal Studios)
- Various props used in the films, as well as authentic replicas
- Interviews with and commentaries from Bob Gale and Robert Zemeckis, particularly:
  – www.bttf.com/bttf-myths-and-misinformation-debunked-by-bob-gale.php
  – www.mentalfloss.com/blogs/archives/97285
  – www.empireonline.com/interviews/interview.asp?IID=1084

APPENDIX II ◀▉▍▎▏

A Fine Line Between Genius and Insanity

"It works! It works! I finally invent something that works!"
—Emmett L. Brown

Emmett L. Brown's brilliance was matched only by his eccentricity. Throughout his life and across multiple timelines, the scientist created an astounding number of innovations, ranging from the trivial and silly (sawdust pancakes and crying potatoes) to the amazing and paradigm-shifting (time machines and doorways to other dimensions). Presented below is a list of Doc's known inventions. See also the "Video Encyclopedia" entry in the lexicon.

APPAREL, HEADWEAR AND FOOTWEAR:

- Booster belts, designed to enable Doc to wax the roof of his car without using a ladder [BFAN-18]
- Full-Body Oven Mits—human-sized, heat-resistant gloves capable of protecting a wearer even from the heat of molten lava [BFAN-15]
- A metal body framework connected to laser-tracking eyeglasses, enabling a baseball player to practice hitting homeruns, with the glasses tracking the ball, and the framework manipulating his arms; the device, also programmed for fielding, pitching and kicking dirt at an umpire, could fold up into the shape of a baseball [BFAN-8]
- A propeller helmet enabling Doc's younger son, Verne Brown, to fly [BFAN-1]
- A coonskin cap for Verne, also containing a built-in propeller [BFAN-18]
- The Haircut Omatic, a helmet containing comb, brush and scissor attachments, designed to groom a wearer's hair in one of three settings (high school football buzz cut, bald-man wash and wax, and executive clean-cut and trim), but more likely to result in constantly changing haircuts (including punk, beehive, bouffant, powdered-wig, and other styles, both male and female) [BFAN-25]
- A binocular helmet enabling Verne to spot objects from great distances, with a pair of large yellow lenses that slid down over his eyes [BFHM]
- The Telescope Hat, an over-sized, helmet-mounted device for use in viewing the arrival of Comet Kahooey [BFAN-23]
- Jet-powered sneakers for Verne [BFAN-21]
- Rocket-powered skates for Doc's older son, Jules Brown [BFAN-1]
- Electro-guide boots, a type of hover-technology-based footwear that Vern frequently wore indoors, despite being told many times not to do so [BFAN-3]

- Magneto-sandals, enabling Doc to walk on walls and ceilings [BFAN-10]
- Waterproof tennis shoes, created using high-top sneakers, a can of lard and electrical current (which failed to catch on since the footwear ended up deep-fried—and, thus, un-wearable) [BFAN-11]
- Fance-o-Dance Memorizing Shoes, programmable to let a wearer perform a variety of dance types (including waltz, swing, fox trot, cha-cha and the Bobby Van hopping dance), and customizable as pumps, loafers, sneakers, or pumps that looked like sneakers [BFAN-17]
- Steam-powered snowshoes, which Doc invented circa 1888 [BFAN-21]
- Booster-boots, enabling a wearer to increase one's height (by being lifted off the ground), outrun moving vehicles and jump over tall buildings [BFAN-24]
- The Atmo-Processor, a personal atmospheric enhancement unit worn on a person's head and torso [RIDE]
- Mag-lev hover boots, a type of fusion-powered footwear intended for use with the Timeman personal time-travel suit [RIDE]

ARTIFICIAL INTELLIGENCE AND COMPUTERS:

- A robotic servant known as the 15-Tube Mechanical Home Butler, which became a common household appliance in an alternate 1985, making Doc extremely wealthy [BTF1-s1]
- A five-armed, cylindrical robot with a rolling base, known as an Automatic Housecleaner [BFCM-1]
- Another robot, the remnants of which he stored within his workshop [BTF1-n]
- The Mechanical Psychoanalyst, consisting of a bed wired to monitor its occupant, as well as a robot seated nearby, designed to resemble, speak like and use the psychoanalytical techniques of Doctor Sigmund Freud [BFCL-3]

- A monitor in the DeLorean's dashboard that a time-traveler could summon to gain information about his or her destination era and location, from an onscreen narrator who addressed Doc by name [**BFAN-7b**]
- The Sub-ether Tracking System, a computer program installed at the Institute of Future Technology's Anti-Gravitic Laboratory, used to confirm space-time coordinates [**RIDE**]
- A visual database used to educate science students, known as the Video Encyclopedia [**BFAN-1 to BFAN-26**]
- A universal linguistics translator, built into the DeLorean's grill, able to instantly translate any language—including that of evolved dinosaurs [**BFAN-3**]
- A handheld computer called an input device that could be utilized for multiple purposes, including science experiments and video games [**BFAN-1**]
- An inflatable computer console that emerged from the DeLorean's dashboard at the push of a button [**BFAN-7a**]
- A handheld iPad-like tablet device that proved impractical and non-portable since it was as large as Doc and could not fit into his DeLorean [**GARB**]
- A laptop-style computer that was too unstable to use since it was powered by plutonium instead of a standard battery [**GARB**]
- The Sub-ether Time-Tracking Scanner, located aboard Doc's Eight-Passenger DeLorean Time Travel Vehicle, enabling occupants to track the temporal movements of other cars [**RIDE**]
- The Doc Brown Blackboard, which produced moving images designed to look as though drawn with chalk, accompanied by voice narration [**BFAN-3**]
- The ELB Video Message Center, attached to the Brown family refrigerator, and used to record and play back messages [**BFAN-6**]
- A holographic teacher that Marty utilized to study for college [**BFAN-1**]
- A three-dimensional holographic projector [**BFAN-5**]
- A board game based on the layout of Hill Valley, with miniaturized versions of each building, as well as holographic representations of vehicles and citizens—including a giant Biff Tannen serving as an obstacle to players [**BFAN-6**]
- A projector mounted to the front of Marty's hoverboard, enabling him to watch three-dimensional movies while in transit [**BFAN-10**]
- The ELB Life-on-the-Edge Facsimulator, consisting of ultra-realistic video game simulations of racecars, airplanes and other scenarios, designed to help develop hand-eye coordination on a level equal to actual experience [**BFAN-19**]
- A pull-down screen inside the DeLorean that displayed videos explaining scientific principles (such as how to make a battery out of lemons) [**BFAN-3**]

CAMERAS AND PHONES:

- An oversized snartphone prototype with a built-in camera and GPS system, made from a 1980s telephone, a Polaroid instant camera, a fax machine, a satellite antennae and other electronic devices, which proved to be a failure since modem service at the time utilized dial-up Internet access [**GARB**]
- A camera able to create optical illusions of those photographed, allowing Doc's family to appear to be wearing clothing appropriate to various eras, without actually having to change attire [**BFAN-2, BFAN-10, BFAN-13, BFAN-25**]

- A device enabling a user to photograph any person from any era in history, with one touch of a button [**BFAN-6**]
- The Magnascope 4000, a camera with an extendable lens, enabling a user to snap a photograph at extreme distances [**BFAN-15**]
- A camera attachment resembling a small figure of Admiral Richard E. Byrd, that moved back and forth so those being photographed would "watch the Byrdie" [**BFAN-25**]
- A camera optics device known as an auto-iris, used to film his Video Encyclopedia [**BFAN-4**]
- A balloon-mount, to which Doc could attach a video camera in order to document his travels in a hot-air balloon [**BFAN-2**]

CANINE-ASSISTANCE SYSTEMS:

- A pair of robotic gloves enabling Doc's dog, Einstein, to use a computer, play cards and perform other manual tasks [**BFAN-1, BFAN-6, BFAN-22**]
- A sensor that recognized Einstein's paw-print, enabling the pooch to enter the Brown family home unaided [**BFAN-2**]
- A machine allowing Einstein to receive a robotic massage whenever he felt like being petted [**BFAN-2**]
- A mechanical dog-washing tub for Einstein [**BFAN-4**]
- A pair of scissors, stored in Einstein's collar, that could be activated at the press of a paw in order to cut a rope [**BFAN-7b**]
- A contraption combining a baby stroller and a pulley, with which Einstein could raise himself to the roof for fresh air [**BFAN-9**]
- The ELB Super-Sniffer Snout 4000, which amplified Einstein's canine sniffing ability via a large, nose-like contraption attached on one end to the dog's snout, and on the other to the front of Doc's DeLorean [**BFAN-20**]
- The Canine Retrieval Apparatus, built to rescue dogs from great heights, such as on a roof [**TLTL-v**]

FOOD PRODUCTS:

- Sawdust pancakes, produced by Doc's Automated Flapjack Maker, which failed to catch on [**RIDE**]
- Sawdust dog food, which proved more successful than the sawdust pancakes [**RIDE**]
- Banana pizza, created using Emmett Brown's Digi-Chef digital food molecularizer, by combining bananas and pizza at the molecular level [**RIDE**]
- A hybrid vegetable called self-watering onion-potatoes; the onions made the potatoes' eyes water [**BFAN-20**]
- A genetically engineered strain of popping corn developed with help from his wife, Clara Clayton-Brown, which the couple dubbed Super-Growth Mondo-Corn, given its size—a single ear nearly filled their garage [**BFAN-21**]
- Full-course Food Pellets that, when added to water, provided a complete meal [**BFAN-26**]

HOME APPLIANCES—EXERCISE:

- Auto-Jog Mechanical Running Shorts, enabling a wearer to run not only on ground, but up walls; settings included "Rest," "Jog," "Run" and "Gentle Trot" [**BFAN-1**]
- A floor-to-ceiling contraption of pulleys and gears powered by a stationary bike, purpose unknown [**BFAN-c**]

- A workout machine consisting of a pair of mechanical legs running on a treadmill that, when wired to a person's actual legs, enabled that individual to experience the health benefits of running without physically having to exercise [BFAN-2]
- An exercise bike with mechanical arms to hold a book, as well as feed hotdogs and a beverage to the person operating the device [BFAN-19]
- An exercise device called an electric perpetual portable trampoline, which could fold up and fit into a person's pocket, and be activated to instantly unfold at the push of a button [BFCM-1]
- A contraption that paced in circles to help calm a person's nerves [BFAN-21]
- A homemade Nautilus machine that could also chop wood [BTF3-s1]

HOME APPLIANCES—FOOD AND BEVERAGE:

- An alcohol still built from the shell of an old washing machine [BTF1-s1]
- An automated toaster, coffee maker and dog-food dispenser, used to serve Doc and Einstein breakfast each morning [BTF1]
- A contraption set to automatically fry eggs and bacon, as well as toast bread, built during his stint as a blacksmith in 1885 [BTF3]
- The ELB Hot-Diggity Dogger, designed to boil and serve a thousand wieners per hour, as well as apply mustard and ketchup, and supply a beverage [BFAN-22]
- A massive cooling unit built using the technology of 1885, including pulleys, pressure valves, pipes and other pieces of equipment, for the purpose of creating ice—one discolored cube at a time—so Doc could enjoy iced tea [BTF3]
- A simple toaster that browned un-toasted bread pushed through a slot on one side of the device and ejected toast from the other [RIDE]
- The Automated Flapjack Maker, one of his earliest creations, capable of cooking more than 300 pancakes per hour on a rotating griddle—which failed to catch on since it produced sawdust pancakes [RIDE]
- The Digi-Chef, a digital food molecularizer able to combine various foods (bananas and pizza, for example) into a single substance (banana pizza, in this case) at the molecular level [RIDE]
- A drill-like device used to make peanut butter inside the shell [BFAN-15]
- A device for canning homegrown tomatoes—which failed to work properly, instead propelling the fruits across the Brown kitchen at high speed [BFAN-14]
- The ELB Quick-o-Popper, a room-sized machine for popping the massive kernels of Doc's super-growth mondo-corn [BFAN-21]

HOME APPLIANCES—HAIR CARE AND HYGIENE:

- A model of electric hair dryer that was a failure since it set fire to a stuffed doll placed beneath it during testing [RIDE]
- The Static-o-Matic Electric Hair Chair, which harnessed 200,000 volts of static electricity to make human hair stand up, thereby making it easier to cut [RIDE]
- An automatic hair-washing device, worn over a person's head and utilizing a small pair of robotic arms [BFAN-14]
- The Son-o-Dent ultrasonic tooth-care system [BTF1-s1]

- A type of headgear that automatically brushed a person's teeth while simultaneously cleaning his or her face with a washcloth [BFAN-14]
- Another set of robotic headgear for automatically washing a face, combing hair and brushing teeth [BFAN-22]
- The Perpetual Motion Foot-Massage Unit, intended to cure athlete's foot fungus [BFAN-7a]
- The Auto-Infant Cleanser, created in or before 1888, designed to help Doc and Clara automatically bathe Jules [BFAN-21]

HOME APPLIANCES—OTHER:

- Steam-powered household appliances, for use in the event of electrical blackouts [BFAN-6]
- The Dyno-Matic Spray Gun, a handheld tool for bronzing children's shoes or other items, such as hats [RIDE]
- The Suc-o-Matic, a self-propelled, energy-saving vacuum cleaner powered by the very dust it picked up [RIDE]
- The Ozone-Friendly Freon-Free Cooling Unit—a type of ceiling-mounted air-conditioner designed to produce no chlorofluorocarbons and not damage the ozone layer of Earth's upper atmosphere [BFAN-10]
- A conveyer-belt contraption incorporating mechanical arms ending in blue hands, used to crush tin cans and collect them in a receptacle [BFAN-20]
- An automated, crank-driven sewing machine for Clara's use, built during the couple's Old West days [BFAN-21]

MIND-READING, MIND-CONTROL AND TELEPATHY DEVICES:

- The Brain-wave Analyzer, enabling a wearer to telepathically hear others' thoughts, and consisting of a mass of vacuum tubes, rheostats, gauges, wiring and antennae; Doc deemed it a failure after being unable to discern what Marty McFly was thinking—but it may have worked better than he realized [BTF1-n]
- The Brain Wave Analyzer, used to monitor a person's brain patterns and determine whether or not that individual was mentally healthy [BFAN-12]
- The Deep-Thinking Mind-Reading Helmet, which harnessed electromagnetic impulses created by synaptic responses from the cerebrum and the cerebellum, transmitting mind waves into the helmet's interpreting circuitry, thus translating the impulses into written language [RIDE]
- The Deep-Thought Mind-Reading Helmet, which enabled a wearer to hear the unspoken thoughts of others [BFAN-1]
- The Thought-inducing Auto-pacer, intended to help an individual focus on a problem at hand [BFAN-1]
- The Memory Archive Recall Indexer and Enhancer (M.A.R.I.E.), enabling a user to recall any memory, fact or information learned during his or her lifetime, by donning a large helmet wired to a computer [BFAN-15]
- The Flashback-o-Matic, enabling a user to recall forgotten memories by typing words onto an old-fashioned typewriter, triggering a helmet-mounted projector to display those memories on a screen [BFAN-17]
- The Projecto-Recollector, a helmet-mounted device built in or before 1952, enabling a wearer to project thoughts onto a nearby screen [BFAN-24]

- The ELB Pediatric Policer, a helmet-mounted device that operated similar to a lie-detector, which determined if a child was misbehaving by measuring sudden changes in blood pressure, skin temperature and pulse rate, and triggering alarms in the event of bad behavior [**BFAN-26**]
- The Mental Alignment Meter (M.A.M.), created in an alternate 1931 and able to measure a person's affinities, including what that individual finds attractive or repulsive [**TLTL-4**]
- The Mind Mapping Helmet, a type of headgear used to record a test subject's mental patterns for analysis by the Mental Alignment Meter [**TLTL-4**]
- The Mind Map Printer, a special typewriter used in tandem with the Mind Mapping Helmet to print out a punch card pronouncing judgment on an individual's mental state [**TLTL-4**]

POWER SOURCES AND CONTROL SYSTEMS:

- The Flux Capacitor, affixed inside a DeLorean DMC-12 sports car, which facilitated time travel; the device required 1.21 jigowatts of electricity (generated either via plutonium or a bolt of lightning) to trigger a temporal reaction [**BTF1**]
- The Photo-Electric Chemical Power Converter, developed from 1949 to 1985, and designed to efficiently convert radiation into electrical energy [**BTF1-s1**]
- A homemade nuclear reactor, made from an old furnace, a hot water heater and boiler-room parts—which, when combined with the Photo-Electric Chemical Power Converter, could be used to create a working time machine [**BTF1-s1**]
- An automobile engine that ran on salt water, developed in 1954, which never went to market since the scientist sold the design to Standard Oil for $5 million [**BTF1-s4**]
- A set of replacement time circuits for the DeLorean, built using 1955 technology after the system was struck by lightning and rendered non-functional [**BTF3**]
- Homemade Pres-to-Logs, constructed from compressed wood with anthracite dust chemically treated to burn harder and longer; Doc used these so he wouldn't have to stoke his blacksmith forge in 1885, and later to increase Locomotive No. 131's speed to 88 miles per hour, enabling the damaged DeLorean to achieve time-travel [**BTF3**]
- The Agro-Waste Fuel Conversion System, which transformed ordinary manure into clean-burning fuel pellets; a single marble-sized pellet could heat a typical house for an entire winter, but the odor was overwhelming [**RIDE**]
- The Super-Electromagnet, powered by the Mr. Fusion to create a mega-magnet capable of incredible strength—but once activated, it attracted every steel object within its immediate vicinity, causing the device to be pummeled and damaged [**BFAN-1**]
- A variation on Francis Hauksbee's frictional electricity machine, which Doc and Marty used to generate fake lightning in order to entice Benjamin Franklin to conduct his famous kite and electricity experiments [**BFAN-6**]
- The Environmental Adjuster, a wheeled contraption with a large emitting dish, used to create customized environmental conditions, such as thunder, lightning or fog [**BFAN-12**]
- The Hydrolunarsolarwinderator, a portable power plant that transformed, at the press of a pedal, from a device small enough to fit in a wheelbarrow to an entire building that could link to a city's power lines, drawing energy from wind, water, sunlight and moonlight to provide free, unlimited power [**BFAN-22**]

- A pan-dimensional field generator, used to power Doc's extradimensional storage closet [**BFCL-3**]
- A glowing, hovering coil called a Static Accumulator, used to generate a static charge [**TLTL-5**]
- A component of the Static Accumulator known as the Oscillator Gigathruster [**TLTL-v**]
- A homemade cyclotron (a particle accelerator used to speed up charged particles utilizing a high-frequency, alternating voltage), which he dubbed a proprietary ultrasonic subatomic molecular redistributor [**BFAN-3**]
- The Mr. Profusion, offering safe, efficient fusion power for the home [**RIDE**]

TIME MACHINES:

- A time-traveling DeLorean DMC-12, powered by the Flux Capacitor [**BTF1**]
- An exact duplicate of the DeLorean, created when the vehicle was struck by lightning in 1955, which Doc later discovered while visiting the future [**TLTL-5**]
- A foldable version of the DeLorean time machine, with greater capacity to fit the entire Brown family, as well as audio-activated time circuits [**BFAN-1**]
- A miniature time-traveling mail truck built while Doc was trapped in 1692, to deliver a call for help to Marty McFly in 1991 [**BFAN-4**]
- An Eight-Passenger DeLorean Time Travel Vehicle—an experimental, energy-efficient, convertible upgrade from Doc's original time-traveling car, capable of carrying eight occupants in two rows of four [**RIDE**]
- The *Jules Verne Train*, a flying, steam-powered locomotive containing a Flux Capacitor, built sometime after 1885, while Doc lived in the Old West [**BTF1**]
- A series of devices called Diagnostic Modules, utilized to troubleshoot problems with the DeLorean's time circuits [**TLTL-5**]
- Flux Synchronization Modules, maintenance devices enabling Doc to sync up two DeLoreans in order to link both sets of time circuits and override one car's time destination via the other's computer [**TLTL-5**]
- A trio of devices called Flux Emitters, enabling the DeLorean to achieve time travel—two attached to the hood, on the vehicle's front passenger's and driver's sides, and a third affixed to the roof [**TLTL-5**]
- The Chronometric Analyzer, a diagnostic device built by Doc's future self in 1931 to analyze and repair the DeLorean's damaged time circuits [**TLTL-4**]
- The Timespan, a technology involving holographic place/time projection [**RIDE**]
- The Timeman personal time-travel suit [**RIDE**]

VEHICLES, MODES OF TRAVEL AND ADD-ON DEVICES:

- A model of flying car called the Aero-Mobile [**BTF1-s1**]
- Another flying vehicle known as the Rocket Car, a prototype of which he built in 1931, intending to unveil it at that year's Hill Valley Exposition [**TLTL-2**]

- An Airborne Personal Transport Device, built in an alternate 1931 as a follow-up to the failed Rocket Car, but powered by static electricity [TLTL-4]
- The Electrokinetic Levitator, an early-model flying vehicle also based on the Rocket Car prototype, utilizing the Static Accumulator to achieve lift [TLTL-5]
- A makeshift hang-glider capable of carrying three people, which Doc used to rescue his son, Verne, and mother-in-law, Martha O'Brien, in 1850 [BFAN-13]
- The Flying Observatory, a vehicle resembling a flying saucer and powered by a stationary bicycle, that achieved lift by creating a negative magnetic charge; Biff Tannen mistook it for a spacecraft in 1967, and again in 1992, inciting mass hysteria and convincing others that Doc was an alien [BFAN-23]
- Several different apian (bee)-powered aircrafts [TLTL-v]
- A flying bicycle, built in 1931 by affixing parts of Doc's Rocket-Powered Drill to the back of a two-wheeled bike [TLTL-1]
- A jetpack designed to be worn on a person's back [BFAN-3]
- A purple-cushioned, hovering chair that could carry a person around a room [BFAN-13]
- A zeppelin that unfolded from the roof of the DeLorean, enabling the vehicle to fly [BFAN-11]
- A miniaturized helicopter with a mounted video monitor, which Clara sometimes used to summon her sons to dinner [BFAN-6]
- A slingshot that extended from beneath the DeLorean's hood at the pull of a lever, and hammered two metal stakes into the ground, anchoring a thick rubber-band with which Doc could then propel the flying car into the air [BFAN-3]
- A device for launching the DeLorean out of Doc's garage, designed like a giant pinball-machine's ball-serving mechanism [BFAN-17]
- Another launch system consisting of a massive boxing glove attached to a tension-loaded spring that punched the rear of the DeLorean, causing it to quickly accelerate [BFAN-8]
- A remote-controlled crane to carry around the foldable DeLorean [BFAN-1]
- An inflatable raft affixed to the bottom of the DeLorean in case of water landings, activated by a pull cord beneath a dashboard panel, enabling the vehicle to rise to the surface and travel back to shore [BFAN-4]
- A system for reconfiguring the DeLorean as a covered wagon, for use during the Hill Valley Pioneer Days Parade [BFAN-13]
- An automatic-retrieval feature for the DeLorean, enabling the car to return to a specified set of four-dimensional coordinates in the event that the scientist failed to return to the vehicle within an allotted time [TLTL-1]
- A handheld auto-remote device enabling Doc to summon the DeLorean to his location over long distances [BFAN-4]
- A train-track extension for a horse-drawn wagon, built in 1885 so that Doc could guide the damaged DeLorean over the vehicle's tailgate and onto the local Central Pacific Railroad tracks [BTF3-n]
- A large set of extendable chain cutters attached to the bottom of the DeLorean [BFAN-4]
- A system enabling the DeLorean's driver to expel an occupant by extending the passenger seat through the door and discarding him or her on the ground [BFAN-7b]
- The ELB Autogroom 5000, a robotic shaving and grooming system built into the DeLorean's dashboard [BFAN-7b]
- A pair of robotic arms inside the DeLorean's trunk that could pick up items and automatically place them within the vehicle's storage compartment [BFAN-7b]
- An automated, subterranean tunnel-car system located beneath Doc's home that carried his family to the *Jules Verne Train*, along with a ramp enabling the locomotive to launch from belowground [BFAN-1, BFAN-9]
- A Utility Box Car for the *Jules Verne Train*, large enough to carry a young Apatosaurus [BFAN-26]
- A souped-up Roman chariot for Marty to race against Bifficus Antanneny, with a mechanism for automatically replacing damaged wooden wheels [BFAN-5]
- A boat with flapping wings, used to carry Doc and Clara up to the roof of the Brown family home, for the purpose of stargazing [BFAN-9]
- The Junkmobile, a three-wheeled vehicle for his sons, comprising a bathtub attached to a snow sled, and powered by manually turning a bar attached to two eggbeaters at high speed, thereby causing the tires to spin [BFAN-13, BFAN-21]
- A self-cooling suit for use while riding a bicycle [BFAN-23]
- The Thru-Haul, an interdimensional large-item auxiliary transport vehicle that could be attached to the back of Doc's time-traveling, eight-passenger DeLorean, for the purpose of hauling belongings [RIDE]
- The Crash Repel and Avoidance System Hardware (C.R.A.S.H.), a technology enabling Doc's eight-seat DeLorean to push off any vehicles in danger of colliding with it [RIDE]

WEAPONS, ALARM SYSTEMS AND PROTECTIVE GEAR:

- A four-barrel shotgun known as the Terminator, constructed in 1885 and loaded with double-aught buck, nails, broken glass and shiny new dimes [BTF3-sx, BTF3-sp]
- A rifle that expelled a net for use in capturing animals, such as the *Bufo marinus* toad [BFAN-7a]
- The Tow-Bar Torpedo, built into the front of the *Jules Verne Train*, enabling Doc to stop a fleeing vehicle by firing a towing cable [BFAN-15]
- The ELB Aqua-Ammomatic, a scientifically perfected water-balloon system that could propel balloons more accurately, at greater distances and with a better burst ratio when heated to 82 degrees and expanded to a pressure of 1.2 pounds per square inch (psi) [BFAN-18]
- A burglar alarm to protect his safe in 1885, consisting of a rat trap wired to a lever that, in the event that someone tried to rob him, released a net from the ceiling, along with several pots and pans, thereby capturing the perpetrator and producing a great deal of noise [BTF3-sp]
- The ELB Lunchbox Burglar Deterrent, consisting of an extendable arm and mallet to attack anyone attempting to steal his Come-and-Get-It Lunchbox [BFAN-15]
- A burglary-thwarting device, built in or before 1944, designed to frighten off would-be trespassers by blurting out "Hold it right there, buster!" upon sensing intruders within his home [BFAN-17]
- Voiceprint-activated locks for dresser drawers [BFAN-17]

- An alarm system in the Brown family garage, installed to protect the DeLorean from theft, by sounding sirens, photographing the thief and using robotic arms to awaken and dress Doc [**BFAN-26**]
- The CLB NightVision Prototype 85 helmet, enabling a wearer to see in the dark [**BFAN-1**]

MISCELLANEOUS:

- A computerized chess set, built sometime in or before 1955, with each playing piece connected to a complex set of wires designed to move the pieces around the board mechanically [**BTF3**]
- A machine that turned newspaper pages automatically, enabling Doc to read the news without his fingers becoming blackened by ink [**BFAN-2**]
- A system for automatically folding newspapers that Verne delivered on a daily route, consisting of a conveyor belt—sometimes powered by Einstein—and various mechanical arms [**BFAN-19**]
- The Hydraulic Scrapbook, an electronic scrapbook used for preserving personal and family-history memorabilia, such as photographs and news clippings, with pneumatic cylinders to automatically turn the pages [**BTF1-s1**]
- The Write-o-Matic, a writing utensil consisting of a pen with a wire-attached suction cup [**BTF1-s1**]
- A machine enabling Clara to electronically grade students' assignments and tests from across the room, using a stylus [**BFAN-2**]
- A giant guitar amplifier for Marty McFly, which overloaded and burst when Marty turned it up to full volume [**BTF1**]
- The Ronco Aroma Amplifier, consisting of a funnel connected to an electronic box, with a hose running out the other side and attaching to a wearer's nose, enabling that person (or dog) to track someone based on scent [**BTF2-s1**]
- A tree-house for Jules and Verne, built from car, school-bus and airplane components [**BFAN-c**]
- Scratch 'N' Listen postcards, enabling a user to record voice messages on a chip affixed to the back of a paper postcard; a recipient would then scratch the chip to activate the recording [**BFAN-4**]
- An underwater breathing apparatus made from two large milk cans, a bellows and rubber tubing [**BFAN-4**]
- A large, multi-lensed telescope, mounted on the roof above the Browns' home, through which Doc and Clara sometimes gazed at the Moon [**BFAN-9**]
- Another telescope that could be folded up like a compact [**BFAN-3**]
- A device that automatically rocked Jules' crib when he was a baby [**BFAN-21**]
- A large-format television known as the Megascreen TV [**BFAN-23**]
- A large-format flatscreen TV, invented before such televisions were commercially available, that could be built into the wall of a house—which shorted out during rain, since the back of the TV protruded outside the home due to the absence of microelectronic components in the 1980s [**GARB**]
- A videotape recorder with full 14-day programming capability, which Doc created for the 1932 Hill Valley Junior Science Fair; although the device worked perfectly, it was a failure since the television had yet to be invented [**BFAN-13**]
- A remote-controlled set of wipers for cleaning gunk off television screens [**BFAN-14**]
- A conveyer-powered contraption consisting of a treadmill, various gears and belts, as well as a large spinning piece of wood, which Clara used to remove a tattoo from Verne's belly [**BFAN-14**]
- The Fly Trap, Rehabilitation and Release Center, intended as a humane alternative to a traditional fly-swatter, and consisting of a glass capsule containing a miniature bed and overstuffed chair [**BFAN-15**]
- The ELB Sunshine Umbrella for Rainy-Day Tans, which emanated a very bright light source when opened, and emitted a stream of water, serving as a sunny-day spout for those who enjoy walking in the rain [**BFAN-15**]
- The Heat-Seeking Rat Trap, a windup motorized mousetrap on wheels, with a miniaturized dish used to track vermin [**BFAN-15**]
- The Perpetual-Motion Hula Hoop, also known as a "Perpa-Hoop," which utilized a battery and internal gyros to eliminate the stress and injuries often caused by what Doc saw as a "wacky fad" [**BFAN-15**]
- The Come-and-Get-It Lunchbox, designed to loudly summon its owner at lunchtime [**BFAN-15**]
- A system for awakening Jules and Verne in the morning, consisting of a large wall-mounted timing device, a mechanical hand attached to a rod, and a recorded message in Clara's voice [**BFAN-20**]
- A chlorophyll and enzyme booster engineered to prolong the leaf life of Jules' money-tree [**BFAN-20**]
- Yo-Bub No-Stub Folding Chairs, containing a sensor dish programmed to move them out of the way if a passerby were in danger of stubbing a toe; the chairs could walk unassisted, and could be summoned via a clap to follow a user [**BFAN-22**]
- A sign in Doc's laboratory that flashed "DINNER" when it was time for him to join his family for the evening meal [**BFAN-c**]
- An ointment for making warts disappear—which had the unexpected result of rendering Doc invisible [**BFAN-7a**]
- Super-Sudsy Soap, a concentrated, lemon-scented cleaning solution, two drops of which could fill an entire yard and home with suds [**BFAN-22**]
- The Mr. Gin, created while Doc was visiting 1927 Chicago to find a cure for Einstein's cat-aracts; the invention, resembling a Mr. Coffee with a beaker for a coffee pot, was used to brew a cure from fermented juniper berries [**BFCM-1**]
- An all-purpose cleanser capable of wiping grime off any surface, which Doc used as a young man to keep his fancy suit clean—but which, due to an inherent instability in its chemical makeup, broke down into its component enzymes, rendering it unsuitable for commercial use since it then acted as a highly corrosive acid [**TLTL-4**]
- An extradimensional storage closet that was larger on the inside than on the outside since it contained access to multiple dimensions [**BFCL-3**]
- Custom power-tools with an oversized plug requiring greater power than could be supplied by a 110-volt non-grounded outlet [**BFAN-22**]
- A Rocket-Powered Drill, a patent for which Doc applied at age 17, which never went beyond the prototype stage [**TLTL-1**]
- Radio-transmitted odors [**TLTL-v**]
- Self-cleaning windows [**TLTL-v**]
- Personal tunneling devices [**TLTL-v**]

APPENDIX III ◀◀◀◀

Relatively Speaking

*"So, you're my great-grandfather, the first McFly
born in America... and you peed on me."*

—**Marty McFly**

One recurring theme throughout the Back to the Future mythos was that Marty and Doc, in the course of their temporal adventures, inevitably met their own ancestors and descendants, as well as those of other characters—frequently Biff Tannen's. In addition, the duo often traveled incognito, hiding their true identities to avoid temporal contamination.

Presented below are all known members of the films' recurring families, in all known realities, along with aliases that Doc and Marty assumed during their travels. Also included on the list are any animals owned by the main characters—and Biff's car, which he cared for and even named. Consult the lexicon for further information about particular entries.

Relatives: Martin Seamus McFly

- Baines, Ellen (aunt)
- Baines, Joey (uncle)
- Baines, Milton (uncle)
- Baines, Sally (aunt)
- Baines, Sam (grandfather)
- Baines, Stella (grandmother)
- Baines, Toby (uncle)
- Doris (great-aunt, surname unknown)
- John (uncle, surname unknown)
- McFly, Arthur (grandfather)
- McFly, David R. (brother)
- McFly, Electra (descendant)
- McFly, George (father)
- McFly, Harold (ancestor)
- McFly, Jennivere (ancestor)
- McFly, Jim (ancestor)
- McFly, Jules (descendant)
- McFly, Linda (sister)
- McFly, Lorraine Baines (mother)
- McFly, Maggie (great-great-grandmother)
- McFly, Marlene (daughter)
- McFly, Marta (great-granddaughter)
- McFly, Martin (great-great-granduncle)
- McFly, Martin Jr. (son)
- McFly, Martin III (grandson)
- McFly, Pee Wee (fifth cousin, thrice removed)
- McFly, Seamus (great-great-grandfather)
- McFly, William Sean (great-grandfather)
- Mickey (great-uncle, surname unknown)
- Miskin, Delores (ancestor)
- Miskin, Sylvia (grandmother)
- Parker, Daniel Jr. (father-in-law)
- Parker, Jennifer Jane (wife)
- Sussex McFlys, The (ancestors)
- Tannen, Biff Howard (alternate-reality stepfather)
- Tannen, Hepzibah (temporary fiancée)

Relatives: Emmett Lathrop Brown

- Archimedes (horse)
- Brown, Emmett Jr. (fictional son)
- Brown, Erhardt (father)
- Brown, Jules Eratosthenes (son)
- Brown, Verne Newton (son)
- Clayton Brown, Clarabelle (wife)
- Clayton, Daniel (father-in-law)
- Copernicus (dog)
- Einstein (dog)
- Galileo (horse)
- Lathrop, Abraham (uncle)
- Lathrop, Sarah (mother)
- Newton (horse)
- Newton (dog)
- O'Brien, Martha (mother-in-law)
- Oliver (uncle, surname unknown)
- Shemp (monkey)
- Strickland, Edna (alternate-reality wife)
- Strickland, Gerald (alternate-reality brother-in-law)
- Tiny (sons' dinosaur)
- von Brauns, The (ancestors)
- Wooster, Jill (ex-girlfriend)

Relatives: Biff Howard Tannen
(a.k.a. "Biffsters")

- Antanneny, Bifficus (ancestor)
- Biffingham, Lord, Earl of Tannenshire (ancestor)
- Chopper (pet German Shepherd)
- McPhips, Oz (great-great-granduncle)
- McFly, David R. (alternate-reality stepson)
- McFly, Linda (alternate-reality stepdaughter)
- McFly, Lorraine Baines (alternate-reality wife)
- McFly, Martin Seamus (alternate-reality stepson)
- Shiela (pet name for his car)
- Strickland, Edna (alternate-reality stepmother)

- Tanén, Biffando de la (ancestor)
- Tannen the Barbarbain (descendant)
- Tannen, Beauregard B. (ancestor)
- Tannen, Biff Jr. (son)
- Tannen, Bob (ancestor)
- Tannen, Buffy (descendant)
- Tannen, Buford (great-grandfather)
- Tannen, Cliff (brother)
- Tannen, D.W. (ancestor)
- Tannen, Ebiffnezer (ancestor)
- Tannen, Frank (ancestor)
- Tannen, Gertrude (grandmother)
- Tannen, Goodman (ancestor)
- Tannen, Governor (descendant)
- Tannen, Griff (grandson)
- Tannen, Hepzibah (great-great-grandaunt)
- Tannen, Irving (father)
- Tannen, Jimmy (ancestor)
- Tannen, Mac (ancestor)
- Tannen, Mercy (ancestor)
- Tannen, Mongo P. (ancestor)
- Tannen, Mugsy (ancestor)
- Tannen, Officer (alternate-reality dinosaur Biff)
- Tannen, P.T. (ancestor)
- Tannen, Riff (brother)
- Tannen, Thaddeus (great-great-granduncle)
- Tannen, Tiffany (daughter)
- Tannen, Tim (uncle)
- Tannen, Wild Bill (ancestor)
- Tannen, Ziff (great-great-grandson)

Relatives: Clarabelle Clayton Brown

- Brown, Emmett Lathrop (husband)
- Brown, Erhardt (father-in-law)
- Brown, Jules Eratosthenes (son)
- Brown, Verne Newton (son)
- Clayton, Daniel (father)
- Clayton, Grandpa (grandfather)
- Clayton, Polly (ancestor)
- Clayton, Ulysses S. (uncle)
- Einstein (dog)
- Jehosaphat (uncle, surname unknown)
- Lathrop, Sarah (mother-in-law)
- O'Brien, Martha (mother)

Relatives: Jennifer Jane Parker

- Lapinski, Betty (grandmother)
- McFly, David R. (brother-in-law)
- McFly, Electra (descendant)
- McFly, George (father-in-law)
- McFly, Jules (descendant)
- McFly, Linda (sister-in-law)
- McFly, Lorraine Baines (mother-in-law)
- McFly, Marlene (daughter)
- McFly, Marta (great-granddaughter)
- McFly, Martin Seamus (husband)
- McFly, Martin Jr. (son)
- McFly, Martin III (grandson)
- Norman (grandfather, surname unknown)
- Parker, Daniel J. (grandfather)
- Parker, Daniel Jr. (father)
- Parker, Genevieve (great-great-grandmother)
- Parker, Peter (grandfather)
- Parker, Wendel (great-great-grandfather)

Relatives: Gerald (S.S.) Strickland

- Fanny (aunt, surname unknown)
- Brown, Emmett Lathrop (alternate-reality brother-in-law)
- Miss Prettywhiskers (sister Edna's cat)
- Strickland, Blackout Warden (ancestor)
- Strickland, Clay (descendant)
- Strickland, Dean (relationship unclear)
- Strickland, Edna (sister)
- Strickland, Irene (mother)
- Strickland, James (grandfather)
- Strickland, Ricky (relationship unclear)
- Strickland, Robert (brother)
- Strickland, Roger (father)
- Strickland, Vice-Principal (relationship unclear)

Relatives: Douglas J. Needles

- Needles, Amy (daughter)
- Needles, Darlene (relationship unclear)
- Needles, Frankie (ancestor)
- Needles, Lauren Anne (wife)
- Needles, Roberta (daughter)

Relatives: Goldie (Muhammed) Wilson

- Wilson, Clara (descendant)
- Wilson, Goldie Jr. (son)
- Wilson, Goldie III (grandson)

Relatives: Marvin Berry

- Berry, Chuck (cousin)
- Berry, Marlin (descendant)

Aliases: Marty McFly

- Anthony
- Callahan, Harry
- Corleone, Michael
- Courageous Clyde
- Crockett, Sonny
- Dances With Frogs
- DeLorean, Marty
- Eastwood, Clint
- Ghost of Christmas
- His Royal Hairness
- Klein, Calvin
- Klein, Marty
- Lewis, Marty
- Mac the Black
- Marticus
- Nephew Martin
- McFly, Martin "Zipper"
- McFly, Marty "Blackeye"
- Olsen, Jimmy
- Smirnoff, Yakov

Aliases: Emmett Brown

- Brown, Brain Buster
- Brown, Daredevil Emmett
- Brown, Doc
- Brown, First Citizen
- Brown, Goodman
- Mega Brainman
- Sagan, Carl

APPENDIX IV

Cover Gallery: Every Picture Tells a Story

"No wonder your president has to be an actor. He's gotta look good on television."

—**Emmett L. Brown**

f you're looking to expand your *Back to the Future* collection, the following section should facilitate the hunt. This gallery should not be considered entirely comprehensive, as the wide range of formats, designs and foreign-market versions released over the years, and from one region to the next, make it virtually impossible to be aware of every single variation. For more information about individual titles, see Appendix I.

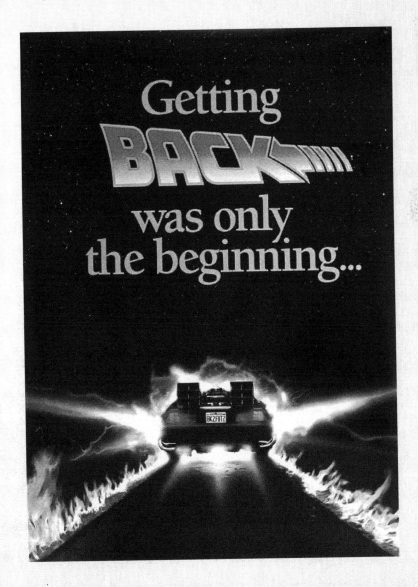

THEATRICAL AND TELEVISION FILMS

Back to the Future (VHS)

Back to the Future Part II (VHS)

Back to the Future Part III (VHS)

*Back to the Future:
The Complete Trilogy* (VHS)

*Back to the Future
Trilogy Boxset* (VHS)

*Back to the Future: The Trilogy—Limited
Edition Set* (VHS)

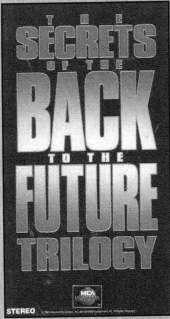

The Secrets of the
Back to the Future Trilogy
(VHS, Universal Pictures)

The Earth Day Special
(VHS, Time Warner)

Back to the Future (Betamax)

Back to the Future Part II (Betamax)

Back to the Future Part III (Betamax)

Back to the Future (LaserDisc)

Back to the Future Part II (LaserDisc)

Back to the Future Part III (LaserDisc)

Back to the Future Trilogy (LaserDisc)

Back to the Future (DVD)

Back to the Future (DVD)

Back to the Future (DVD)

Back to the Future: Universal 100th Anniversary (DVD)

Back to the Future Part II (DVD)

Back to the Future Part II (DVD)

Back to the Future Part II (DVD)

Back to the Future Part II: Collector's Edition (DVD)

Back to the Future Part III (DVD)   *Back to the Future Part III* (DVD)   *Back to the Future Part III* (DVD)

Back to the Future Part III (DVD)   *Back to the Future Part III* (DVD)   *Back to the Future Part III: Collector's Edition* (DVD)

Back to the Future: The Trilogy (DVD)   *Back to the Future Trilogy* (DVD)

Back to the Future Trilogy (DVD)

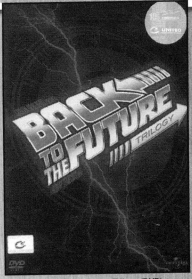

Back to the Future Trilogy (DVD)

Back to the Future: The Complete Trilogy (DVD)

Back to the Future: The Complete Trilogy (DVD)

Back to the Future Trilogy: 3 Disc Anthology (DVD)

Back to the Future 4 Disc Collector's Set (DVD)

Back to the Future 20th Anniversary Box (DVD, Japan)

Back to the Future (Blu-ray)

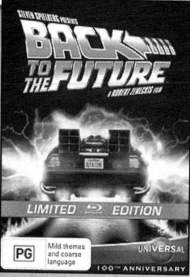

Back to the Future: Limited Edition (Blu-ray)

Back to the Future (Blu-ray)

Back to the Future Part II (Blu-ray)

Back to the Future Part II:
25ᵗʰ Anniversary Edition (Blu-ray)

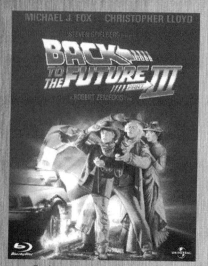

Back to the Future Part III (Blu-ray)

Back to the Future Part III:
25ᵗʰ Anniversary Edition (Blu-ray)

Back to the Future Trilogy (Blu-ray)

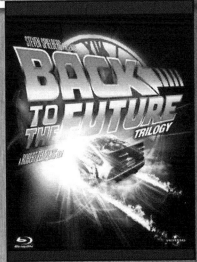

Back to the Future Trilogy (Blu-ray)

Back to the Future Trilogy:
Collector's Edition (Blu-ray)

Back to the Future Trilogy:
Limited Collector's Edition (Blu-ray)

Back to the Future Trilogy:
25th Anniversary Set (Blu-ray)

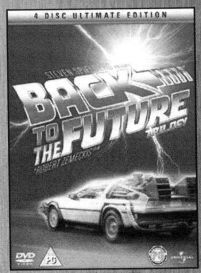

Back to the Future Trilogy:
4 Disc Ultimate Edition (Blu-ray)

Back to the Future: The Trilogy (Blu-ray)

Back to the Future: 25th Anniversary Trilogy (Blu-ray)

Back to the Future: 25th Anniversary Trilogy (Blu-ray)

Back to the Future: 25th Anniversary Trilogy (Blu-ray)

Back to the Future Trilogy: Limited Edition (Blu-ray)

UNIVERSAL STUDIOS THEME PARK

Back to the Future: The Ride

Doc Brown's Chicken

ANIMATED SERIES

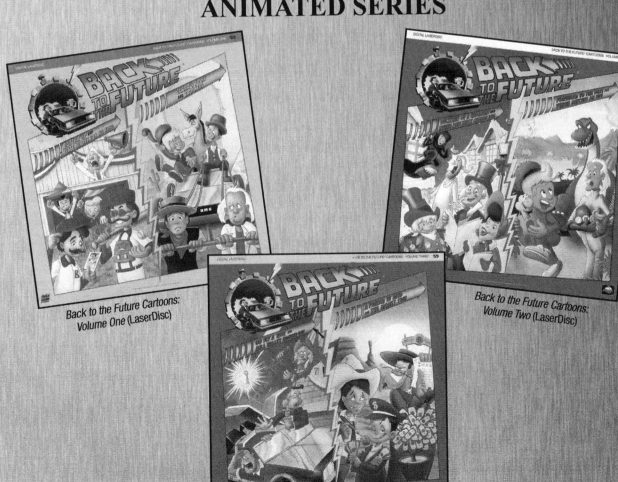

*Back to the Future Cartoons:
Volume One (LaserDisc)*

*Back to the Future Cartoons:
Volume Two (LaserDisc)*

Back to the Future Cartoons: Volume Three (LaserDisc)

Back to the Future: Volume One (VHS)

Back to the Future: Volume Two (VHS)

Back to the Future: Volume Three (VHS)

Back to the Future: Volume Four (VHS)

Back to the Future: Volume Five (VHS)

Back to the Future: Volume Six (VHS)

Back to the Future: Volume Seven (VHS)

Back to the Future: Volume Eight (VHS)

Back to the Future: Volume Nine (VHS)

BOOKS

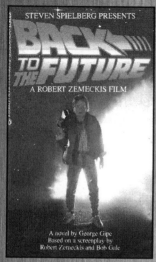

Back to the Future novelization

Back to the Future novelization

Back to the Future Read-Along
Adventure (Rainbow, U.K. only)

Back to the Future Part II novelization

Back to the Future Part II novelization

Back to the Future Part II novelization

Back to the Future Part III novelization

Back to the Future Part III novelization

Back to the Future: The Story

Back to the Future: The Official Book of the Complete Movie Trilogy

Back to the Future Part II photo book (Japan)

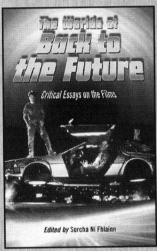

The Worlds of Back to the Future: Critical Essays on the Films

Hollywood SFX Museum Back to the Future Exhibition book (Japan)

Film Classics: Back to the Future

Back to the Future Screenplay: Complete Scenario of the Acclaimed Movie

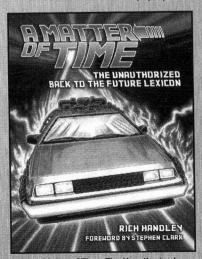

A Matter of Time: The Unauthorized Back to the Future Lexicon

Back in Time: The Unauthorized Back to the Future Chronology

MAGAZINES

Back to the Future Fan Club Magazine #1

Back to the Future Fan Club Magazine #2

Back to the Future Fan Club Magazine #3

Back to the Future Fan Club Magazine #4

Back to the Future Annual

Back to the Future Souvenir Magazine:
Official Collector's Edition

Back to the Future Book 1

Back to the Future Book 2

Back to the Future Book 3

600 g

FREE INSIDE

MALTED

Shreddies

WHOLE WHEAT CEREAL WITH VITAMINS

Nabisco
Shreddies box
containing
booklets

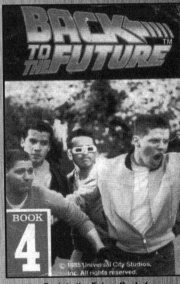

Back to the Future Book 4

Back to the Future Book 5

Back to the Future Book 6

COMIC BOOKS (HARVEY COMICS)

Back to the Future #1 (preview issue)

Back to the Future #1 (monthly series)

Back to the Future #2 (monthly series)

Back to the Future #3 (monthly series)

Back to the Future #4 (monthly series)

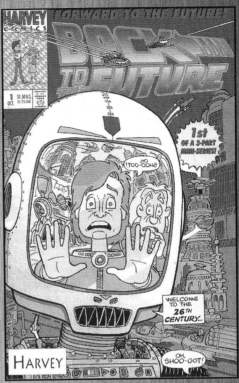

Back to the Future #1 (miniseries)

Back to the Future #2 (miniseries)

Back to the Future #3 (miniseries)

IN-UNIVERSE TITLES

A Match Made in Space,
by George McFly

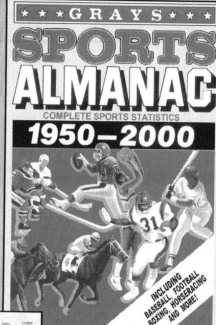

Grays Sports Almanac: Complete
Sports Statistics 1950-2000

Oh LàLà

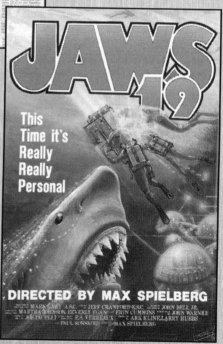

Jaws 19

Hill Valley Telegraph

EMMETT BROWN COMMENDED

Local Inventor Receives Civic Award

Reagan to Seek
Second Term
*No Republican
Challengers Expected*

Mayor Wilson
Vetoes Zoning Bill

Hill Valley Telegraph
(May 23, 1983)

Fantastic Story Magazine
(Fall 1954)

Amazing Stories (October-November 1953)

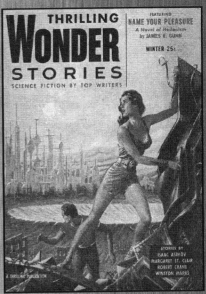

Thrilling Wonder Stories
(Winter 1955)

USA Today
(Oct. 22, 2015)

Tales From Space #8 (August 1954)

Headline Comics #67 (Sept./Oct. 1954)

VIDEO GAMES—CLASSIC

Back to the Future
(Commodore 64, Electric Dreams)

Back to the Future Adventure
(Commodore 64)

Back to the Future
(Nintendo NES, LJN)

Back to the Future Part II (Atari, Image Works)

Back to the Future Part III (Atari, Image Works)

Back to the Future Part II
(Sega Master System, Image Works)

Back to the Future Part III
(Sega Genesis, Arena)

Super Back to the Future Part II
(Super Famicom)

Super Back to the Future Part II
(Toshiba EMI)

Back to the Future: The Ride
(Nintendo GameCube, Kernco)

Back to the Future Part II & III
(Nintendo NES, LJN)

Back to the Future Part III
(Sega Master Drive, Image Works)

Back to the Future Part III
(Sega Master System, Image Works)

Back to the Future Part III
(Sega Master System, Image Works)

VIDEO GAMES—MODERN (TELLTALE GAMES)

*Back to the Future: The Game
Episode 1 (iTunes)*

Back to the Future: Blitz Through Time (Facebook)

*Back to the Future: The Game
Episode 2 (iTunes)*

*Back to the Future: The Game
Episode 3 (iTunes)*

*Back to the Future: The Game
Episode 4 (iTunes)*

*Back to the Future: The Game
Episode 5 (iTunes)*

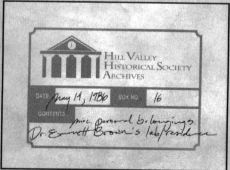

*Back to the Future: The Game—
Collector's Edition (PC & Mac DVD)*

*Back to the Future: The Game—
Special Deluxe Edition (PC & Mac DVD packaging)*

*Back to the Future: The Game—
Special Deluxe Edition (PC DVD cover)*

Back to the Future: The Game (Wii)

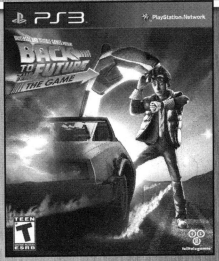

Back to the Future: The Game (PS3)

OTHER GAMES

Back to the Future Video Slots
(International Game Technology)

Back to the Future: The Pinball
(Data East)

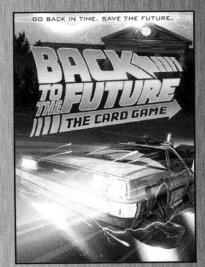

Back to the Future: The Card Game
(Looney Labs)

Back to the Future: The Board Game (Movie Licensing Games)

Back to the Future Pachinko (Cross Media International)

MISCELLANEOUS

Back to the Future Part II trading cards
(Topps, single pack)

Back to the Future Part II trading cards
(Topps, full box)

Back to the Future Happy Meal box #1, front (McDonalds)

Back to the Future Happy Meal box #1, back (McDonalds)

Back to the Future Happy Meal box #2, front (McDonalds)

Back to the Future Happy Meal box #2, back (McDonalds)